MW00817037

THE
EVOLUTION
OF SIN
TRILOGY

USA TODAY & WSJ BESTSELLING AUTHOR
giana darling

THE
EVOLUTION
OF SIN
TRILOGY

USA TODAY & WSJ BESTSELLING AUTHOR
giana darling

Copyright 2021 Giana Darling
Published by Giana Darling
Edited by Jenny Sims
Cover Design by Najla Qamber

This eBook is licensed for your personal enjoyment only. This eBook may not be re-sold or given away to other people.
This book is a work of fiction. Any similarities to persons living or dead are purely coincidental.

THE AFFAIR

THE EVOLUTION OF SIN, #1

USA TODAY & WSJ BESTSELLING AUTHOR

giana darling

For all the romantics, I'm proud to be in the same boat as you.

"Les émotions les plus belles sont celles que tu ne sais pas expliquer."
The most beautiful emotions are the ones you can't explain.

Charles Baudelaire

Playlist

"The Night We Met"— Lord Huron
"Come Fly With Me" – Frank Sinatra
"Lover Undercover"— Melody Gardot
"Mar De Suenos"—Mark Barnwell
"Sinnerman" — Nina Simone
"Black Mambo"— Glass Animals
"Le lac" – Julien Dore
"Pleasure This Pain"—Kwamie Liv, Angel Haze
"Open" —Rhye
"Can't Help Falling In Love"—Ingrid Michaelson
"New Amsterdam"— Pink Martini
"Transformation"—The Cinematic Orchestra
"This Is What It Feels Like"— BANKS
"Le Vie En Rose" — Edith Piaf
"Leave Your Lover" – Sam Smith
"One Last Night" —Vaults
"Ne me quitte pas" — Carla Bruni
"Non, Je Ne Regrette Rien" – Edith Piaf
"Bleeding Love" —Leona Lewis
"Broken Strings" — James Morrison, Nelly Furtado
"Are You Hurting The One You Love?" — Florence + The Machine

"I Get Along Without You"— Chet Baker

"Dead Hearts" – Stars

"Baby I'm A Fool" — Melody Gardot

"Come Together" – The Beatles

"Anchor" – Novo Amor

"Painter Song" – Norah Jones

"Toes" — Glass Animals

"Late Night" – Foushee

"Love Love Love" – Of Monsters and Men

"Piano Sonata No. 16 in C" – Mozart

"Let it Be Me" – Ray LaMontagne

"All About That Bass" – Meghan Trainor

"Desparado" —Diana Krall

"To Love Somebody"— Lindi Ortega

"Quelqu'un M'a Dit" – Carla Bruni

"For Your Precious Love" – Otis Redding

"I Don't Wanna Love Somebody Else" – A Great Big World

"Generique " – Miles Davis

"Only You—Matthew Perryman Jones

"Exile Vilify" – The National

"Setlla By Starlight" – Miles Davis, John Coltrane

"Make You Feel My Love" – Adele

"It's Always You" – Chet Baker

"Turn Me On" – Norah Jones

"Fix You" – Coldplay

"I'll Be Good" – Jaymes Young

"Fever" –Peggy Lee

"Perfect" – Ed Sheeran

"All I Want" – Kodaline

"Often" – The Weeknd

"I Do" – Susie Suh

Chapter One

RAIN POUNDED AGAINST THE STEAMING TARMAC, AND THE FORCE OF THE WIND slapped each raindrop against the oval window beside my head so that the gray of the runway, the rolling clouds, and the Vancouver skyline blurred into one. The rain calmed my nerves, and I closed my eyes to better hear the tap and whistle of the weather outside the tin machine that had—somewhat precariously—carried me from Paris to Vancouver in just fewer than seven and a half hours. We were deplaning a third of the passengers, then refueling to make the last leg of the journey to my final destination of Los Cabos, Mexico.

I took a deep breath and tried to focus on my happy place while the economy passengers filed off the plane. The flight was necessary, and after twenty-four years of traveling, I should have been used to the bump and grind of air travel.

In theory, I was. Before every flight, I waited calmly in the endlessly snaking line to check my bags, greeted the attendant with a genuine smile, and agreed that yes, I would have a pleasant flight. It wasn't until I was on the plane, secured in my seat by the tenuous hold of the belt, that my fear kicked into supercharge. I was intensely grateful to my younger brother

Sebastian for loaning me the money for the first-class flight. At least now, if the plane went down, I would have a bigger seat to cushion the fall.

"You still look a bit green, *chérie*." The middle-aged gentleman beside me leaned forward and offered me his unopened water bottle. "The worst is over, though. I hope someone is picking you up in Mexico. You are in no shape to drive after all of..." He waved politely at the remaining travel sickness bags the flight attendant had passed to me twenty minutes into our flight.

I managed a weak smile for Pierre. He was a fifty-year-old bachelor, quite distinguished really, with steel gray hair and cunning brown eyes. And maybe, under different circumstances, he would have propositioned me. As it was, he had offered to pay someone to switch seats with him when he discovered how sick I was. Failing that, he had settled in with relatively good grace and lectured me on the tricks of international trade law to distract me. Everything considered—I had managed to drool on his Hugo Boss blazer while I dozed between throwing up—I was grateful to him.

"No, but I'll catch a taxi to the resort." At the moment, I wasn't looking forward to my enforced vacation. All I wanted was to step off the plane back in my familiar Paris and slip into the small wrought iron bed in my studio apartment in *St-Germain-des-Prés*.

Pierre nodded and shot me a sidelong look. "Are you going to be all right now?"

He was getting off now to visit his daughter and newborn grandson. He didn't like North America, and I got the feeling he was lingering just to eke out a few more words in his native tongue before switching to English.

I nodded meekly, but before I could respond, the deeper voice of someone behind us spoke. "If you will allow me, I think you are leaving her in capable hands."

I opened my eyes when Pierre nudged me indelicately with his elbow and cleared his throat. Immediately, I blinked.

The man who stood before us dominated the entire aisle. His dusky golden skin stretched taut over his strong features, almost brutally constructed of steeply angled cheekbones and a bladed nose. I had only the vague impression that he was tall and lean because his eyes, a deep and electric blue like the night sky during a lightning storm, held me arrested.

The way he held himself, the power of his lean build, and the look in those eyes reminded me of a wolf caged within the confines of civility but eternally savage.

"I'm sure she would be delighted." Pierre sent me a barely concealed look telling me to pull it together.

I smiled hesitantly at the gorgeous stranger, aware that I was a mess of clammy skin and melted makeup. "I'm fine, really."

He nodded curtly, his eyes devoid of any real sympathy. "You will be."

Pierre hesitated as his eyes searched my face for reluctance. I smiled at him and took one of his hands between my clammy palms. "*Merci beaucoup pour votre aide. J'espère que vous passez un bon temps avec votre fille.*"

I was rewarded with a broad grin before he hastily collected his things and moved toward the front of the plane. I watched him go instead of focusing on the stranger as he took Pierre's abandoned seat, but after a few moments with his eyes hot on my face, I turned to him uneasily.

His thick hair was the color of polished mahogany and appeared overdue for a trim as it curled at the base of his neck. My fingers itched to run through the silken mass, but instead, I smiled.

"There really is no need to look after me, monsieur," I continued in French. "I am quite well now."

I squirmed in my seat when he didn't immediately reply. "It's silly, really. I've been afraid of planes since I was young."

"Oh?" He clasped his hands, and I noticed that he didn't wear a watch, that his fingers were long and nimble. The freckles on the back of those strong hands surprised me, and I found them strangely appealing. I wanted badly to dig into the bag at my feet for my sketchpad.

Because I was uncomfortable, I nodded empathetically. "I was four when we moved to Puglia for a year, and I don't remember the logistics of the move very well, but I remember the plane." I looked at him from the corner of my eye, and he nodded for me to continue with his hands steepled in front of his beautifully drawn lips. "It was with some budget airline, and the plane itself was barely held together by rusty bolts. I think the captain might have been drunk because we dropped and dipped the whole way through."

"Which airline?" His voice was silky and cool, like the brush of a tie against my skin.

"I don't remember now." I frowned at him. "Why?"

He waved my question out of the air with those deep blue eyes focused on my face. "Tell me more."

Those are magic words to hear from a man, I think. It unfurls something hidden deep within a woman, something that is habitually scared and insecure. *Tell me more.* It was somehow intimate to hear those words, even from a stranger, *especially* from this stranger.

"My father was in debt, so we were basically fleeing." I shrugged, but the sharp ache of terror still resounded in my chest when I thought of my mother's despair and my brother's desolation. "Maybe I had caught the flu, or maybe I was scared, but I spent most of the flight losing the contents of my stomach. Needless to say, it wasn't a pleasant trip. Since then, I've traveled a lot, but the feeling never goes away."

"Ah, but flying is a pleasure." He did not smile, and I had the sense he rarely did, but his eyes grew dark with pleasure. "Close your eyes."

"Excuse me?"

"Close your eyes."

I pressed back in my chair when he leaned into me slightly in order to reach the button on my armrest. My chair tilted back, and I found myself looking up into his lean face, his shoulder still warm against my front.

"Close your eyes," he repeated firmly.

I swallowed twice before doing so. I didn't know his name, where he came from, or anything personal to mark him with. But somehow, it was thrilling. To be in the hands of a perfect stranger and trust him enough to surrender my sight and allow him to make even the simplest decision for me.

So I hardly flinched when a blanket covered my chilled feet and was pulled up under my chin. His fingers, ridged with slight calluses, brushed against the tender skin of my neck as he tucked me in.

"You are flying," he said quietly, but it felt as though he spoke the words against my ear. "And if you relax, let every muscle loosen and breathe deeply. Nothing is more soothing than being in the air."

Instead, the pit of my stomach coiled, and I found myself wishing I was another kind of person. Someone who flirted with handsome strangers, who would lean into that firm mouth and take it without any qualms.

"We aren't in the air," I pointed out. "We are in a machine made of metal that has no business being in the sky."

"Ah, it is the machine that frightens you." I wondered where he sat and if he remained leaning over me. "Let it be a bird then, a swan."

"Okay," I mumbled, suddenly exhausted. "But only because swans are mean."

I smiled at his husky chuckle but fell asleep before he could say anything else.

When I woke up, it was to the delicate tapping of rain against the window and the brisk click of fingers on a keyboard. Deeply rested and disorientated, I moaned and stretched across my seat before righting it. Blinking away the sleep, I looked up and met the searing eyes of my stranger.

"You had a good rest," he noted, and for some reason, I flushed.

He was even more handsome than before if that was possible. In the darkening night, his hair was mostly black, kissed red by the artificial overhead lights. He seemed like some creature of the night, something dark and too sexy to be true.

"Yes, thank you." We spoke in English now, and I couldn't remember if we had switched over before I fell asleep. His voice was smooth and cool, enunciated perfectly with just a hint of French charm.

"We land in twenty minutes." He watched my surprise and handed me a plastic cup of sparkling liquid. Our fingers brushed as he passed it off, and a current of electricity made my grip on the cup shaky. Quickly, he righted it with his other hand and pressed both of my hands to the plastic. "You've got it?"

I nodded and flexed my fingers under his hold, but he continued to hold my hands against the cup for a beat too long. He stared at me with a slight frown between his thick brows, but I couldn't begin to discern if it was out of displeasure or surprise. I had never been so attracted to a man in my life, and I wondered if I imagined the tension between us. My tongue darted out to coat my dry lips, and his eyes followed its path intently. Then suddenly, his hands were gone, and he sat back in his seat, his fingers flying on the keyboard of his phone.

I blinked and slowly sank back into my chair. Obviously, I had misread the signs. I took a sip of the sparkling liquid and discovered with delight that it was ginger ale. Sipping it slowly to savor the sweet pop of bubbles on my tongue, I turned my attention to the early evening turning into twilight the color of a bruise outside my window. The sparkling lights of Los Cabos could already be seen ahead of us, and instead of wondering about the intrepid stranger beside me, I focused on my excitement. I had one week of paradise before I met with reality in New York City.

After five years in Paris and only a handful of visits in that time, I would finally be reunited with my family. The last time we all lived under the same roof, I was nineteen years old. My twin siblings, Cosima and Sebastian, had been the first to leave. Cosima when she was eighteen in order to model in Milan, and Sebastian just months later to England with Cosima's money in his pocket and a fierce determination to become an actor. I had lived with my mother and eldest sister Elena after that.

I squeezed my eyes shut and refused to think about those years. It had been nearly five now since I had left our small life in Napoli to attend *L'École des Beaux-Arts* in Paris. Though I was close to my family, it had been good for me to spend those years apart from them. I returned home a better person than when I had hastily fled, and I was both excited and anxious for them to see the new me.

"What are you smiling at?"

His question was faintly brusque as if he was irritated with me. When I turned to him, though, his eyes were on the glowing screen of his phone.

"I haven't been home in a long time, and I'm looking forward to seeing my family again."

"Your husband?" he asked tersely.

I laughed, and it felt so delightful after hours of sickness and sleep that I laughed some more. He watched me with twisted lips as if he wanted to smile but couldn't understand why. "Was that funny?"

"Oh, not really." I leaned forward conspiratorially. "But one needs a boyfriend to get married, and I haven't had one of those in years."

"Now, that is funny." He put his phone back in his pocket, and I felt a flash of triumph when he once more focused on me. "It is incomprehensible to me that you would be single." His eyes sparkled as he leaned forward, and a lock of hair fell across his golden forehead. "Tell me, other than your obvious fear of flying, what's wrong with you?"

I laughed. "We're almost in Los Cabos. I don't have time to list all my flaws."

"I have a feeling there aren't many," he murmured and stared at me in that way I was discovering he had, looking through me and at me all at once. "But perhaps it's better that you don't tell me. A woman of mystery"— his voice was low and smooth, so captivating I didn't register the pilot preparing the plane for landing—"is a seductive thing."

"You had better tell me about yourself, then." I leaned back in my seat as the plane began its steep descent into the city. "You're handsome enough already."

His loud chuckle surprised us both. It was husky with disuse, and his expression, though inherently beautiful, was almost pained. When the sound tapered off, it left him frowning. "What would you like to know?"

"Something repellent," I demanded cheerfully.

"Repellent? That's a tall order." Though I usually was uncomfortable under the eyes of others, those baby blues against my skin invigorated me, and I beamed back at him as he spoke. "When I look at you, I can only think of lavender and honey."

His fingers found a lock of my auburn hair, and he rubbed it between his fingers to release the scent.

"Well." I cleared my throat. "Happily, we are talking about you."

His grin was wolfish as he leaned back in his seat again. "I make a very good living."

"Ah, you're one of those." His silver cuff links shined even in the dim light of the descending plane. "That helps. I'm more the starving artist type."

"Hardly starving." His eyes raked over my curves even though I wore a modest cotton shift.

Despite myself, I flushed. "No, but an artist all the same. Let me guess, you work with money."

"In a sense," he said, and his eyes danced. "Is this twenty questions?"

I laughed. "I haven't played that since I was a kid."

"Not so long ago."

"Long enough," I corrected and shot a look at him from the corner of my eye. "How old are you?"

"Thirty-one. I'm also six foot one, and I've broken my right arm three times." His small smile was a boyish contrast to his sharp, almost aggressively drawn features. I wanted desperately to trace the exaggerated line of his jaw and dip a finger into the slight hollow beneath his cheekbone.

"Twenty-four." I pulled the bulk of my wavy hair to one side in order to show him the tattoo of color, making a whirlpool design behind my ear.

When I didn't explain its significance, he frowned. "What is it?"

"A mark," I said simply.

I jerked slightly when his fingers brushed over the swirled ink. "I like it."

"Thank you." My voice was breathy as I draped my hair once more over my shoulders.

"What brings you to Mexico? I take it your family doesn't live here." His finger ran down my arm lightly, highlighting the paleness of my skin.

"My family is much more exotic than I am." I thought of Mama and the twins with a slight grimace; years of hero worship were hard to completely eradicate. "My best friend booked the trip but couldn't make it. I was only too happy to take her place."

He nodded, his eyes intense as he contemplated me. The connection between us thickened and hummed like the air during an electrical storm.

Disturbed, I shifted away from him to look out the window as we swooped low over the ground above the runway. Strangely, I didn't feel my usual apprehension as the plane tentatively brushed the tarmac once, then twice before landing smoothly.

We didn't speak as the pilot announced our arrival, and it was only when the plane came to a slow stop at the terminal that I turned back to him. He faced forward with a furrow etched deeply between his brows and his mouth firm in concentration. I wondered what he thought of me, of this strange meeting.

Sensing my gaze, he said, "I've been trying to decide if I should see you again."

"What makes you think I would want to?" His eyebrow arched in response to my attempt at sassiness, and I gave in to his silent reproach with a little shrug. "What's stopping you?"

The seat belt sign turned off, and we both stood at the same time, suddenly almost touching; the slim space between us charged with electricity the color of his eyes. He looked down at me, his deep chestnut hair softening the dangerous edge of his features.

"I have never wanted someone the way I want you." His hand skimmed over my hip and sent a deep, throbbing shock through my system. "But I don't like the idea that you could very well change my life."

My heart clanged uncomfortably against my rib cage, and though I desperately wanted to say something, I couldn't find the words to untangle the jumble of hormones and desires I had been reduced to. So instead, I watched a serious smile tilt one side of his closed lips as his eyes scraped over my face one last time, and then, without a word, he left.

Chapter Two

My cell phone rang just as I emerged into the muggy Mexican heat to hail a taxi. I shook my head at the many men eager to help me with my suitcase for a few pesos and stuck my cell between my ear and shoulder.

"Giselle, darlin'." Brenna's husky Southern drawl warmed me. "How is the drug runner city treating you?"

I smiled and nodded enthusiastically at a sweet-faced Mexican man who pulled up in his beat-up yellow cab. "I just got off the plane, B, but so far no drug runners."

She laughed, but it wasn't the full-bodied sound I was used to. Brenna Buchanan was Hollywood royalty and my best friend from Paris. It was thanks to her that I was here in the first place, due to a scheduling conflict with an upcoming film. But something about her tone had me second-guessing that.

"How are things on set?"

There was a telling pause, and the creak and bang of an old door slamming shut. "Great."

"You must be in..." I paused and raked my foggy brain for the details. "Verona now?"

"Mmhmm." A whistle in the background sounded suspiciously like the call of a boiling kettle. "Listen, darlin', I don't have much time between scenes, but I just wanted to call to square away the details at the resort."

I sighed wearily as I got into the warm interior of the car. "You wouldn't be lying to me, would you, B?"

"No." Her own sigh echoed my own. "Maybe. I just needed to, um, take some time off from the fans."

"Don't let all this fame go to your head." I leaned my head back against the sticky leather and gave the driver directions to the resort. "I miss Brenna Buchanan, curvy misfit, not the Glamazon on red carpets in couture gowns."

She made a humming sound. "Fair enough, darlin', and for you, I will always be that girl. But admit it, I rock haute couture."

I rolled my eyes and laughed for the second time in weeks. "I wish you were here with me."

"I know." Her voice softened into a croon. "How are you holding up?"

"Fine," I murmured as the cab flew past brilliantly painted low buildings and old trucks lagging under the weight of debris in the peeling cabs. "I'm happy for the time to paint."

"It will be good for you to relax," she agreed before a cacophony of falling metal erupted in the background. "Listen, I should go. But don't worry about anything. I've got a handle on the situation over here, and I set up everything with the resort under my name. Just relax, drink the tequila, and find a man who makes your heart beat."

I smiled wryly as I thought of the handsome Frenchman I'd met on the plane. He had my heart racing the moment I caught sight of those electric eyes.

"Will do. Take care of you and your gowns."

She laughed and kissed me through the phone, but I held it to my ear for a minute after she hung up. Brenna had lived in Paris for the past three years with her husband, Franklin Robinson, a wealthy Brit with business in France. She had taken me under her wing as soon as I arrived, and she was the first one I had turned to when Christopher had shown up in Paris to destroy my life.

We pulled up to the Westin Resort and Spa in Los Cabos, and I was immediately blown away by the sheer size of the resort. The multistory tangerine building sprawled across a massive lot dotted with palm trees and dense green shrubbery. Women wearing expensive jewelry and small bathing suits wandered in and out of the hotel, and a group of men in exquisitely cut suits exited a huge black SUV ahead of me.

"Brenna," I muttered as a bellboy took my luggage with a smile.

"Ah, Brenna Buchanan." The man behind the grand marble desk smiled warmly at me. "Will Mr. Robinson be joining you later?"

I blushed at the mention of her handsome husband. "No, I'm here alone."

He frowned, and his fingers clattered across the keyboard ominously. "We have you booked into a deluxe suite with the couples package. I'm afraid it's nonrefundable."

Of course.

I smiled prettily. "I completely understand. Thank you."

He nodded briskly and printed out the necessary documents, but as he handed me the key cards, he winked. "I'm sure you'll find someone to share it with before the week is out."

I laughed lightly. "I don't think so. Have a nice day, *señor*."

Despite my disavowal, the Frenchman's silken voice wound through my thoughts as the swift elevator carried me to the twelfth floor. He had been so perfect that I doubted the reality of what had occurred between us. It felt like one of my childhood fantasies come to life.

It was just as well, though. I was in Mexico to relax before the inevitable rockiness of my family reunion. Just thinking about seeing them again made my heart race, so I was glad to open the door to my room to find the A/C cranked and the fan on. It was a lovely space echoing the soft colors of the sea with large French doors leading to a small patio overlooking the beach. I waited anxiously for the bellman to drop off my things, and then, with a squeal like a preteen girl, I jumped onto the brightly dressed bed.

Later that night, after an invigorating shower and a quick rest, I walked through the resort just as they were lighting the torches lining the walkways. The light south of the equator was different. Sunlight poured like honey, fragrant and gold across the brilliant tropical gardens, and as the sun brushed the horizon, gem-toned hues exploded across the sky. I raised my camera to my eye and allowed my instinct to take over, capturing shot after shot as I walked the darkening paths. Being somewhere so beautiful soothed my ragged heart, and though I was hyper-aware of the couples strolling past and scrutinizing my lack of a partner, I felt more at ease than in years. I had one week to unwind before my family reunion, and I intended to make the most of it.

There was a large outdoor dining room beside the beach with a mariachi band in full swing beside a roaring blue-green fire. A few couples swayed gracefully on the dance floor, but I was drawn to the quartet of men toiling away in the intense heat. As I drew closer, I saw one of them with his eyes closed, the body of his large guitar cradled against his round stomach. Sweat beaded on his forehead, the damp fabric of his thick cotton outfit clung to his chest, but there was pure rapture on his features as he swayed in time with his music.

I inched closer and took a picture of his passion.

"*Señorita!*" Another Mexican man, handsome and young with his glittering black hair slicked back, noticed me crouching awkwardly at the side of the stage and walked over with a large smile. "What is a beautiful woman doing on the ground? You must be dancing!"

"No, thank you," I demurred as the semicircle of well-dressed diners turned to look at me. Somehow, I had become a part of the evening entertainment.

"Come, *señorita*," he continued to coax, his hips swaying to the beat of the candle flames. "A beauty like you must dance."

I could feel a blush flame across my cheeks as I shook my head, mortified by the multitudes of paired diners staring at me.

"Maybe I can persuade you."

My breath left me in one long whoosh as I looked up at the man before me. The candlelight was at his back, illuminating his tall physique and casting shadows across his features. It could have been anyone really, and his English was flawless, but I knew who it was by the palpable energy pulsing between us.

A thrill ran up my spine, and I shuddered.

The Frenchman extended his hand, and the moment I took it, I was in his arms, pulled there seamlessly as I rose. I was overwhelmed by the smell of him and the strength of his body against mine. Unconsciously, my hands tense on his broad shoulders, mapping the shift of hard muscles between the silken fabric of his skirt.

His eyes gleamed in the shadows, night dark yet shining with predatory satisfaction as he whirled me away onto the middle of the dance floor with the other couples.

"The lady is dancing," the emcee cried, prompting a polite round of applause. "My job is done for the night, ladies and gentlemen. Please enjoy."

The music grew louder, filling the heavy night air with beats and vibrations. I felt them thrum through the soles of my feet, and I laughed when a couple beside us spun gracefully across the floor.

"It's good to see you again..." He waited for me to supply my name, and I realized with a start that he hadn't known it on the plane.

I bit my lip and considered my options. It was exciting, my interaction with the stranger, but I wasn't willing to give too much away. So with sudden confidence, even though no one had ever called me by the nickname, I said, "Elle."

He repeated the syllable, and the way he tasted my name was sinful, like biting into a slightly overripe fruit, sweetness bursting from his lips.

I looked up at him and smiled wryly. "I wouldn't have thought you'd be so happy to see me. You practically sprinted from the plane this morning."

A small smile twisted his lips, but his hands tightened, one in mine and the other on my hip. "Any man with sense runs from a siren."

"Good save." I looked up at him from under my lashes and was rewarded with his sparkling blue eyes. "I don't see you running now."

"No." He seemed just as perturbed by the idea as I was. "I'm here to work, and usually, I'm not the type of man to mix business and pleasure, but when I saw you standing there..." He shrugged, irritated by his lack of control even as he moved us masterfully across the dance floor. "I'm also not the type of man who denies himself when he wants something badly enough."

The music pulsed quickly now. I could feel the beat at my core, and any questions I might have voiced were lost to my breathless enthusiasm as the Frenchman spun me faster. We were doing some version of the tango. I had watched enough movies growing up to know that, but the more we moved together, the less formal it became. One strong hand hiked my leg up over his hip, and I slid inch by delicious inch down his steel thigh until he pulled me upright once again. With my arms on his chest, I undulated like the wavering flames low to the ground, his hands on my shoulders guiding me down. I was short of breath but not from dancing. I was moving intimately with a man I hardly knew, and I could have sworn nothing had ever been so erotic. The music reached its rapid-fire crescendo, and I was sent spinning across the floor in tight circles guided by his strong hand. It was only when the music suddenly slowed and ended on a breathless whimper that he stopped me with his body flush against my own.

He was basically unfazed by the most sensual experience of my life, cool and composed with not a gorgeous strand of hair out of place. But those electric eyes dilated as they stared down into mine, and his body was tense with unease. I melted further against his marble edges, and for a moment, I thought I might have had the courage to kiss the perfect stranger until hands descended on our shoulders, jarring us apart.

"Very beautiful couple, very beautiful!" the emcee cried, inspiring a round of applause. With his arms on both of us, he grinned at the crowd. "I think we have a winner for best couple tonight, *si*?"

There was some outcry and a smattering of agreement from the other diners, and he taunted them to take the dance floor and show us up.

"And these two, they will dance again!"

A hand snatched his mic out of the air, and my Frenchman looked down into the much smaller man's face with inscrutable coolness. "No. We will not."

The emcee nodded and laughed nervously, but I was forced to mask a chortle as I was led from the dance floor.

His table pressed up against the beach, close to the fire but on the other side of the sweltering music. Its twangy refrains faded away as we approached, replaced by the gentle crash of waves on the shore. It was an utterly romantic setting, but I had a feeling my Frenchman could have made an industrial waste plant sexy.

"I have people joining me," he muttered almost petulantly even as he pulled out a chair for me.

I hesitated, awkwardly poised over my seat. "There is no need for me to join you."

Strangely, my coolness seemed to amuse him. Even in the wavering light, I could see a grin cut into his left cheek. "Excuse me, as I said before, I'm not used to mixing business and pleasure. My objection is to my pending associates, not you. Please, eat with me, Elle."

I bit the inside of my cheek but finally settled in my seat. I was silent as a waiter came to take our drink order even though I was usually very opinionated about wine. It was obvious when he began to order in heavy, polished Spanish that he knew what he was doing.

When we were alone again, he sat back in his chair languidly and stared at me with such carnality that heat flared across my skin, and my nipples puckered shamelessly against the frail fabric of my dress. He was so sleek and powerful it was hard not to relate him to a jungle cat, something dark and solitary stalking the woods at night looking for prey.

"You know..." I attempted to make casual conversation, anything to lower the temperature between us. "I don't even know your name."

His mouth pursed, and his hands flattened on the table as if he was bracing himself. I shifted impatiently in my seat while I waited, but when he did look up, the desire in his eyes paralyzed me. "Have you ever had a holiday affair, Elle?"

I blinked and licked my lips nervously. "Would you believe me if I said yes?"

He smiled again, small and almost too fleeting to capture. "You are a stunning woman, so there can only be two reasons for your inexperience. Lack of opportunity or lack of gumption."

Even as I blushed, I tilted my chin and gazed down my nose at him. "I think we both know the answer to that."

"Yes." He leaned forward on his forearms, and his eyes caught the flame, glittering like sapphires caught in a fire. "The question is, now you have the opportunity, but do you have the gumption to take it?"

"Are you propositioning me?" I teased. My heart was racing, and my hands were damp as they tangled in my lap.

He nodded somberly. "I am."

"I see." I swallowed and tried to ignore the intensity in his eyes as our chemistry crackled in the hot air between us. "And if I say yes?"

"A girl who thinks ahead." He grinned, suddenly carefree. "Very good, Elle. You should always protect your interests."

I raised an eyebrow, prompting a short bark of laughter from him.

He held up his hands innocently. "You are here for the week?" When I nodded, one of his fingers began to trace the outline of my hand where it lay on the table. His eyes were hot on mine, and his voice dropped lower, smoke rubbing itself sensuously against my skin. "Well, I imagine we could find a number of things to do in seven whole days."

It was hard to believe this was happening. I had been such an ugly duckling my whole life, especially compared to my glamorous siblings, that I couldn't imagine what this beautiful Frenchman saw in me, but it was obvious he did see something. Something he liked very, very much.

My tongue darted out to wet my lips, and his eyes darkened as he followed its path. "One week with a perfect stranger, no complications, no surprises. Just..." He turned my hand over and feathered his fingers along the sensitive skin of my wrist where my pulse beat madly. "This."

"If I say yes, will you finally tell me your name?"

He blinked, and a slow smile spread across his hard features as he chuckled. "Yes, Elle, but I'll warn you now, you won't get much else."

I understood. If I entered into this holiday affair, as he so casually offered, he would remain a stranger. The only part of him I could know was his body. My eyes flickered over the strong width of his shoulders and the firmness of his hands on mine.

Was it enough?

My sister Cosima's voice rang out in my head; yes!

I opened my mouth to respond when a small group appeared at the entrance to the restaurant.

He leaned forward, an urgent desire in those blue eyes. "I want an answer by the end of this meal."

When I nodded mutely, still overwhelmed by the moment, he flashed me a genuine smile and traced one finger behind my ear and down my neck.

"You have beautiful hair," he murmured before sitting back in his chair, looking utterly unruffled and almost bored when his guests arrived at the table.

I stood to shake their hands when he introduced us and was met with surprised smiles. Cage Tracy lingered over our handshake with flagrant approval. I recognized him, of course, as the lead singer of Caged, the absurdly popular French band that was just becoming a phenomenon in America. He grinned down at me with gorgeous nearly black eyes and thick black hair he kept secured in a messy braid over his shoulder. I wondered how a rising rock star knew my French businessman.

"It's a pleasure to meet you," he said as he pulled out my chair for me and leaned forward familiarly when I sat down. "Sinclair always did have the most exquisite taste in women."

Sinclair. I tasted the name, rolling it on my tongue so that it split and reformed like mercury. It was an old-fashioned name, formal even, but dark too and inexplicably sexy. I looked over at him to find him staring at me, his eyes midnight blue in the darkness. A shudder rolled through my shoulders. *Oh yeah*, it suited him.

"She's only a friend, Cage," he said mildly as the other three men and a woman sat down around us.

"Of course," the woman––a plain brunette with slightly protruding front teeth––demurred. "Do stop interfering, Cage. You always hit on Sinclair's women. It does get boring, you know."

Cage smirked at me, but when Sinclair raised a cool eyebrow his way, his smile tripped and slid off his handsome face. I hid my smile behind my wineglass. Obviously, the Frenchman demanded obedience.

An older man, though no more than forty, with brilliant silver hair who introduced himself as Richard Denman leaned closer to Sinclair in order to politely inquire, "What happened to the other one, your girlfriend––"

Sinclair cut him off with a sharp glare before quickly looking at me. I feigned nonchalance, picking up my glass of water and smiling at Cage as he charmingly related his love for Mexico in his thick French accent, but I had heard.

Tension knotted the muscles between my shoulders.

I didn't know anything about this man I was considering sleeping with. And I *was* considering it. The idea of a holiday affair was not new to me— I'd read books and watched movies—yet it went against every conservative bone in my body. Not to mention the addition of a girlfriend, a woman from his real life who probably expected his love and fidelity.

I snuck a glance at Sinclair and frowned. He didn't seem like the type of man to love easily, and I wondered about the nature of his relationship. Were they close, and, if so, how long had they dated? I bit my lip. It would drive me crazy to render a picture of the unknown girlfriend, so I resolved not to consider her any longer. It was cold of me, and I felt a pang as the idea rebounded off my morals, but I would do it.

I would do it for me because, for the first time in my life, I was faced with the possibility of something I wanted that was actually within my grasp to take. All it required of me was, as Sinclair had said, gumption.

I settled back in my seat while the wine was poured. When our waitress began to take dinner orders, Sinclair made eye contact with me as he ordered and raised one reddish brow. I understood his question, and though I raised both of my own eyebrows, I also nodded slightly, giving him full rein to order my meal. His eyes sparkled as he did so, and it gave me time to think over his proposal.

There was no doubt I was intensely attracted to him. Honestly, a woman would have to be dead not to be moved by his fierce looks. But I had never dated an overtly attractive man. In fact, I had only dated one man, and he had not been a hunk by any stretch of the imagination. Mark had been sweet-faced with thick-rimmed glasses and distinctly Canadian manners. We had dated a full month before he worked up the courage to even kiss me.

I watched Sinclair speak easily with one of his associates. After a moment, his posture changed infinitesimally, and I knew he was aware of my gaze. Immediately, heat pooled at the base of my stomach. I knew that saying yes to this man would rock my world, and honestly, I wasn't sure that I was sophisticated enough to deal with it. Catching my eye, he stared at me, desire blazing so brightly I was sure everyone at the table was aware of the fiery air between us.

"So, Elle..." Cage leaned over to me with a boyish grin on his exotic features. If I hadn't been so inextricably caught up in Sinclair, I'm sure I would have been bowled over by both his good looks and star power. "Tell me about yourself. What brings you to Mexico?"

My stomach fluttered, and I realized that my anxiety had been laid to bed by Sinclair's charm. I hadn't thought about the horror I had left behind in Paris or my family reunion in over an hour.

"I'm here to paint."

His eyebrows shot into his hairline, and a flicker of suspicion flashed across his face. "You're an artist. Would I know any of your work?"

I shrugged when I felt Sinclair's gaze on us. "Maybe."

"Well, where did you study? A friend of mine is one of the proprietors at MoMA." The woman beside him snorted derisively, but he ignored her. "I know quite a bit about art."

"European." Robert Corbett, the only man over sixty in the group, slapped his thick hand on the table and then pointed at me triumphantly. "Irish?"

"I thought French like Sinclair," Duncan Wright countered, his glasses iridescent in the candlelight.

"Not quite French, are you, *chérie*?" Cage frowned at me thoughtfully.

Before he could press me further, Sinclair chuckled darkly. "Elle is difficult to know. Leave her be."

It was said with good humor, but I knew it was a warning. No one was to press me for details, and I wasn't to offer any.

I should have been angry, or at the very least indignant over his privacy clause in our looming holiday affair, but I only felt a secret thrill of excitement. I wanted to know how his caramelized skin tasted and trace my fingers over the line of the muscles in his torso as it arrowed to his groin. If I could have that, I assured the more conservative part of my conscience, the personal details wouldn't matter.

"And what about you, Cage?" I spoke quietly as if I had a secret to share so that Sinclair could only wonder at our topic of conversation. *Let him worry*, I thought with an inner smile.

Cage threw his head back and laughed heartily, his glossy hair catching the candlelight and highlighting his heathen good looks. "Unless you've been living under a rock, I think you're playing dumb, Elle."

I smiled at him over the rim of my wineglass, pleased and surprised by my ease with the singer.

"And how do you know Sinclair?" I took a careful sip of my wine, savoring the robust flavors of the Cabernet Sauvignon he had ordered for me. It was delicious, and another current of arousal sparked through my system. The Italian in me loved a man who knew his wine.

"It's a long story. Let's just say we met through a mutual friend a very long time ago." His tone implied he and that friend had shared some very intimate times together, and once again, the woman beside him with the buck teeth rolled her eyes.

He laughed and winked at someone over my shoulder. "Isn't that right, Sin?"

I looked over my shoulder and up to find him standing behind me with a frown. Goose bumps rippled along my skin, and I rubbed my exposed arms even though the breeze off the ocean was tacky with warmth.

"If I remember correctly, I introduced you to our 'mutual friend,' and you took off with her," he said as he put a warm hand on my shoulder. The heat from his contact seared through the thin material of my dress and made me shudder.

Cage gasped in dramatic objection. "Me? Never. Elle, who do you believe? This French gypsy or the hunky rock star?"

I laughed, at ease with Cage's mock arrogance. It reminded me of my brother Sebastian's public persona, and unexpectedly, I felt a pang for home. "I'm not the right person to ask."

I tilted my head so that my eyes could meet Sinclair's over my shoulder. His were dark and troubled, his other hand clenched by his side as he fought to control the emotion in his features. I could sense his pain, his discomfort over Cage's carelessly worded humor.

"Oh?" he asked quietly.

"Because she clearly favors me," Cage declared smugly, leaning back in his chair like a king on his throne.

"No," I spoke softly and ran the fingers of my right hand gently down the outside of Sinclair's leg nearest to me. "Because I have a soft spot for gypsies."

His nostrils flared, and without looking at Cage, he said, "Trade places with me. Duncan has something he wants to discuss with you."

Cage looked at the man in question, who only shrugged, but Cage did as he was told with a roguish grin.

"Can't blame him for wanting you all to himself." He gave me a kiss on the cheek and chuckled when Sinclair took him by the shoulder to pull him firmly away.

"I liked him," I protested mildly as Sinclair settled in beside me.

"You'll like me more." His hand landed heavy and hot on my bare knee, branding me. "Now, are you done trying to distract me? I really do have business to discuss, and I want you to think long and hard about my proposal. Can you do that for me?"

His voice was so seductive. No one else I knew had such powerfully sexy speech. It might have been the undercurrent of French in his pronunciation or the depth of his baritone, the fact that he never spoke loudly, yet every word vibrated throughout my body. Whatever it was, I was almost certain I would do anything that voice commanded.

So I nodded mutely and watched a slow smile tip his firm lips.

"Good," he said and turned immediately to Richard Denman.

The sluggish ocean breeze carried his leather and smoke scent to my nose, and I sucked a lungful deep into my lungs. His hand on my bare thigh seemed to throb against my overheated skin, and when I squirmed slightly, he squeezed me into stillness.

"What brings you to Mexico, Elle?" The woman beside Sinclair leaned forward and smiled at me with closed lips. I wondered if she was self-conscious of her buck teeth.

"My best friend booked the room but was unable to make it." Brenna would have loved the luxurious resort, and I worried she was working too hard under the direction of her new manager.

"Lucky girl." She extended her hand. "Candy Kay."

My eyebrows rose by their own volition, but she was kind enough to laugh at my rudeness. "I know. It's misleading. I gave up introducing myself as Candace years ago. People refuse to call me anything but Candy."

"It's a lovely name," I offered politely, trying to recover from my earlier faux pas.

She laughed loudly, her teeth flashing in the candlelight. I found her rather beautiful actually when her features relaxed with good humor, and she forgot to pull her lips closed.

Her insecurities reminded me all too vividly of my own as I grew up. It was only recently that I had come to terms with myself, with the red hair and olive skin, the freckles and the lack of Italian spicing my speech. I was the only one in our family without a discernable accent, and though Elena shared my red hair, it was dark, almost black, and she had the long, lithe body of the twins while I remained stunted, shorter, and too curvy. For years, I had hidden behind baggy clothes and dyed my hair an unnatural black. I fingered a wavy lock of auburn hair nervously.

"Did I hear you say you're an artist?" she asked. "I'm hopeless with any form of creativity, but I so admire artists. You must have an awfully romantic life."

I laughed as I pictured the cramped apartment in an old servant's quarters where I had lived for the past five years. "Not exactly. But I do love what I do. I'm lucky to have had the opportunity to pursue it."

"I think it's wonderful when people follow their passions." Candy spoke in a low mumble, the better to hide her teeth, I thought, but Sinclair looked over abruptly as if she had yelled.

"Not everyone is so lucky," I agreed, thinking of my twin siblings toiling away in London and Milan for years; two young people alone in a foreign country trying to scrounge together enough money to support a family of five.

"That's why I respect Sinclair so much, of course," she said. "His passion is boundless."

He chose that moment to look over at me as Duncan Wright spoke animatedly to him about stock options. His eyes were dark, and the shadows cast his features in stark relief. The sharp jut of the bones in his face was almost cruel, and the intensity of his expression was near to savage with desire. A shiver trembled across my shoulders. *Boundless passion.* The look he gave me promised just that.

"I haven't known him for very long," I exaggerated smoothly; prying my eyes from his in order to smile at Candy. "Tell me about the work you do with him."

I watched her come alive, her lips pulled over her teeth, her eyes sparkling, and I knew she too shared a passion for her work. "I'm the vice president of the company, and while I love the thrill of closing a land deal, I won't lie to you. My favorite part is working with Romani International, Sinclair's charity. That's one of the reasons we are here."

"Oh?" I scoured my mind for any information on the Romani people but found I was sorely lacking in knowledge. I knew it was the politically correct term for gypsies and that they were nomadic people with somewhat vagabond lifestyles.

"He doesn't like to talk about it much." She cast a quick glance at the man between us, but Sinclair was busy debating something animatedly with the other men. "But every year, he rewards his closest colleagues and associates with a week-long all-inclusive vacation. Of course, it's not really a vacation. We are here to close a deal on a resort while simultaneously milking our fellow travelers for donations to the Romani Foundation. Business never sleeps even when Cage crashes the party," she said with a sigh and a quick glance at Cage, who was leaning across the table shouting in faux outrage at an unfazed Sinclair.

So Sinclair was in real estate?

I was quiet as the food arrived, and a beautifully presented glass of fresh shrimp ceviche was placed before me. I looked over at Sinclair as I raised a spoonful to my mouth and hummed in delight as I took the first bite.

His hand tightened around my thigh, and his lips parted on a small gasp at my expression. I was dazzled by his desire, and emboldened by it, I deliberately swept my tongue across my bottom lip.

His blue eyes flashed. "I need you to say yes, Elle."

His smoky voice made me dizzy, but I shook my head slightly to clear it and smiled demurely at him as if I was used to this degree of male attention. "I'm still thinking."

"Well, stop talking and eat up then. I'm an impatient man."

I giggled quietly so as not to draw the attention of the other diners. "I would never have guessed."

His resulting smirk was self-mocking. "You are too observant for your own good."

"I'm an artist." I shrugged because, to me, that explained everything.

He stared at me intently for a moment, leaving his food untouched. "You look like a piece of art."

My eyebrows shot into my hair at the romantic thought, but Sinclair abruptly pulled his hand from my thigh and turned to Candy as he tucked into his chicken mole dish. I was almost glad for his dismissal as his words continued to ring in my head. No one had ever said something like that to me, and coupled with our electrifying chemistry, I was worried that despite my conservative upbringing and the fact that he obviously had a girlfriend back home, I was undoubtedly going to agree to the conditions of his holiday affair.

Chapter Three

"DID YOU ENJOY YOUR MEAL, ELLE?" SINCLAIR'S VOICE WRAPPED AROUND ME and tugged my focus from my conversation with Richard Denman, a fascinating man with his own architecture firm in New York, to the handsome Frenchman sitting on my other side.

For some reason, I blushed. "Yes, very much. Thank you."

We had made our way through four courses, ending in a rich Mexican chocolate mousse that had made me weak in the knees. I took the last decadent spoonful of sugar in my mouth and closed my eyes briefly as I savored it. When I opened my eyes, Sinclair's were blazing.

"Tell me," he gritted out between his teeth. "What will it be, Elle?"

It took me a moment to find my breath. He was so achingly handsome that I couldn't believe he was real, let alone that someone like him would be interested in me. His eyes narrowed at my hesitation, and I laughed breathlessly at his impatience.

I straightened my spine and looked him in the eye, trying to convey the weight of my answer. "Yes."

He blinked as if he had misheard. "Say it again."

"Yes."

The grin that split his face was the first unreserved expression I had seen on his hard features since meeting him, and it attracted the attention of Cage, who stopped his animated storytelling, which included an air guitar, to frown at his friend.

"What's cause for such a smile, Sin?"

"I've been smiling like that all night, and I'd wager it's for the same reason as Sinclair." Richard Denman slapped a powerful hand on my back. "This is one intriguing lady."

I tipped my head down in embarrassment, but Sinclair's hand found mine under the table and squeezed.

"Margot won't like her, that's for sure." Cage guffawed at the idea even as the rest of the table shot him disapproving looks.

"His personal assistant," Candy explained. "She's a bit... protective."

"Nothing will do it for that woman unless it's Sin. Not even me," Cage divulged with a wicked wink that made my heart sink farther.

And he had a girlfriend back home. I wondered what these people thought of the arrangement; if they knew Sinclair had decided to take me as a lover or if, perhaps, this was routine for him when abroad.

He must have caught the apprehension on my face because suddenly, he stood, pulling me with him. "Good night, everyone."

No one batted an eye at his rude farewell, and we were already walking away when they began to call their own goodbyes. I tried to wave at them and smile, but Sinclair's long legs ate up the ground, and I finally just gave up.

"That wasn't very nice," I pointed out as we emerged from the restaurant onto the torch-lined path to the rooms.

"I don't have the time to be nice," he said as we made our way swiftly through the lobby.

"Oh." I was struggling to keep up with his brisk pace, and my quip was slightly breathless as a result. "But you have time to cheat on your girlfriend?"

There was barely a hitch in his stride, but a muscle in his jaw clenched menacingly. He maintained an arctic silence as we took the elevator up to the top floor. I bit my lip, nervous that I had overstepped my bounds but angry with myself for succumbing to his charms. Whatever conflicting feelings I might have had fled when he opened the door to his room.

Glass doors dominated the entire far wall of the cream-colored living room, exposing the obsidian waves of the Pacific lacquered by the moonlight as they rolled gracefully onto the shore. I moved immediately to the sight, inexorably drawn to the power of the scene. Even as the beauty overwhelmed me, I was aware of Sinclair a step behind me. It felt almost like he was indulging me, allowing me to enjoy the view for a moment before the icy cold of the elevator ride descended once more.

"Are you ready to have a mature conversation about this now, Elle?" His voice was disarmingly soft, and the hand that skimmed down my arm was gentle, but when I turned slightly to face him, his deep blue eyes were frosted with censure.

"Mature?" I repeated, shocked by his rudeness.

He remained calm and grabbed my hands as they came up to push him away. "How old are you? Twenty-two?"

I glared at him, but he only raised one cool brow in the face of my defiance.

"Twenty-four," I muttered.

He kissed the center of one of my trapped palms. "That wasn't so hard, was it? Clearly, you have never had an affair before, of any kind, and I admit that is part of your considerable appeal." The way he stressed the word considerable, tilting his hips slightly so that they were pressed against mine, unraveled me. "And obviously, you have a problem with the idea of my infidelity. What would make you feel better about it? If I said that I had never cheated on her before? I haven't. That our relationship is rocky, that she is bitter, and we haven't slept together in months or years? Lies." His turbulent eyes locked onto mine with utter sincerity. "The truth is, she is steady and whip-smart, beautiful. I've been with her for a very long time."

I could feel my heart beating too slowly, too heavily. It knocked monotonously inside my chest like the dooming toll of an old clock.

He seized me suddenly, pressing me against the wall and lifting me slightly so that I was suspended between his warm body and the cool glass. One hand supported my back, and the other delved into the thick hair at the base of my neck so that I was completely entangled with him. Suddenly, I couldn't bear the idea of not being with him.

"But I want you. I want to know the flavor of the skin behind your knees and the way you smell when you're aroused by my touch. I've never wanted anything as badly as I want you against my skin."

I was flushed by the heat of his praise, of his steely body against mine, and I almost moaned with lust, but my resolve still wavered. Could I really do this?

He took a deep, almost frustrated breath, and for a moment, his handsome face was suspended in heart-wrenching uncertainty. "Don't say no. I don't think I could let you go."

Oh my.

That did it.

How could any woman resist such a powerful man genuinely yearning for her?

I brought my hand up to his strong face and placed my forehead against his. "I'll stay."

He stiffened and sucked in a ragged breath. "You don't have to."

"I know." I smiled, joy blooming in my chest. "I want to."

His mouth was on mine before I had finished speaking, hard and rough in his haste. I moaned as his tongue swept into my mouth and plundered. My hands sank into his thick hair and tugged him closer; my legs wrapped around his torso so that I was locked onto him.

His lips moved from my mouth to my neck, sucking lightly at the tender skin there as the hand in my hair tilted my head back.

"Ah," I breathed.

Urged on by my exclamation, he deftly undid the pearl buttons of my bodice to reveal my pale lacy bra. He groaned at the sight of me and bent his head to suck at my puckered nipple through the thin fabric. I arched into the wet heat of his mouth and groaned. The solid length of him pushed against the apex of my thighs, and I imagined what he would feel like inside me, stretching me and filling me until I burst with pleasure.

Suddenly desperate for the feel of his skin against mine, I fumbled with the buttons of his ivory shirt and pushed it from his shoulders. His skin was stretched tight across his lean cut muscles, and when I opened my mouth over the skin of his shoulder to bite down lightly, the manly, slightly salty taste of him exploded in my mouth.

With a growl, he reared up and trapped both of my hands in one of his, pinning them to the foggy glass so he had unfettered access to my breasts.

"God, you're beautiful," he rasped, his hot breath wafting over my nipple as he deftly undid my bra and plumped my breasts between his capable hands. "Keep your hands there. I have to taste you."

I almost choked on my sharp inhalation of surprise when he dropped to his knees and tugged my dress to the floor. He grasped my hips in a vise-like grip and pressed his nose to the apex of my thighs, breathing deeply. It was unbearably erotic, seeing him on his knees before me, his dark head against my pale thighs. He ran his nose down the inside of my thigh, nipping the skin there so that I jerked. His soft chuckle fanned across my sex and further inflamed my arousal. I was quivering putty in his hands.

"What do you want?" he asked as he pressed his closed lips to my panty-covered clit and hummed lightly.

"You," I panted.

"Here?" He pressed an open-mouthed kiss to the inside of my thigh.

"No," I groaned in frustration. "Higher."

"What?" he practically purred, swirling his tongue in my belly button.

"Your mouth." I had never begged before for anything, but all reservations had melted off me at the first touch of his lips to my skin. "On me."

I groaned as he slowly began to peel off my underwear.

My head fell back against the glass, and I squeezed my eyes closed in anticipation. But instead of the lush feel of his mouth against me, the dull thud of vibrations against the wooden floor jolted me from my stupor.

With a vicious curse, Sinclair wrenched himself away from me and pulled his phone out of his pants pocket. He stared at the screen, taking tight, controlled breaths before looking up at me with rapidly cooling eyes. "I have to take this."

I nodded mutely.

He strode through the room into the adjacent bedroom as he answered the phone, "Hello."

It was her—the girlfriend—obviously. I took a shaky deep breath and closed my eyes. My sweat-dampened skin was stuck to the cool glass, and my underwear hung off me in disarray. I had never been this girl before, and the realization of what I had almost done shocked my system.

Suddenly freezing in the air-conditioned room, I pulled together my clothes and got dressed. I considered running away, but the thought of it chilled me, like a thief or a whore stealing away in the night.

Berating myself for not bringing a cardigan, I stepped through the glass door and onto the massive patio. The breeze was ribbon soft and smelled fresh, faintly of Mexican honeysuckle. I took a deep, bracing breath and leaned over the railing to gaze at the graceful sea.

I had never met anyone like the Frenchman. The moment I had laid eyes on him, I'd known something was inextricably compelling about him. I was in over my head. Sinclair was older, coupled off, and the head of an obviously successful company. But there was something else below all of it that called out to me. It might have been naïve of me, but I believed him when he said he hadn't cheated on his partner before. It didn't make the situation any better or worse, but maybe it was something.

"Have you been to Mexico before?"

I closed my eyes and didn't turn around to face him, but I could picture him leaning against the doorjamb with his arms crossed, protected and casual.

"No." My voice was quiet, but I had no doubt he could hear me. "I've lived in Europe all my life."

We lapsed into silence. I didn't think either of us really knew what to say, and it made me feel better to know that the sophisticated Frenchman was at a loss too.

"Look at me," he said softly. When I didn't, he repeated himself firmly, ordering me this time.

I turned around, and he stood exactly as I had imagined, propped against the doorframe with the light from inside silhouetting his mouthwatering physique. He looked cool and unruffled despite our almost lovemaking, but something in his silence was as vulnerable as me.

"Stay."

It wasn't a question or a plea, but I knew how badly he wanted me to stay because I felt the same inexplicable need.

I shrugged helplessly. "I don't know how to do this. I've never had a holiday affair or sex with a stranger, let alone someone in a relationship. I'd probably just screw it up and say something too intimate or do something to cross the boundaries."

"Try it," he coaxed, stepping forward into the moonlight.

His beauty caught me like a sucker punch to the gut. I braced on the railing to steady my resolve.

I couldn't find the words to refuse him, though. I knew that if I opened my mouth, I would say yes to this man, this man with the electric blue eyes and the ability to turn me into live nerve endings with only a look. So I smiled at him with my lips closed and my eyes downcast as I moved, carefully in a wide arc, away from him and back into the suite.

He didn't follow me as I crossed the palatial room to the front door, but when I turned around, unable to help myself as I opened the door to leave, he was standing in the darkness just outside the door, watching me with an impassive expression but for the telltale tightness in his jaw. Quickly, I stepped out of the room and closed the door behind me.

Only once I was in the elevator did I close my eyes, bang my head against the wall, and moan.

Chapter Four

I HADN'T SLEPT WELL. HOURS AFTER I RETURNED TO MY ROOM, I TOSSED AND turned, tangled in my sheets, wishing they were Sinclair's sinewy limbs. Finally, around six thirty in the morning, I threw the covers off and dragged myself out of bed. I spent the morning creeping around the resort, swimming in the ocean instead of the pool, walking down the beach past other resorts so that if, by chance, he happened to be looking for me, it would be nearly impossible to find me.

When the sun began to blister in the midday sky, I retreated to my room for a siesta instead of finding a shady spot beneath a palapa on the sand. I woke up restless around four o'clock, too eager to catch the last of the sun's rays to continue my childish hiding. I was in Mexico to relax, and I wasn't going to let some inconsequential, albeit extremely gorgeous man, ruin it.

As I assembled my beach bag, I dialed the one person who could help me make sense of something like this.

"Cosima," I gushed when she answered the phone in her lilting accent. My youngest sister was the only woman on the planet who sounded just as gorgeous as she looked.

"*Bambina*, I miss you too much." The sound of city life interrupted her speech, and I could imagine her floating down the streets of New York on her way to a photo shoot. "I cannot wait for you to get here. How is Mexico? Any hot men come up to you on the beach?"

I blushed even though she couldn't see me.

She laughed delightedly at my pause, clapping in the background. "Oh, tell me everything. And I mean everything. People always skip the best parts without realizing it. Is he unbearably handsome?"

"Oh God, Cosi, he is the most beautiful man I've ever met." I sighed and flopped on the bed in my bathing suit and cover-up.

"Oh, don't let Sebastian hear that," she whispered, referring to our good-naturedly arrogant brother, her twin, who took his good looks very seriously.

I laughed but was too distracted with the thought of Sinclair to really mean it.

"Wow, he must be something," she murmured, picking up on my emotional state. "When did you meet him?"

"Just yesterday," I said, still incredulous that all of this could have happened in only one day of knowing someone.

I stood from the bed and grabbed my oversized bag, propping my sunglasses on my head as I left the room. "Listen, have you ever had a holiday affair?"

My little sister, only twenty-two and already light years ahead of me in the romance department, laughed her throaty chuckle. "Oh, Gigi, you surprise me! I highly recommend it."

I bit my lip as I walked down the four flights of stairs to the lobby. "Have you..." I hesitated. "Have you been with a committed man?"

She paused, and I could almost hear the cogs whirring in her head. "You mean like a married man?"

"Not exactly. Someone with a girlfriend, though, a long-term one."

"Hmm." She thought for a few moments, but it felt like hours before she finally said, " Never a married man. I demand a certain level of attention, and married men just can't provide that."

I smiled as she had intended, but I knew it was more than that. Cosima was one of the most honest people I knew; it would have been impossible for her to live a lie like that.

"But I have cheated with a man before. I didn't know until the deed was done, but I also tried to avoid him after that. As impossible a feat as it was..." She clucked her tongue, a habit she had inherited from our mother. "Why do you ask, *bambina*?"

"The man, he has a girlfriend back home." I smiled at one of the Mexican bartenders as I claimed a lounge chair and shed my cover-up.

It was a beautiful day with clear blue skies, and I settled down to get some sun on my pale limbs. I closed my eyes and allowed my sister's voice to counsel me, soothing me from my frenzied state of the night before.

"Listen, Gigi, normally I would say stay away from an attached man, especially for you. Given your lack of experience, I would urge you to think carefully about how far you are willing to go with a man you hardly know in a foreign land. But, at the same time, I think this could be good for you to have some fun with a handsome man. It won't be serious, and you won't get hurt. As far as the girlfriend is concerned..." Her voice was strained, her Italian accent much thicker, and I frowned with worry over her change in tone. "If he wants to cheat on her, then he will."

It wasn't exactly reassuring advice, but it was true, and I could always count on her for that. I took a deep breath and felt the sun soak into my skin like a balm.

"So you think I should do it? Have a holiday affair?"

"Gigi, from the sounds of him, I think you'd be crazy not to."

I smiled into the phone and accepted the acute pang of homesickness that pinged in my chest. It had been thirteen months since I last saw my sister, and before that, eighteen months since I had visited with any other member of my family. I was nervous about moving to a new city to rejoin my entire family after over five years of being separated from them, but hearing the familiar strains of Cosima's liquid voice reminded me why I was so desperate to see them.

"I love you," I said.

My little sister laughed loudly, no doubt stopping people on the street with the sight of her joy. "And I you, always."

I hung up feeling lighter than I had in a long time, and coupled with a brisk half an hour swim in the cool waters of the pool, I was happy and pleasantly lethargic when I emerged from the water to bask once again in the sun.

"Can I get you a drink, *señorita*?" a sweet-faced man asked.

"She'll have a sex on the beach," a strange voice answered for me.

I turned to my left to see a man stretched out on the lounge chair one over from me. His skin was the color of mahogany, and it rippled across his gym-toned body. He wore small black briefs and nothing else. I blushed and looked away quickly. The waiter nodded and left to place our orders.

"What if I don't drink?" I asked with soft reproach.

"Ah, but I am usually a very good judge of character." He swung into a seated position and leaned forward to offer me his hand. "Stefan Kilos."

I took his smooth palm in mine and smiled into his beautiful face. "Elle Moore."

He had startling green eyes in such a dark face, and his thick coffee-colored hair fell to his broad shoulders in glossy waves. I wondered briefly if he was gay, considering how beautifully maintained he was, but one flash of those perfect, pearly white teeth dissuaded me.

"You are the artist, yes?" He moved his lounge chair closer. "I saw your exhibit in Paris last month. In fact, I purchased one of your pieces, *Le Solitaire de Nuit*."

"You're kidding?"

It still astonished me that my art was becoming well-known, particularly in France. My mentor at *L'École des Beaux-Arts* had thought me crazy for moving out of the country just as my career was gaining momentum. I agreed with her, and it was only one of the many reasons I was nervous about New York.

"No." He shook his head and captured one of my hands in his. It was an overly familiar gesture, but it was something one of the twins would have done, and I beamed back at him. "I absolutely love it. It hangs in my bedroom at home in Greece. The light reflecting off the dome of Sacré-Cœur is masterfully done. I really am a big fan."

Pleasure unfurled in my stomach and sluiced through my veins like a drug. This wasn't the first time someone had approached me about my work, but it was the first time outside of France, and it gave me a flicker of hope for my artistic future in America. I allowed him to keep my hand and beamed into his face as I launched into my favorite kind of talk: the art world.

Thirty minutes and three sex on the beach cocktails later, a sharp prickle of foreboding tickled the base of my spine. I rolled my shoulders to rid myself of the teeth-gritting apprehension, but it remained for the next five minutes as Stefan made me howl with laughter over the antics of a mutual friend.

"Stop," I gasped, wiping the tears rolling down my cheeks. "Really, Stefan, you have to stop, or I'll die."

"Well, we can't have that." He chuckled then frowned at something over my shoulder, squinting into the high sun to discern the intruder. "Can I help you?"

"No." I closed my eyes briefly at the sound of Sinclair's smooth French-minted tone. "But I believe Elle can."

Stefan frowned, catching my weariness and Sinclair's obvious animosity. "I'm not sure if she can. We were just in the middle of sharing a drink, actually."

"One of many, it appears," he countered coolly.

I flushed at the collection of glasses on the plastic side table even though I was more than capable of holding my liquor.

"Listen." Stefan was getting irritated now, though he only rested back on his hands, exposing the mighty breadth of his chest like a gorilla sizing up his competition. "I don't know who you think you are—"

"Stop it," I said as I stood to face Sinclair.

I blinked hard at the sight of him. Though it had only been a few hours since I last saw him, his astonishing beauty took my breath away. He wore a white linen shirt and light gray swim shorts that exposed his muscular calves, and a pair of Ray-Ban aviators were propped casually in his mane of deep red-brown hair.

"Stop it," I repeated. "Sinclair, stop being such a bruiser."

"A bruiser?" His eyebrows rose almost comically into his hairline.

"Yes." I nodded adamantly. "A bruiser. I was having a delightful time with Stefan before you barged in, and I would like to return to it."

He stared at me for a moment with dangerously still blue eyes before directing his gaze to Stefan. "I think it best that you leave."

Stefan ran a hand down my arm, but it was more friendly than sexual, and I knew he only meant to reassure me. He would stay if I wanted him to and maybe even go so far as to tell Sinclair off. After half an hour of conversation, I had the distinct feeling that I had made a friend.

"You know my room number," he said softly in a way that conveyed undeniable intimacy, and I knew it was for Sinclair's sake. "Call me if you want to get a drink."

I nodded as he collected his things and left with a final wink even though I didn't really want to be alone with Sinclair. Cosima's advice had given me a new lease on the idea of a holiday affair, but I still wasn't sure if I could face sex without intimacy. Even with a man like Sinclair.

When I remained facing away from him for a few moments, and he didn't speak, I wondered if he had left. But two knuckles drew delicate lines down the bare skin of my back, and a second later, his front pressed into me. One hand pressed against my hip, pushing us gently together, and he placed a heartbreaking kiss where my neck met my shoulder.

"I've made a decision." I could feel him hard already against the small of my back, and a violent shudder wracked my frame. "Would you like to know what it is?"

His hand moved from my hip up over the curve of my waist between my breasts to my neck, where he wrapped his fingers one by one over my throat to tip it back for better access to his lips.

"Yes." I was too enraptured with him to be aware of my surroundings, but I was vaguely conscious of the fact that we stood in public beside a very crowded pool. When I tried to pull away, his hand tightened slightly around my neck.

"I've decided we are going to have an affair." He ran his nose up the side of my neck and gently nipped at my ear. "I know you want me, Elle; I can feel it in your lush body. I know you're scared that I'll ruin you for other men." His other hand made its way around my back and down over my rump to tickle the skin of my inner thigh. "It will be worth it."

Oh, I didn't doubt it. I was already damp with arousal and trembling with need. My mind was whirring with thoughts of his lean fingers on me, in me, how he would taste in my mouth and feel inside me.

"Do you believe me?" he crooned.

I nodded my head slightly and dropped it back against his shoulder. As I did so, I caught the eye of a tall, willowy woman walking by herself over to the bar. She was pretty, but it was the expression on her hard features that doused me like a bucket of ice water. Condemnation. Of course, she couldn't have known anything about our situation, who Sinclair or I was, but her look of disgust still quieted my lust, and I shoved away from Sinclair abruptly.

He stared at me expectantly as I swirled to face him, and when I glared, he lifted his palms in surrender. I almost laughed.

"I know the sex will be great," I said, surprised by my own boldness. He rewarded me with a slight smile. "But I told you last night, I just don't think I'm comfortable sleeping with someone I know nothing about."

He tucked his hands in his pockets and sighed heavily. "What do you want to know?"

I had so many questions that it took me a moment to make sense of my thoughts. I gestured for him to take the seat next to mine, and when he hesitated, I narrowed my eyes. With an exasperated shake of his head, he sat down, bracing his forearms on his knees so that he was still too close for me to think clearly.

"I don't need to know the specifics. In fact, I don't even want to." His eyebrows arched incredulously, but I ignored him. "I want you too badly to care if I know your last name or where you live. But I feel uncomfortable. Like if I ask you the wrong question, you'll be angry with me."

"You want boundaries," he confirmed, his eyes suddenly effervescent with intrigue. "Rules."

I nodded even though the look in his eyes gave me pause. "Exactly."

His slight smile was wicked, his voice like smoke. "Rules I can do. Number one: no personal specifics such as full names, location, family, etc. As we are both here for work, I think some discussion on the matter is acceptable."

I sat down across from him with a sigh. "So we can talk about business and sex?"

At my less than enthusiastic tone, he grinned. "Trust me, both are infinitely interesting. Number two: if we do this, we do it my way." Automatically, I frowned, but he placed one hand on my knee, lightly brushing the tender skin on the inside of my leg until I was soothed. "You belong to me for the next six days."

My mind protested loudly at such a possessive statement, but my body reacted positively, warming and liquefying until I was as pliant as warm dough.

"Before you argue with me, think about the practicalities." His fingers were moving softly, teasingly over the inside of my trembling thighs. "You don't have someone else in mind for a holiday affair, do you? No, I didn't think so. As you said, you don't have much experience with these things. But you're eager to learn, aren't you, Elle?"

I was too focused on his fingers—now at the apex of my thighs, lingering over my bikini-clad core—to answer. We were tucked into a reasonably unpopulated corner of the pool, and I was grateful for the rock formation concealing us from most of the swimmers.

"It turns you on," Sinclair continued in velvet tones, "to have me touch you here." His fingers slipped under the elastic of my bathing suit, and he hummed at finding me wet. "When anyone could walk by and catch us."

I shook my head, but I wasn't fooling anyone. My knees quivered slightly as the pad of his thumb feathered lightly over my clit.

"Be mine for the week, Elle. Let me show you how many ways I can make you come."

Without warning, two fingers plunged into my wet core, and I moaned involuntarily. He shifted slightly to block the view of me from across the pool and tilted his fingers to find my sweet spot while his thumb drew tight circles on my clit.

My orgasm descended quickly, a short, sharp burst of exquisite pleasure radiating from beneath Sinclair's skilled fingers. My knees quaked, and I let out a soft cry before slumping forward. He caught me on his shoulder and ran his free hand down my back soothingly. To anyone watching, we probably looked like a sweet couple embracing. No one could see his hand skillfully bringing me down from my high with delicate finesse. My nose was at his warm throat, and his scent, coupled with my post-orgasm state, made me dizzy.

After a minute or two, he gently pulled his hand away from between my thighs and righted me. I stared at him with drowsy half-lidded eyes as he brought his fingers to his mouth and sucked. A tremor sparked at the base of my spine, and I shivered.

"You taste like honey," he murmured. His eyes burned so bright a blue that I blinked.

I knew I should say something, but my mind was dumb with bliss, and when I opened my mouth, all I could find was, "Thank you."

His eyes widened, and one corner of his mouth rose in a smirk. "You are most welcome, Elle."

I laughed. "I'm sorry, I just don't normally do things like this. Not to mention, I've never orgasmed so quickly in my life, I think I'm a bit stupefied."

I closed my legs and reached for my cover-up. It was easier to concentrate when I was covered.

"But you'd like to, wouldn't you?" he asked darkly.

I licked my lips nervously and watched his eyes map the path of my tongue. My body was still soft and warm from coming, and while I couldn't believe he had just skillfully brought me to climax beside a very public pool, or that I had allowed it, there was no denying that it had been the most exciting experience of my life. *It was only a week*, I reminded myself, and nothing irrevocable could happen in such a short time.

"Yes."

He nodded, not surprised this time by my acquiescence. "Don't play with me. I need you to mean it."

"I do." I stared at him with earnest eyes and watched as his stern features relaxed into a slightly boyish grin.

"Good. Now, I'd like you to accompany me to a business party I have to attend tonight."

"Oh." I hadn't expected that.

Detecting my disappointment, he widened his grin. "Trust me, Elle, I would love nothing more than to spend the rest of the day in bed with you, but duty calls. I promise to make the wait up to you."

I blushed, embarrassed that he had discovered my eagerness, but his smoky laugh made me smile too.

"I have some work to do, and I realize I interrupted your sunbathing. I'll meet you in the lobby at eight." It wasn't really a question, but he waited for me to nod before he stood to leave.

He hesitated for a moment before leaning down to brush a swift kiss to my cheek. "Until then, siren."

I sat there after he left, stunned by the turn my vacation had taken. Brenna had sent me to Mexico to relax, the only person who knew why I was so hastily leaving my beloved Paris, and here I was, more stimulated than I had ever been in my life. With a large sigh, I flopped back against the chaise lounge and closed my eyes. I knew next to nothing about the devastatingly handsome Frenchman, but already, I was hooked.

Chapter Five

THE HOME OF SANTIAGO HERRERA WAS THE KIND OF PLACE I HAD ONLY EVER seen in movies about drug cartels. It was a low sprawling building made of butter yellow stucco and roofed with the traditional red tiles, but that was where the classic Spanish style ended. The interior was modern-day opulence. The kitchen, which I had accidentally wandered into after getting lost on the way back to the reception from the bathroom, was larger than most restaurants, and the bathroom boasted a talking toilet. We had been at the party for two hours, and Candy had assured me I'd only seen one-quarter of the massive home. I found it all a little bit off-putting; the modernity was something out of a science fiction book, and by the time I found Sinclair, I was a little flustered.

It was hard to believe the movie star handsome man sitting at the bar was waiting for me. Sinclair wore light gray trousers and a deep blue dress shirt with a cobalt blue tie that matched his eyes. He had discarded his jacket at the door even though most of the men at the party were dressed more formally in suit jackets and tails. I preferred his look and so too, it seemed, did the slinky brunette leaning against the bar so close to him. He seemed unperturbed by her attention, but his expression was only politely interested, and he turned his head briefly to check the hallway leading back from the washrooms. I smiled, and as if he had sensed it, he froze, his glass suspended between his lips and the bar. I held my breath as he slowly turned his head, unerringly finding me across the large, crowded floor. I could feel his eyes scorch a path of fire across my body, and when his gaze finally met mine, it flared with desire.

I had worried the whole afternoon about what I should wear to a Mexican soiree, but the minute I saw Sinclair's reaction to the dress, I knew I had chosen well. The gossamer-thin fabric draped itself elegantly across my shoulders and crossed over my breasts, exposing a deep slice of plump cleavage. The soft lavender color suited my sun-kissed skin and auburn hair, which I had left simple, just curling softly down my back.

Sinclair strode forward without noticing the sour expression on the face of the now lonely brunette at the bar and brushed a chaste kiss against my cheek. "Have I mentioned yet that you look absolutely lovely, Elle?"

"So do you," I murmured after dragging in a deep lungful of his leathery scent.

His smile was small, his conservatism back in place after the more playful man I had seen by the pool that afternoon. "Thank you. I was worried you had run away when you didn't come back straight away."

"I got lost," I explained with a small laugh. "I don't have the best sense of direction, and this is a big house."

"Of course," he allowed smoothly, his hand on the small of my back as he moved us out of the way of foot traffic and into a more private corner of the room. "I should have texted you the floor plans."

I looked over at him sharply to see if he was teasing. "Would you have?"

His expression was practically inscrutable, but I was beginning to know where to look for telling signs of emotion in his sharply cut jaw and expressive brows. I was about to tease him when someone called his name from across the floor and started over to us.

My smile slipped slightly, but Sinclair pressed his palm to the small of my spine and leaned in to whisper, "Poor girl, you were hoping for a more exciting evening, weren't you?"

"This is delightful, Sinclair, really." I gestured to the opulent surroundings and the glittering Mexican magnates littering the hall like discarded jewels. "I've never been to an event like this before."

"I wish I could say the same." His hand was warm on my hip as he tucked me into his side, but his smile was gone, replaced with his normal implacable mask as the guest arrived at our side. "Santiago, it's good to see you again."

Santiago Herrera was younger than I had imagined, with thick black hair slicked back from his broad forehead to reveal large obsidian eyes. He wore a burgundy dinner jacket and shoes with tassels. Despite his obscene wealth, something was amazingly approachable about his demeanor.

"And the same to you, my friend." He took Sinclair's hand and turned immediately to me. "Please, introduce me to your lovely date. It's not often I have the pleasure of meeting a beautiful redhead."

"It's not often I have the pleasure of meeting a man brave enough to wear a velvet dinner jacket," I teased, surprised by my boldness. It must have had something to do with being next to Sinclair, who made me feel tingly with female power.

He guffawed, a strange chortle of amusement that made me giggle. "My last wife complained about my fashion sense." He flattened the lapels of his jacket carefully. "I divorced her over this jacket."

I looked up at Sinclair to validate the outrageous claim, but he was staring at me with a slight frown between his chestnut brows as if we were discussing complex physics.

"Well, I think you look dashing," I asserted.

Santiago beamed. "Tell me you speak Spanish, and you will be my next wife."

"Don't make promises you can't keep," I scolded lightly and watched him laugh again.

This time, Sinclair smiled slightly too, and that small expression of humor warmed me more than a room full of laughter. I wondered what had made Sinclair so reserved, but it was undoubtedly part of his appeal too. Every insight into his carefully concealed mind and spirit felt like a major victory.

"I'm sorry, Iago, not only is Elle French, but she's unavailable to you," Sinclair said smoothly, his hand still lightly resting on the swell of my hip.

I opened my mouth to correct him about my nationality before I remembered the rules. No personal details. And truth be told, being French and everything that represented—refined, contained, and witty—was preferable to me than the gritty, poverty-stricken image my Italian upbringing invoked.

"What a waste." The Mexican magnate spoke in flawless English, only slightly spiced with an accent. "You had the drop on me, though, Sinclair. It's hardly a fair playing field when you are French as well."

"American," he corrected with narrowed eyes, all amusement gone.

Santiago pursed his lips but nodded, obviously understanding the gravity of his tone. What was so wrong with being French?

"I saw Dylan Hernandez by the buffet. We should discuss business now rather than later so that you can enjoy your party," Sinclair said.

The feel of his hand smoothing down my back distracted me. With that simple touch, the desire that had lain tamely at the base of my belly all night flared to life.

"Of course." Santiago squinted at us, his lips still pursed, but finally, he nodded. "We'll go up to my study. Katarina can hold down the fort while I'm gone. You should meet her, Elle; her beauty is your only competition tonight." His grin flashed again. "She is my sister."

"Good idea. Kat will no doubt be on the patio on a clear night like this. She is an astronomer. You'll like her. But first," Sinclair turned to me, his gaze strangely intimate, "I was telling Elle about your remarkable collection of Frida Kahlo's work."

"Kat will show her," he said, with a dismissive wave of his hand as if such a collection was nothing to brag about.

Considering she was a longtime idol of mine, I couldn't believe that I had the opportunity to view her work outside of a museum. Sinclair noted my smile and matched it with a small one of his own.

"I thought you might enjoy that."

I nodded, my tongue tied with anticipation.

"If you'll excuse us for a minute, Iago, I will just show Elle the powder room, and then I'll meet you in the office."

I frowned slightly as I had just returned from the restroom, but his fingers stroked the skin at the base of my neck tantalizingly, and I forgot to protest.

"Of course." Santiago nodded and leaned forward to grasp my hands. "I wish Sinclair always visited me with such a beautiful companion. He never mixes business and pleasure. Such an awful separation, don't you think?"

"I'm not so sure. He hasn't been divorced three times," I joked.

He laughed and squeezed my hands. "Touché." After brushing a kiss against my cheek, he stepped back and looked at Sinclair. "Five minutes?"

"Better make it ten."

Santiago's thick brows raised, but he acquiesced with a shrug before turning away.

As soon as he did so, I turned fully to Sinclair with my own arched brow. "The powder room?"

Amusement and something darker sparked in his eyes. "Yes. You are bored with this party, and I'm sorry for it. Let me try to ease some of the tedium. Come."

With sure feet, he led me out of the main hall and through twisting, turning corridors. I had no idea how he could have known where he was going in such a maze.

"You made Iago laugh within thirty seconds of knowing him," Sinclair said, almost to himself. "I haven't seen him open up to a stranger like that in years."

I shrugged. "He seemed very friendly."

"Oh, he is. But he doesn't enjoy life much anymore." At my searching look, he explained, his hand warm in mine as he led me through the house. "His brother was killed two years ago, gang violence in Mexico City. He moved himself and Kat here soon after."

I felt sympathy pang in my stomach and shrugged off the brief thought of life without one of my siblings. Even my eldest sister, Elena, whom I had never been particularly close to, was vital to me.

We had stopped in the middle of a narrow room fronted in glass paneling, standing beside an open door in the gently rushing breeze. There was barely an inch separating our bodies, but Sinclair carefully maintained the distance.

"I didn't mean to make you frown," Sinclair said. "Santiago is a very rich man, with many things to take his mind off it."

Money couldn't erase heartache, I wanted to say but didn't. I had the feeling Sinclair would have argued with me, and I was too curious about why he had brought me to this room to fight with him.

"Enough of that," he said, somehow sensing the change of direction in my thoughts. "I have something much more enticing in mind at the moment. We only have a few minutes, so do as I say." He looked at me sternly, but I could tell he was amused and aroused. "Stand against the wall."

My belly was already fluttering with anticipation, and I hastened to do as he asked.

"Spread your legs and clasp your hands behind your back." His voice was like a physical caress. Instantly, I moved to do as he bid me. "Don't move."

He admired me for a moment.

"You really are the sexiest woman, Elle." Swiftly, he moved to stand in front of me, but frustratingly, he didn't touch me. "I've been hard all night thinking about what you are going to let me do to this sinful body of yours."

My nipples beaded against the thin material of my dress, and I arched forward slightly, willing him to notice. His lips twitched in acknowledgment, but he ignored them.

"Have you been thinking about it too?"

I nodded, wishing my legs were together so I could alleviate the throbbing in my core.

"What did you imagine me doing?" Finally, he touched me. He ran a finger down my chest between my breasts. "Touching you here?"

Lazily, he circled one breast with his finger, narrowing in closer and closer to my furled peak. My chest felt heavy with sensation, and even though he had only just started caressing me, I was panting. I jolted when his fingers found both aching nipples and pinched. The flare of painful pleasure made me moan. Sinclair shifted on his feet uncomfortably, and I was grateful to find evidence of his own arousal.

"Or maybe here?" he murmured, running one hand up the inside of my left leg. His fingertips trailed like fire up my sensitive skin, and I whimpered slightly, begging him to touch me properly.

Heeding my silent plea, he crouched to his knees before me and lifted the front of my skirt to gaze at my lace-covered sex. I trembled when he pressed an open-mouthed kiss to the skin just to the left of my center.

"We were interrupted last time." His hot breath fanned over me, making me shiver. "I was going to wait until we got back to the resort, but I have to taste you."

His mouth closed over my clit through the flimsy cloth and suckled. I gasped and pressed my hands against the wall to support my shaking knees. Pulling aside my panties, he slicked his fingers across my wet flesh. He groaned against me, heightening the sensation of his tongue against my sensitive nub.

"You want this badly, don't you?" he questioned, sitting back on his haunches to look at me. "You want to give yourself up to me."

"Yes," I breathed, nudging my hips against the fingers circling my entrance. "Please."

I felt no embarrassment, only knee-weakening lust. At that moment, I would have done anything for the orgasm looming large in the distance.

He smiled triumphantly and lowered his head to me, once again finding my clit, but this time without the barrier of lace between us. His tongue laved at my bundle of nerves as two fingers entered me, twisting to reach my sweet spot. I was so incoherent with lust that it took me a moment to realize that he was pushing something inside me other than his fingers. I looked down abruptly, but his dark head blocked my view.

"Trust me," he ordered hoarsely as a small vibrator nestled inside me.

My legs tensed as I hesitated—I had never played with sex toys before —but his ministrations increased, the pace of his fingers devastating against my swollen flesh. The moment I relaxed, the device inside me switched on, buzzing softly within me. I cried out loudly as my orgasm came crashing down, and Sinclair reared up to swallow my loud cries, his fingers still strumming my clit. I had never tasted myself before, but I found it surprisingly erotic, and when he pulled away, I protested weakly before laying my head against his solid chest.

I squeezed my eyes against the overwhelming sensation, and I was grateful for Sinclair's large body holding me upright when he turned the toy off, and my legs turned to noodles. My love life with Mark had never been anything close to as mind-blowing as this, and Sinclair and I hadn't even had sex yet.

"Best. Party. I've. Ever. Been. To," I said between shallow breaths as I recovered.

Sinclair's dark chuckle ruffled my hair, and I could feel his solid length pressed to my hip. "I have to agree with you."

"I've never…" I hid my face against his chest, and murmured, "I've never done that before."

"Which part?" he asked dryly. "Had a tryst at a party? A man kiss you here?" His fingers gently swept over the curls between my thighs. "An orgasm?"

"All of the above," I whispered.

Gently, he pulled my face away from him and took my flaming cheeks between his palms. His blue eyes were darkly serious. "You are beautiful. I didn't realize how inexperienced you are."

It was a vague probe into the state of my virginity, I knew. I wondered if it would matter to him or if it would make him change his mind. I didn't take the bait.

"Oh." I squeezed his arousal in my hand, causing him to hiss loudly. "Do I have time to take care of this?"

He raised a brow, and I bit the inside of my cheek, wondering if I was being too bold, but he smiled reassuringly and smoothed my hair in a surprisingly tender gesture that seemed so at odds with the in-command man of minutes before.

"Unfortunately, our ten minutes are up; though, I'm sorely tempted to forget business and whisk you back to my hotel room right now."

I grinned and interlocked my hands behind his neck, pushing up against his erection. "Why don't you?"

His eyes were electric with suppressed desire.

"Another thirty minutes tops, and we will leave." He pulled his phone out to check the time and grimaced. "We've taken too long already." Swiftly, he leaned down to readjust my underwear and smooth the skirt of my dress. "Come on."

"But, um." The sex toy was still inside me. "Aren't you forgetting about, erm, something?"

One eyebrow rose coolly. "I don't believe so."

Oh, okay.

So he wanted me to walk around the party with a sex toy inside me?

I thought about arguing with him, but his aloof, almost daring expression and my warm glow dissuaded me.

"Okay, we should hurry to your meeting," I said, taking his hand to lead him out the door.

He might have chuckled, but as soon as I opened the door, the sounds of the party reanimated. After a minute of indecision at an oddly shaped corridor, he took the lead from me, gently guiding me to the kitchen where he thought we might find Katarina.

"I'll be in the room next to the library if you need me," he said as we paused to the side of the kitchen doors, out of the path of the hustling wait-staff. At my blank look, his lips twitched. "Kat will know the way."

I nodded, but the idea of being without Sinclair in the twisty-turvy house was unpleasant. Unlike my siblings, I had never been particularly good with large groups of people, and outside art showings and gallery openings, I rarely went to parties.

"You'll be fine," he assured me, reading my thoughts. "You and Kat will get along brilliantly. Think of me when I'm gone?"

There was a devastating twinkle in his eye as if he knew something I didn't. I narrowed my eyes at him suspiciously, but he only shrugged innocently and put his hands in his pockets. When he turned to leave, he started to whistle. I watched him move through the crowded room with the grace and power of a wild cat, his broad shoulders straight and his long legs eating up the space. Women turned to watch him, but he remained oblivious, and I knew few would approach him. His carefully controlled expression, almost cruel due to his hard features, would discourage even the most ballsy women.

With a sigh, I turned away from him. Sinclair was the sexiest man I had ever met, the kind of man who only inhabited women's darkest fantasies and Hollywood movies, yet he was here with me. It was enough to make any girl feel like a million dollars. Of course, my recent orgasm didn't hurt either.

Chapter Six

Santiago's collection of art was staggeringly comprehensive and outrageously expensive. A room three times the size of my studio apartment in Paris was dedicated to the works of renowned Mexican painters like Diego Rivera and Frida Kahlo, but it also paid tribute to local artists and some contemporary American talents such as Julie Combal.

"I know I'm in the minority, but I find Kahlo's drawings almost more haunting than her paintings," I murmured as I took in her 1926 sketch *Accident*, which depicted the artist bound in a body cast besieged by images of the car accident that had left her with multiple broken bones and lifelong pain.

"Honestly?" Katarina's thicker accent made all her words run together like a song. "I prefer the American style."

I smiled at her, once again struck by her likeness to Cosima. Though Katarina was not particularly attractive, she shared the same effervescent spirit that kept me smiling and laughing.

"My brother is much more interested in the arts than I am." She shrugged. "I find it hard to understand the beauty in living things. Planets are much easier."

We moved along to another image, this one a satirical reimagining of a Del Monte ad by Minerva Cuevas, a contemporary Mexican artist.

Kat gave me a sidelong look. "I think we have been friends long enough now—what has it been, fifteen minutes?—for me to ask you about Sinclair."

"What about him?"

She laughed at my coyness and shrugged. "If you don't want to discuss him, I understand. But as I understand it, you are here alone. Sometimes it's just nice to talk to a fellow woman about a boy, no?"

So true. I had been itching to call Cosima all day, but there was no way she could really understand the magnitude of my holiday affair without knowing anything about the gorgeous, composed man who was Sinclair. Kat was a gift, really, given to me by the man himself. I wondered if he had thought about just that when he paired us together.

"We met on the plane coming down." I flushed, remembering it. "Planes make me nervous, to say the least, and I was making a fool of myself. Sinclair was nice enough to keep misery company."

She looked me up and down clinically with a critical eye that only women possess. "I would say he was only too happy to help."

"Trust me, it's the makeup." I laughed.

Katarina pursed her lips, a habit that she and her brother shared. "Beautiful and bashful. I can see the appeal."

"Oh, stop embarrassing her, Kat." Cage Tracy's familiar French melody had me turning around to face him.

He looked dashing in a white silk shirt that contrasted with his developing tan and impenetrable black hair, but it was his smile that made him so disarming, and I could tell from Katarina's startled little gasp that she thought so too. The murmur of voices around us spiked slightly at his arrival, but he was still relatively obscure enough that no one bothered him for autographs. I realized it was his ungodly beauty that drew their attention more than his fame.

Cage gave me a warm kiss on the cheek. "Though she does have a point. You look absolutely edible tonight, Elle."

I swatted his compliment out of the air, but the feel of the toy between my legs was a constant reminder of just how desirable Sinclair found me. "You are such a tease."

"Me?" He feigned horror. "How dare you? Kat, vouch for my character, please."

"I certainly will. Cage only ever acts like a bad boy if someone leads him astray, isn't that right?"

I looked over my shoulder as the statuesque blonde who had spoken came up beside Cage and took his arm. She was very beautiful but in a sharp, almost menacing way like something from a Grimm fairy tale. Her blond hair was so pale it was almost white, and her frosty eyes found mine instantly, regarding me with cool reserve.

"You must be Elle." She presented her hand to me as if it were a gift.

I was usually pretty easygoing with people, but something about the studied haughtier of this woman set my teeth on edge. I didn't take her hand, but I did smile at her, thinly. "I must be."

Cage guffawed, despite her withering look his way. "And this is Margot Silver, Sinclair's executive assistant."

She looked far too glamorous to be someone's assistant, but I let that slide. Katarina cast a furrowed glance at Margot's slim arm resting possessively on Cage.

"Margot, maybe you would like to look at Diego Rivera's works with me while we get to know each other better?" I asked, my voice carefully devoid of anything but sugar sweetness.

Her pale eyes widened slightly, but she bared her teeth in a semblance of a smile. "Of course."

I winked at Katarina as we walked away, and Cage turned to regale her with a funny story. She seemed surprised but quickly blushed and mouthed, "Thank you," over his shoulder. I didn't know what chance the sweet girl had with the rock star, but I was willing to do my part to foster the flames.

"So, Margot." I smiled demurely at her as we came to a stop out of hearing distance from the others. "Why don't you say what you have to say?"

Her large eyes widened, and my candor exposed a moment of vulnerability. It took her a second to bare her fangs. "Sinclair has a long-term partner."

She waited for me to react, but I only blinked at her and crossed my arms. If she had expected Sinclair to lie to me, then she didn't know him as well as she thought.

"Listen." She sighed sharply and adjusted her stance on her ridiculously high and absurdly lovely heels. "Despite what you may think, I'm not warning you off to be a bitch. I'm doing it because Sinclair, for all his coolness, is still a man, and a beautiful woman is any man's weakness. He's had a rough life, and the past few years have been good to him, so he doesn't need some random strumpet messing that up for him."

Okay, even though I objected to her use of the word strumpet, I had to admire her mettle and loyalty. Sinclair deserved people like this in his life, and even though Margot Silver was far too judgmental and cold for me to genuinely like, I tipped my hat to her.

"I appreciate that." I dropped my defensive pose and ran a hand through my hair in frustration. "But I have no designs on Sinclair other than as a friend. Not that it's any of your business."

"A friend?" She snorted. "Sure."

Fair enough.

"Our friendship will end when the vacation does," I amended.

Margot stared at me for a long minute, seemingly taking note of everything from the color of my hair to the shape of my fingernails. "See that it does. Under other circumstances, we could have been friends."

I inclined my head even though I didn't really share her sentiments. It wasn't her fault, I thought as she walked away, that she had touched on those icky feelings within me, on the idea that I was being a whore and a home wrecker.

As I made my way back over to Cage and Katarina, I gasped. The egg inside me began to vibrate, jolting my dozing nerve endings with a burst of electricity.

"Are you okay, Elle?" Cage asked as I came to a sudden stop two feet away.

I nodded, my throat working past the moan in my throat. Surreptitiously, I searched the room for Sinclair, but he was nowhere to be found. How was he doing this?

"Did Margot put the fear of God into you?" Cage asked, hiding his smile behind his glass of whiskey. "She can be a fearsome woman."

"Evidently," I said dryly. "Thanks for the warning before I wandered off with her."

He laughed. "I had a feeling you knew what you were doing."

I smiled slightly and subtly rubbed my legs together, trying to ease the sensations at my core. The conservative side of me, the one that had always dominated, urged me to go to the bathroom and remove the toy while the other side, the one embraced by my more passionate twin siblings, delighted in the sensation of being teased unbeknownst to the crowd of people milling around the multi-million-dollar mansion. It was the cherry on top of an utterly decadent night. The only thing that would have made it complete was Sinclair.

As if summoned by my desire, a warm hand slid over my bare shoulder and down my back possessively. "Have you been thinking about me?" he whispered darkly in my ear as the vibrator ceased its motions.

Cage seemed taken aback by his friend's grin, but he recovered quickly with a wink at me. "It's a good thing you came when you did, Sin. I was just thinking about asking your date here to leave with me."

I rolled my eyes, but Sinclair remained unmoved, his voice cool. "I should have known you would find her tonight."

"In that dress? She's hard to miss."

I reached out to Kat, who had taken a step away from us, and lightly tugged her closer to me. "Katarina has been the most wonderful guide."

"Of course, she has." Cage squeezed her shoulder as a brother would. "Our Kat's a real gem."

She blushed, but Cage was too oblivious to notice how she reacted to him, and when I looked up at Sinclair to see if he noticed, his eyes were on mine, twinkling with mirth.

My mouth fell open when the vibrator started again, this time at a higher intensity. I wobbled slightly, and Sinclair smoothly tucked me under his arm.

"I think Elle has had too much to drink." I frowned at him as he spoke

—I had only finished two glasses of wine—but he looked down at me with unmasked desire, and I bit my lip. "I should be getting her home."

"How did the meeting go?" Cage asked as he leaned forward to double kiss me on each cheek in farewell.

"As can be expected. Santiago assures me the deal will go forward as planned."

I tuned them out in order to say goodbye to Kat, but when I tried to get out from under Sinclair's arm, he tightened his hold. He did stop the vibrator, though, and I was grateful when the thick fog of desire cleared slightly from my thoughts.

I shrugged at Kat helplessly, and she giggled.

"I've never seen him like this," she whispered in her lovely accent. "He is very interested in you, no?"

I shook my head. "We just met."

She waved my statement out of the air. "This is no problem. I just met you, and already, I know that we are friends."

I beamed at her. Yes, I had felt that instant connection as well, and I was sorry to be saying goodbye to her already.

"If you stay with him, I mean, after this vacation, then maybe I will see you again," she said, ignoring my look of doubt.

"Why don't you give me your email?" I suggested instead of hinging my hopes on something that would very likely never happen.

Kat grinned, and we exchanged information. Sinclair finished his conversation with Cage and patiently waited for me to hug her goodbye before tugging us away. Immediately, people converged on us to talk to Sinclair as we made our way from room to room and into the main reception hall. When the man walking swiftly beside me ignored a particularly adamant older gentleman, I frowned.

"Shouldn't you stay and talk to these people?"

He continued his brisk pace without looking at me. "No."

"Because you don't have time to be nice?"

"Exactly."

I assumed he had already said goodbye to Santiago, so I felt less guilty about leaving so hastily. But honestly, I was burning from the inside out because of the infernal toy, and now, with my hand in Sinclair's and the knowledge he was taking me to bed, that he simply couldn't wait, I was incoherent with lust.

I shivered as we stepped into the cool night air, and Sinclair took off his jacket without any hesitation to slip it onto my shoulders before he went to secure a car. The blazer smelled strongly of his musky, leathery scent, and I pressed my nose into the collar in order to get my fill. He caught me when he returned, but he only gave me a funny look as if he couldn't understand me. I shrugged and took his hand once more in mine. He tensed at first, but when I squeezed his large palm, he squeezed back.

I stared up at him as we waited for the car to come around. He was so dashing with the bright moonlight in his thick hair, burnishing his bladed nose and sharp cheekbones like a lacquered mask.

He sensed me staring at him and looked down at me with smoky eyes. We stared at each other, and my breath hitched as desire spiked down my spine straight to my sex. I'd never known a single look could spark an inferno of longing in my gut.

The chauffeured black car stopped in front of us, breaking the connection, and Sinclair helped me in before moving around to the other side. The moment we were settled and the car took off, the vibrator started again. I squirmed, but Sinclair stilled me with a firm hand on my knee.

We sat like that in silence for a few minutes while I struggled with the building sensations. Then, almost indiscernibly, his hand began to draw patterns on my knee, inching higher up my leg. I watched his tanned hand trace my paler skin and closed my eyes on a breathy sigh when he reached the junction of my thighs.

He hushed me as one finger pressed against my damp panties. "Did you enjoy the party, Elle?"

I nodded my head with my eyes squeezed shut.

"Open your eyes." He waited for me to do so before plunging two fingers into me, jostling the vibrating toy.

I gasped loudly, and my eyes flickered to the front, where the driver listened to soft classical guitar.

"Obviously, you can't stay quiet." He frowned at me and lightly slapped my sex.

I bit off my moan. "I'll be quiet."

"Too late," he whispered before taking his hand away from my heat and turning off the vibrator.

He pressed a button, and a partition slowly closed between the front and back of the car. His eyes were dark and serious as he stared at me, taking in my flushed cheeks and tumbled hair.

"Take my cock out," he ordered.

Desire rolled through me and made my mouth suddenly parched. "What?"

"Don't make me ask you again."

I swallowed rapidly and turned in my seat in order to reach his zipper. A sizable erection strained against the front, and I almost groaned again when I took it in my hand through his pants. His strong grip clutched my wandering fingers, and I understood that I had disobeyed him yet again. I took a deep breath to settle my nerves before I unzipped him and reached inside his boxers to grab his naked length. He was large and thick, the head plush and red. I licked my lips.

"Suck it," he commanded, but his voice was less demanding than it had been.

I took the crown slowly in my mouth, swirling my tongue along the sensitive underside. The taste of him was potent, musky, and all man. I moaned as he thrust forward, pressing the head against the entrance to my throat. I braced my hands on his thighs and tried to relax in order to take him deeper.

"You love this, don't you? Taking me in your mouth," he rasped as his strong fingers wove into my hair so he could hold me still while continuing to thrust gently into my mouth.

I leaned farther down, eager to feel all of him. It felt right to do this for him. A heady sense of power and arousal rushed through my blood, and when Sinclair suddenly pulled me away, I was disorientated.

He looked at me with electric blue eyes, his fingers on my chin. "We're here."

I blinked and nodded. "Right."

His chuckle followed me as I scrambled out of the car, suddenly embarrassed about going down on Sinclair with someone in the front seat. I kept a few feet between us as we walked into the lobby, and I didn't think he noticed. But the moment we got into the elevator, I was pressed hard against the wall.

His hand lifted one of my legs, curling it around his waist while the other took a fistful of my hair and tugged, forcing my chin back. He stared down at me with hard eyes.

"Don't pretend you don't want this, Elle. I can feel how you respond to me." His hand traveled up my thigh and over my hips and quivering belly until he could cup one of my breasts. My nipple was sharp against his palm, and I shuddered when he rolled it between his fingers. "I could see these puckered on the plane. Your breathing hitched just like this." I gasped when he lowered his head to nip my bottom lip. "And when I leaned over you, your eyes begged me to kiss you."

I remembered it vividly, how his charm had made even the dreaded plane ride feel sexy.

"Do you still want me to kiss you, Elle?" His breath fanned across my neck as he placed a kiss there and another at the edge of my jaw.

I moaned and pressed my hips against his, but he only laughed and lightly bit my chin. His tongue swept across my pouting lower lip. "Tell me."

"Kiss me," I begged shamelessly.

The elevator pinged, and before I could capture his lips, he was pulling me gently from the wall. My legs were less than steady as I followed him from the elevator into his palatial suite. He must have called ahead because the lights were dim and Latin music wafted through the room on the sweet-smelling breeze from the open French doors.

"I even get music?" I looked over my shoulder at him, where he lingered by the door. "I'm a lucky girl."

My teasing smile faltered slightly when I saw the depth of intensity in his eyes. He walked toward me slowly with long, predatory steps. I didn't realize I held my breath until he was in front of me, and his knuckles skimmed my cheek.

"You deserve much more than music." His voice was quiet and slightly forced as if the admission cost him. "Flowers, and jewels, and romance."

I pressed his lingering hand to my cheek, and murmured, "I just want you."

He stared at me intently, and for a moment, I wasn't sure if he would continue our holiday affair. It made me aware of how very much I wanted it.

"I'll hurt you."

He wasn't being arrogant, and honestly, I couldn't say that I would emerge completely unscathed from our romance. I wasn't the kind of woman to sleep around, and I had only ever been romantically involved with one very sweet man who was just as naïve as me. And Sinclair was not naïve. He was coolly confident, full of smoky secrets, and sexy as hell.

"I'll forgive you," I assured him, but he remained frozen before me, the only sign of his desire the burning light in his lightning blue eyes.

So, I took matters into my own shaky hands. I stepped closer until his arousal pressed into my belly. On my tiptoes, I planted an open-mouthed kiss on his fragrant neck, sucking lightly at the skin before scraping my teeth across it. His entire body tightened with need, and I smiled against his throat, emboldened by his reaction. Slowly, I worked my fingers against the buttons of his shirt, popping them open so that his torso was bared to me. My hands slid down his smooth stomach, trailing the deep V leading to my final destination. He sucked in a sharp breath when my fingers wrapped firmly around his fabric-covered erection. He was long and thick in my hand, and I wondered how he would react if I dropped to my knees to take him in my mouth again. Just remembering how he had tasted made heat unfurl deep in my belly. I squeezed him harder, and he groaned.

I squeaked when he moved suddenly, plucking me from the ground. Automatically, I wrapped my legs around his waist, and his hand cupped my bottom. He tilted my head in order to plunder my mouth with long, bold strokes of his tongue. His teeth gently nipped my bottom lip, but his tongue soothed over the small pain before I could register it.

He carried us to the bedroom and placed me on the edge of the bed. I watched from under my lashes as he crouched before me in order to slip off my shoes. His eyes found mine as he cradled my foot and ran his teeth along my instep, then placed a kiss below my ankle. I shivered and tried to reach for him, desperate to have him on me, in me, any part of him, but most specifically, the appendage straining violently against his gray trousers.

He tugged my hand so that I was standing and then turned me to face away from him. His fingers found the center zipper of my dress and slowly tugged it down. The sound of yielding fabric had never been so erotic, and when his tongue lightly traced the path of the parting dress, I sighed in warm arousal. Only when the dress pooled at my feet did he press himself against my back. His erection rested against the crest of my bottom, and I wiggled back against him. He nipped at my earlobe as a warning. This was his seduction, and with only a moment of hesitation, I yielded to his direction. When I became pliant against him, he growled his appreciation, and his hands trailed up my stomach to cup my breasts through my bra.

"You have amazing breasts." His voice was hot against my neck, and I dropped my head against his chest to give him full access to them. "You would blush if you knew all the things I wanted to do to these."

I did flush as one hand deftly undid my bra, and I shrugged my shoulders so that it slid down my arms. His warm palms against my bare flesh seared my delicate skin and made me gasp. His fingers circled my nipples, so close but not touching. I arched into his palms, but he only chuckled darkly. "You seem so quiet and prim, but I knew the moment I had you naked under my hands, you would come to life. My siren."

His fingers finally found my nipples and pinched firmly. I moaned and pressed my bum hard against his arousal. Too soon, his palms left me, trailing down my hips to grab the sides of my underwear. He pulled them down slowly, descending to his knees as he did so. I felt naked and vulnerable, faced away from him as I was. I could feel his eyes on my bare posterior, and the unadventurous Giselle protested.

"Bend over and place your forearms on the mattress." Sinclair's voice was hypnotic, and I swayed under his persuasion, his sinuous tone banishing my bashfulness.

I did as he asked without hesitation even though I was now open to him. Oddly, it didn't feel clinical or even embarrassing. It was sexy to present myself to his gaze, and I knew by the way his breath hitched that he was impacted by the display. One finger reached out and ran lightly from the top of my buttocks down to my wet sex. I shuddered at the forbidden sensation.

"You look gorgeous like this," he mumbled slightly as he leaned close to me. "Pink and wet and open for me. This is what you need."

I groaned my agreement and wiggled my backside slightly, encouraging him to explore further. His gentle laughter, more an exhalation than anything, fanned across my aching core before he pressed a chaste kiss to my right cheek. His hands caressed the round orbs firmly and moved down my thighs to lightly skim the backs of my knees. My legs shook and almost failed me.

He continued to plant open-mouthed kisses down the inside of my thighs, closer and closer to my dripping core. I whimpered as he sucked on the tender skin beside the apex of my thighs.

"Sinclair." My voice was breathless, needy, and I barely recognized myself. "Please."

"Please what?" Cool air blew gently against my overheating sex, and I pushed my bottom backward, shamelessly hoping to connect with his mouth.

"Touch me." I knew what he wanted. He was pushing me to voice my desires, to explicitly describe my needs. It was terrifying and exhilarating at the same time to hear my voice beg him for contact. "Please, put your mouth on me."

"Good girl." The smile in his voice and the bold sweep of his tongue against my core soon overtook my excitement at pleasing him.

I cried out loudly, and my legs shook as he pushed two fingers inside me and began pumping them slowly in and out. One hand found my lower back and pushed it down so that I was arched up, even more exposed, my legs farther apart to balance. His lips found my clit and gently sucked.

I yelled into the duvet as my climax bloomed, building and building until I thought I would die.

"Sinclair, stop, it's, I …" I said incoherently, but he ignored me, his fingers moving faster now as he added a third.

The blankets were clenched tight in my damp fists, and I bit into my thumb as the pleasure spiraled higher, and my womb clenched almost painfully with pleasure. I had never experienced anything so blinding, so beyond normal sense, and I was almost afraid to let go and dive into the deep well of bliss his fingers coaxed me toward.

"Come for me." His voice was tight with control. "Come for me now, Elle."

His demand pushed me over the edge, and as I went tumbling into the darkness, his voice kept me anchored to reality. The orgasm overwhelmed me, my legs shaking, sex convulsing, and it took all my strength just to stay conscious through the powerful onslaught.

"Are you okay?" he asked between gritted teeth as he stood behind me. His arousal brushed against my buttock, hard and pulsing, and I realized at some point while I recovered, he'd shed the rest of his clothes.

I was exhausted, but the feel of him against me spurred me on. "No, I need you. Inside me."

Anxiously, I waited as he recovered a condom from his discarded trousers. He groaned as he took my hips between his palms and brought himself to my drenched entrance. I gasped when he pressed forward slightly and moved his hips gently, just kissing the inside of my sex. Passion reignited violently in my belly, and I tried to push back against him, but his strong hands held me firmly. He planted a kiss on the middle of my back before placing his hand there, gently pressing me down once more so that my rump was raised in invitation. I tightened on the tip of him embedded in my core, causing his fingers to twitch on my hips.

"I want to feel you inside me," I almost whispered, embarrassed by my bold desires but too stimulated to ignore them.

His fingers tightened an instant before he thrust inside me, wrenching an animalistic moan from him and a cry of pleasure from me. He was so large inside me that, at first, despite my wetness, there was an uncomfort-able stretch. I winced slightly, hoping that he wouldn't notice. He paused, and I held my breath until he began to slowly pull out. My breathy sigh must have satisfied him because he moved forward again. His strokes were slow and sure at first, pulling almost all the way out before thrusting inside my aching depths. The pain was gone, drowned in a tidal wave of pleasure as wave after wave of sensation coursed through my blood.

"You feel incredible," he rasped as he leaned over my back to play with my hanging breasts. His fingers rolled my taut nipples until I was breathless with pleasure.

"Come for me like this," he ordered, pressing an open-mouthed kiss to my damp shoulder. "With me deep inside you."

One hand dropped from my breast and unerringly found the sensitive nub at the top of my sex. His fingers circled it, mirroring the ministrations of his other hand on my right nipple. The tremors began at my core and vibrated through my entire body as my orgasm took me. I crested the wave on a broken cry, and my sex clenched tightly around Sinclair inside me, milking him until he groaned and climaxed too. I could feel the kick of his dick as he climaxed, and it drew out my orgasm. Minutes later, I was still panting and shaking slightly when we had both collapsed to the bed in exhaustion.

Sinclair rolled over, propping himself on his rippling arm to look down at me as I recovered. He was covered in a thin sheen of sweat that made him glow golden in the low yellow lights. "Please tell me you aren't a virgin, Elle."

It would have been too good to be true if he hadn't noticed.

I considered how to respond, fingering the white duvet as if I wasn't concerned with our conversation or my very exposed position.

"Not anymore."

Chapter Seven

HE CURSED UNDER HIS BREATH AGAIN AND WAS SILENT FOR A FEW MINUTES. He flopped to the bed beside me and dragged an arm over his forehead as he stared at the ceiling. Tears pricked the backs of my eyes, but I reminded myself that I had wanted this. I had been completely naïve my entire life, and I didn't want to arrive in New York as the same meek girl I had been when I left to go to Paris years before.

"You should have told me," he said, not accusing but firm, as if he was scolding a wayward puppy.

"I thought this was supposed to be just physical."

I propped my head in my hands in order to look at him. He didn't sound very angry, and I was inordinately glad about it. I was still flushed and joyful from our lovemaking, and I wasn't ready to argue yet.

"An affair is an intimate thing, Elle. I didn't propose one night of sex with a stranger. As I told you on the plane, I've never been so drawn to a person in my life. I'm not interested in having sex with a stranger; I want to be with you. And that includes knowing pertinent information about you, like the state of your virginity."

I nodded. "I'm sorry. I realize it was deceitful of me."

His brow furrowed, and I somehow resisted the urge to smooth it with my fingers.

"I don't know if it would have changed anything," he admitted softly.

Joy unfurled in my chest, and I smiled at him prettily. "It doesn't have to change anything now. I quite liked it."

He lifted his head to raise a cool eyebrow at my attitude, but I only grinned at him.

"You quite liked it?" he repeated in a deceptively reserved voice.

I giggled as he leaned once more on his elbow to look at me. "Well, yes. Didn't you?"

He shook his head at me and ran his other hand through the tumbled mass of chestnut hair falling around his ears. "I more than liked it. Despite myself, I'm already thinking about all the other ways I can have you."

I noticed his frown, and this time, I didn't quell the urge to iron it away with my touch. He allowed me to touch him, though he tensed under the caress and grabbed my hand.

"I may have been a virgin, Sinclair, but I wasn't completely inexperienced. I have had a boyfriend before, and we did do things." It was not pleasant to think about my sexual encounters before Mark, but I wanted him to know. "And before that, I did things with a man. Things I'm not really proud of and would prefer not to talk about, but I just want you to know. I'm not pure or anything."

Sinclair rolled over me. Bracing his weight on his knees, he straddled my legs and bracketed my face with his forearms. His gaze was somber, but one hand played almost absently with a strand of my hair.

"Not pure? Regardless of whatever happened before and heedless of your conventional virginity, I noticed your purity right away." He pressed a finger to my lips when I tried to protest. "I don't mean you seemed young to me or naïve. I mean that there is a grace, a serenity to you that speaks of purity. It has nothing to do with sexuality." His grin was self-deprecating. "Though obviously, I noticed that too."

"You are just being nice." I squirmed beneath him, uncomfortable with his compliment.

"I don't have time to be nice," he reminded me curtly, but his eyes were dancing as I looked into them. When I smiled back, he sighed happily. "There. You are mine for five more days, Elle, and I fully expect you to smile and graciously receive my flattery whenever I desire it. Understood?"

I laughed. "Yes, sir."

His eyes darkened suddenly, and I felt him twitch against my thigh. "Are you sore?"

I mentally checked my erogenous zones for discomfort, but other than a slightly swollen, pleasantly achy sex, I felt fine, extraordinary even. "No."

I slid my arm around his neck, aware for the first time that he was naked in my arms. My fingers boldly explored the play of muscles in his back, my nails scratched lightly down his sides so that he hissed, and when I brought them between us to run my hand down his beautifully defined torso, he hummed with pleasure.

I squealed as he wrapped his arms around me and flipped over onto his back so that I straddled him. I blinked down at him a few times as he smiled and placed his arms behind his head.

"You wanted to explore," he reminded me. "Feel free."

I bit my lip, and he frowned, his voice hardening. "Do not be shy with me, Elle. We have six days together, and I assure you, this will be the tamest of those nights. There are so many things I want to do with you, for you, to you." His hand reached up and cupped my full breasts, his thumbs flicking my distended nipples.

Emboldened by his words, I leaned over and softly kissed the hollow at the base of his throat. I readjusted my position over him so that I could reach one of his small brown nipples with my lips. Sucking it into my mouth, I gently ran my teeth over it and was rewarded with his hands sliding into my hair, urging me on. As I trailed sweet kisses down his chest —my nails raking his skin harder now so that his breath came in pants—I realized how powerful sex could be. There was nothing in my world but Sinclair's body laid out like a dusky-skinned Adonis for me to worship.

My lips found his jutting erection, and I mirrored my other chaste kisses by my softly pursed mouth to the flared crown. A bead of moisture rested there, and as Sinclair looked down at me with fevered eyes, I deliberately licked the salty-sweet substance, smacking my lips as I hummed my approval. His hands tightened in my hair, but the mild pain only heightened the experience. I was his, to do with as he pleased, and the idea aroused me further. I moaned around him as I took his length past my lips and deep into the back of my mouth. His taste was intoxicating, tempting me to reach one of my hands down to play with my soaking sex, but I was too dedicated to his pleasure to do so. Instead, I wrapped one hand around the base of him, squeezing firmly each time my lips descended to my grip, and with the other, I cupped his soft sack drawn up with desire.

"Make me come this way," he said through his teeth.

I murmured my consent as I took him from my warm mouth to run my tongue along the length of him, wondering at his size and loving his girth. I hesitated at the root and wondered if he would like his balls touched in the same way. At the first tentative brush of my tongue, his muscles contracted, and when I rolled one in my mouth cautiously, his groan reverberated through my core.

"Yes," he hissed, and he tugged on my hair almost painfully, causing me to moan too.

I could feel my wetness trail down my leg, but I was so focused on Sinclair that I barely registered my own needs. His release would be better than my own.

Suddenly desperate for the taste of him spilling into my mouth, I took him swiftly to the back of my throat, relaxing so that I wouldn't gag as he began to pump back and forth in my mouth. I relaxed my jaw, flicking my tongue over his tip whenever he retreated and waited breathlessly for my reward. I could feel his climax the moment it shuddered through his body. The muscles in his legs and stomach grew taut, and his fingers twitched before clenching tightly in my hair. A feral groan ripped from his chest as he spent himself across my tongue. I quickly lapped up his release, surprised by how much I enjoyed it.

He lay exhausted as I straightened from my slightly uncomfortable position, but his arms tightened around me, and he brought me to his chest to press a kiss into my hair.

"You are magnificent," he murmured, and I wondered if I imagined the reverence in his words.

I closed my eyes and absorbed his praise. We lay silently for a time, and I wondered if he had perhaps fallen asleep. *Maybe I should leave*, I thought with sudden anxiety. This was a holiday affair; he wouldn't want to spend the night with me. I chewed the inside of my cheek as I considered my options, but his sleep-roughened voice interrupted my reverie.

"What are you thinking about so loudly?"

I sighed, deciding to tell him the truth. "I was wondering if I should leave now."

Instantly, his corded arms tightened like a vise around me, but his voice was casual as he said, "If you'd like."

My heart dropped into my stomach, but I nodded against my chest and tried to push from his embrace. "No problem."

"But," he continued mildly, and when I looked down at him, his eyes were still closed, "I would prefer it if you stayed."

Relief flooded me, reheating every place that he had spent the night coaxing to life inside me. My hand splayed across his chest, burrowing in his sparse chest hair. I could feel the calming beat of his heart against my palm.

"I'd like that too," I whispered, looking down at the most handsome man in the world.

His thick, dark eyelashes rested on his sharp cheeks, casting long shadows over his dusky gold skin. He wasn't too tanned yet, but there was a depth to the color of his skin that suggested his forefathers had been something other than white, and his hair was a richer shade of mahogany than I had ever seen. My throat ached from his beauty.

His eyes fluttered open, and I froze under his brilliant gaze. "What are you looking at?"

"You," I said simply. "I love the way you look."

His smile moved slowly across his face, tilting his firm lips and creasing the corners of his eyes with crow's feet. "Let me take you on an adventure tomorrow."

I laughed at his abrupt change of subject and the boyish glee in his eyes. "An adventure?"

"Yes."

"What kind of an adventure?"

"One that is a surprise."

I looked down at him with wide eyes, delighted by his carefree mood. "And if I don't like surprises?"

His shrug dislodged me slightly from the side of his body, and he was quick to tuck me back into his arm, pressing my head gently against his chest once more. "You'll like this one."

I didn't doubt it, and as an unattractive yawn completely distorted my features, I wondered sleepily if it was possible for me to dislike anything about this man.

"Sleep," he encouraged, a hand smoothing over my hair. "I'll wake you up in the morning when it's time to go."

I snuggled closer to him and wondered if I had ever been happier. It was silly, I knew, to think such things when I only had another six days with him, but it was hard to ground myself in reality when Sinclair could show me such wicked fantasies. As sleep descended, I remembered the girlfriend waiting at home for him, and my heart jerked uncomfortably. It didn't matter if I was emotionally battered at the end of the affair. I would let him go back to his partner, and I would move to New York with no regrets. But even as dreams began to flicker behind my closed lids, I knew that wouldn't be the case.

Chapter Eight

I woke up slowly, stretching my arms over my head and twisting my hips to work the kinks out of my lower body as I groaned into awareness. Without opening my eyes, I smiled because I knew what had awakened me.

"Hi," I said softly.

Rough tipped fingers traced the side of my face, and when I opened my eyes, Sinclair was looking down at me. "Elle, are you ready for our adventure?"

I smiled, gazing at him from under my lashes, and gently pushed the duvet back in order to expose my breasts, which instantly drew tight in the cool air. "I had a different adventure in mind."

He shook his head, and his voice was almost sad when he replied, but I could tell he was pleased with me too. "I've unleashed a monster."

I pouted playfully. "That doesn't sound very flattering."

"A siren, then."

He sat on the edge of the bed, already fully dressed in a thickly knit, light blue sweater that complemented his eyes and white linen shorts. His overlong hair was still damp from the shower, and his rich and manly fragrance drifted over me.

My mouth watered, just looking at him. Though I was slightly sore, my sex clenched at the thought of being with him again. And again.

His eyes sparked on the fire in my gaze, but he only shook his head again and moved off the bed, walking away into the bathroom. "We have to leave in twenty minutes. You're welcome to have a shower here, and we can swing by your room on our way out."

As much as the idea of a shower in his room, preferably with him, appealed to me, it made more sense for me to return to my room to shower and change. When I told him so, he nodded and patted my bottom as I walked past him to dress.

"Meet me in the lobby in fifteen. Wear something comfortable," he ordered over his shoulder before leaving the bedroom.

I walked back to my room in a state of hyper-awareness as if my happiness magnified my senses. My bare feet kissed the cool marble floor of the lobby, and the soft skirt of my dress swished over my tingling thighs. Despite my lack of sleep, I was awake and eager for more.

Sinclair consumed my thoughts as I peeled off my party clothes and stepped into the shower. The hot water stung the sensitive skin between my legs, but the pounding spray massaged my aching muscles.

I was amazed by the way he had undressed my conservatism and laid bare the heart of my sexuality. With Mark, I had been awkward and bumbling under his sweetness, and it was a revelation to have someone so confident and experienced drive the action. I thought about the way he had ordered me to bend over and commanded me to orgasm. I shuddered at the memory as I lathered my hair with my honey-scented shampoo. His cool words echoed in my head, and a resulting tightness in my gut confirmed my attraction to his controlling nature.

I was also grateful for his reaction to my virginity. Really, I had been sexually active for years, and it had felt wrong to misled Sinclair by labeling me a novice. But I was also loath to validate those sexual experiences, the hands and face and acts of a man who had used me for years. I closed my eyes and pressed my forehead against the tiles, letting the water sluice down my head and back. Was it foolish to believe that Sinclair could erase those memories? I could still feel his hands on my skin, so it was easy to believe in their potential power to eradicate all touches before them.

Regardless, I had five more days with the man, and ignoring the shadow of foresight at the corner of my bliss, I vowed to enjoy every moment of it.

When I arrived in the lobby ten minutes later, Sinclair was frowning at the screen of his Blackberry. I stopped for a minute to study him, the way his gleaming chestnut hair fell over his forehead and the deliciously narrow set of his hips.

He looked up suddenly, straightening to his full height as if he was a hunter that had just scented his prey. The look that sparked in his blue eyes was just as feral, triumphant. If I could have torn my eyes away from the sight of him, I would have checked to make sure no one was staring. As he stalked toward me, I could feel my heartbeat kick up, and the absurd desire to flee seized me.

"Hi," I breathed when he came to a stop just before me. I had to tilt my head to continue looking into his vivid gaze, the only windows into his otherwise inscrutable expression.

"Hello, yourself." One of his fingers smoothed down my neck, tickling the heavy beat of my pulse there. "Nervous?"

My laugh was unusually shrill, but I rolled my shoulders and forced myself to relax. This man had just been inside me; why the hell was I behaving like an awkward stranger?

Sinclair's eyes narrowed, and his fingers threaded through my hair, tugging until my head was forced back and he towered over me. "Tell me what is going on behind those grays, Elle, or I'll take you over my knee, and we can forget all about the surprise adventure."

A shiver of excitement raced up my spine, and I bit my lip at the thought of being spread over his lap, exposed like I had been last night. He must have felt the shudder, and his brows rose in silent question, but I shook my head.

"I don't know why, but I feel shy around you this morning," I said.

His head tilted as he studied me, his fingers now firmly massaging my scalp. Each stroke of his fingers released one of the knots of tension pinching my shoulders together.

"We are no longer strangers, but we aren't lovers yet, not after one night.

Normally, this might be awkward, but not for us, not when I own you." He marked the downward quirk of my mouth and responded with a sharp tug on the roots of my hair. "You are embarrassed because you liked being taken by a stranger and ordered to come."

I shifted restlessly on my sandaled feet as liquid desire pooled between my legs.

A slight smirk tilted his lips as he leaned forward to speak against my lips. "Are you wet now, Elle? Just from hearing my voice?"

I groaned, unwilling to admit the power he held over me.

A couple passed by us, talking happily as they dragged their suitcases into the lobby. The man, a short, older gentleman with a thick helmet of gray hair, turned to us sharply, and his nostrils flared as if he could smell me. Sinclair turned his head slightly to stare at him and used his free hand to tug my bottom until I was pressed against him. The gray-haired stranger smiled and winked at me before patting his own partner's bum affectionately.

When he was gone, I tried to push Sinclair away. "I can't believe you just did that."

His grip was firm, and the lines of his body against mine were made of steel. I wanted to rub up against him like a cat, scratch him and nuzzle him until he stroked me.

Somehow, he read my thoughts. "I can do whatever I want to you. The night you agreed to our holiday affair, you knowingly entered into my world."

I briefly remembered his words, *"You belong to me for the next six days,"* and my anxiety upped another notch.

I licked my parched lips. "That doesn't sound very fair."

"No," he mused. "It isn't. No mortal man should hold a siren in his arms, but you've given me the opportunity of a lifetime."

My heart tapped a quick dance against my rib cage, delighted and surprised by his poetry, but as I watched his eyes darken, the beat moved lower, pulsing now in my belly.

"I want to push you, Elle, see how far I can take you. By day seven, you'll be begging for me to take you in ways you can't even imagine now."

I gasped as my mind raced with possibilities. I was so preoccupied that I almost stumbled when he suddenly pulled away from me. He frowned at me, catching my hand and winding it around his arm.

"Sore?" he asked, and though there was no hint of emotion in his beautiful profile, he sounded a little amused, maybe even smug.

I blushed and tried to take my hand from him. "Not a bit."

Unable to even wriggle under his strong fingers, I sighed and allowed him to pull me outside the main doors to the front of the resort. The same long black car from the night before idled in front of us. Sinclair opened the door for me to slip in so that I faced him, backward to the momentum of the car. He was quiet for the duration of the drive, his eyes on the glowing screen of his phone as he read emails and conducted business, but I was glad for the reprieve.

I rested my head against the plush seat and stared out at the blurring colors of Los Cabos slipping by. My camera was strapped across my body, and without hesitation, I swung it into my hands to snap the abstract smear of Mexican scenery.

We stopped at a light beside a bus station where a young woman, only a few years younger than me, slouched against a pole, a soft roll of brown belly exposed by her small white shirt and tight blue jeans. Her skin was dewy with sweat, and her slightly unkempt hair stuck to the dampness between her breasts. She stared at me insolently with large eyes the color of molasses, and when I raised my camera to capture her strangely erotic sloth, her pale tongue poked out and caught a bead of sweat from the downy hairs of her top lip. My shutter clicked, and my heart palpitated with triumph as the car pulled into the traffic a second later. I recalled the photograph to the screen of my Canon and found exactly that moment of lazy sex, her belly exposed, sweaty breasts plumped up.

I wasn't sure if I would have normally found sexiness in the image, in the girl, but the darker recesses of my mind were cracking open. I wondered how many kinds of sultry there were, how many types of sex and fantasy.

I peeked up at Sinclair with my tongue unconsciously mimicking the slow lick the Mexican girl had stroked against her top lip. He was staring at me, his head still slightly bent to view his phone as if he had become entranced by something after briefly glancing up at me.

The electric heat in his eyes shocked something within me, and without really thinking about it, I scooted lower in my seat, spreading my thighs wider as I did so. It was cool in the car, but I could suddenly feel the Mexican heat press heavily against my body, warming my breasts until they ached and slowing my heart rate until it thumped lazily, only strong enough to pump languid arousal through my veins.

I stared at Sinclair from beneath lowered lids, my tongue caught between my teeth as my hand found my breasts and squeezed, stoking the fire there. He was completely still. I pressed on, following my own pleasure. My palms slicked down my smooth thighs and slowly pulled my legs farther apart until I was bared to him. Slipping off my flip-flops, I planted my feet on either side of him, my toes curling over the cool leather to steady myself. His Adam's apple bobbed as he swallowed, and I smiled slightly, my fingers lightly dancing over the ticklish skin of my inner thighs.

It was so unlike me to explore myself like this, even in the privacy of my own bed under the cloak of night, but Sinclair made me feel wanton, just as damp, and obviously as sexual as the woman at the bus stop.

I groaned when my hands finally found the edge of my swimsuit and slipped inside. I wanted to tell him how wet I was, but my voice was stuck somewhere around my toes, and I didn't want to push myself too far. Desperate for his involvement somehow, I pried my eyes open and looked up at him.

He was staring between my legs with burning eyes, but almost immediately, his gaze found mine and rapidly read what I had written there. His eyelids lowered, and his voice was rough with longing, so potent it arrowed desire straight to the wet place my fingers played over.

"Feel how wet you are, how ready you are to have my cock inside you. Circle yourself with your thumb, place two fingers at your entrance, and pretend they're my cock, pressing against you."

I struggled to keep my eyes open, but I wanted to look at him as I did this, as I touched myself for him.

"You look so sexy playing with yourself. I could watch you all day," he said.

I groaned, increasing the pressure of my fingers across the slick folds of my sex.

I could see the long, mouthwatering length of him press against his shorts and I imagined crawling between his knees to take it out, the feeling of him in my hands, against the roof of my mouth as I took him to the back of my throat. I shuddered.

"That's it." His voice was so deep it reverberated throughout my body, strumming me until I vibrated. "Push those fingers into your sweet pussy for me. Feel how tight you."

I could hear myself, the wet suck of my fingers plunging inside my aching core, but it only drove my pleasure higher.

"Do you think you can come like this, Elle? With only your fingers and the sound of my voice."

I whimpered and finally closed my eyes against the growing pressure in my groin, but the snap of his words sliced across my flesh with the force of a whip. "Open your eyes." His firm lips moved sensuously, deliberately over his next words. "I own you. When you come, you will look at me. Add another finger."

The additional finger stretched me wide, reawakening the ache of last night. Now, I really could imagine his thickness inside me, sliding forcefully into my depths over and over again.

"Don't come yet," he said, and when my eyes flashed open in a panic, he hushed me. "You can't come without my permission."

I was desperate for it. My orgasm was so close I could taste it, metallic, at the back of my tongue. My blurry eyes watched as he grabbed himself through his shorts, and I wasn't sure which one of us groaned. Maybe it was both of us.

"Do you want me to take my cock out, Elle?"

I nodded, my head lolled back against the seat. My breath came in short, hard pants, and my chest was tender, heavy with sensation. But Sinclair was not unmoved by my display. His slashing cheeks were taut with control as he spoke through gritted teeth, fighting to keep his cool. I knew he was doing it for me, allowing me to explore, to discover how to pleasure myself, but it cost him.

My breath hitched when he exposed his erection, curved and severe with desire for me. I licked my lips and watched as he wrapped a strong fist around himself and pulled up. A pearl of liquid shimmered at his crown, and already, I knew how it would taste, remembering the unique flavor of him on my tongue.

"I want you in my mouth," I whispered, my dry mouth flooding with saliva as I thought about it.

"I know you do." His lids were heavy. Only thin slits of blue gazed at me. His thick lashes brushed his cheek. "Which would you prefer, Elle? To come on your hands or to have this"—he brandished his cock, his fist pumping it from root to tip and his thumb rolling over the slick head—"in your mouth."

His eyes widened slightly as I shivered, and a small smile warmed his mouth, his question answered. "On your knees."

Inelegantly in my haste, I dropped to my knees in the spacious town car and reached forward, eager for my prize. When he caught my hands in one of his, the other still on his throbbing length, I frowned up at him.

He looked so handsome staring down at me, his bottom lip lush beneath the firm top, his jaw tensed but his eyes sucking and hot with excitement. He was a paradox, my Frenchman, hot and cold, stern but poetic, mine but not mine.

"I don't want you to use your hands. Clasp them behind your back and take me with your mouth. I won't be easy on you. You have no idea what you do to me." His fingers threaded in my hair and slowly pulled my mouth toward him.

I tentatively licked the sensitive underside, and when he hissed, I opened my mouth, sheathing my teeth, and took the flared head of him inside. My tongue traced over his flesh, greedy for the taste of him, the saltiness of his fluid and the musky smell of his arousal. I breathed through my nose as I bore down on him and swallowed rapidly when he pushed through the back of my throat. I almost gagged on my triumph when my nose pressed into his groin, and a primal groan ripped from his lips.

He kept me firmly planted there for only a few seconds, lessening the pressure for my ascent long before I was uncomfortable, and after a brief circle of my tongue over the head, I opened my throat and took him all the way again. And again.

Heady on the pleasure, I could feel my own wetness slide down my thighs, and the orgasm that had receded with the absence of my fingers hovered over me. I knew I only had to press the pad of my thumb delicately to my pulsing clit to come, but I didn't.

Sinclair hadn't said I could.

He swelled in my mouth, and his strong legs tensed. I prepared for his orgasm, tipping my head to allow a deeper angle of penetration even as my eyes sought his face, desperate to see his expression as he spilled into my mouth. But his hands clenched my hair and pulled my face away roughly. His chest heaved as he breathed in and out through his mouth, trying to control his desire. I blinked at him in confusion, but after a moment, when he was under control, he rasped, "Are you very sore?"

I nodded. "I'm aching."

He detected the wantonness in my tone, and suddenly, he was lifting me and easily fit me on top of him with my knees straddling his legs and his pulsating erection at my entrance. His fingers found me drenched with desire, and he let out a long, ragged breath.

"So wet for me." He seemed awed by it, and the smokiness of his voice made me wriggle, rubbing against him. "Stop." His fingers bit into my curved hips, and his eyes bore into mine. "This is going to be quick. For both of us. Put your hands on my shoulders and hold on."

His dark promise thrilled me, and I grabbed his shoulders, clenching his sinewy muscles and the soft fabric of his shirt in my fists. As soon as I latched on, he breathed deeply like a warrior before a battle and thrust into me. I screamed, my head falling back on my shoulders, but he was already lifting me to slam back inside. He was so big that I couldn't take all of him. The size of him inside me ached as it was, but it was a delicious pain, and I began to throw my hips down as he manipulated me over his rigid length. I was moaning, babbling incoherently, so lost in the pleasure I momentarily forgot where I was.

His thumb shifted and found my needy clit, gently brushing it with the pad. My orgasm lay before me, and I was greedy for it, gagging for it, but he hadn't said the words, and after a few more battering thrusts, I was worried he wouldn't.

"Do you want to come, Elle?" His voice was somehow still cool and controlled, only slightly cracking through with desire.

I grated my hips against him, taking another inch, and heard him gasp with pleasure. "Please, I need it."

"I know you do. I can feel you milking me. Desperate for my cum, aren't you?"

I loved listening to his cultured voice speak such dirty words, they made me wetter somehow, and the next time he plunged into me, it was to the hilt.

"Oh God, please, please, please," I begged, quaking with the need to release.

"Yes," he hissed. His hands raced up my torso, holding my plump breasts between his hot palms and scraping both callused thumbs across my puckered nipples. "I am your god. Come hard for me. Now."

I shattered. Currents of pleasure raced over my body, undoing my particles and liquefying my bones. I was vaguely aware of Sinclair's bark of triumph, like a rutting animal, and the sound intensified my pleasure. The heat of him releasing inside me tipped me further over the edge so that I clawed at him with both hands and leaned forward to bite his shoulder. He shuddered at the contact and twitched inside me even after he had finished.

I lay exhausted on top of him for a minute before he lifted me gently off him and placed me on the seat beside him. My eyes were closed, but I could hear him fiddle with something in the side door, and then my lids sprung open when I felt the slightly abrasive cloth against my sloppy sex. He concentrated on his cleanup, a furrow marring his habitually smooth forehead. I reached up to touch it, and he flinched.

"What's wrong?" I asked, too fatigued to feel embarrassed by his sudden aloofness.

He shook his head, the reddish hairs at the back of his neck sticking there. "I shouldn't have lost control like that. You must have been in pain."

I snorted and shrugged when he stared at me with a cool raised brow. "I was overwhelmed with pleasure. When I'm with you, I, well, I feel electric, like there is a pulse between us."

He nodded curtly as if he understood. When he finished his gentle cleaning, he closed my legs and disposed of the damp napkin in the door garbage.

"I came inside you." A thrill punched me in the stomach, and I placed a hand there, shocked by my reaction. "And you obviously aren't on birth control." He shook his head, and a muscle in his jaw clenched. "There is a pharmacy near the resort. I'll get you something on the way back."

"I am," I whispered, suddenly embarrassed. "To regulate my, um, periods."

"Good." He nodded curtly. "I am tested regularly, and I assume you are clean, but that won't happen again."

My lips pursed, but I nodded, unable to speak past the constriction in my throat. It was stupid of me to be so emotional, but I was wrung out, physically and mentally, by the lack of sleep and the whirlwind nature of being with Sinclair. I closed my eyes and sighed.

"Hey." His hand was on my chin, turning it to look me in the eye. "You should know, I've never seen anything sexier than you touching yourself like that for me, except maybe the sight of you on your knees or the excitement in your eyes as you took me in your sweet mouth."

It was hardly romantic, but his words ignited joy deep within my chest. I was proud, so proud of having pleased him and having pleased myself. Despite what my first sexual partner had said, I was capable of doing it right, and the knowledge gave me new life. I beamed at him and watched as he blinked as though he was staring at the noon sun.

"Magnificent," he murmured before shaking his head slightly, his features once again stone cold. "Now, are you ready for the adventure?"

I continued to grin at him. "Hell yes."

His eyes narrowed. "A simple yes would have sufficed."

"Yes, master," I teased and watched as his eyes turned molten. I couldn't believe I had such power over him, and I giggled.

He relaxed; a small grin tucked into the left corner of his cheek. "Siren."

Yes, I thought, leaning back against the seat, allowing my bones to liquefy, *your* siren.

Chapter Nine

I DON'T KNOW HOW HE DID IT, BUT THE SECOND WE STEPPED FROM THE CAR into the Mexican sunshine, Sinclair, the entrepreneur, was back, enigmatic and vaguely disinterested in everything around us. I wondered if that distance would apply to me, but when I hesitantly waited a few feet away from him after the car pulled away, staring at him instead of where he had taken me, he turned to me with warm eyes.

"This is the reason I love Mexico," he said, and I stepped closer to read the excitement in his eyes. They were such a glorious blue that even my artist's vocabulary came up blank and so expressive they almost entirely made up for the blank mask he always wore. I thought of his wild cry as he came in the car, blushed at the thought of the driver hearing us, and then flushed with pleasure.

"Insatiable," he scolded gently, taking my hand and winding it around his arm again.

I gasped as we moved forward. "How did you know what I was thinking?"

He chuckled darkly. "You blush beautifully when you think about sex."

I tried to control my flush and failed, so I tuned out his amusement and absorbed our surroundings.

The Pacific stretched before us; a swathe of silky azure waves topped with broken fragments of golden light. Pelicans crowded around a corner of the busy dock, eager for scraps tossed by the brawny fishermen, competently slicing open the fish being pulled in by wheelbarrows from incoming boats. The mild sea breeze kept the air from reeking of putrid fish guts, and I marveled at the exotic specimens lying on the broad marble tables, their long, silver bodies and sword-like protrusions reminiscent of prehistoric creatures.

Sinclair led me through the fanfare, the intense Spanish repartee and busy dockhands with a sure hand and widened eyes. He was enjoying himself, happy to point out the different types of fish—marlin and wahoo and dorado—all so exotic, like jewels scattered carelessly across the giant slabs.

"They don't waste any of it," he explained, his voice lower than the racket but still excited. "What the tourists or professionals don't take home, the dockhands use to feed their families. Fishing is a serious sport in this part of the country. Most families have made their living from the sea for generations."

We were past the fillet station and out into the open air of the docks, walking swiftly between the boats in search of our own.

"We're going fishing?" I asked, slightly incredulous.

His lips twitched at my lack of enthusiasm. "Trust me, you'll love it."

"I really doubt that," I muttered, but he ignored me.

"I'll tell you what," he said, biting down on the corner of a smile. "Whoever catches the biggest fish dictates what we do tonight."

"Oh okay, I have this couple's package—it's a long story—but a massage might be ..." I trailed off with a gasp when Sinclair tugged me into his arms and leaned down to delicately trace the edge of my ear with his tongue.

"I had something more intimate in mind."

"Oh." I sighed. "In that case, you're on."

We were still smiling as we finally came to a stop at a boat that was not what I would have called luxurious. It was an oddly shaped powerboat with a blue awning and a small upper deck. The name scrawled across the old but carefully maintained hull was *Rosa,* and despite my reluctance, I laughed.

When Sinclair raised a brow at me, I flapped my hand in the air. "My middle name. It must be a good omen."

He frowned at me, but the arrival of a small, deeply tanned Mexican man distracted him from questioning me further.

"Antonio." Sinclair's mouth trembled as he suppressed a smile, but he did allow himself to reach down and warmly clasp the short man's hand. "*¿Qué tal?*"

"*Bueno, bueno obviamente.*" Antonio responded jovially.

He had enormous eyes that sparkled like onyx as he beamed up at me, his mouth full of crooked but bright white teeth.

"Elle." Sinclair's hand wound around my side and swept down the length of my hourglass curve. "This is my friend, Antonio, the best fisherman in all of Mexico."

Antonio chortled loudly and took my hand in both of his. "Beautiful."

My laugh was more air than sound, and we both blushed happily at each other as I thanked him. He kept my hand, tugging me along like a child as he led us onboard the *Rosa,* and gave me the grand tour of the compact two-story boat. He enthusiastically described the mechanics of the down riggers, the huge weights anchored to both sides of the stern that would drag the fishing lures to the depths of the sea where massive, almost otherworldly fish liked to swim.

Slowly, because I was unsure and deeply interested, I helped Antonio and Sinclair prepare the lines. I even took a brief turn at the wheel, but the stress of keeping the boat straight on the rolling waves had me laughing hysterically, and Antonio soon took over again.

When everything was set, Sinclair ushered me to a low fold-up chair facing the rods and handed me a Dos Equis beer before taking a seat himself. His legs were outstretched, long and partially bare in his long khaki shorts, and I devoured the sight of him like that, spread out and casual like unfolded laundry. I wanted to lie on top of him and drag his masculine scent deep into my lungs.

He stopped chuckling at something Antonio was explaining, and his features collapsed into their usual impartiality when he caught me staring. "Can I help you with something, Elle?"

He was using his coolness to tease me, I thought, but still, I blushed and focused on peeling the label from the green bottle in my hands.

"I just like seeing you relaxed. It's different."

"Relaxed? The only thing I feel around you, siren, is desire." As if to prove his point, his eyes set flame to every inch of my skin, burning me like a witch for the spell I had cast over him.

The thought delighted me.

"I think your passions bring you comfort. Me"—I cleared my throat—"I mean my body, fishing, your business deal with the failing resort. It's like that for me with my art; like having an itch, that constant stimulation, but being too comfortable to scratch it away."

He pursed his lips. "It is certainly an interesting analogy."

I shrugged because I knew I could be clunky with English; it was much easier to wax poetic in French or Italian.

"I see only one problem with that," he continued, looking out at water that matched the same striking shade of blue as his eyes. "You are unlike anything I have ever dealt with before; therefore, there can be no frame of reference, no precedent to compare you to."

I frowned at the beer in my hands. "That doesn't exactly sound like a good thing."

"The unknown; it has stalked mankind since the beginning."

"Are you trying to say I'm stalking you?"

"Is it stalking if the recipient is eager to be followed?"

We stared at each other with barely contained smiles bright in our eyes and wobbly on our lips. Eager questions bubbled in my throat, the pressure building until I was sure my lips would pop open and a stream of embarrassing neediness would erupt.

What were we doing?

Why did I like you so much?

Wouldn't it be great if this was more than a holiday affair?

Happily, Antonio's sudden shout shattered our connection, and the Mexican hastily pulled me to my feet as he dashed by to take the bobbing fishing rod in his hands.

"You take, you take!" he urged, reeling in the line rapidly.

I watched skeptically as he tugged fiercely at the trapped fish. It looked much too strong for me.

"I'll guide you." Sinclair's presence at my back calmed me, and I was instantly obedient, allowing my hands to be manipulated into the proper position on the rod.

The waves undulated under my feet, and it was hard to find purchase on the slippery deck, but I ground the soles of my shoes into the floor and squatted lower.

"Place it just below your belly button and keep the rod tilted up. You want the line tight," he coached. "Brace your feet, pull the rod up and back slightly, and then quickly reel in the slack."

The blunt end of the fishing pole dug painfully into my gut as I struggled to reel in the fish. My right arm was already weak from exhaustion, but adrenaline coursed through my veins. The hard pulse of my heart was the epic soundtrack to my big catch.

"Steady." Sinclair's strong voice grounded me. "Don't pull too hard. You need to play the fish. Coax him closer to the boat with a firm hand."

My mind flashed to his firm hands, bringing me to orgasm the night before, and I slipped slightly when the fish zigzagged to the left. Before I could right myself, he was there, his strong arms cupping my elbows and his steely chest pressed to my back. I leaned back against him, settling my bum against his groin.

"Behave," he ordered quietly as Antonio darted around the deck, preparing to net the fish while trying to drive the boat at the same time. "You wouldn't want to lose this monster fish just because you couldn't keep your focus."

I gritted my teeth. "Says the man who is distracting me."

His warm chuckle ruffled my hair, and he slid it off my sticky neck. "Do you have an elastic?"

"Left pocket," I mumbled as I frantically reeled in the tiring fish. A flash of scales a few meters from the boat thrilled me.

As did Sinclair's gentle hands as they gathered my hair and put it rather adeptly into a high ponytail. "Much better," he murmured against my damp neck, skimming his teeth from my ear down to my collar. "Easy access."

I moaned slightly but narrowed my eyes and wriggled my hips, trying to get away from him. He was so arrogant, thinking that he would win the bet, and I would spend the night sprawled across his bed completely at his mercy. More determined than ever, I pushed him away with a firm thrust of my hips and adopted the position Antonio had taught me.

"Antonio," I called. "Sinclair is a terrible tutor. Would you mind helping me?"

Sinclair's smoky chuckle sounded from somewhere behind me, but I was glad he was giving me the space I needed to concentrate. It was so easy to become distracted by thoughts of what he could do to my body. The mere sound of his lightly accented voice whispering dirty promises into my ear was enough to...

I shook my head. *Snap out of it!*

"Is a big fish!" Antonio yelled close to my ear as he came up to adjust my grip. "Very big. Maybe the man should take over?"

"No, no, no," I growled, leaning all of my weight back to keep the fish somewhat close to the boat. How long was it going to fight me? "I can do it."

There was condescending amusement in the Mexican fisherman's voice when he said, "Okay, you do it. But this marlin is a very big, very strong fish."

I almost broke into a dance. Sinclair had said marlins were the biggest fish and the hardest to catch. Imagine the things I could make him do to me if I caught one ...

"Concentrate, Elle." As always, Sinclair sensed my thoughts, and his stern voice cut through my fantasies. "This fish could feed Antonio's family for a week."

My tongue peeked out between my lips, gently clamped against my teeth as I concentrated. Antonio's excited voice babbled in my ear as he checked my progress. I was at the stern of the little boat for forty minutes playing the fish, reeling in fast, then pulling back on the rod in an undulating motion exactly like the sea beneath my braced feet. I had never thought of fishing as a sport, but I soon realized just how taxing it was. My arms and legs felt like jelly, and the rod bit painfully into my stomach even as I shifted it around, trying to find a more comfortable position. But it was thrilling too. At one point, the marlin jumped high into the air, flashing its sapphire ridge and sharp nose. My cramped fingers itched for my camera, and I seriously considered giving up, unsure how much my weak body could take.

"Little closer, closer! Steady, steady," Antonio yelled while dangling over the side of the boat with a large net in his hand.

In one sharp jerk, just a twist of his wrist, he snagged the marlin, calling for Sinclair to help him. The rod was super-glued to my aching fingers, and I watched dumbly as the men wrangled the massive fish into the little hull of the boat. Antonio retrieved a small baseball bat-type instrument and hit the fish over the head until it stopped flailing. Despite my revulsion and the intense swell of empathy I felt for the magnificent creature, I watched rapt as they killed it and heaved it into a water cooler built into the boat. It made me uneasy to realize that I had never seen the process involved in killing the food I so easily shoved into my mouth each day.

Sinclair came over to me somewhat cautiously, and I realized that my confusion must have shown on my face. Gently, he unpeeled my fingers from around the rod and set it aside before taking my hands in his. He rubbed each finger, stroking down to the base and back up to the next finger until they tingled pleasantly.

"I'm very impressed with you, Elle." His voice was quiet but intense. "You have remarkable endurance, and not every fisherman can say they caught a 125-pound marlin."

My eyes widened comically. "I did that?"

"You did." He nodded and ducked his head to press a firm kiss to my lips. "I should have known a siren would have mastery over the sea."

His words ignited my previous excitement, and I squealed, jumping into his arms. He hesitated before his hands slid under my bottom to hold me up. I rained kisses over his face then pulled back to beam into his pleasantly surprised face.

"I'm basically a master fisherman now, aren't I?" When he didn't answer quickly enough, I leaned back to call to Antonio. "Aren't I, Antonio?"

His resulting grin was wide and toothy. "You can fish with me anytime, señorita!"

The rest of the trip was glorious. I lay down on the small upper deck in my bathing suit, recovering from my exercise in the sun. At some point, Sinclair came up to check on me and rubbed sunscreen sensuously into my skin. I dozed in and out of sleep, catching tidbits of Sinclair and Antonio's easy Spanish banter. The language was close enough to French and Italian that I could make out the gist of what they were saying, but I was happy just to drift as they chattered excitedly to each other like little boys.

Sinclair yelled with triumph sometime later, rousing me from my sleep, and I smiled. It was a privilege, I think, to see him so unbound from the tight restraints he kept himself in. Out on the sea, he was less reserved, and when he came bounding up the stairs to where I lay, I cracked open one eye to see him crouched before me with a wide, devastating grin.

"Did you catch one?" I asked sleepily.

He nodded, bouncing slightly on the balls of his feet. "I did."

"Is it big?"

His hand reached out to adjust my floppy white hat. "Don't worry, Elle, you'll have what you want tonight."

I closed my eyes and hummed. "Good."

I fell asleep to his soft chuckle.

When we returned to the docks, people waited with ancient wheelbarrows to take our large haul in so that they could be weighed and filleted. First, Sinclair ordered a picture of me with my huge marlin, strung up beside me from a pole where it dwarfed me twice over. A small smile played over his handsome features as I grinned into the camera and laughed with some tourists who peppered me with questions. Thanks to

Antonio and Sinclair's sage advice, I was actually able to answer most of them, and when I returned to his side, Sinclair kissed my hair, and I knew he was pleased that I had enjoyed fishing so much.

We stayed to watch them fillet the fish, and I frowned when a large silver fish, a wahoo, I thought, was heaved onto the bloody slab. It was huge, fat and long, and with growing dread, I realized it might be bigger than mine. I twisted my head to look up at Sinclair and gasped when he stared down at me with sparkling eyes.

"You lied to me!" I accused, pointing a finger into his strong chest. "You said I caught the biggest fish."

"No." He shook his head slowly. "I said you would have what you want tonight." He leaned close into my outraged face. "And you will enjoy the things I am going to do to you very much."

I harrumphed and fisted my hands on my hips, but a smile cracked through when Sinclair barked with laughter. His head tipped back, exposing his brown neck to my hungry gaze. He was so beautiful it made something in my chest ache.

We thanked Antonio and gave him most of our spoils, but I was happy when Sinclair held back some marlin to cook up back at the resort. I dozed on his shoulder in the car, exhausted from the combination of sun and fishing, while Sinclair murmured in Spanish into his phone. He woke me up with a gentle shake when we reached the hotel.

"Hi." I smiled up at him, blinking the drowsiness from my eyes.

He looked down at me with an almost unnerving intensity that caused my heart to pound. "Hi."

We stared at each other for a long minute until I became discombobulated by the brilliant azure of his irises.

"I have business that I have to take care of tonight." His features hardly moved as he spoke, and I clung to the passion in his eyes as my nerves started to set in. "I won't be back until late."

I waited for him to suggest a late-night rendezvous, and when he didn't, I swallowed my disappointment and nodded. "Right. Well, I could use a good night's rest anyway."

He nodded, carefully studying my reaction. When I remained expressionless, he turned away from me. "Good. I'll contact you tomorrow then."

I shivered at the coldness of his words. We had just spent a fantastic day together, and when I thought about the night before, I was instantly alight with desire. Why was he doing this? Had I done something wrong?

Through my confusion, I took a page from his book, tightening my expression and deliberately cooling my words before saying, "I had a very pleasant day. Thank you for allowing me to join you."

I turn to get out of the car, but I looked over my shoulder to see his reaction. My heart shuddered painfully when he only nodded curtly without looking at me and returned his attention to his phone.

The moment I had walked around to the entrance, the car took off. I watched it swerve onto the palm tree-lined drive until it disappeared through the gates. I hadn't felt so alone since I was nineteen, and my twin siblings left the house one after another without a word. Tears pricked the backs of my eyes, and it took me a moment to realize that I held the parcel of marlin that Sinclair had saved for us. I sucked in a deep breath. I hadn't come to Mexico to moon over a man, however handsome and devastating he might have been. I came to relax, to steel myself for the tumult of returning to my family. I didn't care if I saw Sinclair again, I assured myself. And buoyed by my lies, I entered the lobby with my chin tipped into the air like a princess.

"I'd like the kitchen to cook this for me," I said to the concierge. "I'll eat at Arrecifes at eight p.m."

"Excellent, Mrs. Buchanan. Will anyone be joining you?" he asked with a pleasantly bland smile that did nothing to help my mood.

Someone coming in from the beach caught my eye, and I turned to a brief-clad Stefan with a broad smile.

"Stefan," I called, my confidence revived by his appreciative smile. "How would you like to join me for dinner?"

Chapter Ten

THE FISH WAS FANTASTIC. THEY SERVED IT WITH THREE SAUCES, BUT THE RICH, spicy mole was my favorite. It was easy to focus on the delicious meal because each time I tuned into Stefan's Greek accent, I found myself thinking about another accent spoken by another man. I wondered as I pushed a flaky piece of marlin across my plate, what the business was that he had to conduct so very late at night.

"I know I opened with the dullness of sport," Stefan spoke louder, trying to draw my attention, "but I switched to the art world just for you, Giselle, and still your eyes pass through me. If I was a less beautiful man, I might be insulted."

I smiled at him, grateful for his easy charm. "I'm sorry, Stefan. I had a tiring day. It wasn't considerate of me to invite you to a meal when I can hardly stay awake."

His brown fingers drummed against the tablecloth as he studied me. "No, I don't think it is sleep you want. Might it have something to do with the man down by the pool yesterday afternoon?"

I stared at my empty wineglass as if it was fascinating.

He chuckled as a server came to refill our glasses and take our plates. I hadn't finished my meal, but my stomach was in knots from thinking over what I could have possibly done to send Sinclair away.

"You are here alone, Giselle." Stefan reached forward to take my cold hand in his and squeezed it warmly. "I mean only to be a friend if you have need of one."

The tension that had been building in my chest loosened, and my shoulders sagged slightly with the release. I hardly knew anything about the Greek before me, but that wasn't saying much because I hardly knew anything about the Frenchman I was sleeping with. Had been sleeping with. But Stefan was kind and pleasantly vain, so I knew he would offer me insight over judgment and probably find genuine amusement in my situation.

"I'm having a holiday affair."

He nodded and sat back in his chair, his posture straight but regal, like a king lounging on his throne. "How exciting."

"Yes." I nodded, pretending to be someone confident and experienced —someone more like my sister than me—but I could tell by the shrewd brightness in his eyes that Stefan didn't believe me. "It's more complicated than I thought it would be."

"Affairs always are," he mused. "Is he married?"

My shoulders hunched near my ears as he hit the nail dangerously close to the head. "Longtime partner."

He frowned slightly and raised his glass but didn't drink from it. "I see. But this isn't something you normally do. Why now? Why him?"

And not me, his question seemed to imply. I knew he was attracted to me, but I also got the impression he could have been attracted to anyone with good looks, be it a man or woman. Stefan had the kind of fluid sexuality that was both sexy and scary in a man. I wished I could be as free as him.

"Do I sound childish if I say it was a feeling I had?" When Stefan rolled his eyes in gentle mockery, I laughed. "Fine. Well, he was unbelievably handsome, for starters. And I guess this sort of thing"—I waved my hand abstractly—"was the next step in my evolution from self-conscious frump to a somewhat sophisticated woman."

"From a duckling to a swan?"

I thought instantly of Sinclair, assuring me that the airplane was something beautiful and full of power—a swan. "I guess," I murmured.

"How is it working out for you so far? I must say, you have a glow in your cheeks, and if it weren't for the tension in your shoulders, I would say you look remarkably well."

"We don't talk about anything specific; those are the rules. But he took me to a business party and out fishing today. I feel like I'm getting to know him in a way, but when we returned to the resort, he was cold and dismissed me so easily."

I remembered so clearly the feeling of shame as he left me at the entrance. Just another person disappointed in me.

Stefan was staring at me with narrowed eyes, his lips quirked down in concern. "I could hit him if you'd like?" When I laughed, he glared reproachfully at me. "You wouldn't laugh if you knew how much I value my hands."

I wiped a tear escaping from my eye and swallowed the giggles still hovering in my throat. "I'm sorry, Stefan. That was a very gallant offer, but I think I'll pass."

"What is it that you want to do then? Are you happy to let him dismiss you?" He leaned forward, his bared teeth glinting in the low light. His face had contracted, and I could sense the sudden hostility in him. "Maybe you bored him in bed, Giselle, or maybe you shattered his expectations. Are you happy never to know? This is the problem with women, you know? They think men know everything, that we are unmoved by their charms. The truth, my French-Italian beauty, is that you bombard us with desires. And a woman like yourself should never be dismissed, even if the man in question is 'unbelievably handsome.'"

"What are you saying?"

"I'm saying, if you aren't ready to end your holiday affair, then don't let it end. Go to him, seduce him all over again." His eyes skimmed my form in frank admiration.

The idea of seducing Sinclair was deeply appealing. I could picture him before me, his dazzling blue eyes burning with desire, his head tipped back as he groaned at the feel of my mouth on him.

"There you are." Stefan smiled at me, tipping his wineglass and at last taking a long sip. "Your gumption is back."

I took a sip of wine to hide my coy smile. "Any ideas of how I should surprise him?"

Stefan grinned broadly and rubbed his hands together in glee. "Now we are getting to the good stuff."

Hours later, when the moon was swollen in the dark sky, and all the diners had long since retired to their beds or downtown prospects, I stood at the door of Sinclair's room with my fist closed and poised over the wood.

Despite Stefan's pep talk over more than a few glasses of wine, my confidence was dissipating with each breath. Sinclair had dismissed me for a reason, I reminded myself. Who did I think I was just showing up at his room in the middle of the night? What kind of woman did that?

Me, a small but remarkably powerful voice in my head cried out. *I do that!* The kind of woman I wanted to be, had always dreamed of being, wouldn't hesitate to take what she wanted.

Besides, I had spent over half an hour in my room freshening up for my seduction. I didn't own any beautiful lingerie, so I had opted to go nude beneath the thin white summer dress fluttering against my upper thighs, and Stefan's hands had artfully mussed my hair into something indefinably sexy. I remembered his words of encouragement and sucked in a final deep breath.

No one stirred within the room. I knocked again, with more force, and considered the very real possibility that Sinclair was still at work, or worse, that he was with someone else. I was surprised I even cared. Of course, he could be. What claim did I have on him as a stranger who had known him for three days and knew nothing of his origins or even his last name?

With the last ounce of my courage, I knocked once more before turning on one of my highest heels to leave. I had only taken a few steps away when the sound of the door opening behind me prompted me to look over my shoulder.

Sinclair stood in the frame clad in a dismantled suit, his white shirt untucked and slightly wrinkled and his feet bare. The sight of those naked brown feet had me swallowing past a swell of unexpected desire, but the instant I caught his eye, I almost choked on his expression. His beautiful blue eyes were bloodshot, and his features carefully guarded as if I had come to trick him out of something precious. He didn't say anything as he stared at me, his posture rigid but not hostile. I doubted my purpose for a second as he waited for me to speak, but when his thick brows rose daringly, I straightened my spine and dug deep for some confidence.

On slightly wobbly legs, I slowly walked back to him, only stopping when my high heels brushed his toes. I had to crane my neck to look up into his expressionless eyes.

"Have you eaten?"

He frowned, and I was thrilled that my question threw him off.

Jerkily, he nodded.

I bit my lip in genuine nervousness and noted the way his eyes lingered over the motion. "Do you have room for dessert?"

Slowly, both to heighten the anticipation and to calm my jittery heart, I slid the flimsy straps of my white sundress off my shoulders. No one was in the hall. It was too late for returning diners, and anyone out clubbing wouldn't return home for hours yet, but still, the vulnerability of my almost nakedness as my dress slipped easily off my shoulders to pool at my feet was intense. I kept my eyes on his the entire time, watching as first shock and then excitement flared in those azure depths. I tried not to fidget as he took in my bare breasts, heaving slightly under my anxious breath, and the white cotton underwear blocking me from total nudity.

A thin hiss streamed through his clenched teeth, and he shifted uncomfortably on his feet, but his eyes left blazing trails across my skin. "Jesus Christ."

I raised an eyebrow and shakily joked, "I'm not sure he would approve."

A startled smirk twitched his lips, but he shook his head. "Elle, I shouldn't do this."

I watched his Adam's apple bob convulsively in his brown throat, and it distracted me from the itchy scratch of guilt that prickled up my spine. "You promised me seven days." I cleared my throat, but my voice remained husky with nerves and desire. "You don't seem like a man to go back on your word."

"I made a promise to the woman waiting for me back home," he countered, but his voice was quiet as if even he didn't want to hear the truth of his statement.

I nodded slowly and opened my palms, aware of every ripple of air across my bare flesh. "I know, and I respect that."

It seemed so surreal to be having this conversation in the open, wearing nothing but my modest panties.

His gaze flashed across my exposed skin once more before settling on my eyes. He stared at me for a long moment, his expression hardened with uncertainty. I kept my features open and honest, radiating the simple desire I had for him and allowing some of the other feelings—the ones I was too scared to analyze—to slip in around the edges. Finally, he seemed to find something in my face that he had been desperately searching for, and he let out a ragged sigh.

Feeling brave, I placed my hand against his slightly stubbled cheek. "I want you."

His groan reverberated throughout the still night air, and before I could move, his lips were on mine, his tongue swiping across the closed seam of my lips persuasively until I opened for him. He bent and grasped the backs of my thighs to hoist me into his arms. My frantic hands dived into his thick chin-length hair and tugged, pulling him even closer to me while the hands that cupped my bottom squeezed. Vaguely, I was aware that we were in his room now, the door kicked shut behind us and that he was moving us quickly toward the bed. When he softly deposited me on the mattress, I mumbled a protest against his lips as he moved away.

I stared up at him with pleading eyes, my body physically shaking with my desire for him. His eyes burned as he looked down at me, and I was pleased to see the swell of his dick tightening against the zipper of his slacks.

He licked his bottom lip unconsciously, making me gasp. "You are glorious."

His words infused me with sensual confidence. My heart beating erratically as I allowed my closed knees to flop open, revealing my underwear-covered center. His breath hitched, but he gently pushed my hands away when I reached for him. I watched with questioning eyes as he sank to his knees on the plush carpet and ran his hands up the outsides of my legs to my bottom so that he could tug me closer to the edge of the bed. I leaned up on my elbows to watch him as his fingers ran up one of my legs, lifting it into the air.

Whether it was the fact my seduction had worked or that I had never seen such carnality in a man's gaze before, I felt more confident and infinitely sexier than I ever had before.

I sighed as he kissed the arch of my foot.

"I think we'll keep these on," he husked as he ran his tongue lightly over the seam between my exposed foot and the outrageously tall high heels.

His eyes caught mine, and I sucked in a deep breath at the wicked intent there. Moving up my legs, he sunk his teeth lightly into the soft skin of my inner thigh while holding my gaze. My head collapsed back on my shoulders as I shuddered out a groan.

I squeezed my eyes closed as he lifted my rump to pull off my underwear and splay my legs farther apart. I might have exposed myself to him at the door, but the thought of him staring at the most intimate part of me still made me immensely self-conscious.

A finger dipped through my wet folds, and his smoky voice ordered, "Look at me."

I did as he asked; my eyes wide with apprehension as they landed on his face just an inch away from my aching core.

He blew cool air onto me, and whispered, "You are beautiful."

My entire being flushed hot and prickly with embarrassment, but his strong fingers clenched my thighs until I stopped wriggling. His tongue flicked out over the most sensitive part of me, and desire spiked through my system. Wanting to touch him, I whimpered and grasped at his strong shoulders to pull him toward me, but he resisted, and the gentle scrape of his teeth against my drenched flesh was a warning to let him continue. But the memory of him against my tongue, the unique taste of him, and the wonderful power I felt as I took him inside my mouth spurred me on.

"I want to taste you."

He froze at my words and then groaned against me. I squealed as he lifted me into his arms and flipped around to lie down on his back on the bed. He lifted me over him easily and spun me around to perch me over his face. Panic seized me, and I started to mumble my reluctance, but his firm hands yanked my hips lower until I could feel his tongue swirl over my clit. I trembled and braced my hands on his lower stomach.

I could feel the bunch and pull of the steely muscles under his skin as he moved under me, and I followed the tapered V of his abdomen to my prize. His arousal pressed into his stomach, and when I slid a thumb over his tip, it was wet with desire. I moaned as I leaned down to lap it off him, and his thighs flexed under my palms in reaction. I was beginning to think there was nothing I craved more than the intimacy and the power that came with having him in my mouth.

I had never gone down on Mark. He had respected my reticence in doing so, and the only time I had before was with Christopher. My mind contracted around his name, and I forcibly shoved it out of my head but not before I tensed over Sinclair.

Sensing my distraction, he gently pulled me to the side and turned to lie beside me on the opposite end of the bed from the pillows. He licked his lips as he settled against me, slipping an arm under my head to support me, and my eyes followed the path of his firm mouth. I leaned in to kiss him, but he pulled slightly at my shoulders so that I couldn't.

"What happened?" he asked. His voice was still pure sex, but a flicker of concern wavered in those expressive eyes.

I shrugged. "I don't know what you mean."

Anger clamped down on his features, turning his face into that distant, cold mask. "I'm not going to sleep with a woman who keeps secrets from me."

I couldn't help but snort at that. "We don't have anything but secrets between us, Sinclair."

His frown was fierce, knotting the skin between his chestnut brows in a way that I was beginning to find strangely adorable. "Not here. In my bed, I want you to be honest with me." Something like pain crossed his expression before he could hide it, and I wondered, not for the first time, about his partner back home. "I need you to be honest with me."

He hitched my leg over his hip and settled so close that his hard length pressed against my heat. My breath caught and released on a thready sigh. This was what I needed, I realized as I looked into his beautiful face, this intimacy. I had been without male comfort for most of my life, and to have someone like Sinclair desire me like this was beyond my wildest fantasies, my most hidden dreams.

He pressed against me slightly so that just the tip of him rested inside me. I clamped down on him, and the fire that flamed in his eyes unlocked my reticence to speak.

"I told you I wasn't a virgin," I whispered, closing my eyes so that I didn't have to see his reaction, "and I was telling you the truth."

He stilled against me and stroked my hair in silent support.

"We had a family friend, almost like an uncle, who helped us financially. We were pretty poor, especially for a while there, and he was almost like a guardian angel. When he started to date my sister, I think the family was relieved even though he was old enough to be her father. He was handsome and nice and everything." I clenched my eyes tighter until spots interrupted the memories playing across my lids. "I didn't really think anything of it when he started to seduce me."

Sinclair was so still and silent beside me that I wasn't sure what to make of it, so I slowly peeked out from under one lid. He was staring at me with the telltale muscle in his jaw jumping, and his eyes blazing so blue that I closed mine again.

"He was careful not to hurt me, and he was really kind, but we did some ..." *Horrible, disgusting, immoral, degrading?* "Unpleasant things together. No one ever found out, and when my mother and sister moved to America, they left him behind. I haven't seen him since, but"—I gestured back and forth between our bodies—"it feels strange to actually want to do some of those things with you."

"You don't have to do anything—" he started to say, but I opened my eyes and pressed my palm against his mouth to silence him.

My throat ached with sorrow, but I was grateful for my dry eyes when I whispered, "You don't understand. I want to do those things with you so badly I tremble."

I showed him my slightly quivering fingers and pressed them to his firm chest, trailing them down his skin until I reached his still semi-hard erection.

I wrapped my hands around his base and squeezed firmly. "I need this."

When I looked back into his eyes, they glowed with understanding and, thankfully, desire. He wasn't repulsed by my anxiety or my sketchy past, and I blew out a deep sigh of relief.

At a loss for what to do now, I was grateful when he said, "Taste me, Elle." When my eyes widened, he nodded, and his tone grew stern. "Take me in your hands, between your lips, and do what you want with me. Make me come."

The dominance in his voice left no room for argument, but I could tell by the gentle stroke of his hand over my hair that even though I would be pleasuring him, this was for me too. He was commanding me to step past my fears and do what I wanted desperately and secretly to do. He nodded at me, seeing the understanding in my expression.

With trembling fingers, I pushed him onto his back and straddled his thighs in order to run my fingers over the bumps and muscular curves of his torso. Sinclair was built powerfully but lean like a runner, and I traced the map of his muscles with reverent fingers. Soon, that became inadequate, and I dipped my head to sketch the texture of his abs under my tongue. His groin vibrated under my lips, and I smiled against his skin as I took his rigid length tightly in one hand.

I was surprised by how badly I wanted to take him in my mouth, but I withheld. Twisting my hand over his length slowly but surely a few times, I then flicked the head with my tongue. His fists bunched in the duvet as I parted my lips and pushed him into my mouth. It was impossible to take all of him in this position, but I tried anyway, relaxing my throat and swallowing to fight my gag reflex, but mostly, I swirled my tongue across his luscious head and even lightly scraped my teeth across the base of him.

I could feel my own desire drip down my inner thighs, and by the time he pulled me off him, I was perilously close to orgasming, and he hadn't even touched me. So, when he finally settled between my legs and plowed into me, I screamed in pleasure. I hadn't realized how I would ache for him even after less than twelve hours without him inside me. It didn't bode well for me if I was this desperate for him after only four days with our inevitable end rushing up to meet us.

He shifted the angle of my hips and captured both my hands in one of his to press them above my head. The feeling of helplessness, the texture of his coarse chest hair against my aching nipples, and the fire he stoked so skillfully between my legs banished all rational thought. I threw back my head and groaned.

Sinclair watched me with eyes on fire. His taut jaw and the beads of sweat crowning his forehead were the only other signs that he was not completely in control. He dipped his head and took one of my peaks between his lips, sucking hard. My legs tightened, crossing against his flexing buttocks until the sharp point of my heels dug into his tender flesh. He hissed against my skin and took my nipple gently between his teeth. Unbearable heat swirled through my body, and I clenched my teeth, desperate for release from the tension.

Sensing my need, Sinclair's free hand slipped down my damp belly to the soft curls of my sex, unerringly finding the button of pleasure at my center. I gasped as he flicked me.

I was so close that stars burst across my vision.

"Sinclair, please," I begged, my head thrashing from side to side at the myriad of sensations he evoked in my body. I was so close, but I wanted—no, needed—him to give me permission to tumble over the edge.

"Yes," he growled against my breast, and with my nipple still between his teeth, he clamped down almost viciously.

I let out a hoarse scream as the seams of my body unraveled, and the brutal climax overtook me. Releasing me, Sinclair reared up and began to move for himself, pounding into me with short, hard strokes that drove me higher and higher. When he finally groaned and released inside me, I was heavy and saturated with pleasure, unable to even drop my freed hands from above my head.

He collapsed beside me, his breathing uneven and his dusky skin covered in a sheen of sweat so that he seemed to glow in the soft lamplight. It was late, and I felt more liquid than human. My lids weighed ten tons, but I so loved to look at Sinclair, especially when he wasn't aware of it. I noticed the faint stubble lining his sharp jaw and wondered idly if I would have beard burn painted across my sensitive skin. The thought of being branded by him made my recently sated desire stir its sleepy head.

As if sensing my thoughts, he smiled slightly with his eyes closed. "You are insatiable."

"How did you know what I was thinking?" I laughed.

One lid cracked open, revealing a vivid blue iris sparkling with humor. "I might not know you very well, but I do know your body." His left hand smoothed over the curve of my hip, and I turned on my side to face him. "I know how much I turn you on."

I blushed, but he chuckled and chucked me softly on the chin. "Nothing to be ashamed of. If anything, I'm flattered." His lips twisted as if he couldn't believe it himself. "I know it isn't in your nature to be so bold."

"No," I agreed, fiddling with the edge of the silky pillowcase. "I wasn't sure you'd be pleased."

He raised a brow and indicated toward his satiated organ. "Despite evidence to the contrary."

I smiled, but self-consciousness had reared its ugly head again, and it was hard to put it back to bed. Even though I might not know him very well, I knew enough about his dominant predilections to question whether he had truly enjoyed my assertiveness.

"You don't believe me," he said, and though I wasn't looking at him, I could feel his frown.

"Well, I know you like to be the one in control," I murmured.

The sudden silence was thick and electric with tension. I hadn't expected him to react so strongly to my simple observation, and when I looked up at him, he seemed frozen, staring woodenly at the ceiling.

"I didn't mean to offend," I said softly, but I wasn't really sorry because what I had said was true.

I remembered Cosima telling me about the world of sex and games, glossing over the finer details but still too knowledgeable to be inexperienced in their arts. She had mentioned domination and submission, the thrill some people got from administering punishment and controlling another's pleasure. I wasn't sure how far Sinclair's kink went, but I was pretty sure he was into some degree of BDSM.

He sighed heavily and dragged his arm across his forehead, almost as if he wanted to shield his eyes from me. "I'm overreacting. I was the one who said there should be no secrets in our bed."

A little thrill from hearing him call the bed "ours" raced up my spine.

"I ..." He rubbed a hand over his face. "I used to be involved in the BDSM scene, years ago now, but when I met E... When I met my current girlfriend, I gave it up. She wasn't interested." He laughed harshly. "In fact, she was repulsed by it."

Tenderness swelled in my chest, and I reached out tentatively to touch his arm. "Most people are afraid of things they don't understand."

He turned his head to stare at me, his expression fierce. "You don't know anything about it."

"No." I nodded slowly. "But I'd like to."

His dark brows shot up, but his eyes were stilled guarded. "You don't know what you're saying."

It was my turn to sigh. I propped up on one arm in order to look down at him.

"I do. We've already broken so many rules, yours and mine. If we are going to have a holiday affair, why not live out those fantasies? I can't say I know much about all of that, but I'm curious." I looked down at the crumpled bed sheet, suddenly bashful but unwilling to admit it.

"We aren't talking about squash here, Elle." He was angry now, his voice smooth and steely. "BDSM isn't something you can dabble in. You need complete trust and honesty in order to be safe, and you hardly know me."

And shouldn't trust me, I read in his gaze.

Yes, I thought stubbornly, *I can.*

"I'm not saying I want you to tie me up and gag me every time we sleep together." My skin pulsed with hot and cold pinpricks of lust and fear. "I'm not even saying I want to do this for you." He raised a brow at that but allowed my white lie to go uncontested. "I was shy and miserable with it for so long, declining every indulgence that came my way because I thought I didn't deserve it." I tilted my chin and tried to stop my stomach from quivering with nerves. "This is something that I want, Sinclair. Something that I need."

He stared at me for a long time until my elbow ached from my awkward position, and my skin cooled. I watched his implacable expression, searching for the tells I was now so familiar with, but only his eyes gave him away; the intense blue depths were dark with troubled thoughts.

Finally, he spoke, but his lips were strangely unmoved so that, at first, I didn't know he was talking. "It's intimate, Elle. For some, there is no turning back."

His eyes were locked onto mine, emphasizing his point. I blinked through my surprise because the thought that I may be converted to the lifestyle had not occurred to me.

He nodded, and I wondered if I had spoken aloud. "You acted on impulse, but you didn't really think this through. As a man who has become enchanted by the siren's call, let me at least warn you before you take the plunge."

"Show me." When his lips pursed to argue with me, I placed my palm over his mouth. "How will I know if I like it or not if you don't show me?"

I knew so little about what to do, so I followed my desires, folding onto my knees and scooting closer to him. Taking his angular face between my palms, I composed my features and hoped that I sounded, well, irresistible.

"I want to submit to you."

Why was saying it out loud so arousing? I felt the power of those vulnerable words pull my shoulders back and blaze behind my gaze.

He touched my chin, pinching it slightly in his fingers. I waited calmly as he studied me and felt a thrill course through me as he shuddered with acquiescence. My eyes fluttered closed as I waited for him to kiss me, ravish me in some way, but his chuckle made them spring open. He was smiling at me with something close to tenderness as he drew two fingers down my throat, hovering over my throbbing pulse.

"Not tonight, siren. As I said, this isn't a game, and if we are going to do this, then we will do it properly."

He looked into my eyes with the kind of intensity meant to scare me, and honestly, I felt a shiver of apprehension race across my skin, but before I could react, he was pulling away from me and swinging to his feet with feline grace.

I watched his small, firm buttocks as he bent over to pull on his charcoal gray lounging pants. When he turned back to me, the shutters were once again pulled down over his emotions, and his gorgeous blue eyes were only vacant pools.

"I have work to do," he stated, coolly staring at me as if I was a business associate and not his lover.

In some ways, I supposed, I was no more than an agreement, a pleasurable one certainly, but still just an equal investor in a mutual asset. The thought made me suddenly sick to my stomach.

An angry flush burned my cheeks as I scrambled out of bed and into the other room to search for my discarded summer dress.

He entered just as the cool fabric dropped down over my damp skin. I knew that he watched me as I adjusted the skirt and ran my fingers through my hopelessly tangled hair. I didn't know why he stood there when it was obvious he wanted me gone. It only made it more awkward to have him wait impatiently at the doorway to his bedroom.

Resentment fizzed across my skin, infusing me with sudden shame-fueled hatred. I turned to him, mouth open and ready to snap at him for treating me so callously, for being the most mercurial man I had ever met, but something in his face arrested me. His hands flexed restlessly at his sides, and he rocked lightly back and forth on his feet while his face—the devastating face I was coming to like entirely too much—stared at me with that wolf-like hunger I had only caught glimpses of before. But this time, after a round of passionate lovemaking, the expression was skewed by something other than lust—tenderness, maybe, and an undercurrent of regret.

As if he knew my thoughts, he nodded and cleared his throat to softly bid me good night. "Get a good night's sleep, Elle. You'll need it."

The fight left me. There was indecision in his stance, and in my heart, I wondered if it had been the right thing to come back to his room. It could have ended so amicably if I had just stayed away, but now it was too late, I was invested, and as I nodded curtly at my Frenchman, I could already feel my heart clench painfully with foreboding.

My hand was on the door handle when I felt him grasp my arm. Without turning me, he pressed himself against my back and placed a gentle kiss on the side of my face.

"Sweet dreams."

Chapter Eleven

"So," Cosima practically yelled, "how are things going with the married man?"

I hushed her even though I sat alone on the sand, and no one could hear her through the phone. The midday sun beat down on the landscape, hammering everything into gold. It had been a productive morning, swimming followed by a few hours of photographing and sketching the surrounding area. Now, I lay pleasantly exhausted in the sun slathered with sunscreen. The heat was the only thing I really missed about Naples, and despite being a redhead with freckles, my skin loved a good golden tan. Even though I hadn't heard from Sinclair, I was beyond content, especially listening to the familiar spiced tones of my sister through the phone.

"He is an enigma," I murmured, shifting sand through my hands.

"Oh no, you never have been able to resist a mystery. And I'm sure the sex is fantastic. You must have it bad."

"Cosi!" I protested through my laughter. "I haven't even told you about our sex life."

"I know." I could hear her smile. "Which tells me it's excellent. Otherwise, you would have a million questions and complaints."

Fair enough.

"I do still have a few questions." I took a deep breath and fought the flush I could feel flaming across my skin. I stood to walk to the water, hoping the cool ocean would steady me. "He is, well, he's a bit into domination."

"Oh." The single syllable was loaded with meaning. I could picture my beautiful sister pursing her lips, trying to decide how to approach this. "And are you into it, as well?"

"Yeah," I whispered. "A bit. With him."

"Well, I honestly never thought I would be having this conversation with my older sister. No offense, Gigi, but I also figured you for vanilla all the way."

"Me too. But with him, it's different. *I'm* different. I know it's only a holiday affair, but I want to please him. He is almost totally cut off from everyone, cool and remote. One minute he is so tender with me, almost as if he really likes me, and the next, he's telling me to get lost."

"He sounds like a *bastardo*."

I laughed. "No, he's too well-mannered to be that."

"Your life is your life, *bambina*, but I do have to say it. Don't do this just for him. BDSM isn't something to dabble in." Her voice was weighted, and I wondered what exactly my little sister had experienced in her short twenty-two years. She had left home so young, alone and in a business that often sexually abused women.

"Miss Buchanan?"

I looked over my shoulder to see a young waiter standing hesitantly on the sand. "One second, Cosi." I walked up the beach to address him. "Yes?"

"I've been asked to give you a message." His dark eyes skimmed over my exposed curves quickly before landing on my face. At least he had the decency to blush.

I smiled warmly at him as I took the envelope. "I'm sorry, I don't have any cash on me."

He once again noted my bikini-clad form. "No problem, *señorita*, enjoy the sun."

With my phone tucked between my ear and my shoulder, I ripped open the envelope and sighed when I read the compact script written inside.

"What?" Cosima asked impatiently.

I fingered the letter and smiled hugely. "I have to go; my Frenchman is waiting."

He had been waiting for me on the other end of the beach just off the shore in a small, sleek motorboat. A man offered to drive me out to him on the Jet Ski, but I ignored the offer, giving him my bag to take out to the boat while I walked into the ocean, eager to swim the distance.

Sinclair watched the entire time, his eyes a physical touch on my skin. I was a skilled swimmer, and the velvety brush of the azure waters against my skin gave me confidence. When I reached the boat, I grasped the ladder and paused, tipping my head back as water streamed off me. He didn't offer a hand as I swung onto the deck, and I had to hide a giggle behind my hand when I saw the lust written across his stern face. My eyes flickered down his linen shirt to his worn denim shorts and noted the bulge there. It had only been a dozen hours since I had last seen him, yet the sight of Sinclair, strong legs braced against the rocking waves and skin kissed gold under the sun, stirred something intense inside me.

"Hello, Sinclair," I said, surprised by the huskiness of my tone.

My voice snapped him out of his trance, and he strode over to me. Gripping the backs of my thighs, he lifted me swiftly, easily into his arms. His hands were hot on my bottom, and his lips were instantly on mine, sweeping possessively into my mouth. I groaned against his tongue.

"I missed you last night." His voice heated my skin as his lips skimmed across my throat and down to my shoulder, where he sank his teeth lightly.

My heart warmed like a small furnace in my chest. God, I hadn't realized how much I wanted to hear those words from him. I tipped my neck to the side, giving him greater access and shuddered as he took advantage, sucking and nipping on the delicate skin.

"Me too." I sighed, sinking my fingers into his lustrous mane. "Don't send me away again."

"No," he agreed, his hands flexing on my ass.

We made out like teenagers, his fingers traveling up and down my body, eager to touch every square inch while his mouth worked wonders on mine. When we finally broke apart minutes later, we were both panting. We were so close, staring at each other, that we breathed the same breath. Electricity crackled in the air between us until finally, I grinned. I watched his features crack and break out into a glorious smile. Giddiness bubbled in my chest until I couldn't contain it, and giggles frothed over. He began to laugh too; rich, throaty laughter that made him squeeze his eyes shut.

We were being stupid and silly, just like teenagers fresh in lust—in love —but I didn't care. My heart raced, and I could feel my skin glow. My holiday affair had just become something so much more. And though he didn't verbally acknowledge it, I knew somehow that Sinclair felt the same way.

"What are we doing out here?" I asked as he let me slip down his body to my feet. His erection pressed into my belly, and I shivered at the familiar feel of it.

"I thought you might enjoy going snorkeling with me." He looked down at me, a small smile lingering on his lips.

"You thought right." I smiled, filled with happiness.

The future, those thoughts about going back to reality where he had a girlfriend, and I wasn't bold, were pushed firmly to the back of my mind. I was determined to enjoy the rest of my time with him, no matter what.

He nodded and took my hand to lead me to a small seat beside the wheel. I realized that the resort staff had already dropped off my bag, and I quickly checked on my camera. We were the only people on the boat, and it appeared that Sinclair intended to drive it. He winked at me as he started the engine, obviously catching the surprise on my face.

We didn't speak as he drove us, but he looked over at me sometimes with that slight Sinclair smile. I studied him, pleased with his preoccupation. He stood easily behind the raised control panel, his legs braced and his hand loosely on the throttle. The wind whipped his chestnut hair back from his face, revealing features that were uncharacteristically soft and open. It thrilled me to know he was relaxed in my company, enough so to shed the hardened exterior that he wore for everyone else. Was he like this with the girlfriend? I shoved the thought aside with a frown and focused on the passing coastline instead.

"Can I take your picture?" I yelled over the noise.

Sinclair frowned slightly but relented when he looked over at my eager expression. I snapped a dozen pictures of him, too many really, moving carefully across the hull to get a full-frontal picture of my captain. I knew they would be beautiful photos, and I was happy to have a permanent piece of him to pull out after our holiday ended.

When he turned off the engine, I looked up from my viewfinder to take in the beauty of the small cove we bobbed in. Large reddish rocks bracketed a secluded white sand beach, and the turquoise water was so clear that I could see the multitudes of fish passing by our boat as if through a magnifying glass. I looked over at Sinclair with an overexcited smile.

He placed a hand against my cheek and leaned down to press a kiss to my smiling lips. "It's good to make my siren smile."

I fought the urge to swoon and won.

I shrugged. "It's okay, I guess."

He blinked and barked with laughter. Tugging me to my feet, he swatted my rear. "Ungrateful brat."

We continued our banter as he outfitted us both with flippers, goggles, and a breathing piece. I shook my head at the offer of a life jacket, and he took my hand as we stood at the stern of the boat, ready to jump in. He was so playful and open that it was hard to contain my enjoyment even though I knew better. Logically, I knew he was mercurial, and the situation was temporary, but I felt myself falling, tumbling almost brutally and certainly clumsily, in love with him.

The surf was calm and silky as we moved through the cove. Sometimes, we swam together amidst a school of yellow and silver fish, their touch like cool kisses against my skin, but after a while, we abandoned the serious snorkeling and began to horse around. Sinclair was an excellent swimmer, and when I asked him about it, he divulged that he had been a swimmer since high school and all through college, which explained the delicious cut of his lean body. We swam for over an hour before I dragged myself to the beach, collapsing in exhaustion on the caramel sand.

Sinclair laughed as he emerged from the waves, pushing his wet hair back from his forehead as he stood over me. "My siren can't be tired already."

I wanted to close my eyes, but it was difficult to take them off him. "A certain someone tired me out last night. I didn't get much sleep."

His lips curved softly as he bent down, running two fingers down my chest to collect the drops of water lingering there. "You won't get much rest tonight, either."

No, I wouldn't. The promise in his shaded eyes drew the heat of a different kind across my bare skin.

"You could be a model," I murmured, sitting up to run my fingers over the rippling mass of muscles in his abdomen.

His fingers froze at the line of my bikini bottoms, and a cold anger settled into his previous contented features. I watched his mouth twist before he sighed and dropped to the sand beside me.

His shoulders were rounded as he stared out at the ocean, and he let me take one of his slack hands in my own. "I was a model actually."

My eyes widened comically. I was thankful his gaze remained riveted on the sea.

"My foster mother discovered me; she was my agent before she became my mother." He shrugged as if he didn't care, but I could feel his sadness seep into my skin where we touched. "I only did it for a handful of years. When they discovered I had a sharp mind too, they decided that could be put to better use."

I shifted on the sand until I sat behind him, my legs spread wide by the sheer width of his body between my thighs. He tensed as my arms slipped around him in a gentle embrace, but when I pressed a kiss to his salty skin, he sighed raggedly and relaxed.

"Parents shouldn't make their children sad," I said because I could remember the despair that my father, Seamus Moore, always left in his wake.

"You are very sweet and very correct, but that does not stop it from happening."

"What did they do to you?" I whispered, almost afraid to press him when he was being so inexplicably open.

He was quiet for a long time and utterly still but for two fingers that slid back and forth gently over my forearm.

"Nothing so bad. They used me mostly to position themselves in society. Sometimes it was as easy as making friends with the right sons of important men or modeling to help make enough money to support my father's campaign." His knuckles swept up my wrist and over the back of my hand so that he could link our fingers. "Sometimes, it was about seducing the right person. As I said, it wasn't so bad."

"That's not funny, Sin."

"No." He pressed a kiss to our combined hands. "*Mais comme des gens disent, c'est la vie.*"

But as people say, this is life.

"Not anymore," I said with more ferocity than I intended.

"Not anymore," he agreed. "Perhaps it is easier to understand my need for control now."

It was. My heart ached with the influx of love and sympathy. If there had previously been any hope of emerging unscathed from this affair, it was gone.

"Are you still in touch with them?" I mumbled against his salty shoulder.

"It's complicated."

"Why do I have the feeling most things with you are?" I teased, poking him in his unyielding stomach in an attempt to lighten the mood.

He lifted one of my hands and pressed it to his slightly smiling lips. "Just be grateful you are rid of me in four days."

"More like three," I retorted flippantly even though my chest tightened dangerously. "And for all you know, I could be as complicated as it comes."

He snorted, an undignified sound that was so at odds with his sophisticated persona that it made me laugh. "I highly doubt that. Your straightforward innocence is one of the reasons I find you so irresistible."

"Irresistible, huh?"

He bit gently into one of my fingers. "No man can resist the taste of this skin." His tongue darted out to soothe the fading pain, inciting a sigh from me.

I was tempted to cave to his seduction, but if he was going to speak freely, then this was too good an opportunity to pass up.

I pressed my cheek to his back once more, and murmured, "My family has been broken for a long time."

Sinclair pulled my arms closer around him so that I was flush against his back. His lips against my open palm urged me to continue.

"My father was a drunk and a gambler," I said as if that explained everything. Why my sister had run away, why my brother had moved soon after to America, why my eldest sister hated me—all of it.

"Is he ...?" His body tensed so that I felt like I was hugging a wooden board. "Is he the reason you weren't a virgin when we met?"

It took a moment for his question to settle in. I shuddered but shook my head vigorously. "In a way. If you're asking if he sexually abused me, he didn't. But maybe if he had been around...?" I shrugged.

We were quiet for a few minutes, just holding each other. We were both sticky with salt and sweat from the brilliant afternoon sun, but I was so happy my blood fizzed and danced like champagne. It was hard to tell what Sinclair was feeling, especially when I couldn't see his face to search for his tells, but it was probably better that way.

Three days. Only three more days with this brilliant and beautiful man. My arms tightened around him.

Sensing my mood, he gently reached back to swing me around to his front, settling me over his lap. The feel of his large hands spanning my waist delighted me.

"Are you mad?" I asked, reaching up to run a hand through his silky hair. Under the blazing Mexican sun, it was an astonishing shade of copper.

He lifted his knees so that I could rest my back against them and leaned back on his hands, presenting his long, flat torso to my other wandering hand.

"For?"

"Well, we haven't exactly adhered to your rules. Dunkard fathers and exploitative foster parents aren't business talk or sex."

The left side of his mouth quirked as he said, "No, not exactly. But if you haven't noticed, I gave up on the rules relatively quickly." When I pursed my lips, he shook his head as if I was dense. "Sleeping beside you, taking you fishing, fucking you last night after I promised myself I wouldn't ..." His hand slipped up the curve of my waist, over my breast, and up into my tangled hair. "I think it's pretty obvious I can't control myself around you."

I snorted. "You're never not controlled."

His eyes flared, and I gasped when he sat up and sank both hands in my hair, holding me tight so that even if I had wanted to, I couldn't move.

"Challenge accepted," he murmured darkly before slanting his firm lips over mine.

I moaned into his mouth, opening eagerly for the feel of his hot tongue against mine. My nails raked up his back and locked around his neck, tugging him closer as I wrapped my legs around his torso. I rocked over his erection so that the fabric of my suit rasped against my clit.

His hands plucked at the sides of my string bikini and tugged it off quickly so that his fingers could find me, already weeping with desire for him. There was desperation to our movements, a neediness that inflamed me. It didn't surprise me that I was already aching with want. When two fingers played through my damp curls and swirled at my opening, I groaned and ground down on them. He trapped my bottom lip in his teeth, warning me to stay still as he teased me.

"I don't want to come without you inside me," I panted into his mouth before skating my teeth along his jaw, tasting the salt of the sea and of him against my tongue.

His jaw tensed under my lips, and he quickly undid the tie to his swimsuit, exposing his cock to my waiting fingers. I placed him at my entrance and wiggled over the tip, waiting until his dark eyes met mine to slam down hard onto him.

We both groaned at the sensation. There was some pain, but it only contrasted the pleasure, heightening it. Sinclair took my hips in his hands and tilted my pelvis, hitting a new angle inside me that made my legs tremble. Somehow, I was already close to an orgasm.

Seamlessly, Sinclair rolled me onto my back, spreading my legs open with his palms on my inner thighs, his thumbs teasing me where we were joined together. He was watching himself plunge in and out of my slick depths, his eyes glazed with arousal and two streaks of pink slashed high on his cheekbones. I had never seen anything more attractive.

I shuddered when he picked up the pace, and one thumb found my clit. He circled it firmly, pushing me into a sudden and intense climax that wracked my entire body. I cried out long and low, repeating his name like a chant. I was still out of it when he tilted my hips and began to plow into me, scraping against the sweet spot deep inside me with each thrust as if he was desperate to claim all of me. His features were warped with pleasure, and the sight of him lost in rapture, knowing that I was capable of making him lose control, made me dizzy.

"Elle," he groaned, bottoming out inside me and burrowing his face in my neck as he came.

Afterward, we lay in the sand. His body was too hot and heavy on top of mine, but when he tried to move, I whimpered in protest and linked my legs with his. I could feel him smile into my shoulder, and when he raised himself onto his forearms, I was rewarded with the sight of his smug satisfaction.

"Now, did that seem very controlled to you?" he asked, playfully tweaking my nipple.

I scrunched up my nose. "No. In fact, that was almost barbaric."

He laughed and licked a bead of sweat between my breasts, smacking his lips. "I told you, the taste of you is intoxicating."

"Mmm." I tightened my inner muscles against his softening length, watching his mouth open and his eyes unfocus slightly. "As is this."

When he began to harden again inside me, it was my turn to gasp. "You're insatiable!"

He nodded solemnly. "I only have three days left to enjoy this body, you better bet I'm going to take advantage of it."

I closed my eyes against the dual sensation of panic and desire that bloomed in my chest when he dipped his head to take my nipple in his hot, sucking mouth.

Three days. Only three more days with him.

Chapter Twelve

I SAT ON THE DECK OF SINCLAIR'S EXPANSIVE RESORT SUITE, WRAPPED UP IN AN overlarge fluffy white robe with my feet tucked underneath me and my freshly washed hair curling dry in the light breeze off the ocean when Sinclair's phone rang. We had been suspended in the kind of natural silence that usually takes years to form, only occasionally breaking from his work and my painting to smile like fools at each other.

The entire day had taken on a slightly hazy, almost dream-like nature. After taking me again on the shore, we swam back to the boat and returned to the resort. He had spoken on the phone while we crossed the grounds to his room, but he caught my hand in his, tucking his fingers into mine so I wouldn't feel ignored. I blushed when heads turned to watch us, their eyes lingering on Sinclair with varying degrees of lust and envy. He squeezed my hand when he caught my wide-eyed stare roving over them all, and the side of his firm mouth twitched in a private smile just for me.

After a quick shower where we mostly refrained from inappropriate touches, he led me to the patio without hesitation, swinging open the French doors to reveal a large wooden easel laden with a fresh canvas and the basic tools of my trade. When I had turned to him, my mouth slack with surprise, he shrugged and suggested that because he had to work, it was only prudent that I had something to occupy myself with too.

Now, I sat before the canvas with a soft lead pencil and a nearly completed outline of the Frenchman sitting across from me. It was a three-quarter profile to showcase the strong cut of his jaw and the slashing lines of his high cheekbones. I hadn't even brought his face to life with color or depth, but I could feel the intensity of his eyes and the texture of his twitching lips as they struggled to hold back a smile under my fingers as I feathered them over the canvas. There was a gaping space to the side of his slightly parted lips where I knew a woman's face would appear, head tilted at a desperate angle, mouth open beautifully but tired like the fading bloom of a rose, unfurled and red. I closed my eyes to imagine the heat in her gaze, her flaming sexual intent. Though he appeared to be the aggressor, dark and overwhelming in blacks and shadows, it was she, this woman on the very precipice of desire, who brought the passion into focus.

The sharp trill of the phone cut through my imagination, and for a moment, I wasn't sure where the noise was coming from. Sinclair frowned at the cell phone vibrating on the table beside him, the white light from his computer screen casting his features in stark relief.

I knew immediately who it was when he looked up at me with compressed lips.

I tried to shrug casually as I returned to my work. "You should get that."

His eyes were hot on the side of my face. "I'll leave."

"No. I don't mind if you stay." I turned to look at him even though I was worried he would see the sadness in my eyes.

He looked hard at me before nodding curtly and sweeping across the touch screen to answer the call.

"Darling," he answered.

My lips twisted involuntarily. Darling? That didn't seem like a pet name Sinclair would use. But I guess it suited his buttoned-up personality.

"The four thirty," he confirmed. "I understand. I'll catch a cab in ... No, it's important you are at the party when she gets there, and I really don't care." He paused, and I snuck a look at him. He tugged at a longish lock of hair, a nervous gesture that made him seem vulnerable, and when his eyes met mine, they were foggy with confusion and strain.

I stood, aware that my movement toward the door made Sinclair tense up.

When I returned to the deck a few minutes later, he was still speaking with her. His head snapped up, and I could tell he wanted me to look over at him, but I reclaimed my seat with a calm expression and took up my palate, swirling a cerulean blue with a dab of bright chartreuse in an attempt to replicate the electricity of Sinclair's blue eyes.

"I'm looking forward to meeting her," Sinclair was saying, his voice cool and modulated. "I know it will be hard on you, but seeing your family happy will more than make up for it … Yes, I know. You'd be surprised by how resilient family ties are to the passing of time."

Was it just me, or could the girlfriend sense the sorrow in his tone? I wondered how much she knew about Sinclair's particular brand of sorrow; if she took special care to distract him on Father's Day, what they did together on Christmas, and if he was close with her family. These questions sloshed between my ears like leftover seawater, making me nauseous and unbalanced.

"I don't know, darling."

There it was again. *Darling.* I tried to picture her, conjuring up someone with golden hair and a golden smile, tall of course, with legs for days and perfect breasts. If we met or if, God forbid, she found out about me, she would sneer at the sight of me. *This*, she would say, *is who you chose*?

"I have to go now, but please try to enjoy the meeting. It's not often you get to meet a Clinton."

A Clinton? Oh great, so Darling was not only beautiful, but she had a glamorous job that was also intellectual. I sighed heavily, indulging in my self-pity for one more minute before resolving to obliterate it completely. Sinclair wasn't mine, and it was unfair for me to take my frustrations out on him over that fact.

So when he came to stand behind me, close but carefully not touching, I leaned back into him and tipped my head back to smile.

"Hi."

His eyes were guarded. "Hi."

"Sit down," I urged, glaring at him when he hesitated to do so. Only when he was seated did I follow him across the deck and fold onto his lap.

He stared down at me in surprise, but his arms wrapped around me instinctively, and after a moment, he relaxed, sighing into my hair.

"I wish you hadn't heard that."

I wish you hadn't had to take it.

"It was fine, Sinclair. I know how this is ... How it ends."

His arms tightened around me almost painfully, and he only let go when I wriggled uncomfortably. I wanted to move on, to keep my promise to myself and enjoy the moment with him while I had it, but niggling questions about his girlfriend continued to plague me.

"A Clinton, hey?"

He adjusted in the chair, pulling me closer and tilting me so that I was more comfortable. One hand stroked through my hair, and he watched as the sunshine caught the strands and turned them into fire.

"She's a new associate at a top law firm and fairly political." He waited to see if I wanted to hear more and continued when I nodded. "She works most of the time."

"What's she like?" I asked quietly, paralyzed with apprehension.

He pressed a kiss to my crown. "Elegant, composed, extremely intelligent. When we first met, through her glamorous sister, I couldn't believe they were related."

"I know what that's like. My sisters and I couldn't be more different."

I thought of the inscrutable Elena, composed and tragic like a queen forced to abdicate her throne, and Cosima, sunlight incarnate. I'd been envious of them for years, striving to emulate every one of their formidable attributes.

"I can imagine. You are unlike anyone."

My heart contracted, and I had to bite back a moan. "It hurts me when you are so sweet."

He snorted but pulled back from me to stare into my face. "I'm hardly sweet. I don't have time to be nice, remember?"

I nodded, but I could tell he was surprised and maybe even a little disconcerted by my comment. "I still don't really know what you do, you know."

"No, you don't."

"Do you want to give me a hint?"

"Maybe." He leaned forward, bending over until his lips were just an inch from mine. "But that information comes with a price."

"What if I'm willing to pay?" I darted forward to nip his lip playfully and laughed against his mouth when he caught my lips in a punishing kiss.

Things were just heating up when the bell to his suite rang. When Sinclair didn't immediately pull away, I pushed at him and stood, righting my robe as I moved inside.

"I'm not done with you yet, Elle," he called from the deck as I reached the door and let the waiter in with the cart of aromatic Mexican food.

"I know you are new to this," he began to explain, his voice drifting closer as he made to come inside, "but disobedience will result in punishment."

I'm sure I was the exact shade of my flaming hair when Sinclair rounded the French doors and saw the flustered young waiter and me standing awkwardly side by side. His cool eyes swept over the scene without emotion, and I gasped when he casually leaned against the door-frame and crossed his arms, one eyebrow raised.

"I ..." I cleared my throat as my eyes darted back and forth between Sinclair and the young man. "I ordered food."

"I can see that." Sinclair nodded, the picture of banality with his bare feet peeking out of unbuttoned jeans and his overlong hair curled chaotically around his handsome face. "You need to keep your strength up for what I have in mind tonight."

My throat worked convulsively to swallow my shock. The waiter appraised me with a new kind of interest, his dark eyes lingering over the deep V exposed by the robe. Despite myself, I found desire surge through my blood. When I looked back at Sinclair, he nodded as if he could see my arousal from across the room.

"Pay the man, my siren. Where are your manners?" he reprimanded softly as he padded over to me and took the receipt from the waiter.

He watched me as he signed it and tugged me into a silken embrace, his arms wrapped around my form so that I could feel his entire length even through the thick robe. He sunk deep into the kiss, tantalizing me with deep strokes of his talented tongue while a hand pushed my robe daringly low on my shoulders, exposing the tops of my breasts. Forgetting myself completely, I submitted to his possession and moaned quietly as I melted into his arms.

When he finally pulled away with a slight but very smug smile, I had to blink rapidly for a minute to reorient myself.

"Oh," I squeaked when I saw the waiter shift uncomfortably, adjusting a very discernable bulge in his pants.

Mortified, I dashed into the bedroom and closed the door on Sinclair's deep chuckle as he addressed the poor young man. I closed my eyes and banged my head lightly against the wall to dislodge the lingering desire cluttering my thoughts. How could I have been so ... slutty? I could feel the dampness between my legs, slicking my thighs as I rubbed them together. I had been so turned on by Sinclair's possession, by my exposure to another man. What if I hadn't freaked out? Would he have taken it—me—further? The idea of being laid bare before a stranger as Sinclair manipulated my body brought on a molten wave of desire.

"Oh my God," I murmured, sinking to the floor before the bed with my head in my hands.

That was how Sinclair found me minutes later. Immediately, he swooped down to pick me up and took me out into the main room, where he had set up the small table on the deck with some candles and our food. I was mute as he settled me in the chair and turned on the soothing twang of Spanish guitar over the speakers. He maintained the silence as he served us, and I was grateful for the space to calm my whirring thoughts. Even though I enjoyed the food immensely, I was hot and cold with shame throughout the meal.

It wasn't that big a deal, I knew. So what if we had made out in front of an audience of one, and Sinclair had made a few innuendos? No big deal. But I was so inexperienced with both sex and being in the spotlight that I didn't know what to make of my embarrassment and, even more so, my excitement.

When I reluctantly gave up on the creamy rice pudding after only three bites, Sinclair tugged my chair closer to his and pulled me onto his lap. He loosened the front of my robe, ignoring my sudden tension, and softly began to stroke my neck and shoulders.

"Talk to me."

I sighed deeply. "I don't know what to say."

"There is no right or wrong thing to say here, Elle. I just want to know what you think about what happened?"

"I ..." I sighed again. "I liked it."

He tilted my chin up so that I could see his smile. "I thought you might. You like it when I make the decisions. When you aren't responsible for the shame of your sexual desires."

I hesitated but nodded. My hand was resting on his chest over his heart, and I found a much-needed sense of calm in his steady pulse.

"What I would do with you if I had more time." He shook his head, but his voice was wistful and amused. "But as it is, we only have three more nights. And I have plans for this one. As I remember it, you owe me a fantasy."

I gulped as our fishing bet came back to me. My skin tingled with desire in anticipation of Sinclair lighting me on fire. It was astonishing how ready I was for him all the time; I constantly felt in danger of bursting into flames.

His fingers skated down my neck and squeezed gently. "Your pulse is racing. What are you hoping I will do to you?"

I stared up into his achingly handsome face while ideas stampeded through my mind. My lips parted, and he dipped his thumb into my mouth so that I could gently nip at it.

"Tell me."

Banked fires stirred in his eyes, and I was suddenly determined to ignite them, to take hold of the passion he felt for me and coax it into a livid blaze. I knew what this man liked. I might have only known him for five days, but I knew how to touch him, how to tease him. My submission was imminent, but that didn't mean I couldn't first take pleasure out of seducing him.

"I want you"—I paused, watching the flicker of surprise in his eyes at my boldness and the way I lightly tugged his roguishly long hair—"to undress me."

Immediately, the rope holding together my robe was pulled into his hands, and the fabric gaped open across my chest, not quite revealing my pebbled nipples. I watched his eyes dip into the hollow between my breasts and his Adam's apple bob as he swallowed hard.

"Do you see how my body reacts to you?" I breathed, too timid to speak in the husky tones I imagined would better suit my sensual words. To make up for it, I swept one hand from my neck, between my breasts, to the top of my curls. "Feel how wet I am. Dip just a finger inside me."

He did as requested, one long finger tracing the folds of my drenched sex. I swallowed my moan, determined to remain in power for as long as he would let me.

"Take your clothes off and lie down."

His eyebrow quirked, but he did as I asked, slowly pulling his white T-shirt over his head to reveal the stretch of his lightly tanned abdomen that always made my mouth water. He undid the clasp of his linen pants, staring at me with blatant desire as they dropped to the floor to reveal his hardened length. All moisture left my mouth.

He lay down without touching me, but I didn't care. As soon as his back hit the bed, I straddled his lean thighs and notched his cock against my center, sliding along it slowly, methodically. His hands fisted in the bed sheets at his side, and I was thrilled with his discipline. When he was slick with my moisture, I shimmied down farther and took him firmly in my hand, my eyes on his as I languidly licked a path up his shaft.

"Elle," he groaned, his legs shifting restlessly as I drew circles across the tip of him with my tongue. "Careful."

I was so turned on, especially knowing that my heady power was given only out of graciousness, that he could and would rip it away from me in a second. Eagerly, I drew my lips over my teeth and took him to the back of my throat. I echoed his strangled moan with one of my own, reveling in the salty, manly taste of him.

Until then, I hadn't been able to take him fully inside my mouth, but as I pumped the rest of his length, damp with my salvia, I knew that I had to.

"Elle," he growled again in warning. "I am not coming in your mouth."

I hummed in agreement, which only made his hands come to my shoulders and clench firmly. I was still in control but barely. Before I lost my nerve or Sinclair took the situation out of my hands, I swallowed his length down my throat and moaned in triumph, careful to breathe through my nose.

"Jesus Christ," he barked, jackknifing into a sitting position. His hands suddenly gripped my hair, both forcing me off and farther onto his cock.

I fought his hold and tentatively swiped my tongue along the base of his shaft before rising slightly for breath and lowering again. He allowed me time to find my rhythm, and in less than five minutes, I was rewarded with the first taste of his warmth in my mouth. I pulled back to take the rest on my tongue, laving him gently even after he had finished and collapsed on the bed.

I crawled up to lay beside him, just an inch apart but not touching. Even satiated, the thin wedge of air between us hummed with tension as if our molecules were magnetic, pulling inexorably and almost painfully toward the other's.

"Don't get too comfortable."

I shifted to look up at him. His eyes were closed, but his voice had deepened, darkened into the velvet ropes that bound me to his will.

"In two minutes, I'm going to get up and leave the room. You will completely disrobe and wait for me on the bed. Do you remember how you were positioned on the bed our first night together? I want you like that."

My muscles twitched with memory, and before he had even fully left the room, I was shedding the rest of my clothing and falling into position on the end of the bed. My bum was high in the air, propped up by my folded and spread legs while my hands gently grasped my ankles. Even though my dampening sex was fully exposed, there was a certain comfort in being so contained, small and perfectly parceled for Sinclair to unwrap at his leisure. I could smell us on the sheets, and even though it was harder to breathe, I pressed my nose into the silky fabric to inhale deeply.

After a few minutes, my breath and pulse slowed slightly, and I fell into an almost meditative state. All my senses heightened, from the greedy throb of desire at my core to the abrasion of the sheets against my aching nipples.

I pictured the things he might do to me. My imagination conjured whips and chains, strange instruments of pain and torture that would set my teeth on edge as he forcibly extracted pleasure from my body. A shiver slapped the small of my back and vibrated up my spine.

The door opened with a soft breath, but Sinclair didn't say anything as he moved into the room. I almost jumped when something soft trailed between my legs and up over my back. The sensation didn't last long, and I realized as he tied it firmly and carefully around my head so that our skin didn't brush that it was a blindfold. He smoothed a hand down my spine, his fingers splayed in a possessive move that made my teeth rattle with a deep shudder.

"I'm going to tie you up, Elle." His cool voice was as glossy and impassive as a still water lake. "Would you like to know why I'm doing this?"

I whimpered as another tie brushed over my weeping sex on its descent to my ankles, which he gently secured to each wrist so that I was in a kind of depraved yoga pose.

"Use your words," he reprimanded.

"Yes, please."

He had barely touched me, and I was already a tight wire suspended over a dizzying abyss.

"You need to be punished for making me come in your mouth without permission."

The last tie was secured, and he moved away from me to somewhere else in the room where I could hear him prepare something.

"You need to understand how to control yourself."

Without warning, a resounding smack rang throughout the room. The pain was so shocking that it actually took a moment for my bottom to erupt in fiery pain. A cry rose in my throat, but I swallowed it with a barely discernable gargle.

He blew across my stinging right butt cheek, and crooned, "You are not a good girl, are you?"

I wasn't sure if I should answer, but just as I opened my mouth, his hand came whipping down on the other side of my ass. This time, I cried out.

"No, I know you are not." Another delicious wave of cool air wafted across my aching skin and sent tingles shooting straight down to my sex.

Again, his hand went swinging down on me, releasing endorphins and sweet-edged pain. I gasped into the sheet and moaned.

"A nice girl doesn't get turned on by a spanking," he scolded, his fingers dipping into the pool of desire beneath my burning bottom.

He dragged one knuckle down over my clit, and I jerked in my bonds at the roar of pleasure it released. With one hand still on my center, he spanked me again, pushing me further into an unfamiliar basin of shimmering pleasure. My fingernails dug into the thin skin of my ankles as I tried to find the ground beneath my floating body, but the sharp tingle of pain only elevated me further.

"How many do you think you deserve? Ten, twenty? Your ass is already a beautiful shade of pink."

I groaned, desperate for him to go on but incoherent with pleasure. My brain was too busy trying to process the waves of desire pounding down on me to form actual words.

Two fingers sank into my heat at the same time that his other hand landed.

"Ahhh!" I screamed.

My entire body was coiled so tightly that there didn't seem to be any space between my skin and bones, my blood and muscles. I was reduced to quaking flesh, an organism entirely dependent on pleasure to survive.

"Sinclair."

"You may not orgasm."

"Ugh!"

"*Silence*," he ordered in French. "*Si tu restes juste comme ça, je te donnerai ce que tu veux.*"

If you stay just like this, he said, *I will give you what you want.*

I gritted my teeth.

Two slaps landed in quick succession.

"You took me in your mouth without permission."

Slap.

"Splayed your naked body on a public beach for my pleasure."

Slap.

"You begged me to dominate you, to take your pleasure and make it all mine."

Slap, slap.

I was panting heavily now like a feral animal, and my wetness was coating the inside of my thighs, pooling on the silk sheets.

He paused for a long beat, his fingers still inside me and his thumb poised just over my clit.

"You seduced a taken man."

My racing heart tripped over itself, and I lost my breath completely. Shame swirled with my desire until they formed something new, something brighter and more powerful. It built in my pulsing body until my tongue throbbed with my confession.

"Yes," I groaned. "I did."

"Good girl," he crooned.

He pulled his fingers from my clenching sex, and I opened my mouth to scream at him to put them back, but his words interrupted me.

"Would you do it again? Seduce a taken man, give him your sweet pussy and let him make you his?" he asked.

The blunt edge of his erection brushed against me, and I bucked back against my bonds in a desperate attempt to get him inside me. I was so close to orgasming. All I needed was one of those beautiful gusts of his cool breath against my heat, and I would have shattered.

"Don't make me ask you again."

Slap, slap.

I groaned raggedly, too aroused to worry if I sounded sexy or not.

"Yes!" I hissed. "I would do it again, and again and—" My litany was cut off with a hoarse shout as he thrust inside me to the hilt.

My sightless world erupted in pinwheels of brilliant color as I fell completely into the darkness, free-falling past the bold shards of my devastating desire. I vaguely felt Sinclair's fingers tighten on my hips, his length dragging deliciously, almost too roughly against my firing nerve endings and his almost silent shout of release before I blacked out.

Chapter Thirteen

I FIDGETED IN MY CHAIR, TRYING TO TAKE THE PRESSURE OFF MY PLEASANTLY sore backside. Though the café had padded chairs, I could still feel the warm pain, and each movement I made forced my thoughts back to last night and the things Sinclair had done to me.

I looked up from my half-eaten bagel to find him staring at me with a raised brow from across the table. He was speaking with Richard Denman and Robert Corbett about the resort they were in the process of securing; a place twenty minutes down the beach that had been abandoned due to financial strain. Sinclair had shown me pictures yesterday, and I had to agree with his instincts; the thick slice of land right on the white sandy beach was well worth the price.

I took a sip of my latte and deliberately allowed the foam to kiss my top lip. As I watched him, my tongue made a slow sweep across my mouth. His other eyebrow joined the first, marring his usually fathomless expression. I laughed softly and broke eye contact, turning to the left to see Candy observing us. Immediately, I ducked my head and fought the blush crawling across my skin.

Her hand found mine on my thigh and squeezed lightly. "You look as though you've enjoyed your trip, Elle."

"I have, very much." I nodded but refused to meet her eyes.

There was no doubt in my mind that she knew about my holiday affair with Sinclair, but I didn't want to make her any more uncomfortable with the knowledge of it.

"So has Sinclair."

She nodded her head toward the Frenchman now locked in a heated debate with Duncan Wright. Well, Duncan was heated, speaking animatedly with his hands while his mouth twisted around his frustrated words. Sinclair just sat there with his hands placed loosely on the table, posture straight but professional, not hostile under Duncan's anxious focus. I scoured his face for clues and found nothing but calm.

"You leave tomorrow, right?" Candy continued, and I finally turned to her. "Time flies."

I tried to breathe through the sudden depression gripping my throat and shrugged. "It will be good to see my family."

"Uh-huh." She slanted me a long look, waiting for me to say something more. When I didn't, she sighed and turned fully to face me. "Listen, I've been working this whole trip, and I'd love to take a break to do some shopping. Would you go to town with me this afternoon?"

Immediately, my eyes sought Sinclair. He had mentioned going to the failing resort to look around with some building inspectors and Richard Denman, who I found out was a revered architect from Chicago. I had been invited along, but after learning that Margot would be there, I had begged off.

"It will be fun," Candy trilled. "I promise."

I laughed at my hesitation and shook my head to clear it of the Frenchman. I had no obligation to Sinclair; he was busy, and though I should have been photographing, I figured I could do that in town.

"I would love to."

Candy nodded curtly. "Good."

I had my purse and my camera, so we decided to head out right after breakfast, but I lingered, trying to get a private moment to say goodbye to Sinclair. I knew it would only be a few hours until I saw him next, but being away from him still made me slightly anxious. I groaned into my hand.

God, I had it bad.

"What are you moaning about?" His trademark small smile brightened his handsome face as he looked down on me. "Personally, I can't think of anything to bemoan. I am in Mexico on a beautiful day the morning after sleeping with a gorgeous woman."

His words wooed me, and I stepped so close to him; we were almost pressed together. I knew the others stood just to the side, but Sinclair didn't seem to mind. In fact, his grin widened, and he pressed my hips to his with a firm hand on my lower back.

"You'll miss me this afternoon."

It wasn't a question, but I nodded anyway. "When will you be back?"

His thumb inched under my shirt and rubbed over the bare skin at the base of my spine. "Not soon enough. In time for dinner."

I smiled at the domesticity of his comment, unsure if he realized it or not. "No worries. If you are late, we can skip right to dessert."

"Mmm, lavender and honey. My favorite." He leaned close, bending down to look me straight in the eyes. I thought he would kiss me, but he only smiled, his firm lips parting to reveal nearly perfect white teeth. "Be safe and have fun, siren."

I swallowed and braced my feet farther apart, afraid that I would float into the air on cloud nine. "Will do, sir."

He chuckled and lightly brushed his hand over my bottom as he let me go and stepped away.

"Are you done hitting on my lady, Sinclair?" Cage demanded as he stepped away from a shell-shocked young woman who stared after him and slung an arm around my shoulders.

I laughingly shoved him away with my hip, but he held on, his face collapsing into sorrow. "Look what you've done, turning her against me."

Candy hit him none too lightly on the back of his head with a binder. "Let her go, you oaf."

Cage winced, rubbing the back of his skull. "You guys are no fun."

"I assure you, that's not the case." There was a trace of humor in Sinclair's cool tones.

His colleagues blinked, shocked by his innuendo. Robert Corbett cleared his throat and shifted uncomfortably, but Richard Denman grinned broadly at me and winked. Sinclair was the one to break the silence by raising a condescending eyebrow at his dumbstruck friends and winking—actually winking—at me as he walked past us to the waiting car.

"Wow," Candy breathed, a hand to her lower stomach. "I'm surprised I'm still standing."

I flushed but didn't try to contain my laughter.

"What have you done to that man?" Richard clapped a hand to my back, his silver hair gleaming in the sunlight. "Whatever it is, keep it up. I haven't seen Sin so light at heart ..." He frowned and then threw his head back to chuckle. "Ever."

Their compliments were slightly awkward. I had wondered what Sinclair was like with Darling back at home; if he was so charming, so passionate. It seemed that I now had an answer, but it only led to so many more haunting questions. Like would I ever see him again after I got on the plane tomorrow?

Cage, surprisingly, didn't say anything. Instead, he squeezed my shoulder and released me, taking a step back to study me. He was wearing distractingly bright green spandex swim shorts, and the sight of his muscular thighs and the bulge in the thin material momentarily distracted me. After a second, he grabbed a piece of paper off the receptionist's desk and scribbled something on the back of a card before pressing it into my palm. Distracted by his sudden departure, I tucked the folded paper into my purse without reading it.

When the men and an unseen Margot had left, Candy and I decided to walk to town. It was a half an hour trek in the hot sun, but we were both up for it, and it gave me the opportunity to photograph the small stretch of local boroughs before we hit the market. Candy kept up a constant stream of pleasant conversation, happily pointing out things I might find of interest, and she flat-out giggled when I insisted on taking a picture of an old Mexican man wearing nothing but a long pair of dusty shorts. He was sound asleep and practically rolling out of his seat before a small but carefully maintained pink house.

"How long have you been doing photography?" she asked me, wiping off the crown of sweat beaded on her forehead.

"My sister bought me my first camera when I was sixteen." I could still remember the feel of the secondhand Canon in my hands and the hard click of the shutter as it closed over an image. I still had the camera, carefully wrapped in my suitcase because I hadn't wanted to risk shipping it to New York with the rest of my meager things from Paris.

"Did you train?"

The mouth of the marketplace loomed up ahead, and the colorful cacophony made my finger twitch over the lens of my camera.

"Five years at *L'École des Beaux-Arts* in Paris, mostly in painting."

"Wow. I've always loved art. Obviously, working with Sinclair, it's a prerequisite. But I cannot paint to save my life unless you count splatter painting."

I laughed, but my mind was caught on her earlier comment. "Sinclair likes art?"

She frowned at me over the rim of a large ceramic pitcher she was inspecting. "Well, he should. He owns one of the more prestigious art galleries in the city."

What city? I bit back my question and nodded. "Right."

She must have caught my sigh because suddenly her hand was on mine.

"Listen, Elle. I know we don't really know each other, and under other circumstances, I'm sure the classy cultured artist would have nothing to do with the dumpy businesswoman." Her smile was sharp with self-deprecation. "But I feel as if we are friends. And as a friend, I can tell you that I've never seen my boss like this. He's lightened. Usually, he walks around like a living sculpture, beautiful and untouchable, but you make him come alive."

Tears stung the back of my eyes. "Why are you telling me this?"

It was brutal to hear about his possible affection when I knew it would end tomorrow. Besides, no matter what other people might have said, I knew that Sinclair only wanted a holiday affair, no personal attachment and no strings. But God, it felt good to pretend, if only for a minute, that he felt something more than lust toward me.

Candy's grip tightened over me. "Because I think you should tell him how you feel. If you have feelings for him, fight for him. I like his girl-friend"—she paused, and guilt flashed across her strong features—"but that doesn't mean I can't see what is so clearly happening between you and Sinclair."

I shook my head and pulled my hand away from her. "Stop."

Her dark eyes were wide with sincerity, but she held up her palms in surrender. "Fine. I had to say it, but I understand if you are too afraid to act on it."

I flinched as her arrow found the bullseye. The new Giselle wasn't timid, or afraid, or meek. But—I bit my lip and took another step away from her—that didn't mean I was stupid.

She sighed deeply and picked up the pitcher again. "So what do you think? Too garish?"

WE SPENT THE NEXT FEW HOURS TRIPPING AROUND DOWNTOWN CABO SAN Lucas; all talk of Sinclair clearly off the table. Instead, Candy told me about her start in business, interning for large corporations and subsisting on ramen noodles and business lunches before she met Sinclair at a confer-ence. They had hit it off right away in the Q&A session of a famous real estate broker who they reduced to a blubbering mess after ripping into his flimsy business model. She laughed as she recounted the story, and so did I, imagining them tag-teaming the poor man.

I told her little about my past beyond Paris, and if she noticed my evasion, she didn't let on. It was difficult to explain my splintered family and the fear that had driven me first from Italy and then my beloved Paris. It felt strange not to tell her about my siblings, though. Usually, when someone questioned me, I automatically spoke of their more glamorous lives, casting my own dull existence into shadow. Instead, we talked about art and France, both of which Candy was an expert in.

By the time we decided to head home, the light was syrupy as the sun began to sink in the cerulean blue sky, and Candy was laden with shopping bags.

"I can't believe you didn't get that bracelet," she said between each labored breath. "Seriously, Elle, it was gorgeous."

I sighed, picturing the Mexican silver and turquoise cuff that we had seen in the jewelry store. It had been a beautiful piece of jewelry, but I couldn't afford it. The credit card Cosima and Sebastian had given me practically burned a hole in my pocket, but I refused on principle to use their money for anything less than essentials.

"Starving artist," I said by way of explanation, though that wasn't exactly the truth either.

"You don't look it." Candy eyed my curves with good-humored envy. "I'd give my right arm to have a figure like that."

"It took me a long time to be okay with it," I admitted, running a hand over the exaggerated flare of my hip. "I have two tall, thin sisters."

Images of Cosima in *Sports Illustrated* flashed through my mind, but I repressed my old habit of comparing us, burrowing it deep beneath the confidence that Sinclair had newly gifted me.

Candy pursed her lips. "Damn, there are more of you?"

I laughed and felt warmth suffuse my chest as she linked her arm with mine. It felt good to be lighthearted and girlish, to laugh too loudly at Candy's impressions of Cage and snigger together over details of her last lover who had a thing for woman sucking lollipops.

"No, seriously," she had said, eyes wide. "I ended up with three cavities."

I had never really had many friends unless you counted my family. Brenna was my only true friend, and I couldn't even remember the details of our relationship in the beginning. After she had invited me for coffee the first time, who had called whom next? Either way, it had always been easy, and I realized that I felt the same unself-conscious ease with Candy.

We were laughing when we entered Sinclair's suite using the spare key card he had given me. I pretended not to notice Candy give it a significant glance, and happily, the low murmur of chatter in the room distracted her.

Obviously, the inspection had gone well because the men involved each clutched a flute of frothing champagne, and they all cheered when we entered.

"You got it?" I asked, breathless from the excitement crackling in the room.

Sinclair dropped the unopened bottle he'd been holding—which Cage caught hastily—and strode over to me before I could even blink. He hefted me in his arms and beamed into my face. "Oh yes, siren, we got it."

I squealed and hugged him, too aware of the others to do anything more. Cage, apparently, shared no such qualm because he was on Candy, his lips slanted over hers before she could protest. When he finally broke away with a loud smack and a cheeky grin, she was the color of a vivid sunburn.

"You ass," she snapped.

Cage only chuckled and turned to me, trying to plant a kiss on me as well.

When Sinclair raised an eyebrow at him and hugged me closer, he only shrugged and murmured, "Spoilsport."

I ignored him. "Are we going to celebrate?"

"We are." Duncan adjusted his glasses and indicated his champagne flute.

"Santiago and Katarina are coming." Sinclair spoke in his normal muted tones, and though everyone could hear him and see us, I knew he was absorbed by me. "Do you want to go out with them?"

"Dancing?"

His eyebrows rose over twinkling eyes. "You like to dance?"

I shrugged, thinking about our first night together when we had moved sinuously across the dance floor. "I'd like to dance with you."

His arms tightened around me before he loosened his hold. I slid down his body, feeling his half-hard bulge press against my stomach when I finally landed on my feet. He was still staring at me with the small smile I was coming to think was just for me.

Cage coughed loudly and took a long chug from the champagne bottle he had caught from Sinclair. "Are you sure you want to go out? We can get out of here if you want to"—his eyebrows waggled—"stay in to celebrate. In fact, if you really beg, I'll stay for that party too."

Candy dug an elbow into his ribs. "You're such a child."

"Prude."

"Asshole."

I smiled at their exchange, still looking up at Sinclair. His face was relaxed, his hands loosely clasped around my waist. I caught Richard's eye over Sinclair's shoulder and watched him nod his approval, lifting the flute in a silent cheer.

"Cage is right," I murmured, rolling onto my tiptoes into order to speak against the corner of his jaw. "We did have other plans for tonight."

He groaned, his hands flexing on my hips. "Don't tempt me, minx." He leaned down, running his tongue along the delicate shell of my ear. "I could take you right now, in front of all these people, and you wouldn't say no, would you?"

A shudder wracked my spine, and his dark chuckle was warm in my ear. I shoved him away playfully and battled with my blush.

"Sinclair," a feminine voice snapped.

I turned to see Margot standing in the open door to the suite, momentarily distracted by how lovely she was in her vivid green dress with her silky blond hair gleaming. She was staring at us with haughty indignation as if I was some whore who had lured Sinclair to the dark side.

He tensed, but his voice was cool when he addressed her, "Yes, Margot, no one will force you to go if you would rather stay here. Alone."

She bristled and took a few steps into the room, oblivious to the ominous silence that had descended as everyone watched the exchange in rapt attention.

"I know you better than this," she said, waving her hand disdainfully in my direction. "You don't do messy. Cut her off now before she deludes herself into thinking this is anything more than a holiday affair."

Each word struck me in the chest like a poisoned dart. I took a step back, right into Sinclair, who clamped an arm around my waist.

My skin burned with shame, but when I tried to wriggle free, he leaned down to growl, "Stop it."

"Stop being such an Ice Queen. Can't you see he's happy?" Candy said, her teeth bared.

Margot raised one pale brow and looked me over, cataloging everything from the rubber flip-flops at my feet to the volume of my humidity-infused hair.

"She leaves tomorrow. Can't you see the consequences?"

"Enough." His voice cracked like a whip. "You will not ruin the night for everyone, M. Is that understood?"

Her throat worked as she swallowed, and her eyes were wide as she tried to silently appeal to his logical side, but I could tell by the weight of his arm across my stomach that he wouldn't yield.

Strangely, I felt bad for Margot. Even though I hated to think about it, she was right. Even if I made Sinclair happy now, was it worth the guilt he would feel returning home to his girlfriend? I wasn't so sure.

I placed a hand on his arm and gently removed it, deciding to give them a minute to speak without the awkwardness of my presence.

"Come on, Candy, help me pick out what to wear?"

I extended my hand to her and smiled when she happily interlocked out fingers, shooting a withering glance at Margot as she did so.

"Your things are in the bedroom." Sinclair spoke softly, but I heard him even from across the room as we opened the door to leave for my room.

"Excuse me?"

I didn't turn around, but I could tell by the sudden silence that everyone was as confounded as I was.

"I said your things are in the bedroom."

Finally turning around, I glanced helplessly at our audience. He had a girlfriend, for God's sake. What was he doing announcing to them that we were sleeping together? Obviously, we hadn't been completely discreet, especially tonight, but still.

My frantic eyes found his, and I opened my mouth to speak but clamped it shut again when I saw the stern expression on his face. He was daring me to protest over his lack of respect for my privacy or my individuality. *I own you*; his words from the drive to the marina echoed in my head. I swallowed past the rising fear that he did, and he would continue to own my heart long after we left this place.

He sighed, tucking his hands in his pockets as the shutters slammed down over his features. "Go get dressed, Elle. We will wait for you."

I stood there for a minute as he turned to talk to the men, ignoring the last ten minutes of public affection and humiliation as if it had never happened. Margot watched me curiously with her head cocked to one side as I hesitated.

"Are you okay?" Candy whispered.

"I'm just not used to being controlled," I hissed, even though this seemed like the millionth time this week that Sinclair had done so.

"What are you going to do about it?"

I pursed my lips as Cosima's accented voice echoed through my head and urged me to follow her example. I picked out the tiniest dress in my arsenal, one that Cosima had bought me for Mama's restaurant opening two years ago, and held it up for Candy with a smile.

"I'm going to make sure he doesn't regret it."

Chapter Fourteen

THE DANCE FLOOR VIBRATED WITH THE PULSING BEAT OF THE TECHNO MUSIC blaring through the five feet speakers surrounding the dance floor at the Pink Kitty nightclub. Scantily clad dancers ground against each other, their bare skin glistening in the blue and pink lights flashing overhead. My long hair was tangled and damp against my exposed back, so I lifted it from my skin, wishing fruitlessly for a breeze to pass through the open front of the club into the back where we moved to the throbbing beat.

My eyes sought out Sinclair over at the bar talking to Santiago and Candy. I had politely implied that if he could distract those two, then maybe Cage and Kat would dance together. He had raised those strong brows but done as I requested, and now Kat stood close to me, laughing as Cage danced around her with the flair of the expert performer he was.

Smiling to myself, I pushed through the crowd, desperate to get some air. My feet were sore from dancing so long in my only pair of high heels, a ridiculously tall pair of nude pumps that I had purchased in Paris when Brenna invited me to the premiere of one of her movies. Sinclair had seemed to like them, though, if his dark promise to fuck me with nothing else on was anything to go by.

When I had emerged from the bedroom, everyone but Sinclair had left to wait for us in the lobby. He apologized with a twisted smile for Margot's inappropriate behavior. I didn't correct him—our behavior was far more inappropriate than her concern—mostly because the way he looked at me in the short, tight white dress I wore was enough to distract me from the truth.

The cool air hit my sticky skin as soon as I pushed open the heavy door to the fire escape, and I breathed a sigh of contentment as I lifted my hair from my neck.

"You've got a beautiful smile," a hot voice breathed into my ear.

I scrunched my nose against the foul smell of the stranger's breath and tried to step farther down the stairs so that he could get by. When he didn't move, I turned to look up at him, finding a vaguely attractive frat boy leering down at me.

"Thank you," I said coolly, drawing my arms across my chest to hide my ample cleavage from his gaze. "My boyfriend thinks so too."

The deception fell from my lips too easily, and for a second, I allowed my mind to go there, to imagine what it would be like to be Sinclair's girlfriend. I wondered if he would call me darling and give me space to express my independence, or if he would be the man I knew him to be now, deliciously possessive and spontaneous.

"Come dance with me, babe."

The man's voice rudely interrupted my daydreams, and I looked up at him sharply, noticing that he had closed the distance between us and now stood only a step above me.

"I'm good, thanks."

I turned to walk farther down the steps, thinking I could make my way around to the front of the club where there would be more people, but his arm snagged me just as I was taking a step. A squeak punctuated my fall as I slammed into the railing, and the air collapsed from my lungs. Taking advantage of my position leaning over the iron banister, he pressed into my back and slowly righted me so that I was flush against his front.

He groaned. "This is nice. What do you say we skip the dancing, and I take you back to my hotel?"

My heart was beating painfully hard, but I knew how to think through the fog of panic, thanks to my experiences with Christopher.

"As I said, I have a boyfriend." My voice was surprisingly calm, and I was thankful for it. Some men did this for the thrill of the fear, I knew.

I attempted to step free from his arms, but they constricted around me like a boa.

"We don't need a hotel." He spun me around and clamped down on my lower back, pushing my hips tight against his arousal.

His head descended, and I frantically fought for a way out of this situation. My arms were held tight at my sides, and without leverage, there was no way I could dislodge a man almost a foot taller and eighty pounds heavier than me.

So, I did the only thing I could.

When his lips slanted over mine and his greasy tongue stabbed into my mouth, I bit him. Hard. The taste of blood blossomed against my tongue, and his hoarse cry rattled my eardrums. He shoved me away, and I stumbled on my stupid heels, falling back with a crash against the railing. Pain exploded in my head as it cracked against the metal, but I stood as quickly as I could, fighting the wooziness. The pervert was bent over, his hands folded over his heavily bleeding mouth.

"You fuckin' bith," he mumbled and took a menacing step forward.

I kicked off my shoes, leaving them on the landing, and took off down the rest of the stairs. I could hear him lumbering after me, but I knew I was quicker because he was crippled by pain. I stepped on something painful as I tore around the corner to the front of the club, but I ignored it, stopping only when I saw a large Mexican bouncer. I bounded into him, and he caught me without question, pushing me behind him when he caught sight of the man trailing behind me.

"Ignacio." The bouncer nodded at another man guarding the door, and he took off toward the creep who had assaulted me.

Finally, the bouncer turned to me, his large face creased with concern. "Are you okay?"

I nodded, but my body was shaking, and I could still taste his blood against my teeth.

"Can you tell me what happened?"

There was shouting down the street, but the bouncer took me gently by the shoulders and bent down so that his large brown eyes were all I could see.

"I need you to tell me what happened. Can you do that?"

The cool air off the ocean made me shiver and gave me the wherewithal to shake my head and request the one thing I really needed. "My boyfriend is inside. He's tall with reddish hair and really pretty blue eyes. Can you get him?"

He stared at me for a minute before nodding tersely and moving me to the stool that he probably sat on when the line was slow. I started when he slipped a coarse blanket around my shoulders, but he smiled kindly at me and moved away a few steps to speak into his walkie-talkie. I could hear the man I'd bitten groan as the other bouncer dealt with him, but I didn't look over at them. I knew I would cry if I did, and I wanted to be stronger than that. So, I sat on the stool and dragged deep handfuls of air into my lungs, counting to seven before I released each breath.

A few minutes later, my group burst through the door to the club, and Sinclair was suddenly before me, crouched on his knees in order to look up at me.

"Elle," he croaked, two knuckles skating down my cheek to the corner of my mouth. They came away with blood on them, and I realized that he thought it was mine.

"His," I explained through my chattering teeth.

His eyes were large, the color of wet blue velvet, and his voice was unbearably soft when he said, "*Désolé, ma sirène.*"

I swallowed a sob and wrestled one hand out of the blanket to clutch his damp button-up. "Hold me?"

I was in his lap before I could blink, nestled in the cradle of his arms with his firm lips pressed to my forehead. The bouncer was speaking with Candy and Richard Denman, both of them yelling at him for answers.

"Stop," I called and cleared my throat when my voice didn't carry as well as I wanted it to. "Stop asking him questions."

They turned to me, blinking widely, struck dumb by my insistence and probably my awful appearance.

The bouncer bent down before me, and I realized that despite his impressive bull-like size, he had a handsome face made sweet by large eyes the color of melted chocolate. "Can you tell me what happened now?"

I nodded and took a deep breath, drawing comfort from Sinclair's arms as they squeezed gently around me. Santiago, Kat, and Cage all appeared while I told my story but quickly turned away to speak with a policeman who had shown up, interacting in rapid-fire Spanish. Sinclair's body grew increasingly tense as I recounted the incident until I felt like I was sitting in a cage. When I finished, the bouncer asked me a few questions before going to join the conversation with Santiago and the policeman.

I looked up at Sinclair, but he gently pressed my head back to his shoulder, and I knew it was because he didn't want me to see the anger on his face.

"Cage, get her some water to wash that cretin's blood out of her mouth. Candy, I want you to take her home now. Go straight back to the resort and take her to my room," Sinclair said, once again the cool and controlled businessman.

I was mute as he placed me carefully on my feet and moved a few steps away. The sudden distance was like alcohol in an open wound. Why was he leaving me?

Cage reappeared with a plastic cup of water I used to swish out my mouth, spitting the pink liquid into a street grate as I kept an eye on Candy stalking after Sin.

"What are you doing?" Candy hissed, her large teeth flashing as she bared them at her boss. "You should take her back."

He shook his head but didn't look at me. A muscle in his jaw spasmed, and I watched his fists clench and unclench as he fought to remain calm. For some reason, the sight of him made me want to weep.

"Do it now, Candace," he ordered before turning around and striding over to the conversation with the police.

Candy turned to me, her angry eyes dulling with empathy as she took in the miserable sight of me. With a gusty sigh, she placed an arm around my shoulders. "Come on, Elle. Let's go back."

We were silent in the cab, but she held my hand the entire time. I didn't cry, but my body was weak with the effort to hold in the tears, and my left foot throbbed brutally from a deep slice on my instep. The stupid incident, coupled with Sinclair's continued hot and cold attitude, the fact that I was leaving tomorrow and he would go back to his darling girlfriend, sent the careful walls compartmentalizing my life crumbling down.

When we reached Sinclair's suite, I hesitated in the doorway. He had ordered Candy to take me home, and my heart throbbed as his words echoed in my head.

"Come on, I'll make you some tea while you take a shower, okay?" Candy placed a hand on my back, and I winced when she pressed into tender skin from where I had fallen backward on the stairs.

My head and heart pulsed in painful tandem, and I was grateful to her for leaving me to my own chaotic thoughts.

"You don't have to stay," I still offered.

She looked at me like a headmistress, her expression deeply at odds with the tight blue dress I had encouraged her to wear. "Don't be selfish. I want to be here with you."

I ducked my head and nodded, warmed and shamed by her gesture. I quickly made my way to the bathroom and shucked my clothes, waiting until the temperature was close to scalding before stepping into the spray. I brushed my teeth twice, then let the water pound the thoughts out of my head and pressed my cheek to the tiles as sobs finally wracked my aching frame.

I didn't know where Sinclair was or why he hadn't taken me back to the resort. He could have been angry with me for disappearing alone, and I wouldn't have blamed him; it was incredibly stupid of me. It was our last night together, and I had ruined it.

Otherwise, my encounter with the drunken horn dog at the club didn't disturb me as much as it might have. I was used to men taking what they wanted, and their aggression didn't surprise me anymore. Which was why, I think, I was so deeply enthralled with Sinclair. He was such a contradiction to the little I knew about men. He struggled to do the right thing, to remain in control and logical despite the desires that burned brightly within him. He was a deeply passionate man beneath the calm resolve, and I admired him for it even though I was the one to take that calm from him. The pain increased in my chest when I thought about what I was doing to the woman who loved him back home and to the man Sinclair struggled so hard to be—a good man with morals.

Self-loathing bloomed in my chest until I almost couldn't breathe. Everything awful that I had done in my short life welled up from my memory banks and flooded me. It was a strange and bone-numbing feeling to realize you were the villain in your own life story.

Later, after I had finally expelled all my tears and the water had beaten my body and psyche free of all hurt, I lay in the king-sized bed with Candy sound asleep beside me. She had insisted on staying until Sinclair came home, but he had been gone for over two hours now. I turned my head to look at the glowing face of the alarm clock.

2:43 a.m.

I sighed, bone-tired but unable to sleep.

I bolted upright when the door to the suite opened and closed a few minutes later. The sound of male conversation wafted in through the open door, and I strained to make out what they were saying.

Candy stirred beside me, and I quickly turned on my side, my heart galloping as I feigned sleep. I felt her sit up and the gentle scratch of her gaze on my face before she slipped out of bed to join the commotion in the living room. As soon as she had gently closed the door behind her, I was up and at the door, cracking it open noiselessly for better audio.

"It was fucking stupid, Sin," Cage was saying as he took a seat on the couch.

"And you know when Cage says something is stupid, it's really idiotic," Candy added dryly as she curled up sleepily on the couch.

"It was fucking necessary," Sinclair snapped as he poured himself a snifter of brandy from the bar. "You know the police wouldn't have done anything."

Cage shrugged as he snagged the drink from Sinclair, who promptly poured himself another, but his voice was tight when he said, "You didn't need to beat the guy to a bloody pulp."

"And you didn't need to help."

I covered my mouth to muffle my gasp.

Sinclair poured more brandy into his now empty glass and prepared another one for Candy before he went to sit beside her. She waved her hand at the glass, dismissing it as she uncurled from her position.

"This is a talk between men, I think." She placed a hand on his shoulder and squeezed tightly. "Not a long one, I hope. It's late, and that girl in there needs you."

She smiled with her mouth closed tightly over her teeth as she moved toward the door. Her hand was on the handle, gently swinging it closed behind her, when she muttered, "And don't underestimate how much you need her too."

Sinclair's back was to me as he stared after her, and I had the pleasure of watching him peel off his blood-soaked shirt and throw it onto a nearby chair, every movement jerky with anger. I had never seen him so thrown off, and despite myself, attraction sizzled over my skin as his naked back came into sight.

After a few moments of silence, Cage leaned back against the cushions, his leather pants creaking, and slanted his friend a look. "We have a problem here."

I watched Sinclair's jaw work as he chewed his thoughts over. Finally, he tipped his glass back and drained the scorching liquor. He placed it on the table and braced his hands on his thighs.

"I know."

"What are you going to do about it?"

They must have really hurt the creep if they were talking so seriously about the consequences. I shivered and rubbed my bare legs together.

"I honestly have no idea." He thrust both hands into his hair and tugged harshly. "How did I get myself into this fucking situation?"

"Do you really want me to answer that? Because I've been wanting to say some things for a while now."

"Since when have you censored yourself?"

"Fair point." Cage nodded. "*D'accord.* I think you're in a relationship for the wrong reasons. Yeah, she's smart and beautiful, and your parents love her, and you guys get along well, but that's not what love is."

"And you would know?" Sinclair barked, but immediately, he shook his head. "Sorry."

"*Mon ami*, I'm not exactly a relationship guru, but I've known you for years, and no matter what you try to tell yourself, you can't control everything. Hell, you shouldn't be able to. You and Elle ..." He shook his head, and I sucked in a deep breath. "It's the first time I've seen you cut loose like this. She's good for you."

"She can't be."

"Bullshit."

"I don't know anything about her." He stood in an explosion of movement and began to pace back and forth. "Where she lives, who her family is ... nothing. And she sure as hell doesn't know anything about me. If she did ..." He shook his head as his voice petered off.

"If she did, she would be just as into you," Cage asserted. "She's a strong girl, Sin. Look at how she reacted tonight. She gave that guy exactly what he deserved and didn't even break down."

This seemed to take the wind out of Sinclair's sails. He sat down with a ragged sigh. "She's too good for me."

"Probably," Cage agreed easily. "But any girl worth being with always is."

They were silent for a few minutes, each lost in their own thoughts. I stood against the wall just inside the bedroom and struggled to unravel the thread of my thoughts. Did Sinclair feel even half as much as I did for him?

"She scares the fuck out of me," Sinclair muttered. I had never heard him swear so much.

"You've never been one to back away from fear."

"I knew the minute I saw her that she would do this," he said, and I felt a pang in my chest for causing him so much undue pain. No matter what he felt, I knew I would be getting on the plane alone tomorrow.

"I think that says more than enough about your connection with her. For once, take something *you* want. Not what Willa and Mortimer want. Not what you think society expects you to have. You've made it. You're successful as fuck and respected. You've earned a little trouble, especially when it comes in as beautiful a package as Elle."

Sin was quiet, staring into the bowl of his glass as if he could divine in the brandy for answers. "I have obligations."

Cage sighed dramatically. "Why do people tie themselves to things that make them miserable, hmm?"

My Frenchman didn't seem to have any response to that. Instead, he leaned back against the cushions and expelled an exhausted breath.

"I'll leave you with her." Cage unwound his large body from the couch, flipping his long braid over his shoulder as he did so. He leaned down to clap Sinclair on the back and brought him close, touching their foreheads together for one long minute. I held my breath at their intimacy. Who was Cage Tracy, lead singer of France's hottest band, to be so close to Sinclair, a man whose icy barriers seemed nearly impenetrable?

When they broke apart, Sinclair was calmer, his shoulders relaxed. He followed his friend to the door and stood in the middle of the living room for a few minutes after Cage left, tugging a hand through his tousled dark red locks until they were in utter disarray. I longed to go out to him, wrap my arms around his trim waist, press my breasts to his naked back and slide my hands over the moguls of muscle crossing his stomach.

But the truth was, I had no place in his world. It was just as it had been all my life. I was a meteor in a universe of floating stars as bright and beautiful as diamonds, secure in their function and place while I zoomed by.

A noise from the living room alerted me to Sinclair's movements toward the bedroom, so I scrambled back into bed and tried to breathe calmly through my clattering heart. I knew I had to talk to him even though I had no idea what I would say, but I kept my eyes closed when he came into the bedroom and paused just beside the bed, looking down at me.

His fingers brushed a few stray hairs away from my face and lingered against my parted lips. I wondered if he knew I was faking sleep, but I kept my breathing even just in case, and a minute later, he turned and padded softly into the bathroom. The light spilled into the room from the open door, and I opened my eyes as I listened for the sound of his movements. When I heard nothing, I got up to investigate.

He stood with his arms braced on the sink, his chest bare, and his head dipped so that long strands of glossy mahogany hair obscured his face. I hovered in the door for a moment until I was sure he could sense me by the slight shiver that rippled through his stiff shoulders.

Slowly, he tilted his head to the side to look at me. When our eyes met, I gasped. I felt our connection as painfully as if an anchor had rooted its sharp, sure hooks deep in my heart, linking our two souls with a thick, unyielding chain. It was not a delicate hold or a whimsical emotion. Love gripped me tightly, wringing me out until I wasn't sure I breathed.

Sinclair's eyes were large, but his expression guarded as I took the few steps necessary to reach him, then bring my hand to his face and trace the sharp angle of his cheekbone. After a second, he let out a short, sharp breath and turned his head to press a kiss into my palm. The gesture almost undid my fragile state, unzipping what would surely be a sloppy mess of emotions, but the sight of his raw, bleeding knuckles distracted me.

I tsked as I took one of his hands in my own and turned on the tap to wet a washcloth resting on the marble counter. He watched me carefully as I gently pressed the hot cloth to his scrapes.

"No chastisement?" he asked.

"Disappointed?"

"No, surprised. I assumed you would be a pacifist."

My eyebrows rose, and I purposely placed my tongue between my teeth after reminding him, "I bit the bastard's tongue."

He held the corner of his smile back so that it was adorably lopsided. "That you did. I hope you don't mind that I added a few ... touches to your masterpiece."

"Oh?"

"Just a black eye, maybe some purple near the jaw." He shrugged. "Black and blue are really his colors, you know."

It was my turn to fight my smile, laughter bubbling up and escaping before I could help it. Sinclair being uncharacteristically playful was impossible to resist. "I agree."

We grinned at each other like idiots, my hands now holding each of his. I looked down when he did to see his fingers twine slowly with mine, and when I met his gaze again, those electric eyes were bright.

"Will you do something with me?"

My belly fluttered with desire despite myself, but he laughed and shook his head. "Get your mind out of the gutter, Elle, and help me with the blankets."

Curious, I dutifully followed his orders as we deconstructed the bed, pulling off the heavy blanket and pillows to move them out onto the balcony. He pushed the two lounge chairs together and set up our makeshift bed, presenting it to me with twinkling eyes.

"Bored of the bedroom?"

He walked around to me and ran his knuckles down my cheek before pushing my hair over my shoulder. "Would you like to know the first thing I noticed about you?"

I was oddly breathless, so I just nodded.

"It was all this creamy skin. I imagined what it would smell like." He leaned down and ran his nose along my jawline. "Lavender and honey. What it would taste like under my tongue." His tongue smoothed over the shell of my ear before he nipped the lobe. "Even though you were ill, I could imagine how it would look in the sun and underwater. I had all these fantasies."

He tipped my chin up and rubbed a thumb over my pouting bottom lip. "I wanted you under the stars."

"Why are you doing this?" I whispered.

Something flickered across his eyes and was gone. He cocked his head in question.

"Why are you making it impossible for me to walk away with a whole heart?"

A light shudder ran down his spine, and I knew it wasn't from the balmy sea breeze.

"I told you I would hurt you," he murmured.

I flinched, and his hands slid down to my arms so that I wouldn't turn away. "You did. I guess I'm the villain in this love story then."

His eyes blazed in the low light. "You are not a villain for caring. I gave you no choice."

I snorted and tugged my arms from his grip, needing space.

"There is always a choice. And I'm not mad at myself for making it." Anger flared through the heartache, and I stepped so close I was almost standing on his toes. "I would make it again."

I could see the insecurity in the quirk of his unsmiling mouth, and I badly wanted to eradicate it, to burn away all of his considerable self-hatred and replace it with my love.

"Let me love you tonight." I took his frozen face in my hands and tried to smooth away the distress. "Let me pretend that I'm allowed to love you, that I'm yours. That tomorrow, instead of getting on a plane alone, I'll go back to a life we share."

My boldness left me shaky but strangely confident. I could feel my old dull and sensible skin slide away completely, leaving me raw and new and shiny. Even if he rebuffed me and told me to leave right now and never see him again, I would have this—the new me—and that would be enough.

I listened to the breath of the sea on the shore and of Sinclair's against mine for an interminable time until he sighed deeply and pulled me against him. One hand pressed to my lower back, and the other cradled the back of my head as his fingers threaded through my damp hair. Though it was only a hug, and I still had no idea how he really felt about me, somehow, it was enough.

I pulled away and pressed a hand to his chest to let him know I wanted him to stay there. When I was sure he understood, I began to slowly undress him, tugging off his expensive scuffed shoes and deftly undoing the catch to his pants that had so eluded me the first night in his bed. When he was gloriously naked, I started to pull my own clothes off, but he caught my wrist in his hand and shook his head.

"I like you in my clothes," he said, taking the hem of his T-shirt in his hands, "but it covers too much of this skin."

I let him pull the fabric over my head and tried not to quiver when he took a step back to stare at me with burning eyes. I could feel his gaze all over my body, caressing the generous curve of my breasts and tickling the gentle slope of skin down to my heated core. The power of his appreciation bubbled in my blood until I felt woozy like I had imbibed too much champagne.

He groaned and reached for me, tugging my body into his arms with a strong pull that robbed me of breath. It was my turn to moan when he fused his lips to mine, stroking me with hot strikes of his talented tongue. I was ready for a rough fuck, something dirty that would make me flush with embarrassment and lust, but he changed the angle of the kiss, pulling back to suck lightly at my bottom lip, then the top. His hands held me delicately, as if I weighed nothing, and when he pressed a knee onto the makeshift bed to lay me down. My descent was so gentle I felt like I landed on a cloud.

I had wanted to show him how much I loved him, but he was on top of me, sweeping long strokes of his broad fingers up and down my skin and planting gentle sucking kisses next to my aching core and heavy breasts. He was worshipping me with his body, playing mine like the finest instrument, and I wondered if this was his way of telling me how he felt. If he was loving me with his body in the only way he knew how. When he finally placed an open-mouthed kiss on my pulsing center, I unraveled long and slow like a ball of yarn rolling across the floor.

When I opened my eyes a minute later, he was looking down at me with an inscrutable expression and mildly frantic eyes. I didn't know what was bothering him, but I knew how to help him. Grabbing his ears to pull him in for a long, tangling kiss, I opened my legs and wrapped them around his pelvis, tipping my hips in order to open myself to him. He pulled back when he was poised at my entrance, panting slightly, his eyes unfocused but intent on mine. Only then did he slowly push inside me, not stopping until he was as deep as I could take him.

Eyes locked, he moved inside me, long, slow thrusts that had me feeling every inch of him. It was hard not to feel wholly owned by him at that moment, caught up in his arms, thrust down on his erection, invaded by him with all my senses. Even the sixth, that elusive sensory element that was more spiritual than visceral. Every time he slid inside me, his head kissing the every end of me, I felt stamped by him. It was a mark I knew I would wear inside me for the rest of my life even if I never saw him again. Even if I never had his smoky scent in my nose, his lean muscles under my hands, his gleaming red-brown hair hanging around us like a curtain as he kissed me.

I started crying, silent tears that leaked from the corners of my eyes and slide into my hairline. Sin didn't hesitate as he made love to me, dipping down to lick the trail from cheek to temple. When he kissed me again, it was bright with salt.

"I want you to remember this," he ordered in that cold voice that encased burning intent. "I want you to remember the feeling of me in this tight pussy, the way we fit together my edges against all your lush curves. I want my body imprinted on yours forever."

And my heart? I wanted to call out in anguish. *What about that?*

Instead, I lurched up to catch Sin's lips in an all-encompassing kiss, and then, when the slow, massive crest of a tsunami-like climax loomed over me, and Sin's thrust increased with his own need to come, I breathed into his mouth the truth of my heart, "Forever."

Chapter Fifteen

I woke the next morning with the gentle ocean breeze tickling a lock of hair against my cheek. The sun was just cresting over the horizon, spilling handfuls of glitter over the calm cerulean sea. I would have sat up to watch it properly, but Sinclair was a heavy weight plastered to the right side of my body. Carefully, I turned my look at him, aching at the sight of his peaceful expression and the softness of those hard features in repose. Daringly, I traced my fingertip gently over the straight reddish brows, down the strong line of his nose, and over the defined, scruff lined edge of his jaw.

It was impossible not to feel stirred by him as both a woman and an artist. If he had truly been mine, I would've spent years drawing the planes of that handsome face, discovering how it morphed in shadow and sun, as it evolved over the years with deeper creases in those hollowed cheeks and across the broad forehead. I wished I had the time to memorize every random freckle and mole, every inch of that beautiful darkly gold flesh so unique on a man with mahogany hair.

But I didn't.

This was my last morning with my Frenchmen, and I was determined not to be morose. I had one day left with him, and I would relish every perfect moment.

Carefully, I slid out of our makeshift bed so I didn't disturb him and then tiptoed back into the room to call for breakfast and plan our day with the concierge. While I waited, I showered and readied myself, still pleasantly shocked and amused that Sin'd had all my things brought to his room. It was over-the-top bossy, but I continued to find myself endeared by the quality instead of annoyed as I maybe should have been.

The truth was, Sin's dominance brought me peace and made me feel safe. I could recognize that more clearly in the wake of my assault the night prior. It felt good to know he was taking care of me, ordering Candy as my keeper while he dealt with the aggressor the way the smothered alpha male in him needed to. I'd never had anyone, but Cosima stand up for me before, and it felt unbelievably poignant to know that this man would after only six days of knowing me.

What might he do for me after years?

I pushed the thought out of my mind as I smoothed sunscreen into my tanned, freckled face and product into my curling damp hair. It was easy to choose my skimpiest bikini, a high-cut vivid blue color that reminded me of Sinclair's eyes that cupped and plumped my heavy breasts to best advantage. Satisfied he wouldn't be able to keep his hands off me, I donned a loose lavender linen cover-up and answered the knock on the door for room service.

He was still asleep when I carried the massive tray out to the terrace, and I took delight in placing it out of the way so I could straddle his hips and wake him up by peppering kisses all over his face.

"Good morning," I sang lightly as his lids fluttered open to reveal those deeply pigmented blue eyes. "Time to wake, sleepyhead."

His brow furrowed as he stretched beneath me, almost dislodging me in the process. I giggled as he grabbed my hips to keep me secured. "What time is it?"

"Nearly eight o'clock."

His brows lifted. "I can't remember the last time I slept so late."

I laughed. "It's hardly noon, Sin, I think it's okay. You didn't get to sleep until three in the morning anyway." I smiled shyly as him, aware of his warm grip sliding up my waist. "Besides, I liked watching you sleep."

"Ah, yet another clue to the mystery of Elle. You are a closeted somnophile," he teased.

I was grateful for his good mood and playfulness so I leaned into it, nipping at the tip of his nose, my hair a curtain around our smiling faces. "Not yet. But I'm discovering I might have a masochistic streak."

"Ah," he said somberly, one hand moving over my hip to grasp my bum cheek hard in his grip, making me hiss. "Maybe we should spend the morning exploring that."

"Nope," I crowed happily, flopping onto my side off him to grab for a piece of bacon on the tray. "You're always making plans, so I thought today, it was my turn."

He arched a brow as he sat up, the covers falling from his beautifully carved chest in a way that had me frozen with the bacon raised halfway to my mouth. Catching my look, he twitched his lips in that small, wicked grin, and he leaned forward to steal a bite of bacon from me.

"Excuse me," I accused, but laughter suffused my tone.

He ignored me, chewing his bacon then reaching for a cup of black coffee on the tray, but I detected the hint of a smile behind the lip of the rim as he brought it to his mouth. "So, what does the siren wish to do today?"

"We're going to go snorkeling, then get massages in a cabana on the beach and have an early dinner on the beach so we can get an early night." I blushed as I thought about what we may be retiring early to do together.

Sin considered me carefully. "I don't like the thought of another man's hands on you. In fact, it makes me irrationally angry. Do you see what you do to me, Elle? You make a sane man mad with passion."

It was hard not to take his words as a sublime compliment. No man had ever spoken to me in such a way, as if he was helpless against my pull, willingly throwing himself in my thrall.

It was heady, but it wasn't about the power for me.

It was about the vulnerability it expressed in a seemingly invulnerable man.

Maybe it was about power dynamics, I thought as I remembered how beautiful I felt when I submitted to Sin's demands. I made myself vulnerable sexually in ways both new and profound to me, and Sinclair was doing the same emotionally. The ebb and flow of our relationship seemed as timeless as the tide over the sand, and I wondered how I could ever recover from such an elemental connection.

"I've lost you," Sin murmured, studying me with keen eyes.

He had red-brown stubble roughening the skin at his jaw, around his firm mouth, and it made him look roguish and tousled, the well put together gentlemen that he normally presented a far cry from this morning's relaxed man.

"Not yet," I quipped, but the joke was stale and fell with a thud between us.

"Elle," he breathed on a sigh as he sat up to reach for me.

I didn't meet his eyes as he grabbed a loose curl spiraling over my chest and moved it through his fingers like a silk ribbon.

"Admittedly, this has become more complicated," he confessed softly before using his other hand to tip my chin so I was forced to look at him. When I did, his gaze was so clear, I could map the striations of different blues in his irises. "Let's have today. Teach a man set in his ways to relax and let us have some fun. Tomorrow at breakfast, we'll talk, yes?"

It was like a life raft tossed into the storm of emotions threatening my composure. I clung to it as I clung to him, reaching up to wrap my fingers around his wrist so I could bring his hand to my mouth for a soft kiss. Our gazes locked over our joined hands, and I smiled at him, giving us both some grace from turmoil.

"*Je suis d'accord*," I said, agreeing with yet another of his proposals. "Let's go."

WE WENT SNORKELING. I'D NEVER BEEN BEFORE AND DIVING INTO THE DEEPER waters between small mountains of coral where unknown creatures lurked was slightly frightening, but it felt right to push my boundaries when I was with Sinclair. He had proven last night that he would protect me and he had proven every day of the last six that he was eager to expand my horizons.

As if sensing my nerves, Sin held my hand as we pushed off the boat we'd rented and descended into the clear turquoise waters.

"Follow me," he said, that fleeting boyish excitement making him so much younger than his thirty-one years.

It was easy to follow his lead. I tried not to take too much symbolism from the way he guided me through the waters, deeper and deeper, farther from the boat, holding my hand the entire time as he pointed out the myriad of species that flashed and floated by us. Whenever we breached the ocean to breath and take a break, he explained the varieties, parrot fish, angel fish, yellow pork fish, and brilliant blue damsel fish the color of Sin's vivid irises.

It was breathtakingly beautiful.

I'd been born by the ocean in Napoli, a town as defined by the ocean as it was by its famous pizza, but I had never explored the waters from below. We were poor without the opportunity to do so, but also, the bay of Napoli was polluted beyond repair.

This was a sacred oasis. A hushed kind of reverence existed between Sinclair and me as we swam for hours in the bay. It was clear that he was deeply moved by the ocean and its inhabitants. As we floated on our backs, staring up at the almost blindingly bright sky, he recalled fishing trips he'd been on, and his company's focus on environmental sustainability.

It was the most I'd ever heard him speak at one time, and when we decided to drag our exhausted selves back to the boat, he seemed surprised to still be recounting a story to me.

"I'm sorry," he said, slightly startled. "I've been talking nonstop."

"I wish you'd go on," I told him honestly because I'd long ago given up any chance of being coolly aloof with him. "I love to hear you speak. You have a lovely accent and vocabulary for someone whose first language isn't English."

A shadow crossed his face as he'd helped me into the boat and turned to ready it for our return to the resort.

"As do you."

I recognized it for the subject change it was and sighed lightly as I took my seat and tied a lavender scarf around my hair so it wouldn't turn into Medusa-like dread locks in the wind.

"My father was a native English speaker," I explained but didn't go on.

This was one time when I was happy for our rule about revealing too much of our lives. Talking too much about Seamus always depressed me.

Sinclair left it alone, and we didn't speak again as we motored back to the resort for our massages.

In fact, the cool Frenchman was back in full force as he checked into the spa and followed our masseurs down the beach to the private section used exclusively for the spa. It was getting late in the afternoon, and we were the only couple on the sand. It should have been romantic, but he hardly looked at me as we were left alone to disrobe and make ourselves comfortable on the table.

I wanted to say something to break the strange static energy emanating from Sin, but I didn't know what to say, and I couldn't find the words before the two male masseurs returned.

Happily, he was incredibly skilled at massage, and I was soon emptying my mind to make room for the languid pleasure of having my sex-sore and previously assaulted body worked over by knowing, strong hands. Lulled by the massage, the lyrical rush of water against the shore, and the soft strains of guitar music funneled through hidden speakers, I soon drifted into a kind of half-sleep.

So, I only faintly heard the conversation that took place in Spanish over my head. I didn't speak the language, and I figured the masseurs were allowed to banter while they worked.

I didn't even flinch when my masseur moved away for a moment, thinking he was retrieving more oil.

It was only when another minute passed that I thought to lift my head from the hole in the bed, but just as I did, a soft touch to the back of my crown had me lowering again.

I obeyed the silent comment and relaxed into the rough, strong hands as they moved from the small of my back, framing my spine, all the way to the nape of my neck. Once there, one hand collared the column tightly, working thumb and fingers into the tight muscles.

It was a firm, almost possessive grip that sparked something low in my gut and turned the massage from passively pleasant to heighteningly erotic. It was hard not to squirm as those firm hands cupped the outside of my ribs, thumbs rolling down until they reached the dimples in the small of my back and then began slow, strong circles over them.

A moan escaped my mouth, followed by a long sigh as I melted further into the bed.

"That's it," a smoky voice said close to my ear as the man massaging me leaned over my back, hands still working. "I am the only man to make you moan. You should remember that, my siren, even when you leave this place."

I startled slightly at the sound of Sinclair's voice. "Where are our masseurs, Sin?"

"Dismissed."

"Sin!"

"With a very healthy tip," Sinclair amended with humor in his tone. It disintegrated in the heat of his next words. "I told you this morning I had a difficult time imagining another man's hands on you, bringing you pleasure. It seems the reality was even worse. I would have paid even more than I did to banish him and take his place."

I was a dazed mess of flattered, aroused, and bemused, but with Sin's hands still working over my body, I quickly succumbed to arousal. He chuckled low as I squirmed when he ran this thumbs under the sheet covering my bottom up onto the high swells.

"I don't think we need this anymore, do you?" he asked rhetorically as he tugged the sheet off with one hand.

The cool breeze whistled through the gap in the curtains of the cabana and smoothed over my suddenly feverish skin. I gasped as Sinclair moved lower, his hands unyielding against the dense flesh of my bum as he massaged it.

"Such a gorgeous ass," he hummed appreciatively, the way one would after sampling good wine.

When I tensed as his thumbs dipped between the crease and pulled me open to his gaze, he hushed me softly. "Relax, my siren. There is no part of you that isn't beautiful and tempting to me."

I shivered lightly as he pulled my cheeks apart, my hole exposed to him.

He groaned at the sight as he continued to knead my bottom, opening and closing my cheeks like a perverted game we were both enjoying entirely too much.

"If I dip my fingers down just here..." he muttered darkly, a finger running from the inside of my crease down to the wet leaking from me like an overturned jar of honey. "Ah, yes. I shouldn't be surprised anymore to find you so ready for me. All you need is my voice in your ear, isn't that true, Elle?"

A whimper was my only answer. I'd never known a massage could be so sensual that the mere press of his hands into my muscles could ignite such a burning need to climax.

"Please, Sin," I whispered, no longer surprised that he could raze my inhibitions so completely to the ground.

We were in a loosely concealed cabana on a public beach within sight of the resort beachgoers only twenty yards away.

Yet, I was willing to bare myself to him completely. To fold and bend and contort into whichever shape might please him best because in pleasing him, I was pleasing myself, knowing he would bring me only toe-curling satisfaction.

When he moved away from my core, I groaned in protest, but he only hushed me and worked those steely fingers down my legs all the way to my toes, where he wrenched gratification even out of my pinky toe.

"Flip over," he said finally in a rough voice that abraded my skin until it pebbled into goose bumps.

It felt good to know he was affected too, and when I turned onto my back, I caught sight of the glorious erection tenting the white towel affixed around his hips. I went to grab it, but he clucked his tongue at me. I waited patiently as he moved around the table to my head and then leaned up as he gripped the headrest and took it out of the table.

"Drop," he ordered, waiting until my head fell backward, my upside down gaze fixed to his groin. "Move forward so there isn't as much strain on your neck."

I obeyed, scooting forward so that more of my shoulders were over the edge of the table. The adjustment brought me perfectly in line with the lower half of his groin.

My mouth watered, and I wondered mildly if I had an oral fixation.

Sin stepped forward so that the rough toweling over his dick brushed my lips. I stared up at him into his burning blue eyes and sucked in a breath at the savage desire there.

"I had a feeling you would like playing behind such a flimsy veil," Sinclair taunted me, almost cruelly, yet I was utterly aroused by it. "You love the thrill of discovery. Of someone finding you consumed by me and the pleasure I can bring you. Do you want to be consumed now, Elle? Do you want to take my aching cock between those sweet lips and into that tight throat while I play with your gorgeous breasts?"

I was panting, sweat beading on my forehead, saliva pooling on my tongue. Reduced completely to flesh and womanhood.

"Yes, please," I whispered hoarsely, licking my dry lips and catching the towel in the act.

Sin jerked his hips forward slightly. I couldn't resist the impulse to cup his shaft through the material, tonguing it until it was warm and wet over his hot flesh.

When he'd had enough, he unhooked the towel so that it fell to the floor at his feet. He kicked it away, gripped the base of his erection in one fist, and painted the wet tip along my lips. The smell of him, musky and briny, invaded my senses and made my head swim.

"Open," he commanded, and I was obeying before he could finish the word.

His flesh was silken heat across my tongue as he tunneled instantly to the back of my throat, then paused while I worked to swallow around him. The position made it shockingly easy to take him into my throat on a smooth glide and I hummed in contentment around him when he was seated to the hilt.

"That's it," he said in that kingly tone that implied my pleasure was his to own. "I know how much you love my cock in your mouth."

I did so much it was almost worrying. I felt close to climax, just feeling the texture of his shaft between his lips and up over my tongue, from the salty taste of him exploding over my taste buds. When his hand, still slick with oil, found my breasts and began to roughly massage the flesh and play with my nipples, I groaned long and low in warning.

I'd orgasm in seconds.

Playing my body like a maestro, Sinclair sensed my impending climax and thrust harder between my lips. He caught my nipples between his knuckles, and twisted until twin bursts of pain radiated through my breasts and arrowed straight to my sex.

I gasped around his dick, bracing into orgasm, and then...nothing.

Sinclair was suddenly sliding from my clutching mouth and hauling me upright before twisting me around to face him. I was puddy into his hand, limp with longing, and when he finally had me as he wanted me, butt perched on the end of the massage table, legs hooked over his arms, he notched his head at my sex and thrust inside me to the hilt.

Air exploded from my lips of a garbled cry as he started a punishing pace, the force of his thrusts pinning me ot the table. I clutched him closer, fingers slipping on his oiled shoulders, nails scratching when I lost purchase so that I was clawing him. He didn't seem to mind. Instead, he grunted and forced me even closer, the end of his cock hitting the end of my channel in a way that had pain splintering into pleasure.

"God, the thought of filling you up with my cum," Sin rasped before he claimed my mouth in a ferocious kiss that completely eradicated my composure.

I came.

I came with his tongue in my mouth, his shaft in my swollen pussy, his body all around me, and his heart so close to my own, separated only by our flesh and bone, and our flimsy promise that tomorrow we would forget each other completely.

I sobbed at the savagery of my climax, only vaguely aware of Sin chanting something over and over until he came himself on a ragged groan.

We held each other after that for long minutes, the breeze swirling around us, the light growing hazy outside the linen curtains as the sun dropped and broke open on the horizon like a spilled yoke.

I had Sinclair's softening breath in my air, his hand moving lazily through the ends of my curls, along the warm expanse of my lower back. His heart pounded against my chest as he held me close, and I closed my eyes to count the beats.

Filled with acute longing and something I couldn't swallow that felt a lot like love, I clenched him hard to me and borrowed my nose in his neck. He let me. He let me because I liked to think, he felt the same desperation for me, the same pain at our inevitable parting.

He didn't say a thing until my hold loosened, and then he pulled back to drop a small kiss to my forehead. When we locked eyes, his were carefully guarded.

"Well," I said, clearing my throat as I attempted to gather my shattered willpower to me once more. "That was certainly the best massage I've ever had. What do you I owe you?"

Sinclair blinked once, then a smile tore across his chiseled features, and he laughed at the roof of the tent, clenching me in a hug that vibrated with his mirth.

Chapter Sixteen

I WAS LAUGHING SO HARD, MY BELLY ACHED, AND TEARS LEAKED FROM MY EYES. In fact, I was laughing so hard I rolled away from Sinclair so he wouldn't see the way my eyes crinkled, and my skin went red with the effort of my rolling giggles. Happily, there was no one on the private beach the resort had ferried us to for our romantic dinner for two. Behind us, palm trees swayed, their branches rattling softly in the wind while the lit candles on the small table laid out with our meal guttered gently.

"Yes, Elle," Sinclair drawled coolly from beside me on the blanket we had spread out over the sand on the white beach. "It was highly amusing."

"I think," I gasped between chuckles. "It may have been the funniest thing I've ever seen."

There was a soft laugh, and then Sinclair was rolling me back toward him and pinning me down with his large, lean body. His gorgeous face loomed over me. The hard planes cracked through with that small smile that seemed to illuminate the entire sky.

"He was just speaking the truth," he told me pragmatically.

I laughed harder.

The masseur Sinclair had so perfunctorily dismissed from the cabana had greeted us back in the spa when we were done with a knowing smirk and said, "Maybe *señor* can massage *me* some time. The lady is glowing."

Sinclair's response to the innuendo had been a shocked blink and a minute shrug of his shoulders as he feigned humbleness over his sexual gifts.

I'd kept my laughter contained until now, recounting the situation with him over the candle-lit dinner we had just sat down to enjoy at sunset.

"And would you massage him?" I teased.

He ran his nose down the length of mine, then shrugged a shoulder. "I am only interested in women, but I have no fear of male praise emasculating me. I am flattered."

It was my turn to blink in shock. Sinclair was so typically masculine and so buttoned up in some ways that it was often difficult to discern where the reserved gentleman began and the roguish deviant began.

"Though, it should be said," he murmured as his nose trailed off the cliff of my jawbone down to the hollow of my neck where he breathed me in as if I was some fragrant bloom. "Massaging anyone after having my hands on your gorgeous body would be a serious letdown."

"Oh, stop it." Praise still made my skin prickle like fire ants crawled over it. Compliments were for impressive boss ladies like Elena and gorgeous, loving superstars like Sebastian and Cosima.

I was ordinary.

Even my body, curved and plush, was normal compared to my siblings' lithe grace.

But Sinclair's sudden, fierce scowl had me reconsidering that.

"Listen to me," he demanded, his voice cold and powerful as he righted himself enough to grip my chin and pin my gaze with his. "You are nothing short of a siren. I do not care what passes as beauty in some magazine or movie. This is *real* life, and in it, there is no reality in which you are not a living, breathing dream of stunning perfection. If you do not believe my words, believe my actions. Would I be so helpless against your pull, so willing to deviate from everything I've ever stood for if you were not so lovely?"

My eyes burned so hot that they blurred. It took me a moment to realize I was crying and then another to realize I'd stopped breathing.

"But, Elle," Sin whispered, moving even closer so that those blue eyes were my world, and I was utterly submerged in their depths. "It is not so much this hourglass body or the flaming curls of your hair that hold me so captive. It is the soul shining in your eyes and peeking from your sweet, shy smile. You have so much to give the world. It is remarkable to me that you should not see that. I have known you only a week, and I am blinded by it."

"Stop," I whispered, and if I flipped a switch, the last of the sun slipped over the horizon, and the entire sky dimmed.

"No," he said adamantly, his hand on my chin moving into the back of my hair so he could fist it just tight enough to bring my scalp alive with tingles. "No, I hope you never stop hearing my voice say those words for as long as you need to hear them. Even when I am gone."

"When you're gone," I croaked, crying hard even though I didn't want to show him such weakness.

It couldn't be helped.

I was a goner for a man I should never have known.

A man who was never mine to have.

Determination set his jaw, his eye dark with intent as he pulled back to sit beside me, leaning back on his hands.

"Undress," he told me coolly, but his eyes? They burned. "Show me that beautiful body."

My fingers trembled as they went to the buttons on my thin floral dress as I fumbled to undo them. I watched Sinclair as he watched me, loving the tension in every inch of his posture as he held himself back from ravaging me. It was that contrast between his verdant desires and ironclad control that I found so endlessly arousing.

"Watch yourself," he coaxed, the words a sinuous coil of smoke wrapping around me like a drug that made me light-headed. "Look at that golden skin, freckled and smooth. I want to taste each one with my tongue."

"You should," I agreed eagerly.

I was very freckled. It would take him a very, very long time.

His lips twitched into a smile as fleeting as a shooting star. "Be good for me, Elle, and you'd be surprised what I would do to you."

A little shiver rippled through my shoulders as I undid the last of the long row of buttons and pushed the parted fabric open. I wore a gathered white bikini underneath that had always reminded me of seashells.

"A siren, indeed," he murmured, then went to his knees to move between my parted thighs.

I watched with my heart beating hard in my throat as he used one finger to slowly, achingly slow, draw one bikini strap down my shoulder and then the other. The light tickle of his flesh against mine drew my skin into tight bumps. It was so delicate, a whisper, yet it vibrated through me like a gong strike.

"You are the most magnificent woman," Sinclair admitted, almost to himself.

Jealousy flashed through me before I could quell it, and of course, it was my bad luck he was observant enough to catch it.

"You want to ask if I think you are more magnificent even than her," he noted, his voice devoid of feeling.

I cursed him for his infallibility. For once, I wanted to be so unmoved.

"I want to ask a lot of things," I confessed with a blithe little shrug.

I didn't fool him.

Sin sat back and pulled my legs over his as he faced me, then tugged me up into his lap. My hair made a dark curtain around us as I leaned my forehead against his and stared down into his eyes.

"Maybe one day, my siren, I will let you ask them," he said opaquely.

I tried not to let it give me hope.

"But for now, you must know, the only two people in the entire world to me are you and me," he promised.

And then he sealed that promise with a kiss as lush as spring rain in a blooming garden. I had no choice but to respond, melting into him, wanting to give him every inch of me one last time before it was too late.

Because he could skirt around the inevitable, but we both knew the truth.

This was the end of us.

The termination of a relationship that we had only begun to sketch into something I knew in my bones could be have been the masterpiece of my life's work.

I swallowed the tears that surfaced and dived deeper into Sinclair's molten embrace.

The energy built between us, a desperation that hummed and sparked like electricity against our skin. I tore his linen shirt as I pulled it from those broad shoulders, needing his flesh under my hands, and he threw my bikini top first, then my bottoms far down the beach as if the sight of them insulted him.

I was wet when his fingers found me and slid like a brush through paint from my clit to my entrance.

"Please, sir," I begged, embarrassed of my cries but beyond that, lost to the current between us. "I need you now."

"Do you ache for me?" he asked in that cold voice that made me shiver. "Do you need me to fill up this tight pussy and remind you that I am the first man to take it?"

"Yes," I hissed sharply as he began to fuck me with his long, nimble fingers.

"Ride them for me, and I may let you ride my cock later," he promised.

I tossed my head back on my shoulders as I set my hips to the ancient rhyme of the sea on the shore, rocking back and forth, up and down. The friction was sweet and building, clenching my womb, my legs, and toes, sending sparks to my swollen breasts. I felt filled with the fire of our passion, but still, I wanted more.

Reading my restless need or perhaps feeling his own, Sin used his fingers, still wet from my sex, to quickly lube the head of his swollen dick then slotted it at my entrance.

"Watch me," he barked almost harshly.

The second our eyes locked, he impaled me, thrusting up into me at the same day he brought me down onto him with both arms wrapped tight around my torso, a hand clenched in my hair to pin me down.

I screamed at the resulting burst of pain-tinged pleasure and immediately set my hips to a punishing pace. There was this gluttonous need in me to come as if I could baptize him with my orgasm and claim his spirit for my own.

Sin grunted softly, sweat beading on his forehead, dampening the thick russet hair I ran through my fingers.

We watched each other, mirroring the expressions of the other.

Joy, lust, ecstasy, desperation and even fear.

I wasn't sure who felt what or when, only that on that beach joined together like two halves of a shell I felt we joined in perfect union, and it made me want to cry.

You were meant to be mine, I wanted to say and didn't, the words burning my throat.

A whimper escaped, a noise Sin recognized as something other than lust.

"Tell me," he ordered softly, reading my mind in that way he had, pressing his forehead to mine as he rolled his hips.

I gasped.

"Tell me," he repeated, withdrawing from me completely, leaving me achingly empty.

I rolled my hips down to bring him back to me, but his pained expression made me realize what he wanted from me. Still, I waited until he thrust into me again, all the way. He waited for me to speak, keeping me on the edge with those long, smooth strokes until finally, when I was quivering and whimpering with need, I whispered the truth that had been scorching my tongue for days, since almost the first moment I saw him.

"I love you."

He slammed back into me with a guttural moan, triggering my orgasm and his own. I clutched him to me, unwilling to relinquish the feel of his body against my own. He murmured something against my hair and pulled me into his arms as he rolled over. I wrapped one leg between his and tucked my head under his chin, bringing as much of my body into contact with his as I could. Because I already knew that in a few hours, as soon as the sun rose, I would be walking away from Sinclair forever.

The End.

THE
SECRET

THE EVOLUTION OF SIN, #2

USA TODAY & WSJ BESTSELLING AUTHOR
giana darling

To everyone who read The Affair and understood that love is complicated and all the more beautiful for it.

Everything carries
  Me to you
  As if everything
  That exists,
  Aromas, light, metals,
  Were little boats that said
  Toward those isles of yours
  That wait for me.

Pablo Neruda

Chapter One

THE WAITING AREA IN FRONT OF THE ARRIVAL GATES AT JFK AIRPORT WAS crowded with people waiting for loved ones. Before I was even fully past the sliding glass doors, a wonderful voice—rich and decadent like a spoonful of chocolate ganache—called out to me.

"Giselle, *mi amore!*"

Cosima Lombardi was one of the lucky ones. Easily the most beautiful person I had ever seen, she crossed the crowded space with strong strides, her waist-length onyx hair floating behind her and attracting the glances of everyone in the terminal. Oblivious to it, she enveloped me in her long, thin arms and pressed me close to her body so that I was flush against her famous curves. This was the way a woman like Cosima Lombardi hugged – no boundaries and no embarrassment, just passion.

She pulled back to regard me with startlingly long-lashed eyes the color of melted butter. "I've missed you, *bambina.*"

It was still hard to believe a woman like this could be my sister.

"I missed you too, Cosi." I dragged in a deep breath of her spicy scent and instantly felt at ease. "But you didn't have to pick me up. I thought you had some work thing tonight?"

As one of the hottest young models on the fashion scene since Karl Lagerfeld championed Cara Delevingne, she was constantly working.

She swished one caramel hand through the air, the gold bangles on her wrist just as musical as her mild Italian accent. "My sister comes before work, Gigi. You should know that. I haven't seen you in seven months and two weeks." Her frown was fierce, and it was obvious to me why photographers loved her face as devotedly as they did.

"Excuse me." A teenage girl, no older than fifteen, approached us with barely concealed excitement, dragging her embarrassed father behind her. "Are you Cosima Lombardi?"

My sister smiled genuinely at them and extended her long-fingered hand. "Hello, darling."

She winked at the awkward father and leaned over to give the strange girl a kiss on each cheek.

"Wow," the teenager gushed, and I smiled as my sister obligingly took a picture with both father and daughter.

There was no one in the world I loved more than my sister. It felt good to watch her interact with the people who approached her for her face and fame only to become enchanted with her warmth.

I was still smiling when she returned to my side and pressed a kiss to my cheek. "I'm sorry about that. Now, tell me absolutely *everything* I've missed in the past seven and a half months."

The shadow of Christopher crossed my thoughts, but I stubbornly refused to acknowledge it. There were only two other people in the world who knew the truth about why I was moving to New York after years abroad, and I intended to keep it that way, no matter how much I loved my sister.

"Your life is much more interesting, Ms. Sports Illustrated."

Cosima laughed at my teasing, and it felt good when she took my arm in hers to march me over to the baggage claim.

Yet I found myself casting my gaze around the airport in search of a certain man with electric blue eyes. I knew that he wasn't on the same flight, but I had done three laps of the plane just to make sure. For the rest of the journey, I had alternated between staring blankly at the seat in front of me and bursting into intermittent tears. The poor man beside me hardly fared better than Pierre on the flight from Paris. At least this time, the Dramamine tablets I had taken kept me from throwing my guts up. Still, I knew my eyes were probably still red from crying, and I was pale from lack of sleep. Thankfully, Cosima was too excited to see me to notice the telling signs.

"It was very weird," Cosima was saying. "The fact that people pay me just to pose for a camera is still strange to me. Do you know how much I got paid for that shoot?"

"Do I want to?" I winced, thinking about how much my studies at *L'École des Beaux-Arts* cost. Though I had been slowly climbing my way to success in the Parisian art scene, uprooting my life cross continents was bound to take its toll, and I was reluctant to rely once again on my sibling's generous financial support.

"Probably not," she agreed cheerfully and casually reached out to smooth my wayward hair. "Let's just say it was enough to put a down payment on a two-bedroom apartment in Tribeca!"

It still surprised her, I knew, that her face could buy such an opulent lifestyle for herself and our family. I would never understand what it had been like for her, running away to Milan from our small town in Southern Italy in order to raise enough money for us to leave our impoverished life behind. Sometimes, there was sadness in her eyes that I knew no one would ever reach.

"That's amazing, but you know I'm not surprised. You work so hard."

She made an unattractive sound and easily swept my luggage from the carousel. "Modeling isn't work. At least compared to what you do. I loved the print you sent me for my birthday. It's in the office of my new apartment."

We pushed out into the parking lot, and I was hit with a burst of bracing air. Greedily, I gulped in deep breaths because I knew the quality of the city air would be far from this clean, far from the pastry-scented, Seine-flavored breeze of my beloved Paris.

"I'm thrilled you're home, Gigi, but I think I should warn you." Cosima peeked at me from the corner of her eye as she handed my bags to a cab driver. He was an older, East Indian man with a particular smell and lovely brown eyes who stared at my gorgeous sister with nervous appreciation. "Elena is going to come down on you like the hammer of God for not coming home in four years."

"I saw her two years ago," I protested weakly, but I couldn't meet her eyes as we got into the yellow cab because I knew that was a lame excuse and so did she.

"I know you two have..." Cosima struggled for diplomatic words, but they did not come easily. "A distance between you, but you are sisters, and it hurts her that you never come home."

"I'm home now." But I leaned my head against her thin shoulder and sighed because I knew though she was talking about Elena, she was really speaking on behalf of the whole family. Four years was far too long, especially for a family as close as ours. "And I brought Elena her only vice, Bonnat chocolates. I took the train to Voiron for the weekend just to pick some up for her."

Our eldest sister was one of those women whose work was their life, which was the main reason, I think, that she liked America so much more than our native Italy. She had enrolled in law school as soon as the twins had enough money to bring her over from the motherland, and now, only four years later, she was an associate for one of the top firms in the country. For her to take time out of work to make room for a man in her life was a pretty big deal.

"So I guess she and this guy are pretty serious," I said with a massive yawn.

Cosima clucked and took my hand in her bronze one. We looked so dissimilar that no one ever believed we were related. The twins, Cosima and Sebastian, were mirror images of each other while Elena hovered somewhere in the middle with deep red-brown hair and stormy gray eyes similar to my own.

Cosima snorted inelegantly. "They've been together for nearly the entire time you've been gone. Elena wants them to adopt a baby."

"What about marriage?" I sat up, startled.

Marriage was a huge thing for our very traditional Italian mother. I couldn't imagine her reaction to a baby born out of wedlock.

"Daniel doesn't believe in marriage." She shrugged, but the sadness flashed in her eyes, and I wondered what she knew about the mysterious Daniel. "Mama might not understand that, but she loves Daniel enough to forgive him for it. Besides, it's already hard enough for Elena. You weren't here, but she had a meltdown when they realized she couldn't have children."

I pursed my lips and looked out the window at the passing blur of lights in the night. Elena had always wanted to be a mother. Of all of us, she was the most traditionally Italian, lusting after the family life at the cornerstone of the culture. It was ironic, I had always found, that she was the least maternal person I knew. Despite my reservations about my older sister, I felt deeply ashamed that I hadn't been there for her.

"Ah, the city." Cosima tugged my hand. "She won't welcome you, *bambina*, but I promise you, in time, you'll come to love her."

I sighed and rested my head against the stale-smelling headrest to watch the vibrant lights of New York City come at me. I had the feeling that Cosima was talking about more than the city. I hadn't realized until now how much I had missed in the past four years, and maybe, how hard it would be for me to come home.

MY ANXIETY FLED THE MOMENT COSIMA AND I PULLED UP TO MAMA'S townhouse on the border of Soho and Little Italy. It was an old brick affair with black trim and red flowers in the window boxes. Mama had lived there since she and Elena had moved to America four years ago, but I had only been inside once when Cosima had flown me in for Mama's restaurant opening.

As soon as Cosima opened the door, we were hit with the pungent smell of Mama's Italian cooking and the warmth of many bodies. We shuffled through the small entrance area and into the long living room where, to my slight horror and surprise, a small gathering of people stood and yelled, "Surprise!"

I laughed delightedly at Cosima as she propelled me into the many waiting arms. "I can't believe you did this!"

"Giselle."

My mother's voice, the thickly accented, heavy sound of it, froze me in my tracks, and without knowing why, tears came to my eyes. Hers was the only face I saw in the crowd, and I realized with sadness that I had forgotten what she truly looked like. The twins had inherited her coloring – the inky waves, and caramelized skin – but her figure, a classic hourglass like Sofia Loren but softened with good food and kind age, was like mine. A silent sob escaped me when she wound me up in her warm arms, and the scent of rosemary and sunshine enveloped me.

"Giselle, my French baby," she murmured over and over as she held me, her fingers pulling gently through my tangled hair.

"Mama," I breathed once before tucking my face into her hair.

We stood like that in the middle of a room full of people for a few minutes before I could compose myself. Though we had talked almost every day on the phone or by email, it felt unspeakably good to be with my mother again. As with my other siblings, she was everything to me, and it astonished me—now that I was home—that I could have ever been comfortable staying away.

"Quit hogging her, Ma." A rich voice, the male equivalent of Cosima's, but deeper, darker, resounded throughout the room, and with a shriek of joy, I threw myself from Mama's arms into Sebastian's.

He chuckled as he caught me and lifted me easily into his arms. "You've grown, *mia sorella*, and your hair..." He tugged a piece. "I think this is the first time I've seen you red since you were twelve."

I pulled back and smiled into his ridiculously handsome face. "God, I missed you."

Mama tapped me on the bottom and *tsk*-ed at my use of God's name, but Sebastian and I only laughed as he placed me once more on the floor.

Seb had visited me last year in Paris while he shot a movie, and it still wowed me that my two younger siblings were doing so well in their respective careers. Two years ago, Sebastian had written and starred in a low-budget indie movie about an impoverished Italian immigrant in New York during the 20s. It had won three awards at the Toronto International Film Festival, and now, my baby brother, the same person who used to run naked through the grimy streets of our home in Napoli, was a burgeoning movie star.

"I missed you too, *bambina*." Though I was older than the twins, they both called me baby because I was decidedly shorter than their towering heights.

"I like it better this way." Elena stepped forward, suddenly in front of me, her hands awkwardly extended for an embrace. "Your hair, I mean."

My eldest sister shared my coloring but little else. Her auburn hair was darker than mine, a red so black it was the color of wine, cut short and chic around her angular face, showcasing a creamy expanse of freckle-free skin and sloe eyes the color of storm clouds. Her body was lean and small-boned where mine was softer, curved like the other women in our family, and I knew, as her eyes fell over my breasts and tucked waist, that she felt a pang of isolation at seeing me again. Whereas I took comfort from knowing that we looked at least vaguely similar, Elena saw only the things in me that made her different. She was the spitting image of our father, and we all knew that was hard on her, but I always found her heartrendingly beautiful anyway, somehow sharp and romantic all at once.

And though she was also the smartest person I knew, and despite my deep respect for her, our embrace was awkward. Something between us had wilted years ago, and I was still unsure how to recover it.

"You look beautiful too, Elena."

We both took a large step back after our hug, but the twins and Mama filed in around us.

Though I was tired and still mildly queasy from the long flight, it felt good to spend time with my family and the close group of friends they had made over the years. I met Sebastian's girlfriend, Kayla, who I had recognized immediately as a model for Calvin Klein. It wasn't serious, Seb assured me later as he refilled my wineglass, but she was a good lay.

There were also my mama's three best friends, all chefs like herself, and Cosima's friend, Erika, a Dutch model with cheekbones that could cut glass, and Elena's assistant, Beau, whom I had known for years and was closer to than Elena herself.

"So," Cosima began as she caught my arm and spun me through the doorway into a dark room off the main hall.

I had only visited the house once on my prior trip to America after the twins had officially moved Mama and Elena here three years ago, so the layout was still unfamiliar, but I thought we were in the guest bedroom.

"Tell me how things ended with the Frenchman," she said before she flicked the light on and gracefully collapsed on the deep red covered bed, patting the space next to her so that I would sit.

I sighed and placed my head next to hers on the pillow, comforted by her spicy scent and the way she casually took my hand in hers. "I left."

"Oh?"

"I left before he woke up this morning. I just couldn't say goodbye. What was I going to say? Thanks for the hot sex and amazing adventures. I love you. Catch you never?"

I held myself still in the ensuing silence and resisted the urge to turn over to look into her expressive face for her response. Cosima was careful with her words—when she wasn't in a rage—and I knew she was meticulously shifting through them like individual grains of sand.

"I was worried you would love him. You didn't tell me much about him. I don't even know the mystery man's name, but I know you." Her thumb swept back and forth over my palm. "And intimacy for one so passionate cannot be untangled from love."

I scoffed. "You're the passionate one, Cosi."

She propped herself up on one elbow in order to glare down at me. "Can there be only one passionate woman in this family?"

I pursed my lips but said nothing.

"Exactly. Now tell me why you left like this You took away his chance."

"His chance to what?" Break my heart in person?

"To ask you to go home with him."

She said it as if it was a simple choice, as if it was only natural that he would want to take a complete stranger home with him.

"He didn't know anything about me." But I winced even as I said it because I knew it wasn't true.

"You can know a person without knowing the trivialities."

"I don't even know where he lives. That's a pretty big omission."

She snorted inelegantly, and I couldn't help but smile at her. Before Sinclair, I had never loved another human being like I loved Cosima. To me, she was the essence of beauty and life, full of volatile emotions and overwhelming love.

"You would have liked him."

Her expression softened, and she smoothed a piece of hair away from my face. "I'm sure I would have."

We both turned to look at the door as it creaked open, revealing Elena, who blinked owlishly at us cuddled on the bed before muttering an unintelligible apology as she closed the door.

"Get in here, Elena," Cosima scolded and jumped up to tug her forcibly into the room.

Our eldest sister looked uncomfortable but allowed herself to be maneuvered by Cosima so that we lay in a row with Cosima at our center, connecting us but tactfully giving us the space we needed from each other.

"We were talking about men."

"Ah."

"Giselle had a little fling in Mexico."

"Really?" Elena's brows almost touched her hairline. "That doesn't seem like you."

Anger rushed through me like a brush fire before I settled it with a deep, careful breath. "It isn't, but I'm glad I went through with it. I want to be bolder."

"There's a thin line between bold and reckless," Elena said in her schoolmarm voice, the same tone I had heard countless times as a child and the same tone I still heard every time I faced a potentially thrilling situation, always cautioning me to stay safe.

"Oh come on, Lena, it's only a harmless fling." Cosima winked one of her golden eyes at me. "And besides, you of all people can't blame a girl for falling for a pretty face."

"True."

"Daniel was a model for a few years." Cosima laughed at the expression of prudish disapproval on our sister's face. "That's how we met."

I remembered Sinclair's terse expression when he brought up his own short-lived modeling career, and even though I didn't know his foster parents, a flare of hatred burned up my throat. I was grateful to Mama for not pressuring Cosima into the profession, but that didn't mean my little sister didn't carry invisible scars on her pretty gold skin.

"Wait till you meet him. Over the past few years, he's become even more stern." Cosima made a face, comically constipated looking, before dissolving into laughter. "If Elena didn't make him have Bran cereal every morning, I'd think he was having serious issues."

I laughed, scooting from the bed as I did so. I indicated pouring some wine and moved toward the door when I got their nods of approval. It was a rare conversation amongst our family that didn't include a bottle of wine.

"Very funny." Elena smiled indulgently at our favorite sibling. "I should get out there. He'll be here soon."

"Where was he this time?" Cosima asked, idly running a hand through Elena's short, elegantly curled tresses.

"Mexico," she said as I closed the door behind me and made my winding way back into the large kitchen at the front of the house.

It was an open space punctuated with a large wooden island over which Mama's prize copper pots and pans resided on a sort of rustic trellis. The cabinets were an unfinished birch, and the gleaming countertops were cool under my questing fingers as I sought out the clay pitcher of red wine Mama kept filled at all times.

I smiled at the sounds of laughter from the main room, and for the first time that night, I relaxed enough to stop worrying about Sinclair. The decision to leave him without a word would plague me for the rest of my life, I knew, but at least for this first month in a new city, surrounded by my loving family, I would have plenty of opportunities to take my mind off it.

I was pouring out three glasses of wine when I felt the prickle of awareness race up my spine. There was the soft fall of shoes crossing the wooden floors, and then the heat of another body pressed close to my back. Somehow, though I didn't know how it could be possible, when I turned around to face the stranger, it was my Frenchman.

"What are you doing here?" he snapped, his eyes blazing.

He looked at ease in the space. His crisp shirt was still pristine and tucked into his charcoal gray pants, but it was open at his throat to reveal a deep slice of brown skin. The cuffs were rolled hastily over his forearms, and his jacket hung across his shoulder casually as if he had just taken it off to relax. Even though I had just seen him this morning, the sight of him in my mama's kitchen threw into stark relief just how absurdly good-looking he was.

"Well?" he growled when I didn't immediately answer.

I couldn't believe he was here. My mind spun wildly, trying to confirm his presence. It seemed more probable that I was imagining him. I had the strongest urge to reach out and run my fingers through his glossy red-brown hair.

"What are you doing here?" I whispered, afraid he would disappear.

Confusion crossed his face but something like horror came over his features, and he croaked, "Elle... Giselle Moore."

I opened my mouth, but no noise would come out, probably because my thoughts kept running into themselves and collapsing. I cleared my throat, about to ask *something,* when Elena came in from the hall, obviously looking for him. "Oh good, you're here."

She walked briskly over to him and planted a perfunctory kiss on his cheek. He was still staring at me, wearing a stunned expression on his arresting features. And as Elena tucked herself into his side, I finally understood why.

"Giselle, this is my partner, Daniel Sinclair." Her voice was cool, carefully devoid of the Italian accent the rest of the family still maintained.

A loud sound thrummed through my ears, a crackling, creaking, and thunderous noise akin to a burning building falling in on itself. I hadn't known that heartbreak was audible, but—I swallowed hard against the rise of sobs in my throat—I discovered that, apparently, it was. I didn't have time to fully absorb the behemoth emotion because Elena stared at me as if I had grown three heads.

An awkward moment ensued where we all stared at each other but finally, my face flaming with embarrassment, I stepped forward with my hand extended.

"It's a pleasure to meet you."

"You are supposed to be a scrawny brunette," Daniel asserted as he quickly took my hand in his.

Even though the connection was brief, desire vibrated through my core. Irritated, I took a step forward and fought the urge to bare my teeth. I couldn't believe this was happening.

Things like this didn't happen in real life.

My heart crashed against my ribs, and I gritted my teeth as I said, "When I was eighteen maybe."

He plucked a framed photo off the windowsill behind him, demonstrating a familiarity with Mama's house that unnerved me.

Thrusting it into my hands, he said, "Eighteen?"

It was a picture of me two years ago, the last time Mama and Elena had visited me in Paris. We stood before the Eifel Tower, and I had to admit, it was easy to mistake me for someone else. My first few years in Paris, alone, after everything that had happened, were hard on me. Though somehow the family had scrounged up enough money to send me to school, there was little else to spend frivolously on clothes and accessories. I'd always been shy and awkward in my body, the ugly duckling in the gorgeous Lombardi flock. As a result, the twenty-one-year-old me was too skinny, pallid, and adorned with hair dyed an unnatural shade of black.

"Twenty-one," I demurred, unable to look up into the blue eyes bearing down on me.

"She went through an awkward phase, Daniel." Elena took a fresh glass from the cupboard and poured wine as if she was completely oblivious to the tension between us. "All girls do."

She and Cosima hadn't, but I didn't bother to say that.

"I've never seen a picture of you," I spoke quietly, desperately wanting this to be a private conversation. "I don't have Facebook."

"Who the fuck doesn't have a social media account?" he growled, his voice low and dangerous.

Shame flared through me because it was an omission that my mentor at *L'École des Beaux-Arts* had harped at me about, but growing up in Italy hadn't instilled a great love of technology in me, and honestly, the current social media frenzy kind of freaked me out.

I opened my mouth to snap at him defensively when I noticed that we were close, only a step away from being pressed up against each other as if we couldn't stand the space between our bodies even as we reeled from the shock of our reunion. My heart was fluttering madly, but I wasn't sure if it was with desire or some heady mixture of anger and fear.

I raised my voice and felt it liquefy with rage. "So, Daniel, you've been with my sister four years. What an amazing *commitment*."

Suddenly, he loomed over me, and I lost my breath when I saw the electricity in his eyes. Thrilled to be sparring, I looked up at him, ready to volley a return when Elena came between us. She pressed a wineglass into Daniel's hand, frowning at him when he didn't immediately take it. Finally, with a scowl, he took the glass, put it deliberately down on the table, and poured himself a tumbler full of the brandy Mama kept hidden behind the flour in the pantry.

Elena watched him with concern but didn't say anything. Instead, she tilted the bowl of her wineglass around and around so that it caught the light and cast a red-tinted gleam against the white wall.

"So, you're back for good," he muttered over the rim of the crystal glass as he came to stand before me once again.

I nodded, even more sure of it than I had been before this exchange. I was giddy with nerves, hot with shame and lingering desire for the man who had been my sister's for the past four years.

"And you are going to help make that happen," Elena reminded him with a gentle hand on his tense arm and steel in her tone. "You promised to introduce her to Rossi, remember?"

Daniel's features softened when he looked down at her, as did hers, and I was struck by how perfectly compatible they seemed. Obviously, they shared a powerful ambition and an iron-hard exterior that was impenetrable to most but the very, very lucky.

I swallowed hard. I knew Sinclair better than that.

"I'm sorry, Lena, I'm exhausted. Of course, I will." He patted her hand and smiled tightly.

Her smile was wider, and I noticed how full and red her mouth was. "Mexico was hard?"

He nodded and ran a hand through his thick russet mane. Just last night, my hands had pulled on those silky strands as I climaxed around him, hoarsely calling his name. "It was necessary."

"Well, I'm glad it's finished." She turned to me and stepped closer against his side for comfort. "It's so good to have you home after so many years, Giselle. But I have a case going into mediation tomorrow, and I'm afraid I have to be off."

We embraced each other again, and Daniel snared my gaze over her shoulder. We stared intently at each other with my heart thrumming against Elena's as if we could somehow discern the beginning of our inexplicable bond and sever it at the base.

"It really is nice to have you home," Elena murmured once more as she moved away, and I caught the flicker of insecurity in the quirk of her lips.

"I'll get your coat," Daniel offered, already strolling purposely across the room, but she stopped him with a tired wave.

"You just got back, Daniel, and Mama made your favorite Kobe meatballs. Stay." She walked over to him and placed a tender kiss on the corner of his lips. "I'll see you at home."

Daniel's eyes barely flickered my way, his intractable jaw clenched before he nodded and pressed a kiss to her forehead. "I won't be late."

She nodded. "I'll be up."

After a quick glance and half a step in my direction, she pushed her arms into a gorgeous black trench coat and left through the front door without looking back.

And I was left with the one man in the world I most wanted to avoid.

Chapter Two

OBVIOUSLY, HE WASN'T PLEASED. HE STARED AT ME WITH A SEVERE SCOWL, and it disturbed me that I felt a shiver bite into the sensitive skin at the small of my back. I could hear the murmur and explosion of passionate chatter from the other room, but it was muffled in my ears as I strained to remember every detail of our week together. There must have been clues, but my lust-saturated memories were hazy. The only thing that kept coming to mind was Sinclair, his laughter as we rolled through the waves, his cool commands as he directed me for his pleasure, the way he had held me so tenderly our last nights together. My eyes stung with tears and my throat burned, but I kept my jaw locked against the emotions, only taking a moment to acknowledge the irony of my constraint. I had learned it from Sinclair.

"Jesus Christ," Daniel Sinclair groaned. "I should have known."

"I can't believe this is happening," I murmured, and my voice came to me as if I was underwater.

He paced away from me, putting the counter between us before he faced me again.

"I don't know what to say."

"Then don't say anything," he growled, still unwilling to look at me. "This is too fucked for words."

My mind was whirring, stuttering, and smoking like a failing engine, making my eyes tear. I coughed to clear my throat and tried to assemble some rational thought. "I don't know what to say."

He spun around and swooped down on me, his fists clenched by his sides. "You ran off."

"Excuse me?"

"You left this morning without a word, Elle." His breath hissed through his clenched teeth, and he took a large step away from me. "Not a bloody word."

"I thought it would make it easier."

"And is this what you had in mind?" He glowered at me, those striking brows pulled low over his blazing eyes.

He took my breath away, even in moments like this.

"I didn't know." I shrugged, trying to ease the load of guilt off my shoulders. "I didn't expect to see you ever again."

Something powerful darkened those blue eyes I had grown to love so much, and I held my breath, wondering if my words had hurt him. But before I could say something, he was in front of me again, his cool mask in place.

"Giselle?" Sebastian called from the other room.

We leaped apart, and I let out a shaky laugh, pulling a hand through my hair self-consciously.

"Be out in a second!"

"We can't do this here," Sinclair said.

I fisted my hands on my hips and corrected him, "We can't do this *anywhere*. You are dating my sister!"

"I'm aware of that. But we need to talk about things before we pretend this never happened."

Never happened?

My heart faltered and almost gave out. How could I forget about him? I caught a glimpse of one of the many family photos lining the wall beside the massive dining room table. Sinclair stood with his arms around Elena and Cosima, his smile small and tight. Anger surged through my blood, but I was already so weak with guilt that my voice wasn't as condemning as I wanted it to be.

"You cheated on my sister, Sinclair. Or should I call you Daniel?"

"It takes two to cheat, Giselle."

His dark eyes narrowed, and I flinched away from the truth of his words.

"I'm not the one with the partner!" I bit out between my gritted teeth.

"Doesn't matter," he said in that damn slippery smooth voice. "You knew there was a woman. You just didn't know who it was."

Guilt surged through me, tripling my anger. I stalked toward him, my eyes glinting as I caged him in the corner of the kitchen.

"Are you saying this is some kind of lesson in karma?"

He cocked his head slightly, a piece of burnished hair falling into his eyes. "Yes."

"How can you be so fucking philosophical and calm right now?" I hissed.

I had never been so full of poison in my life. My thoughts were gathering speed, hurling into my conscience, sending straight shots of shame directly into my heart. I reached out to grab him and noticed my hand shaking.

He stared at it too before dragging his eyes across the rest of my body. My face flamed as each pass of his gaze evoked a memory of his skin against mine, and when his eyes finally met mine, they were bright with something other than hatred or horror.

The murmur of voices grew louder, and I heard Mama heralding people into the kitchen to search for me. Sinclair looked at the door, his jaw hardening again. He took a bold step toward me so that my breasts just brushed his lower chest. Despite myself, desire furled deep in my belly.

He stared at me for only a second, but to my sluggishly beating heart, it felt like a lot longer. I sucked in a quick breath when he lifted his hand and brought it with astonishing tenderness to my overheated cheek, dragging his knuckles down the slope of it in a gesture I had come to yearn for.

"I never stood a chance." He smiled thinly and brushed his lips against my forehead so lightly I couldn't be sure he actually touched me.

When he stepped away, I trembled with a heady combination of longing, regret, and anger, but before I had a chance to voice it, Sinclair was striding from the room. He collected his coat in the main hall, and I heard him run into Cosima. They spoke too swiftly to hear, in voices too low for me to understand. I was still standing there when the front door closed behind him, and Sebastian strolled into the room with Mama on his arm.

They both took one look at me and frowned. Mama rushed to my side and settled me against her soft body, cooing softly in familiar Napoli dialect while Sebastian immediately refilled the empty wineglass beside me on the counter. It was Elena's, but I didn't protest when he pressed it into my hand. My gut clenched when I realized how much more we had unintentionally shared. Now that Sinclair was gone, I felt hollow and rotten like an old house creaking in a tunneled wind.

Cosima swept into the room with a large smile that immediately dropped into a scowl when she took in the room's temperature. She glided over to my side and took my face between her warm, dry palms.

"She said something to you, didn't she?"

Oh God, I almost moaned. Of course, they would think Elena had said something to upset me. It was usually the case. But now, after what I had done, it hit me like Thor's hammer in the stomach.

"No." I tilted my face into her left hand and tried to smile. "Jet lag."

There was silence in the kitchen as my family debated whether or not to press me. They knew better than to believe my deception, but I was hoping they would accept it anyway.

Cosima pursed her lips and shared a look with Sebastian, but it was Mama who turned me in her arms and hugged me tight again.

"You go home with Cosima now, *bambina*, unless you want to stay here with me?" She pulled back to look down at me. Her beauty settled the turmoil currently twisting my stomach into knots.

"No," I murmured, because even though I wanted to be alone, I knew Cosima would be upset if I spent my first night home without her. "I'll go."

Mama nodded and pressed a kiss to each cheek. "You will feel better in the morning. Come by the restaurant when you have a minute, *si*?"

My acceptance turned into a squeak as Sebastian lifted me easily in his arms and squeezed me tight.

"I'm glad you're finally home, Gigi."

Tears pricked the back of my eyes, so I buried my face in his neck and clung to him hard before he let me down. He smiled down at me with those large amber eyes but I could tell it was just a mask so that I wouldn't pull away from his searching gaze. He wanted to know what was wrong, and it went against his nature not to question me further. The only reason he was letting me go at all was because he believed Cosima would press me for answers.

I said goodbye to the rest of the party, claiming jet lag as the cause for my early departure, and left with my sister. We were quiet in the cab, and Cosima's uncharacteristic silence made my distress all the more acute. A part of me wanted her to hit me so hard with questions that I cracked open and spilled all my secrets. It would feel so good to come clean, confess about the mess my life had become, but I knew that it would be selfish to indulge myself. Elena was our sister and expecting Cosima to keep my secret was asking her to pick sides.

Besides, I was more than a little afraid she wouldn't be on mine.

She watched me as we entered the tall, elegant building near Central Park West. I took in the sweeping lobby with caramel-colored marble floors, and the older man with brilliant white hair manning the desk. It was a soothing, sophisticated place that didn't seem to suit my sister, but I realized the last time I had really spent any quality time with her was back in Italy at our small house on a wild plot of salty land in Napoli. She was a model now and a successful one at that.

We traveled up to the eighth floor, and I knew she had made a deliberate choice to live on this level as it was her lucky number. For some reason, I held my breath while she opened the large door at the end of a short hall. I was worried that her apartment would be much like the building, aesthetically pleasing but impersonal, glossed over with glamour instead of warm with personality. The idea that I might not know my sister like I had always assumed made my skin prickle.

I let out a sigh of relief as soon as I stepped inside. Large black bookcases stuffed with novels sectioned off a small office behind the living room where twin chocolate brown leather chairs and a mahogany sofa bracketed a large fireplace. The walls were painted a deep warm red, and the dark wood floors extended all the way back into the kitchen, where I could see glass-fronted cabinets and a dedicated shelf overflowing with herbs. It was so true to the Cosima I knew, brilliant and warm and secretly introverted, that the sight of it instantly settled my stomach.

"You like it." She grinned at me and slipped off her ridiculously tall heels, putting them in the mirrored closet beside the door.

"I love it," I agreed.

"I bought it over a year ago, and I've been slowly trying to make it my own," she admitted. "I had to flirt shamelessly with the building committee in order to paint the walls—they were beige." She made a face, prompting me to laugh. "But I think it's coming along nicely."

She took my purse and jacket from me, hanging it up amid the myriad of designer items in the closet before taking my large suitcase in hand.

"Hades is around here somewhere," she said over her shoulder as she led me through the apartment to the hallway where my bedroom would be. "He can be a little hostile with strangers."

Hades was her black cat, a feline with more attitude than his mistress.

"Oh, Cosi." I gasped when I saw my room. Blues and lavenders dominated the scene, inspired by the massive painting over the white wrought-iron bed. It was one of my own pieces that I had sent to her after my first gallery showing. Tears brimmed over my lashes, my emotions unable to take another hit, no matter how slight.

"I decorated with you in mind. I know you want to find your own place, but I want you to feel at home here, and if you want to stay, well"—she shrugged—"that would be fine too."

I laughed weakly and hugged her. "*Sei carinissima.*"

"I'm not sweet at all. I just love you."

There was no *just* about it, so I squished her harder.

"And when you are ready to tell me what happened with you and Elena, I hope you'll come to me. No matter what, I'm yours. I'm here for you," she whispered, stroking a hand down my hair.

I only nodded as the tears came freely, dripping soundlessly down my face.

Chapter Three

I HAD MADE A LIST ON THE PLANE. A LIST OF THINGS I HAD TO ACCOMPLISH MY first week in the city. But at eleven o'clock on my first day in New York City, I sat at Cosima's kitchen counter staring blankly at the paper, my eyes stuck on the first item lining the top.

Contact Elena's boyfriend about DS Galleries.

Cosima had left at the crack of dawn for a photo shoot in Central Park, her beautiful face bare of makeup but glowing even at four thirty in the morning. I had shuffled out of my room on two hours of restless sleep and pressed a kiss to her cheek. At the time, I was happy to have the morning to myself, but now, as the afternoon crept closer, I found myself still paralyzed in my chair.

I tried telling myself a million different things. That I couldn't love a man I had only known for a week, that it didn't matter because I couldn't love him enough to hurt my sister, that even *that* didn't matter because he didn't feel the same way about me and how awkward would it be at family dinners knowing that he had done things to me and I to him that I had never dreamed about before meeting him.

I tried to luxuriate in the love I felt for my sister, but the material felt rough, abrasive against my skin. Elena and I hadn't been close in a long time, and I wasn't sure if that should alleviate my guilt or deepen it.

But it didn't matter, and honestly, I knew no rationale would make the problem go away nor my overactive feelings about it or him. I was stuck, well and truly stuck between a rock and a hard place.

I was just about to drag myself out of the apartment to walk aimlessly around New York, hoping to absorb my new hometown, when the landline trilled. I hesitated for a second before answering and immediately regretted it.

"Giselle Moore? This is Margot Silver." I recognized her professional disdain immediately—Sinclair's personal assistant was hard to forget. "I'm calling on behalf of DS Galleries. We would like to set up an appointment for you to meet with our curator Isa Rossi at your earliest convenience."

Was she going to pretend she didn't know who I was? I swallowed loudly before answering, "My schedule is relatively open as I've just moved to the city. I can be available whenever is convenient for Mrs. Rossi."

"Very well." Her tone had warmed fractionally. "She has a cancelation tomorrow at one o'clock. If you'll come to the gallery, she will see you then. Oh, and you may want to think about investing in a cell phone and joining the modern age so that it is easier to get in touch with you."

My hand was slightly unsteady as I replaced the old-fashioned phone back on its cradle. I let out a whooshing breath and dragged my hands through my hair. Sinclair had kept his promise to Elena to introduce me to the New York City art world, but he wouldn't be doing it himself, that much was sure. It was for the best, of course, but my heart still panged pitifully in my chest as I stalked into the bathroom to shower before lunch with my family.

THE STREETS OF NEW YORK WERE NOT AT ALL LIKE THE STREETS OF PARIS. The French city was the most visited in the world, yet even at the height of tourist season in the summer, it did not feel half as crowded as New York City on any given day. I was thrilled by the bustle as soon as I descended from Cosima's quiet apartment. My senses tingled as they were assaulted with every smell from bagels to smoke and choking exhaust, and my eyes flitted across hundreds of beautiful, varied faces. My dilemma was momentarily trivial in comparison to the hugeness of New York, and I allowed myself to bask in humanity.

Unfortunately, as soon as I reached Osteria Lombardi in Soho, my good mood gave way to anxiety. I had been inside my mother's restaurant only once before when Cosima had flown me in for the big opening party. So, it felt strange to stand in front of the brick façade, staring at the family name I had forsaken scrawled elegantly across the massive glass window beside the red-painted door.

I wrung my hands together as I realized the truth of my situation. A childhood of poverty and frequent, violent visits from the mafia had adhered my siblings, Mama, and me together like paint on canvas, but after I left Italy years ago, I had purposely kept my emotional distance from them. I had needed the space to recover from Christopher.

Now, I was paying the price. I had no idea what was going on with my siblings, and worse, I hadn't even known Elena's goddamn boyfriend.

I dragged a deep handful of city air into my lungs and opened the door.

Soft Italian opera floated on the fragrant air, and the murmur of late lunch diners lent the rustic, elegant interior a homey feel. The exposed brick walls were lined with shelves full of Italian wines, and the wood-beamed ceiling perfectly matched the dark chocolate stain of the table and chairs.

Loud throaty laughter drew my attention to the back of the long rectangular room to the table where the Lombardi family sat.

"Giselle," the twins and Mama called out at the same time, their musical voices chiming.

Mama got up to wrap me in her sweet dough-scented arms, and I felt myself relaxing a bit. It had been a long time since my mother held me.

"I order for you," she said as I settled beside my brother.

He quickly placed a kiss on my hand in greeting. I watched him check the screen of his buzzing phone and smile roguishly.

Mama swatted at him with a fierce frown. "You know the rules, *patatino*. Phone down."

Seb chuckled, but his phone disappeared with a cool sleight of hand. "I'm a grown man, Mama. I think we can stop with the nickname."

I cocked my head playfully and squinted at him. "I don't know. You do kind of look like a potato."

He bristled because his beauty wasn't something he took for granted, but he surprised me by saying, "That is Mr. Potato Head to you. Who do you think they modeled those suckers from?"

Elena remained absent as the food was brought out, and we all tucked into Mama's delicious meal, but I decided not to remark on it. Instead, I teased Cosima about the makeup she still wore from her animal print-themed shoot in Central Park, and Sebastian told me about the development of a film he was intent on directing and starring in. After three glasses of wine and a heaping plate of Mama's pillow-soft ricotta gnocchi, I felt as if I had never left the family table.

"Where is she?" I asked because my tongue was loosened from the Chianti.

They didn't have to ask whom I was speaking about.

"Appointment with the adoption firm."

I looked sharply at Sebastian. How had I forgotten that Elena wanted to adopt? My stomach flipped, and I placed a hand over my mouth, certain I might be sick.

"How far along are they?"

I could feel Cosima's careful gaze as Seb answered. "Early days. They've been approved but no matches yet."

"No wedding?"

Cosima had mentioned over the phone that Sinclair didn't believe in marriage, but perversely, I wanted to hear them talk about him.

"He is a handsome man, but the family idea is"—Mama pursed her lips as she fought to translate her words into English—"broken. Marriage for him is a cage."

"And a baby isn't?" My voice was remarkably calm even though my heart thudded loudly inside my rib cage. Any sister would ask questions about the boyfriend, so I didn't think I was being too conspicuous.

Mama shrugged. "They do it differently in America."

"He's French," I automatically corrected her.

My nails dug into the skin above my knees as punishment for my stupidity.

"I know what you mean, though," Cosima said. Her golden stare made sweat fizzle under my skin. "Honestly, I think that he wants a baby to please Elena. He would do anything to make her happy."

I was careful to school my features into a pleasant but unconcerned expression and gave a noncommittal, "Mmm."

"I'm not a fan."

"Sebastian!" Mama scolded him, slapping the back of his hand even as her wide mouth smiled.

He winced and rubbed his hand dramatically, but I wondered if he wasn't delighted with her. He and Cosima had been without parents for so long that I thought it would either be irritating or incredible to have a mother, especially such an involved one like Mama, in their lives again.

"What? I don't. He does not know how to properly love a woman. If he did, Elena would be a much happier woman, no?"

"Have you ever thought that might be Elena's problem and not his?" I asked before I could help myself. When everyone's eyes swiveled to me, I swallowed harshly. "I mean, you can't rely on other people for your own happiness."

I really needed to try to remember that. I'd been walking around like my former self, the pre-Sinclair Giselle who smiled only timidly and still felt like a scrawny, unappealing youngster. Just because I couldn't have him didn't mean that I had to revert to that. I had fallen in love with two people that week in Mexico, Sinclair and the new version of myself, one that I was genuinely proud of.

I sighed into the contemplative silence at the same time that Cosima did, and we both smiled at each other.

"I've known him for years. You forget that I introduced him to Elena, and I wouldn't have done that unless I had faith in his character," Cosima said as she glared at her male equivalent, but he only shrugged casually, throwing a wink my way when it only made Cosima more irritated.

"Me? I like him. He is very cold. I can say this? No hugs for him, you understand?" Mama tried to explain even as she stroked my hair, twirling it around her fingers and draping it against her palm. She had always loved my red hair, and I knew she was happy I had stopped dying it black.

I thought about the Sinclair I knew and tried not to take away too much hope that the warmth I had experienced with him was a one-off, reserved not even for his girlfriend but just for me, his weeklong mistress, his holiday affair. He had *wanted* me to love him, making love to me until the wealth of my affection for him was all I felt, all I could articulate. Why had he done it?

I couldn't decide now who the villain was. Me, for pursuing him, for allowing myself to love another woman's partner, or him, the gorgeous devil who had so thoroughly, so easily seduced the simple European girl on the way to a fresh start?

"I'm late," Elena announced by way of apology as she slid into the vacant chair at our table. The rich material of her cashmere coat whispered as she swung it off her delicate shoulders and around the back of the chair. In a high-necked lace blouse and stovepipe black pants, she looked like an Italianate Audrey Hepburn.

"Yes, and I don't believe I forgive you," Cosima warned.

A reluctant grin tapped Elena in the cheek as she immediately moved forward to place warm kisses on her youngest sister's cheeks.

"Better."

This time she actually laughed, a sound I was pretty sure I hadn't heard in years.

"You are such a dork." She shook her head and reached over to take Mama's hand in hers. "Seb, how are you and flavor-of-the-week?"

He snorted but didn't take offense. "How did you know her name is Flavor?"

"Easily, all your bimbos clearly had unintelligent parents. That kind of stupid is genetic."

"Just because they aren't rocket scientists doesn't mean they aren't highly imaginative in... other areas."

"Slut."

"Prude."

"*Ragazzi!*" Mama scolded tiredly. "Enough. I must go to the kitchen and help men there. You sit, Elena, and eat, *si*?"

"*Si, Mama,*" we chorused.

"What happened to Savannah? I thought I saw you two talking the other day outside your building." Cosima asked as she topped off our glasses of rich red wine.

Sebastian's reaction was immediate. His thick straight brows crashed down over his molten eyes like boots stomping out a fire.

"Nothing."

"Who is Savannah?" I batted my eyelashes at my brother. "Your lover?"

"Shut up."

"Oh, someone is touchy." Elena frowned at her nails, smoothing down a slightly ragged cuticle on her otherwise delicate and perfectly manicured hands. "And I don't see why. Savannah Richardson is one of the most well-respected women in the city, Sebastian, hardly a dirty little secret."

He bared his teeth, and—I almost couldn't believe it—growled.

"Oh right," Elena continued smoothly. "She is recently married, isn't she? To some hotshot Hollywood producer."

"Elena," Cosima warned softly, her shoulder pressed hard into Sebastian's side in an effort to stabilize him.

"Fine, I'll just say, it's probably for the best. She should be with someone her own age. Tell me, what is it like to have sex with someone the same age as Mama?"

"Elena," Cosima snapped this time, but it was too late.

Sebastian was out of his chair, looming over the table in Elena's calm face.

"I think you've proved to all of us that age doesn't equal maturity." He ripped the leather jacket from the back of his chair and took a moment to stare at her, his features softening slightly. "And you would not be nearly as cruel if you understood love yourself."

"Sebastian," I called after him as he stormed away from the table, the consummate actor, exquisitely dramatic.

"What is wrong with you?" Cosima asked, somehow keeping her irritation firmly under control. I was surprised, to say the least. The teenage girl I had lived with years ago was not capable of such self-restraint.

Elena shrugged, causing Cosima to bare her teeth and repeat her question with more force.

She sighed and scraped her dark hair behind her ears. "Daniel has been acting strange since he came back from Mexico."

I stilled, every muscle in my body paralyzed by my inner conflict, the half of me that wanted them to know and the other half of me that was terrified to death of the discovery.

"I'm not sure if he really wants this baby," she continued.

"Oh Lena." Cosima reached across the table and clasped her hands. "You know how Daniel is. He will love the baby just as soon as it arrives. Abstract thought isn't his biggest strength."

"True."

"He'll be a great dad."

My sisters stared at each other for a second before collapsing into giggles. I bristled a bit at their humor, though I *did* think Sinclair would be a great dad.

"What about you, Giselle?" Elena turned to me. "What was your first impression of my partner?"

Partner? What a stuffy way to refer to a lover, reducing it to something almost platonic and certainly boring. I took a deep breath, realizing that I was unfairly judging my sister for how she related to *her* boyfriend. Hers, not mine. It wasn't my place to even think about them, let alone allow my bias to further taint my strained relationship with my sister.

"He seemed..." I paused to consider—gorgeous, enigmatic, too controlled? "Professional, maybe a bit aloof."

Elena nodded, satisfied and maybe even a little proud of my impression, but Cosima scoffed. "If you met his parents, you would understand."

"His parents?" I assumed he no longer saw any of his foster parents.

"Willa and Mortimer Percy."

I frowned, the names tickling something half-forgotten at the back of my brain.

"Mortimer Percy is the governor of New York," Elena explained with quiet pride.

My mind bubbled and spun like soapy water between my ears. I took a breath and then another one. Had Sinclair *lied* to me?

"I thought, I mean, I think someone mentioned to me that he was in the foster system."

"Oh yes, until he was sixteen. They found him in France, you know? Willa is with Looking Glass Model Agency, and she spotted him on the streets of Nice. A few days later, they were taking him back home to America." Elena sighed happily. "It really is an amazing story."

And total bullshit. I was certain of it. Though it did make sense that this Willa woman would work in the fashion agency if Sinclair had been telling the truth about his time spent as a model.

"He modeled for a time, but after a year or so, the Percy's decided to adopt him."

"Elena's making it sound like this fairy tale, but really, they are not good in the heart, you know?" Cosima stroked the stem of her wineglass, staring into the bowl as if it were a crystal ball. "They found Cage too but didn't bring him back to America."

"Don't be so dramatic, Cosi. They paid for his living expenses and visited him. Cage is just ungrateful." Elena sniffed.

"I don't know what your problem is with Cage, but you need to get over it. He's practically family."

"Oh, so we are letting just anyone into the family these days?"

"Elena," I protested softly because I could see Cosima was gearing up for a throwdown.

Her lips thinned, and she reached out to pat my hand as she said, "I wasn't talking about you, Giselle. Obviously, the twins and Mama are very happy you're in New York now."

Her words slammed against the soft spot in my rib cage and cracked bone. My breath whooshed out of body, but I shook my head when Cosima leaned forward to take a bite out of our older, callous sister even though my own rage was burning the back of my tongue.

I knew there were reasons behind Elena's attitude; excuses and psychological scars that could provide invaluable context to her insults. I knew it, but I didn't care. The bottom line was, I didn't like her, and I could barely remember a time when I had.

When we were younger, it was easier for me to take the passive-aggressive put-downs, the scathing reminders of my flaws. But it was different now, not least of all because I was in love with her boyfriend.

It made the situation so messy I could only stare at it, unwilling to dirty my hands even if it meant cleaning it up. I hated my sister, and I was in love with her boyfriend. Even if the two had once been separate entities, they couldn't be mutually exclusive now that I had made their connection. Once combined, they yielded an infinite number of questions, but the most important one flashed before my eyes like a neon For Sale sign.

Was hating my sister justification for ruining her life?

Chapter Four

OSTERIA LOMBARDI WAS THREE BLOCKS FROM DS GALLERIES, AND I MADE IT A point to walk past the artful stone façade on my way home from the restaurant. I even peered in the windows, but I told myself I wasn't looking for anything in particular. A massive abstract painting done in brilliant glistening oils hung over the reception, and before I had made a conscious decision, I was through the wide doors into the cool interior.

The receptionist smiled as I approached, but she left me in silence to stare at the piece for a moment longer.

Anyone who inquired at the front desk was immediately submerged in the painting. I was underwater looking up through layers of cerulean, lazuline, and pastel blues to the heart of the sky where it winked white and yellow as if behind a pane of mottled glass. It was deeply disorientating yet strangely serene, imbuing me with the kind of calm that comes from holding your breath underwater for a little too long.

When I finally blinked, surfacing with a physical shiver, the young woman behind the desk smiled kindly at me. It didn't surprise me that she was used to such a reaction. It was a stunning piece.

Since I was already there, I strolled through the gallery, a collection of large and larger rooms made cohesive by the exhibits on display. Though there were some stunning pieces, including an array of weepy watercolors depicting haunting scenes of solitude, there were no more paintings like the one in the reception.

"Who is the artist?" I asked when I rounded back to the front room.

The petite Asian woman smiled, but the sound of approaching footsteps distracted us both from her answer. I felt overheated and conspicuous in my green dress, like Gatsby's beacon. My embarrassment was short-lived, though, because it was true. I had come into the gallery hoping to see him, and my wish had been granted.

"Sinclair," I greeted calmly as I turned around, proud of my composure.

It shook dangerously when I took in the tall, cool sight of him standing before me with his hands in the pockets of his gray tweed pants. He was dressed casually, the sleeves of his oxford blue shirt rolled up, and his suit jacket disposed of to reveal a gorgeous flannel vest cut perfectly to his tapered torso. My mouth was parched by the time my eyes reached his, the blue of his irises smoky with an indecipherable emotion.

"I wondered if you might stop by."

I blinked, which only made his beautiful lips twitch slightly in amusement.

"Thank you, Eddie." He nodded toward the receptionist. "I'll take it from here."

Without turning to see if I followed, Sinclair strode briskly down the hallway that I had just emerged from. I hesitated. Now that I was actually in his presence again, my determination to tell him off wavered precariously. Just the sight of him, the feel of him in the same room as me, unbound me from the tight moral constraints I knew were necessary.

"He wants you," the Asian woman explained, startling me out of my blank stare.

"Excuse me?"

"He wants you to follow him," she explained kindly, and I realize she was probably used to clients staring dumbstruck after her hunky boss. "His office is on the top floor of the building. I'll let his assistant know you are on your way up."

"Isn't that office space?"

She smiled sympathetically at me. "Yes, for Mr. Sinclair's primary business, Faire Developments."

I felt nauseous. How could I know so little about him when every thud of my heart seemed to echo his name? I smiled tightly, thanking her in a small voice before following Sinclair's path down the hallway to the large chrome elevator.

The doors whooshed open on the sixtieth floor to reveal a large reception done in cool grays and blues and punctuated by the large glass-fronted desk displaying the name of the company in bold navy letters, *Faire Developments.*

It wasn't a genuine surprise. After all, I had known in Mexico that he was there to buy a failing resort, but every piece of information I garnered still felt like a nail in the coffin of our relationship. *Relationship?* God, who was I kidding here? There was no relationship between us, but foolish ex-lovers and a long future as potential in-laws stretched ahead of me. I placed a hand on my queasy stomach and straightened my spine, determined to bowl over the awkwardness between us no matter what.

His assistant, a surprisingly young man with brilliant red hair and a smattering of large russet freckles, waved me through with a large grin, and I wondered briefly where the frosty Margot was. I followed the fluid sound of Sinclair's voice around the corner to a set of slightly open frosted glass doors.

I hesitated in the doorway, watching him stare out the wall of glass at the street, the pale autumn light beautifully highlighting the planes of his face. He was speaking Spanish, and it took me a second to notice the black Bluetooth headphone in one ear. I was just about to leave, painfully uncomfortable, when those blue eyes punctured me, pinning me to the wall like a preserved butterfly.

"*Sit,*" he mouthed. And there was no room for disobedience in his stern expression.

I sat but made sure to level a hefty glare his way as I did so.

While I waited, I tried to distract myself by studying the office space. It continued in the modern aesthetic of the rest of the building, but there was warmth in the white, brown, and cream color scheme, the depth of the leather chairs, and matching low-level couch. The entire length of the far wall was glass as well as most of the back wall by the chairs. It offered a stunning panorama of the bustling city streets and made the office seem like the Crow's Nest of the civilized world. There was a conspicuously blank space suited for a painting behind his desk, and not a single photograph graced his work surface. I searched for any sign of the man I knew and found none.

I smoothed the hem of my short skirt over my thighs and tried to steady my breath. It was nerve-racking to sit in front of him like that as if I was a lowly student waiting for an interview and not an angry ex-lover with righteous concerns. But each moment I spent sitting there diluted my fury. I wondered if he had planned for exactly that.

When I tilted my head up to see if he had finished the call, he was looking at me with his hands folded across his desk. I didn't know how long he had been done with his conversation, but I also didn't really care. The moment our eyes met, whatever resolve I might have amassed went up in flames.

"Giselle."

Hearing his voice caress my full name did something funny to my pulse.

"Daniel," I said with considerably more venom.

He stared at me impassively from over his steepled fingertips, and I couldn't help but notice what a picture he made, the handsome prince on his urban throne. For some reason, the image made me remember my previous anger.

"So, you came to have a mature conversation about this."

My eyes bugged out of my head, and it took me a second to find my voice. "Are you kidding me? I came here to tell you to *go to hell!*"

His lip twitched infinitesimally, just enough to let me know he was joking with me.

"This is hardly the time to develop a sense of humor, Sinclair," I chastised him, but when he broke out in a small boyish grin, I couldn't help but smile back at him.

"There is a thin line between comedy and tragedy." He opened his steepled hands wide.

I shook my head. "I have no idea how you can be so calm right now. We betrayed Elena."

The light in his eyes flickered and dulled as his gaze turned out the window. He was silent for a few long minutes, but I didn't know what to say to fill the quiet.

When he finally turned back to me, Sinclair, the businessman, was gone, and I was once again faced with the man I had grown to know in Mexico.

"The irony isn't lost on me, Giselle, and of course, I know the information hurts you." He leaned forward, bracing his forearms on the desk, his eyes blazing. "You think it's easy for me? I feel the same guilt you do."

I was shaking my head without even realizing it. "Then how can you even ask me to be here?"

Didn't he feel the same physical ache that I did, looking at him, being in the same room, the same city, on the same god-forsaken continent?

I was speaking before I even fully understood what I wanted to say. "How is it possible that you didn't recognize me?"

I knew it wasn't fair to blame the situation on him, even though he had decided to cheat on Elena, but it felt good to unleash some of the raging emotions trapped in my chest.

"You were a scrawny, timid brunette in every family photo, and honestly, Elena doesn't speak about you very much."

I flinched from his words even though I should have guessed as much.

Sinclair's eyes were sharp against my skin, slicing through my mask until I felt raw and abraded. "I can live with the guilt, Giselle, and I know what I want. The only question is, what do *you* want?"

"What do you mean, you know what you want?" I whispered, almost afraid to ask but willing to delay answering his question by any means possible.

How was I supposed to respond to that, anyway?

Well, Sinclair, I love you, and the thought of spending the rest of my life seeing you with my sister, loving her, starting a family with her... I forcibly swallowed the sob that rose in my throat. No, of course I couldn't say that to him. Not only was he dating my sister, but even when I had bared my soul to him our last night in Mexico, he remained stoic. It was clear that he wanted to resolve the situation as quickly and cleanly as possible. I wondered, with sudden dread, if he would suggest I move back to Paris.

His lips flat-lined as he stared at me. "Why did you sneak out that morning?"

"It seemed like the easiest option," I muttered, suddenly embarrassed by my flight, especially in light of the fact that he was constantly questioning my maturity.

"I see." His words landed heavily on my ears. "Well, if you want things to be easy, Giselle, I have nothing to offer you but avoidance. Is that what you want? To coexist in this family, see each other at dinners and birthdays while ignoring the chemistry between us?"

No! my mind screamed, but I only shook my head slightly. "That does seem like the best option."

My eyes were clouding, but for a brief second, I thought I caught a flash of disappointment cross his stern features. But before I could double-check, Sinclair was back in control. He nodded curtly and leaned back in his throne.

"Fine. You will deal exclusively with my business partner then, and we will limit our interactions to polite small talk at family functions. Obviously, we will keep what happened in Mexico between us."

"I don't have anyone to tell."

The corner of his firm mouth softened momentarily. I straightened my shoulders before he could take pity on me.

"Well, thank you for making this as simple as it can be." I stood and smoothed my slightly shaking hands down my skirt, aware of his gaze taking in my every movement. "I just want to finish by apologizing for my behavior in Mexico. I knew you were involved, and even when you tried to leave me, I threw myself at you." I smiled slightly, black humor twisting my lips. "Maybe we even deserve this."

I heard his carefully controlled breathing, but I didn't have the strength to look up at him before I turned to make my way out of the office. My hand was on the door, my damp palms almost slipping off the handle when I felt him behind me. I tried to swallow the cry bubbling up from my chest, but a strangled moan escaped from my clamped lips.

"Oh, Elle." He sighed.

His hands clamped gently around my shoulders and slowly turned me around to face him. I kept my eyes trained on the floor, taking in his polished leather loafers. I knew if I looked up into his handsome face, I would lose it. He waited for my gaze before sighing, and when he didn't get it, carefully, as if I was made of tissue paper, he wrapped me in his arms. My head was tucked under his chin, my cheek pressed to the fabric of his blue button-up, and I could feel his heartbeat, slow and measured, beneath my touch. His scent overwhelmed me, and the feel of his hard lines cushioned by my curves reminded me of every touch and tryst we had shared in Mexico. My heart trembled, my resolve crumbling until finally, I shifted in his hold so that I could press my arms around his lean waist. We both let out another sigh as we melted into the embrace, and though it was just a hug, it was the most heartrending embrace I had ever experienced. My tears stained his expensive dress shirt, but I knew he wouldn't care.

This is going to be so hard, I thought.

Sinclair's arms tightened around me, and I realized I had spoken aloud.

"I don't want to hurt you."

"You promised me you would." I laughed weakly and tried to put some distance between us, but he only let me pull back slightly so that one hand could tilt my chin up to meet his gaze. Those blue eyes burned into me, making me shiver.

"Tell me this is what you want, Elle." His voice was hoarse.

Could he possibly want to be with me too? I allowed myself to think for one insane, amazing second.

"No," I murmured, honestly, "but I'm not willing to ruin my sister's life."

He raised his eyebrows. "And if it wasn't your sister you were hurting, what would you do then?"

I shook my head adamantly and tugged myself out of his grasp. "It is. There is no point in pretending otherwise."

This time, he let me open the door, and I was already halfway down the hall when his voice followed me.

"I'll miss you."

I didn't turn around to let him see how freely my tears fell, so I just paused and whispered, unsure if he could even hear me, unsure if I even wanted him to, "Me too."

Chapter Five

We managed to avoid each other for two and a half weeks. It's amazing how productive my period of misery became. Almost every day, I made an effort to paint or walk around the city with my camera, and coupled with long conversations and hours of reconnecting with the twins and Mama, I was able to maintain my façade as a content, single girl.

If Cosima noticed my misery at home, the effort it took me to rouse myself in the morning, the times my eyes unfocused as I was tugged into the current of my memories with Sinclair, she didn't say anything. She had always been perceptive, but I suspected she wasn't willing to talk to me about my private life because she wasn't ready to speak about hers. She spent very little time at the apartment, and sometimes, when she arrived home, she seemed hollow; her beautiful eyes like gold lame over her turmoil.

I also met with Sinclair's DS Galleries business partner, Rossi, surprised to find an incredibly friendly woman waiting for me at the chic French bistro where we had scheduled to meet. She was one of the most beautiful older women I had ever met, with fine light blond hair that softened her handsome face and large tilted eyes like a cat. Despite her inherent glamour, she was extremely well versed in the New York City art scene, and the tight ball of insecurity I felt about my lack of artistic abilities loosened under the weight of her professional wisdom. Eddie, the pretty Asian receptionist I had met the day of my confrontation with Sinclair, was often present at our discussions, and I found their odd couple chemistry—Ms. Prim and Proper and witty, coolly bored Eddie —refreshing.

Despite the distractions, it sucked not having someone to talk to about Sinclair. I knew where to find Candy now, and the temptation to make contact with her was strong, but I decided it wasn't fair to drag her into my mess, especially not when she worked with Sinclair. And I was convinced that he had told no one about the horrific connection we had. Which was why I was both suspicious and thrilled when I received a call on my new cell phone from Cage late one Friday afternoon as I was exiting the gallery.

"How's my beautiful European?" he asked into my shocked silence.

I cleared my throat and found myself looking around the busy street conspicuously as if even talking to Sinclair's best friend was a crime. "It's good to hear from you, Cage, but how did you get my number?"

There was a pause and my heart clenched in worry before he laughed. It was such a familiar and infectious noise that I found myself smiling.

"Sin might have slipped up a bit a few days ago, and you know me, I couldn't lay it to rest until I found you, so"—I could hear the triumphant smile in his voice—"here we are."

"As good as it is to hear your voice, I don't think Sinclair, er, *Daniel*, would like it very much if he knew we were talking."

"That's probably true," he mused, and even though I knew I was right, disappointment settled in my chest. "Which is why we won't tell him about it."

"Cage..."

"Good, I'm glad that's settled. I'm starving. Meet me for an early dinner?"

"Cage—"

"*Génial*, there is a really great French bistro near the gallery. I'll meet you there in fifteen."

He rattled off the name and address before I could protest and hung up the phone.

I stared at the slim piece of technology for a few minutes, debating the pros and cons of meeting Cage for lunch. On the one hand, Sinclair would be furious if he ever found out, and it was definitely not fair of me to be seeing his best friend when we had agreed to stay out of each other's lives as much as possible. But on the other, I was desperate to talk to someone about him, and I didn't doubt Cage's sincerity or ability to lie to Sinclair.

Before I had even fully made up my mind, I looked up to find myself in front of the intimate French restaurant. Just as I was about to chicken out, I noticed the crowd of young women next to the entrance and the lovely sound of Cage's heavily accented but perfect English. Their bodies parted enough to reveal him in all his superstar glory, using his white teeth, deeply tanned skin, long braided hair, and formfitting leather pants to their distinct advantage.

He noticed me shyly lingering a few feet away, and his bad-boy grin stretched into a true smile. Excusing himself quickly from the giggling mass of breasts and hips, he strode my way. Giddiness and genuine pleasure propelled me forward, sending me walking and then running into his arms.

He chuckled into my hair as he caught me and squeezed me tight. "It's good to see you too, Elle."

I pulled away, blushing with embarrassment, which made him laugh again.

"It's good to see you just the same as ever." He winked and threw an arm around my shoulders to usher me into the cool interior.

Even though I knew I shouldn't, I secretly delighted in the feel of Cage's arm around my shoulder, the security and the comfort it afforded me as we stepped into the trendy restaurant filled with the crème of New York society. The hostess smiled warmly at him and ushered us immediately to a table against the far wall. I was grateful too that he remained silent until we were seated.

"I hear you are settling in well," he began, but his eyes sparkled as if he were a kitten toying with a mouse before pouncing.

He sat easily in the chair, slouched slightly with his leather jacket open to reveal a tight gray T-shirt embossed with the name of his band in upper-case black letters. The end of his thick, perfectly mussed braid hit his sternum, and his slashing brows covered large, almond-shaped eyes that denoted him as something other than purely Caucasian. His body was massive, surpassing six feet by numerous inches, and the hand that tapped out a tune on the table was large and powerful. I almost snorted at my former analogy. Cage was nothing like a kitten.

"Oh, what leads you to say that, Cage?" I asked with a small smile because I had honestly missed his games. "In fact, if I remember correctly, I never gave you any of my information."

"I have my ways, Giselle." He winked and broke into a wide grin when I laughed. "Just as you have yours."

My smile dissolved into a sigh. "Sure, the ways of a freaking adulterer."

Cage's laughter prompted the tables closest to us to look our way, but my charming companion waved them away with a smile. "So hard on yourself, Elle. As they say, it takes two to tango."

"In this case, there were too many people on the dance floor," I muttered, playing with the short hem of my purple dress. Sinclair had loved me in purple; he once said it was the color of my scent. I swallowed hard and put on my auto smile for Cage. "I hope you didn't ask me to lunch to talk about him."

"No," he spoke carefully. "Not exactly."

The waitress chose that moment to take our drink orders, and I waited impatiently for Cage to stop flirting with her. His eyes twinkled as he did so, and I knew he took some satisfaction from annoying me.

When he was finished, he turned to me again. "You know, we have never spoken my language together."

"*Non, je ne savais pas si tu aimeras cela,*" I said.

We grinned at each other.

"For future reference, I do like it. Sinclair and my bandmates are the only ones I know in America who speak French with me."

"How long have you been here? Despite all the time we spent together in Mexico, I don't know anything about you." I realized that with sadness. How could I have spent such an endless week with such fascinating people and know so little about them?

"And I, you."

My gaze snapped to his, and something locked in place with an almost audible click. It was a comforting thing, and I recognized it immediately as friendship.

Leaning across the table, Cage took my hand between his two large ones. "Sinclair is like a brother to me. I have known him through everything, and he will always be family. But that doesn't mean I don't have room for a friend."

The waitress arrived with the bottle of Burgundy we had ordered, and I grinned, ignoring her hostility, as I raised my glass. "I can toast to that."

A BOTTLE AND A HALF LATER, CAGE AND I WERE STILL SITTING AT THE TABLE, swinging from French to English and back as we imbued more of the heady French wine. The chef had even come out to see the faces of the couple that had ordered two main courses each, leaving it to him to decide what they were given. He was entirely too young and handsome to head up a successful restaurant, and I told him as much when he finally agreed to sit down for a moment.

"Ah, well, I was blessed with good luck," Chef Devereaux, or Dev as he had encouraged us to call him, said in an accent as thick as Cage's. "And even richer friends."

I laughed. "And rich friends make great investors."

He tilted his head in agreement. "But I have to say, I prefer the beautiful friends over the rich ones."

"Is that true?" I grinned behind my wineglass. "Then you and Cage should get along just fine."

The two men laughed too loudly, not caring who heard them, and I felt a pang of homesickness for the beautiful country I had fled. Though I loved Italy, it was France that had fostered my soul and turned me into a person I could be proud of.

My nostalgia got lodged in my throat when I dragged in a startlingly familiar smoky scent. I barely had time to swallow my mouthful of wine before I felt his presence behind me.

"It's good to know where I stand with you, Devereaux."

The newcomer's voice ran its fingers down the back of my neck, feathering along my spine like a light caress. I shuddered almost violently and nearly spilled my drink. Cage's heavily booted foot found my heeled one under the table, pushing against it lightly in a subtle show of support.

"Ah, but Sinclair, if it is any consolation, your date is both beautiful and rich, and for whatever reason, she chooses to associate herself with you so"—Dev shrugged charmingly—"that is something, uh?"

I looked up at them as everyone laughed, at least, everyone but Sinclair. He was standing beside his companion, a gorgeously dressed Elena, with his eyes on me, hot and overexposed. Simultaneously, I wanted to tell him to quit being so obvious and lay myself out on the table before him, naked in offering.

I shuddered again.

"Giselle." My sister obstructed our gaze as she leaned down to brush her lips against my cheek, eschewing the Italian custom of kissing both. "What a lovely surprise."

She spoke like that, my sister. It had taken her longer to master the English language than she cared to admit, and she was determined to put her vocabulary and etiquette to good use. No trace of her accent remained, and though her tones were smooth and dulcet, they were missing softness.

In fact, as she stepped away from the kiss, I noticed the lack of softness anywhere on Elena. Her limbs were taut, honed by hours spent running and swimming, and her features were harder than mine, pinched further by a discontent that had plagued her for years. She was only twenty-six years old, a whopping thirteen months older than me, but she carried herself like a woman who covered her gray hairs and wore pearls.

I almost snorted when her hand went to a beautiful string of them at her throat.

"Cage." Sinclair had shifted his focus to the singer lounging in his chair like a god. "I wasn't aware you knew Giselle."

He shrugged and brushed the end of his braid against the plush weight of his bottom lip. It was such a sensual gesture that both Elena and I shifted restlessly. "We met in Paris. We are friends for a while now."

"You never mentioned," Sinclair said, his teeth slightly bared.

Cage shrugged again. "I didn't make the connection between Giselle and your lovely Elena until just now."

The atmosphere between us, already fraught, vibrated with tension. Elena looked between us all with a small smile that was far from genuine. My sister didn't like to be left out of the loop.

"You two are dating, then?" Something like distaste flashed across her face as she looked at Cage and a high flush crept up her neck.

"No," Sinclair barked, at the same time that Cage grinned at me and winked.

"Would it be the end of the world if they were, Daniel?" Elena looked at him with disapproving concern, and I was surprised that we were getting away with the barely-concealed deception. It was so obvious to me that a secret was being—poorly—hidden right before her eyes, but for all her natural curiosity and brainpower, Elena was oblivious.

"Yes." Dev nodded solemnly. "You see, there is already a line."

"A line?"

He nodded again. "A waiting list for the honor of taking this lovely woman out to dinner."

I laughed at the flirtatious Frenchman, grateful to him for reasons he couldn't possibly understand. Playing along, I placed my hand on his arm and leaned in intimately. "Technically, you beat everyone to the punch. You've already fed me dinner."

We both looked at the empty plates littering the white-clothed dinner table and everyone, except for Sinclair, laughed.

"Cheater," Cage accused with playfully narrowed eyes, but I noticed them flick over to Sinclair and held my breath when he stirred restlessly next to me. "Although, if any woman is worth it, it's Giselle. Don't you agree, Elena?"

I kicked him hard under the table. That was taking his twisted game way too far, and I wasn't the only one who thought so. Sinclair glared at his best friend with such concentrated hatred that I thought his blood vessels might pop.

"Daniel." Elena tried to soothe him with a soft stroke down the arm.

If I had been in a position to offer comfort, I would have slid my hand into the back pocket of his slim-fitting trousers and squeezed his pert ass. It would have both turned him on and forced him to recognize my presence. My fingers twitched on the table to do just that, and I wasn't surprised when his eyes snapped to them. I extended my pinkie finger toward him, furious and ashamed that I could offer no more. A muscle in his jaw ticked once before his mask slid back into place.

"You are here for dinner?" Dev asked, standing up to flee back to the kitchen and away from the awkwardness. "Let me show you to your table, *oui*?"

Elena's eyes flicked across our faces, her pink lips pursed. She was clever enough to sense the undercurrents swirling beneath the murky waters, and I wondered if her curiosity would get the better of her instinct to back away from the mess.

"Giselle, I have a favor to ask of you. Do you have a free moment tomorrow morning for coffee?"

I held my breath as my mind raced across excuses, leaping from one to another as if they were hot coals. Nothing seemed suitable, and besides, I had the stupid, crazy desire to see the apartment that my ex-lover and older sister shared.

"Sure."

I risked a glance at Sinclair and found him looking at me with guarded eyes. His lips moved slightly as if he wanted to say something, but Elena tugged him forward and broke our connection.

"Tomorrow then." She smiled slightly at me, the same tiny slice that Sinclair was prone to give out, but she ignored Cage, a snub that was notable if only because Elena prided herself on decorum.

As soon as they were out of hearing distance, my mouth fell open like a puncture mark on a heavy sigh. "That was horrible."

"Hell," Cage agreed. "But interesting."

I frowned at him from behind my wineglass as I downed the rest of the crimson liquid.

"Sinclair couldn't take his eyes off you, and Elena couldn't stand to look at you."

"She doesn't know if that's what you are trying to say. Elena hasn't been able to look me in the eye for years."

He nodded, but his dark eyes remained focused on the remains at the bottom of his wineglass. "I thought it was just me she hated the sight of."

His melancholy surprised me. "Are Mr. Rock Star's feelings hurt?"

My teasing tone had the effect I desired. He gulped back the rest of his wine and grinned at me. "Never. Now, I could use something a hell of a lot stronger than wine after that little situation." He wiggled his fingers over his shoulder at the departed couple. "I could also use a woman. And you could use a man, no?"

My heart clenched painfully, and for a second, I actually thought I was having a heart attack.

"Maybe."

He laughed beautifully. "Good enough. Let's go."

Chapter Six

I HADN'T BEEN TO A CLUB SINCE THE INCIDENT IN MEXICO, AND AT FIRST, I had been nervous, especially when we entered Sinner's nightclub, and Cage was practically assaulted by a group of women. Most of them didn't know he was a rock star, but it didn't really matter. The French singer exuded sex and impossible magnetism. I tried to sidestep away, to give him space to entertain the scantily-clad women, but his hand had reached through the gaggle to snare me and tuck me against his side.

"Ladies," he rumbled in his low, accented voice. "I owe this gorgeous *chérie* a drink, so please, excuse us."

"So smooth." I laughed as he turned us toward the bar.

He shrugged and squeezed my waist. "You know how it is to be beautiful."

I didn't argue with him. As soon as we had left the restaurant, I decided to let Cage take the lead. A night in the life of a rock star had to be a thrilling experience, and I wanted to remember what I had felt like with Sinclair in Mexico, throbbing like a strobe light with sexuality.

"Four shots of tequila," Cage ordered, cutting to the front of the crowded bar without a fuss.

When I raised my brows at him, he lifted my hand and quickly licked my skin before shaking salt onto it. "For Mexico."

I sucked in a shaky breath, tucked a lime into one hand and the shot in my other. "For Mexico."

That had been four hours ago, I thought, or at least three. But I had lost all sense of time in the black space, punctuated only with flashing colors catching on glistening bare skin. My dress was damp with sweat, mine and those I had danced with, both men and women who had felt my body intimately as if being on a dance floor gave them the right.

My current partner, a handsome all-American kind of guy in the last pieces of the suit he had probably worn to his job on Wall Street, ran his hand up my knee to my thigh and hitched it over his leg to bring our pelvises closer. I closed my eyes and focused on the pulse of the bass-rich song and the swirl of alcohol tingling in my blood.

Cage was beside me, somehow dancing equally with three girls at the same time. His dark brow glittered with a crown of sweat that made him appear sexier, less civilized, and more heathen. He was keeping his eye on me, but it didn't feel obtrusive. He was my fun keeper, assuring that every moment I spent with him was filled to the brim with it.

My partner, Tim or Jim, pressed his nose into the damp hair above my ear and whispered, "You are so fucking sexy."

I pulled back, pressing one hand to his damp chest and smiled coyly as I bent at the knees, dragging my hand from his sternum to his hip as I descended. His groan vibrated against my hand.

He wanted me. The shape of his arousal through his slacks was obvious, and the heat in his eyes was blatant, almost pleading. I wondered hazily if it wouldn't be a good idea to go home with him. I'd never had a one-night stand, and Sinclair had awakened a neediness within me that I couldn't quench alone in the dark of my room with my fingers.

I was just opening my mouth, my lips grazing his dimpled chin, when he was jerked away. I lost my balance as I had been flush against him, and it took me a second to right myself and see what was unfolding. A man I had never seen before—massive and currently scowling—drew back one corded arm to pound it into Tim/Jim's nose. Blood erupted immediately and made it almost impossible to discern his curses as he crumpled in on himself.

I watched in a daze and reached behind me to find Cage. His hand snagged mine and threaded our fingers. Still distracted by the fight—it couldn't have been because of me, I didn't even know the guys—it took me a moment to recognize that the hand in mine was too lean to be Cage's, the fingers long and strong. My breath caught in my throat, and slowly, because I feared that he would fade away like an apparition as soon as I laid eyes on him, I looked over my shoulder.

Before I could turn fully, he was off, dragging me through the gathered bodies without issue. We passed close to Cage who was looking at me intently, the end of his braid in one hand brushing the tail against his lips.

Sinclair didn't break pace until we were off the main dance floor and climbing the steps to the open second level. The atmosphere was slower than the strobe light thrum of sexuality downstairs. Here, it was thick with sensuality. People spoke in low velvety voices, close together in semi-private booths obscured by glossy black curtains. A few people mingled on the dance floor, touching each other in slow motion with a deliberateness that spiked blood pressure.

I barely had time to observe the VIP lounge because Sinclair powered across the floor without speaking to any of the people who tried to stop him. Finally, we came to a stop at the far side of the second floor after shimmying through a small door in the bar. Without a word, he swiped a card and pushed me gently into the room. I whirled around to yell at him, but the door had already closed, and I could hear him speaking to someone through the barricade. I tried to yank open the door, but someone on the other side was holding it closed.

Furious, I spun back around to face my temporary prison. It was a medium-sized office, the front wall made entirely of glass in order to overlook the main dance floor below. The floor thrummed slightly with the force of the music, and the dark room flashed with colored lights. Suddenly cold, I rubbed my hands hard up and down my arms and decided to snoop a little. If Sinclair was going to shove me into a room like a freaking Neanderthal, then I was going to take advantage of it.

The large matte black desk was L-shaped, facing both the door and the windows, and it was clear of paraphernalia. Frustrated, I moved around to sit in the high-backed red leather chair in order to open a few drawers. I was just about to close the first one when I noticed the white edge of a Polaroid photograph sticking out between two black folders. My heart picked up speed as I carefully pulled it free and looked at a picture of me. In it, I lay on my back with my red hair a swirling mass around a sleepy, satiated face. My lids were low over slightly smiling eyes, and one hand rested against the creamy top of my breast. I barely remembered him taking the photo. Sometime after we returned to Sinclair's suite from the private beach on our last night together. I couldn't believe he had kept it, but somewhere beneath my shock, a sense of powerful calm was rising.

I didn't look up when the door opened and closed. Instead, I crossed my legs, aware of how high the hem of my dress rose over my thighs, and continued to look down at the picture.

"Pretty risky, having something like this lying around." I was grateful that the tremor in my heart wasn't echoed in my words.

"As I recall, it wasn't exactly 'lying around.'"

I leaned back in the chair, steeling myself to look up at him. "Why do you still have this, Daniel?"

He stood halfway between the door and the desk as if he was unsure about approaching. I had never seen him unsure about anything, and I wondered, hopefully, if I was making him *nervous*.

I sighed when he remained silent. "Fine. How about you tell me how you knew I was here? Or, better yet, what happened downstairs."

Amusement tipped the corner of his firm lips. "Don't feel like it."

"Excuse me?"

He shrugged and strode across the space confidently to take a seat in the chair across from the desk. "I don't feel like talking to you about that."

"Oh?" Indignation vibrated through me. "Well, I don't feel like being here."

Ha! How would he like that?

Again, he shrugged.

"Stop playing games with me, Sinclair. Why the hell am I here?"

His too blue eyes flamed, and he leaned forward, arms on the table so that he could move that gorgeous face closer to me.

"I love it when you say my name."

That caught me off guard, "Daniel?"

"Sinclair. You know, before you, I hated my family name."

"Why does everyone call you Sinclair then?"

"Cage always has, and he has a way of influencing people. It's his way of reminding me where I came from."

"Oh."

He smiled slightly at my lack of eloquence, his confident mask secured firmly over his face. "And you are here precisely because I don't want to play games with you. You're here because I saw you dancing in the pit with a dozen different men wearing my favorite dress and my favorite smile, and I couldn't stand it." Slowly, keeping eye contact with me the entire way, he got to his feet and stepped around the desk to stand in front of me, so tall that I had to tip the chair back to look into his eyes. "You are here, Giselle, simply and complicatedly, because I miss you."

My tongue was pasted to the roof of my mouth, stuck to the back of my teeth so that I could barely breathe, let alone respond. Tears pricked the backs of my eyes, and I realized with mortification that this was where the moisture had gone. But his gaze on me was tender and open, asking to receive whatever response I was able to give him.

A knock on the door jolted us both, and Sinclair chuckled softly as he called for them to come in. The young woman who entered was beautiful and all skin. The tiny crop top and black skirt she wore only covered the essentials. She licked her lips and beamed at Sinclair as she carried in a tray and placed it on the coffee table where he had directed her. They were speaking, polite small talk, but I was too focused on Sinclair's declaration to tune in.

He missed me.

My heart was too warm in my chest, like the sun over my tossing oceanic stomach. I was at once deathly ill and too alive, suspended on the rack of desire and pain with no sense of escape.

By the time the girl left, I was basically breathless.

Without a word, Sinclair reached down to take my hand and led me to the small lounge area toward the heavenly smell of... chocolate. I frowned down at the assortment of chocolates, mini cakes, and candies on the large gold lacquered tray and back up at Sinclair.

He grinned, one of his rare full and boyish smiles that hooked my heart and dragged it through the waters straight toward his net. "The club is called Sinner's for a reason. We cater to all the indulgences here, including gluttony. There is a dessert bar on the second floor."

I mouthed, "*Wow,*" and took a seat on the low red loveseat. Sinclair tugged one of the velvet chairs closer and sat down too.

"Drink." He nodded at the tall glass of water. "And eat."

I took a long drink of the cool liquid, grateful for its effect on my dry throat, and carefully bit into a chocolate-covered strawberry. My eyes fluttered closed at the explosion of bitter and sweet on my refreshed tongue.

When I opened them again, Sinclair was staring at me ravenously. I shivered, poised like a gong waiting for the hammer strike to bring me alive.

"You should be forbidden from eating in public." He shook his head and propped one ankle on his opposite knee. "I'd almost forgotten what a pleasure it is to watch you."

I swallowed hard and fought for purchase on the slippery surface of my morality. "You shouldn't be saying things like that."

"I would amend that statement. I *should* say things like that. Every. Single. Day. But you've assured me that you don't want to hear them so..." He opened his palms wide, at a loss.

"Are you..." I sighed. "What are you doing, Sinclair?"

"I'm renegotiating our agreement."

"We don't *have* an agreement."

He nodded, completely unfazed, and gestured to the tray of bite-sized sins. "Eat, please."

I looked between him and the sweets, both representing tempting threats to my body. I picked up the cocoa-dusted truffle, choosing the lesser of two evils.

"I didn't know you owned a club," I said because I felt impotent in our current line of conversation.

"It was my first asset, actually." He chuckled softly at my expression. "I was twenty-one years old, fresh out of university and still living with my controlling, conservative parents. It was a pretty cliché trope. I hoped, if they wouldn't let me leave, that I could get myself kicked out and owning a club seemed like the way to do it."

"I heard something about them. You didn't tell me they had adopted you."

"I didn't tell you a lot of things. That was part of our agreement. And the subject of my parents and my fruitless rebellions is not something I like to discuss." He glanced sidelong at me, a mischievous light in his eyes.

I found myself leaning forward, mouth slightly open like a fish hooked by the cheek. "So?"

"So what?" he said, a smug smile in his eyes.

"Did it work?"

"Not quite, but I did get a surprisingly profitable club out of it and my first million."

I leaned back with a huff. "So not exactly a classic teenage trope."

He laughed again, louder this time, and I realized this was the most I had ever heard the stirring sound. I wished my mind was clearer, unclouded by the copious amounts of liquor in my system, so that I could better absorb it.

"No, not exactly."

He stood with a grace that made my mouth water and moved to stand over me again. I kept my eyes on the confections but I wasn't sure if it was to ignore him or because the restless submissive was shifting and fighting for purchase inside me.

"Do you want to know what it taught me, Giselle?" His voice was deeper and his faintly accented words tingled like ice sliding down my spine.

He was so close that my cheek was almost pressed to his trouser-clad thigh. I wanted to take off those pants with my teeth and use my mouth, hands and throat on him.

"It taught me the art of patience. Have you ever heard the saying, good things come to those who wait?"

I shook my head slightly even though I had heard it before.

His breath was warm and whiskey scented over my crown as he leaned down to gently tip my chin up with one finger so that my neck was craned and my eyes rested on his.

"Patience is a virtue, virtue is a grace, Grace is a little girl who doesn't wash her face," I said.

I was close enough to see his features collapse, slowly at first like a loose domino tumbling a dozen more, into laughter.

When he was finished, he stared down at me with caged eyes filled with stars. "You always surprise me."

The cell phone on the desk vibrated angrily and he swiftly turned away from me to answer it, leaving me mid-shrug. He picked up and listened without saying a word of greeting.

"I don't care who his father is, get him *the fuck out of my club.*"

My eyebrows shot up at his harsh tone and less than formal language. I was pretty sure Sinclair *never* raised his voice. Triggered by his sudden mood change, the air in the room stiffened and pressed against me until I was locked into place.

He placed the phone back on the cradle with a slow calm but when he looked over at me his face was implacable, his eyes just a color.

"As I was saying, you always surprise me. But tonight, I was not happy with your behavior. Drunkenly dancing with men like that." He shook his head. "I thought you would want to be more careful after the incident in Mexico."

I flinched as his dart landed with deadly accuracy in my breastbone. "Don't talk to me about Mexico. I was perfectly safe and aware tonight, Sinclair. And, if it appeals to your idiotic French misogyny, Cage was close by."

"Still, I did not like it." He wasn't speaking sternly now, in fact, his accent had thickened slightly and he seemed more disturbed than angry.

I shrugged beautifully, as if I wasn't affected by his concern, his potential jealousy. "You have no right to do anything about that."

"I have the right, Giselle, and I will always have that right. I am closer to you than any other man has ever been or will ever be."

"No."

"*Mais oui,*" he confirmed with that infernal, casual arrogance of the French. "I know things about you, the dark places and the deep, that even you do not like to explore. I know the things you hate about yourself, and I? I nurture them because I know them to be beautiful."

"Stop it," I breathed, suddenly aware of the slight tremor wracking my frame.

He lifted one shoulder insolently and tucked his hands in his pockets. "It is not something I can stop knowing."

"What do you want from me?" A scalding tear rolled over my lid and slid down my cheek.

Sinclair reached out to sweep the burning trail with his thumb. "We could be friends."

My laugh was soggy with my tears. "Don't be ridiculous."

"I can't say anyone has every accused me of being *ridicule* before."

"Je ne le crois pas," I said wryly, *I don't believe that.*

"See, this is why we must be friends. You are the only person I have ever met who makes me feel like a boy."

I frowned, unsure if that was a compliment or not.

"You know *le Petit Prince*? There is a quote, it goes 'only children know what they are looking for.'"

I waited in silence for him to explain, but he only stared at me with those inscrutable eyes.

It didn't really matter what the motivation was behind his offer of friendship. I was desperate to grab it, to snare anything that represented time with him. Because he was right, of course. He knew me better than anyone. Even Cosima, who I loved devotedly yet knew so little about, even Brenna, who hadn't replied to my emails in over two weeks. A friendship with Sinclair meant that I could smile at him genuinely, that I could speak with him in front of our family like I knew him and spend time with him casually as if I had a right to.

"Okay."

"Okay?"

"Yes, I mean okay. I think we should be friends too."

We stared at each other without smiling because our joy was concentrated in the eyes. I wrapped myself in the warm blue hues and stopped breathing. He reached out slowly and wrapped his long fingers around my hand, gently pulling me to my feet.

His eyes creased slightly with the effort of holding back his smile. "I'm taking you home."

Desire plucked my strings like a puppet master, my mouth dropping open to gasp.

"Friends don't let drunk friends drive or get into cabs alone," he pointed out, stepping away to gather his wallet and keys from the desk.

I took the moment to suck in a deep, necessary breath. *Right*, friends. I had never needed to memorize and carry a piece of information so badly. I watched his lean form from the corner of my eye, the colored lights flashing against him like the light of a camera. I released the enormous breath and dragged in another to fill myself with my new mantra, *just friends*.

I knew the minute we opened the door that Cosima wasn't home. The air was cool and dark, unpunctuated by the habitual crackling fire and music crooning from the surround sound speakers. I wasn't sure if her absence was a blessing or a curse because the current of electricity that crackled constantly between Sinclair and me snapped with ferocity as soon as we understood our aloneness.

"Drink?" I murmured as we moved toward the kitchen at the back of the apartment.

Without waiting for an answer, I started to rifle through the fully stocked cupboards. I had no idea where Cosima kept the liquor, and I was too frazzled to properly guess at where she may have housed it.

"You sit," he demanded in that quiet, stern voice that made my bones shake with desire. "I'll fix us both a drink."

I nodded gratefully and slipped onto one of the stools at the large wooden island. I watched him maneuver about the kitchen gracefully, locating the ice, tumblers and whiskey as if he himself had placed them there.

"You come here a lot."

"Yes." He poured a perfect two fingers into each glass, one with ice and one without. "It is one of the reasons we can have a friendship. Cosima was my friend before I even met Elena."

An arrow of hatred painted with the name of my eldest sister found its home in the center of my heart. I cemented it there with guilt and shame and felt it throb.

"You know, I would say that I can't see you and Cosima being friends but," I laughed lightly, "she is infectious, isn't she?"

"Yes."

He handed me the glass with ice and watched me intently as I lifted it to my lips and touched the burning liquid to my tongue. I watched his eyes but he was either unaffected or being very careful.

"How did you meet her?" Talking about Cosima seemed as good a topic as any. In fact, it seemed to be one of the *only* topics I could even begin to feel comfortable talking about with Sinclair.

He stepped back to lean against the counter across from the island, giving me a full view of his beautiful suit-clad physique.

"Willa signed her." I recognized his adopted mother's name and noted that he didn't call her something affectionate like mom. "When she was nineteen. I was in Italy with Willa when she discovered her, standing in the rain wearing a long black dress. You couldn't tell where her hair ended and the dress began. She looked like something from Dante's *Inferno*."

He shook his head and stared into his glass as if divining a memory. I waited for him to continue but he remained silent. Cosima never spoke about her time away from home and honestly, I think the rest of us were too afraid to press her into confessing. What exactly did an eighteen-year-old girl have to do to pull her family out of destitution?

I shivered, pulling Sinclair from his reverie. His lips compressed into a flat line. "She was too young to have such sad eyes. I didn't want her living with my parents—she had obviously already been through a lot—so I offered to host her here in New York."

"Wow," I blinked a few times as I tried to process the picture of my vivacious sister inhabiting the same space as the fiercely private and enigmatic Frenchman.

A tiny smile twitched his lips. "It was an interesting experience to say the least. It was just for a short time; within the year, she had enough money to bring over Elena and Mama. Sebastian arrived from London soon after."

And you met her.

What would have happened if I had stayed in Italy? If I had moved to New York with my family and Sinclair had met both Elena and I at the same time?

The hypothetical made my teeth ache.

"You know," I said, to distract myself from that destructive line of thought, "I don't know very much about what happened to my family during the past five years. Cosima and Sebastian never talk about it, and as you know, I am not very close with Elena." I sighed and took a long sip of the burning whiskey. "We all used to be so close."

Sinclair crossed his arms and inclined his head, waiting for me to go on. I was surprised by his readiness to talk about my family when they were the cause of the mile-wide distance between us, but I was even more surprised by my relief at having someone to talk to who would understand.

"Have you been to Napoli?" He hesitated but shook his head. "Well, I can understand why not. Tourists go for the pizza and the history, but they never leave as enchanted as they were with Florence or Rome, Venice or Umbria. Naples is a deeply dirty place, especially if you are poor."

Sinclair nodded to convey that he was still listening before turning around to grab a few things from the fridge and cupboards. I watched him assemble the ingredients for crepes with a slight smile.

"You need to eat," he explained without facing me.

On cue, my alcohol weighted stomach clenched and turned over nauseously. "Okay."

"Continue."

I watched the ice in my glass swirl and tried to collect my thoughts.

"I'm sure you've heard about Seamus? He was an English professor at the university, but by the time the twins were born, he had basically been forced out due to his gambling and drinking problem. He loved Italy, every single thing about it, and it had been his goal growing up as an Irish Catholic in Boston to move to the country." My laugh was forced. "He was ridiculed by his family about it, and when he finally made the move, they basically disowned them. I don't even know their names."

"Would you like to?"

His question surprised me into answering honestly. "Yes, but only because I'd like to know how Seamus turned out the way he did. What made him decide to bury his family in debt to the mafia and disappear without a trace."

Sinclair nodded, and I paused for a minute to watch the surprisingly erotic sight of his strong wrist whisking the crepe batter.

"He disappeared after Cosima moved away. Sebastian moved to England a few months after that. We were almost destitute and so lonely." I could remember the dull vibration of too much silence in our small Neapolitan home and the collapsed look to Mama's handsome face, how her smile dragged and her soft hands trembled.

"It would be understandable if you resented them." He competently swirled the runny batter evenly over the surface of the pan while his eyes remained bolted to mine.

"I don't resent the twins. I never have, and I never could. They did everything to get us out of there, things that I don't know and probably never should." I hesitated, unsure if I should tell him the truth.

He flipped the completed crepe onto a waiting plate, moving with machine-like efficiency. His silence was a gift. I knew he wouldn't judge me because when it came down to the two of us, Sinclair was my musician, skillfully plucking and strumming until I produced just the right tune. I might make the sound, but how could he blame me when he had orchestrated it?

"I resent Elena and Mama sometimes."

Flip, slip, and the sizzle as butter landed in the pan.

"Mama for staying with Seamus for so long, for loving him when she should have left him. And Elena... We stopped being sisters when the twins left."

I wanted to tell him about Christopher, about what had happened between the three of us, and how Elena had never forgiven me. But it wasn't really my story to tell, at least not to Elena's present partner, whatever he might have meant to me.

Sinclair sprinkled brown sugar over a perfectly cooked crepe, folded it, and squeezed a sliced lemon easily in his fist over the top. He placed the plate in front of me but snagged my wrist before I could pick up the fork. With nimble fingers, he plucked the elastic off my wrist and moved behind me to gently gather my messy, still slightly damp hair between his hands. I shivered when cool fingers dragged over my heavy pulse. When my hair was secured in a ponytail, he lingered, and the only sound in the entire apartment was my heavy breathing. My head spun, and I realized I was still pretty intoxicated.

"Eat, Giselle."

I sighed but did as he told me, watching from the corner of my eye as he cleaned up the kitchen and ate his own rolled crepe standing up.

"How did you become interested in art? It doesn't seem like your childhood was conducive to frivolity or creativity," he asked after demolishing his crepe and starting to work rolling another. There was sugar stuck to his lemon juice slicked finger tips that I wished I could suck off with a curl of my tongue.

"No, but I did it anyway. I used sticks and dirt, made rock formations, and even got my hands on a canister of spray paint. We only had standard grade lead pencils and printer paper, sometimes something a little nicer if Seamus had done well at the tables. Cosima sent me my first paint set for my nineteenth birthday, this incredibly beautiful box of Sennelier oil paints. It was one of the only things I took with me to *L'École des Beaux-Arts*."

"That makes me unspeakably sad," he said simply.

I shrugged because it didn't matter to me anymore. I wouldn't let it. "It affected me a lot. I didn't know who I was or what I was allowed to do when opportunities eventually came my way. I felt unworthy, I think."

"You know better now."

"I do," I agreed. "Whatever else happened in Mexico, good or bad, you helped me lock that into place."

"That makes me unspeakably happy," he murmured as if my words weighed heavily in his chest and compressed his lungs.

His phone began to ring, but I wasn't startled or surprised. It only seemed right that our intimacy would be interrupted. I turned away before he could answer it and made my way to the bathroom.

"Elena." I heard him murmur her name before I was fully out of earshot.

I braced myself against the sink basin on wobbly arms and scowled at the mess of a redhead in the mirror. After so many years of staring at my reflection and seeing only how I didn't look like my gorgeous siblings, I was happy to find my own beauty lurking beneath the smudged mascara and sticky hair. It was impossible to view myself as ugly, as average, when a man like Sinclair found me so attractive.

I peeled off my clothes and turned the shower on to scalding hot. The pounding spray further sobered me, and I focused on the individual pricks of water against my skin instead of the gorgeous dilemma waiting for me somewhere in the apartment. After scrubbing myself from head to toe in a lavender-scented product, I stepped from the shower and into the steamy room.

Wiped clean, I felt raw and unprepared to face Sinclair. I desperately wanted to go to him as I was, naked and cooling like an un-iced cake. I wanted him to paint me in his sugary kisses and color me pink with desire.

As I stood in the middle of the bathroom, my hand found its way over my breast and down to my sex. I moved my hand through the downy curls and hissed as I found my clit. I braced one hand on the sink and stared at the slowly clearing mirror while I played with myself.

A reel of memories from our Mexican affair played in my mind; flashes of myself spread open and shockingly wet, the taste of his arousal on my tongue, the sharp string of a slap on the thin skin of my ass.

I was slick and throbbing, my breath fogging up the mirror again. I stretched two fingers past my entrance and moaned slightly, taking my lip between my teeth, biting it like Sinclair would do if he were kissing me, demanding me to come for him. My fingers were too small, too gentle on my skin, and I ached for the precision of his touch, the painful pinch and sexual pull of his hands on my body. I groaned again, loudly.

"Elle?"

His voice exploded against my skin, showering me with hot shards of desire. My fingers worked faster.

"Elle?" He was closer, just outside the slightly open door to the bathroom. "Is everything okay?"

My eyes drooped with the heaviness of my arousal, but I forced myself to keep them open and on the door in the mirror. I was rewarded with the sight of him coming into the room, the steam swirling around his legs and kissing his face with dew. I shuddered violently and pinched my clit hard between my fingers. I was so close.

He stood there, shocked, taking in the view of my pink sex peeking out from under my slightly bent bottom and the hand running over it eagerly. I saw his throat swell and bob as he swallowed hard.

I whimpered.

His burning eyes shot to mine in the mirror, and the fierce desire in them almost brought me to my knees.

"Stop." His voice lashed out across the room and hit me like a whip.

My hand increased its frenzied movements. I was too close to stop now.

"I said," he repeated in that glacial, exacting voice that never failed to make me wet, "stop."

My hand trembled as I took it away and placed it on the sink. I panted as I stared at him in the mirror, waiting for him to direct me.

His lips were pursed into a flat line, and his fists curled before he put them in his pockets. "Go to bed, Giselle."

My heart dropped to the wood floor with an audible splat as he turned and left. The steam had disappeared through the open door, and the cold apartment air grated goose bumps into my skin. I shivered and pulled a towel from the rack to wrap around my body.

Whatever hope I might have harbored that he would be waiting for me in my bedroom was crushed when I slunk into the dark room and found it cold and empty. Tears of humiliation stung my eyes and made my nose tickle.

I ditched the towel and lay on the duvet, letting the cold air bring my lava-filled body back down from its near eruption.

I was an idiot to be caught touching myself with Sinclair in the apartment. Whatever opportunity I might have had to be friends with him had obviously gone out the door with my inappropriate behavior. What had I expected? Did I really think he would suddenly succumb to nefarious desire and drag me into the bedroom like a Neanderthal and have his wicked way with me? This wasn't a romance novel, and Sinclair was certainly no caveman.

My eyes shot open at the clack of ice hitting ice in a glass.

Sinclair stood framed in the door and he maintained eye contact with me as he made his way to the high-backed chair across from my bed. He sat down, planted one foot atop the opposite knee, and took a sip of his whiskey.

I blinked.

He looked entirely comfortable sitting across from me, like a spectator at a movie or, more likely, a man waiting for the show at a strip club.

"By all means…" His voice was thicker than the steam from the bathroom and warmer than the cold air assaulting my bare skin. "Continue."

My breath streamed out through my slack mouth.

Could I do this?

Should I do this?

Touch myself in front of the man dating my sister?

But you have done this, the villainous voice inside me reminded, you've done this with Sinclair many, many times before. And besides, you want to.

Still, I hesitated, my mind whirring louder than my latent desire.

"Don't make me tell you again." Sinclair's voice wrapped firm fingers around my flailing thoughts and carefully bound them, gagged them. "Touch that pretty pussy for me, Giselle. I want to see you come."

A feathery moan escaped me, and my hand found my still damp sex without hesitation. I watched his stern face as I twirled one finger around my clit, not quite touching it, before moving down to my entrance to do the same thing. His jaw clenched, and I knew that teasing myself was teasing him even more. I feathered both hands over my inner thighs, tensing at the resulting tingle at my core, and sighed deeply.

"Spread your legs wider for me."

I pushed them farther with my palms and ran my fingers over my sex to open myself for him.

"Good girl," he crooned. "Do you remember the night I spanked you? Your ass was a beautiful shade of pink, and you begged me to take you, to ease the throbbing in your sweet little pussy."

His words sprinted like a brush fire across my skin, lighting the tiny hairs all over my body until I was scorched and completely bare. My eyes fell closed at the intensity.

"Open those eyes, siren. I want to watch my voice make you come."

I shuddered and pried my eyes open. His blue gaze still blazed, but his mouth was softened by a small smile that warmed my heart.

"Sinclair," I breathed restlessly, searching for the last component to trigger my release.

He stood, drained his whiskey, and made his way to my bedside. When he placed his cold glass over my bare navel, I shivered at its contrast to my feverish skin and held my breath as he leaned over me, bracing himself on one hand beside my left cheek.

"This is the last time, *ma petite voleuse*." He spoke just above my lips, the words slipping into my mouth on his warm breath. "So make it a good one."

I opened my mouth wider, maybe to protest or to beg, but his lips captured mine in a sweet open-mouth kiss. Two fingers trailed down my cheek and rested against my fluttering pulse.

"Come for me," he ordered softly as he pulled away.

And I did, in an explosion of sensation so deep that every muscle in my body contracted hard, so hard that I thought I was seizing. A scream ripped from my throat, and my legs scissored, trapping my hand between my thighs.

When I finally came down enough to open my eyes and release my hand, he was gone. The only sign of him was the empty tumbler on the bedside table and the feel of his control and desire lingering in my spent muscles. I squeezed my eyes shut and felt the tears come before I was even aware I was crying.

I'd wanted some kind of closure, fantasized about a sexual "farewell," and now that I'd had one, wrung from his voice and my hand, I felt despair deeper than any I had known before. Sinclair might have been in my life, a friend now, at least, but knowing I would never have his heart had never been so clear to me.

Chapter Seven

"Really?"

I laughed loudly, but the lunch hour traffic on the busy terrace of the restaurant drowned out my lack of class. "Yes, really."

"I don't think I understand this." Mama's beautiful almond-shaped eyes squinted at me, a habit she had when English confounded her. "*Si vuole dipingere le persone aver fatto sesso?*"

You want to paint people having sex?

Cosima too was squinting, a thinner, younger look-alike. "No, Mama, it's Giselle."

I frowned at my family as they all nodded in agreement. They must be wrong, they thought, because sweet innocent Giselle would never do anything morally ambiguous and definitely not something so crude.

"I'm serious." I took a deep breath and slid my damp palms nervously over the soft jersey fabric of my dress. "I want to do a series depicting private sexual moments, a study of individual sexuality."

Elena blinked at me owlishly before laughing. I took a second to notice how light it was, tinkling like glass wind chimes. I almost winced at the comparison to my own brassy chuckle from a few minutes ago.

"You can't be serious? Who would even want to pose for you like that?"

I cleared my throat because this was part of the pitch that I really needed to nail. "I was hoping you would, for starters."

The second of shocked silence made me fidget. I reached out for my wineglass, almost tipped it over in my haste, and slipped my sweating palm back within the other.

"I can't believe you are asking your own family to pose nude for you." Elena's pretty features scrunched up in horror.

The shame I constantly felt in her presence threatened to overwhelm me, but I swallowed back the bile and forced myself to breathe.

"It's *art*, Elena, not porn, for fuck's sake," Sebastian chastized at her before turning to me with an arrogant grin. "How do you want me? I can give you a few phone numbers if you'd like a woman's opinion."

His wink made me snort, but Elena shook her head. "You are so crass."

"Which one of us is the more American, then, Elena? The crass one or the prude?"

He had a good point, but I covered my smile behind my hand.

"I'd be happy to do it," Cosima said softly, "but you might not like what you get."

I frowned at her. "You model swimsuits and lingerie, Cosi. Honestly, I didn't think this would be a tough sell for you."

She lifted one shoulder in an elegant shrug. "It is still enough clothing to cover secrets, no?"

"You don't want me. This body is old."

I turned sideways to face my beautiful mama. Caprice Lombardi was the kind of woman you dreamed up for an Italian centerfold; lushly curved under swathes of silky olive-toned skin gently creased like pleats at the corners of her light brown eyes, with hair too long for a woman her age in America but exactly right for an Italian, older but everlastingly sexy. She tugged at the end of her thick black braid now and stared at me with worried eyes as if she was letting me down for not being younger or prettier.

"You've been in America too long, Mama," Sebastian scolded, reaching across the table to take her hands. "A beautiful older woman is a delicacy."

Elena snorted softly and received a glare from both of the twins; otherwise, the remark went uncontested. It reminded me of what Elena had said when I had first arrived about Sebastian's affair with an older married woman. I resolved to ask him more about it, but he had been so busy since I'd arrived that I had barely seen him.

"He's right. You are gorgeous, Mama," I said and watched her beam at me.

She turned to Elena and pursed her lips, an indication that she was going to scold our eldest sister. Elena squirmed under the look.

"Of course, you will do this for Giselle too?"

It wasn't really a question, and I could see the darkness descend across Elena's features like a coming tempest.

"Really, Elena, if you don't want to do it—" I began.

"Of course she does!" Mama cried, her hands wildly punctuating the words. "We are a family; we do things, always, for each other, *si*?"

"*Si, Mama*," we choroused diligently.

The twins shared a look, and Elena glared at me.

I sighed and played with the stem of my glass. Despite a few hiccoughs in our past, I still wasn't exactly sure why Elena hated me so much. It would have been awesome to have her on my side. We could have been a team of two like the twins, who were so close that it was easy to feel ostracized from them despite the wealth of their love for the rest of the family.

It had become impossible to think about Elena without Sinclair, and I wondered, in a growing series of what-ifs, whether I would still lust after, love after Sinclair if Elena and I were closer.

"I'm sorry I'm late." As if my thoughts had conjured him, Sinclair appeared beside Elena, bending down to place a kiss on her cheek.

He wore a perfectly tailored gray herringbone suit jacket with silvery gray flannel pants and a matching vest over a black button-up. His chestnut hair had been cut in the hours since I had last seen him, and it was now stylishly cropped short at the sides and longer at the top, softly waving back from his strong features. It softened and refined him, but I missed the length because it spoke of the slice of rebellion in his soul.

"It was my fault," Cage explained, coming up behind him with a wide grin. He took off his mirrored aviator sunglasses with a flourish and tossed them on the table. "The ladies couldn't get enough of me out front."

"I think it was Ryan Gosling they were after," Sinclair corrected dryly as he finished kissing Mama and Cosima's cheek, then shaking Sebastian's hand.

He was before me now, and I held my breath to see what he would do. Would he kiss me on both cheeks, or could we get away with a casual hello? He leaned down without hesitation, barely brushing his cool lips against my overheated skin.

"Hello, Giselle," he said, and I wondered if anyone else could hear the husky timbre in his voice.

"Ah, *ma belle chérie*." Cage swooped in to give me a slightly too long kiss on the mouth. His delicious scent, something like leather and pure masculine sex, wafted over me, and my lips softened under his firm pressure.

Sinclair cleared his throat loudly and thumped Cage on the back. "Sit down, Casanova."

Cage winked at me and sat down in the empty chair to my right, tugging my seat closer to his with a broad grin. He leaned over me to say to Mama, "You make gorgeous children, Caprice."

To my delight, Mama blushed. "You are very dangerous."

He barked with laughter, jutting his chin at Elena, the only person at the table not delighted with his presence. "Me? I wouldn't hurt a fly."

"Pfft, a fly, maybe no, but a woman's heart?" Mama shook her head somberly. "No chance."

We laughed at their banter, and everyone settled in to order their meals and catch up on small talk. I was glad for the reprieve. Being in Sinclair's presence after my embarrassing display of wantonness last night was awkward, to say the least, and I couldn't stop tugging anxiously on a lock of hair.

"Relax, Elle," Cage spoke with his head angled down at his menu, his full red lips unmoving. "You are acting like a thief in the police station."

I consciously slowed my darting gaze and looked over at him again to find his generous smile beaming back at me.

"I'm hopeless."

"Yes, but those in love normally are."

I sighed and rolled my shoulders back, determined to get over my own self-imposed discomfort.

"Much better," Cage murmured.

"You shouldn't have left me with him last night."

It wasn't his fault, not really. If Sinclair had wanted me, he would have succeeded with or without Cage's protests. In fact, I was about eighty-five percent sure that he had paid that guy to start a fight with my cute dance partner just to get him off me.

"*You* shouldn't have left him that last night."

My head jerked sharply over to him, my mouth slack.

Was he really bringing up Mexico in front of my entire family?

A quick look around the table confirmed that no one was listening and that Elena was affectionately fixing Sinclair's tie, but I still lowered my voice when I hissed, "You have no idea what you are talking about."

Cage ceased pretending to care about the menu and looked me straight in the eye. "It is you who has no idea what you could have had."

Before I could question him further, the waiter arrived to take our orders.

"Giselle wants to paint the family nude," Elena said before the server was even out of earshot.

My eyes were hot with embarrassment, but I tilted my chin up and tried to pretend she didn't make me feel like some kind of pervert.

"Oh?"

Oh? I glared at Sinclair. Really? All I get from the art connoisseur and ex-lover was a stupid, oh?

"Can I preorder those?" Cage asked innocently, speaking to me but looking at my older sister.

"Well, at least you know Cage will pose for you," Elena sneered.

"Yes, you might not believe it, but I look even better naked."

Sebastian leaned forward to pound fists with him, the movie star and the rock star bonding over their mutual self-love. It was almost adorable.

"I want to showcase sexuality," I tried to explain the idea that had come to me, fully formed, last night in the dirty wake of passion I had wallowed in after Sinclair left. "Those stolen, private moments that people are the most afraid to share."

"Interesting," Sinclair said. "Could you give us some examples?"

Elena frowned at him, but I continued, "Okay. An older woman propping her breasts up nostalgically, the press of a foot against an erection and the fetishism of it, or maybe a woman alone in a bathroom, staring at her reflection in the mirror as she masturbates."

Sinclair's eyes were on me. I could feel them roll off my face to the flushed skin of my chest like cold marbles.

"It will be tasteful, obviously," I hastened to add. "The point isn't the nudity or the sex; it's the vulnerability and the shame that stems from a person's most private desires."

I knew all too well the shame of desire. I could feel it like a punching glove to the heart every time I looked at Sinclair.

Everyone waited, looking at Sinclair, the man who owned a prestigious art gallery, a man whose opinion they would trust implicitly. I realized for the first time that I should have been anxious about impressing him because he was, in a sense, my *boss* in addition to my clandestine paramour.

I looked up, ready to face judgment, and our eyes locked with an audible *click*.

"Have you heard of Aleah Chapin? We hosted her at the gallery, and her work explores mature women in the nude. It's an interesting take, definitely a feminist one, and it has stirred a lot of interest in the art world." He paused, and a flicker of something like a smile teased the corners of his mouth. "I believe your show would stir a lot more than 'interest.' In fact, I believe you will have people lusting after your paintings faster than you can possibly produce them."

I smiled so hard that my cheeks hurt. "You really think so?"

He nodded curtly. "Without a doubt."

Cosima clapped her hands together. "Of course, they will! Our *bambina* is beautiful and talented."

Sebastian nodded thoughtfully. "You know, if you want to paint the family, would you be interested in including other famous people? I know a few actors who would be interested in posing for something like this."

My mouth dropped open in shock, and he laughed at me. "Close your mouth, *bambina*, it's not a sure thing."

"I think we need a bottle of Prosecco, *si*?" Mama smiled at the server and called him over. "We must have Prosecco, please."

"I'm afraid we only have champagne," he began to apologize, but Sinclair interrupted him.

"A bottle of Dom 2007, if you have it."

The young man nodded gratefully. "Excellent, sir. May I ask what the special occasion is?"

Mama beamed up at him. "My daughter is going to paint the naked people."

He blinked down owlishly at her before stuttering a nonsensical reply and scurrying off to get the champagne.

As soon as he was gone, we all dissolved into laughter. I giggled so hard that my belly ached, and Cosima was in tears. I caught Sinclair's eyes mid-laugh and saw him smiling at me, the rare soft and wide smile I loved so much. We stared at each other for what seemed like a long time, safe to indulge for a second amid the raucous laughter. I tried to convey my thanks for his approval, my guilty apology for my behavior the previous night, and the bittersweetness of sitting at my family table with him sharing a laugh with the people I loved most.

After a moment, he nodded at me as if he had understood every word in my gaze. Then he slowly dismantled the smile on his face so that when the others finally tuned back in, his features were once again perfect and impassive.

Cosima shed her clothes almost the moment we were in the door from lunch. Without a word, she had undone the knot at the back of her elaborately wrapped dress and let it fall to the ground.

"Where do you want me?"

My mouth opened and closed as I took in her scantily clad form, her breasts and lower half covered only in tiny scraps of web-like lace.

"You don't have to do this right now," I said even though my fingers itched to sketch her form, to imprint the beauty of her body and those tragic eyes Sinclair had spoken of onto canvas.

One slim shoulder rose and fell. "Why not?"

"It's just not really how it works, Cosi. I need to know more about your, well, your sexual history and what, well"—I blushed—"turns you on and stuff."

She stared at me with one eyebrow raised, amused and slightly condescending. "And stuff? My God, I hope you pitch this series better to the galleries."

I laughed and relaxed slightly. "You and me both."

"What shall I tell you, then?" She moved into the kitchen, all grace and utter ease as she pulled out a chilled carafe of iced tea.

I took a seat at the island and watched her prepare me a drink, much like I had the night before with Sinclair. In a strange way, I wanted to ask Cosima many of the same questions I wished I could ask him.

"Do you have any sexual fetishes?"

Her nose wrinkled. "Sex is kinky by nature, no?"

"Well, sure, I guess. But I'm referring to specific things, terms maybe."

She was already shaking her head. "I've done a lot of things and rarely disliked any of them. American women might call me a slut."

I opened my mouth to protest, but her wink made me smile. "You're teasing me."

"A little."

I pouted.

"Alright, *bambina*, I will tell you a little something about sex." The word hissed out of her mouth and billowed into the air like steam from some fierce engine. "I've been nothing but this body for almost my entire life. It can be a powerful thing to be beautiful." She shrugged. "But if you don't have a reason to build strong bones beneath it, it is easy to become many very ugly things. Sad, used, dumb, or dead."

"You're strong."

Her slashing brows rose. "Maybe now, but let me tell you, I've also been sad, used, dumb, and very nearly dead."

We stared at each other. My heart was beating too fast, and I felt nauseous as my imagination went to work. What exactly had my little sister done to get us out of our poverty?

"The door was open."

Elena stood on the step below the kitchen, holding her pretty Prada purse in one hand and a bottle of wine in the other. She brandished it now and tried to smile. "I brought a peace offering. Daniel told me I was a bit... rude at lunch."

"You were a straight-up bitch, my darling Lena," Cosima corrected with a smile as she swooped down to hug her, uncaring of her unrobed state. "But I'm still glad you brought us wine."

I smiled slightly at Elena as she was ushered into the kitchen to the seat beside me, but I didn't acknowledge her quasi-apology because there was a much bigger one on the back of my tongue.

"Where are your clothes, Cosima?" Elena asked.

She grinned. "Giselle is going to paint me."

"What, now?"

"Yes," I said. "We were just getting started."

"Where would you like me?" Cosima asked.

I bit my lip as I contemplated what she had told me and gave her a brisk nod when an idea came to me. "I'll start with some sketches so you can keep your underwear on if you'd like. Stand over by the door."

She captured the pose I wanted in less than thirty seconds, her years of modeling experience making her the perfect visual muse. I had her standing astride, facing me like a proud warrior, naked and daring. Her body was lush in all the right places and defied gravity just as Cosima had defied the weight of poverty and then of expectation. I wanted her body in the sun, lit up under the brassy warmth like a trophy while her face, tucked slightly to the side, seeking the shadow, remained in the dark. I'd need to figure out how to catch the glimmer of gold in her eyes, the velvety softness of the color like worn cloth. The challenge excited me, and I trapped my tongue between my teeth as I littered the floor with page after page of sketches.

Every woman in the world wished they looked like that, unblemished golden skin glistening over long muscles and delicate bones. The midday sun was not kind to a body, but the harsh light shone like gilt on the inky waves rippling over her heavy breasts and tickling the bare skin above her pubis. Only three things disrupted her natural beauty; twin gold bars through her dark nipples, visible through the transparent lace bra, and a raised, bizarrely symmetrical scar three inches in diameter on her left butt cheek that she wouldn't really let me look at.

"I'm sorry about that," Cosima had said, dismissively gesturing at the nipple piercings. "Misspent youth and all that."

I wanted to see more of the brand, pepper her with questions until she couldn't help but sneeze out the answers.

Elena, for her part, kept curiously silent and empty of censure. I was pretty sure the nipple piercings had surprised her, and that Cosima's comfortable nudity offended her sensibilities. Still, she only sat perched on the stool with her legs crossed and her arms folded like a debutant at tea.

"You are so untroubled," she finally breathed after a long stretch of pencil scraping and silence.

"I've never had a hard time with nudity," Cosima said in a voice tinged with dark humor.

"How?"

I tried not to look at Elena, but I desperately wanted to see if her expression matched the quiet despair in her tone.

"We were all meant to be naked."

"Maybe women who look like you."

"No." Cosima's arched brows slammed down. "Every person is beautiful naked."

"Even without those curves?"

"Even with them?" I countered softly.

Elena and I looked at each other then and smiled over our shared sense of insecurity.

"You don't believe me because I look like this, but that is why I like Giselle's idea so much. Everyone is naked under his or her clothes, vulnerable under their masks, and a person's sexuality is an extension of their human need and their primitive desires. It is not a shameful thing."

"Who knew the swimsuit model was so wise?" I teased, my strokes on the thick paper looser now to accommodate Cosima's fluid expressions.

"You would be surprised by what standing in front of a camera every day will do to you." Cosima winked, but both Elena and I remained quiet because, I think, we had both wondered the exact same thing.

Elena sighed and propped her delicate face in her hands. "Listen, Giselle, I am sorry I was so negative earlier about your collection. I really would like to pose for you." She hesitated. "It will be hard for me, though, so maybe I could go last? By then, you might not even want me." She laughed awkwardly.

"I'll want you."

"Okay. I'd like to model then."

"Thank you, Elena." I smiled widely at her. "It means a lot to me."

"Well, I was hoping we could do a sort of trade? I'd love to commission you to do a painting of Daniel. His parents' anniversary is coming up, and I know it would make the perfect present."

"Um..." I tried desperately to analyze if it was a good idea or not. "I'm not sure if I'll have time with everything I have to do for the show."

"It would mean a lot to me," she echoed with a pretty smile, and I heard the trap catch around my ankle.

Cosima stifled a laugh at Elena's manipulation.

"Touché," I murmured.

"This is good. You should model for Giselle; you need to be more comfortable about sex. As the only one of us getting it regularly, Lena, I'm surprised you aren't more confident."

My heart stopped and stuttered at the restart.

Elena blushed, actually blushed. "He is insatiable."

A metallic taste flooded my mouth, and I realized that I had bitten clean through my lower lip.

Cosima laughed. "It's good to hear that you two are still going strong after so much time. Gives a girl some hope."

I swallowed back the nausea and focused on soothing my torn lip.

"Last night, he came home and practically accosted me," she admitted with that stupidly pretty blush. "He hasn't been like that for ages."

I stood before I could help it, the pencils in my lap clattering to the ground.

"Bathroom," I squawked before scurrying out of the room.

I pressed myself to the closed bathroom door and squeezed my eyes shut so tight they pulsed. I felt like a sickening swirl, circling the drain, full of dirt and debris.

Breathing heavily, I focused on reducing the thudding pace of my heart and tried to clear my mind.

Elena and Sinclair *lived* together. Of course, they were going to have sex. They belonged to each other; it was only natural.

A sob broke through my silence, and I clapped both hands over my wounded mouth.

Rational thought at the moment was definitely out of the question.

Before my thoughts could catch up to my actions, I had pulled out my cell phone and pressed his contact information.

"Faire Developments, Daniel Sinclair's office, Margot speaking."

Shit, I only had his office number.

"Hello, Margot." I cleared my throat. "This is Giselle Moore. I was hoping to speak with Mr. Sinclair about a recent development at DS Galleries."

There was a long pause as she digested both my name and my stupid excuse to speak to her boss. "Any inquiries about the gallery can be made through Mrs. Rossi."

"I was told to speak to Mr. Sinclair specifically about this matter." *Bullshit, bullshit, bullshit*. Please buy it.

Another long hesitation ended in a sharp sigh. "Please hold."

My breath seemed grossly loud in the small bathroom, and I worried briefly about what my sisters would think I was doing. I thought about going out to tell them I was taking a call, or maybe just hanging up before I embarrassed myself further, when his voice came over the line.

"Miss Moore, how may I be of assistance?"

It was the businessman on the phone, not exactly what I wanted, yet his cool, perfectly formed words soothed me.

"Sinclair," I breathed because I didn't know what else to say.

There was a beat of silence. "Yes, I fully comprehend the seriousness of it. I'm in the middle of a meeting, though. I will call you back."

Click.

I stared at the home screen of my phone blankly for a second, absorbing the rush of disappointment that crashed over me. Of course, he was busy. I had no right to even call him in the first place. He was, at the most, my new friend and, at the worst, my ex-lover. You simply didn't call someone like that to vent, especially if it was about his or her goddamn partner.

"I'm going insane," I murmured to my wide-eyed reflection.

After a few deep breaths and chastisements, I washed my hands and went back to the kitchen where my sisters were chatting away amiably as if nothing had happened.

I guess nothing really had.

"I was just inviting Cosima to the annual Romani International charity gala next Friday," Elena said as I reclaimed my seat. "It's an organization that advocates for the rights of nomadic peoples across the world. I thought, maybe, and I know it is late notice"—she cleared her throat—"you might like to attend too?"

It was Sin's charity. My heart fluttered at the thought of discovering more about it and of seeing Candy Kay again.

"I would love to."

Elena and I smiled at each other for the second time that day, for the second time in over five years, and the tenderness I felt ached like a bruise.

My phone began to ring, and I looked down at the screen with surprise: *Faire Developments.*

"Excuse me." I slipped off my stool again and made my way to the balcony. "I should take this."

Cosima caught my eye as I moved past her, now clad in a robe, and I knew she was suspicious of my behavior. I ignored her and hustled outside.

"Hello?"

"Giselle." His voice was warmer. "I'm sorry about the delay. You sounded upset."

I sighed and leaned against the railing separating me from the nine-story drop. "I was, but that's no excuse. I'm sorry for bothering you."

"I'm flattered that you called me."

"Really?"

"Of course, it means I am the first person you think of when something bad happens. That's no mean status."

"No, I guess it isn't. Although, I was upset partially because of you."

"Ah, I suppose that makes sense." I could hear the humor in his voice. "What did I do this time?"

I smiled even though my words still hurt. "Elena was talking about your sex life. About, well, about how you went home last night and 'practically attacked her.'"

"I see."

I waited for him to elaborate or for me to somehow die of embarrassment, but neither happened.

"I told you it was silly. I'm sorry, I'll let you get back to work."

"Nothing you ever feel is silly, Elle." He sighed. "But what did you expect? Elena is my girlfriend."

"I know." God, I felt like a complete idiot.

"Don't feel stupid," he ordered, somehow reading my mind. "It's the fucking situation that is stupid, not you."

"I'm not making it any better," I admitted.

"And I am?"

We were both quiet for a moment. I stared down at the gorgeous chaos of early evening in New York, the yellow cabs and rivers of pedestrians. It seemed, at the moment, infinitely more organized than my life.

"Go fishing with me tomorrow."

"What?" Of all the things he could have said, I was least expecting that. I told him so.

After he finished laughing, he said, "It won't compare to the Pacific, but autumn fishing in New York is the time to do it. I'll take you out to Manhattan Beach and introduce you to the Antonios of New York."

"There are more like him?" I couldn't imagine the eccentric Mexican fisherman being like anyone else.

"Not quite, but the regulars under the Verrazano Bridge are real urban fishermen. You'll like them. Better bring your camera."

I was grinning so widely it was difficult to speak. "I never go anywhere without it."

"It will be an early start," he warned. "On the water at five o'clock."

"Bring me a caramel latte, and I'm set."

"I'll be by at four thirty-five to pick you up."

"Okay."

"I'll see you then."

"Okay." My heart was beating fast; I didn't want to say goodbye. "I'll see you then."

"Just a thought before I sign off. Do you remember what you said when you discovered who I was? You weren't willing to hurt Elena. Admirable, Giselle, but maybe you should consider this; who else is hurting for your sacrifice?"

He hung up before I could respond, but I had nothing to say, so I guess it didn't really matter.

Chapter Eight

I woke up with a smile before dawn the next morning and sang loudly to Beatles music in the shower as I carefully washed every inch of my body. Though I usually let my hair dry naturally into thick waves, I applied curling product and blew it dry with a diffuser so that the red locks settled into large, messy curls around my flushed face. I knew it would be cold out on the water at the beginning of November, so I layered with care, rolling a gray turtleneck over my silk camisole and tugging thickly knit socks up to my knees over my blue jeans. The shades complemented my coloring beautifully, and when I put on the final touches, a dove gray knitted headband with matching gloves and scarf, I stared at my happy self in the mirror with quiet pride. This was the Giselle I wanted to be, happy and confident. It was hard to be like that under the current circumstances when I felt ugly and villainous with my family and desperate around Sinclair, but Cosima-level confidence took time, and I was happy with my progress.

I had been hoping to escape the apartment unobserved, but as soon as I left my room, I heard the swell of Italian music in the kitchen.

Cosima stood before the stove in thick socks and a pink cashmere robe, her inky hair swinging as she moved fluidly to the music, her voice raised in song.

"A bit early for Verdi, isn't it?"

She spun to face me with a wide smile, her quick eyes taking in my carefully coordinated outfit without expression.

"It is never too early for *il maestro*! Although, I would argue it is way too early to be looking so cute. Where are you off to?" she asked.

I poured myself a glass of water with ice from the fridge to buy myself some time. Sinclair hadn't said to lie about our outing, and was there really anything wrong with my sister's boyfriend taking me out? After all, I was new in town.

"Sinclair." I cleared my throat. "Daniel invited me fishing. I told him the other day at lunch that I had enjoyed it in Mexico, and he got pretty excited about taking me." I rolled my eyes. "Who would have guessed such a buttoned-up guy would be a fishing geek."

Cosima grinned as she stirred the fragrant concoction in her pan. "*Massive* fishing geek. He enters the Bassmaster Elite Series on Oneida lake every August, and I'm pretty sure he always takes his executives to Mexico just so he can get in some fishing."

I laughed, remembering how boyish and carefree he had been out on the water. "I'm looking forward to it."

"He's taken me out before." She scrunched her nose up. "Let's just say I'm more comfortable on land. I'd take horseback riding over fishing any day."

"Why are you up so early?" I accepted a plate of the stewed tomatoes and eggs with glee.

"A model dropped out of the Ralph Lauren shoot in England." She burned herself on the pan and cursed savagely in Italian. "I have to be in Cornwall by tomorrow."

"You don't seem too enthused, and that doesn't really explain the early start."

I had never been to England, but I did know Cosima had worked there after leaving Napoli.

"I hate England." She shrugged with one shoulder. "I leave later today, but I couldn't sleep thinking about it."

"That's a bit extreme, isn't it? I mean the entire country?" I grinned at her. "What did the Brits ever do to you?"

Her smile was uncharacteristically thin. "It's a smaller country than you'd think."

My phone lit up with a text from Sinclair. "I have to go."

I hopped out of my seat, shoveling another spoonful of tomato and eggy goodness into my mouth before pulling on my green gumboots. I spun around to give Cosima a hug, but she was already beside me, arms open.

Love bloomed in my chest like a prize-winning rose.

"If I don't see you before you leave, I'll miss you," I said, stepping into her spicy-scented embrace.

"I will be back in three days. If it was for any other brand, I wouldn't be going at all." She pressed a fragrant kiss to my cheek. "Now, be safe and enjoy your day. Sinclair can be a charming bastard when he wants to, so I'm sure you will have a grand adventure."

I smiled slightly, but her remark hit a little too close to home. She watched me with a curious smile as I collected my bag and slipped into an emerald green raincoat. Even after I had closed the door and descended into the lobby and out onto the street, I could still feel her eyes on me as if she had implanted a tracking device.

Happily, all thoughts of my sister fled when I saw Sinclair in a gorgeous blue Porsche idling at the curb. I squealed as I slid into the low two-seat car and swung to face him with a large grin. "This is *the* coolest car I have ever seen."

His small smile and sparkling eyes made me giddy. "It's a 964 series Singer Porsche 911."

At my blank look, he grinned boyishly as he gunned the throaty engine and pulled into the pre-dawn traffic. "I spent my early years in an orphanage in Nice, Giselle. I practically grew up watching beautiful cars drive by."

"Never close enough to touch," I murmured as I fingered the pale buttery leather seats.

He shrugged, but there was tightness around his eyes.

"I was not poor for long." He changed lanes and shot me a glance.

"They found me when I was sixteen years old. Took me after two weeks of visitation."

"Love at first sight?"

His mouth twisted. "Willa was looking for the next big thing in Paris, and they took a vacation to the South, as if being in Paris wasn't vacation enough. She found Cage and me smoking in an alley and invited us for a drink. She was beautiful." He shrugged, but his muscles were too tense to pull it off. "I thought maybe she wanted to sleep with me. It happened sometimes."

"They didn't have to adopt you?"

"No, not really, and they didn't right away. You know they took both of us in, Cage and me, but I was the one they kept. Sometimes, I wonder if Cage hates me for it, but I'm the one who ended up with their bullshit."

"Wow." I blinked a few times as I digested the tide of information. "So you and Cage really have known each other forever. Did he go to America with you when you moved?"

"No, he stayed in Paris. They let him stay with their maid in their *pied-à-terre*. We visited every Christmas, but I haven't lived in France since I was seventeen."

"Do you miss it?" I asked.

I did every day, and I had only lived there for a handful of years.

"Yes and no. I think of myself as American now. It is this land that has sustained me. I will always love France; nearly everything is better there." I smiled at his typical French patriotism. "But I left many things there that are best left alone."

I bit my lip and stared out the window, debating whether to continue questioning him about his parents. I was so curious to know everything about him, but I didn't want to romanticize him further or make him uncomfortable.

But, as was always the case when I was around Sinclair, I couldn't help myself. "So, Willa represented you?"

His lids lowered. "Yes, but I only modeled for two years. When I turned eighteen, I demanded to be allowed to go to college. I was smart and well-mannered, the perfect young man in their eyes. I think they figured, why waste his potential? They already had Cage, the artistic prodigy and, to some extent, Cosima, who was the real talent in front of the camera and on the runway. Even better if their oldest son wanted to follow in his father's academic footsteps, maybe even follow him into politics."

"It's almost like a fairy tale. I mean, out of all the orphans in the world, they picked you. I would ask myself all the time how it happened. I mean, why you?"

His gaze snapped to mine, and I realized that I had touched a nerve. My hand reached out to brush through the thick reddish hair dangling in front of his face, and I pushed it back from his forehead.

"I know why I would have picked you," I amended softly.

He snorted. "You know, I didn't do anything to earn this face."

My heart twisted. How could he think he was only worth the value of his beauty? I had never met a more accomplished man in all my life, and I doubted I ever would.

"You're right. But you worked hard to develop into the sophisticated, intelligent, driven man you are today. And in my eyes, that's sexier than any six-pack."

He raised his eyebrows at me, and I giggled. "Okay, okay, I love your six-pack too."

There was a slight smile on his lips, and for a few moments, we drove in silence, listening to the deep rasp of Cage on the media system. He sang in English, his voice rising like the howl of the wind over the crashing drums and swooshing guitar. I had always loved *Caged,* and everyone in France seemed to quietly lust after at least one of the gorgeous band members, so I really hoped they could make it in America.

It was amazing to think about how inextricably linked we all were; Sinclair, Elena, Cosima, Cage, and I. They had been together for years, through the kind of experiences that I had only ever read about. Sure, I had known hunger and abuse, crime and drunkenness, but I had been young, shielded by the worst of it by my other siblings. I squirmed in my seat, feeling disgustingly naïve and fresh off the farm.

We finally pulled into a small packed lot beside the water, the lights of the city and Verrazano Bridge reflecting in the deep blue ocean. The combination of the urban and natural filled me with fizzy adrenaline and I quickly slipped out of the car with my camera to my eye in order to take a few pictures before the light picked up. But I was melancholy, sucked into the vortex of self-hatred and doubt that had plagued me throughout my younger years. It was a strange feeling to realize that I was extraordinarily lucky. I felt almost sick with it.

Sinclair was quiet too as he gathered our gear and briefly spoke to some other men going down to the rocky water's edge with their poles and coffee thermoses. I drifted away from him as he set up our stuff and politely asked to take some pictures of the beautifully weathered fishermen already sunk knee-deep in the icy waters. They consented without words, a grunt or nod or maybe a toothy grin was all I needed, and I was surprisingly grateful for their silence. The quiet felt good around me, like a warm blanket over my shivering sense of self.

When I finally made my way back carefully over the slippery rocks to our post, the sky was losing the last of its girlish blush, sinking into an eggshell blue. I stopped just to his left side and studied Sinclair through the lens, the way his hair rustled like liquid copper in the wind, and the slight flush that sat high on his pronounced cheekbones. I could understand why Willa had chosen him; his beauty was a strange thing, rare and almost inanimate, like a statue brought to life.

I don't know how long I stood there before he turned to me. We stared at each other, and I wished hopelessly that he could understand even one-tenth of the turmoil inside me.

He sighed, as if in answer to my unspoken desire, and placed his rod in a crevice between two large rocks. In three long, sure steps over slippery boulders, he was in front of me. I tipped my head to maintain eye contact. I was strangely breathless as his intensity exerted itself like the force of gravity on my lungs.

"Elle." His cool hands cupped my face. "Stop thinking."

I tried to articulate myself but could only shake my head.

"I didn't bring you out here to overthink, to stress or worry about if what we are doing is wrong. I brought you here because this is one of my favorite places in New York, and I wanted to share it with you. Can you please let it be as simple as that?"

I shook my head again, but this time, I found my voice. "Why me?"

His eyes darkened. "You won't like the answer to that."

My heart plummeted to the pit of my stomach so quickly that I thought I would throw up. Somehow, I managed to smile thinly and step away from him instead.

"Fair enough," I said, moving past him to grab my smaller rod.

It was purple with a glittery grip, and I laughed wetly as I took it into my hand. When I looked over at him, he was shaking his head at me in irritation.

"Is this Elena's?" I asked because I was that masochistic.

"If you can't stop yourself from saying idiotic things, don't speak," he barked, striding back over to pick up his rod.

I blushed at his reprimand, but it was true. I was being petty and weak. Why couldn't I just enjoy this gorgeous morning with this gorgeous man? Don't look a gift horse in the mouth and all that. So—I took a deep breath and shoved all the grime in my soul under the rug—I wouldn't.

"You bought it for me, didn't you?" It was a rhetorical question because I knew he was too angry with me to answer. "Thank you, it's adorable."

He nodded curtly and adjusted his stance.

"*Je n'arrête pas de faire l'andouille,*" I murmured just loudly enough for Sinclair to hear me.

I snuck a glance over at him and saw his lips twitch reluctantly.

"I just can't stop making the sausage," I repeated, this time in English.

I beamed as he chuckled, shaking his head at my antics.

"You may be acting like a fool," he agreed, taking a side step to bump me with his hip. "But at least you are an adorable fool."

I laughed too, so relieved that the tension had dissipated that I felt almost giddy.

"I love French expressions." I sighed happily and leaned into him.

"They have to be the most nonsensical idioms in any language," Sinclair noted, but his voice was warm, and I knew he was happy to have someone to speak to about France.

"Well, *les doigts dans le nez* happens to be my favorite, and it makes absolutely no sense. That's the beauty of them. I mean 'the fingers in the nose' does *not* translate well to 'with my eyes closed.'"

"Who do you think knows more?" Sinclair's eyes gleamed with challenge as he looked down at me.

"Me, hands down. You said yourself you haven't considered yourself French in a long time. At this point, I probably speak your language better than you do," I taunted.

He leaned down, so close to my face that I could smell his minty breath, and grinned boyishly.

"You're on."

WE SPENT THE ENTIRE MORNING IN BROOKLYN. AFTER FIVE HOURS IN THE water with three gorgeous striped bass in our cooler, we made our way to a small pizza shop that was already packed at eleven in the morning. The pie was cheesy, greasy, and loaded with fat speckled pepperoni, and we devoured it between sips of Sprite, which we both agreed wasn't nearly as refreshing as the French Schweppes.

He caught me up on the developments with the Mexican resort; Richard Denman was flying into town with the preliminary blueprints, and he was in the process of procuring a decrepit building near the Hudson, which he hoped to turn into high-end condos. I loved the passion in his eyes as he spoke about his work, and I knew that, despite his parents' wishes, he would never go into politics when he could be building things.

I told him about my years in Paris, how I had met Brenna and why my relationship with the Canadian boy had ended. Nothing serious passed our lips, and by the time the check came, my lips were rubbery from wearing a smile for so long.

As we slipped back into the Porsche, I thought about how easy it was to forget about everything else when I was with Sinclair. Our chemistry still sizzled in the air between us, but today had truly felt like a date between friends, our looks full of a different kind of intimacy.

The closer we got to Manhattan, the stiffer I became as reality began to encroach on my thoughts. In an hour, he would be home with Elena, and I would be back to pining for the unattainable Frenchman.

"Stop overthinking," Sinclair ordered, placing his hand on my thigh. "We just had an amazing morning. Let's not ruin it by thinking."

I sighed. "Am I that easy to read?"

"You forget how well I know your body."

His fingers splayed across my jean-clad thigh, and I could feel the heat of his touch through the thick material.

"I *should* forget," I said.

"No, don't ever."

I shifted out from under his hand and looked out the window. How could he so easily balance the morals of this situation? Was it because he really didn't care about me in any way other than as a friend, with only a lingering desire for my body? I knew he wasn't a bad person, that he wasn't hoping to use me for sex or manipulate me into falling further in love with him, but no matter his intentions, both outcomes were entirely possible.

"Why don't we swing by and pick up Cosima?" he suggested, his voice bright for my benefit. "When we first moved to New York, we went to a show on Broadway every Saturday."

"That's a good idea," I agreed, mostly because I knew he suggested it to put me at ease. If Cosima joined us, it wouldn't be so taboo. That he usually hung out with my sister suggested that our behavior was *fine*.

Sinclair waited in the car while I zipped up to our apartment to fetch her. I was pulling the keys out of my purse to open the door when I saw that it was already cracked open. The hairs on the back of my neck stood on end as I slowly pushed the door open.

I cautiously moved through to the back of the apartment and finally caught a glimpse of someone sitting at the island in the kitchen, someone I had never seen before. My gasp must have alerted him because the large, bare-chested man swiveled on the stool to face me.

His broad face was tight with pain, and my eyes quickly crossed the quilted breadth of his chest to latch onto the sight of his hand over a bloody towel pressed to his left side. Through my shock, I noted the thick, wavy dark hair falling into black eyes and bronzed skin. He was so gorgeous that he made my eyes water.

I was just opening my mouth to scream or question him when Cosima came sweeping into the room, her eyes focused on the medical kit in her hands.

"*Cazzo*, Dante, I don't know why you don't just –"

"Cosima," the man named Dante practically purred in a voice like none I had ever heard, thick and pulsating with sexual allure. "We have a visitor."

I was looking right at her when those golden eyes shot to me and widened. Her mouth formed a perfect 'O' of horror, and she dropped the tin box to the counter with a loud clang.

"What are you doing here?"

"Um, I live here. What is a man doing in our kitchen with a *bleeding wound*?"

Dante adjusted in the chair, leaning back as if he wasn't clutching what I was sure was a bullet wound.

"I..." Cosima sighed loudly and pushed her hair back with both hands. "Listen, Giselle, I need you to leave. Right now."

I looked between her and Dante, whose eyebrow was raised at her in curiosity.

"Are you kidding me right now? I'm not leaving you here like this!" I said, throwing an arm out to indicate the burly man in our kitchen.

"You are." Her voice was aflame with surety. "You are going to go out for the afternoon and enjoy the city, think about your show and see friends. You will *not* say anything about this to *anyone,* and I will text you when you can return to the apartment."

"Cosima," I started to yell, but her posture changed, arms crossed under her breasts and eyebrows drawn so low over her eyes I could only see dark pits of determination.

Dante stared at me impassively, but the moment his eyes flicked to my sister, they burned like hot coals. He seemed proud of her for showing me the door and not the least bit distressed that I had walked in on him or, more importantly, that blood was seeping through the towel and the firm press of his fingers, coating them a lacquered red.

"Cosima..." I tried again, my voice softer because I knew I would leave like she wanted me to.

She shook her head firmly but brushed her hand feather light down my cheek as she moved forward to tend to Dante.

"*Parta.* Go."

I backed away slowly, but they didn't notice or care. Cosima was bent over her wounded soldier whispering passionately in Italian while he closed his eyes and hissed with pain. They were a striking pair, and under other *normal* circumstances, I would have loved to stick around to get to know him better, to see what kind of relationship they had.

Instead, I tip-toed quietly to the front door, slipping past them without trouble, but I froze with my hand on the knob when I spotted the unfamiliar keys tossed on the small hallway table.

Beside them rested a small, strangely innocuous-looking black gun.

"Excuse me."

I turned around to see Dante looming over me, so tall that I had to crane my neck back uncomfortably to meet his black eyes. A shiver started at my ankles and coated every inch of my skin. He brought to mind the men I had known in Naples, the kind of men who took what they wanted regardless of the cost. They were the same ones Cosima had run away from when she left home.

Dante was a Mafia man.

"Uh, yes?" I asked, finally.

A smirk sliced the right side of his lips and gave his beautiful face an almost manic charisma. I held my breath as he stepped closer and slowly leaned toward me. I closed my eyes when his breath fanned across my face, although I wasn't sure what I was thinking in doing so.

His dark chuckle alerted me to the cool air now brushing my front, and

I peeked through one eye to see him standing at a respectable distance again, this time with the gun in his large hand. I let out a sound somewhere between a yip and sigh. His grin stretched wider.

"Shouldn't leave this lying about now, should I?"

I frowned at his accent; somehow, I hadn't placed it before. "You're British."

A snarl tangled his features for just a second before he stared calmly at me. "And you are Giselle, the beloved sister of my Cosima. She wouldn't like it if she knew we were talking but, please, let me just say"—his blatantly sexy smile punched me in the gut with reluctant desire—"it is an absolute pleasure to finally meet you."

"I've never heard of you," I said as I moved closer to the door and twisted the knob.

Dante continued to smile at me. I had never seen a man with so many different kinds of smiles.

"You will," he promised.

I shut the door and fled down the hall to the elevators.

WE SAW *WICKED*. I HADN'T WANTED TO SEE IT. AFTER ALL, A PLAY ABOUT A woman who descends the slippery slope into villainy was a little too close to home for my tastes, but Sinclair, with his slight smile—much preferable to Dante's sinister smirks—had insisted that it was not to be missed.

"Okay, okay," I admitted as we followed the crowd out of the theater. "That was absolutely amazing."

He shot me a sidelong look as we walked into the fading sunlight.

"Don't you dare tell me 'I told you so,'" I threatened, leveling a finger at his twitching lips.

He held his hands up in mock surrender, but his voice seriously lacked sincerity. "I don't even feel the need."

"And I don't want to hear anything about the bad witch being a sympathetic character or anything, okay?" I added with narrowed eyes. "Last time I checked, you didn't have a degree in English."

"No, you're right. Just psychology."

"You're kidding?"

His gorgeous eyes sparkled as his hand found my lower back to gently usher me through the throbbing crowds in Times Square. "And a Master's in Business Administration from Columbia."

I stared up at him, knowing that he would safely see me through the swarms of people. "I really don't know anything about you, do I?"

He shrugged, and I immediately regretted puncturing our beautiful bubble with the sharp edge of reality.

"You know considerably more than most people. The facts you are referring to can easily be looked up online."

"I thought about doing that, looking you up. But I was too nervous," I admitted as I stopped to root through the pocket of my parka for change.

The violinist who swayed to the sound of his own lilting tune nodded at me even though his eyes remained closed. He was so absorbed in his music, his passion, that he had transcended his body.

Art had always been the medium of my sublimity. My love for Sinclair was devastatingly similar, dangerous because it did not recognize right or wrong. It simply existed. I smiled at the violinist with my heart in my eyes before turning to look over at Sinclair, who viewed me with that inscrutable expression.

"I must admit I haven't read my own Wikipedia page. We have someone at the company to manage those sorts of things, but I am reasonably sure that there is no mention of me being a serial killer or something equally disturbing."

I snorted. "I wasn't worried about that. You tied me up and spanked me; if you had wanted to kill me, then you definitely had the opportunity to."

He grinned at me, shaking his head almost reluctantly as if he couldn't quite believe I was real. I beamed back at him and didn't notice the seriousness in his eyes until it was too late.

"You were worried about seeing pictures of me with Elena."

I swallowed painfully and nodded.

He sighed and brought us to a complete stop in the middle of Times Square. The darkness brought out the multicolored lights flashing against his features and reminded me of our strangely intimate time at his club.

"Giselle, I want you to listen to me when I say this because I know you will only let me tell you once." His hands fell heavily onto my shoulders so that he could bring me closer. "You have nothing to be ashamed of. At the risk of sounding callous, I do not regret the time I spent with you in Mexico and neither should you, not unless you truly did not enjoy it."

"Don't be ridiculous." My voice was fainter than I would have liked, but it was hard to speak past the gunk of volatile emotions clogging my throat. "It's not about me, though. It's about Elena."

"Is it?" His hands squeezed my shoulders. "Or could it just be about us?"

I was already shaking my head. "It doesn't work like that."

"We set the fucking rules, Giselle." He stepped back from me and glared, his eyes so cold they burned. I didn't know what he could have been thinking, staring at me with such furious intensity in the crowded space, the bodies bumping into us and the cacophony of downtown New York City completely forgotten.

"No, we don't." I laughed but there was a frenzied edge to it that made me realize I was close to having a panic attack. "I haven't set the rules for my own in life *ever*. And now? When I could ruin the life that my sister has so carefully constructed for herself? It's not the time to start."

Sinclair glared at me for another long minute before stuffing his hands in his pockets. He looked off into the crowd and shook his head.

"I would hate to call you a coward, Elle, but a person who does not pursue their own happiness is definitely that."

"I am happy." When his eyebrows rose coolly as I had known they would, I shrugged gracefully. "I really am. Right here, right now with you, I am happy."

"And when I go home to Elena?" he countered.

It was my turn to look off into the distance at the hundreds of people passing under the colored lights of Times Square.

Finally, I pursed my lips and faced him. "Will you be?"

"You've asked me before not to answer that question."

"You're right. You are still with her, though, so I guess I have my answer, don't I?"

He frowned at me, but I smiled softly at him and linked my arm through his to pull him through the crowd. I was done with heaviness and despair. The regret and the shame would surely visit me in the morning when I woke up heavy with my separation from him. For now, I was content to fool myself into a friendship with him, this man I loved.

"Want a pretzel?"

There was only a slight hesitation before he said, "Only if they have Dijon mustard."

I hid my sigh under a smile and fell just a little bit more in love with him for going along with my charade.

Chapter Nine

"You seem to be spending a lot of time with Daniel."

I paused, my hand hovering over the canvas precariously. I could see my hard heartbeat shake my hand.

"Huh?"

Cosima's gold eyes swiveled my way, but she didn't move a hair out of position. "I said, you seem to be spending a lot of time with Daniel."

I focused carefully on adding a dab of burnt umber to the mixture on my palette, darkening the shadow beneath Cosima's round breasts and between her proudly braced legs. The painted woman who stared out from the shadows of the canvas peered at me with the same expression as her real-life counterpart, unerringly direct and more than a little disconcerting.

I exhaled a breath I hadn't known I was holding when she shrugged and said, "It's nice that you get along. He has been part of my life, of the family, for so many years it is weird to think you two only just met."

Only just met... Well, we had only met two months ago almost to the day, but it felt like so much longer. And we had been spending a lot of time together, too much really if we wanted to fly under the radar. Sinclair had assured me that Elena worked too much to notice and that he often spent his free time with Cosima. Luckily, Cosima had been wrapped up in her own world for the past ten days, probably with the dangerous-eyed Dante.

"Yeah." I forced my voice to be casual. "He is a nice guy, if a little stuffy."

She ignored my attempt at criticism and broke her pose to open the door behind her. We were in her kitchen/dining area again, which had lately served more as my studio than anything else. Canvases were stacked against the island, and sketches were taped to the wall beside the door. In the last two weeks, I had finalized sketches of Cosima, Sebastian, Cage, and even one of Mama, hovering over the stove in a damp robe with the sheen of sweat on her soft skin. She hadn't blushed at all when I suggested the idea. I wanted to explore the tried and true roles of older women and exploit the sensuality they still retained despite the domestication. Mama had laughed joyfully at the suggestion.

"I have to admit, I'm a little surprised. You are one of my favorite humans on the planet." Her smile poured over me like sunshine. "But Daniel doesn't like change. I think the last friend he made was Elena."

My skin itched. I was always careful not to ask too many questions about their relationship, but this was just too good an opportunity to pass up.

"How did they meet?"

"Why don't you ask Elena? She should be here in ten minutes or so, and I have to get ready to leave."

She slipped on the translucent black robe laying on one of the stools, but something in my face made her hesitate on the way to her bedroom.

She sighed and came over to cup my face in her warm hands. "We have all been apart for a long time, Gigi, and we are all used to keeping ourselves to ourselves, yes? So, if you want to know something, you must not be afraid to *ask* it, or else you will never really know."

I nodded but didn't meet her eye as I moved away to clean my brushes before Elena arrived. Cosima's signature sigh punctuated her exit, and I was grateful for the few minutes alone I had before my older sister arrived.

I hadn't seen her since the day Sinclair had invited me fishing, but we had spoken over the phone about her appointment today. Though we hadn't talked yet about her sexual hang-ups, I was already picturing her standing tense and rigid before a background of wood planks, naked but for the magazines, something like *Playboy* or *Sports Illustrated*, held tight to her private areas. It wasn't an unusual feeling, the inferiority complex that could make a woman as stiff as a board, but I knew my sister had it in spades. I wasn't judging; before Sinclair, I had been very much like that too.

After washing my brushes gently in turpentine solution, I set them out to dry and moved my easel to face the wall so that it would remain private until its completion. I grabbed my large sketchbook and my tin of charcoal before settling on a stool at the counter to do some preliminary drawings.

My mind wandered as my hand swooped across the thick page, inevitably settling on my situation with Sinclair. In just over two weeks, we had lunched together twice, gone to see Cage play a solo set at a new bar in Soho, and attended an art show in Brooklyn. We had been careful, though, not to be anywhere private. After what had happened at Cosima's apartment, I think we were both wary of our control. It was also the reason I hadn't asked him to sit for me even though Elena wanted his portrait done in less than a month. Instead, I chose to work from picture and memory. There were enough photos of him on the boats in Mexico and online that I felt confident enough to produce his likeness.

I would see him tonight at the Romani International gala, but I knew it wouldn't be the same. He would be there with my sister, his girlfriend, on his arm. They made a beautiful couple, as immaculate as wedding cake toppers.

Even though we hadn't touched inappropriately since I had stroked myself at his behest after the club that night, the electric current between us was constantly charged, and I wondered if we would be able to mask it well enough to fool our families tonight.

"Giselle."

I looked up at Elena and tried not to sigh in defeat. She stood before me in a gorgeous gray cashmere coat that perfectly complemented her shoulder-length artfully curled red hair. Her heart-shaped face was exactly the same as mine, but her features were more refined, and perfectly symmeterical like a China doll. Only her eyes, a deep gray under slightly heavy lids, could have been anything but classically stunning, maybe even sexy if she let them be.

I shook myself as I stood to give her a kiss on each cheek. "You look lovely. Would you like a cup of tea?"

She shook her head and swallowed. "It's after four, isn't it? I'd love some whiskey."

My eyebrows shot up before I could help it. "Uh, sure. Why don't you make yourself comfortable, and I'll get us some glasses."

We were quiet as I puttered about the kitchen, looking for the alcohol and tumblers, but she was thinking so loudly it rivaled the buzz of the refrigerator.

I smiled gently at her as I sat down and handed over her drink. "I know you might be uncomfortable, but we should talk about your, um, sexual preferences before we get started."

"I don't like it," she blurted out, her eyes enormous with horror. Her hand clamped over her mouth as she shook her head.

I watched her mutely as she took a long sip of the burning whiskey and straightened her shoulders. "I apologize. I meant to say, I don't really enjoy sex."

What!? How could she not enjoy sex with Sinclair? Of all the things she could have divulged, I never would have guessed it was this.

"I understand that men need it," Elena explained calmly as if we were talking about the weather. "But I've never really understood the appeal."

"Have you never orgasmed?" Again, I couldn't fathom that Sinclair, the man who had unraveled me so thoroughly in Mexico, could have failed to bring any woman the ultimate pleasure.

I felt a little sick talking to Elena about Sinclair like that, but I had trapped myself in a corner and could only pray we ended the conversation quickly.

She stared into her nearly empty glass and swirled the contents. Her face was slack with unspeakable sadness.

"Do you remember Christopher?"

A shudder wracked my body. Why was she bringing him into this? I nodded.

"When you left, he came back for me. He still wanted to marry me." Her accent had slipped back into her words, a silk ribbon strangling her speech. "Mama approved. She didn't know about what had happened between you and him." She shot me a look, not accusatory—I could have dealt with that —just sad. "She let me stay with him a lot because we were going to be married. He took advantage of it, keeping me for days at a time."

"What did he do?" I whispered.

I knew what Christopher was capable of.

She shrugged soggy shoulders. "A lot of things. Things that I don't have words for. One day, he went too far. Luckily, Cosima was in town. She came to take us to America." She laughed wetly, her sloe-eyes glistening. "I still don't know how she found me, but that was the last time I ever saw him."

We were silent. My hand trembled as I poured her more whiskey.

"Anyway, I can enjoy sex and, trust me, with Daniel, I do. But the desire for it?" She shrugged. "It's just not really there."

I stared down at my sketchpad for a few minutes as I tried to digest our conversation. The silence wasn't awkward, though, and when I looked back up at my older sister, she was biting her thumbnail like she had done as a child.

"Hey, Elena?" I murmured, waiting until her low-lidded eyes met mine. "Do you want to go out for a drink?"

"Well, what about the painting?"

I stood and winked at her. "I'd rather get drunk."

"Oh, thank God." Elena grinned too. "Let's do it."

WE DIDN'T GET DRUNK. AFTER ALL, I WAS DRINKING WITH ELENA, A notorious stick in the mud, and we were only a few hours away from a highly publicized charity gala. But we had a few glasses of delicious Italian wine at a ridiculously chic bar Elena had chosen not far from the apartment. We talked about work mostly because it was one of the only things on the very short list of acceptable topics to talk about with each other. Her passion for the law came through in her suddenly expressive hands and the way her speech slipped and swayed into broken English in her haste to explain the legal profession to me.

When she tried to deviate, I choked a little.

"Excuse me?"

She shrugged elegantly. "You seem to be very close with him. I was just curious, are you sleeping with him?"

"Elena!" I laughed nervously and watched as she took it the wrong way, thinking it was true, that I must be sleeping with the sexy French singer.

I didn't know what to do. How could I tell her it was because I was sleeping with the sexy French businessman instead?

"You've been spending too much time with Cosima. Her dramatics are rubbing off on you," she teased, only slightly awkward.

"Oh, calm down. I was just shocked that my conservative older sister wants to discuss my sex life. Sebastian would be in hysterics if he heard you now."

She frowned, and I took a moment to notice how the expression barely creased the skin across her forehead beside her eyes. She was so perfectly modulated that it was like interacting with a robot, one dressed very tastefully in a silk sheath dress.

I sighed. "I am not sleeping with Cage. He's just a good friend."

"A very handsome one."

"Are you saying handsome boys and girls can't be friends, Elena? That seems like pretty simple thinking." I couldn't help the little barb. Insulting her intelligence was the weakest chink in her armor.

"I don't believe they can." She sniffed. "And anyway, I don't know why you would want to spend time with such a barbarian."

I laughed. "Cage is hardly a barbarian. Now, who's being dramatic?"

"Who's being defensive?"

I glared at her. "Listen, Elena. I'm not comfortable talking about my sex life with you, but that doesn't mean I'd lie about being with Cage. I'm not."

She pursed her lips and stared at me intently as I swung my coat over my shoulders and collected my bag.

"Please don't tell me I'm the only one in our family without some weirdo fetish."

My head snapped back so quickly it hurt, but I masked the pain and my horror so that I could look at her unaffected. I wondered briefly if Sinclair was rubbing off on me.

"Weirdo?" I echoed.

When she remained unfazed, her eyes wide and filled with insecurity-infested waters, I realized that my older sister, a pillar of strength, was terrified of being found wanting.

I sighed and leaned over into her personal space to press a warm kiss to her cheek. It was something Cosima or Seb would have done, but I was beginning to understand how much more eloquent touch could be than the spoken word.

"You're perfect, Elena. No comparisons necessary."

She smiled and patted my hand where it rested on the table. I watched her awkward movements with a raised brow, and she sighed lightly before entwining our fingers. A lock of beautifully curled hair fell across her pale forehead like a wine stain on a fancy tablecloth. She was so lovely in her timidity that it took my breath away.

"I'm not very good at this communicating thing," she said, waving a hand through the air to illustrate her lack of eloquence. "To be perfectly frank, you make me uncomfortable. I know you don't mean to, but that's how I've always felt."

"Um, okay," I said, because while I appreciated her attempt to open up, what else was I supposed to say to that?

She squeezed my hand before releasing it. Our increased physical distance seemed to calm her skittishness. "What I mean to say is, family is important to me, and I would appreciate it if we could both make a greater effort to get to know each other again."

The portion of my soul that was supposed to house my moral compass was achingly empty and hollow against the knock her words had rung upon it. My hand shook slightly with the reverberations as I reached for my glass and swallowed the last of my wine.

"I'd like that, Elena. Very much."

She smiled, a slight but genuine tilt of her closed lips. "Good. As an olive branch, I would love to set you up with a wonderful friend of mine. His name is Ulrich Wick. He works in finance, and he has the loveliest head of hair."

I bit my lip against my protest because as far as olive branches went, it was relatively harmless, and honestly, it would probably do me good to go out with someone new.

"That sounds lovely." I leaned in to give her a hug and smiled slightly when she gave me her customary pat on the back.

"Does Wednesday work for you?"

"Sounds great," I said. I donned my coat and began to walk toward the door. "I'll see you tonight."

"Excellent. Oh and Giselle?" she called after me. "Try to wear something more appropriate for daytime when you see Ulrich, he's a tad old fashioned."

I waved my consent at her over my shoulder and pushed through the door into the welcome city bustle.

Despite the awkwardness, I was glad we had spent some quality time alone. It didn't change how I felt about Sinclair. It hadn't lessened or intensified my guilt, and honestly, it hadn't made me feel any closer to Elena.

It was strange how indifference could cripple a relationship just as assuredly as animosity.

Still, I hadn't spent quality time with my eldest sister in years, and it was interesting to catalog her growth and sameness. She went for a manicure every month but still picked at her hangnails when she was nervous, and she spoke with a perfect English accent, but the wrinkle between her brow when people spoke too quickly belied her aptitude with the language. She was such a writhing mass of contradictions I wasn't sure how to read her, let alone get along with her. And I was okay with that.

Did it make me a terrible person that I found my time spent with Elena most lent itself to my relationship, or lack of one, with Sinclair?

Because I could understand now how he could love her, how very compatible they were even if it was artificially. The superficiality of their likeness was exactly the point of their relationship; they both liked to live life behind a meticulously honed mask of respectability and elegance.

LATER THAT NIGHT, I LOOKED IN THE MIRROR AS I CAREFULLY APPLIED THE last of my lipstick, a deep reddish-pink that complemented the dark gray, silver threaded dress Cosima had helped me choose earlier that week. The silk flowed down my curves like rainwater over steel, binding my waist and baring a deep square of flesh between my breasts. My auburn hair, lighter than it had been since my sun-kissed summers in Napoli, spiraled softly around my lightly freckled shoulders.

"It's good," I murmured to myself in the mirror, sucking in a deep breath and adjusting my full breasts in the tight panels to show them off to their best advantage.

But I didn't feel good. My heart was fragile and dry in my chest, something that had been set aflame and with each beat turned slowly to ash. I wished Cosima was here to press a fragrant kiss to my cheek and tell me I was beautiful or Brenna, who would have already popped the champagne and made our preparation into a party. I wasn't used to dressing up, but it felt sad and a little wrong to do it alone, especially when I was already wretched with the thought of facing Éclair (my couple name for Elena and Sinclair).

I grabbed my jeweled clutch and slipped my feet into delicately strapped black shoes before opening the door to leave.

"Mind a tag-along?"

My head whipped up, a lock of my hair sticking to my eyelashes, to see Sebastian decked out in a gorgeous black tuxedo. He held a box of sweets from Dylan's Candy Bar and a small silver flask.

"This is to get us through the night." He indicated the flask and then held up the candies. "And this is your reward for afterward."

"A handsome man comes to my door bearing gifts? I'd be a fool not to take him." I slipped into his arms for a spicy scented hug and closed my eyes for a second to absorb how good it felt to be with my brother again.

We stood like that for a moment before I murmured, "How did you know I'd need you?"

He hesitated and pressed a kiss to the top of my hair. "Cosima might have suggested it."

My heart stuttered. I knew Cosima was perceptive, but how much had she surmised about my relationship with Sinclair? Could she possibly know?

"Come on, Cinderella, you'll be late for the ball."

Sebastian gently pulled me from his arms, placed the candy on the side table, and locked up the apartment with his spare key.

We traveled in Sebastian's luxurious Bentley, whose cream leather interior retained its new car smell. His driver, a short, stocky man with vibrant orange hair, greeted me in a thick Scottish accent before Sebastian put up the privacy screen.

He opened the flask, took a long swig, and passed it to me, watching me with narrowed eyes as I swallowed a burning mouthful.

"You are so different, *bambina*." His voice held only the faintest trace of

Italy, a whisper that suggested he was foreign but gave no indication of his nationality unless you were familiar with the sounds of Naples.

"So are you."

He leaned back in his seat, slinging an arm over the ledge above the in car bar. His thick black hair waved across his bronze forehead and accentuated the pure gold of his eyes. He was so handsome, but the way he held his mouth, even to smile, was off. Crooked in a way that might have been sexy to some but just seemed sad to me. There were so many secrets between my family members that it seemed impossible we could ever regain our childhood closeness.

"I had an affair in Mexico."

It was a huge admission for me, but Seb, the seasoned movie star, only raised one brow, so I barreled on.

"He was amazing." I couldn't keep my voice from turning dreamy. "No one has ever made me feel so safe and so inspired to push past my comfort zone. He was handsome and intelligent and just remote enough to make him seem mysterious." I laughed at myself and shrugged. "So, obviously, I fell in love with him."

"But?" I raised my eyebrows at him, and he sighed dramatically before explaining himself. "As a man, I know there is always a 'but' with women, and it is almost always justifiable."

"Well, you're right. The 'but' is that he is taken."

"Ah, that is a significant 'but.'" His eyes sparkled as he took another sip from the flask. "Is it just me, or have you forgotten what type of butts we are talking about?"

I laughed and hit him lightly in the shoulder. "You are such a goofball."

"Self-proclaimed and proud of it." He winked.

My giggle ended on a sigh as I looked out the window and spotted the Four Seasons Hotel looming ahead of us. I startled when Sebastian reached over to take my hand in his, but I didn't look over at him when he started to speak.

"For whatever reasons, tonight is going to be difficult for both of us. I want you to know that I'm here with you, *bambina*. We are going into this hive of bees together unified. If you want to leave at any time, say the Italian word."

The Italian word was a precaution we had established as children when Seamus would return home twitchy and bloated after days of drinking and gambling. When the fights grew too loud between our parents, and mostly, when the Camorra came to collect their payments from Seamus, whether he had the money or not, Elena would call out *insieme*. We each had our own hiding places; the twins were tucked into the closet behind the water heater while I was placed under the back porch. Elena had taken the worst haven, under the sink in the kitchen, a place that was kept empty by Mama specifically for that reason. I had always wondered how much my older sister had witnessed from her cramped hideaway, how much the violence and conflict had affected her. I knew the hours spent cold and alone outside had led me to detest the feeling of both.

"*Insieme*," I murmured. "Together."

Sebastian nodded and placed a kiss on my knuckles as we came to a stop in front of the gorgeous hotel, an elegant pale stone façade surrounded by modern glass architecture. I was in awe as Seb ushered me from the car into the tasteful lobby and up the sweeping marble staircase to the main event room.

I blinked rapidly when we entered the formal space, blinded momentarily by the wealth of marble and crystal, silk-clad ladies and tuxedoed gentlemen. There couldn't have been more than two hundred people in attendance, but they were some of the richest individuals in Manhattan, and it wasn't hard to feel awed by their hard-won or inherited wealth and grace.

Sebastian chuckled at my déclassé expression and tugged me farther into the room.

"Beautifully dressed sharks in a pretty tank, *cara*. Nothing more," he reminded me as we pulled up at the bar to grab retro champagne glasses.

"Yeah, and I'm Nemo," I muttered, smoothing the front of my dress with a clammy palm.

"Sebastian."

His laughter cut off abruptly at the breathy sound of his name, his shoulders hunching slightly and his knuckles white against the edge of the bar. He let out a deep exhale before turning around to face the woman who had said his name.

She was absolutely lovely, like a movie star out of the 1960s. Her large blue eyes were wreathed in a tasteful ring of kohl, and her tiny mouth was red and full like a rosebud. She was petite in a way I had always desired to be, with fine bones and slim hips emphasized by the fluidity of her gown. Despite her youthful features, the grace of her posture and the fine lines across her pale forehead denoted her age. She put on a good show in the filmy black dress with the long white opera gloves, but she couldn't fool the artist in me. I would have been surprised if she was a day under forty.

I knew who she was even before Sebastian cleared his throat, and said, "Savannah."

They stared at each other for a long, heated moment, completely ignorant of everyone else around them. I was surprised by their chemistry even though Elena had made it apparent in her insults that Seb had had an affair with an older woman. The proper Savannah Richardson did not seem at all like my fun-loving brother's type.

I cleared my throat and stepped forward with a genuine smile. "Hello, I'm Giselle. It's very nice to meet you. I've heard such wonderful things."

One icy blond brow rose slowly as she looked back and forth between my brother and me, but she did deign to take my offered hand.

"The pleasure is mine. I wasn't aware you were in town." Her eyes darted briefly to Sebastian, who remained standing stiffly at my side. "I very much hope you are enjoying being reunited with your family."

"I am, thank you." I continued to smile at her even though the situation was strangely grave. "Sebastian decided to be my white knight and accompany me here tonight." I leaned in conspiratorially. "I've never been to such an opulent event before."

She laughed lightly, and I caught a glimpse of something younger in her, something almost childlike and delicate. Her wide blue eyes slid to Sebastian again, inexorably drawn to him, and I felt a pang of empathy for the older lady. I knew all too well what it was like to love an unattainable man.

"You are in good hands with Sebastian then. I've dragged him to enough of these over the years to make him a hardened veteran, isn't that right?"

Seb grunted noncommittally and shot me a glare when I dug my elbow in his side. I was opening my mouth to appease Savannah, maybe even apologize for my thuggish brother, when an older gentleman stepped up beside her and placed a heavy hand on her birdlike shoulder.

"Savannah, darling, I've been looking for you." He spoke in a loud, gruff voice; a radio announcer from the 50s accompanied by the static rasp of an old stereo. It added to his old-school tails, the cummerbund, and slicked silver hair. He was a handsome man, robust and virile despite his age, and I immediately liked him.

"Seb, my boy." He beamed when he noticed my brother and stepped forward to grab him in a rough hug. "How the hell are you?"

"Fine as ever, Tate." Sebastian's lips twisted in a reluctant grin. "I was just introducing your *lovely wife* to my sister, Giselle Moore."

Savannah flinched slightly at Sebastian's casually spoken truth, and I realized then why Sebastian had said tonight held its own hardship. They were obviously in love, or, at least, they had been, and it had ended on less than auspicious terms.

"Giselle, the artistic one, right?" Tate grabbed my hand between his two mitts and squeezed it gently. "Tate Richardson. Media mogul, producer, director, and the lucky bastard married to this beautiful lady."

Savannah straightened, and any softness I had seen before vanished. She was suddenly the kind of New York matron I expected, haughty and beautifully aloof as if nothing could touch her. Sebastian scowled at the change, and something flickered in her eyes. It was pretty obvious to me that *he* was the only one who could touch her.

"You haven't been by in far too long, son." Tate had turned back to Sebastian. "What ever happened to our family Sunday dinners?"

Sebastian shifted slightly away from me as if the slight distance would make it harder for me to hear this conversation.

"I didn't know you two were in New York, and I've been busy working on a new project." He finished his flute of champagne in one long drink and reached behind the bar to grab something stronger, an expensive brand of whiskey that he poured into a short glass. The bartender eyed him warily, but after a quick wink, she let him be. She was only human, after all.

"Well, I'm sorry to take my brother away from you, but I see our sister over by the windows, and she will kill us if we don't check in," I said with a huge smile.

Tate nodded his head and said something in his booming voice to Sebastian so I took the opportunity to lean in close to Savannah and pressed my hand to her arm. She looked at me sharply but softened when she saw my slight smile.

"He's okay?" she whispered.

I hesitated before responding. "I think you're better equipped to answer that question."

She sucked in a quick breath before looking away. I knew I was dismissed, but I forgave her sudden coldness because it was obvious she wasn't dealing well with her separation from Sebastian.

I badly wanted to ply him with alcohol and attack him with questions about their relationship, but as we left the older couple and Sebastian became more and more relaxed with each step away from the mature blonde, I knew I couldn't. Not only would it be awkward and painful for him but it was also hypocritical of me to question his apparently sketchy relationship when I couldn't even face my own.

"Where did you say they are?"

"I didn't actually see them." I shrugged when he shot me a sidelong look. "*Insieme*, Sebastian. We needed to get out of there."

He looked at me for a long second before nodding curtly. "We did. Should we find our table then?"

We headed over to the table displays and found ours in the middle of the vast venue, far enough away from the live band not to have to shout over the music but essentially front and center given the layout of the room.

"Why would we be at such an important table?" I murmured as Sebastian weaved between the round tables and future diners.

He shot a look over his shoulder. "A movie star, a business tycoon, a lawyer from one of the best New York City law firms, an up-and-coming artist, and a politician? I think that group warrants a good table."

"A politician?" I asked, but we were already at our table, and the sight of the people sitting around it made me forget my question.

Before I could even digest the sight of Elena or Sinclair, someone was in my arms, wrapping me in an embrace that made my heart ache for an earlier time.

"Candy," I breathed as she squeezed me tighter.

"Candy," she agreed, releasing me only enough to smile her buck-toothed smile into my face. "I can see you're shocked I'm here, so I'll give you a second to get over it and be excited to see me again. Although I'm not going to give you too long because I'm furious with you for not getting in touch with me after three long months of separation."

"Two months," I corrected automatically.

She blinked before tossing her head back and laughing. "Okay, the fury lasted for a much shorter time than I anticipated. You are officially forgiven. But you've got to make it up to me by sitting beside me."

She took my hand and finally had the wherewithal to see Sebastian standing beside us, staring bemusedly down at her. She stopped mid-step and gaped openly at him before turning back to play-whisper, "And introduce me to this guy."

It was my turn to laugh, and the distraction of their introduction was a welcome one as the three of us took our seats. I felt warm and safe with the two of them beside me so when I finally looked up at the rest of the table, I did so with a faux confidence I didn't really feel.

My eyes landed immediately on Sinclair, which wasn't surprising given the fact that I had known where he sat at the table as soon as we were in its vicinity. He was already staring at me, those blue eyes electric with intensity as they swept over my body, taking careful inventory of everything about my person. When they reached mine, his mouth softened into something close to a smile.

God, he was gorgeous.

"Giselle." Elena's voice brought my attention to her seat beside him, and I noticed that they matched—his ice blue tie and her velvet dress. She looked like a modern-day Audrey Hepburn, and my hands found my bodice self-consciously before I could help it.

"Elena, you look absolutely lovely. Thank you so much for inviting me tonight."

"Thank you, but I wasn't the one to extend the invitation. Willa and

Mortimer wanted to meet the last addition to my family." She beamed at the older couple I had yet to notice who sat to her right.

"We've heard a great deal about you," Willa Percy said with a close-lipped smile as her brown eyes scraped over my body with the precision of a scalpel, searching for flaws with the gravitas of a surgeon.

Logically, I knew that Willa was a beautiful woman; African American with a light brown complexion smoother than silk and thick wavy hair she wore cut into a chic shoulder-length bob. But I found nothing warm in her expression or any charisma in the way she carried herself. She seemed almost like a doll, perfectly turned out in every way except for the lack of vitality in her eyes.

On the other hand, Mortimer Percy struck me as the kind of man to play Santa at a charity event or roll around in the mud with his sons. He was a broad-shouldered, All-American kind of man with a square jaw and a full head of golden-brown hair streaked with silver. With looks like that, it was no wonder he was a popular politician.

"No one told us you would be so pretty, though." Mortimer smiled broadly. "We just heard some nonsense about you being a fantastic artist or something of the sort."

I laughed because he wanted me to, and his good humor was infectious. "What did I do to deserve such flattery?"

"Don't lay that at my son's doorstep. I'm afraid he's not the effusive type. Is he, Elena?" Mortimer guffawed.

Elena laughed too, but I was uncomfortable with the assertion, and when my eyes found Sinclair, the muscle in his jaw was ticking as it did when he was trying to control himself. Sensing my gaze, he looked up at me. I held his stare, opening myself to any thoughts he needed to purge himself of. I willed him to trust me with the emotions he normally carved up and shoved into the furthest recesses of his mind. His mouth opened slightly on a long exhale, and he shook his head slightly.

"*Later*," he mouthed.

My heart clenched in anticipation of seeing him again.

"It was Mama," Elena admitted. "She never could shut up about you."

"Elena," Sebastian warned under his breath, but she didn't take heed.

"Giselle was always Mama's special girl. She's thrilled to have her back, of course. The entire Lombardi clan together again. Although Giselle still goes by our father's last name."

I watched as Sinclair surreptitiously moved Elena's wineglass over to his side of the place setting.

"Names are so important." Willa stepped in, boredom laced throughout her words. "Daniel never did consent to take the Percy name."

"You never offered it to Cage," Sinclair said quietly. "And it was easier to keep Sinclair."

Willa sniffed, but Mortimer put his hand over hers to quell her. "We understand, Daniel, of course. Names are unimportant in the grand scheme of things. We are a family of choice, not circumstance."

His words set fire to my chest. I wanted a relationship of choice; I wanted Sinclair to choose me.

"There are no reporters at the table, Mortimer. You can stop the politicking," Willa said.

"Mom," Sinclair chastised, and I was surprised to see it had a positive effect on Willa, who straightened in her chair and applied a smile to her smooth cheeks.

"Very well. Elena, darling, how is the adoption process going?"

I almost choked on the sip of delicate white wine I was drinking. Could this evening get any more excruciating?

"Slowly, unfortunately."

"You must use our connections. Why forge relationships if you can't use them to your advantage, hmm?"

"We're in no rush," Sinclair reminded them. "Elena is only twenty-six. We have time enough to start a family."

"He's just nervous." Margot appeared at the table, a sharp smile on her face as she slipped into one of two empty chairs beside Candy. By the way she stared right at me, I knew Sin had warned her of my presence. "As long as I've known him, Daniel has always wanted to be a father."

Candy's hand found mine under the table and squeezed.

Sebastian snorted and muttered under this breath, "This is going to be one long fucking dinner."

I couldn't have agreed more.

Chapter Ten

IT WAS BETTER WHEN THE MUSIC STARTED IN EARNEST, AND PEOPLE BEGAN TO dance. Elena was occupied with Mortimer, so Sinclair took Margot for a spin while my charming brother guided Willa—who actually laughed in delight—around the floor.

It had been a long and stifling dinner, and the sudden absence of tension made the air taste like ambrosia.

Candy gave me a solid thirty seconds of peace before descending on me.

"Okay, I have no idea how you are dealing with this." She stared at me incredulously, but when I didn't respond, she huffed. "That wasn't a rhetorical statement, Elle. How the hell are you dealing with this, this weirdness?"

"I'm not. I mean, I'm not dealing with it well."

"Sinclair briefed me, but you know him."

I smiled because I did. "What did he say?"

"Oh, *pfft*." She blew the bangs out of her face, and I loved her for her artlessness. "Something like 'Candace, Elle is in Manhattan. She also happens to be Elena's sister. You'll come to the gala tonight and see her. I would appreciate your discretion.'"

"Typical." I nodded with mock sincerity.

"Totally," she agreed.

We beamed at each other.

"This is a mess."

"Totally," I agreed.

"What are you going to do about it?"

I shrugged, and the heaviness of my guilt and desire broke the filter I had kept so far over my thoughts.

"Come on, Elle, you *love* him. Don't tell me you're okay with the status quo?"

"Of course not. But what would you have me do? Ruin my sister's life?"

Candy waved her hand dismissively. "That's a bit dramatic. She'd be heart broken, sure, but she would get over it. Anyone can see those two aren't soul mates."

"Soul mates? Honestly, Candy, who can say such a thing even exists?"

"You can!"

I slumped back in my chair even though I shouldn't have been shocked by her words. Was Sinclair my soul mate? I had never really thought about the term or what it could mean. I only knew how I felt about the enigmatic Frenchman I had met in Mexico and the gravitational pull between us. I craved him in a way that was more elemental than addiction but still dangerous, more respectful than reverential but still sacred. I wanted to be with him more than I wanted nearly anything else in the world even though I hardly knew him.

The question fell so easily into my lap that I was surprised I hadn't seen it all along. It really came down to this; did I want him more than I wanted my sister's happiness? Did I want him enough to live with the guilt? And I guess, most importantly, did he love me enough to take those on too?

"Richard said it in Mexico, and I'll say it again; I've never seen Sinclair lighter or happier than I have when he was with you. I didn't know you before, so I can't track the same changes, but I know you love him, and the girl I came to admire the hell out of in Mexico would not let something so precious go so easily."

"She's my sister," I said for what felt like the billionth time.

"Excuses."

"A good one," I amended, but I wasn't sure she was so wrong.

"You don't seem to be behaving yourself, Candace."

I looked up and over my shoulder to see Sinclair. He wore a deep navy, nearly black suit that fit his lean body perfectly and emphasized the crazy blue of his eyes. I was still getting used to his new haircut, but the lock of mahogany hair that fell over his forehead made him almost shockingly gorgeous.

"Do I ever?" Candy asked, baring her prominent teeth in a full smile.

I was happy she had abandoned her effort to keep them hidden, and I wondered what had prompted the change. I made a note to ask her later, feeling a little guilty that I had dominated our conversation.

"Touché." His lips twitched with humor, but when he shifted to look down at me, his eyes blazed with stark hunger. "Giselle, accompany me outside for some air."

It was that question that wasn't a question; the dominance I had come to crave from him. My body was primed and ready, and he hadn't even touched me yet.

I nodded, not trusting my voice, and took his hand to help me up from the chair. A subtle glance confirmed that Elena was still busy, near the bar now and surrounded by a large group of lovely, wealthy people. She was laughing and carefree as she bantered with like-minded elites, and I realized how much she fit into this scene, how much she loved it.

We didn't speak as he ushered me outside, but the light touch of his hand on my lower back radiated like a beacon across my skin. The cool air felt amazing against my overheated skin, and I was immediately seduced by the murmur of traffic and the pulsing thrum of city life.

"New York is louder than Paris, crowded and coarser, but I absolutely adore it." I shook my head and leaned over the balustrade to peer at the darkened garden below. "I didn't expect to love it like this."

"For all its glamour and beauty, there is a certain artlessness to the city that is its most appealing quality."

I beamed over my shoulder at him. "Exactly."

"You are happy here, then?"

I turned back to the shadowed gardens to hide my frown. It was a harder question than it should have been, and the reason for that stood just behind me, exuding a cool sexuality that sent tingles over my skin.

"I am. Despite the occasional awkwardness of being reunited with my sisters and brother after years apart, it's good to feel at home again."

He stepped up to the stone railing beside me and braced his arms against it. His knuckles were white even in the darkness. I could feel his tension as if it were my own, the line he had hooked through my heart pulled taut by the strain.

"I'm jeopardizing that."

"A bit."

He smiled slightly at my honesty. "Before you, I never knew how selfish a person could truly be."

"Because you want both Elena and me?" I ripped the question off my heart quickly like a Band-Aid, but the pain still radiated through me and made my jaw ache.

He was silent for a lot longer than I was comfortable with, but I tried to remain patient and still. This was hardly the place or time for such a conversation, but I wasn't willing to end it, not after weeks of wondering.

"It's more complicated than that," he said finally.

"How?"

His jaw tensed, the muscle skipping in his cheek.

"How?" I pressed.

"I have," he hesitated, "a responsibility to Elena. I owe her happiness."

My throat was being stitched closed inch by inch. "You can't stay with someone because you feel beholden to them."

"You can," he argued firmly, turning to face me with eyes like chips of dry ice. "In fact, I would argue that most relationships are based on exactly that."

"Those relationships fail," I whispered.

I felt like an egg leaning too far over the balustrade, waiting with bone-chilling apprehension for the right breeze to tumble me over the edge.

"What are you saying, Elle?" His hands were suddenly on my arms, grasping them so firmly that I gasped. "You said yourself, you were not willing to sacrifice your sister's happiness, and now this? What the fuck do you want from me? Because when you ask me these infernal questions and when you look at me with those gray eyes, what do you expect me to do? I am no saint, and I won't pretend for one second longer that I'm anything close to a gentleman."

His lips crashed onto mine, and the feel of them went off like a bomb through my body. He tugged my shaking form closer until we were flush against each other, pressed so tightly I could feel him everywhere. His tongue swept between my teeth and took exactly want he wanted; my pleasure, my surrender.

I gasped into his mouth when his hands slid down my curves and grabbed my butt to lift me onto the ledge. As soon as I was settled, he stepped close, pushing my dress up and spreading my legs open to make room for him against my center. I tipped my head back to moan, my eyes absorbed by the sight of the moon as Sinclair's lips found the sensitive skin under my ear.

"You want this," he rasped, pressing even closer so that I could feel his erection against my heat. "Why can't you admit that you want this?"

My head was dizzy with sensation, but the conscious part of me hated his question. Why couldn't I admit I wanted this? More, that I *needed* it. I bit back a sob at the idea of never having him like this again and tightened my hands in his hair.

His hand lowered, finding my heeled foot and running his fingers gently around my anklebone before moving up, cool and fluid as rainwater, to my inner thigh. I panted when he pulled away to look into my eyes, his fingertips lazily swirling across the heated skin just beside my sex.

"Admit you want this."

I moaned because I could still see the people inside, splashes of rich color behind the slightly mottled glass doors.

Elena was in there.

"Even with all those people mere steps away and your sister just inside, you want this, Elle."

I leaned forward, pressing my lips to his neck to lick at his delicious salty skin. But he wouldn't let me escape into the fantasy. Instead, he pulled me back and grasped my chin firmly between his thumb and forefinger.

"Tell me."

"Yes," I breathed.

"Yes to what?" Sinclair's eyes sparkled in the starlight, and I knew he was enjoying this. "You know how much I like it when you use your words."

"Yes," I said, louder this time. "I want you. I *need* this."

I watched my words ignite him, the way goose bumps raced across his skin like a lit fuse toward his fiery gaze.

"*Elle*," he groaned, before simultaneously claiming my mouth and plunging two fingers deep inside me.

He caught my moan between his teeth and echoed it with one of his own. Combined with the roar of my blood rushing through my veins, it took me a moment to realize someone was clearing their throat behind Sinclair. I thought quickly, pulling him to me instead of pushing him away, placing my hands over his hair as I tucked his face into the side of my neck. That way, someone might not notice who I was kissing. Sinclair tensed but allowed me to hide him.

I sighed heavily when I saw Cage standing there with his hands in the pockets of his all-black ensemble.

"You scared me."

"I can't imagine why, *chérie*, when you chose such an excellent place for a clandestine *rendezvous*."

I frowned at him as Sinclair extricated himself from my embrace and smoothed down my long skirt before turning to Cage.

"You're late."

Cage laughed, but it was a hollow sound. "That is the least of our transgressions."

Sinclair's lips thinned, and he stepped forward, barring me partially from Cage's cold look. "Are you judging me, rock star?"

"Are you implying I don't have a right to, gypsy?"

I blinked as the acidity of the atmosphere stung my eyes. I could understand why Cage would be disappointed in us for falling into each other's arms yet again. Still, he had been there in Mexico, and more than that, he had encouraged me to pursue Sinclair again, even knowing Elena was my sister. Why the hell was he being so antagonistic?

"Cage," I began, but he held up a hand.

"No, Giselle, I think I will tell you some things, hmm?" He tugged at the end of his braid and sighed roughly. "I care for you two, and I do not care much for your woman or your sister, Elena. But I just came from talking with her about a baby, a baby she hopes to have with you, Sin. She was smiling, you see, in a way I did not think she was capable of. The idea of family made her smile like that. And you are both her family."

He shrugged with the tired wisdom of someone eternal. "I want you to be together. I'm, as you say, Team Giselle. But you both need to take your heads out of your asses and figure this out before you all get fucked."

I don't know when I started to cry, but by the time he was finished, I couldn't see through the tears, and a thin trail of snot was seeping from my nose. It wasn't because of Cage's cruelty. It was because he had no choice but to speak so harshly; the truth of our clandestine relationship *was* cruel.

"Jesus, Cage," Sinclair said.

His rage was palpable, but instead of ripping into his friend, he stepped back to me and took my face in his hands so that I was forced to look up at him. He pulled out a handkerchief from the inside pocket of his blazer and tenderly wiped my tear-streaked face. Cage was watching us, and people inside were waiting for us, but I realized with growing warmth that Sinclair wouldn't leave without making sure I was okay.

"I'll take you home."

"No." He flinched at my rejection, so I placed a soothing hand against his on my cheek. "No, you need to go inside to Elena. Cage is"—I sniffed grossly, but he didn't recoil—"right. This isn't fair to anyone. We agreed to be friends, and it needs to stay that way."

Sinclair closed his eyes and breathed deeply before touching his forehead to mine and admitting in a soft, quiet voice that mended my heart as quickly as it was broken, "I can't leave it like this. I thought I could but ..." His sigh feathered against my lips. "I need more time with you. Give me more time with you."

It wasn't quite a question, but it didn't matter. I pressed my lips to his nose and whispered, "Okay."

His full smile took my breath away, and I laughed when his lips crashed inelegantly against mine. Pushing a lock of hair gently behind my ear, he bent his knees so that our eyes were level, and when he spoke, his voice was pure smoke.

"Tuesday night, my siren. That's when I'll have you."

"YOU LOOK FLUSHED."

I was startled out of my daydreaming by Sebastian, who had joined me at the bar where I waited for a glass of wine.

"Hmm?"

"I said you look flushed."

His eyes were sharp, so I straightened up self-consciously. It was dangerous to have one's head in the clouds around one of the twins; they saw things most people shouldn't.

"It's warm in here."

"But you were just outside," he countered, too casually. "With Cage?"

"Yes, the poor guy can't keep his hands off me." I giggled nervously.

He didn't buy it.

"Interesting, he can't seem to keep his hands off that one either." He tilted his head to indicate Cage, who was kissing a beautiful woman's neck on the dance floor.

"My heart," I joked, clutching at it dramatically.

Sebastian bit down on his smirk, which made me realize how serious he was about seeing this line of questioning through to the end. I didn't know if it was because I was still high on Sinclair's kisses or if it was because I was so tired of lying and feeling guilty, but either way, I crossed my arms and gave Sebastian my best no-nonsense glare.

"Seems like another poor guy can't keep his eyes off you."

Ah. I knew who he was referring to without following his gaze behind me. I had felt his eyes on me as soon as he and Cage had followed me inside after a short private conversation. I wore that gaze with pride as an invisible mantle across my shoulders, infusing me with a cheeky confidence and power.

"I don't know what you're talking about, Seb," I demurred. "But I may have been distracted by Savannah Richardson's multiple attempts to catch your eye."

We stared at each other for a long moment, and I wondered if yet another of my familial relationships would be reduced to this—acridity and defensiveness.

But Sebastian mocked me for my pessimism by dissolving into full-throated laughter. Still chuckling, he leaned forward to swing his arms around me and tug me closer.

"Ti amo, bambina."

"I love you too," I said as I pressed my smile into the soft fabric of his blazer.

A slight cough alerted us to the arrival of Elena, who stood with her fingers clutched tightly in front of her gorgeous Grecian-inspired velvet gown. Despite her dark coloring and slumberous sexy eyes, Elena conducted herself like an ice queen. I wondered idly if she had ever seen *Frozen.*

"What's so funny?"

"Nothing." I waved away her question and nodded at the older man behind her. "Who is this?"

Elena's eyes narrowed even though her lips automatically formed a genteel smile as she stepped backward to introduce him. "Mr. Paulson, please let me introduce my siblings, Sebastian and Giselle."

Mr. Paulson wore a light metallic silver suit that perfectly matched his coiffed helmet of hair and stern expression. Despite his austerity, deep brackets around his broad mouth indicated he smiled often, and his orange pocket square meant he couldn't take himself too seriously.

"Wonderful to meet you." He clasped my hand in both of his, and even though I understood he wanted the gesture to be warm and welcoming, the feel of his eyes cataloging every inch of me negated the effect.

"Mr. Paulson is the CEO of Dogwood International Hotels," Elena explained with a significant eyebrow raise, trying to convey the importance of this fact. "Daniel and I invited him tonight to meet the family. Unfortunately, my youngest sister Cosima is away at the moment on a photo shoot, but she sends her regrets."

"Ah, Cosima." Mr. Paulson had a surprisingly soft voice, his words carefully spoken. "She is a delightful young woman. I thought for certain she would be married by now."

I frowned and opened my mouth to question his odd comment, but Elena shot me a glare before I could.

She laughed lightly and placed a gentle hand on his arm. "She receives proposals by the dozens, but my younger sister believes in the sanctity of marriage and doesn't take entering into it lightly."

While they smiled at each other, I nudged Sebastian in the ribs, and he shrugged, rolling his eyes.

"You and Sinclair have been engaged for ages now. When are you love-birds going to tie the knot?" Mr. Paulson asked Elena, but his eyes veered toward me.

It was a smart move. It took me at least three seconds to rearrange my shocked features into some semblance of normalcy. Engaged?

Sebastian's hand pressed between my shoulders comfortingly, and I watched him jerk his head slightly from side to side.

Aware of Mr. Paulson's eyes, I swallowed my relieved sigh.

"We are happy as we are," Elena was saying, but she fiddled with the long string of pink pearls at her neck nervously. "In fact, I've never been happier. My entire family is living in the same city for the first time in years."

Seamus wasn't here, but he had long ago ceased to exist for us, so I guess our father's absence didn't really matter. Still, Elena's increasing insincerity made me uncomfortable, and my fidgeting brought Mr. Paulson's attention to me.

"Family is the most important thing in a person's life, I've come to realize. My wife is the most important person in my life. Are you married, young woman?"

I bristled slightly at his condescension but hid it behind a flashy smile. "I am not."

"And you?"

Sebastian laughed. "Happily single."

Mr. Paulson's disapproving frown was nowhere near the magnitude of Elena's glare. A sharp prickle of foreboding lanced my spine.

"Companionship is the greatest treasure in life," he said.

Sebastian's answering grin was glorious. "I assure you, Mr. Paulson, I do not lack for companionship."

The older man's face twisted with disgust. "*True* companionship is about loyalty and commitment. It does not come and go as the changing of the tide."

"Not the best analogy," Seb winced theatrically. "The waves always kiss the shore."

The two men stared at each other, but I couldn't take my eyes off Elena, whose lips were so pursed that I wondered if they would produce a diamond if I put coal between them.

"Paulson, I see you've met Giselle and Sebastian," Sinclair said as he stepped slightly in front of Sebastian to shake the businessman's hand.

I hid my smile behind my hand as my brother glowered at the back of Sin's head.

"Yes, yes, it's good of you to bring your fiancée's family to an event like this. It's important to have your support system beside you," Paulson said with a broad smile that brought out surprisingly charming dimples in his cheeks.

He was definitely a man stuck in the 1950s, but he did seem to genuinely like Sinclair.

"Fiancée," Sinclair murmured softly.

Elena fidgeted nervously, and it was obvious that I wasn't the only one who knew he spoke quietly when he was upset.

Paulson was pleasantly oblivious. "Yes, yes, though I have to say you're making it an awfully long engagement. I had my wife at the altar before she could change her mind, let me tell you." He guffawed.

Sinclair smiled slightly, but when Elena placed a hand on his arm, his entire body stiffened.

"Pauly, please don't tell me you are embarrassing me again," a surprisingly young woman protested in a brassy Brooklyn accent.

Mrs. Paulson was maybe forty, at least fifteen years younger than her husband, with long dark permed hair and acrylic nails painted a vivid red that matched her lipstick. Though her dress was the same demure silver as her husband's suit, it was obvious that she was rough around the edges and not born into the same blue blood stock as most of the other guests in the room. I instantly liked her.

"Never," Paulson assured her with a dramatic wink before introducing Teresa to the rest of us.

I watched him tuck her firmly into his side, how she placed her hand over his heart as if it was meant to be there. I sighed, long and gustily, before I could help it. Seb elbowed me gently, and I realized that she was saying something to me.

"Excuse me?"

"You're Giselle Moore, the artist," she repeated, her brown eyes wide with excitement. "Sinclair told me how wonderful you were, and I just had to look you up. I would be over the moon if you'd do a commission for Pauly and me."

I really didn't have the time with the showcase coming up, but I understood how much it would mean to Sinclair to make the couple happy, and I was delighted he had taken the time to mention me to them.

"I would be honored. Thank you, Mrs. Paulson."

Her laugh was brassy, and I thought, awesome. "Terry, please. We must be on familiar terms if you are going to paint me."

Elena hid her smile behind her hand, and even though it was studied to look like a subtle gesture, it drew the eye of everyone in our little group.

"Is something funny?" Terry asked.

My sister waved her hand airily. "It's nothing really."

But I recognized the sharp edges in that lady-like smile, and my stomach cramped because I knew what was coming.

"No really, what is it?"

Elena sighed. "If you really want to know, I just thought it was funny because Giselle's upcoming collection is a series of nudes."

The Paulsons both turned their heads to me in tandem. If I hadn't been about to vomit, it might have been kind of funny.

The men—Sebastian, Cage, and Sinclair—were all frowning at Elena with varying degrees of condemnation, but it was the latter who wrapped a strong hand around her wrist in warning.

She didn't heed it.

"Yes, I know, that was exactly my reaction at first. It might make more sense if you understand the theme. It's about sexual perversions," she explained as if *a* plus *b* equaled *c*.

"Elena," Sebastian gasped.

Cage just shook his head in disgust.

Mr. Paulson looked at me with unmitigated horror.

I had never seen Sinclair so still, his entire body as hard as marble with restraint. One more wrong word, one breath released the wrong way, and he would shatter into a terrifying fury.

Terry looked at me for a long time. I waited without breathing for her to berate me, to laugh, or even turn on her heel in disgust. But she just looked at me until I felt dizzy.

Then she did the most interesting thing.

She tilted her head to the side, squinted her eyes, and threw back her head in raucous, completely genuine laughter. No one moved an inch as she laughed and laughed and clapped her red-tipped hands.

"How wonderful! How does one paint sexual perversions? I imagine it's something like *Fifty Shades of Gray* but done in paint?" she said, laughter still bouncing through her speech. "I have to admit that I usually find art kind of"—her nose wrinkled adorably—"stodgy, but I could definitely sink my teeth into something like that, couldn't I, Pauly?"

To my shock and mild horror, Mr. Paulson blushed like a schoolboy and patted his wife on the arm. "I'm sure you could, darling."

"Tell me..." She leaned forward to stage whisper, "Would you be willing to paint me like that?"

It took me a few seconds to find my voice again, but I could feel Cage and Seb at my back like the warmth from a fire, and it filled me with confidence.

"I would be absolutely delighted. And to tell you the honest truth"—I leaned forward with my hand over my mouth, imitating her dramatics—"I think art can be pretty boring too."

Terry laughed. "My God, you are a treasure. I'm going to give you my card, and you, you amazing girl, are going to promise to call me no later than tomorrow to make an appointment with me."

"I promise," I said solemnly though my eyes sparkled back at her.

She nodded decisively and patted Mr. Paulson over the heart. "Good. Well, I'm sorry to pull my handsome husband away, but I fancy a dance before we get dragged into another business discussion, so if you don't mind?"

"Not at all," Sinclair said, inclining his head.

Terry laughed at him and actually reached up to pat his cheek. "So polite, Mr. Sinclair, but I see the trouble buttoned up under your coat."

She winked at me as Mr. Paulson said his goodbyes.

We were all quiet for a moment after they left before we turned on each other.

"Are you fucking kidding me, Elena?" Sebastian said, rounding on her with clenched fists.

"Me?" she asked, her eyes wide with faux sincerity. "What did I do wrong? In fact, I think Giselle should thank me. I just secured her a commission."

Even I gasped at that.

Sinclair dropped her arm as if it were a poisonous thing and looked down at her with cool censure. "Giselle's grace just secured her the commission, as well you know. You tried to make her feel little, *non*?"

Elena opened her mouth to protest, but Cage cut in, "Karma's a bitch, uh, Elena?"

Her lips pursed with delicate displeasure, but her eyes flashed as they swept over me, striking me with the force of a tiger's paw. I stepped back as pain radiated through my chest.

"Daniel, I really didn't mean anything by it." She looked up at him from under her lashes. It wasn't until that moment that fury took root in my heart. Was she really going to try to bamboozle him out of his anger?

I vibrated.

Cage put a hand on my arm to calm me. I was surprised when it helped a little.

"I don't care what you intended," I said before Sinclair could completely lose what little resolve he had left to keep calm. "Either way, it was a thoughtless thing to say. I am not painting sexual perversions, and if you feel that way about my work, please keep it to yourself or, at the very least, don't speak about it with potential patrons."

She stared at me with storm cloud eyes just a few shades darker than my own, and I stared right back. It was the first time I had really stood up to her passive-aggressiveness, and it felt scary but really good.

Finally, she gave a little nod and said, "I misspoke, I shouldn't have called them perversions, but I don't know the language of these things. Of course, Giselle, if you don't want me to speak about you, I won't."

It wasn't really an apology, but I nodded anyway before turning to Cage and Sebastian. "Well, I think we've had enough of tonight, don't you?"

Sebastian laughed softly and slung an arm over my shoulder. "Hell yeah."

"We'll see you Thursday for Thanksgiving, though," Elena reminded us sharply as we began to walk away.

"Oh goody," Sebastian murmured drolly, and we walked out laughing even though we had both left our hearts in the Four Seasons ballroom.

Chapter Eleven

My heart was beating like a mad thing in my chest, hammering against the ribbed walls almost painfully.

It was finally Tuesday.

Sure, it would probably be the last night I would ever spend with him, but I was grateful for the closure and maybe just the teeniest bit hopeful that it wouldn't be the end.

I smiled at my reflection, pleased to find the Giselle I had unearthed in Mexico smiling back at me. My entire day had been decadent, mostly thanks to Candy, who insisted on a girls' day at the spa. I had been steamed, plucked, manicured, pedicured and, for the first time in my life, waxed bare. I'd run my hands over the ultra-sensitive flesh as I pulled on my carefully selected lingerie—art nouveau-inspired high-waisted satin panties and a balconette that barely contained my breasts. My waves were brushed out until they gleamed, the usual mascara and blush was applied, and I had anointed my pulse points with lavender oil, knowing how much Sinclair enjoyed the scent on me.

It was fun to take a day to pamper myself, and it wasn't something I would have done even six months ago. So, I made a promise to myself that even if this was my last night with Sinclair, I wouldn't let it impact the positive changes his presence had made on me.

But I also promised myself that I wouldn't ruin the night with heaviness and questions, and even though I was so incandescently happy that I felt like I could float into space like a rising star, there was no accounting for how the night would evolve, and I wanted to be prepared.

I was just putting on some music after finally deciding between John Legend and Nora Jones when my phone vibrated violently and fell off the kitchen counter.

"Hello?"

"I'm sorry, I was so nervous I had to call! Is he there yet?" Candy's voice chirped through the phone as if she was yelling in my ear.

"Obviously not, or I wouldn't have answered."

"Right." She paused sagely. "So, what's up?"

"Candy!" I laughed. "Why are you bothering me?"

"Oh come on, it's not like you don't need the distraction. He isn't due for another fifteen minutes, and don't you dare tell me you haven't already fluffed the pillows, plumped up the girls, and turned on some sultry tunes. I bet you're practically itching with restless anticipation."

She wasn't wrong, so I sighed and flopped down on the mahogany leather loveseat in the living room with a clear view of the door.

"I fluffed the pillows twice actually."

She snorted. "I don't doubt it. This is your big chance to show him that you're the right choice. It's a pretty big deal."

I hummed into the phone, but a niggling question kept popping into my head. "Candy? How do *you* know I'm the right choice? I don't even know if I believe that."

"Oh, Elle, I know your naïvety is part of your wonderful charm, but I do wish you could see yourself the way other people do. You are, I don't know," she huffed, "lovely. Just natural and kind and charming. Everything that Sinclair has a hard time emulating."

It was my turn to snort. "I've completely fucked up his life."

"Well, yeah, that too," she agreed cheerfully. "But in a good way."

"This conversation is giving me a headache."

"Really? I think it will be the highlight of my night."

"Maybe we should spend more time talking about your love life then." I paused. "I saw you dancing with Cage at the gala."

There was a long stretch of silence. I stared at my pale lavender manicure while I waited.

"That's an entirely different can of worms," she said finally. "Don't get me wrong, I'm fantastic. But Cage is going to be an American rock star, and he will never think of me as anything besides Candy Kay, Sinclair's trusty sidekick."

I wanted to argue with her, but the thing was, I didn't want to lie either, and I wasn't sure if Cage ever *would* see Candy in a romantic light. Truthfully, I had seen him look at Elena with more passion than he had ever expressed with Candy.

"Wow, now that I've finished being a Debbie Downer, tell me what you're wearing."

I almost choked on my laughter. "You helped me pick them out this afternoon!"

"Right, damn. Okay, you are officially no fun. I'm going to get back to my riveting night of Netflix binge-watching and rabid popcorn eating."

"What show is it tonight?" I asked through my chuckle.

"The new season of *Succession*. Is it wrong that I think Logan Roy is a total hunk?"

"Cage *and* Logan Roy? You have eclectic taste. I'll give you that."

She snorted. "Yours is better."

A brisk knock on the door struck my heart into a staccato beat. I jumped up from the couch and was halfway to the door before I realized I was still on with Candy.

"It is," I agreed, already beaming as I hung up and swung open the red door.

Sinclair was smiling too. My favorite smile, the one that curved his cheeks and broke the ice in his blue eyes so that they flooded with warmth. We stood staring at each other like that for a long time, and even though I felt stupid just standing there staring at the too-good-to-be-true man in front of me, I was too giddy to care because he was doing the exact same thing.

"Hi," I finally said, a little breathlessly.

"Hi." His grin deepened. "Are you going to invite me in?"

"Yes, of course." I blushed, which made him chuckle, which, of course, made me flush even further.

We had been alone together for thirty seconds, and it was already the best night of my life.

I stepped to the side as he moved into the apartment and inhaled deeply when he leaned forward to press a chaste kiss to my cheek. I pressed my hand to his chest, felt the beat beneath my splayed fingers, and grinned up into his face.

"Can I say that I'm so happy you're here?"

Sinclair's face was neutral again, perfectly held in repose more beautiful than Michelangelo's *David,* but his eyes gleamed with contentment.

"Only if I can say it back."

I tipped my head back and laughed. "God, that was cheesy."

One of his dark brows arched. "Oh, really?"

His hand slipped between my breasts, down my belly, and around to the base of my spine, where he flattened it and pulled me against his groin. I groaned when I felt the hard ridge of his erection against my belly.

"Is this cheesy?" he taunted before capturing my mouth in a deep kiss, his tongue sweeping past my lips in a way that made my knees buckle.

I didn't worry, though, because a second later, his hands were under my butt, lifting me into his arms. I wrapped my legs around his waist as he pushed me against the door, gasping against his lips when he ground his hips into me.

It took me a moment to reorient myself when he suddenly pulled away, setting me gently on my feet as he stepped back. I blinked at him, my swollen lips open over my panting breath.

His chuckle was deep, a frequency that made me shiver compulsively. "Don't fret, my siren." He brushed his cool thumb over my bottom lip. "We have time. We have all night."

"What?"

"We have all night," he repeated casually, but his lips twitched.

"Elena's out of town?"

His thumb dipped between my teeth and rested on my tongue. Automatically, I closed my lips over it and sucked. I watched his eyes darken and felt myself throb.

"We have all night," he said again.

My cheeks ached with the force of my grin, and even though I was desperate to touch him after weeks of careful avoidance, I didn't. There was still so much between us that if I pressed my hand to the gap stuck between us, I knew it would push fruitlessly against the clotted air. There were ways to cut through it, but most were so dangerous, so scary in ways both good and bad, that I didn't know how to take action.

So, I just stared at him with a dumb smile while I cataloged the fall of his dark hair over his forehead, barely red in the low light of the entryway, and the way his tailored Oxford blue button-down conformed to the honed muscles underneath. He stood with both hands in his pockets, fists clenched, and even though his face was as implacable as always, I knew that tell. He wanted to claim me just as badly as I needed to be taken by him. He could have been hesitating for so many reasons, but I hoped it was because he feared that he'd lose his eternal control.

I looked at the floor, happy that my hair fell forward to cover my suddenly shy smile. "Can I take your coat?"

He slipped out of the heavy black coat and handed it to me without letting our fingers brush. My heart was beating strangely, sliding and skipping over beats in my chest. I was breathing erratically, too, in anticipation.

Sinclair toed off his beautiful leather loafers, and on some strange impulse, I ducked down to grab them, thinking to put them in the closet with the rest of the shoes, but Sinclair's hand on the top of my head froze me in a crouch. My body hummed under his touch.

"What are you doing?" His voice was liquid, and when I looked up into his face, it was taut with desire.

I swallowed convulsively. "I thought I would put your shoes away." I laughed nervously. "I actually don't have a clue."

"I have to disagree with you on that. You seem to know exactly what you're doing."

My heart clipped briskly against my ribs, and I licked my lips, wondering if maybe I did know what I was doing. If I had subconsciously known how being on my knees before him would affect him. I shifted from my crouch to my knees and sat down on my heels, spreading my legs slightly and placing my hands demurely before me. My heart beat so quickly it fluttered, a hummingbird knocking on my pulse points. My hair fell in a soft curtain around my face as I tilted my gaze to the floor. I knew how I looked sitting like that because I had practiced the traditional submissive pose in the mirror in preparation for tonight.

It was astonishing to me that I could enjoy being so bold, taunting him as I just had, yet so deeply crave my submission to him. Six months ago, I hadn't known anything beyond the bounds of sexual abuse and timid sexuality. Now, I felt like a live wire, still beneath the plastic coating but always thrumming with a vibrant sensuality.

His sharp intake of breath filled me with triumph.

"Yes, siren, I think you know exactly what you are doing."

His hand slipped from the top of my head, down the side of my cheek to grasp my chin and raise it gently to meet his gaze. "I am in a shockingly good mood, so I am going to give you a choice. You can get up, hang up my coat, and lead me into the kitchen where we can continue the night as if we were on our first real date, with all the sweetness and awkwardness that accompanies that..." He paused, and his eyes glittered as his hand sank deep into my hair to tilt my head back almost brutally. "Or you can take me between those sweet lips like you've been wanting to do for weeks. I think you missed pleasing me almost more than I missed the feel of your wet mouth around my cock."

I moaned, both shocked and overwhelmed by his words. My body was already changing, my muscles melting into pliability, ready to mold themselves into whatever position he desired. Saliva flooded my mouth, moisture pooled between my legs, and my nipples furled atop my heavy breasts. In two sentences, Sinclair had turned me on more than anything else ever had.

"Tell me what you want."

I wanted to moan again, but I knew he loved the words. "I want you in my mouth."

"Who do you want me to be?"

I opened my mouth to ask what he meant, but one look in his eyes showed me the dominant caged there, yearning for release even as he gave me the keys to the lock.

I hadn't planned on starting the evening this way, but I should have known we wouldn't be able to resist. It had been too long since our last night together, and even though we had only ever been together sexually for one week, my body was trained to respond to his like this. More than that, I wanted his dominance and control because they were intrinsically married to *my* power and pleasure.

"You," I said firmly. "My Sinclair."

His hand clenched in my hair, and his nostrils flared as the Dom was unleashed. "Very well. Clasp your hands behind your back. You may only use your mouth."

I threaded my fingers together at the base of my spine obediently while he undid the buckle of his leather belt and lowered his zipper. I was already panting. The rough sound of the zipper was like a physical caress against my overheated flesh, and I shuddered when his hand disappeared within his loosened slacks to reappear with my prize.

He was already magnificently hard. The sight of his swollen flesh within his fist, slowly stroking, made me whimper.

"So eager," he murmured. "I've dreamed of you, Elle, exactly like this. I love knowing that I put that flush on your creamy skin, that you're wet just sitting like that for me, waiting for me to touch you. I love knowing that even this"—his fingers trailed from the edge of my jaw to the hollow of my collarbone—"turns you on. You want me with every breath you take."

He stepped closer until he was almost brushing my lips. A bead of moisture adorned his crown, and I licked my lips unconsciously. My tongue caught the edge of his flesh, the salty taste of his skin making me moan. He brushed the tip of his erection against my open lips, painting them with his arousal like lipstick. When I tried to take him into my mouth, he pulled back, stroking himself faster but still in control.

"Please," I breathed, embarrassed by my supplication until I saw his hand stutter mid-movement.

He stopped stroking, letting his hands fall to his sides so that I could take control of his pleasure. I let out a breathy little sigh and nuzzled the hot flesh with my cheek. I drew my nose down his long length before taking one of his silky balls into my mouth. I rolled my tongue around it, humming with pleasure as I did so.

My sex was dripping down my open thighs to the cold floor beneath my knees, and the front door to my apartment was still slightly open two feet behind me. Someone could catch me like that, wanton and exposed.

"Anyone could come in and find you like this," Sinclair rasped, reading my mind as only he could. His hands threaded through my hair, pulling slightly but not manipulating the movement of my lips across his shaft. "But you wouldn't stop, would you?"

I groaned deeply, taking him between my lips to the very back of my throat in answer.

His hands tightened in my hair, forcibly pulling me off his cock with a popping sound so that I had no choice but to look up at him from a painful angle. He was so tall, towering over me with a dark gleam in his eyes that thrilled me.

"I want you to get up and go into the kitchen. Take off all of your clothes and wait for me in front of the balcony doors," he directed, his clipped, cool words trailing across my skin like ice.

I hesitated, old habits overriding my instinctive desire to obey.

"You wanted *your* Sinclair, Elle," he reminded me. "You only have to say stop to make it all end."

My gut clenched at the thought of it ending, of him leaving. I needed this, his dominance, almost as much as I needed his love.

"Yes, sir," I murmured, lowering my gaze respectfully.

His hands pulsed in my hair at my submissive gesture before he let go.

Without another word, I scrambled to my feet and headed into the kitchen. I quickly shucked my clothes, leaving them in a messy pile, and positioned myself before the doors with my head lowered and my hands lightly clasped, my bare back to the kitchen behind me.

I became absorbed in the soft colors of the setting sun melting like candle wax between the iron spikes of the city skyline. The contrast reminded me of Sinclair and me, the soft with the hard, the warm and the cold. So opposite but so perfectly matched.

I didn't know how long I was zoned out for, standing nearly pressed to the cool glass, but I startled when Sinclair's hands skimmed down my arms.

"Trust me."

He wasn't asking, but I had the power to say no, and it was a heady realization.

"Always."

"If you want me to stop, you need a safe word."

I'd thought about that while I had been researching the ins and outs of submissive life. I wasn't sure I liked the idea of a safe word. It seemed almost like a prenuptial agreement; it took the edge out of the scene and created a different sort of tension. Would he go far enough for me to have to use it? Would I break his trust by uttering it in a moment of knee-jerk panic before I could adjust to the boundaries he pushed me past? But I knew the serious necessity of it, and I was ready with an answer I hoped would please him.

"Heartbeat."

There was a question in the way he stilled behind me.

"Because even if I need you to stop, you'll still own me. When we're like this, you own every beat of my heart."

"My siren," he breathed, planting a delicate kiss on my neck to express his pleasure with me. "You are a constant delight to me but..." He shifted behind me, firm and tall once again. "I am in the mood to punish you."

I shivered as he raised my arms in front of me and stepped flush against my back, reaching around with a long red scarf to competently bind my hands together. Once I was secured, he looped the end of the fabric over the curtain rod above the doors, jerking it twice to check its stability, before securing it once more to my tied hands. He stepped back, giving me room to test the bonds. I found that even though I couldn't lower my arms, I could move side to side.

"Legs apart," he said even as his knee slipped between my thighs and forced them open.

I sighed when his hands came around to cup my breasts, pressing the nipples firmly between his fingers until they burned. Too quickly, he moved on, smoothing his palms over my soft belly, around to the firm flare of my hips, and to the inside of my thighs. His chin rested on my shoulder, his lips against my pulse.

"You've tortured me. Having this body so close but unable to touch you"—his lips parted, and his tongue swept over my skin—"has been agony."

He pushed on the inside of my thighs until I spread them even wider, my muscles burning with the effort. I could feel my arousal trickle down one thigh and shivered.

"Did you mean to do that to me, siren? Did you wear those short skirts and lick your pouty mouth knowing how hard it would make me?"

He trailed his fingers in my wetness, running them back and forth like laps in a swimming pool. I throbbed for him, greedily sucking at his finger as he dipped one inside me. He circled my opening and then thrust to his first knuckle, repeating the movement over and over again until I was a panting mess, writhing in my bonds.

"Hush," he demanded. "Stay completely still and do not make a sound."

One hand continued its excruciating rhythm on my sex while the other disappeared beyond my vision. Two seconds later, both hands were on my breasts, smearing my wetness across my nipples and rolling them brutally between his fingers.

"You have gorgeous breasts," he said. "So responsive to the simplest touch."

He flicked one nipple and then the other, making me gasp despite my vow of silence. His dark chuckle stirred my hair. "Don't make a sound."

My body screamed when he snapped two clothespins over my already aching nipples. I wanted to buck and moan wildly at the intense sensation, but I wanted to please Sinclair even more. I bit my lip until it pulsed with pain. I needed to be in control of myself just as much as Sinclair was if I wanted to be his sub. This was my audition; this was what I had been planning for since the gala. There was no way in hell I was going to be anything less than perfect.

"Good girl," he murmured. "Do you like being displayed like this for me and for anyone with the good fortune to look out the window across from us?"

I focused on the buildings across the way, on the sliver of sunlight fading slowly over the horizon, and I shivered. The idea of someone watching us made me flush with pleasure.

"You have to be punished for being such a tease, and I can make your body sing in so many sweet ways." His hand lifted and came slapping down over my core, the other arm already wrapped around my belly to hold me up when my knees wobbled.

He circled my opening and then entered me to his first knuckle, repeating the movement over and over again until I was a panting mess, writhing in my bonds.

"Hush," he demanded.

He swatted my heat again, harder this time, jiggling my clamped breasts. I bit off a whimper.

"I said, quiet," he warned.

He slapped me again, and the force radiated through me. I was so close to the edge, my toes on its very precipice, but I had nothing to rub against, no voice to beg with, no power to do anything but accept the pleasure Sinclair doled out to me.

His hands left me for only a second, but I immediately missed the contact, my body bowing uncomfortably in an effort to follow his touch.

"I'm going to taste you now, but remember you are being punished. You are not permitted to come, and if you do so without my permission..." He trailed off, and I knew enough to fill in the blanks.

If I hadn't wanted to impress him so much, I might have orgasmed on purpose just to see what kind of punishment I would get.

His cool lips fluttered over the inside of my damp thighs, traveling gentle as a breeze to my center and over to the other thigh, where he bit down firmly on the flesh. I groaned loudly and was rewarded with a slap on the ass.

"Quiet," Sin said and then blew cool air across my sex.

His tongue lapped at me carefully, following my folds like a cartographer, and when my knees grew weak, he placed them over his shoulders so that I was practically sitting on him. The sensation of being suspended, reliant on Sinclair for my balance and my ultimate release, was so arousing that I was sweating and grinding my teeth after only thirty seconds to keep from orgasming without his consent.

"Please," I panted finally, as pins and needles of painful pleasure assaulted my body.

Instead of answering me, he grasped my bottom tightly in both hands and pressed me closer to his mouth. My legs started to shake as I was wracked with pleasure and a scream gathered speed, collecting in my gut and surging through my lungs.

"That's right, siren," Sinclair said against the inside of my thigh. "Let go. Show me how much you missed me."

I was so grateful for his permission that I could have kissed him. But my body reacted before my brain, seizing my pleasure and ripping it from the seams of my body until I spilled open, achingly exposed. I only noticed that I was sobbing when Sinclair stole my breath with a demanding kiss and entered me in one fluid motion. He caught my gasp between his lips, biting my lip and angling his hips as he pumped into me. I tried to lock my legs around his waist, but he held them up and out, stretching me until I could feel the delicious burn between my legs.

"The world is watching, Elle," he panted against my damp neck. My aching sex clenched hard in another brutal orgasm, or maybe the first one had never stopped.

He growled and bit firmly into the base of my neck as he came inside me. I couldn't see his face, but I could sense the impression of it on my closed lids like the imprint of sunlight, glowing so brilliantly it left a scar on my retinas.

Chapter Twelve

I WAS GLAD I HAD PLANNED A COLD SUPPER BECAUSE IT WAS AFTER MIDNIGHT before we dragged ourselves from bed—where we ended up after the kitchen—to refuel. Sinclair carried me to one of the barstools and retrieved a blanket from the living room to wrap around my naked shoulders so that I wouldn't be cold. I watched him silently as he moved through the kitchen in only his black boxer briefs, collecting the gazpacho I had made that afternoon, the skewers of prosciutto-wrapped melon, a bundle of deep red grapes, a baguette, and a gorgeous round of Camembert cheese. His brow was wrinkled in concentration as he arranged everything on two large platters, and he frowned further when I laughed at him.

"Yes?"

I covered my mouth with a hand and said, "I won't judge you on presentation, Sin."

He shrugged, but I caught the sparkles in his eyes before he lowered them back to the work at hand. "You are an artist. Of course you will judge me on presentation."

I tucked my tongue into my cheek and gave his half-nude form a lascivious once-over. "Trust me, baby, it's an A plus every time."

He blinked at me before laughing freely, tipping his golden throat back to bark at the ceiling. I smiled, too, and leaned forward to watch him.

"You make a man feel like a god."

"You are one."

His eyebrows slammed down, and he leaned against the counter to cross his arms and stare at me disapprovingly. I knew it shouldn't have, but that look always made me wet.

"Don't put me on a pedestal. I don't belong up there."

"I didn't say you were a god to everyone, Sinclair. Just to me," I amended.

"After what I just did to you, I'm surprised you would equate me with anything so holy."

My body tingled with the imprints of his lips, teeth, hands, and cock. Even against the softness of the bed our second time around, the sex had been rough, two animals locked in heat and only conquered by the eventual need to sustain themselves on something other than flesh.

He took the plates in hand and placed them at the small table beside the little balcony. I followed with a nearly empty bottle of crisp Pinot Grigio.

"I don't think there is anything really dirty about what we do together," I admitted as I popped a grape between my lips. "It's honest and sometimes a bit brutal, but I think that is what makes it special."

"You are very poetic."

I frowned and leaned forward over the table to accept a grape from Sinclair's fingers. "It doesn't make what I'm saying any less true."

"No, I suppose you're right. It's been a long time since I heard anyone speak about BDSM like that." He looked out into the brightly lit nightscape; the glimmer of red and white lights highlighted his puckered forehead and soured mouth.

"When did you start experimenting with it?" I asked, unsure if I was phrasing the question in an insulting way.

His lips twisted, and for a moment, I wasn't sure if he was going to say anything.

"I've always had the desire to control. A number of therapists have surmised that it has everything to do with being powerless as an orphan and then under the thumb of very authoritarian foster parents." He rolled his eyes, illustrating how little he thought of their theory. "The truth is much simpler, and it might offend you. I have always had the desire to control, to manipulate and weld the will of others into forms of my own making. BDSM is the physical manifestation of those desires."

"That sounds very super villainy," I admitted.

His small smile surprised me. "On the contrary, I believe it to be soothing. As the Dom, it's my responsibility to provide exactly what my sub needs, even if they are unconscious of those desires. It is about finding the balance, that golden edge between pain and pleasure, reluctance and desire. Love and hate. It is on that fine line between those extremes that I might find the true you, the one that no one but me will ever see."

"You already have that."

"No, I don't." He smiled that small, warped smile that I hated so much. "Only when you really belong to me can I know you like that."

Silence descended, but it wasn't uncomfortable. These moments were inevitable between us, I thought, because there were so many dead ends in a conversation where the future was not to be discussed or changed. If I was a different person, better maybe or worse, I would have used the moment to tell him that I wanted to belong to him more than I wanted my next breath.

Instead, I slid my hand over his lightly, pulling his attention back to me. "Tell me what it would be like if we were in an actual relationship type thing."

Despite myself, I blushed at the thought of discussing such things, and despite the dark, Sinclair could see that.

"You can beg me to make you come, but you can't actually say the words Dominant and submissive?" he asked.

I shrugged and spooned a helping of gazpacho into my mouth so that I wouldn't really have to answer.

His eyes crinkled with suppressed mirth, but he sat back in his chair and studied me thoughtfully. I loved that about him—how he took everything I gave him and mulled over it as if I was special, important, and worth consideration.

"Alright, Elle, why don't we start with the basics? There are different D/s relationships with varying degrees of control. On one end of the spectrum, there are the slaves and Masters. A slave is expected to obey commands at all times, to be controlled in all aspects of his or her life by the Master."

"That sounds horrible," I said. The honesty burst from my lips like the grape between my teeth.

Sinclair chuckled easily, and I loved that I could coax that from him. "I think we can safely rule out that kind of relationship. I have no desire to control your life." He reached across the table to run two calloused fingers along my jaw. "Not when you live so beautifully."

"Now who's poetic?" I said softly.

His eyes darkened to wet blue velvet, and I gasped when his fingers tightened on my chin. "Submission is poetic too. Get on your knees, siren."

I was sliding out of my chair before I had even fully absorbed his words.

"Come closer."

I hesitated. My inclination was to stand and walk over, but I knew what a real submissive would do, and the idea of crawling to him lit a fire in my belly. I kept my eyes on the ground as I moved forward on my hands and knees, ass swaying.

When I settled at his side, he spoke again. "This is something we might do in a real relationship. I might have you eat at my feet, only by my hand."

His fingers appeared in my lowered line of sight with a purple grape in his grasp. I immediately parted my lips and tilted my head back to receive the morsel, taking care to swipe my tongue against his skin as he fed me.

"Behave," he warned mildly before continuing in an almost bored tone. "There would be rules, of course."

He waited, but I had the feeling I wasn't supposed to respond.

I could hear the smile in his voice when he finally said, "Exactly. You would not speak unless expressly ordered to, and when you did, how do you think you would address me?"

"With appropriate respect, sir," I said.

My voice was breathy, and he hadn't even touched me.

"Very good. I cannot count the things I want to do to you, not least of all because you would blush to your toes to hear me give voice to them."

I could feel that full-bodied blush, how my blood ricocheted through my veins and my heart knocked brutally against my ribs. Idly, I worried about heart failure.

"Please, tell me," I whispered hoarsely because I was so filled with desire that even my throat was swollen with it.

He studied me dispassionately for what felt like a long time. The more his gaze cooled, the warmer I grew. I couldn't think when he looked at me like that, not of Elena or the stress of my upcoming showcase, not of my lifelong insecurities or even my own name. When Sinclair looked at me with those aloof and commanding eyes the color of lightning, my very soul felt electrified.

Finally, he stood, so close to me that my nose was pressed into the inside of his lower thigh. I breathed deeply, so intoxicated by his smoky, masculine scent that I almost felt high.

His hand lowered heavily to the top of my head, and he said, "I would rather show you."

I let out a breathy little sigh before I could help myself. His hand slid over my crown and threaded through my hair, pulling firmly at the roots until pain prickled deliciously down my spine. My back arched to release some of the tension. Slowly, he tugged my head back until I was looking up at him. With his other hand, he placed his thumb on my bottom lip, rubbing back and forth until my mouth blossomed open under his touch.

He was so masterfully made, his features so perfectly chiseled that they were almost brutal to look upon, especially now when he loomed over me like the statue of a god.

My God. Oh, how I wanted to devote myself to him, venerate him with everything I had.

I swept my tongue along the ridge of his thumb, staring into his eyes through my eyelashes as I daringly took him into my mouth and scraped my teeth across the pad of his digit. His eyes flared.

"This lifestyle is not always about pain and restraint," he explained. "It is about worship."

His ability to read my mind no longer surprised me.

"I worship you," I breathed.

He pulled his thumb from my mouth and drew two fingers tenderly down my cheek before saying, "And I you."

Without another word, he reached down to pull me into his arms. Cradled securely against his chest, I let myself listen to the beat of his heart as he led me into the bedroom and gently laid me on the bed. Languidly, I watched as he went into the bathroom, re-emerging with a bottle of lavender-scented massage oil and the same red scarf he had bound me with earlier. Warmth pooled between my legs just at the sight of it.

I studied him silently as he straddled my prone body on the bed and blindfolded me by gently secured the fabric around my head. I gasped in disappointment when his body left mine once more, but he returned to me quickly after plugging his phone into the music system. Glass Animal's "Toes" beat sexily from the speakers.

"This is about you, my siren. I control you to discover you, to unlock the secrets of your heart and the hidden desires in that brilliant mind of yours." His voice was as smooth and warm as the massage oil he heated between his palms and applied to my shoulders.

I hummed with pleasure as he began to knead my neck and chest, my mind empty of everything but the exquisite pressure of his hands against my skin. His fingers moved down my arms to my very fingertips, where he released an uncanny amount of tension just by pinching the pads of each digit. After working his way from my stomach to the bottom of my feet, he tenderly rolled me onto my stomach and began to caress my back.

A moan built deep in my gut. It was in no way a sexual massage, but I felt restless with desire nonetheless. Each press of his strong fingers into my muscles molded me further and further into a creature of his own making, as supple and easily manipulated as clay beneath his touch.

I was mindless, made only of sensation by the time his thumb found the pronounced curve of my bottom. He pressed hard into the muscles there, almost painfully so that I sucked air between my teeth. I wasn't sure where the massage oil ended and my own wetness began.

"On your knees."

His voice slithered into my subconscious. I raised my heavy body as quickly as I could, tucking my knees underneath me, arching my back so that my ass was raised with my hands grasping my ankles and my face pressed into the sheets. Cool air drifted deliciously over my overheated flesh.

The slow, arousing massage continued, but this time, it was punctuated by the sound of his cool voice washing over me. "I remember the first time you displayed your pussy like this for me. You were so wet." His thumbs dipped down the crease and pulled apart my lips to expose my wet, pink core. "I could smell you from across the room."

I groaned softly into the bed and wriggled, desperate for more stimulation.

He punished me with a swift, brutal spank that left my skin singing out for mercy. His hand squeezed the smarting skin, clenching it under his strong grip until I whimpered.

"I wanted to punish you just like this for bewitching me."

Another painful slap, my skin even more sensitive under the sheen of oil.

"I wanted to take this perfectly plump ass in my hands, warm these cheeks, and spread them open for my tongue."

I tensed in anticipation as he spanked me twice more, harder than before, and slowly spread my burning cheeks so that my most forbidden place was exposed to his gaze. His thumbs commenced their massage over my abused flesh.

I shuddered when his hot breath wafted over my center. "I'm going to take your ass, Elle. Would you like that?"

My answer was the bestial groan he wrought from me as his hot, velvet tongue stroked heavily over my asshole. I shuddered at the depth of pleasure, the heat of my embarrassment only providing further kindling for the fire raging inside me.

He slapped my ass again. "Use your words, siren."

"Yes, sir," I breathed.

"Yes, sir, what?"

"Yes, sir, I want you to take my ass."

Saying the words out loud set my oiled skin aflame. I wasn't mortified. I was desperate. Desperate to show him how much I could take, how eager I was to be physically and emotionally splayed open before him, used by him.

His finger slowly followed the track of my wetness from the inside of my knee to its source at my center.

"So wet for me."

"Yes," I hissed, locking my knees to keep from rocking back against his gently questing fingers.

I needed more. My tender flesh missed the pain; my mind craved debasement.

"Please, sir," I begged.

His tongue was back at the tightly furled entrance between my cheeks. He circled my opening languidly, his hands roughly suppressing the undulation of my hips.

I wanted to buck back at him like a bitch in heat, howl at the sky, force Sinclair to break his control and take me like an animal. Instead, he enforced my stillness, my silence, and caged the sensations roiling through me, heightening them until I was a churning mess of incoherent need.

"You've done this before," he reminded me, and I was momentarily surprised he remembered that. "But you've never had me here." His thumb firmly circled my anus before plunging inside. "No one will ever own this ass but me."

The tightly knotted mass of shame that had lain at the core of my psyche since the moment Christopher had initiated contact with me began to unravel. With the mental release came a flash of gut-wrenching memories; Christopher's pale hands as they coaxed me onto the bed, his casual suggestions that I might please him as payment for his kindness to my family and his sincere promise to keep my "virginity" intact. He was never physically forceful, but his emotional manipulation of my teenage self had been perfectly calculated.

Goose flesh rippled across my skin, and I pressed my teary eyes harder into the bedsheets until the scent of Sinclair and me, of our intimacy, killed the images like mustard gas.

I gasped as Sinclair pushed forward with two fingers, pumping and twisting them firmly inside me. It was so decadent, these dual feelings of fullness and taboo, that I was drunk from it.

Sin's hand pressed hard on the base of my spine so that my bottom was steeply arched into the air.

"What are you thinking of, siren?"

His fingers inside me, stretching. His smoky scent braided with the smell of lavender, the smell of me. His words saturated every conscious thought so that they fell into a heavy sleep, and I was only my body.

"You," I said.

"Yes, me. When we are together, you only think of me."

"Even when we aren't."

He swatted me again.

"Who is in this room? Only you and me, Sinclair and Elle. A Dom and his sub." His voice lowered dangerously, and his touch left me. I felt his absence more painfully than any spanking. "I will ask you again. What are you thinking of?"

"You, only you." I jerked my hips back at him. "Always you."

His hands were back on my ass, powerfully clenching and pulling them apart to make way for his cock. He nudged my slicked opening and paused.

"I could own you, all of you."

"Yes."

The head of his cock slid slowly, only an inch, inside me.

"Do you know how I know that?" he asked, his voice softer now, smoother than the hand that stroked down my back as he pushed farther inside me. "I know because you own *me*, my siren."

I buried my face in the blanket and groaned raggedly as he seated himself fully inside me. The pain was like a heated blade cutting through me, and my bottom was raw from the spanking. I was surprised by how much I liked the pain, loved how it unlocked my mind and sent it reeling into velvety darkness. Loved that it was Sinclair in this most private part of me. The feeling was so intense that I wanted to wriggle away from it, but each undulation of my ass only pressed him further against me.

"Ah," I said, chasing after each elusive breath.

"Hush."

His hands were all over my skin, soothing away my restlessness by lighting fire to my nipples with firm twists and tugs, dipping into my drenched sex to pinch my clit. After endless minutes, he rooted one hand in my hair and tugged until my neck was craned back, and he was hunched over me with his tongue on my ear.

"I'm going to fuck you now. I expect you to ask permission before you come."

I didn't know if I could orgasm like that, but I held back my concern.

His hands rubbed roughly over my ass, reawakening the ache there. "You can, and you will come for me like this."

The first sinuous glide of his cock leaving my body was strange and wonderful, and as he began to saw in and out of me at an infuriatingly slow pace, my clit began to throb like a strobe light.

The calloused fingers of one hand plucked at my nipples while the other flattened across my stomach and urged me to sit back against his thighs. I whimpered and moaned, ugly little animal sounds as I churned up and down, grinding and bucking in any way I could to relieve the ache swelling uncomfortably inside me.

"Ah, Sinclair," I begged, unable to speak but desperate to convey how much I needed more, more, more.

He turned my head, fusing his mouth over mine to absorb my cries into himself as his fingers grew cruel against my breasts and his hips jutted punishingly against mine. I screamed against his lips as his hand slid lower and rhythmically pinched my clit to the beat of his savage strokes.

I tore my lips from his, the separation painful as if Velcro secured us. "Please, let me come."

He hummed but continued the torment.

"Please, please."

His mouth found my ear, nibbling at the lobe before his tongue slid down my salty neck. His voice filled me like a second cock. "What are you thinking about, siren?"

The feel of his sweat-slicked skin against mine, the powerful clench of his hands on my hips, the sound of our bodies slapping and panting... Him, him, *him*.

"You."

"Yes," he hissed, and three of his fingers plunged into my sex. "Come for me."

I had never been so happy to obey anyone in my life.

Chapter Thirteen

I'D NEVER HAD A VISION OF THE KIND OF MAN I MIGHT FALL IN LOVE WITH.

My sisters always had. Cosima imagined herself with an Italian, someone who worked with their hands and came home smelling of earth and wine. They would love passionately and fight passionately and have a brood of gorgeous children who constantly got underfoot. I had yet to see her with such a man, but I knew she kept that dream sewn into the lining of her soul.

Elena's prince was a little more typical and a whole lot more modern. She didn't want to be treated like the timeless woman the way Cosima did, like a sexual creature and a domestic goddess. Elena wanted a relationship of equals, a partnership that afforded her individual power and independence. Her man was eloquent, elegantly opinionated, and urbane.

And technically, that man stood before me right now, his lean back gold and black in the acidic sunlight streaming in through the windows of Cosima's kitchen. He was Elena's ideal; smart, classy, and eternally composed. Hell, he even wore three-piece suits on a daily basis. They were practically made for each other.

Yet I was watching a completely different man cook me breakfast. There was boyishness in the chestnut hair flopping over his forehead and gentle humor in the way he rolled his shoulders to the beat of Meghan Trainor's "All About That Bass." He had laughed when I blasted it from the speakers, shaking my booty so that the bare skin winked at him from under the tail of his dress shirt. I could count the number of times I had heard Sinclair laugh on my fingers, but this was the best yet because he kept laughing as he reached out to tug me into his arms. I smiled into my coffee at the memory.

This man, the kind that only laughed at the really good stuff and looked at me with a heady mixture of authority and awe, was *my* kind of man.

"I better be the reason behind that gorgeous smile, siren."

I looked up to see him looking at me, his electric eyes sparking with mirth even though his lips remained smooth and impassive.

I shrugged one shoulder as he slid a plate laden with bacon and avocado studded scrambled eggs in front of me. "I wouldn't say that exactly."

His eyes narrowed. In less than a second, the soft Sinclair, the one with the boyish curl and the wide, almost awkward smile, was gone, and in his place was Sinclair the Dom. He wore his icy control like a king's mantle across his shoulders, and when he moved around the island to stand before me, the liquidity of his gait froze the air in my lungs.

He didn't touch me, but he might as well have. The thin slice of space between our bodies vibrated with palpable tension and set my body's rhythm to his like a tuning fork.

"What would you say then?" he said in that quiet voice that echoed through my entire body.

I swallowed hard before answering. "You're more than the reason behind one smile. You hold the lease on my happiness."

The tic in his jaw was the only sign of his shock. He stared at me for a long time, caging me against the island with his arms braced on either side of me.

"I want to *own* your happiness," he said, finally.

I sucked in so much air my lungs expanded to the point of pain.

"I want you to own me," I whispered.

We had never been this forthright, and even though it felt good, scary and good, *scary good*, I wasn't sure it was a good idea.

Sinclair shook his head, and a piece of his newly shorn hair fell across his forehead. My fingers itched to smooth it back, but I resisted because, despite our sexual proclivities, we didn't have the casual kind of intimacy that came from dating.

So instead, I watched the battle in his eyes as he fought between taking me right there on the stool and storming out of the apartment, never to return. Maybe it was overdramatic, but in a situation like ours, nothing was understated.

"I do," he said in a tight voice because there wasn't enough air in his lungs.

Hope—the scrappy kind that you fight for with every pounding beat of your heart—could leave you breathless like that.

I shook my head, mute with emotion, but he pressed a finger to my lips.

"I own you in the dark. The moment you turn off the lights, I own your thoughts and your body. I dictate your touch." His hand skimmed too lightly down the exposed skin between the panels of my shirt. "When you touch yourself, it is because I want you to. You're only echoing my thoughts in the dark, reading my will from across the city. So perfectly obedient. And after you come, my name on your sweet lips like a prayer, you'll dream of me because the entire night is ours, and I won't give you up for one second of it."

I was hot and cold with arousal, but tears still pressed at my eyes. "I'll still wake up alone."

His eyes softened, and the hand that had been tickling the upper swell of my breasts moved up to take a firm hold at the base of my neck. It was almost scary how both actions brought me utter calm.

"Greedy girl," he teased, but when I didn't smile, his grip flexed tight. "There isn't much more of me to take."

Only the part of you in Elena's grip, I thought. But even that poignant reminder didn't hold the same weight as it had as little as two weeks ago. I was turning into a different kind of person, one who didn't care about the consequences of my desires. I couldn't tell if it was a devolution or not. Only the fittest survive, and only those with the selfishness to go after their ambitions succeed.

"Your eggs are cold." He ducked down to press a kiss above his grip on my neck, right on my jumping pulse, before releasing me.

I stared down at the yellow curds without thinking while he cleaned up in the kitchen and came around to sit beside me with his own breakfast. His hand fell heavily onto my thigh, jerking me out of my trance, but when I looked up, he was focused on his tablet, rapidly reading and responding to a deluge of emails. The hand was a reminder of his authority, his presence lest I forget it, and it released me from my worries the way nothing else could.

Happily, I dug into my cold eggs.

We ate silently, and even when I squirmed to relieve the tension at my pleasantly raw core, he only had to squeeze my leg to relay his satisfaction with my discomfort and his will for me to sit still. It was the intimacy of our secret tryst merging seamlessly, beautifully like a watercolor sunset, into something more mundane but just as meaningful. It felt really, really good.

When I was done with the eggs, I made us both another coffee and retrieved my sketchbook before sitting down again. My mind was beautifully vacant, the kind of mental state artists strive for, but only the best are capable of achieving on a regular basis, and I wanted to take advantage of it. My pencil twisted over the paper in loose, languid strokes.

I wasn't surprised when something distinctly sexual emerged from the gray mass of swirls, but the dark taint of the image, the stark disobedience of it did bewilder me. A woman with shadowy hair wrapping around her arousal swollen flesh like bindings yelled across the page, her mouth invitingly wide but dangerous, temperamental.

I realized as I stared at her that she was me. This woman who dared you to fuck her, dominate her, and then dared those who would condemn her to resist her charms. It was so ironic that the more sexually powerful I became, the more I wanted someone to leash me.

"What are your plans for the day?" Sinclair asked.

He had been watching me. I knew because I had harnessed that scorching gaze and locked it around the fierce woman in my drawing.

"I need to paint."

"Of course, your exhibition is coming quickly. January is not so far off."

I stared at him for a second. "I didn't think you knew."

He frowned at me. "Elle, not only is it my business to know about the goings-on at *my* gallery but it is also your first show in America. I assure you, the date has been noted on my calendar since it was decided upon."

I smudged the shadowy lock of hair falling over my drawn woman's face with my thumb and mumbled, "I just remember you saying that you didn't want anything to do with it."

He sighed, and a second later, my stool was tugged toward him so that I was between his spread legs. His fingers threaded through my hair and tilted my head until I was looking up into his eyes. Instantly, I relaxed as my ricocheting thoughts bounced against his palms and slunk back into my skull like chastised dogs.

"How can you be so confident under my hands and otherwise so unsure? Giselle, I said that because you had upset me. You came into my office looking gorgeous and unflappable, and then this soft-spoken woman told me to *go to hell*."

I blushed because that *had* been a little unfair. "I didn't mean it."

"We both said a lot of things we didn't mean that day."

I felt the hook that connected my heart to his sink deeper into my left aorta.

"I do not want to stop seeing you."

My eyes fluttered close to better savor those edible words. When I opened them, his lips were ever so slightly tilted in a bemused smile.

"We see each other all the time," I reminded him.

Just because his admission made me ecstatic didn't mean I was going to be an easy catch.

His gaze narrowed. "It's difficult to play hard to get when you've already told me that you are in love with me."

I bristled, but he did have a point. Instead of answering, I gathered our dirty dishes and put them in the dishwasher, taking my time to completely avoid his burning stare. I was just walking past him to get my sketchbook when he grabbed me around the waist and tugged me between his legs, wrapping his limbs around me so that I was trapped.

"Get off me," I ordered in my haughtiest voice.

"Don't feel like it."

"Sinclair," I said, laughter seeping into my tone. "*Tu es con*, let me go!"

"Nope, maybe if I keep you captive long enough, you will remember that time you said you loved me. In fact, I think you said it *multiple* times."

I rolled my eyes, and even though he couldn't see me do it, he gave me a tight squeeze.

"I have no idea to what you are referring."

His fingers dug into my sides and began to tickle me. I writhed in his grip as laughter exploded from my lips, huge unfeminine guffaws that made my entire body shake.

"Stop... please... Sin," I begged breathlessly, tears streaming down my face.

He spun me around in his arms, smiling that boyish smile that made my heart forget to function.

"I want you to tell me again," he explained, pouting adorably.

A part of me was floating near the ceiling, buoyed by his good humor and obvious affection, while the other part, smaller than a sandbag, kept me tethered to the earth. I cupped his achingly handsome face in my hands because it made me feel better about what I had to say.

"Daniel." He flinched slightly, but I tightened my hands on his cheeks. "I haven't asked you to leave Elena, and I'm not going to. I have no right to ask you, and I can promise you right now, I will never ask me that. But in return, I need you to promise me that you will never ask me if I love you again. I can deal with this." I rolled my head around to indicate our fucked-up situation in the most eloquent way I knew how. "With Elena keeping you, but only if you let me keep a part of myself to myself."

With a heavy sigh, I took a moment to collect my thoughts and project them clearly through my gaze when I met his eyes again.

"You could take it." I thumped my chest. "You could take everything I am. And you know what? A part of me wants that like crazy."

His hands found my hips and rested there, just gently on the curve. I was grateful for it because he was letting me know that he understood what I was trying to say.

"But I have to be realistic, even if I don't want to be. You aren't going to leave Elena, and I refuse to put my heart in a cage I don't have the key to open."

His lips were screwed tight like a lid over the emotions bubbling up at his center. I could see some of it rise to the surface of his gaze, but he was looking over my shoulder, shielding most of it from me.

I swallowed hard and decided to throw in the last of my grenades. "Also, I have a lunch date today."

His eyes snapped to me, flashing like neon lights. "Excuse me?"

"You heard me."

His hands flexed painfully on my waist, but the silence was worse than the physical discomfort. It stretched long and torturous before us like a road littered with mines.

"You're going to sit across from another man when your ass is still sore from my hand?"

I raised my eyebrows. "You're going to go home to my sister when your hand is still sore from my ass?"

Fury emanated from him like dry ice, and I instantly regretted my barb.

I sighed. "Sin, it's just a lunch date. Elena basically insisted on setting us up, and I wanted to seem like a normal girl, one who was interested in other men." I laughed a little. "We both know who I would rather be with."

"Do we?"

"You're kidding, right?"

But he wasn't. He sat utterly rigid on the stool, and his eyes had been reduced to icy shields.

"I want to be with you," I said slowly and maybe a little condescending because I thought it was blindingly obvious.

His jaw clenched, and he stared at me hard for a long moment before standing up and stalking away to the balcony doors.

"Sin?" I stayed where I was because I wasn't sure how to deal with an angry Frenchman even after all my time in Paris.

He continued to stare broodingly out the window. In only his low-slung jeans with the sunlight kissing his skin, he looked like stolen artwork, something far too glorious to ever belong to me.

"You cut a dashing figure standing there, but maybe you could talk to me?" I asked as I scooted onto a stool to make myself comfortable while I waited.

He looked over his shoulder at me, but his face was cast in shadow. "Come here."

I slid off the stool before I could even process his request, and I hesitated when I realized how easily my body revealed his dominion over me. He was in front of me before I could make a decision one way or another, his fingers sinking into the hair over my ears while his thumbs tilted my chin up.

"I have done nothing in my life to deserve you, Elle. Absolutely nothing. I've fought to be a good person when it is not in my nature to be kind or good, not like you." He shook his head, and his thumb brushed against my lower lip. "I do not deserve to hold something so precious in my hands."

I turned my head, dislodging one of his hands so I could kiss his palm, leaving the imprint of my love for him like a lucky coin. I closed his fist over it and held it with both my hands. There was no way to articulate the toxic cocktail of emotions rolling churlishly through my veins, and I knew if I couldn't, my enigmatic Frenchman probably couldn't either.

Besides, we hadn't really spoken about where we would go from here, but as it stood, this was my last morning as Daniel Sinclair's lover, and I wanted to make the most of it.

"Can I show you something?" I asked, my girlish excitement making me bounce on my toes.

Without waiting for his answer, I turned around to grab the large canvas tilted to the left of the French doors. My heart trilled with nerves as I turned to prop it on the easel. I avoided looking back at Sinclair as I stepped back into line with him so he could see the painting unobstructed. It was the one I had been slaving over between my projects for the art gallery opening, but I had only finished it yesterday.

It was based on the sketch I had started in Mexico, the one with the two contrasting lovers a breath away from a kiss. It was my favorite piece in my growing collection because it was so clearly Sinclair and me, lost in the murky shadows but burning so brightly our features were nearly obscured in the blaze.

I looked up at him, bouncing maniacally now, but his gorgeous face betrayed no emotions.

"Well?"

His lips twitched, and he crossed his arms. "Well what, siren?" His grin broke free when I hip-checked him. "It's simply remarkable."

"You think?"

He turned to face me, taking my hands in his so that he could stare down at them. My nails were industriously short, and charcoal was smudged across the thumb and forefinger on my right hand from sketching earlier, but Sinclair gazed down at them as if they were precious gems. He brushed each finger with his lips, slowly and reverently, before looking down into my eyes.

"I know. You are extraordinarily gifted, Giselle, and beyond that, you are brave. Exploring the hidden side of lust and longing is not for the faint of heart."

"No," I agreed, thinking of us. "It isn't. But I'm hoping that it's worth it in the end."

Chapter Fourteen

OTHER THAN MAMA'S, PRUNE WAS MY FAVORITE RESTAURANT IN NEW YORK, particularly for the insanely busy Sunday brunches, so I was pleased when my blind date suggested the restaurant for our outing. I decided to walk there even though it was on the opposite side of Manhattan, which meant I had to say goodbye to Sinclair earlier than I wanted to. He had stayed over longer and ended up heading into the office over three hours later than usual. His tardiness delighted me.

The Indian summer was finally ending, and the breeze was cool between the tightly packed buildings, but I welcomed it. Since Sinclair had left, my heart had stopped racing, but my body was still flushed with the memory of his touch. My nipples scraped against the lacy material of my bra, sensitive from his mouth and the clothespins. In the aftermath of last night, my skin was so responsive that it was hard to resist the urge to touch the swell of my tastefully exposed breasts or the delicate inside of my wrists where Sinclair had nibbled just that morning.

The only thing that intruded on my memories—apart from the occasional New Yorker's elbow—was the prickly feeling at the base of my neck.

At first, I thought it was a stray itch, one that I scratched until the skin was raw, but as I neared the restaurant, the feeling grew until I was almost certain someone was following me. Looking over my shoulder and finding unfamiliar faces every time didn't alleviate my growing anxiety.

I pulled out my phone and dialed the first number on my speed dial.

"Hello?" Cosima's throaty voice was breathless. "*Bambina*, what's the matter?"

"Would you think I was crazy if I said someone was following me?"

There was a long pause and a vague cacophony on the other end of the line.

"How long?"

I exhaled loudly, grateful but unsurprised that she believed me. Cosima had always had a suspicious mind, and given her close association with the Camorra in Napoli and the black-eyed Dante, I knew she had experience with this kind of thing.

"About fifteen minutes," I guessed, walking a little more quickly as the heat of paranoia lit me on fire.

"Okay." Cosima spoke calmly, but I could still hear the mess of her movements in the background and the low register of a male voice. "Stay on a busy street. Where are you going?" I told her, and she thought about it for a second before continuing, "I hope you are wearing something cute, *bambina*. You have been too lonely since your mystery lover in Mexico."

"Shouldn't I cancel if someone really is following me?"

"No, it's best if you keep to your normal schedule and go to lunch. You should be fine once you get into the restaurant, but call me before you leave."

There was more noise as she spoke with someone in the room with her. It could have been my imagination, but I thought I heard a British accent.

"I can't be home for a while more, and I don't want you to be at the apartment alone," she said. "So, I just texted Elena, and you are going to stay there tonight."

"No," I blurted out before I could stop myself.

"Gigi, now isn't the time to pull the sibling rivalry card. Mama is working tonight, and Sebastian is in Toronto. Until we figure out what is going on, it is safer for you to stay with family." She hesitated before adding, "There have been a few strange phone calls to the apartment. A man asked for you the first time, but otherwise, it is always silent on the other line. Please, stay with Elena tonight and let me take care of this."

I chewed on my bottom lip as I focused on the pink awning of Prune in the distance. I really didn't want to stay with Elena and her Daniel after I had just spent a remarkable night with *my* Sinclair. But I didn't want to worry Cosima or be one of those stupid girls in horror films who went against common logic and got murdered.

So I promised Cosima I would and hung up just as my phone buzzed with an incoming text.

Elena: Guest bedroom is made up. Left a key with the receptionist, please let yourself in.

I sighed and was about to put my phone away when another text came in.

The Frenchman: *Please don't worry about tonight. And, more importantly, please think of me during your 'date.'*

I grinned, shook my head, and tucked my phone in my bag just as I reached the long line leading into Prune.

ULRICH WICK WAS AN INCREDIBLY NICE GUY.

He was also incredibly dull.

"I tried to explain how important the discrepancies were to the overall dynamic of the company's infrastructure," he continued, "but of course, it was beyond comprehension for someone with such a pea-sized intellect."

"Of course," I murmured, looking down at the salad he had ordered for me without my consent. Prune had so many delicious things on the menu that I had felt robbed when I arrived to see him already seated and our orders in place. I had spent the past twenty minutes watching him daintily consume a plate of *spaghetti alla carbonara,* and it was torture.

Not to mention the endless conversation about corporate accounting.

"You wouldn't know either, though, I suppose, being a painter." He smiled at me, and the worst thing was that it was a pretty smile, a truly kind one despite his patronizing words.

"Oh, excuse me for a moment, but I believe that is Willa Percy coming this way." Ulrich pushed ungracefully out of his chair, exhibiting more passion in the single movement than in our entire hour-long brunch. I couldn't understand his enthusiasm. I had met Willa Percy, and she was not passion-inducing.

"Mrs. Percy, it is lovely to see you again," Ulrich gushed, reaching out with both hands.

Willa's eyes weren't on my date, though. Her stare pinned me in place so that she could get a really good look at every inch of me, finding fault with my freckled skin, overdramatic curves, and harlot red hair.

But instead of burning shame, of comparing myself to my flawless sisters, I thought about Sinclair, the only person in the Percy family I cared about. I thought about the map his hands, lips, and body had drawn over my skin in the past twenty-four hours, and suddenly, Willa's scrutiny didn't matter anymore.

Ulrich was still talking, and Willa was indulging him with minuscule facial tics, but eventually, he noticed the tension and petered off.

"Giselle," Willa began, her voice cool as silk wrapping around my throat. "You will wait with me while they bring my car around."

It wasn't a question, and normally, I would have protested, but Ulrich looked ready to swoon at the privilege I was being bestowed. I didn't have the heart to tell him that Willa Percy was a self-serving heartless bitch, so I grabbed my purse and followed her outside.

She didn't speak for a moment, opting to fix her lipstick in the mirror of a Chanel compact instead. Her elegance was absolute, from the tips of her pale pink painted nails to the bottoms of her low-heeled cream pumps, and I felt worse than bohemian next to her. I wondered if she had ever known poverty, how she would have judged my perfect older sister or me if she had witnessed the desperation of our childhood.

"You think I don't like you," she began in a cool voice like poured cream, "and you are mostly correct. It is obvious that you lack elevated social graces, a sense of fashion, and the common sense not to get involved with a taken man, let alone a man pledged to your very sibling."

A thin smile punctured her cheek, cutting off my protest before I could even open my mouth.

"I know my son very well, Miss Moore, and it does not escape my notice that he seems to be very much in lust with you. You do not need to protest because I do not blame either of you. My son is quite simply an incredible man, and you have your..." She hesitated and gestured vaguely to my body. "Obvious charms. So, I do not blame you for your initial bad judgment, but I am encouraging you as civilly as possible to cease and desist."

My lips twisted into something like a sneer, but she only laughed softly. "Abandon your pride and think for a moment. If you love my son, as I'm certain you think that you do, then you know that Elena is the best choice for him. Her elegance, intelligence, and stature are perfectly suited to Daniel's pursuits. You know, one day he wants to run for office, just like his father."

My insecurity vibrated as Willa hammered her point home. I didn't want to listen to her, but it was hard to ignore the truth of her statement, especially when she spoke so calmly, so rationally. It was tricky to argue against a lack of passion.

"Daniel had a rough beginning, and I, for one, believe that he deserves happiness now. You may believe that you are the one to bring him that happiness, but you're mistaken." Her eyes swept over me dismissively. "You do not have what it takes to stand by my son."

A beige Town Car rolled up to the curb, and a handsomely dressed young man with skin like roasted coffee beans came around to open the door for the governor's wife.

"Go back inside, enjoy the rest of your meal with Mr. Wick, then go home and call my son. End it. I'm asking nicely, my dear, but the Lord knows I have other ways at my disposal."

I stood silently, stupidly, while she slid into the car, closed the door, and rolled down the window so she could stare at me as they pulled into traffic. I stayed there for a long moment after she was gone, my eyes closed and my senses open to the riotous noises of a New York City afternoon. The cacophony calmed the turmoil churning through me, and when I opened my eyes again, I started off down the street toward my next destination with renewed confidence.

DESPITE MY EARLIER DETERMINATION TO SEE HIM, I WAS NERVOUS GIVING MY name to the receptionist. The young ginger-haired man smiled warmly at me and complimented my choice of dress, but his recognition of my discomfort only heightened my nervousness. If it was that apparent, I wondered if the entire office might know about our secret affair?

I was obviously being paranoid, but not without reason. Sebastian and

Cosima already suspected, and I wouldn't be surprised at all if they'd figured it out for themselves. It seemed almost ridiculous that anyone could remain oblivious to the sultry, heavy air between Sinclair and me when we're together, but the mind was a powerful thing. It was easy to believe what you wanted to believe.

I was still dwelling on it when I was ushered into the office, so it took me a moment to recognize the slick dark-haired man grinning at me with his arms outstretched. Of course, the outrageously loud burnt umber blazer helped.

"Santiago!"

He laughed richly as I stepped into his arms. "Beautiful Elle, the New York smog does wonders for your complexion."

I laughed with him. "You're just being kind."

He nodded solemnly. "I am. But this is easy with such a beautiful woman before me. Isn't it, Sinclair?"

We both turned to smile at the Frenchman who was staring at us with his arms crossed and his feet braced. He looked every inch the successful property developer behind his glass and chrome desk, his hair perfectly smoothed away from his broad forehead. I wanted desperately to tousle it with my fingers.

"She is lovely, though I don't believe that gives you the right to fawn all over her, Iago."

Santiago's laughter was a series of quick, high yips that made me grin. I allowed him to usher me to the seat beside his across from Sinclair's desk.

"I have to say I am pleasantly surprised to see you. Last time I spoke with Sinclair, he was cursing the fact you had abandoned him in Mexico. There must be a good story here," Santiago said.

I bit my lip and looked at Sinclair to answer his friend. I was surprised that my decision to flee had perturbed him, but the longer I thought about it, the more it made sense. Sinclair was a man who appreciated closure and neatly tied-up ends. Even more, he was a man of power, and I had unwittingly stripped him of that power by leaving before he could say anything.

God, was it outrageous to think that he might have wanted to stop me? That he might have wanted to solidify the bond between us with facts and figures, the where and who of it all so that we might have really been together?

My head pulsed painfully in time with my heart.

"...so I would appreciate your discretion on the matter. You know how much I dislike mixing business with pleasure," Sinclair was saying when I tuned back into the conversation.

Santiago was frowning, though, his thick brows knotting together in one long black smear. "This is ridiculous."

I laughed weakly. "You can't make stuff like this up."

"No, no, you cannot. The situation is ridiculous, but what I really meant was that you, Sinclair, are ridiculous. The only reason Elle isn't Mrs. Santiago Herrera right now is because you were there first, but if you insist on being ridiculous about it, then..." He petered off with a shrug as if he couldn't be held accountable for what happened next.

Something like a growl emanated from Sinclair's direction, but before he could calmly slice his friend into ribbons with a steely retort, I said, "Let me assure you, that is not the only reason I'm not your wife, Iago." I sniffed dramatically. "Now if you bought me a ring bigger than your second wife's... then we could talk."

He laughed again, and even Sinclair's lips twitched, which effectively defused the atmosphere.

"Anyway, I hate to interrupt business," I said with wide, innocent eyes as I waited for them to protest.

Santiago opened his mouth to do so, but Sin's chuckle caught him off guard.

"She's just fishing for compliments. You weren't interrupting. Iago has been here for much longer than his allotted appointment, and if I'm not mistaken, he is keeping a lovely woman waiting in his hotel suite uptown."

The Mexican magnate shrugged. "She may be my fourth wife if Elle won't have me."

"Is Katarina with you?" I asked, jumping slightly in my seat at the thought of seeing his wonderful sister.

"Alas, she is back home. Had I known you would be here, I couldn't have stopped her from joining me. She has remarked a number of times with sadness that you did not exchange information."

"Give her my card," I said, pushing one of my newly minted business cards toward him. "I'm actually having a showing the second week of January at DS Galleries. I don't suppose you'll still be here for it?"

His large obsidian eyes lit up, and his smile was overlarge, goofy, like a kid with a candy bar. "I wouldn't miss it."

"If you are in town, you have to come to our family Thanksgiving tomorrow."

"If you insist," he agreed easily.

We beamed at each other until Sinclair cleared his throat, and then we both laughed before turning to look at him.

"Yes, sir?" I asked mildly.

He raised one haughty brow at my innuendo, and the simple gesture was enough to send an arrow of desire straight to my core. God, but that man could imply a lot with a simple look. It probably helped that he was already sinfully attractive.

"If you'll excuse us, Iago, I have plans to show Elle around the office."

It was my turn to raise my brows, but Santiago leaned forward to take both my hands in his for lingering kisses.

"Of course, but allow me to request Giselle's company on my walk to the elevator. One does get lonely in a foreign city," he added sagely.

Sinclair would have snorted, I think, if it wasn't such an undignified thing to do.

I linked my arm through Santiago's and smiled over my shoulder at Sin as we exited. "Be back in a moment."

Margot was at her desk outside his office when we passed by, but happily, Santiago blocked her view of me, and we escaped unscathed. He must have sensed my relaxation as soon as we were out of hearing distance because it was only then that he patted my hand where it rested on his arm and leaned in close to say, "Are you a religious woman, Elle?"

I startled a bit at the randomness of the question. "Um, no, not particularly. My parents used to be Roman and Irish Catholics, but we all kind of abandoned religion when we felt God had abandoned us to poverty and abuse during my childhood."

He frowned down at me, not in sympathy as I might have expected, but appraisingly. "I sensed poverty in you. It gives a person a certain quality, a greedy ruthlessness."

I tried to step away from him, but his clutch on my arm only tightened, and he tutted me like an old matron. "Now, now, don't shy away from the truth. I didn't mean it as an insult. Only when you've known true hunger and desperation are you willing to go after what you want, consequences be damned. It is, if not an admirable quality, then certainly a successful one."

He gave me a moment of silence in order to digest his words while we waited for the elevators. The unpalatable thing was, I agreed with what he was saying. Only the ruthless succeeded. I truly believed that. The only thing I remained unsure of was if I had the balls to submit to my brutal instinct to steal happiness away from my own sister.

Santiago was watching me as if he was asking himself the same question. "You are no longer the person you thought we were before you met him, Giselle. That woman, one whom you undoubtedly thought was good and moral? She has already been murdered by the new you, the one who went after a taken man knowingly, even if it wasn't without qualms." He held up a single finger to hush my protest. "There was strength in making that decision. Do not be weak and unkind now by not going after what you want. In my experience, it only leads to misery for everyone."

My throat was swollen and aching as if I was responding to his words with anaphylactic shock.

"Besides"—he cast me a sidelong glance—"wickedness looks good on you."

I was mute as he leaned forward to press a kiss against my cheek, smelling like heat and expensive cologne. He stepped into the elevator without breaking eye contact, and we watched each other as the doors slid close.

Just before he winked out of sight behind the metal partition, he lifted his hand to his throat and said, "You would look even better in a collar."

Chapter Fifteen

I DIDN'T GO BACK TO SINCLAIR'S OFFICE.

He would come looking for me, I knew, but I still needed a moment to digest Santiago's words. Besides, I reasoned as I fled the sixtieth floor in an elevator of people dressed in impeccable business attire, I had business to conduct in the gallery, and I might as well take care of it while I was in the building.

I made my way to the storeroom where my completed paintings were housed, too preoccupied to notice the woman following in my wake. It was only when the door closed with a slam that I twirled around to see Margot Silver standing against it with her thin arms crossed over her chest.

I sighed. "I don't suppose you came down to help me move these?"

"Don't be cute with me, Giselle. We both know it's just an act."

I crossed my arms to mimic her pose and raised my eyebrows Sinclair-style.

She rolled her eyes at my demonstration. "I'll get to the point because spending any amount of time with you rubs me the wrong way. Stop fucking around with Sinclair."

"I hate to break it to you when you've been so nice to me, but I don't care what you think. You don't know anything about the situation."

"I know that Daniel Sinclair is the best man I know, yet he's acting like a moronic dickhead chasing after your nice pair of tits."

"Aw, thank you, Margot," I said with faux delight.

"If you think I'm the only one who has noticed you two, you're an idiot."

That gave me pause. I had wondered about the twins knowing, but the people Sin worked with? I didn't want them to think less of him.

She practically snarled at me. "I'm not being a bitch because I enjoy it. I'm doing this, whether you choose to believe it or not, because what you two are doing is going to hurt everyone involved. Are you really willing to tank your career and lose your family over what God only knows has to be admittedly pretty damn good sex?"

I gritted my teeth. Those words were my own, the ones that echoed in my head every goddamn day since I'd discovered Sin's Darling was Elena. Yet hearing them voiced with such vitriol made me defensive. Her darkness brought to light all the wonderful things I had experienced with him. We were so much more than the (admittedly damn good) sex.

"I'm not willing to lose anything, including Sinclair. If you're his guard dog, shouldn't you consider the fact I make him happy?"

"Are you so sure that you do?"

Okay, that arrow found its mark.

She grinned like a viper, her small teeth like shiny, poison-slicked weapons. "I'm asking you as nicely as I know how. Back *the fuck* off. You don't have the balls to see this through to the end. If you don't care about ruining your own life, what about his?"

I shivered at her icy tone. She didn't understand that it wasn't just my choice not to follow through on my attraction to Sinclair. He was just as reluctant to fuck up his life as she was.

"If you talked to him, you'd realize he doesn't want anything more. It's over now, anyway," I said.

She snorted. "If you knew him, you would realize that Sin is about the things he doesn't say."

My brow tangled before I could mask the expression from her. She was right, but it didn't sit well with me. Had I been focusing too much on his uttered protests and not enough on the sweet touches and longing kisses? The fact that he still couldn't get enough of me.

My heart fluttered like a hummingbird between one extreme and the next. I broke out in a confused sweat and blinked up at Margot without malice.

She sighed heavily and dropped her arms. "You're a nice girl, Elle. So do the right thing."

I turned away from her as she left. My paintings lay carefully propped and concealed against the wall. I ran my fingers over them lovingly, taking comfort from my art while my emotions rolled on ten-foot waves of indecision within my gut.

"Giselle?"

I startled at the sound of his voice even though I caught a whiff of his smoky scent seconds before he spoke. When I didn't respond, he came to stand behind me. Goose bumps broke out over my skin as he gathered my hair and moved it over one shoulder. He wasn't touching me, but his lips hovered close to my neck, his hot breath like a kiss.

"I thought you'd run away."

I huffed. "Apparently, I can't stay away."

"I don't want you to."

"Sinclair..."

"Giselle..." I could hear his amusement. "Stop worrying, stop hiding. Come out and let me introduce you to some of my team upstairs. I have at least another hour of work to do before we go back to my place, but I'll leave you with Candy. She would love the distraction."

I turned around, tipping my head back to look up at his phenomenal face. "Okay."

"Okay? I was expecting you to protest."

I shrugged. "I want to meet the people you work with. I don't know much about what you do."

"I'm a property developer, and you have actually met most of my core team. Duncan Wright is my CFO, Richard Denman is one of our chief architects, Candy is my right-hand woman, and Robert Corbett is head of our construction division."

"Do they all work in the building?"

"No, most of the time, they are out on location working on projects, but Duncan should be here. Would you like to say hello?"

"Would that be okay?" I asked, unsure about the etiquette.

He shook his head and took my hand to lead me out of the back room. "Haven't you realized by now that I can't deny you anything?"

I was tempted for a moment to test his words by asking him to leave Elena for me. Happily, Rossi found us a moment later, and the opportunity was lost.

Éclair's apartment suited them. Tucked into a beautifully maintained Greek revival townhouse in Gramercy Park, it was luxurious without being ostentatious, and stylish and classy without being too cold. I recognized the art on the walls as pieces that Sinclair would have chosen himself, and the large pearly grand piano in the corner was Elena's most prized possession, a housewarming gift from the twins. It was an older space with soft, glossy dark floors and a slightly cluttered floor plan that was so at odds with today's open-style living spaces.

I loved it.

But it felt unspeakably strange to be in the belly of the beast, the place

Sinclair and Elena shared as a couple. Especially after my previous night with him and the wonderful afternoon I had just spent at his office. As he introduced me to more members of his team and joked with Candy about my distracting capabilities, it felt almost as if I was his girlfriend. Candy had tried to emphasize exactly that point, but I'd convinced her to move the conversation along to less complicated things like her new boyfriend, Gregory, whose Russian accent was so thick that sometimes she could barely understand him. Apparently, it had made for some confusing situations in the bedroom.

Sinclair had stood silently by as I explored the place, but now he stepped forward to slide his hands down my arms and link them through my fingers.

Pressing his nose to my hair, he murmured, "Is it terrible of me to say that I like seeing you here? In my space."

I shrugged helplessly. "I think it is safe to say that we are not the best people."

His hands tightened in mine. "You are very good, Elle. Your lightness, your kindness are what drew me to you in the first place."

"I don't feel like a good person," I said and felt him stiffen behind me, knew that my words hurt him. I spun around to place my hands on his cheeks, my thumbs against his cut-glass cheekbones. "I feel selfish and gluttonous, but I can't help myself. Whenever I'm without you, I trick myself into thinking I can survive without *this,* and honestly, I know if I was strong and good, I could. But I don't want to, and it's getting hard to remind myself why I should care."

Sinclair's electric eyes blazed down at me. I wanted to fidget or drag my gaze away, but I forced myself to stay still, willfully trapped in his snare.

"What are you saying?" he said roughly. "Tell me I am not insane, *d'accord*? Tell me you mean what you say."

My mouth was beyond parched. I felt as if I had swallowed a pound of sand, and when I parted my lips to speak, I could hear them rasp apart like Velcro.

The rattle of a key in the doorway had us springing apart before we could even rationally make sense of the warning. Sinclair cleared his throat and shoved his hands through his hair before turning on his heel toward the kitchen while I quickly settled onto the stone suede couch by the fire-place. That was how Elena found us when she came through the door, looking as beautifully put together as always.

"Giselle, I'm so sorry that you had to go through that today. New York is wonderful, but unfortuantly it is filled with unsavory characters. I'm sure it was just some deviant who took a liking to you then got bored," she said immediately, making her way over to me after carefully hanging up her coat, scarf, and briefcase.

I accepted her soft kiss on the cheek and hoped she couldn't hear my hammering heart. Immediately, she made her way to the sound system and plugged in her phone. A moment later, Chet Baker's smooth tones spilled into the room, and I was reminded of how much Elena loved music. As a girl, she had spent hours at Signora Donati's house playing the piano, and I'd often trailed her, ducking in the dry brush beside the window to the living room to hear the music that pooled beneath her eloquent fingers.

"I decided to host dinner this year," she continued, moving around the room to straighten the already immaculate pieces of furniture. "It's Thanks-giving tomorrow, Daniel. Did you remember to take the day off?"

"You've reminded me every day this week. Of course, I did," he called from the kitchen.

She turned to look at me, narrowing her eyes as she took in the swell of my breasts in the brightly patterned neckline of my dress and the mass of curls that fell artlessly around my shoulders. I took the time to admire how beautifully ladylike she looked in her high-necked lace blouse and black pencil skirt. I tried not to compare her to Lady and me to the Tramp.

"Is that what you wore for your date with Ulrich?" she asked with a surprisingly playful pout. "No, don't frown, this is very much my fault. I should have lent you something. Not that I don't love the whole Parisian artist look, but Ulrich works on Wall Street."

"Trust me, I know," I muttered as Sinclair came back into the room carrying three wine glasses and a bottle of Pinot Grigio. It was the same label we had shared together just last night. I wondered if he knew, and if he did, why he had chosen to drink it now.

"You had a date with Ulrich Wick?" he asked after he had placed the glasses on the table and a brief kiss on Elena's proffered cheek.

I caught the amusement in his eyes as he popped the cork on the wine and began to pour. With my chin tilted high, I replied haughtily, "I did, indeed."

"Elena, how could you?" he scolded lightly.

She sat down beside me on the couch, perched on the edge with her hands in her lap like a princess waiting to be served. But her eyes smiled too, sparkling back at Sinclair with warmth and good humor.

"What? Ulrich is a very intelligent and kind man."

"He is also extremely dull, darling."

Darling. I so clearly remembered him calling her that while we were in Mexico. I had wondered what kind of woman she was. Though I couldn't have known Elena was Darling, it was eerie how close my imagination had come to conjuring her exact image based on the little I had known in Los Cabos.

Elena was laughing, her true light and trilling giggle that made her eyes squinty. "He is not boring, Daniel. You think any man without knowledge of fishing, art, or travel is a bore."

He shrugged one shoulder and handed her a glass of wine. Her fingers brushed lingeringly over his, and he bestowed her with a beautiful smile.

It was hard to listen to their conversation over the roar of blood rushing through my head, but somehow, I managed to.

"It is not so specific. A man, or a woman for that matter, must have passion, or else they are a shell of themselves," Sinclair said.

He was looking at me now, but I couldn't bring myself to meet his gaze.

"Passion is messy," Elena said, waving a dismissive hand through the air. "I think this was one of the first things we bonded over."

He nodded his agreement, but his lips were tight over his teeth with restraint. I fought not to let out a bitter little laugh. Passion was the first thing Sin and I had bonded over too.

"Yes," I managed to say. "How did you two meet?"

"Cosima introduced us." I watched Elena's features melt under the warmth of her recollections and felt my lungs tighten. "I was infatuated with him on sight, I think. He was wearing this gorgeous navy blue bespoke Brooks Brothers suit, and it was before he let his hair get so long and unruly. He looked like such a gentleman."

A wolf in sheep's clothes, I thought.

"I offered to help with her English," Sin explained. "It was as good an excuse as any."

"Well, I certainly couldn't resist my gorgeous tutor, now could I? After our 'study' date, I was hooked, and the rest is history."

It was a cute little story, one that they had obviously shared countless times. I thought about my meet-cute with Sinclair, how I must have looked after puking for hours on the plane. The relationship that followed wasn't exactly picture perfect either.

Once, making the comparison between the perfection that was Elena and little old me would have induced coma-like melancholy and self-doubt, but I knew myself better now. I loved myself more. And I knew that despite our imperfect origins, Sin was inexplicably drawn to *me*.

For the first time since I found out who he really was, I wondered if that was enough to make him choose me over her.

"Oh, by the way, we have an appointment with Miss Hertz this weekend. One o'clock on Saturday. I already let Margot know, and she said it wouldn't be a problem with your schedule," Elena said.

Sinclair grew exceptionally still beside me, the kind of immobility that somehow seemed more obvious than a shout in an empty room. I found myself unconsciously clenching my muscles, freezing in the act of bringing my wineglass to my lips. The air grew static as a storm began to brew.

"Elena," Sinclair said softly. "I thought we spoke about this."

As if to make up for his lack of movement, Elena stood and became a flurry of activity, placing coasters under our glasses and fluffing already plumped pillows.

She didn't look at him when she said, "I know we did, but one conversation that came from absolutely nowhere should not derail our plans to have a family."

Oh, *my God*. I was paralyzed by my urge to flee, the rush of adrenaline through my blood causing some kind of overload in my nervous system. I prayed fervently, with a passion that would have rivaled Mama's, to any god who would hear me, that they wouldn't talk about this in front of me.

I'd never been a very lucky woman.

"We should discuss this later when we can be alone. For now, please call Miss Hertz and cancel the appointment," Sinclair said, so reasonably that even I wanted to punch him.

But Elena didn't rage against his condescension. Instead, she retracted into herself like a threatened sea anemone. It was almost amazing to watch her grow cold and distant, mostly because Sinclair reacted to conflict precisely the same way. I wondered, horrified, how they ever overcame difficulties when both of them gave in to the urge to flee instead of fight.

"I will not. It took us months to get this far, Daniel, and I will not cancel this appointment on one of your whims."

"One of my whims?" Sinclair asked with one eyebrow raised.

Elena stuck out her delicate chin.

Slowly, he rose out of the chair with such controlled discipline that I imagined his joints clicking into place like an automaton. There was something so absurdly terrifying about the calculated movements and the way he cocked his head just slightly to the side to study her. This was the businessman, the Dom, the predator. Someone who dared you to fuck with them so they could have the pleasure of ripping you to shreds.

Suddenly, I felt terrible for Elena.

"We aren't happy, Elena. That is no atmosphere to bring a child into," he said.

"Speak for yourself," she snapped, hands on hips. "I am happy."

He only stared at her. I'd never met anyone who could use silence as a weapon like Sinclair could.

"I want a baby."

"Do you want me to say yes only to please you?" he asked in that cool, quiet voice.

My heart was beating so loudly that it was a wonder they didn't hear it.

"You agreed, Daniel. You agreed years ago when..." She paused, and sadness flared across her features, "When we first got together. You promised that one day we would have kids. It's important, isn't it? That you agreed? I know you never wanted them. You don't think I don't know that? You don't want kids, you don't want marriage, but you want me, don't you? And I *need* this."

My eyes swiveled in my frozen face just in time to see Sinclair deflate. His features softened, and his eyes took on that electric glow that I had once thought was reserved only for me. Wordlessly, he breached the space between them and took Elena into his arms, one hand locked firmly on her neck as he tucked it into his shoulder. Almost immediately, she let out a gusty sigh and wilted into his arms.

I stared at their embrace for a long moment, cataloging the way she fit against him like a tailored suit, how beautifully and tenderly they clutched each other. When I finally wrenched my gaze away from my worst nightmare, my eyes overcorrected and flew to the opposite wall of the room, where a portrait picture of Éclair hung over the mantel. In it, Elena sat in a rigid chair with Sinclair standing behind her, one hand on her shoulder. It was the kind of painting I expected to find in a royal museum, and the sight of it punched me right between the eyes.

I might have murmured something as I peeled myself off the couch and zombie-walked down the hallway to my bedroom for the night, but I couldn't be sure, and either way, they didn't notice me leave. I closed the door softly behind me and felt my way toward the bed in the pitch dark. I flopped on top of the many-pillowed bed and stared into the darkness as if it was a prophet sent to deliver answers. When none proved to be forthcoming, I turned on my side, clutched my knees to my chest, and cried and cried and cried.

Chapter Sixteen

AFTER FINALLY FALLING INTO A TEAR-SOAKED COMA, I WOKE UP THE following morning before the crack of dawn in order to escape the apartment without having to face either my sister or her boyfriend.

Her boyfriend. That was how I was going to refer to Sinclair from now on. Not my Frenchman, not my friend, not even Sinclair but as Daniel, Elena's boyfriend. If I could force myself to think of him as this other person, as I might have known him had I met him properly, I might have a chance in hell of getting over him. I imagined meeting him for the first time at a family dinner and found it easy to believe I would have found him haughty and remote, condescending and one-dimensional. His beauty would have imprinted itself on my psyche—it simply couldn't be helped— but I wondered if the chemistry between us would have remained caged and hidden behind the bars of acceptable social norms.

As of this morning, I was turning over a new leaf. It didn't erase the sins I had already committed, but it would keep Elena happy, my family intact, and Sinclair firmly embedded in the kind of lifestyle he coveted. As I straightened the bed and vainly tried to smooth the wrinkles from my slept-in clothes, I considered moving back to Paris. Christopher had found me there, but by now, he might have moved on.

My thoughts were still spinning with possibilities as I tiptoed out of the bedroom and into the living room. I was just peeling open the front door when the overhead light flicked on, freezing me like a thief in the spotlight.

To my surprise, when I turned around, it wasn't Sinclair who stood there, silently contemplating me, but Elena.

She wore beautiful black silk pajamas with white piping and a matching eye mask pushing back her softly tousled curls. There were dark shadows beneath her eyes, and she wrung her hands in an unusual display of nervousness.

"Morning," I said into the awkward silence.

She blinked. "You look like you are getting ready to do the walk of shame. If you have to leave right now, at least borrow a jacket."

My spine straightened painfully under her casual censure. "I'm fine like this, Elena, but thank you."

"You look like a siren. Do you want men propositioning you on the street?" she snapped.

You look like a siren. It took monumental effort not to collapse into tears right there on my sister's living room floor.

"Fine, if you don't mind, then I would love to borrow a jacket."

Elena nodded curtly and went to the closet to pull out a long Burberry trench coat, the same one she had been wearing the night of my welcome home party. I let her help me into it and tried to breathe through my mouth to avoid the aroma of her Chanel Number 5 perfume. She lingered over the collar, turning it up against my throat and smoothing my wayward hair around my cheeks.

"You are very beautiful," she said, almost as if it pained her.

"We have good genes."

To my utter surprise and dismay, Elena's lower lip curled into a pout and wobbled.

"Daniel doesn't want to be with me anymore," she whispered so quietly that I was almost sure I had imagined it.

"*Scusi?*" I asked, my muddled brain devolving back to Italian.

Her dark eyes shone like polished graphite. "He doesn't love me anymore."

My heart hiccupped in my chest, but I fought down my own feelings with a Herculean effort and gently took hold of her limp hand in order to lead her to the couch.

"First of all, where is he now?" I asked.

"Work. He went in around four thirty this morning. To get away from me." She sniffed wetly and tugged her knees to her chest like a little girl in need of comfort.

"I'm sure that's not true."

"It is. He always goes in to work when he needs to get away. Even on Thanksgiving."

I actually knew that was the truth, but I kept my mouth shut.

She placed her pert little chin on her knees and looked down at her perfectly painted toes. "Things were fine before he went to Mexico. I swear. I mean, we weren't having sex much, but he never seemed to mind before."

"What?" I cleared my throat and fought to be there for my sister despite the absurdity of the situation. "Why do you think things changed?"

She shrugged. "I honestly don't know."

"Have you asked him?" It was too surreal to be having this conversation with her, my sister and his Darling. A small nefarious part of me wondered what would happen if she ever found out that it was *me*, that her belittled younger sister was the one who changed things between them. Would she think back to this conversation and hate me even more for guiding her through a storm of my own making?

The obvious answer was a resounding *fuck yes*.

"He said Mexico woke him up, that he had been numb for years, and he missed pain." Elena scrunched up her perfect nose. "Who misses pain?"

I shrugged as if I didn't understand. "Some people think that pain amplifies life, that it heightens pleasures that would otherwise seem mundane."

My elegant sister snorted.

"If you think about it for a second, it makes sense," I tried to explain, suddenly eager to make her realize how pivotal hurting was, that it was an essential part of the human experience. Maybe if I was eloquent enough,

she could finally understand me. "Why would God give us so much misery
if it wasn't for a reason?"

"We aren't religious," she argued with the second-nature exactitude of a
lawyer.

"I was just trying to help."

"Yes, well, as pretty as the words are, they don't work. Not when I'm in
so much..." She waved her hand around, unable to even articulate the
messy, passionate mass of feelings clogging her system like so much hair in
a drain.

"I think you should call Cosima or maybe even Mama."

I clearly wasn't the one to talk with her about this.

She looked off over her shoulder into the city beyond the windows. The
apartment overlooked the meticulously maintained Gramercy Park, a
private garden accessed by fewer than 350 keys and one of New York's first
attempts at city planning. I knew it was the reason Elena had been drawn to
the house even though she hadn't told me. The beautifully tempered
greenery and exclusivity of the place would have appealed to her obsession
with prestige and control.

"I want you to paint me."

"Pardon me?"

"I want you to paint me," Elena reiterated, turning to face me with a
face made of granite. "I want you to paint me like this, like I am right now."

"Elena..." I hesitated, not only because of the space she was in at the
moment but also because I didn't know how to depict this sister on canvas.
She was an enigma to me, something unknown and frankly terrifying. I
could paint her in four hundred different ways, and it still would not do
justice to the contrary nature of her personality. I only understood one
thing about Elena—she was so desperate to be everything at once, perfect
in all ways, that she had no definitive identity.

She visibly deflated at my hesitation, but my sympathy, my *villainy*,
wasn't enough to make me paint her. I refused to dishonor my art and us
both by combining the three.

"One day soon," I promised. "When you are feeling better. You obviously had a terrible night's sleep, and I would need you to hold a pose for
hours."

She pursed her lips but seemed to believe me, sagging back into the couch cushions like a discarded wind-up doll. My heart throbbed with the echo of hers, a sympathy beat that made it difficult to catch my breath.

"Are you all set for Thanksgiving tonight?" I asked, fully expecting Miss Organized to have everything ready to go.

"I ordered everything from Dean & Deluca. They should be here by four o'clock to deliver it."

"Did you order dessert?"

"A pumpkin pie. Why?"

I stood and walked over to her, offering my hand with a smile. "Come on, why don't we make tiramisu?"

Her lips wobbled before forming a smile. "We haven't made one of those since we were teenagers."

"Exactly," I said, strangely happy with the idea of spending the morning baking with my sister. "Why don't I call Mama, and we can make one together?"

Elena took my hand, coming to her feet before me. We smiled shyly at each other for a moment with our hands clasped.

"Thank you," she mouthed.

I wanted to say *I'm sorry*.

Instead, I squeezed her hand and asked, "Do you remember the recipe for the homemade ladyfingers?"

WHEN SINCLAIR ENTERED THE KITCHEN, CAGE AND SANTIAGO WERE CLOSE ON his heels, and the morning had passed into the late evening. The gorgeous mahogany dining table, which I couldn't help but notice was the same shade as Sinclair's hair, was laden with flower arrangements stuffed into pumpkins Elena, Mama, and I had carved ourselves that morning. Lindi Ortega's bluesy country music threaded through the speakers, lending itself to the candle-lit atmosphere and the heady scent of Dean & Deluca's Thanksgiving dinner warming in Elena's underutilized double wall oven.

I knew he was in the kitchen the moment he crossed the threshold even though we hadn't heard the front door open over the swell of our voices raised to sing along to "Desperado." Elena froze beside me a few seconds later, bent over the open oven to check on the turkey. She shot me a frantic look as Mama warmly greeted the men, and I nodded at her because I didn't know what else to do. She took comfort from the gesture and straightened, self-consciously patting her frilled apron. She hadn't changed into something formal yet, and I knew that bothered her.

"Daniel," she greeted quietly before going to place a soft kiss on his cheek.

He wound his arm around her waist and tugged her into a quick hug. "The place looks beautiful."

"Thank you." She blushed. "Mama, Giselle, and I spent all day decorating."

"We also made tiramisu," Mama said, beaming proudly at the sight of Elena and Sinclair together.

"Oh, where?" Cage asked, darting forward to open the fridge in search of the treat.

Mama *tsk*ed him and slapped at his hand as it shot forward to taste the cocoa-covered mascarpone top. "You wait!"

He pouted dramatically, batting his eyelashes at her. "But I promise to share with Iago. You know, Caprice, he has never had the privilege of your cooking."

"We helped too," I reminded him.

He made a disgusted face. "In that case, I hope you ordered something else for dessert too. Just in case, of course."

"Of course," I repeated mildly.

I squealed when he lunged at me, pulling me into his arms for a smacking kiss on the lips.

"In any case, you look good enough to eat, so I could always have you for the last course," he growled lasciviously.

I laughed and tugged at his thickly braided hair. "You rogue."

"You flatterer."

"Put her down, Cage," Sinclair ordered with his arm still looped around Elena. "And try to behave tonight, will you?"

Cage pursed his lips and stared at me with sparkling eyes as he lowered me slowly to the ground so that our bodies brushed intimately. My eyes flicked over his shoulder to Sinclair, whose jaw was clenched as he played with the ends of Elena's hair.

"Stop it," I whispered to Cage. "Don't make this harder than it already is."

"It's not nearly hard enough, or one of you would have made a change," he retorted, but he released me nonetheless.

"What time will the others be here?" Santiago asked me as he came forward to press a kiss to my cheek.

His fingers brushed lightly over my neck, reminding me of our conversation yesterday about how pretty I would look in a collar. I shivered.

"Cosima should arrive around eight," Elena said.

"This is quite late for Thanksgiving dinner, no?" Sinclair asked.

"We're European, Sin," I reminded him. "It's basically blasphemous to eat before eight."

Humor tightened his lips, but he didn't smile, and I wondered if it was because he could feel Elena's anxious energy pulsing like a warning beacon.

"You're right, of course, Daniel. Happily, though, Sebastian should be here shortly, so we can start with some drinks and appetizers," Elena said. "I'll just go change."

"*Ragazzi*, you follow me into the living room for drinks," Mama ordered with the grace and confidence of a woman who had been beautiful all her life.

Santiago and Cage happily complied, each already trying to charm her with stories from their childhoods living abroad.

When I turned around, Sinclair was leaning against the island counter with his shirt stretched taut between his lean shoulders and his russet head hanging low. I stepped up behind him to place a gentle hand on his back.

"It will be okay," I said, despite my nerves and despite my resolve to treat him with indifference.

"*On a des casseroles au cul,*" he muttered without turning around.

I pursed my lips to buckle in the pain. "You really think our affair is haunting you?"

He sighed. "It is the haunting I take issue with, Elle, not what I did to warrant it."

We were silent for a long moment. I didn't have anything new to add to the conversation. The affair had happened and, arguably, was still happening. It was deeply immoral, not only to deceive another person—in fact, my entire family—but because we were actively, consciously betraying my sister. I loved Sinclair with a severity that obliterated all obstacles in its path, and he, at least, was enchanted enough with me to heed my siren's song over the practical call of reality. Apparently, he had even voiced his reservations to Elena.

I knew the components. I just couldn't make out the full equation.

Sin spun around, one hand plunged into my hair and the other on my hip, pressing me up against the fridge. He pressed his forehead hard against mine. "I'm not going to do this anymore. Do you understand?"

I didn't, so I remained quiet.

"I will not put the people I love through this for one second longer. Regardless of you and me, what kind of person would do this to their partner?"

Again, I didn't know, so I remained quiet.

He sighed heavily, then ran his thumb across my cheekbone to take the sting out of his anger and impatience. "I'm not going to do this anymore, Elle. Do you understand?"

This time, I nodded even though I still wasn't certain what he meant.

The delicate chime of the doorbell sounded, and Sinclair's jaw clenched fiercely when I moved to answer it. His hands flexed against my skin painfully before letting go.

I answered the door to find Sebastian speaking with the young woman delivering the alcohol Elena had ordered. Sebastian was speaking to her easily, taking the bags from her and handing them off to me so that they could take a selfie together. I watched as he whispered something in her ear that made her burst into unattractive and beautifully genuine laughter. Mama and I smiled at each other as they said their goodbyes.

"You charmer," I teased Sebastian as he leaned down to give me the customary kisses.

"Yes, Seb, are all the older ones taken?" Elena said as she breezed into the living room, now wearing a lovely black sheath dress. I could smell her Chanel perfume as she swooped in to give him a kiss.

"Elena," Mama chastised while embracing Seb herself.

She shrugged one delicate shoulder. "It was a joke."

"It's all right, Mama. Elena has never had a very good sense of humor," Sebastian said as he swung off his leather jacket, tossed it onto the side table, and grabbed my hand to tug me farther into the apartment.

"Hang up your coat, you ape," Elena called after us before we disappeared around the corner into the kitchen.

Sinclair was still there, decanting the mandatory red wine while he listened to someone on his phone.

"I want at least three options by the end of next week, Margot," he was saying as we swept into the kitchen.

Sebastian grabbed the extra bottle from Sin's hand and poured himself an overfull glass.

I raised my brows. "Tough day?"

His shoulders were nearly at his ears with tension, and I watched as he tugged his hands through his hair so that it stuck up at funny angles. "Tate wants to produce my film."

"And that's a problem because?"

He didn't answer me immediately. Instead, he leaned against the fridge and stared out the window into the darkening cityscape.

"Rumor is, she's sleeping with Jace Galantine."

I winced because even I knew who Jace Galantine was, award-winning actor, modelizer, and all-around stud. He graced the cover of so many magazines, gossip rags, and movie posters that I hardly went a day without seeing his gorgeous face plastered to something.

"I'm sorry, Seb," I murmured, placing a hand on his tensed arm. "I mean, she is married too, so how much more can this hurt?"

I knew it was the wrong thing to say as soon as it left my lips.

He swung his vibrant gaze to me and glared. "Well, I guess I know where you stand on infidelity."

I bit my lip and focused on not looking over at the silent Sinclair currently assembling the meal from Dean & Deluca's on to serving plates.

"I'm sorry," Elena said as she came into the kitchen with Mama's arm tucked through her own. "I wouldn't have invited Savannah if I knew you two were fighting."

"What?" Sebastian snapped, rounding on her like a provoked bear.

I placed a gently restraining hand on him again and spoke softly, "Why would you invite Savannah Richardson?"

"She is a good friend, no?" Mama asked. "She used to come for the dinners always, and now, we never see her."

I peered up at Sebastian. His face was deeply etched with pained anger, and I suddenly understood the need for Sinclair's perfectly composed mask. How horrible it must be for Sebastian to have his emotions so clearly displayed for others to see.

Elena noted it with triumph, a sly smile corrupting her pretty mouth. "Should I call and ask her not to come, Sebastian? Her husband is away on business, so she would be banished to a Thanksgiving dinner for one..."

I squeezed his bicep and watched him swallow hard before saying, "You've already asked her. We wouldn't want to be rude by uninviting her now."

Elena nodded curtly, but her lips twitched down, and I wondered, not for the first time, how she could be so callous toward her own family.

"Why doesn't everyone sit down?" Sinclair suggested. "The food is hot, the wine is breathing, and the last of our party should arrive soon."

As if on cue, the doorbell rang, and Sebastian shrugged off my hand to go answer it. I followed him, eager to escape the messy atmosphere leftover like an oil spill in the kitchen.

"Cosima!" I cried out when I saw her step through the door and into Seb's enthusiastic embrace.

Despite my cry, the twins hugged silently for a long minute, dissolving into each other more and more with each second as the tension they had both been holding dissipated. There was that deep understanding of another person that I so badly craved. It didn't need to be romantic, but the closest I had ever come to elementally knowing someone like that was with Sinclair, and as I thought of him, a yawning abyss of loneliness blossomed in my heart.

I noticed someone emerge from the other room in my periphery and turned slightly, surprised to see Elena standing mute in the other doorway. Her expression was soft, almost soggy with longing, and I knew it reflected the same emotions in my own face. I didn't feel a kinship with her over our mutual exclusion, though, mostly because I had spent years wanting the same closeness between us and only been met with failure.

"*Mia famiglia*," Cosima cried as she stepped away from Sebastian and grinned at the rest of us. "It wouldn't be quite the party without me, would it?"

She stepped forward to embrace me next and spoke softly for my ears only. "And I had to rescue my sister from spending another night here, hmm?"

I tried not to stiffen at her insinuation, but she only laughed and squeezed my frozen shoulders reassuringly before moving on to kiss the next family member.

Within minutes, everyone was listening raptly to the story she told about a frazzled mother's young children asking to braid her hair into corn-rows on the flight, and the previous uneasiness in the apartment was banished by laughter.

DINNER PROCEEDED WITHOUT A HITCH, AND I DIDN'T KNOW WHO WAS MOST surprised by it. Savannah Richardson arrived demurely. Sebastian was able to keep his calm and react neutrally, even excellently, to her presence by becoming the life of the party. After an initial comment about the food not being as excellent as her own, Mama settled into her matriarchal spotlight with good grace and bantered hilariously with Cage and Santiago, who both seemed to delight in flirting outrageously with her.

Even Elena was quiet, smiling instead of contributing, even though I knew Cage's outrageous arrogance and bawdy humor grated on her nerves. She sat beside Sinclair, and at one point, she reached over to take his hand, but otherwise, the two didn't talk. It didn't give me much hope because Sinclair barely looked my way. Instead, he spent most of the evening talking to Cosima. I felt a curious kind of jealousy when she made him laugh.

We had already presented the pie and tiramisu when the first bomb dropped.

"Katarina would love to be here for your showing, Elle," Santiago said to me, his grin wide with pride as we spoke about my upcoming showcase. "I will have to fly her out specially."

"I would love to see her," I admitted. "And not just because she would make sure you didn't wear this awful chartreuse blazer again."

He laughed, drawing attention to our side conversation.

"How do you know Kat?" Elena asked casually.

And that was when I realized we should not have been talking about Mexico at the dinner table.

"Um..." Sweat broke out across my brow, but surprisingly enough, Cosima stepped in to save me.

"They met in Mexico," she exclaimed with just enough enthusiasm. "Giselle was feeling a little lonely so I sent her Iago's information."

"Where did you stay, Giselle?" Savannah asked.

My mouth opened and closed, but again, Cosima saved me by saying, "I recommended the Westin. Sinclair, weren't you there too? I'm surprised you two didn't cross paths."

Savannah laughed lightly. "It's a small world we live in."

"Yes," Elena said immediately, leaning forward in her seat to smile sweetly. "Savvy, did I hear that Tate is producing Seb's new film?"

I watched Savannah's round eyes widen with shock. "I wasn't aware he was interested, but I'm not surprised. Sebastian is wildly creative."

My brother snorted softly but refrained from retorting. I tried to curb my selfish relief at the turn in conversation, but I couldn't resist looking over at Sinclair, who was looking at me with those fathomless blue eyes.

"Weren't you considering Jace Galantine for a role?" Elena continued, casually taking a sip of her wine.

Sebastian grew still, his fists clenched in his lap while Savannah's comically wide eyes blinked owlishly.

"Giselle, how is the exhibition shaping up?" Cage asked, his black eyes sparkling with rage as they swept over Elena and on to me.

Elena pouted slightly, her attempt to derail the evening once again rerouted, but I had no doubt that she would find something disparaging to say about my artwork too.

"Very well, thank you. I'm nearly finished. Sebastian was one of the best little brothers a girl could ask for. He sent me Kayla Kensington, and my friend Stefan Kilos is visiting specifically to be a part of the showcase." I laughed. "He was offended that he wasn't my first call."

"Stefan Kilos, the Greek shipping magnate?" Elena asked with her eyebrows raised in a haughty semblance of respect as if she couldn't believe her dubious bohemian sister could have such a connection.

"Exactly the one."

"Will he stay with you?" Sinclair asked coolly, his eyes focused on Elena's hand as he ran his thumb along the back of it.

My heart twisted painfully, but I fought to keep my expression neutral. When had the dinner table turned into such a passive-aggressive war zone?

"What the hell are those?" Sebastian asked loudly, leaning over the table to grab Cosima's outstretched hand as she accepted a new bottle of wine from Santiago.

She tried to wrench her hand out of his grip, but his other hand snatched her wrist and shoved down her long sleeve to reveal deeply purple bruises encircling her forearm.

Everyone gasped, but Cosima stood without embarrassment and snapped her arm away. "Nothing that concerns you."

"*Nothing that concerns me,*" Sebastian mocked in a high imitation. "You are kidding me. I think my sister wearing such ugly bruises would obviously concern me."

"It's nothing," she insisted between clenched teeth.

I could see the anger rise in her like a tsunami, the receding calm before the rush of vicious fury.

"Cosima," Mama tried, "who does this to you?"

"No one."

"Cosima–" Elena said.

"No. I do not want to talk about this. I'm fine. Nothing was done against my will."

"What can you mean?" Mama asked.

My eyes snapped to Sinclair, and the same horrified understanding dawned in his eyes.

"I liked what was done to me, understand?" Cosima explained haughtily. Her chin jutted forward like an arrogant boxer's, daring someone to hit her with censure. "These are reminders of pleasure, not abuse. It is no concern of yours anyway, but especially because these"—she bared her bruised wrists—"do not concern me."

Awkward silence reigned at the table as her meaning sank in. Despite my own experience with mild pain in the bedroom, the livid color of her markings scared me. Sinclair had never deliberately hurt me, his spankings were just firm enough to entice, and I couldn't imagine true pain ever entering into our partnership. The idea of Cosima brutally bound as she must have been to incur those bruises made me angry despite myself.

"I will kill him," Sebastian growled.

"You will not. You cannot find him, and I do not want to choose between you or him," Cosima retorted calmly. "Now, if we are done discussing *my* sex life, I think we should all get back to this delicious treat, hmm?"

I was surprised when Savannah Richardson was the one to clear her throat and swallow a large mouthful of tiramisu. "It really is delicious."

There was a smattering of agreement from Cage, Santiago, and me before everyone decided to take her lead and tuck into the cake.

I was so concentrated on acting normally that it took me a moment to notice the tension between Elena and Sinclair. She had removed her hand from his and angled her body fairly obviously away from him. As for him, his face was immobile, his body perfectly rigid. He was furious.

Finally, after a few minutes, he couldn't take it anymore.

"Jesus, Elena, I'm not going to bite." He reached over to tug her seat closer to his once again.

Elena flinched.

"For fuck's sake," Sinclair swore, his face morphing into intense disgust. "I'm not a monster, Elena. I didn't do that to your sister."

"No," she murmured, genuine fear in her eyes, "but you could have. You like that kind of thing."

"I do not!" he roared, heedless of the half dozen other people at the table. "I have never hurt a woman like that in my life. I would never do that to you."

"Only because I don't allow it," Elena whispered.

Sinclair pushed to his feet, his face slack with horror as he stared down at his partner. I couldn't imagine how he must have felt, faced with a girl-friend who was disgusted by his sexual proclivities and who flagrantly denounced them in front of her family. I was just as horrified by Cosima's confession as the rest of them, and I could even vaguely understand Elena's irrational terror, but to fight with him like that in front of other people? I shuddered with sympathy and revulsion.

"I am not Christopher," Sinclair said softly after a long minute of silently staring down at her. She still didn't face him. "I am not that man, and I have never treated you with any degree of violence. I worshipped you, Elena, and still it is not enough."

He sighed, his hand lifting to tug at a lock of hair that was no longer there. "All these years and I still disgust you. I, for one, am tired of it." He stared at her, waiting for her to respond, but she only stared off into the distance. Finally, he turned to the rest of the table and smiled thinly. "I'm sorry for disrupting dessert, but if you'll excuse us, I think Elena and I need to be alone."

"Don't be dramatic, Daniel." Elena straightened, suddenly remem-bering her aversion to drama even though she was so often the cause of it. "Everyone, please stay and finish the cake. It's Thanksgiving, for goodness' sake."

Everyone remained seated, paralyzed by the frozen air between Elena and Sinclair.

"Yes, I'm sorry. Of course, stay and enjoy the cake. I have business at the office, so I have to go, but…" Sinclair tried to smile, but the result was more of a grimace. "Please, stay and enjoy."

Without another word, he crossed to the front door, unhooked his overcoat, and left, closing the door softly behind him. All heads swung from the closed door to Elena, finding her dark eyes filled with tears.

"Oh, Elena," Cosima scolded softly. "Why do you do this to yourself?"

"You don't understand," she tried to explain.

"No, I think we do," Cage said, standing up to look directly down into Elena's face. "You are a coward, Elena Lombardi, and you do not even try to hide it well."

She opened her mouth on a gasp, but Cage was already bending down to kiss Mama on the cheek and say his goodbyes. I accepted a kiss and a shoulder squeeze from him as well before he was out the door, Santiago following quickly in his wake.

Savannah was just standing up to do similarly, I think, when Elena finally croaked, "Please stay, Savvy. I know I'm wretched, but please, stay for a while."

The older woman looked quickly at Mama, who was thoroughly shocked into silence, and then at Sebastian, who seemed to teeter between disgust and sympathy for his older sister.

"Okay," Savannah said slowly. "But only if we can play charades."

Elena's lip trembled fiercely before she finally gave in to a weepy laugh.

Chapter Seventeen

I PLAYED ONE GAME OF CHARADES WITH THE REST OF THE GUESTS, BUT MY mind was hazardously preoccupied with thoughts of Sinclair. After one too many confused glances my way from Mama and Cosima, I said my good-byes with the excuse of a stomachache.

And it did ache, a deep churning that twisted my gut up like a coiled snake, ready to strike out against my impure thoughts. I couldn't help replaying the dinner over and over in my head—Elena's intense disdain and Sinclair's utter defeat. The perfect couple I had constructed of them in my mind was far from reality, but the fractured nature of their relationship —very much like my own with Elena—didn't make my love for Sinclair any more *okay*. We were still two people actively deceiving someone we had promised to love and care for; Elena's bad behavior did not justify our own.

I self-flagellated myself during the entire cab ride, each stroke harder than any Sinclair would ever land, yet I still told the cabbie to take me to the Faire building, still walked the steps to the wide glass doors and buzzed in with the night receptionist who thankfully recognized my name from the gallery. I watched my reflection in the shiny chrome of the elevator doors as they closed and ferried me up to Sinclair's sixtieth floor, and instead of running away from the villain I faced in the mirror, I smiled sharply at myself and strode from the elevator with the confidence of a seasoned sinner.

He knew the moment I entered his office even though I didn't make a sound, and he didn't change his position, angled away from me as he stared out the glass walls behind his desk at the glimmering city rolled out before us. I stayed close to the door because despite my determination to see him, I didn't know how to articulate my desire to comfort him. More importantly, I didn't know if he would even accept it.

"I love you."

That was what I wanted to say. I wanted to smooth it like salve into the wounds Elena had inflicted with her scared and bitter words, wanted to coat him in it until he shone with it for everyone to see.

How many times in the past few weeks had I imagined hearing those words from his lips? Imagined how the power of them would ignite the latent fire in my heart until it raced through my veins, eviscerating everything heavy and dull, the boulders of rationale and pain, the horrors of guilt and yearning. Burning it all clean until I wasn't even a vessel anymore, maybe not even human, just red, smoldering flames feeding on shiny, weightless air.

"I love you."

Sinclair turned to face me, but I tucked my chin in so that the long curtain of my hair would conceal the grotesque longing on my face. He didn't need to see that. I didn't *want* him to see that. It was bad enough that I saw it every day in the mirror, felt it in every single pore of my skin like old sweat and grime. I wanted Sinclair to see me differently, supple and shiny with love.

"Giselle." His cold tone cracked through my simmering thoughts, and I jerked toward him unconsciously. We were suddenly so close that I could see the texture of different blues in his crackling eyes.

"Are you going to say something?" he asked.

He was grinning, but it was twisted badly like a misshapen paperclip rendered useless.

"I'm sorry, I must have been zoning out." I clamped my sweaty palms together in my lap. "What did you say?"

"I love you."

Blink.

Pulse.

Blink.

Pulse, stutter, and pulse.

One hand ran through his hair, and he looked away, slightly over my shoulder as if he couldn't bear to look at me.

"I love you so much that I'm clumsy with it. There are so many times when I stared at you and waited for some sort of poetry to form, words that were worthy of my love for you, the intense, nonsensical, filled to the brim way that I feel about you. I pride myself on being an elegant man. I wasn't born that way, but I was raised it, and when those words won't come, others do. The crass, dirty, and poor part of me emerges like a fucking animal, and all I want to do is claim you, put my scent onto every inch of your gorgeous skin, scream like a psychopath at everyone who looks at you that *you are mine.*"

He was almost panting, his chest heaving and his features cracked wide open to reveal the massive crater I had unknowingly excavated. A yawning darkness filled with his love for me. The heavy sound of his breath and the sight of his pulse fluttering desperately in his throat reminded me to breathe.

"Do you understand, Elle? What you do to me? I want to brand you and fuck you and marry you and breed you and do any goddamn thing I can think of to bind us together so that no one, not one single fucking person, can get between us. Because, *fuck*, ever since I saw you pale and needy and so gorgeous my bones ached on that plane, there have been things between us. Damn important things that just won't go away." He sucked in a deep breath and ran both hands through his hair before his eyes finally landed on mine, sliding into place like a key turning in a lock. "I know you don't want to hurt your sister, and you don't want to cause any more turmoil in your family, but, Elle, my siren, my love, I am being ripped to pieces every day knowing I can't have you."

These words were better than anything I could have possibly thought to long for, to imagine, and they settled around me like fine silk, the softest satin. But instead of luxuriating in the feel of it, I tangled myself up until I couldn't breathe.

"You don't mean it. I mean, not really. It's the excitement, the novelty and mystery of being with someone new, someone so different, and I don't know, maybe younger?" I turned away from the slow freezing of his features; I couldn't bear to watch the ice creep over my favorite blue eyes. "You *think* you want me, but maybe you just don't want Elena, especially right at this moment when she was just so cruel to you, or maybe you're having a midlife crisis, or maybe you just want a submissive or—"

His hand on my arm was firm but not painful as he pulled me around to face him, our hips flush and his breath on my cheeks. "That is an awful lot of maybes, Elle."

"We barely know each other," I lied, and it felt like blasphemy.

"I will tell you anything you want to know. You have free rein to dissect my soul. It is yours to do with as you please."

My heart beat rapidly at the back of my throat, so fiercely that I almost gagged. I had never pictured a declaration of love like this. Everyone spoke of softness and ease as loving words spilled from their lips, of euphoria and the miasmic shift as a yearning heart clicked into place with its soul mate. So why did I feel sick and aching, poised on the edge of an abyss so gargantuan and dark that I could see no means of escape? My fears lived within that crater, the deepest and darkest of them, and as I looked down at them, I knew the decision I had to make—to love Sinclair or not—would mean the difference in facing them.

"They'll hate me," I whispered brokenly as tears slipped over my cheeks and seeped into his fingers.

He pressed his forehead to mine so hard it almost hurt. "They might."

I was both furious and relieved that he agreed so easily.

"How can you know it's worth it?"

His face spasmed with hurt, but he recovered quickly. "I've never been so certain of anything. *Mon amour pour toi est plus grand que le monde.*"

My love for you is bigger than the world.

I sucked in a breath and choked as it fractured in my lungs.

"I just got them back, Sin," I tried to explain.

He lifted his head and stared down at me with eyes that were half-shuttered. He was beginning to understand that I could seriously be rebuffing him.

"They will forgive you. They are your family, and they also understand the ways of the heart. I think they will know that we tried to stay away, but..." He shrugged in that Gallic way that made huge issues seem ridiculously easy.

"They won't."

He stared at me for a long time. I watched his eyes shift through ten different shades of blue. I watched as his heart calcified, and I felt mine crumble in my chest.

"So you will not," he finally said.

I bit my lip, but it was answer enough for him.

With a suddenness that made me gasp, he grabbed my shoulders between his hands and shook me slightly. His beautiful face was twisted into a snarl, his habitually cool mask shattered.

"Why are you choosing heartbreak? It will not stop when you wake up tomorrow, Giselle. It will not stop in a week or a month. This pain will *haunt* you until it devours you whole. You are saving your sister, you think? You are wrong. I had to choose between you and Elena, and I have. I made the right choice. But you had the same choice, and now," he snarled and took an abrupt step away from me, "you are choosing wrong."

He turned on his heel without giving me a chance to speak and disappeared into the darkness of the unlit building behind me.

Chapter Eighteen

I WOKE UP HOLLOW AS A DRIED REED, MY BRITTLE LIMBS CREAKING IN PROTEST as I awkwardly swung myself out of bed. The light slanting in through the gap in the curtains was winter white and dim in the gloom of the early afternoon. I'd slept the day away. Recovering from a crying jag was the worst kind of hangover. The throbbing pulse in my head was stronger than the weak one of my fractured heart.

I tried not to think about him, but everything—from the way the scalding shower water pounded against my skin in a parade of pained and pleasurable sensation to the leftover crepes I ate for breakfast—reminded me of my Frenchman. Finally, after I absentmindedly put dish soap into my coffee for the second time, I succumbed to the cyclone of Sinclair-related thoughts that threatened to dominate my psyche.

I remembered all the beautiful things he said to me that I hadn't been aware of at the time, the many moments he might as well have declared himself to me that I was too stupid to see. I cut myself with memories, strangulated myself with the recollection of his touch. It was easier to wallow in the pain than to conquer it.

When I finally emerged from my bedroom, I was perfectly turned out. I had even painted my nails, something I never did because the chemicals from my paint solutions always dissolved the polish.

I didn't want anyone to have a reason to point out my heartbreak.

Even though it hit me like a punch to the kidneys, I wasn't surprised to see Elena in the living room drinking tea with Cosima.

She looked up at me when I entered and smiled sadly as if I could understand what she was going through. It disgusted me that I did.

"He's done it. He broke up with me," she said.

Cosima didn't say anything, and I had the feeling she hadn't in quite a while. She was perched on the edge of the deep leather chair, her arms braced on her legs as she leaned forward to stare into the bottom of her mug. She looked like she was trying to read her future in the tealeaves.

"I'm so sorry," I said because I was.

She nodded again, her movements heavy with weariness. Despite that, though, she looked even more put together than me in a gorgeous coal gray blazer and matching skirt with every curl perfectly held in place. I noticed the suitcase leaning against the couch and frowned at it.

"I have business in LA for the week."

"Awkward timing, can't you reschedule or send someone else?"

"Why would I? This is perfect timing. I fully expect Daniel to come back to his senses after a week without me."

"Lena…" Cosima murmured, shaking her head as she continued to look into her mug. "You said some terrible things about his character. His pride would take more than a week to recover, not to mention his emotions."

Elena sniffed. "As always, you underestimate Daniel's level-headedness. I apologized to him, and when I get back, I'll show him how sorry I am. Honestly, I didn't even say anything until he acused me. I was just shocked and upset about your wrists and then it all…snowballed."

When Cosima didn't respond, Elena's mouth rolled into a pout. "You don't think he'll forgive me, truly?"

Cosima lifted her head on her hunched shoulders and looked at me for a long second before turning to our sister. "I really don't know. I don't even know if this breakup is about forgiveness. You may hate me for saying this, but really, Lena, are you passionately in love with him?"

She opened her mouth to protest, but Cosima held up a hand and qualified, "I mean the kind of love that sucks all the air out of your lungs so that the only hope of getting your breath back is by kissing the man who owns it."

"Of course," Elena said, too quickly.

I wondered for a wild minute if what Cosima implied was true? Could Elena really not be in love with Sin?

It wouldn't eviscerate my wrongdoings, but it would go a hell of a long way to making my selfish self feel better.

"We've been through a lot together, and in a few months, this crazy period of our lives will be just another thing we overcame. I won't lose him. We are perfect for each other."

Maybe that was the problem. Elena and Sinclair were so perfectly suited on paper that there was no room for improvisation, for growth or movement.

"How did you leave things with him?" Cosima asked.

"He's staying at a hotel, and he says he is moving out." Her lower lip trembled, and she bit it viciously to stop it. Then in a softer voice, she confessed, "I've never lived alone before."

The three of us shared a moment of silence, all staring into the distance absorbed by our own reflections.

"I have to get going," Elena said, standing abruptly.

Cosima nodded, standing too in order to embrace her. I watched Elena step eagerly into her arms, and I wondered at my younger sister's ability to coax the best and most beautiful qualities from everyone. I wondered for the millionth time how she and Elena could have such a better, healthier relationship.

"I'll cab with you to the airport, *si*?" she murmured to Elena, who closed her eyes and nuzzled closer.

My heart squeezed painfully with the keen awareness of betrayal. At this point, did it matter that I had turned Sinclair down when I had already done so much to orchestrate Elena's heartbreak?

My phone lit up from where I'd place it on the coffee table, Sinclair's name flashing like a neon sign. I grabbed it hastily, aware of Cosima's eyes on me, and read the text message.

The Frenchman: Meet me at Devereaux's restaurant in one hour.

I looked up at Elena, small and doll-like in Cosima's arms, and felt the ugliness of my sin saturate my soul.

I texted him back immediately—*okay*.

HE WAS AT THE SAME TABLE CAGE AND I HAD OCCUPIED A FEW WEEKS AGO when we had run into Elena and him on a date. It was cyclical and so totally Sinclair to have chosen it. He stood to greet me with a kiss on the cheek but remained silent as the waiter held out my chair, and I settled in. His quietude left me jittery and intoxicated on the emotional fumes I kept bottled up inside myself. I couldn't even begin to guess at why he had invited me for lunch, especially because he had been too angry, so atypically expressive last night.

"I didn't handle that well," he began, and I wondered for the millionth time how he could do that, switch from human to robot in under a second. "The affair and the secret of it, but specifically, last night when I tried to express my feelings for you."

"Oh?"

His eyes narrowed slightly at my composure. Inside, I was as nonplussed by it as he was.

"The first time I wanted to tell you, we were in Mexico, and you weren't even awake. I had just netted that enormous fish, and I flew up to the second deck to rub your nose in it. You make me feel like a boy, and boys do that kind of thing to girls they like. But you were asleep, sprawled out on your stomach with all that coppery hair spilled around you. I quite literally couldn't breathe as I looked at you and something fundamental shifted in my chest like tectonic plates." He shook his head, shearing himself from the memory. "I was ready to heed your siren song, jump off the side of the boat and into the promise of your arms. But I didn't know if you felt the same, and maybe even more importantly, I take my obligations seriously, and I wasn't ready to entertain the idea of leaving Elena."

He cleared his throat and brought a glass of ice water to his lips. I watched his Adam's apple bob as he swiftly drank half the glass, and I tried not to be endeared by his nervousness.

"Then you told me that you loved me." He laughed harshly. "Or rather, I ordered you to tell me, and as always, you obeyed beautifully. I have never witnessed anything so stunning as the sight of you giving yourself to me, heart and body, with your skin covered in starlight."

God, he was poetic.

My starving soul absorbed those devastating words before I could remind it that we were on a hunger strike.

"After we returned to the hotel and you fell asleep, I called Cage and made a plan."

He waited for me to swallow back the mass of hope that rose like bile in my throat.

"After I broke things off with Elena, I would stay with him while I looked for another apartment. It would take a few months to get all my affairs in order, but then I was coming for you. Robert Corbett had already recommended an excellent private investigator, and I was fairly sure you had told Stefan Kilos who you really were. I was so determined, I even wrote out a to-do list," he admitted with a mocking twist of his lips.

"You didn't," I breathed because this was too good to be true.

"I did. It took a bit longer than I may have liked, and obviously, there is even more in the way than I had originally planned on, but now I'm doing it. I've contacted an attorney to help us negotiate the separation of our assets and told Elena unequivocally that our relationship is over."

"She doesn't think it is." I remembered the determination in her eyes that morning and shivered because there was a storm coming and the clouds rolling across the horizon were the exact color of Elena's eyes.

"To me, it is. It has been for a while now."

"I don't think that changes anything. Elena is still my sister. You are still her boyfriend –"

"Ex-boyfriend."

"Fine, ex-boyfriend. But Sin, you still stayed with her for weeks even after you knew who I was," I pointed out.

Until I said it out loud, I hadn't really known that fact had bothered me. I could focus all I wanted on my reasons for staying away from him, but my heart focused on *his* reticence at the end of the day.

Sinclair adjusted his cuff links, twin circles of silver engraved with the Percy family crest. "I did, and whatever excuses I give you will be exactly that, excuses. But I want to give them to you nonetheless. The first was simply selfish. When I met you on the plane, I told you that I didn't like the idea that you could change my life, and I meant it. My life pre-Giselle was a well-oiled machine. I had a lovely, intelligent girlfriend who loved me and whose aspirations perfectly suited my own. After years of work, my business was firmly established in the city, and I was finally expanding internationally. My parents were proud of me." He shrugged as he said it, but I knew that last point was the most important.

"When I saw you in Caprice's kitchen the night we returned, I wasn't prepared. Mostly because you fucking left that morning before I could tell you how I felt, and I spent the rest of the day searching for you, trying to track down that damn Kilos to beat your information out of him if I had to. When that didn't work, it dawned on me that maybe you didn't want to be with me. It might have had something to do with Margot's incessant scolding on the plane ride home, but by the time we landed, I had already convinced myself that you were just a holiday affair."

"I didn't want to leave you, but..." I trailed off because I didn't know how to explain, in any language available to me, how I had felt that final night, tucked into his arms with so much love to give but no future to give it to.

He sighed raggedly. "There is one more excuse, and it is a big one. In fact, it's the mainstay of why I have been with Elena all this time, maybe even why she feels so dependant on me when she is a capable, independent woman all on her own."

His pause felt cruel, like a commercial break at the climax of a television show.

"About eight months into our relationship, Elena got pregnant."

I choked on my spit and started to cough.

Sinclair waited for me to stop before continuing, "I wasn't thrilled about it. I wasn't ready for children or even sure that I wanted them. But you know Elena. She was thrilled."

I could imagine her excitement, her face made uncharacteristically soft with joy, her voice high and bright and accented because she would forget to modulate her speech. My sister had always wanted children more than anything else. My hand curled into a fist over my heart because I knew the story wasn't going to end well.

The waiter came, having lingered long enough on the sidelines waiting for a break in our conversation, and I happily let Sinclair order for me.

"I adjusted. There wasn't really anything else to do but accept it. Elena wouldn't get an abortion, and even though I wasn't sure if I wanted it, I didn't want her to get one either. The only thing I remained firm on was the fact that I didn't want to get married. She seemed okay with it then, I think, because she was already too preoccupied with being a mom.

"She had a plan. Finish her first year of law school and then take a year off to care for the baby. We moved in together, and she began to buy little things for the baby, onesies with baby animals on them and this little pair of sneakers, each shoe smaller than my fist."

"She lost it," I blurted out because I couldn't handle it anymore.

"She lost it," he confirmed in a hollow voice that matched the emptiness in his eyes.

"C'est tellement triste," I murmured as unbearable sadness flooded through the suddenly open door of empathy I felt for Elena.

"It was horrible," he agreed, unable to look at me. "Only Mama and

Cosima knew. Sebastian was away on location, and Elena didn't want any of her friends to know about the pregnancy until the second trimester."

Sinclair sighed and raked a hand through his hair. "The thing is, she had an ectopic pregnancy. It ruptured her fallopian tube."

"She can't have kids," I concluded in horror. "She always made adoption sound like a choice, not the only option."

Sinclair nodded jerkily.

Fuck.

I couldn't understand why Sinclair would have brought me here to tell me this. I'd already rejected him. Why did he need me to feel the true weight of this guilt? Was it to alleviate some of his own or merely so that I knew all the facts? For one moment, my passion for him flared into hatred so pure I felt electric with it. How could he have done all of this to my sister?

I glared at him with my teeth clenched so hard my head started to pound. He looked back at me, his expression perfectly neutral, his mouth slightly open as if he was willing to breathe in my toxic breath, to house all of my self-hatred and shame within himself so that I wouldn't have to.

He reached across the table to place his hand parallel to mine. I couldn't have withstood his touch at that moment, but his gesture of togetherness was just as comforting.

"I hesitated to tell you because it is really Elena's secret to share, and she is very guarded about it. There is a small chance she could conceive again, but the doctors have assured her not to count on it. She feels defective even though that is far from the truth. The ordeal brought us closer, and I felt compelled to stay with her, to protect her and care for her because I had done that to her. I took away her dream, and the worst part is, I was secretly happy about losing the baby."

"I told you we aren't good people," I said softly. "But not wanting the baby didn't make the miscarriage happen. You aren't to blame either, Sin."

"I know that now. I know a lot of things now." Finally, for the first time since I had sat down across from him, he looked into my eyes and let his pretty, composed mask fall away.

I wanted to reach out and touch that astounding, angular face. Instead, I touched the edge of my pinky finger to his where it lay on the table.

"I know that staying with Elena because I feel that I owe her my love after what happened isn't fair to either of us. I know that it will take a long time to completely separate my life from hers, and I know that she will likely never forgive me. It hurts me to know that, Elle. To know that a woman I have spent the past four years of my life loving will always hate me. I think that pain will stay with me forever, and it's going to ruin me at the most inconvenient times. I may not have been madly *in* love with her, but she was my best friend, my partner, and confidant.

"But I also know that I have never loved anyone the way I love you, and I honestly know that I never will. I understand that this is hard on you, that it's unfair of me to ask you to choose me over your family, but I'm still asking you to make that decision."

I opened my mouth to say something, then didn't.

The waiter arrived with our dishes. When he placed a beautiful plate of seared Dorado in front of me, I blinked up at Sinclair. I felt so vulnerable. I was afraid a slight breeze would dissolve me, scatter me across the air.

"I'm asking you to make the decision, but I don't want you to make it right now, and I don't want you to make it lightly. I want you to know what I know. I have never been so serious or sincere in my life when I say that I want to be with you. I meant what I said in my office. I want to live with you, Elle, and one day, I want to claim you as my wife. Someday soon after that, if you don't mind, I want to have children with you."

"Sin," I said as I tore into the fish with the prongs of my fork but didn't eat. "You can't expect me to think you've done a complete about-face on marriage and babies."

"You're right. That is why I invited you here today. I wanted to give you fair warning that I am going to woo you, Giselle Moore. I am going to show you who I am and how much I love you every day, and I am not going to stop until I've convinced you that I am the only family you need."

"You're killing me."

He nodded curtly and competently cut into his steak, utterly polished and confident once more. "It's part of the process. This is going to kill you. This *has* been killing you all along, but I'm going to pull you out of this hellish situation, and I'm going to love you more than anyone ever has every day after to prove to you how much that pain was worth it. We are going to resurrect each other."

I stared at him numbly. Sinclair's self-assurance might have drawn me to him originally, and his aloofness had tempted me to linger, but it was evidence of this, his boundless passion, which lay waste to my resolve. I tried valiantly to digest everything that he said, but it felt as if I lacked the education, the fundamental principles needed to answer this mathematically, reasonably. Maybe because there was no way to respond reasonably to such a tangled conundrum.

Sinclair finished his steak in silence. A detached part of my mind wondered how difficult it was for him to restrain himself from ordering me to eat. My food grew cold and congealed, ravaged by my nerves but untouched. Still, I stared, my mind so full of thoughts that it shorted out and left me blank.

Finally, after paying for the bill, Sinclair offered me a small, genuine smile.

"I know this is a lot to take in, which is why I am more than willing to give you time to make the decision. The only thing I am not going to do is give you space."

He reached into the breast pocket of his blazer, concealing something shiny in his palm. My skin sizzled uncomfortably under the heat from his touch as he gently took my wrist in his and secured something to it. He raised my hand to his lips, brushing his mouth against my fingertips before releasing me.

I was too caught in his gaze to look at the heavy piece secured to my forearm.

"I own you as you own me, and I'm not going to hide it anymore. When you are ready to stand beside me and tell the world, I promise I will protect you from its censure. And I promise to work hard every day to repair our relationship with your family. I don't want you isolated from them."

We looked at each other, and I felt like his puppet brought to life, a creature with its own will but still tied fundamentally, irrevocably to him.

"I'll be seeing you soon, my siren," he said with a full-fledged grin as he stood and buttoned his blazer. "Oh, and make sure you eat something, *si*? It is hard to make life decisions on an empty stomach."

It took me a few minutes after his departure to clear the fog of my thoughts enough to look down at my wrist. The gorgeous silver and turquoise cuff I had admired in the Cabo San Lucas market with Candy winked at me under the noon sunlight. I told myself it was the glare that brought tears to my eyes, but as I looked down at the gift, all I could really think was *I'm fucked*.

Chapter Nineteen

Sinclair was true to his word.

The following day, a Saturday, I was discussing my finished paintings with Rossi and Eddie in the kitchen of Cosima's apartment when the lavender arrived. Eddie had offered to answer the door because my hands were full of canvases, and the next thing we knew, a team of men and women were carrying arrangements of fragrant purple stalks into the apartment. There were arrangements with white roses in delicately etched glass vases that they placed on every available table, four huge clay pots of it mixed with gorgeous golden grass that swayed in the breeze flowing in from the little balcony, and little silk embroidered sachets filled with the dried flowers that Eddie happily, and nosily, placed in our clothing drawers and closets. By the time they had finished, the apartment smelled like heaven. There was no note with the flowers, of which I was grateful because Rossi and Eddie were forced to accept that it was from Ulrich, the odious man I brunched with at Prune.

I opened the door Sunday to a smiling Santiago who had graced me with a kiss before handing me a brown paper wrapped package. I'd known somehow without opening it that it would be Frida Kahlo's 1926 sketch *Accident*, the very one I had admired with Katarina at Santiago's house party in Mexico. It seemed that Sinclair was calling everyone in my life in his quest to woo me. I wanted to be annoyed by it, but as I hung Kahlo's gorgeous conflicted work of art beside my bed, it was hard to be bothered by such thoughtfulness.

Monday was a framed picture of Sinclair and me from the Romani International Gala with a note that explained how he had paid the photographer for exclusive rights to the picture. I could understand why as soon as I studied it; we looked very much in love, or at least in lust, as I smiled up at him while accepting his hand. It was the moment he had asked me to go outside with him, and I could clearly remember the swirl of apprehension and giddiness that had coiled my stomach into a sailor's knot. Later that day, another picture arrived, this one tucked into an unmarked envelope. It was of me, captured when I was exiting the gallery. My hair was caught in the breeze, the curls fanning out behind me, and my dress pressed intimately to my curves. I didn't know when he would have taken this or why he sent it to me, but I carefully placed it in my nightstand all the same.

Cosima had been deliberately avoiding me, but on Tuesday, when she accepted a delivery of five packages from Dylan's Candy Bar, including their Ultimate Chocolate Sharing Sweet Treat Tower, she finally confronted me about the unmarked gifts.

"The apartment smells like Provence, that sketch in your bedroom is worth thousands of dollars, and now all this candy from your favorite shop?" Cosima stood before me with her hands fisted on her hips, and her yellow eyes narrowed. "Who the hell is this secret admirer, Elle? This is more than a casual crush. Though he clearly doesn't care about cavities..."

I shrugged and tucked my tongue beneath my teeth as I adjusted the shading on the painting of Candy's mouth sucking suggestively at an oversized cherry red lollipop.

"Giselle, talk to me."

"There's nothing to talk about."

"*Cazzatte*," Cosima said, calling me on my bullshit.

I sighed and carefully placed my brush on the palette before putting them both down. "Fine, I should say I don't want to talk about it."

"Giselle –"

"Hey, if you don't want to talk about the Mafia-eyed Dante, then I don't have to talk about this. Okay?"

Hurt flashed across her features before she screwed them shut with a twist of her mouth. "Fine."

I was happy she wasn't home on Wednesday to see the two tickets to watch Miles Davis play in the Rose Theater at Lincoln Center for his ninetieth birthday. I clutched the tickets to my chest and tried to temper the rapidity of my heartbeat with deep breaths.

When that didn't work, I called him.

"Bonjour, ma sirène. Ça va?"

His cool voice flowed over my skin like water, immediately cleansing me of my anxieties even though he was the cause of them.

"Sinclair," I said after clearing my throat and affecting a pretty badass professional tone. "I'm calling to return the tickets."

I could hear the smile in his voice. "I'm sorry, I thought I was speaking to the woman of my heart, Giselle Moore. Not some ungrateful...stewardess is it?"

"They aren't called that anymore, old man," I grumped, charmed out of my demeanor before I could help myself.

"And you've forgotten your manners, young lady."

I shivered at the image his words imparted, picturing myself over his lap for a spanking. He chuckled as if he knew what his words had done to me.

"Why did you give me two tickets?"

"I thought you could take a friend."

"Don't you want to go?"

"Yes. The tickets were originally for me, but I thought you would enjoy it more. I've seen him play twice before."

I shrugged into my gray coat and grabbed my keys from the hall table, unwilling to end the conversation even though I needed to leave for Terry Paulson's apartment.

"I didn't know you liked jazz," I said even though if I had taken the time to think about it, I might have guessed as much.

"We grew up listening to it in the orphanage. Cage actually considered being a jazz singer before the lure of rock stardom called to him."

I laughed, picturing the sexy, leather-pants-wearing Cage Tracey crooning soulfully over a piano.

"I love that sound," Sinclair said casually.

I stopped laughing.

"I won't take the tickets back, Elle. I want you to enjoy the experience. The Lincoln Center has magnificent acoustics, and I like to imagine you there, dressed up in some purple dress with your eyes closed to absorb the music. I only wish I could be there to watch you."

Watch *me*, not the legendary musician.

I swallowed hard and spoke before I could stop myself, "Come with me then."

My words were followed by silence, and I was just about to blurt out something for the sake of speech when he cleared his throat.

"I would like that very much. I have to work until the last moment, but if you could meet me at the office at seven, we can walk to Lincoln Center together. It isn't far."

My smile cut brutally into my cheeks. "Okay."

"Okay."

I knew without confirming that we were both smiling into the phone.

"I'll see you soon then, Giselle."

I nodded even though he couldn't see me and hung up.

I was still smiling when Terry Paulson opened the door for me twenty minutes later. She was clad in a bright floor-length kimono with her voluminous hair twisted into riotous curls. Huge hoop earrings adorned her ears, and her acrylic nails were a bloody red. My fingers itched to capture her particular brand of brazenness, a sexual appeal that was almost crass it was so bold.

"You look happy," Terry said, ushering me into her opulent top-floor apartment. "I hope I am at least partially to blame. Or am I the only one who has been excited for this all week?"

I laughed at her enthusiasm, immediately at ease despite the intimidation of our surroundings. A crystal chandelier the size of a Smart car hung from the foyer ceiling and nearly blinded me.

"At the risk of sounding like a pervert, I've been looking forward to painting you since we first met."

She laughed loudly, throwing her red-tipped hand out to playfully push at my chest. "You are delightful. Now, I hope you don't mind, but I've set things up in the master bedroom. Let Gus take your things for you. Did you take a cab here? I should have sent a car."

"It was no problem," I assured her as I handed off my cumbersome easel and wooden travel kit to the stoic-faced liveried butler who appeared beside me. "It's the only workout I get, so I actually look forward to it."

"You can't be serious." Terry's bright red lips parted over her white teeth, and I found myself wondering what that wide mouth would feel like against mine.

Sinclair had turned me into some kind of sex machine.

"I will have to take you to my tennis club. It's great exercise and good fun. Plus, I think you would look wonderful in a little white skirt." She winked at me, laughing lightly at my blush as she took my hand to lead me through a large corridor, up a set of marble stairs to the second floor and finally, into a bedroom painted a deep, lusty red.

A tarp covered the Persian rug before us, and Gus the Butler had already set up a small table and my easel. I moved over to the station, relieving him of his duties so that I could set up everything to my tastes.

"I did some research," Terry explained as she perched on the edge of her massive four-poster bed, "about sex in the modern-day art world. Pauly loves art, and he's been teaching me about it for the last couple of years, but I didn't really get into it until Elena mentioned your project. It seems like you are doing something similar to Jack Vettriano, yeah?"

I nodded. "There is definitely a similar theme, though there are actually quite a few contemporary painters who explore sexual themes. I really admire Lisa Yuskavage and Jenny Saville too."

"So it was the trendiness that got you interested in sexual fetishisms and fantasies?"

I bit my lip and moved away from the easel with my large draft book and pencil case. Taking a seat on a conveniently provided stool, I began to loosely sketch vignettes of Terry's long face, the deep contours of her collarbones, and the vulnerable recess between her breasts.

"Not exactly. I probably sound cliché, but I recently had a pretty torrid affair that opened my eyes to how many indecent things there are to indulge in. Afterward, I couldn't help looking at people and wonder at their sexual secrets." I looked up at her through my eyelashes, feeling strangely coquettish. "What are yours?"

Terry smiled slightly and edged herself slowly to the head of the bed. "I'm so glad you asked." I watched with lowered lids as she reclined against the heap of silk pillows, legs bent at the knee and braced open to reveal the deep shadows at the apex of her thighs. There was a barely imperceptible rattle as she retrieved something from behind the velvet curtains and produced thick metal and leather cuffs attached to the bed frame. "Would you mind helping me into this?"

I painted the New York socialite like that—bound to the headboard by leather handcuffs, legs spread, and torso raised like the Queen of Sheba languishing on her throne—for nearly four hours. She was a beautiful model, barely a fidget in sight and only one bathroom break. We chatted as I traced her curves across the thick paper and then even thicker canvas. Her New Jersey accent was at odds with her elegance, and I came to realize that even though her husband, Pauly, had taught her the finer graces of high society, Terry was still proud of her Jersey shore roots. She laughingly relayed that Paulson had suffered from insta-lust when they'd locked eyes at a function she was catering.

"He liked my nails and big hair," she explained, wriggling her fingers. "And I may have unbuttoned my top a teensy bit more than was respectable."

I found myself infusing the painting with semblances of her humor, the glimmer within the depths of her brown eyes, the tilt to her harlot red lips. My forehead was hot with feverish excitement, and even as my hand swirled across the canvas, I was thinking of other poses for her.

"Tell me more about your sex life," I coaxed. "Obviously, you enjoy restraints."

"We enjoy a lot of things," she purred, stretching sinuously as I released her from the cuffs.

Without thinking, I gently rubbed the ache out of her wrists. She ran her tongue along her teeth as she watched, her gaze heated. Despite the fact she was fifteen years older than me and, of course, a woman, I was inexplicably attracted to her. Something about her intensity and assuredness reminded me of Sinclair.

"Why don't you come with me to get my daily snack?" she asked after studying me for a long moment.

"Okay."

I let her lead me from the room by the hand after gathering my sketchbook, pencils, and camera.

"I'm so happy we did this," she said, her thumb stroking over my palm. "Your sister called both Pauly and me to discourage us, but she was worried for nothing."

Acid filled my gums. "Excuse me?"

"Hmm? Oh maybe I shouldn't have mentioned it. I think she was nervous that you would scare us off the deal with Daniel Sinclair. Honestly, I can't blame her. Pauly comes across as a real stick in the mud, and he is always bothering them about getting married." She looked over her shoulder to roll her eyes at me as we descended the stairs. "I swear that man could have grown up in Victorian England, all stuffy on the outside but a real perv deep down."

My laughter burst forth before I could help it, but Terry just grinned.

We arrived at a large wood-paneled door, and she knocked three times in a strange rhythm.

"She's a nice woman, your sister, though obviously not very supportive. Do you think it has something to do with that gigantic stick up her ass?" Terry asked me with wide eyes.

I laughed again even though the fact that Elena had once again tried to thwart my project made my belly heat with rage.

A murmur came from inside the room.

"Now, you may come inside and document, but try not to get in the way, okay? Pauly and I have a ritual, you see."

I nodded, my curiosity piqued, and my arousal already high.

Paulson was sitting behind a huge mahogany desk, talking on speakerphone to someone with a Southern accent. His helmet of silver hair glinted in the low light emitted from the antique brass fixtures, and his stern face was tight with frustration. Still, he didn't seem surprised when I entered behind his wife. He even gave us a nod of acknowledgment before turning back to his computer screen.

Terry squeezed my hand before dropping it and stepping farther into the room. I watched her approach the desk with her head bowed and her hands clasped demurely in front of her. When she reached his side, she dropped to her knees in a position of subservience as beautiful as origami.

Paulson ignored her, even when her robe pooled in a small puddle of blue silk around her knees.

Silently, I placed my bag of supplies on the ground and brought my camera to my face. I wondered if I should ask Paulson for permission, but just as I was opening my mouth to do so, he inclined his head at me.

I raised the camera and framed them in the shot. Paulson reached out idly to pet Terry's riotous curls.

Click.

My shutter closed over the sight.

My body digested the image of them like a shot of burning liquor. I placed my hand on an end table to steady myself. This was a real moment in the lifestyle I could have enjoyed with Sinclair. I didn't know how I missed it when I met them; maybe Terry's bold personality had distracted me. I had always assumed that meekness was at the cornerstone of submissiveness, but as I gazed on the couple before me, it occurred to me that personality outside the bedroom had very little to do with it.

Paulson continued to speak on the phone, jotting down notes on a large legal pad with his free hand while the other pulled viciously, casually, at Terry's nipples. I moved unobtrusively around the room, close up to record the way her skin pulled and released like taffy, far away to mark the contrast of the power dynamic.

Finally, he gave Terry some kind of hand signal, and she quickly crawled beneath the desk. From my vantage point, I could only see her bare ass perched almost daintily on her crossed high-heeled feet. There was the soft clack of a belt being undone and the sexual gasp of a zipper.

I zoomed in on Paulson's face, but his jaw barely clenched as Terry paid homage to him. I hastened to take out my sketchbook. For a few long minutes, the only sounds in the room were Paulson's low voice as he spoke into the phone, the infrequent wet suck from Terry's busy mouth, and the scratch of lead over the toothy paper of my sketchbook. I drew ceaselessly, squeezing my thighs together to ease the ache at their center. My mind wheeled with fantasies of performing a similar task for Sinclair, of having an audience the way we did by the side of the pool at the Westin in Los Cabos. A shockwave of arousal pulsed through my body at the idea of Sinclair taking me, using me—however he wanted, whenever he wanted.

Even then, immersed in a real-life D\s scene with another couple, I was thinking of him.

The click of Paulson hanging up the phone brought me out of fantasyland just in time to witness the tensing of his features as he came down Terry's throat. He stared at me the entire time, his expression as forceful as a hand on my throat. I knew next time he would have me on my knees beside Terry in a heartbeat. The thought thrilled me but not more than the realization that I wasn't ashamed by it.

I smiled demurely at Paulson, my tongue peeking between my lips because Sinclair had taught me to be unashamed. He had pried open my reserved cage and exposed the delicious heart of sensuality that now pulsed like a beacon in my belly. He had given me the key to unlock things within myself that I had never known needed to be opened, and that was such an amazing gift.

I knew if I decided to be without him that I would survive. His gift had been unconditional, without strings just like our weeklong affair. But I also knew that if I chose to be with him, I would continue to unfold and bend into beautiful new formations of myself, like origami paper under his artist touch. Thinking about him, about *us*, like that made the prospect of our shared future less selfish and beautifully possible.

Chapter Twenty

He took my breath away.

Standing at his panoramic office window in three-quarter profile, Sinclair had never looked so unattainably gorgeous. His mahogany hair waved back from his broad forehead in a perfect sweep that I was already dying to run my fingers through, and the tailored midnight blue suit highlighted the depth of his tan, the startling blue of his eyes when he turned to look at me. But it was his smile that seduced me completely, the slight but genuine tilt of his firm lips and the way it pleated the skin beside his eyes. That expression meant more than all his gifts combined.

"*Mon dieu*, you are a vision."

I smiled at his breathy compliment, smoothing a hand down the deep plum-colored dress. It was short with a flirty hemline and a high-collared neckline. The torso was sheer, and I wore only a flimsy purple balconette bra beneath it.

"You look like a very classy schoolgirl."

That was the goal, so I rewarded him with a smile and a small twirl so that the skirt floated out and above my lace-topped stockings.

He groaned.

"You make it incredibly hard for a man to behave himself, Elle."

I lifted one shoulder. "You once told me that you were neither a saint nor a gentleman."

He crossed the room in three massive strides so that he was only a breath away from touching me. "With you, I feel like a savage. I want to throw you over my shoulder and have my way with you. I want to handle all that creamy skin with rough hands and brutally push into you before you're quite ready so that you'll feel my mark for hours after I've left your body."

My head tipped back on my weak neck, lips blooming open to make way for my heavy breathing. Less than a minute in his presence and I was already soaking wet.

He stared down into my eyes, looming over me in a way that was both threatening and incredibly sexy. The tension between us grew unbearably taut and vibrated like a struck wire. I was just about to push myself into him, unable to endure the physical space between our bodies, when he broke into a gorgeous smile and began to laugh.

At first, I frowned, but I quickly followed him into giggles when his arms snaked around my waist, tugging me into the air and up against his chest.

"You crazy, sexy, amazing woman. You intoxicate me." He laughed against my cheek as he pressed our foreheads together.

I wrapped my arms around his neck and leaned back in his embrace to smile into his face. "That's probably an apt description. Like alcohol or drugs, I'm not the best choice for you."

His features slammed shut, but I smoothed his frown with my fingers so that he would know I was in a good mood despite my words.

Carefully, he set me down and ran a hand over my hair. "Do not talk like that tonight, *d'accord*? I want this evening to be about you and me only. No ghosts or skeletons from the closet will be joining us. Can you do that for me?"

I nodded because he was asking me for what I was desperate to have.

"Good."

His hand slid down my arm to lace with my fingers, and he tugged me toward his desk. "If we were dating, we would meet here often. I work too much, usually until seven thirty to eight or nine every evening Monday through Friday and frequently over the weekends."

He stopped us both before his desk, pressing my thighs into it and his front into me. I sighed as his hands came around to clasp over my belly.

"That would stop. Or, at the very least, I would work from home so that I could look up whenever I wanted to and watch you paint or sleep or just breathe."

I tilted my head back against his shoulder, settling into the fantasy.

"But at least once a week, we would meet here before I took you out on the town. I want to show you off, do you understand? I want to show the world that I am the man who captured a siren."

He pressed a chaste kiss to my cheek and squeezed me closer to his body.

"Sin," I breathed, not because I had anything to say but because I was full to the brim with emotion, and the only way I could think to release it was by saying his name.

"I wanted to show you a new acquisition I made," he said, tipping my chin up with two fingers so that I was looking at the previously empty space between the two wide bookcases behind his desk.

One of my paintings, *Solitaire du nuit*, now occupied the space. It was a large canvas dominated by a purple-black sky over the tiny lights of Montmartre and the moonlight-gilded dome of Sacre Coeur. A waxy, opalescent moon hung in the deeply bruised night sky like a grotesque pearl. It was one of my first paintings under the mentorship of Odile Claremont at *L'École des Beaux-Arts* and the first to be sold at my opening gallery showcase. Stefan Kilos, the gorgeous Greek I had met in Los Cabos, had informed me that he owned the piece, yet now it hung here in Sinclair's office.

I turned in his arms to gape at him.

He was smiling slightly. "You mentioned that Kilos had bought it. I didn't like the idea of him staring at it while he slept, and I wanted something of you close to me."

I swallowed convulsively.

Sinclair had just made my painting the only personal touch in his office.

"You are very good at this whole wooing thing."

The left side of his smile lifted further. "Thank you."

"I don't know if it's a compliment. I feel overwhelmed by you," I admitted.

"And you didn't before?"

"Touché."

He took my hand, bringing it to his lips in order to kiss my fingertips. "These are very talented fingers. They move my body with your touch and my soul with your art."

I pressed my hand to his chest. "Stop. I don't need pretty words."

"Just because they are pretty doesn't make what I'm saying any less true," he said, reminding me with my own words of our conversation on Tuesday when I'd called him a god.

"But okay," he conceded, sensing my discomfort. "Let's go see the amazing Miles Davis. We can talk afterward."

HE HELD MY HAND.

In theory, it seemed like such a trivial thing. People held hands all the time. Friends held hands, mothers and daughters, linked lines of camp children and people assisting the elderly. It was really no big deal. But I fixated on our clasped hands the entire evening, and not even the incredible Miles Davis nor his bold, brassy music could pull my gaze away from the sight. Sinclair's hands were beautiful, broad palms topped with long, lean fingers all covered in golden skin and lightly dusted with reddish hair. There was a scar on the back of his right hand, a small whitish burn mark that I compulsively ran my thumb over.

We parted for ten minutes at intermission so that I could use the restroom, and for those few minutes, my hand felt almost alien to me. I imagined what it would be like to let myself acclimatize to him the way my body so clearly yearned to do; how it would feel to greet him at the door of our shared apartment at the end of each day and wrap my arms and legs around him koala bear-style, to wake up in bed with my body pressed like a flower between his body and the bed.

His hand was waiting on the armrest, palm up and fingers unfurled when I returned. He smiled at my involuntary sigh when we reconnected and gave me a reassuring squeeze.

Afterward, we were both quiet as we filtered out of the theater and stood before the iconic fountain. I had a feeling Sinclair had things to say, but our companionable silence had created a bubble around us, and we were both happy to stay in it for a while yet.

So of course, some asshole had to come and pop it.

"Daniel Sinclair," a loud voice boomed from behind us.

Sin clenched my hand hard in his before letting it go to slowly turn around. I took a deep breath before doing the same.

An older man with graying blond hair and a beautifully gray cashmere overcoat was striding toward us with a tight smile and a very unhappy Margot on his arm. I sucked cold air in through my teeth, bracing myself for the confrontation.

Sinclair's hand found the small of my back in a surprising show of togetherness.

"Dean, Margot, it's a pleasure to see you. Did you have the gratification of seeing Miles Davis tonight in the Rose Theater?"

Dean looked down at Margot, expecting her to respond. Instead, she continued to glare at me.

"Not a fan of jazz music, to tell you the honest truth. We were watching the ballet." He leaned closer conspiratorially. "Fucking hate the ballet too, but this one loves it, and you know what they say, happy wife, happy life."

Sin and I laughed politely.

"Now, who is the gorgeous redhead on your arm?" Dean asked, dropping the bomb into the middle of our tiny group as if it was a discarded gum wrapper.

I stared at the ground where I imagined it to be, a huge ticking machine with an angry red count down to explosion. Two minutes thirty seconds.

"This is Giselle Moore," Sinclair said smoothly. "She is a Parisian transplant and a very talented artist at the gallery. Her showcase is coming up in January. I think you would be a fan of her work."

"Oh wonderful. You know how I'm always looking for the next big thing. Are you it, Giselle Moore?"

I smiled, but I could still feel Margot's crushing censure, and it took everything I had not to flee from it. "I'm happy to be the next thing, if not the biggest. I'm incredibly grateful for the opportunity."

"The accent, it's not quite French."

"I was born in Naples, actually."

"Enough," Margot spit, finally roused out of her murder plotting and into action. "This is ridiculous small talk. Sinclair, what are you doing here with *her*?"

Her. If I decided to be with him, this man I loved, I would have to get used to hearing that. There were a lot of words for a woman in my position: slut, whore, home-wrecker, mistress, and adulterer. Yet until now, I had never known a pronoun could be so vicious. *Her;* that woman who stole her own sister's boyfriend.

Revulsion rolled through me.

"I enjoy spending time with Giselle, as you well know," Sinclair was saying in that implacable way of his.

It only made Margot incensed.

"Fuck *that*."

"M," Sinclair reproached at the same time that Dean gasped, "Margot!"

She shook off her date's arm, stepping forward to press a finger to Sinclair's chest. She vibrated with righteous indignation. "I was supportive of you in Mexico. I stayed away and let you have a torrid little holiday fling. But we are living in the real world now and fantasies like this"—she waved her hand in my direction as if indicating shit on the sidewalk—"they don't exist in real life for a reason. Sure, she's pretty, but have you even thought about the consequences?"

She wasn't finished, I could tell. But something had shifted in Sinclair's posture, a subtle broadening as his own anger infused him with strength and superhuman intimidation. His anger wasn't even directed at me, and I felt my knees weaken under the pressure of his gaze.

"I wasn't living in reality, M. I was living in the fucking matrix. Nothing had meaning to me but the next meeting, the next deal, how people perceived me in the business world. Have you ever known me to make a decision lightly? Don't come at me like a scorned woman for falling in love with someone other than you or Elena. I'm fully prepared to reap the consequences but only from the people who were really wronged. You can't plan for something like this. It happened. It's done."

There was a pregnant silence. Sinclair's hand slipped from my back to the curve of my hip. He tugged me close to his side where my body settled easily like a puzzle piece. We both sagged slightly into each other.

"I'm happy with my decision," Sinclair said softly.

Margot stared up at him with large unblinking eyes. Sinclair's words had cracked open her hard exterior, leaving her open and vulnerable beneath our scrutiny. I could see the truth of her love in the glazed stare, the trembling lower lip, but I could also read her determination to support him in the way she squared her shoulders and nodded her head curtly at him before turning to me.

"I hope you're half as brave as him. He deserves a lot."

"I know," I said because she was right on both accounts. Sinclair was the bravest man I knew, pursuing what was right for him—which was somehow *me*—despite all the obstacles, moral and physical. Being with him, taking that final step in the betrayal of my sister, wasn't about me being a villain. It was about me being a heroine, his heroine.

This is going to kill you. This has been killing you all along, but I'm going to pull you out of this hellish situation, and I'm going to love you more than anyone ever has every day after to prove to you how much that pain was worth it. We are going to resurrect each other.

Sinclair's words from our lunch date reverberated through my head.

Straightening my spine, I skated my hand under his coat and around his back so that we both clutched each other. "I've always appreciated your take on the situation, Margot. What you've said, what you are saying, isn't wrong. But neither is this."

Her lips rolled under, but after a long moment of intense staring, she shifted on her feet and nodded at me. "Okay. Good luck then."

She turned back to Dean, who was standing with soggy shoulders a couple feet behind her. She hesitated before reaching up on her tiptoes to press a kiss to his cheek. "I'll meet you at the car."

He nodded, but his eyes were on Sinclair. After Margot moved out of hearing distance, he took a step forward to extend his hand to Sin, his eyes sad despite his smile. "Sorry about my girl. You know how she can be, fire and ice and all that."

"I don't know," Sinclair said firmly, deliberately. "But I'll take your word for it, Dean."

The older man smiled again at both of us, dropping the handshake tiredly before putting both hands deep in his pockets and taking off after his wife.

Sinclair and I stood there for a minute or two after they left before he wrapped me up in both arms and hugged me tightly. I giggled into his coat because his affection made me giddy.

"You are so beautiful to me," he said into my hair.

I smiled when he buried his nose in it and inhaled, knowing I smelled like lavender.

"Did you mean what you said?"

I pulled back within the span of his arms so that I could stare up into his electric eyes. "Yes. The affair was wrong and keeping it a secret compounded that, I think. A lot of people—our friends and family included—are going to hate us, and they might never stop." I reached up to run my fingers through his lush hair like I had wanted to all night. "But I would take all the hate in the world if it meant your love."

Sinclair's face broke into a colossal grin, his teeth exposed and shining in the city lights. I grinned back at him, my happiness rushing through me, pushing against my tongue so that I almost gagged with it. Instead, I laughed. And after a moment, he laughed with me, great rolling guffaws that shook our bodies and made my belly ache. It was silly, and it made me feel like the teenager I had never been, impulsive and full of impossible fire.

I moaned when Sin swooped down to capture my smile between his lips. My body melted against him, his strong hold the only thing keeping me steady as he kissed me deeply. I tried to pull away slightly, aware we were in a public, albeit fairly deserted place, but he only brought me closer with a low growl. He gathered my wrists behind my back into one of his hands and pulled me tight against him. I wiggled against his hold, tilting my hips back and forth over the erection I could feel against my belly.

"Come back to my hotel room," he murmured against my skin. "I have a surprise for you."

I giggled, thrusting my breasts into his chest as I wiggled my eyebrows salaciously. "I don't think it's much of a surprise at this point, Sin."

He blinked blankly before chuckling. "Your dirty mind always surprises me."

A few weeks ago, I would have blushed. Instead, I pried one hand out of his hold in order to cup his rigid length through his slacks. "Pleasantly, I hope."

He groaned when I squeezed him. "Most definitely. But that is not actually the surprise I was referring to."

When I pouted, he smiled. "I promise it will be just as fun."

I widened my eyes comically and grabbed his hand to drag him along behind me as I marched to the curb to hail a cab. "Just as fun as sex? Okay, this I have to see."

Chapter Twenty-one

SINCLAIR HAD THE ROYAL SUITE AT THE ST. REGIS. IT WAS RIDICULOUSLY beautiful with heavy velvet drapes, a black marble fireplace, and luxurious furnishings. Yet I could barely take my eyes off Sinclair as he competently removed our coats, hung them up in the closet, and called reception for a bottle of wine to be brought up. He moved through the world with a confidence and discipline that awed me, especially given the way he had grown up before the Percys had found him.

"Please take a seat," he said with a wave toward the two sofas.

"Did you take finishing classes?" I asked, plopping onto the couch with a smile of glee at how comfortable the fabric was beneath my palms.

"Excuse me?"

"I was just wondering if you took finishing classes, or the male equivalent, whatever that may be. You went from a French orphan to a governor's son practically overnight."

"I had a private tutor, and I was enrolled at Trinity." At my blank look, he explained, "It's the best prep school in the country. The summer they brought me over here, I spent every day perfecting my English, learning

Spanish, and improving my standing in every other academic arena. Willa took me through the more delicate etiquette of high society herself."

"I am so sorry," I said somberly.

I was rewarded with his small smile. "So was I, at the time. I lived on a carefully constructed schedule Willa had created for me: schooling, modeling, and dating. Until you, I hadn't realized I'd never stopped living like that even after I rebelled and moved out."

"Dating?"

"Willa and Mort have always expected me to marry well." He hesitated. "They weren't even pleased with Elena at first, but she worked tirelessly to impress them, and now she and Willa are as thick as thieves."

I looked down at my hands so Sinclair couldn't see how those words scrambled my compartmentalized thoughts.

He sat down beside me and tipped my chin up with two fingers so that I had to stare into his intense eyes. "Elle, don't leave me."

"I'm here."

His eyes narrowed, the fingers under my chin turned over to pinch it firmly. "I can't have you checking out of this relationship every time we talk about Elena. We need to talk about her. She's a part of your family and a huge part of my past. If we don't normalize discussion about her, she will come between us."

"I'm sorry. There is just so much... stuff."

I leaned into his hand as he cupped my cheek.

"I know, which actually leads perfectly into the surprise I have for you. I have to be in France on business next week. When we met on the plane to Mexico, I was just returning from an inspection of a recently acquired property in Paris. It's time for me to go back to check on the finishing touches and interview the short-listed interior designers."

My heart sank at the thought of being apart from him just when we had decided to be together but I knew Sinclair's job was his number one priority, and I respected him for his dedication, lusted after him for his drive.

"I completely understand. I'll miss you, but we can talk when you get back," I said.

He was smiling when I looked back up at him. "I hoped you would come with me. It will give us time to figure out how we want to... proceed without the anxiety of lying to our friends and family. But mostly, I love the thought of having you to myself for another seven days, of walking through the streets holding your hand, kissing you when the urge strikes me—which, I'm warning you, will be often."

The idea of being with Sinclair in Paris made me dizzy. My mind rebelled against the image because it was too good to be true. How was it possible that despite everything, I could visit the city I loved by the side of the man I loved? Wasn't the villain in stories like this supposed to end up with nothing and no one?

"When do we leave?" I asked.

"Tomorrow morning. I thought we could stay here tonight."

"I would need to go back to Cosima's and pack."

"I had Candy go over earlier to pack a bag." He grinned at my incredulous look. "Just in case you said yes."

"You are so arrogant." I laughed.

"You love it."

"I do."

"You love me."

"I do." My eyes filled with tears. "I can't believe this is happening."

Sin framed my face in both his large hands and stared at me with complete sincerity, business-like seriousness. "Believe it. Say you'll come."

"I'll come."

"Good girl," he murmured before descending on my lips for a thorough kiss. "Now come here."

He swung me onto his lap to straddle him and gripped my face tightly beneath his hands so that he could maneuver me to his liking as he plundered my mouth. I groaned as he bit into my bottom lip sharply.

"Who owns you, Elle?" he husked against my damp lips.

"You, sir."

I shivered as his hand moved possessively over my curves to land on my flared hips. Just saying the word *sir* triggered my submissive nature, and I found myself edgy with the need to show him how good I could be. I wanted to bend and break under his hands, be reformed into something new and stronger.

"Yes," he hissed, seeing the glazed look in my eyes. "Strip for me. Show me what belongs to me."

I rocked once along his erection, slowly dragging my panty-covered core over him so that he gritted his teeth before I stood, sashaying a few feet away to the space in front of the fireplace. I took a moment to breathe, to absorb the tingling electricity that flowed through our connection. When I looked over my shoulder at him, there were no insecurities or guilt— nothing existed but Sinclair.

I pouted slightly as I swished my hips back and forth for him, the flirty skirt of my dress flipping up to expose my lace-topped stockings and the ends of the purple garters I wore. His eyes burned against my skin.

Suffused with desire, I bent over to bare my ass to him, the two plump cheeks bisected by the thin wedge of my satin thong. I straightened slowly and turned around to stare at him with my lip between my teeth as I painstakingly undid the buttons on my dress. When the fabric gaped open, I rolled my shoulders one at a time until my torso was free of the garment.

Sin made a primal noise in the back of his throat.

I reached back to undo the clasp of my bra and the little zipper on the skirt at the same time. When they fell to the ground, I lifted both breasts in my hands and pinched my nipples hard. I tilted my head back on a ragged moan.

"Show me your pussy."

I shuddered. Framing my hands beneath my breasts, I slid them slowly down my stomach until my fingertips slipped beneath the edge of my underwear. My hips swayed languidly as I bent my knees, dipping low to peel apart my legs and briefly flash the damp gusset of my panties at him.

"Show me," he ordered, and his fierce words hit me like a whip.

My sex throbbed, but I wanted that look of frustrated need on Sinclair's face more than I wanted to relieve the ache. I braced myself on my hands and knees, facing away from him, and reached back to run my fingers lightly over my seam from ass to clit.

"Feels so good," I breathed, rocking my hips into my touch.

"Don't make me ask again."

I bit my lip as I moved my panties to the side, giving my questing fingers access to my cleft while keeping it from his gaze. I groaned loudly as I sank two fingers inside myself.

Pain lashed out across my raised buttocks. I jerked forward to absorb some of the shock, my hand flying from my sex to the ground to brace myself. Another blow landed on the other cheek. I whimpered but kept my head lowered, my body still as Sinclair spanked me hard for my disobedience. When he was done, ten blows later, he looped my hair around his fist and tugged until my back and neck protested the angle.

"Who owns your body?" he whispered harshly into my ear.

I could feel the edge of his massive erection against the hot skin of my ass, and despite myself, I rubbed against him.

He pulled back tighter on my hair so that my eyes watered and a fresh flood of arousal coated my inner thighs.

"Answer me."

"You, sir. You own this body."

"Yet you disobeyed me?" His fingers began to trace back and forth over my swollen sex, just hard enough to stimulate. I tried to rub myself harder against him, but he only chuckled and, releasing his grip on my hair to still me with one firm hand on my hip. "What happens when you disobey me, siren?"

"I have to be punished, sir."

His hand smoothed over the sensitized skin of my ass teasingly. "You want to be punished, don't you?"

When I didn't answer quickly enough—too absorbed by the connection between his hand and my burning flesh—he spanked me again, three quick, powerful slaps to each cheek.

I whimpered and shamelessly ground myself against the air.

"Be still," he barked.

I locked my arms and legs, but I quivered with lust, my swollen breasts swinging beneath me.

His hand dipped into my sex again before he grabbed my hair, lifting my head to paint my lips with my wetness.

"Taste yourself. See how aroused you are?"

I licked my lips, caught his lingering fingers with my tongue, and drew them into my mouth to suckle. He withdrew them too quickly, and I made a noise at the loss.

I wasn't bereft for long. Before I could even process it, Sin ripped my panties off with one violent tug and thrust three fingers deep inside me. I cried out as he began to pump them in and out while his thumb drew tight circles over my clit. My knees began to quake, and unattractive sounds leaked out of my mouth as I lost my mind to the pleasure.

"Sin, Sin, Sin," I chanted between whimpers.

"Yes, siren?"

"Please, please, please..."

"Use your words."

"Please," I burst out as the burn of my impending orgasm rushed like a brushfire over my skin. "Let me come."

"The only way you come is on my cock."

I tried to find the words in my vacant mind to make him understand that I was on the edge, dangling over it, desperate for the final push. "Fuck me then, please sir."

His fingers left me suddenly, and the cool kiss of the air-conditioning made me tremble. If he blew on me, I'd come. But he didn't. In fact, he waited for so long that I finally looked over my shoulder to find him disrobed, sitting on his haunches as he stared at my exposed core, one fist pulling firmly at his cock.

"Please sir," I whispered because my strength had deserted me.

"Are you begging for my cock, siren?"

His eyes were bluer than I'd ever seen them as he stared at me, his face impassive. It turned me on so much to see his tightly leashed control. I wanted to rip his mask off with my nails and teeth, impale myself on him, and rock and rock until he shattered underneath me.

I nearly snarled when I said, "I need you to fuck me. Please, fuck me hard, fuck me like you hate me."

Immediately, he rose and pushed down on my lower spine so that my hips were hitched further into the air, and I was splayed open for him. The tip of his erection burned my wet lips as he placed himself against me. He reached around to grab me by the throat, lifting me onto my knees as he thrust up into me. I groaned as I settled back against him, basically in his lap. He pressed his chest to my back, tightened his grip on my throat slightly so that my airflow was just barely constricted, and bit my ear. "I'll fuck you, Elle. Because you asked so nicely and your pretty pussy is desperate for it. But I'll fuck you like I own you because I could never hate you."

My open mouth clanged shut as he lifted me with one hand and held me securely in place as he began to pound into me. Each time he bottomed out, our skin slapped together. I loved the sound. I bucked back against him, throwing myself into it so that it hurt. I wanted the pain. I needed it, needed *him*, to kill the remaining pain in my heart with physical pain.

"Please," I panted.

He wound my long hair in his hand and tucked it tightly under his arm so that my back was bowed and I couldn't escape the brutality of his thrusts. His hand found my slick clit and clamped it tight between his fingers. It didn't seem possible, but his pace increased.

"More, more," I begged, even though I was already incoherent and my orgasm was looming so large, I was actually a little frightened of it.

"When you come, I expect you to thank me," he ground out.

"Yes, sir."

"Then come."

His fingers released my raw clit, and blood flooded back to it painfully. I screamed. He slapped down once, twice on the abused flesh, and I exploded. My mind fractured, crumbled into ash, and disappeared so that I was only body—throbbing, hot, slicked, and panting, a pink thing of desire. Yet I remembered to scream out, "Thank you, thank you, thank you!"

When I came back to myself slightly, Sinclair was still buried inside me, unwilling to move despite our climaxes. His hands shifted over my scalp where it lay on his shoulder, and I moaned at the comfort of it.

"You are perfect," he murmured against my sweaty cheek. "And somehow, you are mine."

I smiled slightly, too weak to talk. He laughed at me.

There was a gentle knock on the door. Sinclair shifted carefully underneath my prone body until I was in his arms. He stood and swiftly took me to the bedroom where he pulled back the covers and slid me into bed.

"I'll just deal with room service and be right back," he said, pressing a kiss to my forehead.

I nodded, but he had already left the room.

I snuggled deeper under the covers and smiled. In twenty-four hours, I would be in my favorite city with a man who I had loved for months and that now, somehow, I could finally call mine. My upcoming showcase was shaping up to be something I was monumentally proud of and I had friends whom I loved in the city. I knew a wealth of pain and animosity awaited us, but for now, I could afford to languish in the beauty of being newly in love. I tilted my head into the soft pillow and sighed, utterly blissed out.

That was, until I heard the voice speaking to Sinclair in the other room.

"Daniel, we need to talk," Elena said. "I don't care if it's a bad time. I'm not leaving until you hear me out."

The End.

THE
CONSEQUENCE

THE EVOLUTION OF SIN, #3

USA TODAY & WSJ BESTSELLING AUTHOR
giana darling

To the French, who taught me the language of love.

"He used to think he wanted to be good, he wanted to be kind, he wanted to be brave and wise, but it was all pretty difficult. He wanted to be loved, too, if he could fit it in."

—F. Scott Fitzgerald

Sinclair

Le cœur a ses raisons que la raison ne connaît point.

The heart has its reasons which reason knows nothing of.

Blaise Pascal was a fucking genius. Then again, he was French, and my countrymen knew a thing or two about being in love.

Therefore, it should stand to reason that I may have inherently known a thing or two about love as well, but the idea that love could outweigh logic had never occurred to me. It could have been because I couldn't remember much about my birth parents, my Roma mother and her French husband, who both died mere months apart when I was seven years old. Willa and Mortimer Percy had adopted me when I was sixteen, but our family was one of deliberate choice and calculated divination. They loved me in their own way, I think, but it was a secondary emotion. A result of pride and cultivation, the way Frankenstein might have loved his monster.

Then there was the love of Elena Lombardi.

She loved me for the reasons I loved myself: my drive and work ethic, my reasonability and sophistication. I enjoyed her company and coveted her mind; the twisted turns it took to shortcut the obstacles in our road to success. She was dark beneath the veneer, hiding away the same inherent ruthlessness I had been born with, and even though we never spoke about the deep-seated ugliness that poverty had wrought on our souls, it was a comfort to both of us just knowing it existed.

The truth was, we saw in each other the ideal partner for our ideal selves, and for years, it was enough because it never occurred to me to ask for more, for the kind of love my kinsmen waxed poetic about...

... and then I saw her.

It wasn't love at first sight. That implies my response to her was subtle and warm, something easy and quintessentially human.

No, the moment I saw Giselle Moore sitting curled up and vulnerable with sickness and fear in the first-class cabin of that plane, my humanity—the class and refinery that I had cultivated for years—sloughed off me like molted skin and revealed the heart of the animal I secretly knew myself to be.

My heartbeat roared in my ears, and my groin tightened with a desire so fierce, I almost doubled over. Only one thought reverberated through my head like a fucking mantra.

Take her.

Take her.

Own her.

I felt the pulse of the words in my blood as it scorched through my body and ricocheted off the walls of my heart. I wanted her. It was primal and fiercer than anything I'd ever experienced before. It took every ounce of civilization I had left in me to approach her politely, to keep my twitching hands in my lap instead of spreading them all over her luminous pale skin.

At first, she was reserved with me, barely allowing her eyes to slide my way. I took the time to visually devour her, noting how the golden freckles across her shoulders and cheeks contrasted with the olive tint of her complexion, how her auburn hair glowed like copper under the dim cabin lights. And when she finally met my gaze, I stared hard into her eyes, wide and pure as silver dollars.

I found myself jealous of her smiles, wanting to own them for myself.

When I leaned over her, the smell of her lavender and honey fragrance intoxicated me. The soft brush of her aroused breath against my skin nearly made me lose control.

Even as I left her behind on the plane, I knew that meeting her had changed my life, but I could never have guessed how much.

I wasn't a man who believed in fate, but when she showed up at The Westin in Los Cabos, I couldn't say I was surprised. It solidified the proposal that had waited poised on the tip of my tongue since I had first laid eyes on her—a weeklong affair to purge myself of this egregious need for her. Those torturous hours while I had waited for her answer were some of the longest of my life, and they set the precedent for the weeks of indecision that followed, horrific bouts of self-loathing peppered with moments of such clear, bright joy that they obliterated all memory of shame and hatred.

Now, here I was, rearranging everything I had always known and thought I wanted, to make space for my siren, my Elle. The mantra that had infiltrated my head like a siren's song from our first meeting had only intensified, sunk into my bones, and saturated my blood. I couldn't take a breath without feeling her in the previously unused muscles of my heart.

Look at me; she'd even turned me into a fucking poet, a true Frenchman when I'd forsaken my homeland years ago.

I was jeopardizing my reputation and therefore my career, and polarizing the only family that had ever really cared for me. Worst of all, I was forcing the love of my life to choose me over her sister.

Did you want to know the worst thing about this clusterfuck of a situation?

I didn't care.

Everything I had loved before Elle paled in comparison to my need for her. The thought of anything getting in the way of being with her both incensed me and perversely excited me because I knew I would eviscerate it.

It wasn't rational, and it was completely out of character, but as my compatriot Blaise Pascal said, *"the heart has its reasons which reason knows nothing of."* And since the moment I met Giselle Moore, my heart had stopped being mine to reason with.

Which was how I found myself opening the door to my suite and temporary home at the St. Regis with a completely idiotic smile on my face —high on my courage, exhilarated for the first time in my life at the prospect of my future because a gorgeous redhead by the name of Giselle Moore had just promised to be in it indefinitely—only to find my ex-girlfriend at the door.

It was obvious that Elena had come directly from the airport by the large canvas bag she carried over one shoulder. She was still wearing one of her power suits, an inky black ensemble from head to toe that was meant to detract from her femininity. Instead, it highlighted her delicate beauty like a neon pen. She looked polished and gorgeous, and not at all heartbroken.

"Daniel, we need to talk," Elena demanded. "I don't care if it's a bad time. I'm not leaving until you hear me out."

It was a bad time.

The worst.

It was fucking *awful* because I had just shared the most extraordinary night of my life with the woman I had finally convinced to be mine, and she was currently tucked away within hearing distance of this very conversation, wearing only a post-coital smile and the scent of our sex on her skin.

Anxiety pricked my skin like a thousand hot needles. I couldn't afford to lose her, not after tasting, however briefly, the possibility of a future with her.

Giselle Moore was mine. And I wasn't going to let anyone get in the way of that.

Not even her sister.

"I appreciate that we need to talk, Elena, but now isn't a good time," I said, widening my stance so that I blocked most of the doorway.

"Don't be ridiculous. It's eleven thirty at night. You can spare ten minutes to talk to the woman you devoted the past four years of your life to," she snapped.

I gritted my teeth against a brief flare of guilt as she brushed past me into the suite. She stopped in front of the couch, delicately placing her coat, bag, and Prada purse there before facing me again with her hands clasped before her. Even in her righteous indignation, Elena comported herself like a princess. She was heartrendingly beautiful, with a face like a Renaissance painting and a spine made of titanium steel. If I had never met Giselle, I knew I would have stayed with Elena for the rest of my life. It would have been so much simpler that way.

Yet the thought was singularly depressing.

Giselle brought my ordered black and white life into color with her passionate strokes and exceptional love. There was no going back from something like that.

I crossed my arms. "I leave for Paris early tomorrow morning."

"I just got back," she said as if that made it unacceptable for me to leave.

I didn't say anything.

"Fine, that just means it is even more imperative that we talk now."

Stuffing my hands in my pockets, I considered the wisdom of either just kicking her out or hashing it out with her. I was well aware that Giselle was in the bedroom listening to our every word. It might do her good to realize how serious I was about leaving Elena, to hear some of the things I needed to say. And a large part of me realized that Elena needed the opportunity to discuss her feelings with me. When I had ended things with her last week, she barely spoke, barely even moved. She just sat perched on the edge of the couch with her hands demurely held in her lap. I deserved a thorough tongue lashing at the very least and even a good hard slap or two across the face. It was, pathetically, the least I could do to ease her pain.

"Okay, take a seat. Can I get you some water?" I asked, moving forward toward the bar to pour myself a much-needed drink.

I had briefly tidied up the suite before answering the door, more out of habit than anything else, and I was intensely grateful for my compulsion now. Still, I cast my eyes about the room, spotting the neat pile of Giselle's clothes partially hidden under the coffee table on the other side from Elena.

Fuck.

I composed my features and carefully slid my gaze to her. Thankfully, taking her seat and smoothing the immaculate black pants over her thighs preoccupied her.

"A whiskey, please."

I nodded curtly, two cold glasses of liquor on the rocks already in my hands as I skirted the coffee table. I kicked Giselle's purple garter belt farther into the shadows as I moved past to sit on the chair adjacent to Elena.

She accepted the tumbler with a tight smile and a sincere thank you because her politeness wouldn't allow for anything else.

"What is it that you would like to say?" I asked, leaning back in my chair and crossing one leg over the other.

Elena's eyes flickered over the bare skin of my torso as my muscles contracted with movement. She had never been overly effusive about my looks, something I had always been thankful for, but I knew that the sight of me unclothed affected her. Strangely, perhaps, the knowledge did nothing for me.

I wished for Elle's sake that I was wearing a shirt.

"I want to better understand this early mid-life crisis you seem to be having. I've had time to think about it, and I can see that your company's expansion could be putting too much stress on our relationship." I opened my mouth to speak, but she held up her hand. "We both have one-hundred-hour workweeks, and even though our professions have always come first, we need to remember to take time for us."

I knew she must have taken the time to read articles and books about our situation: what-to-do-when-your-partner-leaves-you-unexpectedly and how-to-breathe-life-back-into-your-relationship psychology dissertations and magazine findings. When Elena was faced with a problem, she researched the hell out of it so that when the opportunity arose, she could beat it to death with thought and theory. I knew all of that because even though we weren't married, we had lived like husband and wife for the past four years. I knew all of the things that made Elena Lombardi frequently intolerable and constantly brilliant. I could see the despair she tried to hide in the lines around her pursed mouth and the helplessness she held tightly in her clasped hands. I was actively destroying her, and it was killing me.

It helped to remind myself that it was the least that I deserved.

She offered me a small, shaky smile.

Putain. I was such an asshole.

"It's too late for that, Elena."

"It doesn't have to be. There is no *deadline* on a relationship, no expiration date. We can work this out. A co-worker recommended an excellent couples counselor."

"Not interested."

"Don't be so closed-minded," she urged, her voice still pleasantly modulated even though her hands had unconsciously curled into fists.

"It's not a matter of obstinacy. Counseling wouldn't work for us."

"How can you know that?"

Because I'm savagely in lust and irrevocably in love with your sister, who, coincidently, is lying naked about fifteen feet away from us in my bed.

"Because we don't have any issues to work through. We've never been passionate with each other, which I always thought was a good thing," I tried to explain.

"It is," she agreed eagerly.

I scrubbed a hand over my face, caught the scent of Giselle's sex lingering on my fingers, and fought the urge to lick her off my skin. "It isn't a good thing for a couple. How can there be erotic love without passion?"

Elena's lips twisted, then went lax. "Are you saying that you aren't attracted to me anymore?"

Yes.

Instead, I said, "Have you ever heard the Greek term, *philia*? It describes the love between two warriors or best friends, a partnership based on unswerving loyalty and respect."

Elena blinked at me. "Are you kidding?"

I spread my hands and shrugged. "The Greeks actually valued it more highly than romantic love."

Her eyes, just shades darker than Giselle's, narrowed dangerously. I sounded callous and cruel, as I often did when discussing emotional issues. It was difficult for me to marry the empathy I felt with the logical methodology of my thoughts. Giselle was the only one who gave voice to my mute soul. I wished, irrationally and unfairly, that she was beside me.

"I..." Elena cleared her throat. "I thought we both valued those characteristics. You make our relationship sound so... unfeeling. Maybe I didn't do a great job of showing it, but you mean the world to me, Daniel."

Her words pressed around me like a cold iron fist. Was it possible to feel heartbroken even though I was the one ending things? I wanted, no, I *needed* to be with Giselle, but in doing so, I was effectively antagonizing my best friend. Elena and I had never been as perfect as we thought, but we were still a team. I was losing my right-hand man, and despite how unromantic that might have seemed, it was fucking devastating all the same.

"You mean the world to me too," I said.

But my love for your sister is bigger than the world.

Elena stared at me. She was still waiting for the punch line of a bad joke, for me to laugh and tell her it was all a ruse.

I sat taller in my chair.

It would be unkind to allow her to think she stood a fighting chance of winning me back, so even though doing it sickened me, I slaughtered the last of her hope.

"But I'm not in love with you, and I'm not going to change my mind about this. I want you to have the Gramercy apartment and the furniture. I've moved out the things I wanted to keep and had them put into storage. We never had shared bank accounts or any other permanent assets."

A choked sob escaped her lips like the whistle from a punctured balloon. She clapped a hand over her mouth, cleared her throat, and resumed her enforced dignity.

I had never wanted to hold her more than I did at that moment.

I cleared my throat too. "I am sorry, Elena. It makes no difference, I know, but I need to tell you that you are my dearest friend. Hopefully, after the dust has settled, we can find that again."

Elena stared at me impassively for a long time. It was utterly silent throughout the hotel suite, but I didn't allow myself to linger over thoughts of Giselle and what she thought of the entire conversation. That would come later. For now, I owed it to Elena to be present.

I tried to relax the muscles in my face, open my posture up so that she could see how much I was grieving, and even, if she was perceptive enough, how little I deserved her understanding.

"You're serious," she finally breathed.

I nodded.

She took in a deep, shuddering breath and let it out slowly through a mouth I had kissed a thousand times. It was indescribably strange to look at the woman I had thought myself in love with and feel so devoid of feeling. I was sure it made me a horrible person. I let myself drown in it for a minute.

"Okay." She stood swiftly and strode forward to offer me her hand.

I stared at it before clasping it within my own. She had long, lean fingers that stroked piano keys more passionately than they had ever stroked me. I rubbed the back of them with my thumb, and it felt absurdly *final*.

"I don't want to see you for a while, but I don't see why we can't be amicable about this. You've become a fixture with my family and friends"— I fought the urge to wince—"and I can accept that sometimes, people just grow apart."

"They do."

She nodded curtly and dropped my hand. I watched her pick up her bag, carefully cross her coat over one arm, and begin the slow walk to the door. It was the most surreal moment of my life to watch my former partner walk out of the same space she unwittingly shared with my new lover. If it hadn't been so fucked up, it might have been a little poetic.

So it took me a second too long to realize that Elena had tripped on something and was bending over to examine the purple scrap of lace caught on the sharp edge of her high heel. It then took me a half-second more than that to register the aberrant look of horror on her habitually placid features and the venomous bite of her words as she whispered, "You fucking cheating bastard."

Chapter One

Giselle

I WAS THE PICTURE OF A WELL-LOVED WOMAN.

My skin was still flushed and naked beneath the plush hotel covers, my red hair a chaotic mass of just-fucked glory. I had just enjoyed the most glorious sex with the most glorious man I had ever laid eyes on, and in the morning, after what should have been a night of continued sex and very minimal sleep, I was set to travel to the most romantic city in the world with the love of my life.

But happily-ever-afters were for princesses with hearts of gold and white knights in shining armor, not disloyal Italian artists who got off on being spanked or the morally ambiguous men who introduced them to said fetishisms.

So, it shouldn't have surprised me that Elena had arrived at our door to remind me that this impure princess and tarnished knight did not deserve a happy ending, at least not that easily.

The moment I heard her perfectly enunciated English, I bit my lip so hard the skin broke, and the metallic taste of blood replaced the flavor of Sinclair on my tongue.

It felt too soon after our reunion to ask Sinclair to fight any battles for us. Despite our recent lovemaking and his continued declarations of love and devotion, it was hard not to doubt the man given the inception of our relationship and his initial unwillingness to end things with my sister and his girlfriend, Elena.

Despite my qualms, Sinclair handled the situation with the kind of aloof control that I had come to expect from him. He spoke bluntly, skirting the line between brutality and honesty. I could picture him reclined in a chair, a glass of whiskey dangling from two fingers as he regarded Elena, lazy but powerful like a crocodile waiting in the weeds.

It was harder to imagine Elena's reaction. I didn't know her as well as I should have, and when she responded to Sin's clear dismissal, it was with English words as smooth and emotionless as plastic.

I winced when he spoke about giving her the house, sank further beneath the covers in cringing sympathy when he declared their love platonic, but my empathy felt displaced because Elena didn't seemed perturbed by him. They conducted their breakup like the dissolution of a business agreement.

Like most things that seemed too good to be true at first glance, it all went to hell in a handbasket.

"You fucking cheating bastard." I heard Elena seethe after a long moment of silence.

My mind immediately flashed to my discarded clothes. Before I could consciously assimilate what her words meant, I was hopping up and out of bed. I hovered behind the partially closed door to the main room of the suite, my skin rippled with goose flesh. My body was aflame with the impulse to flee, but there was no place to go.

"Elena," Sinclair began.

"Shut up!" she hissed. "Don't open your lying mouth, Daniel Sinclair. What *the fuck* have you done?"

I heard movement in the other room and darted toward the bathroom. There was no place to hide in the palatial room, so I hurried back into the bedroom.

"Did you seriously cheat on me? Who the hell is she?" Elena was saying, her voice saturated with the sounds of Napoli.

There was no gap to wiggle under beneath the bed. My heart thumped in my ears, pumping so forcibly that my limbs shook with each beat. What would happen if she came into the bedroom and saw me?

"Is she still here?" Elena's voice was just outside the bedroom, high and hard with infuriated disgust.

The door began to swing open just as I dived through the door to the closet. Happily, the walk-in was filled with rows of Sinclair's clothes. I separated the lower level of button-up shirts so that I could nestle between the fabric and the wall. Pulling the hangers back together, I tried to slow my ragged breathing. I hugged my knees to my chest and tucked my chin into the space between my knees; reminded of the times I had hidden as a child back in Naples. I would have taken hiding from the Camorra over my sister any day.

The door to the closet cracked loudly against the wall as it was flung open, and Elena stormed into the room.

"She isn't here, Elena," Sinclair said calmly as Elena stared to rifle through the clothes on the other side of the closet from where I sat.

"Fuck you," she spat. "Like I would believe anything that comes out of your disgusting, deceitful mouth."

Sinclair's sigh echoed throughout the room. "She left just before you got here. I'm sorry you had to find out this way."

My sister snorted so hard, it sounded as if it hurt. "Because there is a good way to find out my fiancé is fucking a *puttana*."

"She isn't a whore, and I am not just *fucking* her."

There was a long pause.

I shifted slightly to peer between a gap in the hanging fabric, unable to curb my curiosity. Elena was in profile, her muscles wound tightly around her nuclear core. I could practically hear her jaw clenching. It was only a matter of time before she exploded.

So, of course, Sinclair lit the fuse.

"And we were never engaged."

My gasp was covered by the horrified, pained noise that those words forced from her. She whirled around to face Sinclair and shoved him so hard that he took a step back. I watched as she advanced on him, pressing him against the wall by the door with both fists clutching his shirt. When she spoke, her mouth was so close to his that for a moment, I thought they were kissing, and my stomach clenched.

"We are common law partners. We live together. We were going to adopt a *baby*. We were going to be a family, Daniel. Don't stand there and tell me we weren't engaged. We were partners in every way that matters."

Sinclair stared calmly down into her face, his hands coming up to cup her elbows gently. "We were *partners*, you are right. We made plans together, supported each other, and navigated our careers together. But we were never partners in the only way that matters." He paused. "I don't believe that we were ever in love with each other."

Elena's hands fell away from his rumpled shirt as she took a shocked step back. Even though it wasn't my nightmare that I was watching unfold, I was acutely aware that our roles could have been reversed. The combination of empathy and relief ran salty, wet tracks down my cheeks.

"Speak for yourself," she whispered.

"I know I'm being..." Sinclair searched for the words and went to tug at his hair in frustration only to realize he had cut it off at Elena's behest weeks ago. "Cruel. But if you will think about it for a while, I know that you will see the truth instead of the brutality."

"Just because I'm not demonstrative doesn't mean I don't love you," she said, her voice weak, fading like the last notes from a wind-up music box.

I wondered if it was because she believed him or if the shock and horror of it all was killing her.

"Tell me, Elena, do you think about me in the spaces between each thought? Do you feel me in your chest like a second beating heart? Do you need me more than your next breath?" Sinclair pounded his fist against his chest and spread his fingers out over his heart. "That is what it is to be *in* love."

"You are in love with the whore," Elena said, her voice once again monotone and without accent. "My God, you actually think you're in love with her."

Sinclair tilted his chin and stared at her coolly. "I am very much in love with her. That doesn't excuse my infidelity, and it doesn't make this any easier to do. But it's the truth."

Elena's pale lips trembled as she pressed both palms to her thighs and smoothed down her trousers. She did it carefully three or four times in a row, her gaze fixed on the movement of her hands over the cloth. Finally, she looked up at Sinclair and stepped forward once more.

"You are the worst kind of bastard, Daniel, because you pretend to be a gentleman. I want you to understand that I won't ever forgive you." She smiled thinly, her face sliced in half by the sharp edges of her mouth.

Sinclair nodded. "I can't expect you to."

"I don't want to speak with you again unless it is through a lawyer," she added.

I understood the spiteful game she was playing, throwing things at him to see how much he could take. I felt sorry for her because I knew he would accept every ounce of bitterness she doled out; no one felt more deserving of hatred than Sinclair.

She was only going to grow angrier when she realized it.

"I understand."

"And I want you to stay away from my family," she snarled, stepping forward to press a finger into his chest. "From now on, you no longer fish with Sebastian, you no longer eat at Mama's restaurant, and you sure as hell stop being friends with Cosima. If I see you with them again, I'll rip your fucking eyes out."

The mass of emotions clogging my throat made it hard to breathe, and I choked on them when I realized that she hadn't even bothered to put a moratorium on a relationship with me.

I knew by the way Sin's jaw hardened that he heard the slight too.

"I was friends with Cosima before I even knew you, Elena," he tried to reason.

"I was your partner before you even knew the whore you've been sleeping with, Daniel," she mocked. "Deal with it. She won't want to be friends with you anymore, regardless. I don't think this is too much to ask for."

For the first time all night, Sinclair softened, stepping forward to lift a tentative hand and place it on her shoulder. She stiffened under his touch but allowed it.

"I am so sorry for hurting you, Elena, and I will do anything to make this easier for you. But I can't promise to stay away from your family. They are my family now too."

A loud *crack* echoed through the room as Elena slapped him hard across the face. "Stop pretending to be reasonable, stop making me feel like the bad guy here. You *cheated* on me, Daniel! If you can't seem to get that through your head, I'll make sure everyone you know understands what a bastard you are so that you don't forget it."

I swallowed a sob, curling my knees into my chest and hugging them, as Elena stormed out of the room. The door to the suite slammed shut with an angry bang behind her.

Sin stood rooted to the spot, his head turned slightly from the impact of Elena's slap. I couldn't breathe without sobbing, so I swallowed convulsively and held my breath. After a long minute, he unfroze, rolling his shoulders back and swiveling on his heel so that he faced my hiding spot. He crossed the space in two huge strides and crouched before me, parting the clothes and lifting my curled form effortlessly into his arms. I was sobbing by the time my cheek hit the overheated skin of his chest.

"I love you, I'm sorry," he whispered, over and over again.

I tried to take comfort from his words, especially because I had yearned for them for so long, but they were only a drop in the ocean of my pain, and I knew I deserved to wallow in it.

Chapter Two

Giselle

I WOKE UP DISORIENTATED AND DISGUSTED. I REMEMBERED SLOWLY THAT Sinclair had ushered me from the tainted suite and onto the private plane that would take us to Paris. The company plane was an extravagant yet practical purchase given how often he had to travel now that the business was becoming an international entity.

I had been delirious and dehydrated when he had gently buckled me into one of the deep cream-colored leather seats, and before we could take off, I'd fallen asleep.

Now, my body ached from the hours I had spent crying. My eyes felt like dried olives, and I knew my breath was disgusting by the gritty texture on my gums. Yet when I turned my head to look over at Sinclair, he was staring at me with uncharacteristic warmth over the pages of *The New York Times*.

"Hi," I said softly.

"Hi."

"Why are you smiling at me like that?"

"I'm not."

"You are too. It is all in the eyes with you."

He lowered the paper slightly to reveal his small grin, and I laughed quietly in delight.

"I was smiling because you are beautiful but mostly, because you are here with me. It reminds me of the first time I saw you, sick and scared on the plane to Los Cabos. The sight of you punched the breath from my lungs."

"I was barfing into a courtesy bag," I reminded him dryly.

He lifted one shoulder in a shrug. "Most women never look so alluring."

I laughed at him. He was being playful with me to make me feel better, to ease the pain of betrayal I felt like a stab wound in my chest. The agony was worse, I thought, because the wound was self-inflicted. Sin's good humor was like pressure on the damage, staunching the blood flow, but I knew the relief couldn't last forever and that there was a very real possibility that the pain would.

"Come here," he ordered softly.

Immediately, I was up and out of my chair. My legs were shaky as I stepped across the small space between us to where he sat on a leather sofa, but I wasn't sure if it was from my flight phobia or the way he ordered me around.

I knew it wasn't very feminist of me, but I loved my bossy Frenchman.

I folded myself in his lap and sighed heavily when his arms cradled me closer to his chest. We were silent for a few moments, luxuriating in our closeness.

"I want to get this out of the way before I move on to more entertaining ways to distract you." He inhaled deeply, steeling himself. "I have made you miserable these past few months, and I hate myself for it. You were always the right decision, the *only* decision. It is almost inexcusable that it took me so long to commit to it."

I made a noise of complaint, but he ignored me.

"Now that I have you, I don't plan to let you go. I mean it, Elle. In a sense, we barely know each other, we haven't even had the time to date yet, but I want you to know that the heavy things, the serious questions and answers that usually accompany a long-term relationship, are on the horizon for us. I'm not a patient man, and I meant what I said about tying myself to you in every conceivable way. I never want to wake up again like that morning in Mexico, knowing I had let you slip through my fingers."

The ragged edges fluttered and settled around my heart. I let out a heavy sigh and replaced the grief with the deep, pleasurable smell of Sin.

"We need this vacation," I murmured.

"We do. I will need to do some work, but I'm sure you will have people to catch up with, and I will make as much time as possible to be with you."

"Honestly? I didn't have many friends in Paris, only my university mentor, Odile Claremont and Brenna." My stomach clenched at the thought of my AWOL friend. I hadn't heard from her since I had returned from Mexico, and her lack of communication was alarming.

"Candy, Robert, Duncan, and Richard are already in the city, and Cage will be there in a few days."

I instantly brightened. "That's great. It will be like a little Mexico reunion!"

Sinclair smiled down at me tenderly. "I shouldn't have been surprised that you made such a good impression on them. By the time we left, you had them wrapped around your pinky finger almost as tightly as you did me."

I strained up to nip his chin between my teeth. "I thought it was a little weird that they were so accepting of our affair, given that they know Elena."

He sighed into my hair. "The only one who ever liked her was Margot, and even then I think it's because they are so similar."

"Sin?" I asked quietly, after a moment of silence.

"Yes, my siren?"

"I love you."

His arms constricted around me. "I will never tire of hearing you say that."

"I don't plan to stop anytime soon."

The plane chose that moment to dip and tremble, which wrenched an anxious whimper from me before I could help it.

"We touch down in under two hours," Sinclair said, his voice transitioning to its deeper, steelier tones. "Until then, I expect you to be naked."

Warmth sluiced through my veins as I immediately lifted my dress over my head. It turned me on to know that my body reacted to his words even before my mind could.

It was awkward to disrobe on his lap, so I slipped to the ground between his knees as I tossed the dress onto my abandoned chair and tugged off my underwear. When I looked up at him through my eyelashes, he was all I could see.

"I want to watch you take my cock down your throat."

I shivered, goose bumps rolling across my skin. My hands fumbled slightly as I undid his belt and tugged the zipper over the straining bulge in his pants. His eyes tracked every detail as I freed his erection, dragging my tongue from the base of him to the tip. His musky flavor exploded on my tongue.

I wrapped my hand firmly around the bottom of his shaft and squeezed, watching the veins pulse. My eyes stayed on his as I flicked my tongue on the underside of his crown and placed him in my mouth before taking him as slowly as I could to the back of my throat.

"You look so sexy like this," he practically growled as his hand slid through my hair before wrapping the strands in his fists. He didn't try to control my pace, but the firm tug was just enough to remind me who was in control.

"Are you wet, my siren?"

I was. My wetness leaked down the inside of my thighs. I groaned around his length, which made him groan too.

Before I could even process the change, Sinclair had switched places with me so that I was sprawled on the sofa. He quickly pushed my legs apart and secured them wide with the seat belts until I was spread open and immobile. I watched him beneath lowered lids as he stared at my exposed flesh, his expression tight with longing.

"You are so beautiful, Giselle," he breathed, leaning in to plant a kiss on each inner thigh.

I trembled when he dipped a finger into my wetness and placed it in his mouth.

"And you taste extraordinary."

I wanted to tell him to touch me harder, sink into me and take me hard, but as if he could read my mind, he shook his head and settled down more comfortably on his knees.

"I need to take my time with you right now. I want to paint your body with mine, map your breasts and thighs with my tongue and trace new paths across your hips and ass with my fingers. I want you incoherent with pleasure, so saturated in me and my love that my name is the only word in your mouth."

I gasped as he softly closed his lips over my clit and laved me with his tongue. From somewhere deep in my sleeping rational mind, I was astonished he could have such an effect on my body. I only had to feel him in the room with me to have my heart racing. A single touch of his skin against mine ignited a furious fire deep in the heart of me.

I watched his dark red head pressed between my thighs as he pleasured me with languid strokes. The sight of such a powerful man, still impossibly immaculate in a thousand-dollar suit, on his knees before me made me feel dizzy with power.

He worked me over masterfully, pausing whenever I grew too excited, licking along every erotic seam of my body until I shook with desire. I tried to press him closer, yanking his silky hair between my fists, but his warm chuckle only fueled me, and the gentle press of his nose against my clit aroused me but failed to satisfy. Curses fell from my lips in a mad torrent as I begged him to make me come.

He ignored me.

A little while later, my muscles had grown slack, and my head lolled on my neck as I murmured his name over and over again, incoherent with an overload of pleasure.

"My sweet siren wants to come, don't you?" he teased against the folds of my sex. "You want to come against my tongue?"

A soft groan was all I could manage.

I could feel his smile against my damp inner thigh. It was the sign he had been waiting for.

With a skillful twist of his fingers and a soft nip of his teeth over the hood of my clit, I exploded at the seams. It was a messy orgasm, my hoarse shouts primal and my body flailing against my restraints as every muscle in my body clenched and unclenched in a mind-blowing release.

Before I could get my bearings, Sin had gathered my bound legs up in his arms and was pushing inside me. A rattling groan escaped me as he slid across highly sensitive tissues. I was about to protest when he ground his hips against my clit and another orgasm was wrenched from me like a waxing strip, edged deeply with pain and all the more intense for it.

I gasped and shuddered as I held on to him, pushing my hips against his as he surged into me. His name was a mantra, a benediction on my lips. I wanted him to come inside me with a savagery that stole my breath away. My nails scoured down his back to hear his moan. I sunk my teeth deeply into that delicious ridge of muscle where his neck met his shoulder to feel him shudder against my tongue.

"I want to feel you come inside me," I begged.

"Fuck," he groaned. "Take all of me."

"More," I demanded, "I need more."

Sin pressed his damp forehead against mine. "Come with me."

"Yes," I hissed as his hips ground into me and my back arched off the couch.

His lips caught mine and muffled my shriek of ecstasy as I pulsed around him, undone again by this man. He breathed my name against my neck and followed me into blissfulness.

When he collapsed against me, and our sweat ruined his beautiful suit, I ran a limp hand through his hair and hugged him as tightly as my spent muscles would allow. Somehow, this gorgeous creature who had mastered my body from the start was now my partner, the love of my life. I could feel our hearts beat in tandem. I let the terror I had held at bay since I had first laid eyes on him in Mexico tear through me on a deep exhale.

"I've got you," my Frenchman murmured against my neck because he always knew the right things to say. "I've got you now, and I'm never giving you up."

I let the tears roll down my cheeks, and I wasn't sure if they were happy or sad, or maybe even a little bit afraid of the things our fragile new bond still had to face.

Chapter Three

Sinclair

I LOVED PARIS THE WAY SOMEONE MIGHT LOVE AN ECCENTRIC, ACERBIC GREAT-aunt who palmed them five-dollar bills and snuck vodka into their punch at family functions. The combination of her gorgeous excess, her calculated haughtiness and secret grim reminded me acutely of my reasons for loving Elena. It was wrong of me to compare my aloof admiration of the city to my feelings for the woman I had just spent the past four years of my life with, but as I rode silently through the beautiful streets of Paris, it was impossible not to think about my ex-girlfriend.

We had never been to Paris together before. Giselle was a large reason for Elena's reluctance to spend any time in the city, but we also disliked traveling together for business. The purpose of such a trip was to accomplish work, not dilute productivity with romantic dinners and afternoon visits to museums.

The irony of my desire to do just that with Giselle was not lost on me.

How could two sisters be so incredibly different and more so, invoke such contrary emotions in one man?

I ran a hand through my hair, a nervous habit I had never kicked. I needed a haircut, but Giselle liked my hair long, and it was finally beginning to curl around my ears as it had in Mexico. I'd grow out my hair to the conceited length of Cage's if it meant Elle would fist it in her small hand while I worshiped every dip and curve of her luscious body.

She was quiet beside me, her anxieties lulled by multiple orgasms and the steadiness of my hand against the bare skin of her thigh. The trust she had in me was evident in my total influence over her body; she was warm, pliable wax under my careful touch, not only ready but willing to be molded into whatever shape and consistency I deemed best for her. No drug, adrenaline sport, or any other false ecstasy could come close to the feeling that power evoked in me.

I wanted this trip to be healing for her, but more than that, I needed it to fortify our bond. We belonged together—this I knew without a doubt—but any relationship, especially one as new as ours, could bow and break under the strain of so much hatred and so many lies. I needed to tie myself to her in as many ways as conceivably possible so that no amount of external conflict could pull us apart. My selfish desire to do this was so great, I was even contemplating a fucking tattoo of her name across my chest. Unreasonably, I wondered if she might consider the same thing.

My fingers clenched unconsciously around her thigh, bringing her bright gray eyes to mine. The serenity in her expression calmed me.

"You are very quiet," I noted.

Her lips twitched. "It's making you uncomfortable."

I raised my eyebrows at her, knowing it would make her laugh.

I wasn't disappointed.

When she was finished giggling, she leaned toward me to press a fragrant kiss to my jaw. "You are so much more volatile than anyone knows."

"Because I want to know every thought that runs through the gorgeous mind of yours? That's hardly unreasonable."

Her lips pursed in an expression of doubt that I was all too familiar with. Giselle wasn't a confident woman at the best of times, and I hadn't given her much reason to believe in me. She might have believed that I loved her, but she didn't trust that I wanted to love her. I'd been fighting it for so long that she obviously still felt like a burden to me.

God, I was fucking disgusting.

"Giselle," I said, tugging her hands so that she was forced to face me. I ran a hand through her copper-colored hair and let it rest on her cheek. "Have I spent too much time telling you that you are mine and not enough emphasizing that I am utterly yours?"

She smiled slightly, but in her reserved mood, I couldn't tell if it was sincere or meant to placate me. Before I could question her further about it, the car pulled up on the narrow street in Saint-Germain-des-Prés where we would be staying.

I watched with the eager anticipation of a child as Giselle laid eyes on the building. Her beautiful features shone with joy as she realized where we were.

"Sin, how did you know?" she crowed, spinning around to throw her arms around me.

I chuckled. "I may have done a little background check at some point. I was starved for information about you when we weren't talking," I explained with a deceptively casual shrug. She didn't need to know how I had spent countless hours poring over everything I could find about her. "I may have stumbled across your Pinterest account."

Her delighted laugh pealed like Parisian church bells through the Town Car, and the sound echoed throughout my body. I was utterly dazzled by her.

"I've always wanted to stay here. Did you know Oscar Wilde died here in 1900?" She pressed her nose to the glass, her hands spread wide against the pane.

I chuckled. "That would explain why our room is named after him."

She spun to face me, her petal-pink lips soft and dewy as they opened and closed in shock. I had to fight the urge to press them to my hardening cock.

"You are amazing," she breathed.

I sank my hand into the silky hair at the base of her neck and pulled her close until I spoke against those enticing lips. "Only for you."

She kissed me with smiling lips and then dove out of the car. I chuckled as I collected our luggage and followed her into the lobby. I found her standing in the small but ornate reception, her face tipped to the ceiling and glowing with joy. It took my breath away to see her like that, especially after months of causing her only pain.

I snagged her hand as I walked past to check in, but she remained blissed out on our setting and didn't clue in to my exchange until I said, "Yes, my girlfriend and I will need a car to pick us up at eight o'clock to take us to *Chez Dumonet*."

She stared at me as I accepted the old-fashioned key to our room, but I ignored her until we were safely enclosed in the elevator.

"Yes, siren?"

"I'm your girlfriend?"

I struggled not to smile, shrugging one shoulder instead. "A bit juvenile, I know."

"No," she whispered after a brief pause. "It's perfect."

"You can call yourself whatever you want, Elle, as long as it implies that you are mine."

She blushed beautifully.

I led her down the hallway to our famous Oscar Wilde room, opening the door for her so I could watch her expression of awe as she passed into it. Cage had an apartment in the city, my parents had a house just outside Paris in the countryside with enough room for us *and* a traveling circus, but I was glad I had decided on the hotel because it meant I got that look on her face.

"It's just how I imagined. Did you know he was a bit of a social pariah? He was cutting edge and sexually progressive for his age, not to mention very gay." She smiled wryly at me. "It's fitting we're staying here."

I raised an eyebrow. "If you're a homosexual, Elle, I'm afraid you should have told me sooner."

She laughed and skipped over to me, throwing her arms around my neck to pull me down for a loud, smacking kiss.

"Thank you for this."

"Mmm?"

"Thank you for taking me away. Thank you for bringing me here, to the second love of my life."

I smoothed a hand down her hair and collected the ends in my fist so I could tip her head back. "Just how thankful are you?"

Her eyes darkened as her pupils dilated, and her voice was breathy when she said, "Why don't you let me show you?"

My cock twitched when she gracefully sank to her knees before me. Her gorgeous red hair shimmered like flames trapped in a silk tapestry. I had to swallow the lump of longing that clogged my throat. I had her, she was right in front of me, begging for me to take her and own her in the exact way I longed to, but the residual panic of loss still haunted me, and it took me a moment to center myself.

I ran a hand down that crazy beautiful hair, pressing her face into my crotch as I did so. She breathed in deeply, moaning at my scent. My fingers flexed against her head.

"Open my pants and take my cock out."

A little shiver ran down her back as her quick fingers undid my trousers and wrapped around my painfully hard erection. There was a bright flush painted high on her cheeks, and her fingers shook slightly with the force of her arousal. It was enough to make any man feel like a fucking king. How could you not when you had a queen worshipping at your feet?

"Hands behind your back. I want you to use that pretty mouth on me."

I'd never enjoyed blow jobs before as much as I did with Elle. It had a lot to do with the sight of her pretty pink lips wrapped lewdly around the width of my shaft, how she strained to take the length of me down her throat, working past her gag reflex to slot me into that tight canal. Don't even get me started on the thrill I got from looking down into her eyes with my dick stuffed down her throat. But mostly, I loved that as soon as I pulled her off me so I could run my fingers, tongue, or cock through her pussy, it would be absolutely drenched with arousal.

My erection snapped back up to my stomach when she let go, but she was quick to run her tongue up the seam of my balls and the underside of my shaft before taking the entire thing in her mouth with one strong downward suck. She moaned loudly, and the sound vibrated through me, sending sparks up my spine.

"You want this, don't you, my siren? You love to take me straight down your throat."

She moaned loudly. Her lips were tight around my tip as she slowly took every inch of me into her mouth. She tipped her head carefully to look up at me, and there was pure, unadulterated rapture in her eyes. The sight was so erotic it made me see stars.

Before I couldn't, I pulled her off my cock, wincing at the intense pleasure of her lips sucking hard as she tried to keep me in her mouth.

"I have plans for tonight, though, and they do not include coming in your mouth."

She pouted then licked her slick, swollen lips greedily as though she couldn't stand the absence of my taste in her mouth.

Fuck, she was phenomenal.

Before she could react, I had lifted her into my arms and was depositing her on the bed.

"Close your eyes," I commanded softly, rewarding her with a kiss to each shut lid as she obeyed.

I got off the bed and went to retrieve the bag of toys I had brought from my suitcase by the front door. Quickly, I grabbed what I needed from the fully stocked bar and shucked my clothes. On quiet feet, I returned to see Giselle lying perfectly still and serene, just as I had left her.

"Good girl," I said as I moved around the bed to secure her hands and feet to the old-fashioned bedposts. "I've waited for ages to have you like this, and now that we have *time*, I will not waste it."

I got off the bed, smiling slightly at her moan of disappointment, and laid out the implements I would need so they were in easy reach on the bedside table.

"I'm going to touch every inch of your delicious body until your skin is singing and you are beyond begging, until you are shaking and mute with pleasure."

I watched a flush sweep over her body, my words like a brush inked with desire and brushed across all that creamy skin. I hadn't craved a paintbrush between my fingers in years, but the urge to paint her like that was nearly as strong as the urge to take her.

So I compromised.

She gasped as I drew the thick, plush head of a clean paintbrush from just behind her ear, down the elegant line of her neck, and into the hollow of her collarbone. Her skin pebbled under the soft, ticklish strokes, and when I passed circles over her tight nipples, her chest arched off the bed to increase the contact.

"I wish you could see all your gorgeous, creamy skin blush with the pleasure that I'm giving you," I said before groaning in the back of my throat. Her breathing stuttered in response as she sank further into subspace. "It is just a pale pink under this brush, but it will be reddened by the time I'm done with you."

I circled her navel, watching her belly flutter in anticipation, but I dipped the bristles in the divot there. She squirmed when I traced the tender intersection of her legs and groin.

"Be still," I ordered.

Immediately, she held herself taut, only her pulse still bouncing madly in her breasts and throat.

"Good girl," I soothed as I wet the end of the brush in the well of her arousal and swirled the dampened end teasingly over her clit.

Her hips shot off the bed.

"I told you to be still," I reminded her, my voice saturated with displeasure.

She shivered, fisting her hands in the sheets and biting her bottom lip in an attempt to control herself.

I passed the brush once more over her swollen button, round and round in progressively harder strokes until her mound glistened wetly in the low light. Leaning over the bed but careful not to touch her with anything other than the brush, I blew cool air across her sex. Her legs quivered in response. I dipped the brush in her dripping pussy once more before I brought it to her breasts. Her nipple pulled ever tighter as her juices cooled and dried on her skin. She moaned loudly when I followed the path of the brushstroke with my tongue and sucked a nipple into my mouth. I drew on it hard, curling my tongue around her peak.

"Ah," she exhaled a long, low gasp when I did the same thing to the other nipple.

"Your pussy tastes so fucking sweet, Elle. Rich and sweet like wildflower honey. Here," I said, bringing the brush back to her sex for more of that sugary nectar. "Try it."

I coated her parted lips in her own wetness and watched as her tentative pink tongue poked out to steal a taste. She hummed once before her tongue completed a full sweep of those plump, pouting lips.

My cock throbbed, bobbing against my stomach and leaving a trail of sticky pre-cum there. Before my control slipped entirely, I traded out the paintbrush for a suede flogger. Carefully, I trailed the soft tendrils over her primed skin.

She shuddered.

"Do you know what this is, my siren?"

"No, sir."

"It's a flogger."

She shivered delicately because she knew what that was.

I trailed the falls teasingly over her entire form, lingering until she writhed.

"So eager. Do you need a little pain, siren?"

"Please."

I wondered if she deliberately forgot to address me as sir in order to be punished or if she was so consumed by anticipation that she really forgot. I decided it didn't matter.

My wrist flicked, bringing the soft tendrils down hard across her breasts. A long, low moan wrenched from her diaphragm.

"Please, what?"

I brought the tails down again, once on the tender underside of her left breast and then again on the right.

"Please, *sir*," she gasped.

"That first night I took you in Mexico, I wanted to do this," I explained, modulating my voice so that it was stripped of the furious arousal churning in my gut. "I wanted to beat your breasts red with a flogger and fuck them with my cock while they were still hot."

A strangled whimper escaped her parted lips. The euphoria that came with dominating a beautiful, strong woman, seducing her so completely that she was at the mercy of your darkest desires, thrummed through me like thunder.

"Would you like that, Elle? Would you like me to fuck you here?" I asked while I continued to strategically lay into her beautiful tits.

I wanted to clamp her rosy, taut nipples, but she wasn't ready for that even though the savage in me didn't really care.

"Yes, sir. Please," she said, the last word dragged out on a groan as the edges of the flogger wrapped around one of her nipples.

Her back came arching off the bed.

"Be still," I ordered.

Her body shook with the strain.

The color of her chest was a deep, ruddy pink when I finally set down the flogger. I reached for the glass I left on the bedside table and grabbed a fat ice cube between my fingers. She hissed as I ran it in light circles around her pain-warmed nipple.

The ice melted quickly against her skin. The next time, I reached for two cubes and held them tightly to each nipple until she murmured incoherently, the pain of the cold sharp against the background of pleasure. When those chips dissolved, I leaned forward to lick up the wetness with my tongue before sucking a nipple deep into my mouth.

She tasted fucking fantastic.

The beast inside me roared his approval.

Simultaneously, I took one nipple between my teeth in a firm grip and twisted the other sharply with my fingers.

"Ah," she moaned.

"Do you want me to fuck these gorgeous tits, Giselle?" I asked.

"Please, please, please, sir."

"What if I don't want to? What if, instead, I want to slide into your sweet pussy and fuck you until you beg me to stop?"

She panted heavily in response.

"What if I want to flip you over onto your hands and knees, take my belt to your ass, and make you come in my mouth before I come all over your back?"

A shudder wracked her body, and a little gasp exploded from her lips. That one. That was the one she wanted. It didn't really surprise me. Elle loved it when I did anything to her sweet, round behind.

Moving quickly, I undid the ties around her ankles and ordered, "Turn over. Hands and knees. Get that ass high up in the air for me, Elle."

She scrambled to obey, planting her face in the covers and curving her back so low it had to be painful. I ran a hand over her cheeks and spread them. Her pussy was so wet that her juices had dripped down her inner thighs. Unable to help myself, I licked the trail up her meaty thigh into her pussy and right up to her asshole.

She tasted like pure heaven.

As I retrieved my belt from the ground, I wondered if I was moving too fast. Her body was utterly pliant under my hands, my commands, but BDSM was about trust, and she was new to the game. It was easy to forget that, given how beautifully she submitted, but I didn't want to take her too far because she was ready. Her absolute trust in me was too precious to squander, her body too beautiful to brutalize, her mind too steeped in past sexual abuse to ever allow me to take her sexual sincerity lightly.

Sensing my hesitation, Giselle wriggled her ass in my face and said, "Sir? Please."

"Please, what?" I asked, running a hand over her buttocks again to comfort her, to comfort me.

"I, I want you to take your belt to my ass. I want you to, um, make me come on your mouth, and then I want you to come on me," she murmured.

Fuck, but she was perfect. Too good for me. But I was a selfish guy, and I was willing to take it despite my merit.

Without further qualm, I looped my leather belt in my hands and gave my siren what she and I both wanted.

I SAT IN THE DARK HOURS LATER, THE LIGHT OF MY LAPTOP SCREEN THE ONLY illumination in our suite. Giselle was asleep on the bed, exhausted from our hours of rigorous play. I hadn't been easy on her—her ass was red from my belt, stripped like a candy cane, and I had left no place untouched by my fingers, tongue, and cock. It was too much when she was already tired from our play on the plane, and I'd acted like a rookie Dominant playing with a shiny new toy. But the truth was, even though I had had her before, I'd never *owned* her. Not like this. My dick stirred in my pants even as I thought about it. The fact that I could mark her now, brand her with sex and pain, my name carved into her voice box with every grateful shout of her ecstasy, wasn't something I imagined I would ever get enough of.

My mind wandered to all the things I could introduce her to in the lifestyle. I didn't want to dominate her outside of the bedroom, not really, but I loved the idea of sending her to the gallery without panties on, of making her touch herself in the bathroom, and of ordering her to wait by the door for me when I came home, her forehead to the ground and her naked ass raised in offering the second I came through the door.

As if conjured by my runaway, deviant thoughts, my email pinged with a note from Elena. I stiffened, my cursor lingering over the notification. I deeply wanted to ignore her and isolate myself from the reality of New York so that I could fully enjoy my time in Paris with Giselle, but I also knew it was my responsibility to Elena to deal with the situation.

So I opened the email.

To: Daniel Sinclair <danielsinclair@fairedevelopments.com>
From: Elena Lombardi <elenalombardi@fieldshardinggriffithllp.com>

Subject: *Your Depravity.*

Daniel,

I meant what I said yesterday. If you cannot respect my wishes regarding your immediate extradition from my family dynamics, I will be forced to divulge not only the nature of our separation (i.e. your infidelity) but also the truth about your sexual proclivities. You may think I know nothing about your disgusting 'scene,' but I'm a lawyer. I've researched and even represented victims of the "BDSM" life-style. Do you not remember my involvement in the Gian Gomeshi trial last year? You like to hit women, Daniel, you get off on causing them pain and forcing them to do things that they normally never would. I don't know how you live with yourself for that. It would be another thing if you tried to restrain yourself, but obviously, you've found some poor victim to take your deviancies out on, and that is why you are no longer attracted to me. I'm not sorry that I never let you beat me, but I am sorry that I thought for even a moment that you were capable of a normal, loving relationship. For her sake, I hope the whore you are supposedly 'in love' with has good health insurance. And I hope she knows whatever sick rela-tionship you have isn't real love.

The bottom line is this; stay away from my family, or I'll let the world know your deplorable secrets. I can't imagine the conservative Mr. Paulson would be too happy to hear about those now, would he?

Cordially,

ELENA LOMBARDI

I SAT BACK IN MY CHAIR AND CLOSED MY EYES AS THE TRUTH OF ELENA'S EMAIL poisoned me from the inside out.

Logically, I knew that properly practiced BDSM could not only be healthy, it could be healing. But I also believed what Elena said about my desires being disgusting. Would Giselle have ever found submission, the pleasure to be had from pain and complete acquiescence, if I hadn't forced them on her? Even now, was she only so interested in the power dynamic because it was the only way she thought she could have me?

I thought back on the four years of my vanilla relationship with Elena and winced. Our relationship had never been about sex, but I could see looking back that I had been deeply unfulfilled by it. Fortunately, it explained my single-minded focus and control as I built Faire Developments from the ground up. If I couldn't have power in the bedroom, I could exert it in all other areas of my life.

Only now, Giselle had alerted me to the possibility of a life as a total Dominant. I wasn't a switch, and I'd also been a powerful force in all aspects of my personality. I didn't want to give up control to anyone; I didn't want to kill the urge to push other people to do my bidding, to see how far I could push someone past their own limits to achieve a goal they had been previously too afraid to attain. Did that make me a sociopath?

The answer, at least at the moment, was a resounding *yes*.

Giselle was what I wanted beyond all things, not just a random submissive to act out my desires upon. I owed it to Giselle to show her that I could love her wholly, without the trappings of a lifestyle that I had missed and longed for. Elena had forced me to give up on the Dom within me, and it had been like living a half-life. Wouldn't that be the same thing for Elle if I forced her to be a sub when that wasn't really what she wanted?

I dragged a hand over my face as my mind surged with doubt and fear. I needed to wake up Giselle so she could have time to get ready for our dinner with my colleagues, but I didn't think I could face her in my current state.

Quietly, I walked over to take a seat on the edge of the bed so that I could look down at her. Her red hair spiraled around her head, bright and glossy like sienna oil paint even in the darkness. Even her thick eyelashes were red, dark against the pale gold of her soft cheeks. My heart ached as I looked down at her. I knew then that a vanilla future was the only way forward for us. It would take some adjusting on both our parts, but Elena was right. I owed it to Giselle to try.

Chapter Four

Giselle

NERVES BOUNCED ON MY DIAPHRAGM, TRAMPOLINING AND CARTWHEELING IN my stomach like circus performers as we walked through the cold night to one of Sinclair's favorite casual restaurants in Paris.

He held my hand, and people gave us appraising looks as we passed them by. It was a heady feeling to realize that they were admiring us as a couple. I squeezed Sin's hand and beamed up at him when he glanced down at me. The soft light of the shops and old-fashioned lampposts spilling into the street turned his hair to pure copper and cast his features in shadow.

"I never thought we would be able to do this," I admitted, somewhat sheepishly.

His eyes were kind, though, his version of a tender smile. "Now you can know that there will never again be a time when you *will not* be able to do this."

He raised our joined hands to place a kiss on my knuckles.

I swooned a little, rocking on my heels, but Sin steadied me with a soft huff of laughter. "Have I worn you out, my siren?"

"The nap helped but yes, a little."

This time his laugh was big and loud enough to attract attention. I stared at his throat, mesmerized by the way it moved with his humor.

He stopped the moment he looked back over at me, his face frozen mid-expression.

"What?" I asked.

"You have this way of looking at me."

"A way?"

"Mmm, a way. A way that tells me that you think of me as the very best kind of man, a person in possession of a very good heart."

"You are that," I agreed easily even though I could tell that he was moved almost to discomfort by the idea.

"I don't want you to be disappointed in me." He said it so softly I had to lean in to be sure of his words. "I will try harder than I ever have before to be that kind of person, but you will have to forgive me my mistakes when I inevitably make them. I wasn't this kind of man before I met you."

His words made my soul ache. I couldn't believe that no one had ever told him how intensely beautiful he was. Though I had met his parents, understood them to be self-serving, I couldn't really fathom how Elena could have refrained from telling him every other moment how special he was. I honestly felt like it was my honor to get to love him, to know him, and take care of him.

I told him so.

He stopped walking and slowly turned to me, slipping one hand through the hair at the nape of my neck and the other around my hip. We stared at each other with wordless feelings in our eyes as he slowly walked me back against a wall and pressed himself close to my body. I relished the heat between us, tipping my head back to maintain eye contact.

"Thank you," he whispered, and I felt, more than heard, the words against my lips.

I pressed a soft kiss to his mouth in response.

When he broke away, he pulled back to smile a ridiculously adorable grin. "Are you ready for some *déjà vu*?"

I frowned but then realized we were in front of *Chez Dumonet*, where we would meet his friends and colleagues from Mexico. It was my turn to grin.

"Lead the way."

I had never been to this restaurant before but only because I had always been too poor for such extravagancies. I loved it on sight for its subtle opulence and quintessentially French features, but I also understood that I was biased by the sight of the Mexico crew sitting around the best table by the window.

"Giselle," Robert Corbett bellowed as everyone stood to greet us.

I couldn't help but laugh as he embraced me in a huge bear hug. Though he was sixty-five years old, he had the kind of virility you would have expected in a much younger man.

When I embraced Duncan Wright next, I couldn't help but note the difference between the two men. The CFO of Faire Developments comported himself with a humble, almost subservient calm and kindness that would have seemed much better suited to a man of Robert's age and slight stature.

Margot only deigned to smile slightly in my direction, but I found myself surprisingly happy to see her. After all, she had been the one to urge me to pony up and claim Sinclair as my own.

Richard hugged me next, but it was a short embrace because Candy was pushing him out of the way before he even had his arms around me.

"I'm the best friend," she explained haughtily as she delicately wrapped her arms around me and then snapped me close with a brutal force that shoved the air from my lungs.

I laughed even as I tried to catch my breath. "Hey, best friend."

"How are you feeling?"

My heart panged. "Like I sacrificed my entire world for the only thing that really matters."

"That was pretty poetic," she said as she pulled away from me and made a face. "But it makes sense. Even though you made the only choice you could, it doesn't make it any less difficult."

"You owe me two hundred big ones," Richard said to Duncan.

I turned to the meek young man and watched him blush furiously.

"I, um, I don't..."

Richard guffawed. "Don't be embarrassed, Wright, you lost fair and square."

"You placed wagers on my relationship with Elle?" Sinclair asked in that perfectly glacial tone that immediately froze everyone in place.

Duncan cleared his throat before stuttering, "Well, logically, you see, I mean, it was obvious to everyone who could see you two in Mexico..."

"Oh, get off your high horse, Sin. We made a bet on you two getting together. Big whoop. Turns out our instincts were correct, which is probably what makes us such invaluable employees too," Candy said.

"And the best of friends," he added, drolly.

Her eyes widened, and she placed a hand over her chest. "You think we're friends? I'm touched, truly."

I laughed at their antics as everyone took their seats. Even though I didn't know the group very well, I felt connected to them because they had been there at the very beginning of Sinclair and me. If anyone could understand the magnetic, inexorable pull between us, it was them.

And they proved their understanding by being nothing but polite and delightful through the entire evening. It was amazing to relax with friends and feel comfortable leaning into Sinclair when he fed me a morsel of beautiful beef bourguignon from his plate and kiss him when I returned from the restroom. Candy coyly commented on the silver and turquoise cuff Sinclair had given me, the very same one that I had admired with her in Mexico, and I was even thrilled when they began to question us about the future as if it were only natural to assume the two of us would be together for a very long time.

"Where will you live when you return Stateside?" Robert asked.

I looked at Sinclair with a deep frown because I hadn't thought of that. We couldn't very well shack up at Cosima's together for a variety of reasons.

My Frenchman didn't look at me, but he squeezed my knee beneath the table. "We'll figure that out when we come to it."

Richard narrowed his eyes at us. "You haven't told anyone yet, have you?"

"No," I admitted, suddenly fascinated with the delicate stem of my red wineglass. "It's a bit easier said than done."

Candy snorted indelicately. "That is officially the understatement of the century."

"Candace," Sinclair warned softly.

"As much as I love to disagree with Candy, she does have a point," Margot chimed in. "What do you do in this situation? Call up your sister and say, 'hello, Elena, you know that man you planned to marry and spend the rest of your life with? Well, I'm sleeping with him.'"

"Boy, I don't envy you that conversation," Robert said with a wince.

"It's not about the sex, though, or at least, it wouldn't be for me," Candy admitted with a guilty look in my direction. "It would be that Sinclair was choosing you to spend his life with and not me."

My heart rattled and rocked on the turbulence of their words. My previous levity drowned beneath the waves.

Sinclair's hand moved soothingly back and forth over my thigh, but it didn't bring me any great comfort.

"It would be the sex for me," Margot countered. "Knowing that my man thought my little sister was hotter? Horrible."

"Quiet," Sinclair ordered, his voice steely. "You are speaking about a situation that is impossible to understand from the outside looking in. More importantly, you are being insensitive to Giselle. She has done nothing wrong."

"Except for having knowingly slept with a taken man," Margot muttered.

Her words found their bull's-eye in the center of my chest.

"You know nothing." Sinclair's eyes blazed bright as a lightning strike as they landed on her. "I will explain something to you which is none of your business even though you seem to think it is. My past girlfriend thought my sexuality was *disgusting*, you understand? She found me repulsive and vile, and when we did have sex, it was never making love. I have great respect for Elena, but she never loved me, not my entire soul. To stay with her would have been a great wrong for both of us. Giselle is my partner now and forevermore. If any of you have a problem with it, I do not care to hear it."

Utter silence fell in the wake of his bitter speech. Even I was a bit afraid of the bristling fury he kept barely contained under that ice-cold façade. Gently, I tangled my fingers with his on my lap.

"I'm sorry," Margot said, more to my surprise. "I didn't mean to cast judgment. I can't say that I fully understand your connection, but I do respect you, Daniel, and if Elle is the woman for you, I won't stand in your way any longer."

"She is the *only* woman for me," he stated imperiously.

I dragged in a shaky deep breath of relief. God, I loved this man.

"Okay." She nodded at him before looking at me. "Okay."

He turned to stare at his other colleagues, daring them to speak out.

Surprisingly, it was Duncan who blinked twice and said softly, "Sinclair, man, we knew she was the one in Mexico almost from the very start. Why do you think we stayed quiet?"

"We want you to be happy. You're happy." Robert shrugged.

It was a lot more complicated than they made it seem, but I could see that their approval meant a great deal to him by the way Sinclair's frown turned to one of confusion and then melted away.

"Now, Elle, how would you feel about a personal tour of the building site tomorrow?" Richard interjected smoothly. "I could always use an artist's eye."

My laughter eased the tension at the table. "I would love to."

"Speaking of an artist's eye," Candy said, "I've had another three offers for the *Dreams Under Water* painting, Sinclair."

"No."

"Sin... At least consider it. You don't even like it."

I looked back and forth between the two of them—at Candy's frustration and Sinclair's adamancy.

"What are you talking about?" I asked.

"Sinclair's biological mother's painting," Candy explained.

"Excuse me?"

Sinclair's mother had been an artist? How was it possible I didn't know that?

"Candace," Sinclair warned.

"Your mother?" I asked him.

Richard let out a low whistle. "Damn, man, you didn't tell her about your mother?"

"When did you expect me to tell her? I *just* made her mine, and you are jeopardizing that by making it seem like I am keeping secrets from her."

Candy bit her lip. "I'm really sticking my foot in it tonight, aren't I?"

"Yes," Sinclair agreed, but his voice wasn't cold because it was obvious Candy was upset.

I was too. "Tell me about your mother."

He closed his eyes briefly to hide the flare of pain that turned them deep and soft as wet velvet. "My mother was an artist. It was how she met my father, Alain Sinclair. She was selling her paintings at a fair in the countryside outside of Nice. She left her family, her caravan, for him without ever looking back. I think they had known each other for only a few days when she took off with him."

"Oh," I said because I didn't know what else to say.

It was a romantic story, a Frenchman falling in love with an exotic, artistic gypsy, but I knew it had a sad ending, one where Sinclair was orphaned at the age of seven. His mother's abilities made it obvious where his love of art had come from, so I wondered why he seemed to be so sensitive about her paintings.

Reading my thoughts, as he so often did, Sinclair explained, "My mother, Apolline, produce a lot of work, mostly nature-inspired abstracts. When I had the means, I tracked down as many as I could. The one that hangs over the reception desk is the only one that I have real memories of. She painted it when she discovered she was pregnant. I remember her telling me that she had dreamed of permanency, of a home, a husband, and a baby since she herself was a child, but she always thought it was an impossible dream."

"Hence the name, *Dream Under Water*," I murmured, getting it.

He nodded.

I looked into his face, seeing the pain at the tight corners of his eyes and the strained press of his lips. Talking about this wasn't easy for him, especially in front of others, but he wanted me to know him, and he was trying to open up in a way I was sure he had never opened up before.

"Love you," I whispered.

The tension in his muscles eased as he leaned forward to press a kiss into my hair.

"*Toujours*," he whispered into my ear.

THAT NIGHT, SINCLAIR DECLARED WE WERE TOO TIRED TO PLAY. I WAS definitely exhausted from all the emotional upheaval, our two previous, rigorous rounds of sex, and jet lag. I also knew that I would *never* be too tired to play with Sinclair. I told him so, but he only smiled slightly before ordering me to get ready for bed.

"Have you seen my pill pack?" I asked, rummaging through my suitcase.

Candy had done an excellent job packing, but of course, she hadn't included my backup pill packet, and the one that I always kept in my purse had temporarily gone missing.

I looked up at Sin anxiously as he popped his head out of the bathroom to stare at me for a long moment before shaking his head.

"*Putain*," I muttered under my breath, but he heard me.

"Is everything okay?"

"Yes, but if I can't find it in the next day, I need to find a clinic to get a refill. It's dangerous to miss more than two days in a row." I bit my lip. "If we want to be one hundred percent careful, we should probably use condoms until I can get this figured out."

Sinclair frowned at me. "Do not be ridiculous, Giselle. You are mine now. What is the point if I can't take you bare?"

I laughed as he meant me to and decided to look again in the morning when I was less disorientated from a long flight and emotional exhaustion.

Happily brushing my teeth beside my Frenchman, washing my face and moisturizing while he took a quick shower and then slipping into bed together in our pajamas was its own kind of distracting bliss. He wore charcoal gray drawstring pants that rode low on his narrow hips. They exposed those ridges of muscle that arrowed straight into his groin. I decided they were the best pants in existence and thought about asking him to wear them every day, all day. But then I thought of him in his three-piece suits and kept my mouth shut because those were incredibly sexy as well.

Suddenly, I was overwhelmed by the fact that if I wanted to dictate his dress, I could because it was something women did when they had a man. They played dress-up with him and for him. I was already planning my outfit for the next day when I would get a tour of the building site for the hotel they were constructing. I wanted to look good to the people we met with because I was a reflection on Sinclair and I wanted them to be proud of me.

On that thought, I tipped my head up on Sin's chest to look at him. "I don't really know much about you."

"You know enough to love me."

I shivered because I was in his arms, and those were good words.

"But I don't know the little things," I stressed.

"The little things are little for a reason. You know what's at the heart of me. Do you need to know what my favorite color is?"

"Yes," I said immediately. "What is it?"

"Giselle..." he said, partly exasperated, partly amused.

"Sinclair..." I mocked him.

There was laughter in his voice when he said, "I'm partial to Titian red."

I blushed as his fingers filtered through my hair. I'd known he loved my hair, and it didn't take a genius to see he was into redheads given he had also been with Elena.

Which led me to my next question. "How many lovers have you had?"

He burst out laughing.

Seriously.

One second we were lying with me tucked into his side, my arm around his belly and his hand around my waist, languid and cuddling. The next, he was frozen mid-crunch, his stomach rock hard beneath my hand and his entire body jerking so much with laughter that my body was thrown off his.

I was so surprised I just stared at him.

When he was finally finished except for the odd chuckle, there were tears at the corners of his eyes.

"Are you quite finished?" I asked, a little enthralled because I had never seen him laugh so hard but also annoyed because what I had asked wasn't funny.

"Oh, Elle." He chuckled before reaching over to tug me back into his side.

I resisted.

He sighed around his smile but gave in, crossing his arms behind his head. I tried not to notice how his biceps bulged, and his abs drew taut.

"Do not be angry with me, *mon amour*. I was only laughing because you bring me so much joy."

"Yeah, right," I muttered, swinging upright so I could cross my legs and fold my arms over my chest.

He bit back a laugh, a chuckle rumbling around stuck in his chest.

"You would really like to know how many lovers I've had?"

"Yes."

"Fourteen."

He searched my face for my reaction, but I was surprisingly relieved. Fourteen wasn't a massive number, and I realized that I wouldn't feel any jealousy about the number anyway as soon as he spoke the words. Sinclair and I were different. He loved me so much that he'd left his orderly life and perfect partner for me, an inexperienced artist.

"Okay," I said as I dropped down at his side again. "What's your favorite meal?"

His arm instantly slid around me again, securing me firmly to his side. His squeeze told me that he was happy with my reaction to his confession.

"Anything with duck."

"I love duck too!"

I couldn't see his face, but I knew he smiled.

"Who are your favorite musicians?"

"Elle, it's been a very long day, and as much as I would love to play twenty questions with you, I also have to be up in four hours to be on-site."

"Okay," I said, a little disappointed.

Sin's hand slid up from my waist into the hair at the back of my head, curling it into his fist so that he could tug my head back in order to look at me.

"We have time now, Elle. There is no need to rush."

Emotion surged up my throat, so just to be safe, I didn't open my mouth to speak. Instead, I nodded.

His other hand slid out from behind his head so that he could gently run his fingers down my jaw. "All the time in the world," he emphasized.

It might have been wishful thinking, but I believed him.

Chapter Five

Giselle

WHEN I WOKE UP THE NEXT MORNING, SINCLAIR WAS GONE. I VAGUELY remembered him pressing a kiss to my hair before getting out of bed, but the jet lag had lulled me into a deep, dreamless sleep, and I couldn't wake up enough to give him a proper goodbye.

There was soft music playing throughout the suite, a throaty French voice that I recognized as Jacques Brel. I stretched the lingering laziness out of my muscles before I rolled out of bed to investigate. A shiny silver iPod was plugged into a dock on the antique rolltop desk with a note tipped against it.

ANY SELF-RESPECTING FRENCHMAN LOVES JACQUES. ANY TEENAGE FRENCH BOY LISTENS TO ENGLISH POP, SO I ALSO ADMIT TO LOVING THE BACKSTREET BOYS AND CHRISTINA AGUILERA AT ONE POINT. NOW, I LISTEN MOSTLY TO JAZZ, AS YOU KNOW; MILES DAVIS, FRANK SINATRA, NORA JONES, AND DIANA KRALL. I COMPILED A PLAYLIST WHILE YOU SLEPT LAST NIGHT.

Bisous,
Sinclair

I grinned down at the note. Even though I knew what he said last night about knowing the important things about him was right, I still longed to know the trivialities, the quirks, and fears, and desires that made Sinclair the love of my life.

I listened to the eclectic playlist as I showered in the gorgeous wood-paneled bathroom, shaking my booty to Britney Spear's *"Oops, I Did It Again"* before crooning along to Edith Piaf's *"La Vie En Rose."*

I had plans to meet Richard at eleven o'clock at the hotel in Saint-Germain-des-Prés, my old stomping ground, and I wanted to make a good impression on anyone I might meet who was close with my Frenchman. Candy had packed my bag, and she had done well. I chose a thick cable knit oatmeal turtleneck sweater with exaggerated braiding and an inky black pencil skirt that I paired with wicked high heeled black leather boots Cosima had bought me as an early Christmas present.

As if sensing my thoughts, my phone rang just as I finished brushing out my curls and stepping into the footwear. My sister's name flashed across the screen.

"Bambina!" Cosima shouted when I answered. "Where are you? There is a sale at Barney's, and when I was walking by the other day, I saw this amazing eggplant dress that would be incredible on you. I don't care what you are doing. Drop it and come shopping with me."

I smiled into the phone. "I would love that, but I'm actually out of town at the moment."

There was a long silence that I felt physically like Cosima had run into the wall of my words and was reeling.

"Out of town," she echoed softly.

"Yes."

I bit my lips as I grabbed my purse and heavy jacket before leaving the hotel room. As much as I wanted to focus entirely on my potentially devastating phone call with my sister, I didn't want to be late to meet Richard.

"Okay," Cosima said finally, still soft-spoken. "Do you want to tell me where you are or who you are with?"

"I can... but I'm not sure you want to know."

Another long pause. My heart was beating in my throat. I always suspected that Cosima knew about Sinclair and me, but this conversation was proving it. I just didn't know what she thought of it, and it wasn't exactly something that I wanted to get into over the phone when we were across the Atlantic from each other.

"Oh, Gigi." She sighed. "Please take care of yourself, okay?"

"I am, Cosi. For the first time maybe ever."

I waited for her censure or a reprimand at the very least.

Instead, I got another gusty sigh, and when she spoke again, her voice was tender as a caress. "You are a beautiful woman worthy of epic love. I've always wanted that for you. But love is hard, the epic kind the hardest."

"You sound like you're speaking from experience." Not for the first time, I wondered what horrors my sister's young life had held.

"I am. When you get back from 'out of town,' I will tell you a little bit about it, and you can tell me a little bit about your vacation," she said.

It was both a threat and a promise.

I had better be ready to divulge everything to her when I returned.

Strangely, the thought comforted me. If she wasn't screaming at me for my adulterous ways now, I had hope that she would be at least mildly supportive of Sin and me when I finally told her the whole truth.

She further confirmed this by saying, "I will tell the family that you took a brief vacation. Say hi to him for me and take care, *bambina*."

Before I could respond, she hung up.

I stared at the dark phone screen as I stood in the underground waiting for the metro to take me to the hotel. There were so many subtle layers to our short conversation that I was still processing them when I arrived at the site of what would be a Dogwood International Hotel.

It was set close to the narrow sidewalk that was characteristic of the neighborhood, but there were beautiful wrought-iron gates and green plants lining the walkway up to the white-stone façade. Sinclair had told me that they weren't building a new hotel so much as transforming two adjacent classic French homes into one building. The small space between the two edifices was breached by a new glass and wrought iron atrium that housed the lobby. I stepped through one of the double sets of tall black wooden doors into the marble foyer and gasped at the beauty I found there.

Drop cloths and building supplies still littered the white-veined marble floors and the huge multifaceted windows were grimy with drywall dust, but I could already tell that the space would be extraordinary and utterly Parisian.

"I was going to ask what you thought, but I can tell by the beautiful expression on your face that you like it," Richard boomed as he strode toward me from the left side of the building.

He was wearing a dusty denim button-up and blue jeans, decked out in a Canadian tuxedo that he somehow pulled off. I laughed as he embraced me in his strong arms, enjoying his scent of stone and fresh sweat.

"It really is gorgeous, Richard. You have fabulous taste."

He nodded as he pulled away, prompting me to laugh again. "Sinclair does as well. He is a very detailed man and, frankly, a pain in my ass most of the time. But the result is always worth his breathing down my neck, ordering me to redo the blueprints a thousand and one times."

My Frenchman enjoyed control in all things. "He's a man with a plan."

Richard gave me an appraising look. "He is, indeed. You should be prepared for that."

"Excuse me?"

He took my hand and tucked it into the crook of his arm. "I have a feeling he has a number of plans for you."

"He dated Elena for four years without much forward momentum. I think we are happy to take things slowly."

Besides, we hadn't even told Elena or the rest of my family about our relationship yet. If I was being honest, I was dreading more than anticipating that. Just because I had decided not to live without Sinclair didn't mean that I was eager to sacrifice my family, especially when we had just reunited.

"I think we both know that Elena wasn't right for him. Now that he has the right woman, I have no doubt that he will want to charge ahead. But don't let him sweep you into anything you aren't ready for. He has a habit of doing that to people."

We walked into the left side of the hotel, where the elevator bank to this portion of the hotel was. The one we took was beautifully appointed with a red velvet bench at the back and wood paneling that harkened back to historic French designs.

"I appreciate that you've known him longer than I have, but I really don't think you are right about this. It was hard on Sinclair to make the decision to choose *me*. I think we just need easy now, probably for a while. It's a massive adjustment for both of us but mostly for him."

I mean, as of under a week ago, Sinclair was living with another woman.

That woman being my sister.

Yes, we were definitely going to take it slow.

"How do you even know that I'm the right woman for him?" I asked softly because, despite his declarations, it was difficult not to compare myself to the elegant and successful Elena or find myself unequal to Sinclair's own brand of movie-star-quality good looks and too-good-to-be-true awesomeness. And I meant that in the traditional sense of the word; I was in awe of him.

"If the only thing I knew was that Sinclair, a man I know to be steadfast, whip smart, and intensely loyal, had left Elena and his beloved well-ordered life to be with another woman, I would know it was the right choice. As much as he has succeeded in his professional life, he lived like a robot for years, and I'm sorry to say, your sister has too. They enabled each other. Now, especially when I have had the pleasure of meeting you and more, knowing you, I can assure you that no woman is more perfect for Daniel. He needs light, love, and creativity. You seem to need the things that he has always been ashamed of; his intensity, his need for control, and his deeply hidden sensitivity."

"Oh," I responded because I was struggling under the beautiful weight of his words.

He grinned at me. "So, I wouldn't be so sure about his desire to move slowly. If I'm right, you let me know if he's speeding too fast for you, and I'll have a word with him, okay?" Richard led me off the elevator onto the tenth floor and into a corridor lined with crown molding and subtle floral-patterned silver wallpaper.

He looked down at me while giving my arm a squeeze. "I've worked with him since he was twenty-one years old and hired my firm to renovate his club. Even though he is technically my boss now, I like to think we are friends and maybe even that he thinks of me as a father figure." He hesitated. "I know I think of him as the son I never had."

It was my turn to squeeze his arm as his words flooded me with warmth. From what I had seen of Mortimer Percy, he seemed like a nice enough man, if not completely self-consumed. In direct contrast to him was Richard Denman, Sinclair's right-hand man and, apparently, a nearly lifelong friend. It thrilled me to know that even though Sin underutilized his loved ones, he had them in spades.

"I'll let you know," I promised.

He searched my face for sincerity, and finding it, he nodded curtly. "Okay, let me show you our latest baby then."

AFTER A LONG MORNING OF TOURING THE HOTEL WITH RICHARD, I LEFT TO walk around the surrounding streets of my old neighborhood while Sinclair finished his meetings somewhere across the city. Habit kicked in, and somehow, my feet took me to *L'École des Beaux-Arts*. It was the safe place I had found, thanks to Cosima and Sebastian's generosity, after the hell I had fled from in Naples. It was the same place that had nourished the creative spirit of masters like Henri Matisse and Anne Rouchette. There was no other place in the world that felt more like home to me than the world-renowned university, and even though my years studying there had been the loneliest of my life, I wouldn't have changed the experience for anything.

I smiled as I slipped through one of the buildings on a whim to find Madame Claremont's studio. It was a large space lined with big square windows on three sides, and currently, a small class of artists-in-training was set up at easels painting a live nude model who reclined comfortably across a raised pedestal. I took a moment to appreciate how technically challenging it would be to reproduce the exaggerated curves and graceful rolls of the large woman on display before I swept the room looking for my mentor.

She stood in the corner farthest from me, but her eyes were already trained my way, studying the changes in me with the highly trained eye of both an artist and a friend. I took a moment to do the same with her, noting with surprising gratitude that she was absolutely in no way changed. Odile Claremont was the daughter of a poor farmer from Alsace who looked more Germanic than French, with long blond hair she braided across the crown of her head and blue eyes so pale that they appeared colorless. She was in her sixties but looked forty, her pale skin unblemished because she never spent any time in the sun.

I finished my examination and nervously waited for her to do the same. She had more changes to the catalog, so it took her a good few minutes. I tried not to squirm and immediately come to the conclusion that she hated what she saw. The last time I had seen her, the day before I left Paris, she had expressed her joy at seeing my natural red hair for the first time, but since then, I had evolved in more than physical ways, and I knew she would see those.

"Continue. I will be outside in the hall if I am needed," she told the class in a French murmur that somehow carried across the room.

I loved the sound of her Alsatian accent, so despite my anxiety, I was smiling at her when she came my way. Without a word, she grabbed my hand and tugged me into the corridor, closing the door behind us.

"Giselle," she said into my hair as she enfolded me in her arms. "You look so well."

I dragged in a deep lungful of her turpentine and lily of the valley fragrance, feeling my worries evaporate.

"I missed you more than I realized," I said as we pulled away.

She kept my hands in hers as she smiled at me. "And I, you. You promised to write, yet you did not."

I blushed under her reprimand. "Things were... absorbing in Mexico and then New York. It would have been impossible to tell you in print how my life has changed."

"Yes," she said, casting another critical eye over me. "I can see it has changed fast and drastically. Tell me about the man."

"How do you know it's about a man?"

She made that French sound, a huff of breath exploding between her lips, a punctuation of sound. "No woman looks like this for any other reason."

"How do I look?"

"Terrified, happy, and *alive*."

I laughed. "Okay, yes, there is a man. You'll love him."

"He's here?" she asked, her pale eyebrows raised.

"He brought me here to get away. Our situation is a little... unorthodox," I admitted.

"*Chérie*, I am French. We are the kings and queens of unorthodox relationships."

I laughed again because that was true. The former president divorced his wife for his longtime lover, a model and singer, while he was in office. Such a thing would have been unheard of in the United States.

"I'll tell you all about it," I promised. "And I have a show coming up at *DS Galleries*. It's a bit different than anything I've ever done before, but I think you would be proud."

"Do you have pictures?" she asked, excitement making her bounce lightly on her toes.

"I do."

"*Parfait*, I will finish with this class in half an hour, and then you and I will go for wine, yes?"

I pursed my lips, desperately wanting to but worried that it would interfere with whatever Sinclair had planned for that afternoon.

Understanding inherently, Odile shook her head in mock exasperation.

"Text your lover and tell him that I insist on stealing you away. I will return you drunk to your hotel, and he will thank me for it."

I laughed again, knowing she was right.

While I waited outside the building in the courtyard, I found out she was right. Sinclair texted back immediately to let me know he would reschedule our afternoon because it was important for me to spend time with my mentor. I loved that he supported me so wholly. Not many men in Sinclair's world, one of business and money, would understand the life and business of an artist, so I was grateful for his mother's profession and for his own investment in the arts.

Our affair in Mexico was also the kernel of inspiration that gave root to my collection. He was the man who had introduced me to the wild passions and delicious shadows of the erotic world, who made it safe for me to explore those depths after Christopher had tainted them.

It was impossible not to think of the Englishman who had ruined my childhood now that I was back in Paris. I had fled to the city because of him and eventually fled from it when he had found me again. I had no doubt that one day he would discover me once more; he was a tenacious but patient stalker. He would never suspect that I had joined my family, though, partially because he had worked so hard to tear us apart.

I mulled over the similarities and differences of the two love triangles I had shared with my polar opposite sister. Christopher had never presented as anything but a gentleman. Mama had loved him, Seamus had relied on him to take care of us when he himself was absent on a drinking and gambling bender, and he had spent considerable time teaching English to us kids. He was all but promised to Elena, a girl nearly eighteen years years younger than him, from the time she was sixteen. With her, he was kind, courteous, and wise, if a bit aloof. They spent hours talking about politics, history, and litera-ture, their heads together over an open book at the kitchen table while Mama cooked, I sketched, and the twins ran around the house playing games.

With me, as soon as I turned thirteen and developed the kind of body that was hard for men to ignore, Christopher was impassioned. It began with innocuous touches, murmured endearments, and encouragements to touch him back and tell him that I loved him. It had taken me years to realize that even though he didn't beat me, he was still a monster, one who brandished love as a weapon of manipulation instead of his fists. He had groomed me to be his since I was a young girl.

The sexual acts didn't start until I was fifteen, and they never escalated to vaginal sex. That, he always said, he wanted to keep for our marriage night. Mama didn't suspect anything untoward when he took me 'out for gelato' or into Rome to see some art gallery or another. I often spent the night with him with my mother's blessing. He never hurt me, but I was always scared, nonetheless.

I didn't know something was really wrong with our relationship until I mentioned it to Sebastian and Elena one day when they were bickering about Sebastian's exploits with a local girl. I'd innocently divulged that kissing was nice, the only thing I liked about sex. Even though I was eighteen at the time, I didn't understand the consequences that my naïve comment would bring. Sebastian had immediately asked if Christopher and I had made love, and when I assured him that we hadn't, not fully understanding the question, he had relaxed slightly but told Mama that I wasn't allowed to be alone with Christopher anymore.

Two weeks later, Cosima had sent a letter telling me that she had the money to send me to *L'École des Beaux-Arts,* and I knew that the twins had orchestrated it to get me away from him.

Elena had reacted differently, obviously. We had never been close, but after that confession, she was cruel to me, calling me names and inviting Christopher over nearly every day but never letting him out of her sight, kissing him in front of me in a way she had never done before. She must have known how desperate he was to get me alone, how much yearning filled his eyes as he stared at me while his lips were locked with hers, but she wasn't angry with him for it. She was angry with me.

I was happy to leave them four months later to start school in Paris. By that time, Sebastian had left, and Cosima was long gone. I was alone in Naples, and I would be alone in Paris, but at least I would be without the two malevolent presences in my life.

Cosima told me years later that Christopher asked for my information all the time, that Mama began to notice his erratic behavior and that she still allowed Elena to move in with him. She also told me that for that half a year our eldest sister had lived with him, he had not been kind to her. I didn't know the details, and I'd never really delved into it before, but it wouldn't surprise me to know that he had sexually and emotionally abused her, taking out his heartbreak and desperation on her because he couldn't have me.

At least, that was the narrative I thought up in order to excuse Elena's blatant hatred of me over the years.

A year after I left, the twins found enough money to move Mama and Elena to New York City, and they left Christopher behind. I didn't know the story there—whether he was happy to see them go or if they fled him like I had. He wasn't something that I had ever talked about with anyone, even Cosima. That was, until the demons he had left me with cropped up in Cabo with Sinclair.

Of course, the situation with Sinclair was different but not totally so. If you wanted to strip it down to brass tacks, the way I knew Elena would when she eventually found out about Sinclair and me, it would be fair to draw the conclusion that in both triangles, the man had chosen me over her. It wasn't as simplistic as that. It wasn't fair to either circumstance or either man. It wasn't even fair to Elena or me. But it was what she would see, and it was one of the reasons, maybe even the core reason, she would never forgive me.

Chapter Six

Giselle

"How was your evening with Madame Claremont?"

I was lying on top of a sweaty Sinclair, my entire body aligned with his, pressed front to front. My fingers were in his hair, threading through the damp strands. We were both exhausted from jet leg and a vanilla but vigorous bout of lovemaking that I'd instigated the second I was in the door from drinks with Odile. As promised, she had plied me with enough wine to make me just the right amount of intoxicated and definitively horny. Sin had taken immediate advantage, but it was the first time in a while that the Dom Sinclair hadn't taken me. It didn't bother me, but I definitely noticed the difference and drunkenly wondered about it before moving on.

"It was amazing. I forgot how libertine the French are. Infidelity and affairs are par for the course, so obviously, she wasn't judgmental about us."

In fact, Odile had been positively *thrilled* about my romance with Sinclair. She had waxed on about how I was finally living my life for me instead of hiding behind ugly clothes, ugly hair, and an ugly outlook on love. It had helped that I'd shown her photos of my paintings for the collection. If the path I'd taken toward sexual deviancy surprised her, she hadn't expressed concern or disgust. Instead, she had informed me that she wasn't one to judge as she was simultaneously dating three *much* younger men. At which point, I had begged her to paint all of them together for the show. She'd agreed, and we set a date for Thursday at her private studio in Montmartre.

I told Sinclair this, my words slightly slurred together from tiredness and a lingering intoxication that made me feel heavy and content.

"Interesting woman," he noted when I was done. "No wonder she helped inspire your talent so beautifully."

I tipped my head up so that he could see my smile, but I was too lazy to open my eyes to see how he received it. Happily, I could tell he was pleased because he slid a hand down the curve of my back to rest it on one of my ass cheeks.

"Are you enjoying Paris then, *mon amour*?"

"Yes. I honestly didn't think I would come back, but I am happy to be here, happier than I thought I would be. I love Paris," I said on a dreamy sigh.

"We could move here if you wanted. It would take me a while to organize the transition of Faire Developments' offices, but it could be arranged, especially as we are doing so much business over here now."

My body tightened with shock. "Are you kidding?"

I let out a squeak as he rolled us before I could protest. I stared up at him with wide eyes, drinking in his intense scowl with mute interest.

"Do I look like I am kidding? I meant what I said when I was wooing you, Elle. I want to be with you in every conceivable way. If it were socially acceptable, I would cuff us together and never let you out of my sight. Not because I don't trust you but because I love every minute with you, watching you react to the world, react to me as if I am some kind of world wonder. It makes a man feel fucking invincible. You give me that? The least I can do is concede to living anywhere in the world that you want to be most."

"When you say things like that, I can't believe you're real," I admitted, placing a shaking hand on his cheek.

He bit the edge of my thumb where it lay against the corner of his mouth. "You have time to get used to it. That is what I have been trying to tell you. Forever, Elle, I mean it."

I let out a shuddering sigh, trying to expel the acidity in my chest that was worry for the future and the pain of the past.

He sensed my struggle, and his hard face softened. "I don't want to go back to the city before you feel secure in this, in us. We will have to face a number of monumental challenges in order for me to give you a happy ending, and if you don't believe in my love for you, we won't be able to overcome them."

I agreed with him, but I didn't know how to respond because I *was* unsure. For weeks, he had seemed content to stay with my sister even though he claimed to love me. I knew he loved me, but I didn't think love was enough. He didn't know me enough, I figured, to see the deep fault lines that ran through my character. He could always change his mind about me, about how well I fit into his beautifully constructed life. The son of the governor of New York, the CEO of a successful real estate development company, and a man of his incredible character deserved the best. I wanted that for him. I wanted to *be that* for him. I just wasn't sure if I was up to muster.

"In a couple of superficial ways, I think Elena is better suited for you," I confessed.

It was hard to do, but I wanted to be honest now that I had the opportunity to be. Sinclair was finally in my arms, in my life in the way I wanted him to be, and voicing my insecurities was a risk to that but not talking them out, giving them license to fester and haunt, was a greater one.

"In no way is that true," he countered immediately. "I told you back in Mexico that I can't say anything bad about Elena. She doesn't like my kink, of course, but that isn't something to hold against her. She is a beautiful, talented, classy woman who I spent four years of my life with. I do not regret those years."

A shiver tore through me, and because I was in his arms, he felt it even though I didn't want him to.

"They led me to you, Elle. You were always my destination, *d'accord*? I feel this, and I know this in every way a man can know that he has found the right woman. I told you that I would fight for us, and I will, even if it means fighting you and your own insecurities."

I stiffened again, but he knew why and addressed it before I could even fully digest the reason myself.

"I am not saying that your fears are baseless. I gave you a reason to doubt me. I am just telling you that I am going to rectify the pain I caused by lavishing you with love and protecting you from anyone who may harm you. Until you feel utterly secure in that truth, I want to stay here in Paris. Are you okay with that?"

Stay in Paris, hidden away in my favorite city with my favorite man so that I didn't have to face the awful consequences of our completely not awful love?

"I can do that," I whispered.

"It may mean being here for Christmas," he warned.

I hadn't thought of that but when I did, I only felt relief. I couldn't imagine spending Christmas with my family when everything was still so unresolved. It would mean either pretending I wasn't with Sinclair or tearing apart my family just in time for the holidays.

"We will have to push back the date of your gallery showing too," he warned.

It was currently scheduled for January, so this was true. If we stayed any longer than a week or two, it would need to be pushed back, and I wasn't sure how I felt about that.

"We could reschedule it for Valentine's Day," Sinclair suggested. "Fitting, no?"

I grinned because it was.

"Let's stay here," I said, going into a crunch so that I could gently bite his chin and then place a kiss there, a physical representation of the apology I wanted to give him for still having so many doubts.

"We'll stay here. I'll contact my office and Rossi to let them know the change in our plans tomorrow," he said, holding me closer for a moment before readjusting us so that I was faced away from him and he was spooned up against me. "Now, get some rest because tomorrow we are going to spend most of the day exploring my girl's favorite place in the world."

"Okay," I said as exhaustion crashed down around me. "Love you more than anything in the world, Sinclair."

"My love for you is bigger than the world, my siren," he said into my ear just before I fell into a heavy sleep.

Chapter Seven

Giselle

I MADE A STRANGER TAKE A PICTURE OF US.

The primary reason for that was because I realized we had no photographs together. As an artist, I collected photos, pictures, magazine clippings, sketches, and swathes of material, *anything* really to document my life and inspire me. I only had the photos of Sin from Mexico when he was driving the boat to our little cove and then a few more that Elena had given me to start the painting she had wanted to commission.

The second reason was more base, selfish, and common in a way that I didn't care to shy away from. We cut a striking image that afternoon. Sinclair was in total black, from the tips of his Italian leather loafers to the button-up he wore beneath a thick black cashmere V-neck sweater and the long Burberry trench he wore over it. He wasn't wearing socks, which may have seemed like a strange thing to notice and like, as in *a lot*, but I did, and I did. The subtle slice of brown skin when the rest of him was covered was so unbelievably sexy that I had actually salivated a little when I met him at the café around the corner from our hotel that morning.

In direct color contrast to him, I wore a pale oatmeal cashmere sweater dress that fit my body like a glove and complimented the knee-high chocolate brown boots that I had splurged on at a small local boutique that morning. I'd also had my hair done at a small hair spa that I had walked past countless times as a student but had never had the money to afford. They hadn't done much but cut in a few layers and form the heavy mass into thick dips and curls across my shoulders and breasts. But I loved it, and Sinclair had responded favorably to the stylish cut if the movie-quality kiss he landed on me was anything to go off.

So, vanity was definitely involved.

But we also had an absolutely amazing day, the kind of daylong date that I never would have imagined happening. After waking up together, we had parted ways so that Sin could go to an early meeting in the 2nd arrondissement, and I could treat myself to the spa and some shopping. I still wasn't rolling in cash so I hadn't seriously thought about hitting any of the city's amazing shopping districts, but Sinclair had pressed his credit card into my hand on his way out the door and ordered me to use it before I met up with him. He didn't give me time to protest, and I was actually thrilled for the opportunity to buy a new outfit to show off for him, so I did as I was ordered.

Later, we met for brunch at an amazing Franco-Taiwanese restaurant, Le 37 m2, before we went Christmas shopping in the Marais. Afterward, Sinclair sent the bags back to the hotel while we walked along the Seine hand in hand, enjoying the surprisingly unpopulated promenade and the crisp bite of the winter air.

In a word, heaven.

Now, we were at the doors of my favorite place in the entire world.

Le musée d'Orsay.

Sinclair was an art lover, but I was fully aware that he watched me react to the multitude of paintings and amazing sculptures more than he viewed the pieces himself. He followed me as I bounced from my favorite work to my next favorite, skipping from exhibition to exhibition like an eager child.

I was too happy to care that I wasn't being chic, and Sin didn't seem to mind either.

"This is one of the pieces that inspired my collection," I blathered on, as I had been since we entered the hallowed halls.

I had already shown him Edouard Monet's *Olympia* with the reclining naked woman with her velvet collar and the famous *Luncheon On The Grass* with the naked woman bracketed by two fully dressed men, but we were now stopped before *L'Origine du Monde*.

"When I was a student, I used to come here every week, nearly every day in the first year I was in Paris. I tried to focus on a different exhibit each time, but inexorably, I found myself in front of Gustave Courbet," I explained, standing to the right and in front of Sinclair so that I could have a minimal amount of privacy. It was difficult to explain my struggle with sexuality, but I wanted him to know.

"Sex had never been a good thing for me, so I had never really explored my own desires. Even when I got up the courage to date Mark in my second year here, we didn't do much more than kiss and fondle each other over our clothes. Pathetic for a twenty-one-year-old," I said, pulling a face.

"Elle," Sinclair protested, but gently so that I would continue.

"I was so drawn to the erotic images here, especially this one. I would just stand in front of it like the closet pervert I was, trying to make sense of the trauma Christopher had left me with and the latent sensuality I felt creep up my throat like bile each time I looked at this painting."

I paused, warring with the echo of that feeling in my gut. It was easy to look over my left shoulder and imagine my younger self—undernourished, swimming in colorless, oversized clothes, and drab under all that harsh black hair. I had been so unhappy and so confused yet utterly oblivious to it.

I turned to Sinclair, finding him braced like a sailor on a rocking deck, and I knew that my confession was hurting him because my pain was his own. He had put himself in charge of my protection, and this was one thing he would never be able to change.

I stepped forward to press my palm lightly to his chest over his heart.

"You took that tangle of angst and desperation, Sin, and you unfolded it for me. You barely knew me, yet you saw my struggle, collected all the broken pieces that I couldn't reconcile, and bound them together. That week in Mexico wasn't just magical because you made me fall in love with you. You made me fall in love with myself."

"Elle," he repeated, but this time the word was a benediction, a prayer of reverence.

He stepped close, bringing both hands up to cup my face lovingly. "We made each other whole, Elle. I was just as broken before you rearranged my life and brought it into focus."

I leaned my forehead against his, grasping his wrists in my hands to feel the strong pulse there.

"I want to inspire that confidence and security in others. That's why my collection is the way it is."

"I know," he murmured.

"I know you do," I admitted. "You know me better than I know myself." I pulled back slightly, but he kept his grip on my face. "That's probably why you make such a good Dominant."

The softness in his expression glazed over with ice, hardening into a mask that hid his true self from me. I frowned up at him because I couldn't understand what I had said to prompt the change.

"Sin?"

But he wouldn't answer me. I knew before I even opened my mouth to appeal to him. When Sinclair decided to close off, it took a sledgehammer to crack him open again, and unfortunately, the middle of a museum was not the place for that messy business.

We continued our tour of the cavernous, converted train station, but we didn't recover our levity. I bided my time, trying to figure out where I had gone wrong, but I kept coming up blank. A part of me wanted to blame myself anyway, but Sinclair had taught me to be strong, and I didn't want to jump to a conclusion where I was in the wrong.

We went for a quick but delicious dinner at *Chez Berber* after watching the sunset from the top of the extraordinarily ugly Montparnasse Tower. He teased me about how effusively I complimented my lamb *tagine* to the waiter and told me stories about his youth growing up with Cage in the orphanage, but it was as if his frequency had changed to another setting, one that threw just enough static into the mix of our interactions that I couldn't fully enjoy it.

It wasn't until we were back in the hotel getting ready for bed that I knew something was seriously wrong.

I had used the half an hour between getting my hair done that day and meeting Sinclair to use the other part of the spa to get a fresh Brazilian wax. So, I was fully expecting a deliciously volatile reaction when I emerged from the bathroom in nothing but a sheer black baby doll and a matching G-string.

Sinclair sat on the end of the bed in those amazing drawstring gray pants, his torso on prominent display as he leaned back on his hands. I wanted to play his abs like a xylophone with my tongue, so I was momentarily distracted from seeing the clench of his jaw and the flash in his eyes that spoke to anger.

When I did look up, I only caught the tail end of it. I was about to question him when he stood abruptly and moved past me, placing a chaste kiss on my forehead like I was a goddamn *child* before he went into the bathroom.

I stood in the middle of the bedroom, stunned and reeling. It was the first time I had really done anything like that, taking the initiative.

And he had totally brushed me off.

My stomach fell out of my body, along with my ability to breathe. I couldn't orientate myself, the room twirling around me, because the foundation I had been building with Sinclair had suddenly, crudely, been pulled out from under me.

"What the fuck just happened?" I whispered, just to hear my own voice.

Oddly enough, it helped.

I said it again louder so he could hear me in the bathroom. "What the *fuck* just happened?"

Sinclair appeared in the doorway and leaned against the frame, his pose deliberately casual as if everything was fine when it so clearly. Was. Not.

"Elle," he said as if beginning a sentence, but then he didn't continue.

"Yes? Are you going to explain why you just brushed me off like that?" I asked, hands on my hips in my own power pose.

"We've had a long day, and I'm jet-lagged."

"*Merde*, Sin, that is a lie and not even a good one. What is going on?"

He stared at me for a long moment.

It struck me how much he looked like one of those beautifully carved marble statues that I admired so much in the *musée d'Orsay*; gorgeously constructed but utterly cold because it was not alive.

"Don't go back to that cold man who treated me like shit in Mexico because he was scared," I breathed, the flaming anger gone and replaced with the glacial chill of fear.

"I know you aren't well-versed in relationships, but most couples don't have sex all the time," he explained calmly, condescendingly.

"I can't believe you would say that to me," I said, pressing my hands to my stomach where I felt the wound that his words had inflicted like a physical agony.

His eyes squeezed shut, woven tightly closed behind his thick russet lashes. I could see the tension in his body and realized how much he hated what he was doing to me. So why was he acting this way?

"Don't you want to touch me?" I breathed, not in despair this time but with feminine authority.

I walked forward with slow purpose as his eyes snapped open at my tone and found me. Those blazing blues carefully cut across my skin like knives, erotic but dangerous. I could sense the tenuous hold on his restraint.

"I'll make love to you," he conceded, but it wasn't enough, and we both knew it.

"I want you to take me," I said, stepping close and up on my toes so that I could drag the edge of my teeth across the sharp angle of his jaw.

His sharp breath gave me confidence.

"Please, sir, I need you to help me."

I ran a finger between my breasts, watching his eyes follow its path as I dipped into my panty-covered mound and emerged with a wet, slicked finger. I tried to bring it to his lips, but his eyes cut to mine with a warning that hit me like a thunder strike.

Instead, I brought it to my mouth, flicking my tongue out to taste myself. My moan was overtaken by the rumbling growl that emerged from his chest.

"I need you to tell me what to do," I begged softly. "I need you to teach me how to make myself come."

A vicious shudder ripped through his body, but he held still. The predator in him, the part of himself that he called savage, called out to me from the cage he had locked inside him. I could practically hear the rattle of the bars, the baying howl at the moon. Each muscle and tendon was starkly delineated under his dusky skin as he strained against his primal urge to take and dominate.

Why was he resisting me?

"Sin," I begged, an edge of desperation to my voice.

He didn't move, but his eyes burned, burned, burned hot but suppressed like the destructive force trapped under the cap of a volcano.

Locking his eyes to mine, I back away slowly to sit in the old-fashioned armchair in the corner by the scroll desk and shed my underwear. I sat down and hooked my legs over each arm to completely expose my pussy to him.

The muscle in his jaw ticked like the secondhand of a clock.

I swallowed the minimal discomfort that my prudish former self might have felt and slid two fingers down to my core, opening myself blatantly under his scrutiny. His regard was so intense that his gaze was a physical caress against my slick folds.

"Should I touch myself here, sir?" I asked, dipping one, then two fingers just inside.

His head tipped further so that he could really watch, but still, he didn't move, didn't speak. I think we both knew that if he did, he would be done. Mine.

"Or here?" I asked on a gasp as I twirled my index finger over my throbbing clit.

I set up a steady thrum across the sensitive bundle of nerves, licking my lips deliberately as I latched eyes on the erection almost comically straining the front of his pajama pants.

"Would it hurt if I pinched it, do you think?"

Sinclair flinched as I did so, and my back arched steeply at the sharp swell of pleasure that arrowed up my spine.

"Do you want to see my fingers inside me?" I asked, trying to channel what Sinclair might order me to do.

It wasn't the same as his commanding presence, but I enjoyed the thrill of playing with a predator, the danger I was knowingly putting myself in. Prey could only dance so long before a true animal before they gave into their nature and *took*.

At least, that was what I was banking on.

My lids shifted to half-mast, matching Sinclair's hooded gaze as I stared intently at the fingers playing over my wet core.

"I need you," I panted.

He jerked slightly, and I knew I had him, just one more little push...

The mechanical vibration of a cell phone cut through the room, bringing us both to a complete halt. We both stopped breathing and looked over at the phone buzzing away on the nightstand.

Sinclair was the first to move, swiftly walking to the phone and answering in a clipped voice. He didn't look at me as he dived into a rapid-fire French exchange and moved out of the bedroom into the suite's living area.

I sat in the chair for a long moment while I listened absently to the exchange. My mind refused to acknowledge that Sinclair didn't want me. He did. I had never doubted that, not through any of the turmoil we had been through. Yet now he denied what we needed?

Robotically, I got ready for bed, letting muscle memory and habit guide me through brushing my teeth and moisturizing before I slipped beneath the covers and turned off the lamp beside my bed. I stared into the darkness for a long time, well after Sinclair finished his phone call and hung up.

Eventually, he came back, stared at my back for a few minutes, and then got into bed. He rolled into me immediately, tucking me tightly into his body so that we were pressed inch for inch, front to back.

"My love for you is bigger than the world," he murmured into my ear after he pushed my hair away from my neck. "I love you more than my need to dominate."

He thought I was asleep, obviously, so I tried to keep my body from going hard with shock and then soft with relief. It wasn't me he was disgusted by but himself. I should have known that, and it irritated me that I was so slow on the uptake when he had been struggling with his sexual deviancy for years before he met me. Now that I knew what the problem was, there was no way in hell I would let it defeat us, not when I finally had the love of my Frenchman after months of longing.

Chapter Eight

Giselle

THE NEXT MORNING, I WAS UP BEFORE SINCLAIR, AND I TOOK IMMEDIATE advantage of the fact. Normally, I wouldn't breach his privacy so flagrantly, and I had a momentary pang of guilt as I checked his phone for any evidence of contact with my sister and his ex-girlfriend. Elena was the only person I knew who had the power to turn Sinclair against himself like he had last night, so I followed my gut and was rewarded when I found an email from her in his inbox.

Rage ignited like a bonfire in my belly, rushing through my blood until it had burned everything clean and clear.

She was officially a bitch.

I didn't care how badly she might have belittled me, but subjecting her lover, former or current, to her unfair biases was absolutely *not* okay.

I worried that the crushing force of my fury would wake up Sinclair, so I carefully closed down his phone and lay in bed beside him as I struggled to digest the news. In a way, it made me feel better to know that at least I hadn't done something to turn Sinclair away, but at the same time, I was disappointed he hadn't shared the email with me so we could talk it through. If our situation had been reversed, he would have expected, no *demanded*, that from me.

Slipping out of bed, I tiptoed over to his computer and fired up the search engine. Before our one night together at Cosima's apartment, I had done a bunch of research on BDSM, but I wanted to know more. I wanted to know everything. The small taste that I'd had of the power dynamic was addictive. It was more than just my attraction to Sinclair that had wooed me. It was the idea of being under his control. The messy mass of desires, shame, fear, and power that made up my complicated sexuality was tamed by the skilled touch of Dom Sinclair. My traumatic history with Christopher also ceased to exist when I was under Sin's spell. I refused to give these things up, especially when Elena's influence was the driving force behind his sudden need to live vanilla and not his desire.

I looked over at him as he laid peacefully asleep, the crest of his thick lashes casting long shadows across his cut glass cheekbones, the fall of his rich mahogany hair across his forehead. He was so achingly beautiful, so deeply perfect for me in every way. I just needed to remind him of that.

Moving into the other room, I made the call I needed to make in order to set my rash plan into action. Thirty minutes later, Sinclair was still in bed with a note I had left explaining that I'd gone into Odile's studio to paint for the day. I met Cage at *Quotidian* to have a tartine and enlist his help.

"Absolutely not."

"But Cage—"

"*Jamais. Pense-tu que je sois con?*" he asked me incredulously.

"No, I don't think you're stupid." I looked up at him from under my lashes, my eyes wide with sincerity. "I thought you were a friend, that you would *want* to help me with this."

He scoffed, unmoved by my act. "You know better than to ask me this, I think, *chérie*. Sinclair would kill me without a second thought if I took you to such a place without him."

"I love Sinclair, but we need this," I leaned in to whisper. "He won't dominate me since Elena sent him that awful email. Last night, he wouldn't even touch me!"

"Even without the kink, he is still more passionate with you than he has ever been with another woman. Maybe he doesn't need it like you think he does."

I gave him a look.

He opened his large palms wide and sighed. "I will not deny that he needs *some* level of control in the bedroom, *d'accord*? But he has lived the past four years of his life thinking it was inhumane to dominate his partner. Do you really think that is something you can bounce back from overnight?"

I hadn't thought of it that way. Elena had been condemning him for years about his sexual preferences. That sort of thing left a mark on someone.

I tilted my chin in the air. It was something Elena did when she wanted to get her way, and even though appropriating her behavior was the least of my transgressions against her, it still felt wrong.

"I'll go without you," I threatened.

Cage glared at me, but humor sparkled in his thickly lashed eyes. "Ah, well that changes things, doesn't it?"

"I think it does."

He chuckled darkly and leaned back in his chair, the big, strong leather-clad rocker in a tiny chair in a feminine French restaurant. A thick fingertip traced his ridiculously full bottom lip as he contemplated me.

"*Je suis d'accord, chérie.* I will let you play, but I will not take you to some club, *oui*? My friend, *Madame* Claire, holds a monthly soiree for like-minded people. I will take you to this, but I have to warn you again, even this is not for the faint of heart."

"I'm not some shrinking violet," I retorted.

He gave me a long, languorous perusal. "*Non*, not anymore, but this change is recent. You may change your mind, and then where will Sin be, ugh?"

"I would never leave him," I said, and I had never meant anything more.

Cage waved a dismissive hand through the air as he knew that already. "He will kill me, you know this? If he finds out I took you out as my submissive."

I frowned. "Your submissive?"

Cage nodded. "I will not take you to something like this unclaimed. As it is, you will garner too much attention as a newcomer and looking like you do. You'll have to be mine for the night. Don't worry, *chérie*, I will try not to enjoy it too much." He winked.

I laughed nervously. "When is it?"

"So eager. We will go this Thursday. Can you get away from Sinclair?"

I bit my lip but nodded. Sinclair was supposed to be going to a business dinner with Paulson and a few other investors in the Dogwood project, so it should be easy enough to slip away.

"Do you have anything to wear?"

"Excuse me?"

Cage sighed dramatically. "I cannot take you to something like this without the appropriate attire. We'll have to go shopping."

He stood and placed a few euro notes on the table before pulling on his beautiful black leather coat.

"Come," he encouraged when I just sat there.

"Oh, right now?"

He grinned, extending his huge hand to help me up. "Yes, right now."

He took me to Agent Provocateur and laughed at my expression of intimidated awe as we swept through elegant displays of delicately webbed lace and gorgeously constructed corsets. Cage stopped briefly at various racks, picking out things that caught his eye and transferring them into the hands of an eager and beautiful saleswoman who followed us around the store. He didn't ask for my size, but I knew enough about Cage Tracey to know that he would make an accurate guess.

It occurred to me that Sinclair would be furious at the idea of someone else dressing me in racy lingerie, of another man taking me to a public playroom. I didn't want him enraged with me or anyone else, but I truly felt that the only way to convince him of my investment in the scene was to pursue it independently of him. If he could only see what submitting did to me, he would have to understand.

And maybe if I were a better sub, he wouldn't be able to keep himself from me like he had been.

"You'll invite him then?" I asked Cage as I followed him into a spacious change room.

I was only mildly surprised when the saleswoman left us alone inside. This was Paris after all, the city of romance and not America, which Sebastian often claimed was run by prudes.

I began to strip, unashamed in front of Cage. He was a rock star, for God's sake. He'd seen way more appealing naked bodies than mine.

For his part, he averted his eyes as he took a seat on a velvet bench.

"I will. We will get you settled first, and then I will let him know you followed me to the event. Give it fifteen minutes, and he'll show up in a rage." His obsidian eyes flickered my way and widened. "Especially if you are wearing that."

I blushed as I pulled up the last stocking and attached it to the garter belt strap. I struck a silly pose for him. "Do you like?"

His eyes smoldered, but his posture was casual as he leaned his back against the wall. "If you do not take your own sexuality seriously, Elle, how can you expect anyone else to? Look in the mirror and tell me what you see."

I swallowed hard past the knot of insecurity growing in my throat but did as he said. Even though I knew Cage wasn't as into the scene as Sinclair was, he still had a very effective Dom voice.

The woman staring back at me wore a tight black corset with stiff lace embroidery and sheer panels that nipped in her waist to extreme proportions and highlighted the creamy swell of her full breasts above the rise of the sweetheart neckline. Inky black thigh-highs encased her curvy legs, exposing a panel of white skin that was somehow extraordinarily sexy against the starkness of the black lingerie. Her red hair spilled like wine across her shoulders and down her back, and her lips grew wet with moisture as she chewed on one.

"Look at yourself and tell me the truth, that you have never seen a sexier woman before in all your life." Cage's voice reached me through the haze of my own self-infatuation.

"I wouldn't go that far," I protested on a breath.

"Then you are wrong," he retorted. "Maybe this will be easier for you. How would Sinclair react if he saw you like this?"

I could picture the exact shade of blue his eyes would darken to, the color of the sky just before it tips into nightscape when it is still just barely electrified with light. His jaw would clench and tick with restraint, and his voice would wind itself around me, seductive and heady as drug smoke.

My entire body shivered and flushed.

"Exactly," Cage agreed, satisfied with my response. "This is the one you will get. And this, you will wear as well."

He got up swiftly and gently tied a length of black velvet ribbon around my neck, like a makeshift collar. It reminded me of the painting from the museum, *Olympia*, with the woman collared in much the same way. My fingers fluttered against the ribbon as my pulse hammered.

"Hopefully, by the end of the evening at Madame Claire's, Sinclair will give you a collar of your own, but for now, this will do."

I swallowed heavily and straightened my shoulders. "I'm going to get him back, Cage."

He nodded soberly. "I've no doubt of it."

Despite both our confidences, my knees shook as I took off the expensive garment and gave it to Cage to pay for as my Christmas present.

If things didn't go the way I needed them to, Thursday could very well be the last night of my new relationship with Sin.

Madame Claire lived, unsurprisingly, in Montmartre, the trendy, artist neighborhood built on steeply curving streets surrounding the *Sacré Coeur*. Her apartment was two floors but oddly constructed because the top level had at one time been the servant's quarters. Now, it was a spacious, open-concept space where nearly everything was visible as soon as you opened the door.

Which was why I froze in the doorframe while Cage moved further into the foray.

My eyes danced over the scantily clad people present, some talking innocuously over glasses of champagne while others took up more daring poses. A man in leather chaps kneeled on the floor on all fours with a tray of drinks balanced on his back. Another man, this one dressed in an impeccable suit, pet him on the head as he spoke with a friend. A woman wearing nothing but scarlet red nipple tassels and a matching leather collar was strapped onto some kind of enormous cross. The man before her was carefully but brutally laying into her with a red leather cane, leaving vivid red stripes along her skin.

My own flesh tingled at the thought.

I jumped when Cage reached out and tugged me farther into the room.

"It's a St. Andrew's Cross," he whispered in my ear.

A quick flash of Sinclair strapping me into such a thing made goose bumps break out over my skin.

Cage chuckled. "A bit advanced for you, Elle."

"Isn't that the point?" I countered.

Sinclair and I had made love once in the four days since Elena had sent him that email. He had done a relatively good job of avoiding me, throwing himself into work and encouraging me to visit with Odile and spend time with Candy and Cage. I knew it was because he couldn't control himself around me, which gave me some level of comfort, but not much.

I missed him acutely.

I had tried to talk to him about the problem, mentioning Elena's cruelty at Thanksgiving, how wrong she was to condemn him for his interest in BDSM. He had shut me down with a flick of the wrist before he removed himself from the room to take a call. I was trying to be patient with him even though he was hurting both of us with his obstinate behavior but having a plan made it easier.

Four days was long enough.

It was time to bring my Dom back.

A slight smile pulled at Cage's full lips, but he ignored my comment in favor of leading me toward an older woman reclining in an antique chair while she used a naked man as a footstool at the back of the room.

As we drew closer, I could see she wasn't very attractive—her features were too broad and plain for that—but the elegance of her bearing and the cutting wit in her dark eyes was enough to arrest me.

"Madame Claire," Cage purred as he inclined his head toward the woman. "May I introduce the lovely Elle?"

"You may," she replied, but her sharp eyes reprimanded me as they trailed over my body. "Is this how you wish to present yourself?"

Without thought, I folded to my knees and tilted my head toward the ground, my hands clasped behind my back. Immediately, my mind cleared of anxieties and I let out a deep exhale of relief when I felt Cage's approving hand on top of my head.

"Better," Madame Claire praised. "It is unlike you to have a pet, though, Cage."

"Yes, she isn't mine. In fact, she belongs to Sinclair."

I didn't have to look at her face to feel the surprise this elicited.

"I have not heard that name in a very long time. As I understood it, he had settled with some *vanilla* American," she said with disdain.

"He has rectified his error," Cage said with faux sobriety. "Elle is both his woman and his sub now."

"Then why is he absent, *mm*?"

"May I speak, Madame?" I ventured.

A pause.

"You may."

"The vanilla American accused his kink of being sexually abusive." Even repeating the words made me irate, but I gritted my teeth and sank further into my pose to find calm.

Madame Claire sniffed loudly, in that quintessentially French show of derision that I had always loved.

"Monsieur Sinclair has suffered from this fear for too long. Look at me, sub," she ordered softly, waiting until I looked up at her before she continued. "We will do what needs to be done to get your Dom back, *oui*?"

My smile was almost painful as it blasted across my face. "*Je suis d'accord.*"

Sinclair was having a late dinner meeting until nine o'clock, so Cage insisted on taking me on an introductory tour around the room to acclimatize myself to the situation. I protested at first, but it was a good idea because the nervous, bouncing tics of my diaphragm like a precursor to hiccups, disappeared after making a few rounds of the room.

We paused before a scene where a Domme had bound her bulky male submissive at his wrists, elbows, and ankles so that he was prone on his knees, ass in the air on the floor. She played idly with his erection, with the beautiful muscular swell of his ass while she spoke to him at length about everything she was preparing to do to him. From his throaty groans, I knew he was ready for whatever she deemed worthy of him.

I was most excited to talk to the woman in red who was now cradled in her Dom's lap after their session. Her eyes were half-closed as if even that effort cost her energy that she no longer had to expend.

"Laurent, Miss Pascale," Cage greeted warmly, clearly familiar with the couple.

"It has been too long," the handsome Laurent noted with a wide, affectionate grin.

I knew better than to judge a book by its cover, especially after witnessing the dynamic between the Paulsons, but I was still surprised that the Dom who had handled Pascale with such deliberate cruelty could have such a boyish, open face. His curls of sandy hair fell into his wide gray eyes, and his smile revealed twin dimples. Of the two, Pascale, with her striking dark features and sharp pixie cut, seemed better suited, physically, for the role of Dominant.

"This is Sinclair's woman, Elle," Cage introduced.

"Sinclair?" Pascale asked, roused from her post-orgasm daze by the sound of my man's name.

Jealousy flared through me.

She noticed, addressing me with a soft smile. "He was a good friend to my Master once, Elle, that is all. I have never had the pleasure of playing with him."

"Good," I said with a smile to dilute the edge of my possessiveness.

She laughed musically and wriggled closer to Laurent. "Sharing is a special thing. Not everyone is into it."

"I am not," Laurent admitted with twinkling eyes. "Pascale is for my hands, cock, and mouth only. But she gets off on sharing me, which is why we come to these soirees."

My eyes widened, comically apparently because Cage and the couple laughed.

"If you are interested, I would love to watch him play with you?" Pascale suggested seductively, biting the tip of her pink tongue.

I stepped closer to Cage, who wrapped a protective arm around me, but it wasn't because the idea held no appeal to me. If Sinclair had been there and deemed fit to share me, I would have been thrilled.

"You like that idea," Cage ducked down to whisper in my ear.

I shivered as his breath wafted over my neck.

"Tell me, *chérie*, what would you do if Sinclair shared you with me?"

Honestly, the thought had never occurred to me. Cage was sinfully beautiful, the kind of handsome that was intrinsically linked to thoughts of sex. I remembered thinking that if I hadn't met Sinclair first, I would have found Cage the most beautiful man who I had ever laid eyes on. We were good friends, so I never would have entered into a sexual relationship with him. There wasn't that inherent chemistry between us, but would I have objected if Sinclair brought him into our bedroom?

I looked up into his glittering black eyes. "If Sinclair wanted it, it would be my pleasure."

I watched with a feminine thrill as desire blasted across his features, stark and harshly highlighted before he could get it under control.

A thought occurred to me, though, an uncomfortable one.

"You like Elena," I said softly because I wasn't sure, but I suspected.

His lips twisted in a cruel mockery of a smile. "Maybe I just have a thing for sassy redheads?"

I laughed lightly because it was clear he wanted me to and that he wouldn't talk about his unrequited crush with me, at least not then.

"Are you ready?" he asked me after another few minutes of conversation with Laurent and Pascale. "Sinclair will be here soon, and we want to be prepared."

I nodded, and before I could fully process what had happened, we had confirmed my goals, limits, and safe word, and I was strapped into the device Cage had called a St. Andrew's Cross. My cheek was pressed to the cool, smooth wood while my back and bottom were exposed to the crowded room. No one was paying me much attention yet, probably because they were used to the sight and also because a powerful tool of domination was denial—of touch, sight, and acknowledgment. I was living evidence of its success; my flesh was raised with goose bumps, my inner thighs slick with my arousal even though no one had touched me.

Cage's dark voice wafted across the back of my neck like smoke. "He's on his way. Just a few more minutes, *chérie*."

"She's gorgeous," another masculine voice said from over my shoulder. "Are you in the mood to share, Cage?"

"She isn't mine to share."

"If she's without a Dom, I'll ask her directly." There was a shuffling sound behind me. I didn't need to see to know what was going on. Cage had stepped in front of the curious man, his chest puffed and legs spread.

"You will do no such thing," Cage growled.

But he didn't have to because I could feel the change in the air, the static current that suddenly zinged through the room like an electrical storm.

Sinclair had arrived.

The room quieted so much that I could hear each sharp clack of his expensive leather loafers cross the hardwood floor. I shuddered violently when they came to a stop just behind me, the space between us thick with crashing neutrons.

"No one will be touching her. We're leaving."

I gasped as the sound of his voice vibrated against my skin. It took me a moment to recognize his words from within my fog of desire.

"No," Cage said, and for a second, my confused brain thought I had said it. "She needs this. *You* need this."

"I do not." Sinclair's voice was glacial.

"Fine, you think you don't need this. You want to be miserable, that's your decision. But Giselle has a choice, and she's made hers."

"I want this," I said, my voice strong and clear despite the awkwardness of my positioning.

"Giselle—" he began, but I cut him off.

"No. If you don't want to be a part of this lifestyle, then Cage is right, it's your decision to make, and that's fine. I need this, though. I need the submission, to be in the hands of a man who will take me through my darkest desires with dominance and calm. If you can't be there for me, then I need to find someone else to take care of those desires."

His body was suddenly pressed to mine, the coolness of his suit against my skin only serving to further fuel my flushed body.

"It doesn't mean I don't love you," I whispered as I strained to move closer to him.

It was also an empty threat. I would never let another man handle me the way Sinclair did. At least, not without him there.

He was quiet for a long minute.

I focused on breathing in tandem with him, craving even that small harmony.

"Do not make me do this," he began, and the pit of my stomach fell out like a false bottom, "unless you truly desire it."

My relief was so acute that I slumped against the hard wooden cross.

"Please," I begged.

Immediately, a new tension overtook him. I shivered at the feel of his entire body hardening with resolve and desire against my pliant flesh. He tilted his head down so that he could speak against my ear.

"You want to be punished before these people, don't you, my siren? You want them to witness my claiming of this gorgeous body." His hand swept down the curve of my hip and roughly squeezed my bottom.

"Yes, please, sir."

"Good girl," he practically purred before he stepped away from me, leaving my skin cold but my insides burning with anticipation.

"You remember your safe word?" he asked.

"Yes, sir."

"Tell me."

"Heartbeat."

My senses were heightened by my lack of vision, pressed up against the wall as I was, and coupled with my knowledge of the dozen other inhabitants of the room, I was already trembling with need. It also comforted, the idea of being claimed before strangers, and a small part of me knew it was because he hadn't yet claimed me in New York.

I wanted everyone to know that this magnificent man owned me.

His breath whispered against my ear. "Are you ready, siren?"

"Yes, sir."

His response was to drag the tip of the bright red cane I had seen earlier down the curve of my cheek, under my neck, and down my spine until it tickled the crevice between my ass cheeks. He paused there, sliding the end back and forth, deeper and deeper until it dragged achingly slow through my wet folds.

"So wet for me already," he noted, loud enough for the entire room to hear. "You always did like the thought of having an audience, didn't you? The room service waiter in Mexico, the door open to your hall so that anyone could see you kneeling before me in Cosima's apartment. So beautiful, so eager for my cock. You want everyone to see what a good girl you are for me, don't you?"

"Yes, sir," I breathed, barely audible because I was so focused on the throbbing under the tip of that leather strap.

"Louder, let everyone hear you," he ordered.

"Yes, sir, I want everyone to see what a good girl I am for you," I said, my words ending on a ragged moan as Sinclair brought the cane up and back down hard across the swell of my right ass cheek.

I squeezed my eyes shut and gritted my teeth as the sting deepened and rushed like a river through a broken dam down to my sex.

He didn't stop.

The cane striped my ass, upper thighs, and the outside of my sex in a continuous rhythm that made me rock and sound like an instrument under his beating hand. The pain was bright at first and then sank to my very bones where it pulsed hotly, building and building to a crescendo that I knew would break me into pieces. There were no thoughts in my head, no words. Instead, the hypnotic crack of the whip, the bass-like moans from deep in my belly, and the harsh sound of Sinclair's excited breathing played behind my closed lids like a symphony of colors, red, black, and gray strobe lights that lulled me into subspace.

My legs were pulled so far apart that my sex was wide open for the bite of the cane. His cadence changed. It grew faster, sharper still, with an emphasis on the wet slick of my inner thighs. The edge of the hard leather caught the lips of my sex and made me jerk hard against the cross.

"Sir," I cried out as my legs trembled in their straps.

I needed something more, something to shatter me so that he could reform me, reclaim and forgive me for pushing him over the edge.

"Yes, my siren?" he asked in that cool, immaculate voice that made the brutal sensuality of his beating even sexier by contrast.

"Please, I need to hear you, need to see you. If it pleases you," I added hastily, panting so much that the words barely came.

Sinclair landed two more hard swats to my burning ass before he stepped away, cool air stirring over my hot, sensitized skin. I moaned, both from the loss of him and the new sensation of air. It astonished me somewhere deep in the lost recesses of my rational brain that I was at the point where a light breeze could tip me over the edge.

"Cage, Laurent, I need your assistance," Sinclair spoke to his friend and the Dom I had met earlier as he stepped close again to undo me from the thick cuffs binding me to the cross.

I slumped forward as I was freed, but Sin caught me on his shoulder and gently turned me around so my back was to the cross and my front was to the audience.

I watched through blurry eyes as Cage and Laurent stepped forward by some unspoken command to take either arm and pull it around their respective waists. Sinclair bent forward to fasten my legs against the cross again, but this time, the men held my arms bound behind them in a tight grip, their sides pressed up close to mine like parenthesis.

I shivered at the contact, and the desire that had begun to ebb away as they readjusted me flooded back in.

Sinclair was suddenly in my face; his wide, lightning-blue eyes the only thing I could see. "Cage and Laurent are going to hold you down and play with your beautiful nipples while I make you come with my fingers."

I trembled violently at his words.

He smiled wickedly. "You are not allowed to orgasm until you receive permission from all three of us. Do not disappoint me, my siren."

"I won't, sir," I promised.

At that moment, I would have laid prostrate on an altar, bared for an entire congregation to gawk at if it meant Sinclair would touch me. I loved knowing that an entire room watched our exchange, how completely I gave myself over to him. I wanted them to watch how explosively he could make me come.

"You look so beautiful like this, *chérie*," Cage murmured huskily in my ear.

I shivered again as two of his blunt, rough-tipped fingers plucked at my left nipple.

"Watch us play with you," Cage ordered as Laurent also reached up to twist and pull at my other nipple.

I looked down to watch their dark fingers brutally manipulate my flesh and shuddered at the corresponding pull deep in my pussy.

"Isn't she magnificent?" Sinclair asked, drawing my attention back to him.

It was impossible to be unaware of him even when I focused on the other men, though, because I knew they were touching me at his behest. That he was in charge of the pleasure I was feeling, even if it was different hands on my skin.

I sank further into the shadowy depths of submission.

I arched my back, pushing myself further into those unfamiliar hands with a guttural noise I normally would have been ashamed of.

Instead, all I felt was overwhelming need.

"So greedy, my woman," Sinclair noted casually.

"*Oui*," Madame Claire agreed, standing just behind and to the right of our scene, her arms crossed like his, as if both of them were viewing a painting at the *Louvre*. "So beautiful in her greed. Will you give her what she wants?"

Sinclair cocked his head, his face impassive. "Eventually."

"Please, sir," I begged, rolling my head on my neck, restless with desire.

"Sin," Cage asked, an edge of pleading in his voice. "May I take her in my mouth?"

Sinclair's eyes flashed, not with anger but with the joy of possession. He liked the effect I had on Cage, the power being his because he wholly owned me.

He inclined his head magnanimously. "You may."

I gasped as Cage and Laurent dipped in unison to take my straining peaks into their hot mouths. They held me tight to their sides so that I couldn't thrash despite my best efforts, and the feeling of being restrained ratcheted my arousal into previously unknown dimensions.

"Are you worthy of an orgasm, Elle?" Sinclair asked conversationally as he stepped before me again. "You deceived me, tried to top me from the bottom by forcing me into this scene. Now, tell me, who has the power?"

"You, sir," I practically shouted as his fingers ghosted between my thighs.

I humped at the air, desperate to bring them back to me when he pulled away.

"Yes," he hissed. "Me. I can do whatever I want to you, even order these men to take you in their mouths. I know you like their tongues on your sweet nipples, but you know that they are really my mouth, my tongue on your flesh, don't you?"

I groaned in agreement because his fingers were back in the dripping pool of desire between my legs. I was so wet that I could feel the trickles of desire slide down the backs of my thighs. The squelching noise Sin's fingers made as he thrust two, then three fingers brutally deep into my clutching sex was one of the sexiest noises that I'd ever heard.

"Very good, Elle, so wet for me."

God, how could I be anything but? I was dialed to ten and still cresting. The orgasm that loomed large and dark in the distance was terrifying. I knew it would obliterate me, crash through me, and eviscerate everything but the bliss he gave me.

The hard smack of his palm hitting against my sloppy, wet pussy brought me back to him.

"Pay attention. I'm going to make you come now," Sinclair ordered.

He dropped to his knees but even in the lowest position of our quartet, he still emanated power. His face pressed into my left thigh so that he could watch up close the way his fingers began to churn through me, driving me higher and higher.

"Beg us for permission to come," Sinclair reminded.

"Please, please, please..." I began to recite, rising from a whisper to a near shriek as I was seized with excruciating tension, suspended in the moment when a glass hits the floor but before it cracks.

"Show us how prettily you can come," Cage spoke with his teeth against my nipple.

"Come for your Dom," Laurent demanded.

Simultaneously, the two men bit viciously into my nipples and chewed.

"Come now." Sinclair's voice lashed out like the cane against my pussy as he added his thumb, slick with my damp, into my ass.

I rocketed into space. My body lashed hard against my restraints as my mind broke open. I tumbled headfirst, screaming wildly into the darkness, distantly aware that Sinclair would catch me when I fell.

Chapter Nine

Giselle

"Thank you," Sinclair said into the early dawn.

We were back in our bed at the hotel the morning after Madame Claire's, folded together with precision and closeness like a carefully wrapped present. My face was pressed so close to his that I had to go slightly cross-eyed to look into his serious gaze, but it was worth it to see the apology there, the need and gratefulness.

After my orgasm, I had passed out briefly, and when I came to, I found myself in Sinclair's arms as he sat on a velvet loveseat talking to Madame Claire and her sub Dominic about the recent French presidential election. He had clutched me tighter in recognition of my wakefulness and gently drawn me into the conversation, trying to normalize things after the intense scene. It worked. I'd happily talked about the National Front and the protectionist leanings of Marine le Pen and the relief we all felt that she had not won. Cage had joined us at one point, winking at me roguishly as he sat down across from us. I'd blushed but felt no real awkwardness about the intimacy we had shared. Sinclair touched me continuously, petting my hair, stroking the slope of my cheek and the swell of my lips. Reconfirming our connection, I knew, and it made me warm with success.

I had brought him back to me.

"You don't ever have to thank me for reminding you that you are safe with me," I said now, after the first good sleep I had had in four nights. "If anything, I should apologize to you. I thought that I had made it clear that I loved you *and* the sexual freedom that being a submissive gave me. Clearly, I didn't do a good enough job of making you feel accepted."

His arms pressed me closer still. "No, it was through no fault of your own. I let Elena's spitefulness get to me. The truth is, Willa came across me fucking one of my girlfriend's bound to my bed when I was in the twelfth grade and laid into me using the same language Elena always had. It was hard for me to believe that a woman I cared about could accept that part of me when the other two could not."

I made a soft whimper of empathy.

He continued, "I caused you pain. That is unacceptable, especially when I promised you that I would protect you from judgment. I turned right around and judged us myself." He made a noise of disgust and buried his nose in my hair. "*Désolé, ma sirène.*"

"You are forgiven," I said because I knew he needed to hear it even though I didn't actually feel the need to do it. "Let's move on from it, okay? From this day forward, we talk about things that concern us instead of closing each other out."

He smiled against my cheek. "Look at you, Elle. When you first came to me in Mexico, you were this unsure, timid thing with a deep well of gumption and fierce feminine power that you had no idea how to tap into. Now, you are a siren come into her own."

"You had everything to do with that," I said because it was true.

"You would have found it eventually."

I disagreed, but I decided to leave it at that because we were having a moment. I knew there would be more trials in the future, so I thought it was important to luxuriate in the peacefulness, the absolute rightness, of our togetherness while I could.

Our phones buzzed simultaneously on the table beside Sin, and he reached for them.

"The day has officially begun," he murmured dryly as we both checked our notifications.

"You were the one who wanted me to have a phone," I pointed out. "I was happy without one for twenty-four years."

"You needed one. How else can I send you orders to ready yourself for me before I get home at the end of the day? You also need a camera phone to send me pictures of all this gorgeousness while I am away on business trips. A phone was a necessity."

I laughed, the sound trailing off as I read the email from Stefan.

"Sin, Stefan is in town," I crowed, delighted for the opportunity to see the Greek shipping magnate again.

"Joy."

"Sin..." I giggled. "He is a very nice man. And, as I told you, he was the one who encouraged me to go after you that night when you had blatantly tossed me aside."

His lips flattened at the memory. "I am so fucking lucky you have the patience of a saint."

I laughed and snuggled closer. "You make it all worth it."

"You read the email, and I'll be right back. I have a meeting in an hour, but I want to have a bath with you before we leave for the day. You must be sore from last night."

He pressed a sweet kiss to my forehead. I watched him get out of bed, his naked body gilded with weak winter sunlight as he walked into the bathroom. My throat was tight with emotions, but I swallowed them back and turned my attention to my phone.

"He wants to meet for lunch," I called so Sin could hear me as I read the note. "He has a proposition for me."

My words were met with a heavy silence, and I bit my lips against my stupidity.

"I think it was something to do with my art," I amended.

No response.

"I still haven't found my pills, so I'm going to head to the clinic I used to go to in order to get a new prescription," I said again, hoping to distract him.

He didn't say anything, so I took the time to quickly send off a response to Stefan agreeing to meet him at noon at *Le Cinq* in the George V Hotel off the *Champs-Elysées*.

When I entered the bathroom, I took a moment to love the rich wood paneling and the emerald-green tiles that encased the deep bathtub that Sinclair was filling with steaming water and a plethora of lavender-scented bubbles.

"Get in," he ordered, moving away to press play on the music system.

The smooth jazzy refrain of Melody Gardot's music flooded into the room.

I was naked already, so I just swept my hair up into a messy bun and stepped into the nearly painful heat of the soapy water. I sank down, hissing from the sting, and closed my eyes to absorb the heat.

When I opened them, Sinclair was sitting on the side of the tub with a soft white washcloth that he dunked into the water. We locked eyes as he leaned forward to softly run the fabric from my neck down over my shoulders and arms, firmly around each finger, releasing tensions that I hadn't even known I harbored.

"That feels so good," I murmured.

"It feels good to care for you," he responded sweetly.

I opened one eye to make sure he was real before closing them again so I could better feel the friction of the cloth against my heat-sensitized flesh.

"I don't want you to wear panties to your meeting with Stephan today."

My eyes flew open. "Excuse me?"

"You heard me. I want you to go without panties."

"Ugh, I would have thought you would want me as clothed as possible."

A smile tugged at the edge of his mouth. "You would have thought wrong. I want you to go feeling the breeze tease your bare cunt under your skirt, knowing that the moment you get back, I will have my mouth on you and that you will already be wet, knowing that is what I have in store for you."

"Oh," I said because that seemed really nice even though it was a little possessive.

Maybe because it was a little possessive.

He grinned fully at me. "Now, lean back and close your eyes again. Let me take care of you."

THERE WAS SOMETHING ABOUT THE GEORGE V FOUR SEASONS THAT WAS BOTH horribly and magnificently cliché. It was a beautiful, quintessentially French decorated building and the temporary home of many rich and famous visitors who came exactly for the cliché Parisian experience. Despite the triteness of that, the hotel was still a joy to strangers and locals alike. It was an institution in Paris that might have been hated once but was now embraced, much like the Eiffel Tower.

I loved that Stefan had chosen to stay there because it spoke to what I already knew about his character. He further delighted me by waiting for me in the lobby in a perfectly tailored, formfitting burnt orange suit that somehow looked utterly fantastic on him.

I threw myself into his arms because he opened them for me.

"Giselle," he said into my hair.

He smelled amazing, some kind of strong, manly cologne designed to cut women off at the knees.

"Stefan," I beamed at him as I stepped away, clutching our hands and swinging them between us. "You look fantastic."

"As do you." He cast a critical eye over my form, encased in black trousers, a Gucci belt that Cosima had given me, and an amazing pearl-buttoned white blouse. I wasn't wearing panties, and the seam of the denim kept rubbing against my clit. I was mildly concerned about the effects of pussy lubrication on jeans. "Happiness looks good on you. Let me guess, the Frenchman won you over?"

I laughed at him as I took his arm, and he led us into *Le Cinq,* but I didn't answer until we had been seated at a table by the window.

"He did," I confirmed. "The painting you sold him helped that. Thank you, Stefan."

He made a face. "I was loathe to part with it, but he told me about your upcoming collection, and I knew I could replace it with something new and inspired by you."

I blushed. "It's different than my normal work."

"I'm counting on it," he said with a wink. "You are a different woman since Mexico, no?"

"I am. Sinclair makes me feel strong and sure of myself."

"You have many reasons to feel that way outside of your relationship with that man. Your art alone is reason for a considerable about of arrogance," he offered as the server came to fill our water glasses and take our drink orders.

Stefan ordered us a bottle of Domaine Romanée Conti.

I didn't object.

"You flatter me," I said when the server swept away.

"I do not. Your art is actually the main reason I wanted to meet with you." He eyed me for a long moment before coming to a decision. "First, you fill me in on your life, then I tell you about what I had in mind."

I was curious, but I hadn't spoken to him since the first and only email I sent to him on my return to Mexico, letting him know that Sinclair was, in fact, dating my sister. So, I settled in to tell him the entire sordid story and was rewarded by his occasional bark of laughter and lascivious comments.

"So, you ran away again?" Stefan concluded, taking a sip from his glass of extraordinary burgundy wine.

I frowned, hesitating to bring a morsel of codfish, spinach, and raisins to my mouth. "We didn't exactly run away."

"Giselle, darling, do not fool yourself. You ran away from Naples, you ran away from Paris, and now you have run away from New York. You are a runaway girl."

Carefully, I placed my fork back down and propped my chin in my hand to think about Stefan's accusation.

He was right.

I was a runner. I had just never realized it.

Was I that cowardly that I couldn't face the consequences of my actions?

I felt, momentarily, ill.

"We're going back," I said.

"I am not criticizing you, Elle. You left behind a steaming pile of *merde* each time you ran away, so the desire to do so was not unwarranted. In fact, I'm looking to enable you." He dabbed his lips daintily with his napkin before replacing it in his lap and leaning back in his chair to commit himself to staring at me.

"Yes?" I prompted after several moments of his unnerving contemplation.

"A friend of mine is one of the senior editors at French *Vogue*. They need a new art editor, and I thought..." He trailed off with a wave of his hand at me. "You would be perfect. Of course, it means that you would have to relocate to Paris, but given the circumstances especially, I do not think that would be so hard."

I blinked at him in total shock. Editor at French *Vogue*? How was this even a remote possibility? I was just a relatively unknown artist from backwater Naples.

"I don't deserve an opportunity like that," I expressed.

Stefan glared at me. "Bullshit. As we spoke about in Mexico, you have begun, and I dare say have now finished, the transformation from an 'ugly' duckling to a swan. You are a competent, intelligent, and talented artist with a degree from one of the most prestigious art schools in the world. You have four successful shows under your belt and another one upcoming in New York that has already generated much talk, even in Paris. You deserve this opportunity and any others that I or anyone else can throw in your path."

"Wow, that was very impassioned," I said stupidly because I couldn't believe he was being so kind.

"I am not saying it to be kind or because I am your friend," he said, reaching across the table to take hold of my hand. "Though, I am that, your very dear friend, I hope. I am saying this because you deserve the opportunity, and I would be doing my other friend a favor by setting up an interview with a promising employee."

It was hard to speak through my suddenly parched mouth, so I took a long sip of water before saying, "Can I think about it? It just... It seems too good to be true."

"Of course, you can. Talk it over with your lover and let me know. Interviews begin the first week of January, so you have time."

I nodded, looking out at the rain-slicked streets of Paris, feeling the love I had for the city and the awe I had at being presented with such an amazing chance. It would mean giving up the purity of being a full-time artist, but it would also give me the ultimate *in* into the art world of Europe.

"Thank you, Stefan," I said, pouring as much gratitude and love into those words as I could.

Somehow, I had landed more than just the love of a good Frenchman on my trip to Cabo. I had also secured the kind of friendships I had never really had before, with people who would always strive to take care of me. It was *awe*some to realize that.

Stefan smiled lovingly at me. "Anything, anytime, Giselle."

"I hope you know you can ask the same of me," I returned.

His smile turned into a grin. "Excellent, then I call first dibs on that new collection of yours. Send me pictures of the completed paintings and expect me to choose at least three of them for my own collection."

I laughed at him. "Deal."

Chapter Ten

Giselle

It was easy to forget everything but my love of Sinclair and the City of Lights. We established a schedule of sorts, where Sinclair would wake up early and work until two in the afternoon before meeting me at the tiny café around the corner from the hotel. From there, we would head out on a different adventure, reacquainting ourselves with the city we both loved but had been forced to leave. We ambled through the steep and crooked streets of Montmartre, bought charcuterie and cheese from *Marché Place Monge* before heading to *Jardins des Arenes* for a picnic among beautiful Roman ruins, and watched films at the *Parc de la Villette* open-air theater, tucked up in blankets with steaming cups of hot chocolate to keep us warm.

While I waited for Sinclair every morning, I practiced the French art of being a *flaneur*, a person who walks through the streets with no goal in mind but observation and meditation. Sometimes, I made friends with people as I ducked into patisseries, sharing my beloved Maison Kayser chocolate chunk cookies with a family of German tourists or dancing with a young Australian couple to the music of the violinist who was a permanent fixture in front of the *Sacré Coeur*.

Most of the time, though, I walked and sketched to my heart's content. Odile let me use her private studio whenever I wanted so I had made progress on my collection even without my usual supplies.

This included three pieces I was doing on Odile and her three delicious younger men. I was calling the trilogy *The Power of Three*. Each canvas depicted a different facet of the relationship, from a tangle of bodies that were barely discernible as female or male to three sets of thick male hands on a dainty female form, and finally a subtle depiction of them out on a date, the view of the men's hands fiddling with her under the table. At the same time, they dined and chatted casually above.

Even Madame Claire agreed to pose for me, using the same man who had been her footstool that night at her party to serve as a prop for my pictures. I loved the audacity of French sexuality and found myself discussing it openly in a way I never would have before Sinclair, before we had come to Paris to explore together.

Before I knew it, we had been there for two and a half weeks, and it was Christmas.

Paris at Christmas was a revelation. The dark latticework of naked trees lining the narrow streets and broad promenades were ribboned with tiny lights, lampposts boasted large red bows and every storefront was tastefully rearranged according to a different holiday theme. Elegantly dressed Parisians walked leisurely through the city, stopping into lesser-known chocolate shops to seek out *chocolat chaud* and Christmas confections between last-minute gift shopping.

The lavishly decorated Christmas tree that dominated Notre Dame Cathedral's main plaza drew tourists and locals alike, especially as they had canceled the installation last Christmas due to the November terrorist attacks. People had placed flowers beneath the tree like presents to those who had passed away, but the atmosphere was jovial nonetheless, the air filled with laughter and ample cries of *Joyeux Noël*.

It was a gorgeous place to spend Christmas Eve, but I couldn't shake the melancholy that had stalked me the past few days. It made me feel ungrateful to feel this way, especially when the love of my life was beside me, currently holding my gloved hand. He had sensed my mood, of course, and taken the past few days off work in order to throw himself into entertaining me. We ice skated at the Trocodero, ate at all my favorite haunts, even the cheap café under Place de Madeleine, and now we were simply walking the crowded streets on our way from meeting Candy and Cage for drinks.

"You are unhappy," Sinclair noted.

I bit my lip, unwilling to spoil our beautiful day with my stupid, self-indulgent thoughts. "Just thoughtful."

His eyes narrowed. "You know how much your thoughts are worth to me. Please, tell me."

"As happy as I am here with you, I still feel restless. Unresolved."

He nodded. "That's understandable. Even though we are finally together, this is a dream world, one where we don't have to reap the consequences of our actions."

I bit my lip. "Well, I am feeling one of them. I miss my family, and the worst part is that I know this feeling won't go away anytime soon because when I see them again, I'll have to tell them about us, and then they will deliberately go away."

Sinclair pressed my hand between his. The gesture reminded me of the way one preserved a flower between the pages of a book, and I knew it meant that he wanted desperately to conserve my relationship with my family, at least with Mama and the twins.

"You don't know how they will react. They might be supportive."

"Honestly, I think the twins know already. At least, Cosima."

"Oh?" Sinclair asked though there was sharpness in his eyes that said he wasn't that surprised. "She does know both of us well enough to sense something amiss."

"Well, I've definitely been distracted, but I can't see you giving yourself away. Obviously, I didn't know you before, but you seemed to act the same."

"I was happy, Elle, incandescently so. That was a change that everyone noticed."

I sucked in a deep breath between my teeth, surprised by his words but more surprised by the impact they had on me. When would I get used to the fact that Sinclair had always wanted me? That maybe he always would?

"Do you miss her?" I asked. "I'm not trying to trap you. I'm honestly just wondering. It's only natural after spending so much time with a person that you would miss them."

Even though I said the words, and a large part of me meant them, there was still an echo in my chest that urged me to compare myself to Elena. I resisted, drawing on the strength of Sin's hand in mind in order to do it.

"I do and I do not," he admitted. "I miss talking to her because she was smart and curious about the world, a great conversationalist. I think our favorite times together were spent reading the Sunday *New York Times* and hashing out the events of the week and doing the crossword puzzle."

I felt a pang but not a large one. Sinclair and I didn't read the paper together like that, but we would establish our own routines, and we had countless topics to talk about it.

"I do not miss how savage she made me feel for wanting to tug her hair or talk dirty to her. She made me ashamed of an essential part of myself. More than that, I don't miss the life we lived together, stuck in these strict routines and bound by everyone else's rules, including my parents. That's not what any relationship should be about. So, mostly, no, I do not miss her."

He slid a thumb down the line of my jaw and pinched my chin to tilt it up, so I was looking him in the eye. "Do you?"

I shook my head before I could even process his question logically. "No, I never had much of her to miss."

His lips flattened. "The way she treats you... I knew she was never your biggest advocate, but for a sister to treat another sister that way, I think it's disgusting."

"You're just protective. I'm sure plenty of sisters have issues with each other."

Sin shot me an eloquent look.

"Okay, maybe not issues as deep-seated and malicious as ours."

"It's good to acknowledge that. And thank you for bringing her up, for sharing with me. I told you that nothing can harm what you and I have as long as we are open with each other. Do you believe me now?"

He was asking if I believed enough in our love to brave the obstacles in our way together. It was a question that he had proven he had the answer to in innumerable ways, from the moment he declared his love for me after Thanksgiving dinner, through his week of wooing me, and the entire time we had been in Paris together. He had stumbled a little after Elena's email, but that was so understandable that it still broke my heart to think of the self-disgust she had instilled in him after all these years.

Nothing was disgusting about my Frenchman.

With that in mind, I answered his question in a way I knew he would understand. "I know we talked about your willingness to move here for me, especially after the job opportunity at *Vogue* came up. I hope you know that I love you for supporting me, but I think it's time we went home. I'm ready to face the music, and our lives are in New York."

"Are you sure?" he asked, and I knew my potential confirmation meant a lot to him.

France had been both of our homes for a long time, but it was in our past. Our future was in the States.

"Absolutely," I said.

He groaned, a sound that seemed to be wrenched from the very soul of him, as he drew me tight against his body and buried his face in my hair.

"Mine," he claimed on a ragged whisper.

"Yours," I agreed.

We stood in the middle of the Notre Dame plaza for a long time, holding each other, and it felt like its own Christmas miracle to have my arms around a man so perfect for me I could not have even dreamed of him before meeting him. Yet there I stood with a man so perfect for me and so perfectly *mine* as much as I was his.

I stood on my tiptoes to murmur, "I have an early present for you. Let's go back to the Wilde room."

"Only if you promise to get wild with me." He chuckled and then groaned. "That was terrible, and I apologize profusely."

I beamed up at him, arms wrapped around his waist. "No apology necessary. As long as you're smiling, I can put up with your shitty puns."

His laughter rang out over the holiday music and made me grin all the way back to our room.

I was folded on my knees beside the bed, a strip of red satin over my eyes with another one binding my hands together in a bow behind my back. I had pre-tied the bow and practiced tightening it around my wrists while they were awkwardly pressed behind me so that I could present myself to Sin as his Christmas present exactly like this.

Of course, I had also gotten him a real gift, a painting that Odile had done of me before I had left for New York. I had posed in a nude workshop for one of her advanced classes, and the painting depicted me from behind, my head tilted so that my riotous curls flooded like a lava spill down one side of my back, and a sliver of my profile was revealed to show me biting my lip. My ass was round and pert with shadows and highlights, and something about the deep line demarcating either side of my back where my spine rested was unspeakably erotic. I knew he would love it even more than I did.

But for now, I was giving him this, me.

I could feel the still air shift, molecules activating with the power he brought to the room as soon as he entered.

"Look at you all wrapped up prettily for me," he murmured as he came to a standstill in front of me. "It turns you on to present yourself like this for me. I can see how wet your sweet pussy is between those thighs, how your rosy nipples strain, begging for me to twist them, bite them, mark them with my tongue."

I began to pant.

"You look pretty as a picture, Elle. I couldn't have drawn you better myself, but I still want to add my mark. You would look magnificent with my come on those flushed cheeks."

"Yes," I gasped because I wanted it.

"I have something else in mind, though, to make this even more beautiful. Would you like it?"

"Yes please, sir."

"So polite," he crooned as I heard him snap something open.

Then he was wrapping something cool and textured around my throat.

My heart leaped into my mouth and stayed there while he clasped the necklace behind my nape.

"Collared," he whispered into the profound silence. "Mine."

I shivered under the power of his ownership. It felt so final to have his brand around my skin. I hoped it was something I could wear every day so that even if strangers didn't know its significance, I would.

"It's a pearl choker, Elle. You never have to take it off if you don't want," he said, reading my thoughts again in that way of his that thrilled and terrified me.

"I don't want," I murmured.

"Good girl."

He pressed his foot between my spread knees, pushing his calf bone hard against my clit. I groaned at the friction of his crisp hair against my flesh. My hips bucked before I could still them.

"Now, you have a choice here, Elle. It is Christmas and I just collared you, so I am feeling generous. I will let you get off on my leg before I do what I want with you or you can wait and see if those plans involve you orgasming."

I shuddered. I didn't really think he would leave me hanging. Sinclair wasn't that kind of man or that kind of Dom, but the thought of getting off on his leg was so dirty, so delicious that I started gyrating back and forth before I had even made a conscious choice.

"That's right, use my leg to get yourself off," Sin murmured.

I pressed my face into his upper thigh, discovering that he wasn't naked and his erection was trapped within the confines of his boxer briefs but angled right at my panting mouth. I moved faster, shamelessly as I tongued his cock through the fabric.

"You want me in your mouth, Elle?"

"Yes, please, sir." My mouth was already dripping with saliva as I imagined the taste of him exploding across my tongue.

"No, I want you to get off on my leg first."

I increased the tempo, humping his leg hard, grinding my clit into his shin.

"You're dripping all over my foot," Sinclair noted, and for some reason, his calm observation drew the coil tighter in my belly.

I loved the debasement of being on my knees in front of him, bound and finding pleasure in the simple act of humping his leg like a dog. I was too deep in subspace to find the degradation anything but electrifying.

I started whimpering, little sounds of pleasure exploding from my mouth as the climax crawled up my back and took hold of my spine before I could even notice its descent.

"Ahhh," I moaned as I thrashed against his leg, almost losing my balance with my hands clasped behind my back.

My sex was still spasming as he abruptly lifted me to my feet and pushed me over the side of my bed. I shouted hoarsely into the sheets as his fingers drove into my clenching pussy, curling and driving deep to draw the orgasm on and on and on. My legs shuddered, unable to hold me up as his mouth sought my clit and clamped on.

"No," I screamed as a terrifying orgasm dropped on top of the first one before it had even finished.

I lost control of my body, my muscles snapping like elastic bands as I collapsed on the bed, only my hips still moving, thrusting back against his fingers and tongue. Sinclair growled into my cunt and ate like a mad man, lapping up the juices that flooded from me.

He adjusted me again just as I was regaining any degree of consciousness, pushing my legs up on the bed and under me so that I was in his favorite position, my hands bound behind my back and my ass presented to him high in the air over my steeply curved spine.

Instead of taking his fingers from me, he added a thumb to the tight pucker of my ass. When I lurched forward, he tugged me back with an arm banded under my belly.

"Does my siren like to be filled?" he asked coldly before biting into the back of my shoulder.

I shuddered against him. "Y-Yes, sir."

"You tied yourself up so nicely for me. Does that mean I can take whatever I want?"

"You can always take whatever you want, sir."

"And why is that?"

"Because you own me," I breathed, a shiver clutching as me as I spoke my absolute truth.

This man totally and completely owned me but only like this, when I was literally twisting myself into a pretzel to please him, did I really feel alive with his possession.

"Yes, I own this pussy," he said, sliding a third finger inside and twisting it savagely so that I moaned and hissed at the pleasure-pain combination. "I own this pretty pink asshole, and I am going to take it as my Christmas present."

I opened my mouth to say something, but only a ragged groan emerged when he landed a hard smack on my ass. He unwrapped his arm from around me and used it to add two fingers to my clutching bottom, twisting and turning them inside me in a sinuous rhythm that had my entire body clenching, quickening again.

"I, oh God," I blathered incoherently as he worked both my holes.

"Hush," he murmured, and I could feel him staring at our connection, watching how I opened and closed around him. "So pretty."

"Please, oh, please," I begged, for what I didn't really know.

"What do you need, *ma jolie fille*?" he husked.

"I need to come again," I panted. "I want to come on you."

"On me where?" he urged me to say. "You know I like your voice."

"Please, sir, take my ass and let me come again."

Before I even had the words out, his fingers were gone and he was surging, sure and steady into my ass. I screamed into the duvet, sweating and moaning and aching as he spread me open over his huge girth.

"Oh God, oh God," I murmured into the blanket at he seated himself fully inside me and then slowly pulled out.

He continued to fuck me tortuously, so slowly that I could feel every ridge and vein in his cock as it entered me.

"Please," I begged.

He pulled out, ignoring my murmured protests and ran his finger around my gaping opening. It was such a possessive, intimate touch that I nearly lost it as he ran his thumb around and around my closing muscle, dipping the tip of his digit into me from time to time.

I could feel the puddle of my arousal at the base of my knees, soaking the bed.

"So fucking pretty," he groaned. "This ass, this pussy, this woman."

"Yours, all of it," I gritted out through my teeth.

"Mine," he agreed, heaving into me again.

This time he set a brutal pace, each time pressing his entire length into me before taking almost the entire thing out again. He pushed and pulled me off his dick, slamming me back and forth against his hips so that I was rocking like an agitated pendulum.

"Work yourself against my cock," he ordered and I threw myself back against him with an athleticism that I hadn't known I possessed.

"Are you going to come with me in your ass, Elle?" he asked me, his cool voice cracking like breaks in the ice at the end of his question.

It spurned me on. "Yes, sir, if you will allow it."

He fucked me harder, slapping my ass with each cruel thrust. The pain gathered at the base of my spine and spooled into golden pleasure.

"I'll allow it. Come then."

A hoarse shout ripped from my lungs as I went completely rigid, the orgasm tearing through me, paralyzing me from the inside out for one shocking moment before it electrified me, shaking and rolling every single molecule in my body together until I was only a churning mass of matter, not even human any more.

Vaguely, I heard his gruff shout of triumph before he released warm and deep inside me.

After a few moments, he gently left me and smoothed me out on the bed so that I was laying straight and tied on the mattress. He unbound my hands and pressed a kiss to each wrist before he undid my blindfold. His hands ran down my back, rubbing and soothing my back, bum and thighs for a few moments before I was a complete puddle of melted woman against the bed. Only then did he go to the bathroom to clean up.

When he returned, he pushed a button for the AC and I sighed softly as it stirred beautifully over my sweat soaked skin.

"Thank you," I murmured as he got into bed beside me.

"No, Elle, thank you for trusting me with yourself. Best Christmas present ever."

I grinned at him even as I fell into a deep sleep.

Chapter Eleven

Giselle

IT WAS ON NEW YEAR'S EVE WHEN I GOT THE CALL.

We were at Cage's massive apartment where he was throwing a 1920s themed party. It had been an amazing night even though my stomach was a little off so I wasn't drinking. Sinclair looked absolutely dashing in a traditional black tuxedo, and his eyes flashed every time he took in the four rows of perfect blush pearls that lined my throat. I had only been collared for six days, and it was still thrilling to both of us.

We were also just straight-up happy. We had found harmony together, living side by side, that I never could have guessed would be so easy or so blissful. I knew we would go back to New York soon. We had talked about going at the end of January, but for now, we were finding our way in our new relationship without the strain of outside judgment.

So happy.

Then I got the call.

"What?" I yelled into the phone, pressing a hand to my other ear to block out the sounds of revelry.

It was long after the countdown, and the party, unsurprisingly as it was populated with musicians and BDSM worshippers, had slipped into loud, jovial debauchery.

"Cosima," Mama cried, "She's in the hospital. They have her in surgery right now, but *bambina*, it does not look good."

My phone clattered to the ground as I stared off into the partygoers thrashing on the dance floor.

Cosima was in the hospital.

It was not looking good.

God, what could have happened?

Sinclair swooped down to pick up my phone, appearing beside me even though I had left him in the kitchen to take the call. He watched me as he spoke into the phone, but I didn't look at him. I was paralyzed with fear and pretty certain I was going to throw up.

"Sebastian?" Sinclair was saying. "Yes, expect us soon. We'll catch the next flight out."

I didn't remember much of what happened after that except for a vague recollection of returning to the hotel to change and pack our bags before catching a taxi to the airport at some time just before dawn. I didn't even remember enough to say a proper goodbye to Paris. When I woodenly mentioned this to Sinclair, he had kissed my hair and promised that we would go back.

Now, I was so afraid that I was physically sick with it. Sinclair had held my hair as I repeatedly vomited on the plane back to New York. I would have been embarrassed, but he sweetly reminded me of how he had fallen under my spell when I was sick on the plane to Mexico and that this was nostalgic somehow instead of gross. It was pure lies, but I appreciated his efforts too much to say anything. Besides, I was too busy making use of the toilet to talk back anyway.

By the time we landed and dragged ourselves into the waiting Town Car, my body felt weak and saturated with grime like a wrung-out dish towel. Sinclair held me tightly against his side as he responded feverishly to emails on his phone. We had to leave in such a rush that he had left a mess of things back in Paris. A part of me was grateful for his distraction, both because it took his mind off Cosima's dire situation but also because it gave me room to think things through unobserved. If he hadn't been preoccupied, he would have easily picked up on the rod of discomfort in my spine that kept me from sinking into his warmth.

My anxiety only increased as we entered the city and headed straight to the trauma ward at St Vincent's Hospital. I hated that my overwhelming fear for my sister was undermined by the drama that had become the cornerstone of my life. Elena didn't know about Sin and me, which meant that as soon as we entered those sliding glass doors, we would effectively cease to exist as a unit at exactly the moment we needed each other the most. I tried to give myself a stern talking-to like a tough coach before a big game, but no matter how much I berated myself for being selfish, reminded myself that this was the least I deserved, told myself that I was a strong, independent woman capable of handling emotional distress without someone else's help, I kept coming back to the desire to whimper like a freaking baby.

Sin pressed his lips to my hair and breathed deeply. "Visiting hours are almost over, but the family will still be there with her. As soon as we are finished here, I booked rooms at the St. Regis."

Of course, because we hadn't talked about what our living situation was going to look like now that we were together. Sinclair was without a home, and I couldn't very well live with Cosima. It would be incredibly unfair to make her choose sides, especially when she couldn't actually speak for herself at the moment.

It took me a moment to understand what he said, but I blamed it on the lingering nausea.

"Rooms?"

Sin picked up his phone and nonchalantly scrolled through his inbox again. "Mmm."

"Why the plural?"

"I need to give Richard a call before we get to the hospital if you don't mind."

"I do mind. Why did you book multiple rooms, Sin?"

He sighed, tugging on a lock of his overlong hair. "I wasn't sure if you would want to stay with me, given the current situation."

Maybe if he had voiced it differently, emphasized his own discomfort with the living situation, with the fact that there would never be a good time to come out to our family but that it most definitely was *not* now, I would have felt insecure about the comment. Instead, my heart melted a little inside my chest because I knew that it was Sinclair, my enigmatic, in-control Frenchman, who was experiencing a moment of doubt.

I got to my knees on the seat in order to take his face in my hands. His eyes were squinted defensively, but their color was pure and velvety with sadness.

"If it wasn't completely callous of us, I would demand to move in with you this very second and take out an ad on page six of the *Times* so that everyone in the entire city would know it," I said.

Sinclair's corresponding grin was so large that I could have counted every single one of his pearly white teeth. "I love you."

"I love you. And I'm going to miss you the second we get inside that god-forsaken hospital," I admitted.

Sin ran his knuckles down my cheek and lifted the hair from my neck to swing it behind my shoulder. I tilted my head to give him access to my throat. The pads of his fingers pressed gently against my fluttering pulse while his other hand slid up my bare thigh, under my skirt, right to the edge of my panties. We both felt the increase in my heart rate.

"Your body and soul, your very heartbeat are mine, Giselle. Remember that even when I'm across the room from you, pretending otherwise. I will still feel every hop and skip of this pulse, feel every emotion that plucks at this chest, and I will remember every single one so that I can console you properly later." He laughed at the flush of arousal that I could feel blooming under my skin. "Such a dirty girl, you know what I meant."

"I do," I said before leaning over to nip his strong chin between my teeth. "I was just hoping you would also console me physically."

His chuckle was deep and smoky as he gripped my chin and brought his lips against mine. "That goes without saying."

The driver pulling in front of the hospital and knocking lightly at the partition interrupted our searing kiss. I clutched to Sinclair, my nails digging into the quilted muscles of his back, my lips sucking hard at his, for one desperate moment before I pulled away.

"Let's go see Cosima," he said, reminding me gently why we were here in the first place.

I was up and out of the car in less than a heartbeat.

IT WAS MY FIRST TIME IN A HOSPITAL. WHEN I WAS GROWING UP, THE HOSPITAL was almost as bad as the police station. No one went because it meant having to disclose why you were injured, and in Napoli, home of the Camorra, death that stemmed from tattling was worse than any other fate.

The whir of equipment and the faint shush of Crocs shuffling across the laminate floor immediately disturbed me. I didn't like the pressurized silence, the forced smiles the nurses gave me as I passed through the lobby, up the elevator, and into the trauma ward. Everything was white or beige, sterile and chemically scented. The antithesis of Cosima.

Sinclair wasn't with me, opting to wait downstairs for a few minutes so that it wouldn't seem suspicious that we had arrived together. I understood the need for duplicity, but I wished fervently that he were beside me, his cool control like a balm to my flustered spirit.

I rounded the corner of the nurses' station, about to ask which room Cosima occupied when I caught sight of a tall, dark, and handsome man emerging from behind a drab curtain.

"Sebastian!" I called out, too loudly, too desperate for the muted ambiance of the hospital ward.

By the time he turned around, I was already barreling into his arms. He caught me in a death grip, squeezing so hard it was hard to breathe. I relished the sensation.

"*Bambina, bambina*," he murmured over and over into my hair.

It took me a moment to realize that he was trembling beneath my embrace, that under his spicy cologne, he smelled like stale sweat and cigarettes. Things were bad whenever Seb picked up his smoking habit.

"Let me look at you," I said, gently extracting myself from his arms.

He kept hold of my hands but allowed enough distance for me to observe his appearance. My heart tightened painfully as I noted his grimy, tousled hair and the deep purplish trenches beneath his glassy eyes. He looked incredibly ill as if Death himself stalked his every move. He might as well have, I figured, because if Cosima didn't pull through, I really couldn't see Sebastian surviving without her.

"You look like shit."

A glimmer of amusement flared in his gold eyes. "You look more beautiful than I have ever seen you."

I'm happy, I wanted to say but didn't. Instead, I shrugged and tugged him by the hand closer to the room he had just left.

"Tell me what happened. Mama only had time to tell me that Cosima was in some sort of accident and that she was in the ICU."

Seb scrubbed both hands over his face, absentmindedly taking mine along for the ride as we were still clasping palms. He didn't notice, and I didn't say anything.

"She was having dinner in the Bronx at this tiny Italian deli she likes even though the prosciutto tastes like shoe leather. According to witnesses, she was eating alone, but she seemed to be waiting for someone. She even bought an extra sandwich and a bottle of Chinotto Neri––"

"She hates soda," I interjected automatically.

"I know, and I can't think of a single damn person in her life who would drink that stuff."

"Only an Italian," I said, because it was our version of Coca-Cola but bitter, the Neri brand quintessentially Italian too.

"Obviously," Seb agreed, his jaw taut with agitation. "I was fucking useless when the police questioned me. She is my twin sister and best friend in the world." His voice cracked, and he cleared his throat. "How can I have been oblivious to this?"

I thought about the secrets our sister kept hidden close to her skin, closer even than her twin brother and best friend in the world could be.

"Continue," I urged because I didn't have anything comforting to say.

"She had been waiting for about fifteen minutes when a black SUV pulled up in front of the shop and opened fire."

I gasped, the scene playing out in my mind like a film reel. My beautiful sister sits at a table near the window and waits patiently for some unknown man like a heroine in a tragic romance novel when the gunfire starts.

I felt sure it was a man she was waiting for, not least of all, because Cosima didn't particularly like women, and they didn't particularly like her. It was clear to me too, that this wasn't a random attack. Who would target a nearly empty Italian deli in the Bronx just for kicks?

If I rephrased the question—who would target a nearly empty Italian deli just to take someone out?—I knew the answer. *The Mafia.*

I swallowed hard and snuck a glance up at Sebastian who was absorbed in his own painful reverie. The face of Dante, the black-eyed mafia man who had appeared one day in Cosima's apartment a few weeks ago, flared to life in my memory. He had something to do with this. I knew it as surely as I knew that it had been wishful thinking by our family to think that Cosima had fled the confines of Naples unshackled. After she had left, and Seamus, our family had been left remarkably untroubled by the local made men. Mama had put it down to God and her devout prayer, Sebastian to the departure of our gambling, addict father, but I had always wondered, and I knew Elena did too, if Cosima hadn't signed away her soul for our freedom.

As we were standing in a hospital with her lying ten feet away, struggling for her life, I was desperately afraid I already knew the answer to that question as well.

"She was just sitting there," Seb said quietly, almost to himself.

"Giselle?" Mama's voice drifted out into the hall, and my heart tripped over the familiar, tender notes.

I spilled through the doorway and tumbled straight into the arms of my mother. She pressed me against her breast, hushing my suddenly laborious breaths and random whimpers of pain. Now that I was there, in the awful hospital that was such a contrast to my vibrant sister, the reality of her situation came crashing down around me. Before I could lose it completely, I pulled away from the faint citrus and semolina scent of my Mama and turned toward the hospital bed.

Cosima under a thin white sheet, thin and pale as a cadaver used in medical school experiments. There were deeply purple bruises under her eyes and a brackish, yellow-brown discoloration over the left side of her face. She had always been svelte, but in the harsh light, she seemed skeletal, impossibly dead.

I gasped and then choked on a bulbous sob.

Mama stroked my hair as I turned and threw up in a bin that Sebastian thrust under my chin.

"*Bambina, bambina,*" she crooned.

"What happened?" I whispered through the bile rising at the back of my throat.

"She was shot three times in the torso."

I tilted my head to stare at Elena. She sat in an absurdly orange plastic chair beside the bed wearing a beautiful turtleneck dress. Her hair was still shiny and supple, curled around her beautiful face perfectly. Hatred rose with the bile to pool at the back of my tongue. How dare she look so composed when Cosima was practically dead beside her?

Elena continued, even though my glare should have eviscerated her. "She hit her head on the way down, and they have her in a medically induced coma until the swelling goes down."

I wrenched my gaze away from Elena and my unfair rage against her to look at Cosima again. Her skin was papery under my fingers when I reached over to brush my fingers against her cheek, and her normally lustrous hair was brittle. Another sob rose in my throat, but I swallowed it painfully. Crying would only prompt my family to do the same.

"*Cane,* let me through!" A roughened voice demanded from down the hallway.

"Get your act together," another voice bit out, "or I won't let you see her."

A moment later, Sinclair led a disgruntled Dante into the room. I gasped at the sight of the Italian man, his inky hair completely disheveled and his black eyes wild with grief. He immediately tumbled into the room and sat on Cosima's bed, his hands shaking as they gently skimmed over her face.

"*Mia bella ragazza,*" he murmured over and over again as he stared at her.

I was deeply surprised and even strangely moved when tears began to roll down his cheeks.

"Who the fuck are you?" Sebastian demanded after the moment of shock passed.

Dante ignored him. Instead, he pressed his forehead against Cosima's and continued to mutter in Italian under his breath.

Sebastian took a menacing step forward but stopped with Dante let out a choked sob. His hand shook as he stroked it down Cosima's brittle mane of hair.

"What happened to you?" he whispered in anguish.

Sebastian vibrated beside me, but I knew he wouldn't rip the mafia man away without asking questions first.

I opened my mouth to do just that, but Elena interrupted me.

"What are you doing here, Daniel?"

It took me a moment to process what she was doing. When I whirled to face her and saw the sincerity in her expression, I was furious for a different reason.

"Elena," I snapped before I could temper my response.

Sinclair held up a hand and stepped forward. "Elena, this isn't the time."

Mama looked between the three of us with sharp eyes that saw too much. "What is going on, *ragazzi?*"

"Daniel and I are," Elena paused delicately, "going through a trial separation."

Sinclair frowned but didn't correct her. I wanted him to so badly that my muscles twitched, but I tried to understand why he remained silent.

Mama barely batted an eyelash. "I agree. This is not the time, Elena."

"No, it is the time for this *cafone* to tell us what he got Cosi into," Sebastian growled as he moved forward to plant a heavy hand on Dante's shoulder.

The made man stilled, his lack of movement filled with threat.

"I didn't get her into anything," he said quietly.

"*Stronzo*, do not lie to me about my sister."

"I would never do anything to harm her," Dante whispered again.

Was it absurd that I believed him? He was looking at Cosima with a tenderness that echoed in my chest.

"Tell me the truth," Sebastian roared, yanking him back by the shoulder.

Dante was on his feet in a flash, his forearm across Seb's throat as he held him against the wall. My brother was tall, over six feet, but Dante was practically a giant, closer to seven feet than six, with muscles defined and bulging like coils of rope beneath his skin.

Dante leaned close to Sebastian's face and calmly repeated, "I didn't get her *into* anything. I *saved* her, *patatino*."

He knew his family nickname.

Who was this guy?

Dante stepped back with a snort of disgust and turned to face Cosima again, his face soft with anguish again. He took her hand but spoke to Sebastian, "I understand your anger but know that I have lived with it for much longer than you, this rage against the people who dare to touch this woman." His fingers tenderly brushed her hair away from her face. "She kept you in the dark because you weren't strong enough to deal with her demons."

Sebastian growled, but I stepped forward to press a hand to his arm.

"She never gave us the chance," I said softly. "Maybe you can?"

Dante looked over at me, his eyes large and wet with tears. For a moment, I could sense his desire to connect with us. There was no doubt in my mind that he loved Cosima and the outsider in him longed to be accepted by her and by association, her family.

But the expression flicked and died a quick death when Elena snorted at my comment and Sebastian bared his teeth.

The family that couldn't even accept their own would never accept him, and by the look in his eye, he knew it.

"It is not my story to tell, not really," he finally said.

"Cut the bullshit," Sebastian said. "I want to know what happened to my sister."

Dante shrugged as if he didn't care, but his eyes were tight. "I can't know for sure. She knows more than one dangerous person, myself included, who could have swept her up into the middle of a feud. She always was too curious for her own good. Too defiant."

"So, you had nothing to do with this?" I clarified because I was pretty sure Sebastian needed to be reminded.

He had the wet black look of murder in his suddenly dark eyes.

"No, but I will find out what happened to her," he vowed, more to Cosima than to anyone else. He leaned closer to her until their noses were almost touching. "And I promise to rip them apart with my teeth, *tesoro*."

Chapter Twelve

Giselle

THERE WAS NO WAY TO PREPARE FOR SOMETHING LIKE THIS. OF COURSE, THERE wasn't a handbook that offered advice to adulterers on how to calmly confront the wronged party about their infidelity. How did a person condense their sinful actions, endless excuses, and genuine apologies into one carefully constructed monologue? Even if you accomplished such a thing, there was no way in hell the person was just going to sit there and listen to you.

"This is impossible," I murmured, my hands clutched around my cold cup of coffee.

Sinclair was cleaning up in the kitchenette after our quick breakfast of croissants, baguette, and fresh plum jam. Or at least, Sinclair's quick breakfast. As soon as I had touched a piece of toast to my mouth, I had run to the washroom to throw up. I was still feeling physically ill from the trauma of Cosima's accident and now, from the stress of confronting Elena, it was impossible to keep anything down.

There was a smudge of purple jelly left on the right side of Sin's mouth that I fixated on as he competently moved around our suite at the St. Regis. I loved to watch the economy of his actions, the contained grace with which he carried his lean build. It didn't disturb me anymore to know that I could spend hours watching him.

Who needed Netflix when you had a hot Frenchman to stare at?

Normally, he was enough to distract me, but I was going to coffee with Elena this morning. To call it a coffee date was misleading and wrong, but I didn't know how else to phrase it except to say that it was a date made to ruin her life, and it didn't have the same ring to it.

We had only been Stateside for three days, all of which were filled with extended hospital visits to a still-comatose Cosima. It felt wrong to tell the family about our relationship during a time like this, but it felt like more of a betrayal to hide it from them during a time like this, so I was meeting with her this morning.

"Elle, we have spoken about this. If you don't want to be the one to tell her, I am more than prepared to do it myself."

I blinked up at him where he leaned over the other side of the island, his gaze direct and strong. I had no doubt he was prepared to do the hard part for me. In fact, I was sure he would have preferred it.

I shook my head. "No. I'm her sister. We may not get along very well, but I owe it to our family bond to tell her about us to her face. I just don't know how to go about it gently, you know?"

"I do know. I know that something like this, it cannot be done gently."

I sighed into my nearly empty mug. It felt doubly wrong to break the news to her, given what was going on with Cosima, but it was for exactly that reason that I knew I had to do it sooner rather than later. If God forbid something worse happened to Cosima, Sinclair and I would need each other. Besides, we were ready to move forward together, and keeping that a secret in the face of everything seemed reprehensible.

"Giselle," Sin said softly, rounding the marble counter so that he could take my cheek in his cool palm. "There is no candy coating this. You are in love with your sister's ex-boyfriend. I do not think words exist in any language that will make that more palatable to Elena."

God, I hated how true that was.

"We made the right decision, the *only* decision, but it doesn't make it seem any less selfish," I admitted.

His thumb brushed tenderly over my bottom lip before he dipped down to press a kiss there. When he tried to pull away, I abandoned my coffee cup to link my hands behind his neck and clasp him closer to me. He smiled against my mouth before kissing me more deeply, his tongue warm velvet against mine.

"The only thing worse than being so selfish, I've found, is not owning it," he said after a minute, pressing his forehead to mine. "We may have acted immorally, but we did it for a purpose. We did it for love, and there is no shame to be felt in that."

"No," I agreed because I couldn't imagine being ashamed of the man I held in my arms.

"Do not show her regret. She is a shark, your sister, and she will sense blood in the water. She will make you pay for that shame."

I sighed loudly against his face and pressed another kiss to his lips. "You're right, of course."

"Of course," he agreed with a smile as I pulled away to scoot off my stool. He gave my bum a playful slap as I moved past him to get ready. "Go get 'em, tiger."

I WAS HAPPY THAT ELENA HAD CHOSEN OUR LOCATION FOR COFFEE BECAUSE I fully planned never to set foot in the place again. Like a nuclear blast site, it would remain toxic for the next forty years. As it was, the place suited my sister entirely, posh and trendy without being hip, with black and white photos on the wall and tons of smartly clad businesspeople milling about even on a Saturday morning. We both sat at a small bistro table in one of the large bay windows, holding our cups of coffee tightly as if to make up for the intimacy lacking between us. We had been sitting there for five awkward minutes in silence while I worked up the courage to begin.

"How have you been?" I finally asked lamely.

"Well, thank you. I've told you before that I'm on the partner track?"

Only a thousand times.

"You may have mentioned it once or twice. That's very impressive."

Elena nodded graciously.

Awkward silence reigned for an excruciating minute.

"Mama told me that you just got back from France. You went to visit friends?" Elena asked.

Her words hit my hollow heart with a dull thud. She was actually trying.

"I did. It was good to go back. It will always be home for me in a way that Naples never was."

She nodded, her eyes glazed over as she looked out the window at the softly falling snow. "I know what you mean. I have absolutely no desire to ever return there, even to Italy. Do you know, I tell people that I am American?"

I wasn't surprised, but she did shock me by elaborating.

"It took me over a year of constant study and practice to rid myself of that common accent. It was the *r*'s that frustrated me. The flat English sound took me forever to master."

"Why is it so important to you?"

She was startled by the question as if I should know the answer. "Italy stands for everything that I abhor. It is gritty, dirty, violent, and fundamentally debased."

"Have you ever thought that you might be substituting the half for the whole? Yes, our childhood could be defined by those things, but does that reflect on our country or only on our circumstances?"

Elena blinked at me. "Does it matter? The half contaminates the whole. The poison spreads."

I swallowed thickly. "You're saying that you cannot forgive Italy for the desperation of your childhood?"

"I see no reason I should."

"Yet you forgive Mama for raising you like that?"

Finally, Elena looked uncomfortable. "She didn't have the power to control it."

I arched an eyebrow at her.

She pursed her lips. "I understand the point you are trying to make, but it isn't valid. Mama tried her best to raise us right. There was nothing more she could have done, and she has more than made up for her mistakes every day since we got out of that hellish place."

I sucked a deep breath into my lungs like a drowning man who knows that will be his last breath.

The stage was set, however poorly, and I couldn't put it off any longer.

"Elena, I actually asked you to meet me here today to talk about something kind of difficult."

She stilled so completely that it brought into stark relief the motion of the coffee shop flowing around us. It was a popular spot at a busy time, and I had to swallow the impulsive panic that everyone was suddenly listening to us.

"I know that you and I have always had a... hard relationship, and I wish so much that it was different." I looked into her eyes and flinched at the lack of compassion there. She shared no such desire. "Our family has been through so much, and it has been our strength and loyalty as a unit that has gotten us through. I admire and respect you so much—"

"Cut the crap, Giselle. What is it that you want to say to me?"

My throat was so dry that it hurt to breathe. Pain shot up my arms directly into my off-beating heart. I wondered if I was having a heart attack.

I gasped for one more lungful of air before willingly falling on my sword.

"I am in love with Sinclair."

Silence.

Total and complete silence.

A non-reaction.

For a moment, I wondered if I had even spoken.

Then she blinked in that slow way of hers that hypnotized you, and when her eyes opened again, they were narrowed with laser-like intensity.

"When?"

The word flung me like a dart through a butterfly's wing, pinning me to the wall, helpless against her scrutiny.

"We met in Mexico. I had no idea he was your boyfriend, and he had no idea I was your sister. We knew each other only as Sinclair and Elle. We, well, we spent a lot of time together that trip, and I fell in love with him. I fell in love with the person he made me believe that I could be."

"An adulterer?" she asked mildly.

I had never been as afraid of anyone, not even Christopher, as I was of my sister at that moment.

"I left him thinking that I would never see him again, but then there he was in Mama's kitchen. There he was as your boyfriend."

"He was more than a mere boyfriend," she hissed.

I nodded. "I know. I knew that he was yours; that this was the man you had been with for the past four years. I knew that you two seemed perfect together."

"We were. We are."

I choked on her words and coughed. "We both refused to acknowledge what had happened. We wanted it to be in the past where it belonged, but..." I chewed on my lip, focusing on the pain there instead of how hurtful it was to look at my sister, to prostrate myself, my heart, before her even though I knew how it would end.

Bloody, with her hand on the knife stuck deep in my chest.

I tried to remind myself that I deserved it, but it didn't ease the pain.

"We became friends again, just friends," I whispered, more to myself than her.

Elena just sat there, cloaked in righteousness and arctic cold disdain.

"But I loved him so much even in those moments. I loved him so much, Elena, that it became bigger than anything else. Bigger than morality and sin, bigger than our circumstances, bigger even than our love for you."

She was staring at me so hard. I could feel the weight of it like punishing gravity, crushing everything inside my body, folding me up into a crumpled little unrecognizable ball of waste. The beautifully pleated lines and contours of the origami figure I had constructed over the past few months with Sinclair, all those beautiful qualities I had grown to know that I had possessed, were destroyed with one slow blink.

I began to cry, which disgusted me because she was the victim, but I couldn't stop.

"I fought it so hard, Elena. We both did. If you believe nothing else, please believe that we didn't want to do this to you. But this wasn't about a choice. If I denied myself my love of Sinclair..." An ugly sob burst through my lips and slapped wetly against the table. "I would have destroyed both him and myself."

"So, instead, you chose to destroy me," she said quietly.

I cried harder, burying my shameful face in my hands. Snot-laced tears ran through my fingers and dripped to the table.

Elena watched me cry.

"You let him defile you, don't you?"

I recoiled at her sharp question, my head flying up so that I could look at her.

She was sneering at me, her red lips twisted like a bloody smear.

"You let him beat you, don't you? You like it when he hits you, when he ruts into you like a wild beast and marks your body as his own." She laughed at my gasp, the sound sharp and high pitched like an auditory weapon. "You stupid slut. Daniel doesn't love you. He is just using you."

A whimper lodged in my throat. I wanted to beg her to shut up, but I deserved her hatred, so I kept quiet.

She leaned forward, her gorgeous face more animated than I had ever seen it, warped harshly with revulsion. "You think he loves you? What is there about you to love? You are just the same meek, stupid, self-centered little girl who always gets what she wants and is shielded like a baby from every bad thing life throws at her. Do you know why Mama and the twins do that? Hmm? Because they know you are weak. They don't love you so much as pity you. If your family can't even respect you, how do you think a man like Daniel Sinclair could ever *love* you?"

She lifted her chin and looked down on me like the queen of hearts condemning one of her subjects to the guillotine. "Daniel is the best person I have ever known. He is an intelligent, successful businessman and the son of the New York State governor. And you think he loves you?"

Her laughter sliced me into ribbons. All I felt was pain, and still, I sat there and absorbed it, ever the masochist.

She sat back in her chair with a comfortable confidence that was somehow cruel. There was a small smile on her lips when she said, "Did you know, when I first found out he was having an affair, I was concerned? Thank you for alleviating my fears. Daniel doesn't love you, Giselle. When he inevitably grows tired of you, no matter how much you let him slap you around in bed, he will beg for a real woman, a woman of power and substance, to take him back. And that destruction you were so afraid of? It will eviscerate you. You will not have your family or Daniel at your side. I haven't wanted you to be a part of this family for a long time, and I always knew Daniel needed to get his perversions out of his system." She laughed lightly and took a sip of her coffee. "Two birds, one stone."

I sat, my mouth gaping wide open like an angry wound. There were no thoughts in my head or emotions in my chest. I was nothing, just as she and I had always secretly suspected.

Elena searched my face for a long minute, her gaze scalping me, before she nodded, assured of my overwhelming pain. She stood swiftly and tugged on her coat.

"Tell Daniel to call me when he's through with you. Oh, and Giselle, stay the fuck away from my family and me. If you don't, every person in New York City will know what a gold-digging whore you are."

Chapter Thirteen

Giselle

I COULDN'T GO BACK TO THE ST. REGIS AFTER THAT. INSTEAD, AFTER ELENA left and I threw up for twenty minutes in the café restroom, I wandered around Manhattan like some kind of urban zombie, both hollowed out inside and rotten to the core. I was empty of thoughts. In a weird way, it reminded me of what it was like to be in subspace, incapable of coherency but eloquent with emotions. They crashed over me in tidal waves, drowning me in dark pools of pain and guilt.

I knew that if I went to Sinclair, he would make it all go away. He would murmur sweet condolences in my ear, stroke my cheekbone in that way of his that made me feel priceless as a statue, more beautiful than anything rendered by Auguste Rodin or Botticelli. He would, as only he was capable of doing, as he always did, soothe my ugly, crumpled edges and fold me back into an origami swan.

I didn't deserve that peace. A small, protected piece of my mind argued that I did deserve it, that I was worthy of Sinclair's love and that maybe all was fair in love and war. But I also knew that if I went back to him before I had somehow disassembled and portioned out the immeasurable mass of self-hatred and grief churning through my system, I would leave him.

Margot had been right when she said Sinclair deserved more than a coward. It was difficult before when no one knew about the affair. We had been disciples of immoral subterfuge and intense yearning, torn between our past and our dreams for the future. We had barely been able to see each other through the mess of obstacles between us.

Now, I had him. The thought sent a zing of happiness down my spine even in the thralls of my guilt. Daniel Sinclair, the beautiful, misunderstood Frenchman with the seemingly perfect life, had risked his reputation, his family, and his career on *me*.

Elena's vindictive words echoed through my head. He was too good for me, on that we wholeheartedly agreed. I doubted that there would ever be a time when I believed myself worthy of his love. So few people ever found their soul mates, let alone had reason to believe in the concept, and there I was, finally, with mine. Whether or not I deserved such luck, I was not going to take it, *him*, for granted.

I had made my decision, and now I had to live with it.

I wasn't surprised when Mama's restaurant loomed before me, the gold lettering of *Osteria Lombardi* glittering in the lower-level window of the brick brownstone. I floated down the few steps to the entrance and entered before I could run away in fear.

One of the servers directed me to the kitchen where Mama was preparing for dinner service. It was that awkward time of day in the restaurant industry when it is too late for lunch and early for dinner, when most of the day's prep had been done by the day crew before the night lineup came in, so Mama was alone at a long stainless-steel countertop hand-rolling *orecchiette* pasta when I pushed through the swinging doors.

She was so absorbed that she didn't notice me, so I took a minute to watch her work. Her long silver threaded black hair was woven into her habitual braid, and her soft features were arranged into an expression that was the foundation of a smile before it springs. Her nimble fingers gently folded the dough into tiny ear-like shapes before setting them aside to dry, and she hummed as she worked. It was a different setting, but the sight of her like that took me back to the hot, dry afternoons in the Naples of my childhood.

For one insane moment, I wished I was back there.

"Giselle, my French baby, what do you do here?" Mama asked, startling me out of my past.

I smiled softly at her, filled with tenderness. I indulged myself by hustling toward her for a hug. Immediately, she opened her flour-coated arms and pulled me close.

This time, when I cried, the tears were silent.

Mama soothed me like a child with indecipherable cooing noises.

"I love you so much, Mama," I breathed.

"*Sempre*," Mama murmured as she brushed my damp hair away from my face. She searched my eyes for a long time before wrapping me up even more tightly. "What has happened?"

Somehow, it was harder to tell Mama, a woman who had raised me to be better than deceit and infidelity. My betrayal meant the end of a relationship with Elena, but did it have to mean the dissolution of the bonds that tied the rest of my family together?

Fuck, I hoped not.

"I have something that I need to tell you," I whispered.

She sighed softly before steering me toward the other side of the counter where she pulled up a steel stool for me to sit on. Once I was settled, she nodded and returned to her pasta making. Love seared my insides as I realized what she was doing, giving me space to confess.

I stared at the way her hands carefully formed the dough, mesmerized by the repetition. It helped me gather the edges of my shredded thoughts.

"Mama," I choked on a sob and cleared my throat. "Mama, I want you to know how much I love you, how much I respect the struggle you've been through in order to keep our family whole and successful. You've been a wonderful inspiration for me, the epitome of grace and goodness. Please, don't let what I'm about to tell you be a reflection on your parenting or how I feel about you."

She nodded but didn't look at me, her eyes fixed on her work even though I knew she would do it blindfolded. Her lack of attention gave me the comfort of a confessional. I knew she was on the other side of the pretend indifference, listening and trying not to judge. It gave me hope.

"I had an affair, Mama, with a wonderful man who I met when Brenna sent me to Mexico. I didn't mean for it to happen, I knew he was in a meaningful relationship, but there was this pull between us that I couldn't ignore. He was the most beautiful man I had ever seen, and he made me feel worthy, good, and free of my insecurities." I sucked in a shaky deep breath. "I fell in love with him even though I never planned to see him again. Only, I did. I saw him that very same day, later that night, in your kitchen at my surprise party."

Mama stilled, just for a beat, in her movements, but it was enough for me to realize that she knew where I was going with my story.

I rushed on.

"I was so ashamed, we both were, when we realized the truth. We avoided each other for weeks, but there was still the agonizing magnetism between us. I really thought we could be friends…"

"Never," she said, so softly that at first, I wasn't sure she had spoken at all.

"I loved him too much for that, and apparently, he felt the same way."

"You began an affair again," she stated.

"We began an affair again," I agreed on a whisper. "We were only physically intimate once or twice before he left her, but either way, it was an emotional affair. I don't know. Maybe that's worse."

"*Si,* it is."

I bit my lip so that it wouldn't tremble, and for the first time in years, I spoke to my mother in our native tongue. "*On posso vivere senza di lui.*"

I cannot live without him.

"And he feels this way?" Mama asked.

The memory of Sinclair declaring his love for me in his office after the horrible Thanksgiving dinner, how impassioned and primal he was in staking his claim on my heart. I knew without having a mirror that the thought of him lit me up like a traffic light.

"He does."

Mama hummed, the way both she and Elena did when they were processing things.

"I love him more than I have ever loved anyone, and"—I swallowed —"he made me love myself too."

A long silence followed my words. I could have said more, I could have definitely clarified who I spoke of and what our future plans entailed, but instead, I chewed on my lip. Meanwhile, mama finished shaping the last of the semolina dough and braced her hands on the table. I waited with my heart in my throat for her to look up at me, yet I was jolted out of my skin when her rich brown eyes found mine.

They were eyes I had stared into for the majority of my life, and her gaze was the one I had grown up looking to for guidance, support, and redemption. So, I think a large part of me was expecting to see the acceptance that I had always found there even though I knew what I had done was at least mildly despicable.

Only, there was no acceptance there.

No, Mama's eyes were filled to the brim with disappointment and condemnation.

"Have you told your sister?"

The urge to weep clutched me by the throat and held me captive for a minute before I was able to nod.

"I should go to her," she said.

A noise of complete distress, something like a dog's yelp, leaped from my lips before I could slap a hand over my mouth. I knew she was right. Elena deserved Mama's time and attention right then more than me. Yet Mama's pure dismissal of my admission and obvious guilt hit me like a freight train on repeat. I struggled not to hyperventilate; I didn't want Mama to take pity on me for medical reasons when she was clearly as disgusted with me as I was by myself.

"I understand," I said.

Mama's eyes narrowed. I sat still, my posture straight and strong despite my innards caving in on themselves. I remembered Sinclair's advice about holding strong, remembering that I had made a *choice*, a premeditated decision to serve the greater happiness of two people, not just myself. It was horrifyingly easy to picture Sinclair five years from then with Elena, his soul subdued, and his work his true mistress.

He belonged with me.

I tilted my chin higher and said, "I'm willing to accept your judgment, Mama. I'm even willing to accept that for, at least a little while, you might not want to see me." I couldn't help the tears that began to race scalding hot down my cheeks, but I didn't let my voice wobble. "I can almost bear the thought of not seeing you and the twins at Christmas and birthdays and for our weekly lunches even though I'll be miserable without you. But what I could not ever bear, what I will never again even entertain, is the thought of being without Daniel Sinclair. He's it for me, and if he is the only family I have now, I can deal with it if I have to."

She stared at me, still for an eternity. At one point, I began to tremble because my body was physically incapable of maintaining its structure under the crushing weight of her scrutiny.

"I am glad for that, *bambina*," she said softly, "because as you say, for a little bit at least, I will not see you."

My lips rolled under my teeth to lock in my scream.

"I do not mean to punish you for finding love. Love..." She sighed heavily. "I know what a person will do for it, and I will never say the consequences are not worth the love. But, Giselle, there will be consequences, and losing me like this temporarily is one of them. I cannot speak for the twins..." Her face crumpled as she thought about Cosima, slowly recovering in the hospital. "But I have a feeling they will feel the same."

I nodded as I slipped off the chair, glad that I hadn't taken off my coat. She was reacting properly. She was right, and I was wrong. I let those words repeat in my mind, finding the words and assembling them so that I grew numb to them.

"Thank you for listening to me," I murmured, ducking my head as I turned to leave.

I had to get out of there before I imploded.

"*Stammi bene, bambina*," she said as I pushed through the swinging door.

Happily, they swung shut before I started sobbing.

I felt mildly better when I was out in the street, absorbed by the myriad of New Yorkers with better things to do than observe my pity party. Even though I had never in my life felt so utterly devastated, so unbearably *raw*, I also felt a profound sense of relief. I was glad that I had put myself through the ordeal of Elena and Mama in one day. I couldn't imagine how long it would take for me to digest this grief, but at least the accusations closest to my heart had been dealt with. Now, I only had to worry about the judgment of my siblings, who I truly believed might be vaguely supportive, and New York as a whole. Daniel Sinclair was a vital part of its high society, and I fully expected them to lend their voice to the criticism laid at our doorstep. The thought of more was frankly harrowing, and for a while there, as I wandered aimlessly around the city, I seriously wondered if I would have a nervous breakdown.

My phone rang in my pocket. I pressed ignore, but not before I saw the lineup of notifications across the screen. Sinclair had called me six times and sent two texts.

Frenchman: No matter what happens. No matter how awful she makes you feel about yourself. Remember the woman I fell in love with. The brave woman with flaming hair and bold eyes who captivated me from the start. It wasn't your beauty that drew me in, my love. It was your capacity to *feel*, to filter every emotion and experience through your body so that you can better understand life. You are so utterly alive that you even succeeded in bringing me to life. Feel for Elena, feel grief for what you have to give up for me (I am more sorry for that than I can say) but then release the grief. If you can forgive me, you can forgive yourself.

Frenchman: Et aussi, je t'aime. Come home to me when you are ready. I have a surprise that I would like to share with you.

My heart ached and throbbed like a mortal wound as I read and reread his words standing in the middle of 7th Avenue as people jostled and rushed past me. The loneliness that had crippled me like a physical condition my entire life seized me in its iron fist. Memories assaulted me: Cosima leaving followed by Seamus and then Sebastian, arriving alone in Paris to make a new life, fleeing it to get away from the threat of Christopher, the distance that remained between my siblings and me. The agony of solitude whipped around me, swirled me into a vortex of pain and then left abruptly.

I placed my hands on my knees and panted lightly from the intensity of my revelation.

I wasn't alone any longer, and if I had the strength to accept the repercussions of my relationship with Sinclair, I never had to be again.

Chapter Fourteen

Giselle

Sinclair was practically vibrating with excitement. His knee bounced up and down under our clasped palms as we sat in the back of the cab that was transporting us to a surprise location. He had seemed incredibly relieved and then uncharacteristically giddy when I'd arrived at the suite, dropped my things, and dived into his arms. He'd held me in silence until I collected myself, and then he had asked me to go with him somewhere. I didn't tell him about the ordeal with my sister and my mother. I wasn't ready to unleash my grief onto him, but I'd sealed the promise that I'd made myself—to devote myself to our future—with a long kiss.

"We're going to Brooklyn?" I asked now, surprised.

His boyish enthusiasm was immediately snuffed out by the incredulity of my tone, and his mask slipped back in place. He raised a cool brow and said, "You dislike Brooklyn?"

"Not at all." I smiled. "In fact, I kind of love it. It's a hipster haven after all."

"You are not a hipster," he said, appalled by the thought.

I laughed. "No, but I am an artist. I like the grittiness that still lingers here, the cool little shops and the community feel. Besides, this is where we spent our first 'date' after we found each other again."

His grin was back.

I shook my head at him as our cab pulled up to a building near the water overlooking the Manhattan skyline. He was out of the car and opening my door before I could pry my eyes away from the gorgeous nightscape.

"I've never seen you like this."

He tugged me out of the car and into his arms, one hand firm on my chin so that I was looking up into his eyes. "I've never been like this."

The air was cold and bitingly fresh in my lungs as he led me to the gorgeous building right beside the Manhattan Bridge overpass.

"Mr. Sinclair," a professionally dressed older woman greeted from beside the entrance. "It's lovely to see you again."

"Meagan," he said, shaking hands with the statuesque blonde. "How are you this evening? I appreciate you meeting us here at such a late hour."

She blushed. "Don't be silly, I'm happy to accommodate you. After all, how much business have you sent our way in the past eight years?"

He inclined his head to acknowledge her words and tugged me forward by our joined hands. "Meagan, this is the woman I was telling you about, Giselle Moore."

To my surprise, she beamed at me and took my hand warmly in both of hers. "It's a pleasure to meet you, Giselle."

"Oh?" I asked, sliding a glance up at Sin.

"Of course. It's not often Sinclair can't shut up about something other than work," she joked.

My eyebrows were somewhere startlingly close to my hairline as I stared up at my Frenchman. He raised one of his reddish brows at me haughtily, as if such behavior was to be expected.

"Who are you, and what have you done to my enigmatic, aloof Sinclair?" I asked.

He chuckled darkly and leaned close to my ear to whisper, "Trust me, your Sinclair is still in here, waiting to have his wicked way with you."

I gulped as his words ignited that ever-ready powder keg of desire in the base of my belly.

"Shall we go in, then?" Meagan was saying as she buzzed through the glass doors and into the lobby.

I followed mutely after her, listening vaguely as she explained the building's amenities and the appeal of living in Brooklyn's trendy DUMBO neighborhood. Sinclair's thumb swooped rhythmically over mine as he conversed with her in the gorgeous glass elevator that took us impossibly high in the converted boxing warehouse. A sense of impending wonder and anxiety churned in my gut as the doors slid soundlessly open to reveal a massive open concept kitchen and living area.

My mouth hung open like a flytrap as I stepped into the space, pulled instinctively toward the massive glass-faced clock at the center of the far wall. Through the wrought-iron face, I could see the entire western layout of Brooklyn. I swiveled around to gape at Sinclair who stood with his hands deep in his pockets, watching me with his usual neutral expression. I caught sight of another identical clock face in the wall perpendicular to me and rushed toward it. This one offered an unparalleled view of the Manhattan Bridge and the sparkling lights of the big city.

I turned again to Sinclair, unable to speak.

He stepped into the recessed living room but kept a wide swathe of space between us. Meagan, the good real estate agent that she was, made herself scarce.

"Sinclair, what are we doing here?"

He pulled a hand through his hair, cleared his throat and shrugged one shoulder. "It is obvious, no?"

"No," I said. "Not so much."

"If you don't like it, we can find something in Manhattan. I would offer to leave the city entirely, but my business is based here, and it would take some time to move the base of operations. I thought Brooklyn was a good compromise, a place close to our family and our old lives but a new neighborhood, one we could explore and learn to love together. We wouldn't run the risk of constantly running into people we knew."

He stepped forward slowly as if he was approaching a cornered animal. When I bristled at his touch, I realized I was giving him reason to act like that. Struggling to relax, I gave him my hand so he could lead me toward the staircase.

"It's rather large; three floors and three bedrooms," he explained as we ascended the stairs to the second level. "I know it might be hard to imagine our lives here, so I took the liberty of labeling a few things."

I moved forward silently to read the large label on the master bedroom door, *Our Room*. Swallowing a sob, I explored further, finding each closet labeled *his* and *hers*, a drawer marked *Giselle's sexy underwear* and another *fishing attire* in Sinclair's neat, sloping script. A sticky note on the main wall was a placeholder for a yet-untitled work of art by Giselle Moore. *I want to sleep beneath your art*—read the caption.

Crying now, I left the bedroom to explore the rest of the floor. The guest bedroom was equipped with a list of approved guests—Cage, Seb, Cosima, Brenna, Santiago, and Katarina but under *no* circumstances Stefan Kilos. There were random red sticky notes on floor-length glass windows, in closets, on the glass elevator doors, and the banister that merely promised *sex here*. I laughed wetly through my tears, aware that Sinclair was following me at a respectful distance. He would be nervous, but of course, he put my feelings first.

God, I loved him.

And that was before I stepped in front of the other bedroom's closed door and frowned at the lack of a label.

"I wanted to explain this one before we went inside," Sin said from behind me, close enough to touch but deliberately avoiding it.

"I want you to understand that this isn't me trying to rush you into anything. Honest to fucking God, I didn't even know if we would survive the night. This is me showing you what I've had a hard time telling you, what I've never had to tell anyone before. I love you, Elle. I love you like there is a second heart inside my chest that beats just for you."

One of his cool hands found my hip while the other pushed open the door before us. I held my breath as we took three steps in tandem into the room.

A purple sticky note on the wall opposite us read—*baby's room?*

I felt my body light up like a flare, leaving only my heart bloody and beating loudly on a pile of ash on the floor. All thought, all reservations, fell away as if they had never subsisted, and all I felt was shock and awe.

"We are going to be faced with a lot of acrimony for making the decision to be together, but I know we can get through it. And on the other side of all those obstacles is a future where we belong to each other, and we can have whatever life we want together. *Mon amour pour toi est plus grand que le monde.*"

My love for you is bigger than the world.

It was. Our love was something colossal, so heavy and uncompromising that it ground to dust everything that stood before it. It had its own gravitational force, wrote its own law of physics and code of morality. It was separate from anything that had ever existed before us and would ever exist after.

How could I ever have thought it possible to walk away from him?

I walked over to the wall and gently unpeeled the sticky note, folding it before putting it in my pocket. Sinclair watched me, his anxiety like static in the air. My Frenchman wasn't used to giving up power, and I loved that he was doing it for me.

My feet carried me back to him as if on a cloud. I placed my hand firmly over his heart, felt the quick patter of his pulse, and smiled up at him.

"Too much?" he asked with a wry twist of his lips.

I canted my hips against him, moved his arms around my waist so that he was holding me. "Never."

"I want to move in immediately," he warned, but his hands clamped over my hips and pressed me closer against him.

"Yes," I agreed, licking at the pulse that was beginning to throb in his neck.

He groaned. "Should we christen our new bedroom, my siren?"

"Isn't Meagan downstairs?"

He leaned back to look at me with cold, demanding eyes. "Does that matter?"

I shivered in anticipation. "No, sir."

"Good girl."

I WANTED TO SPEND THE NIGHT IN OUR NEW APARTMENT, BUT WE DIDN'T EVEN have a bed yet. Sinclair convinced me to go back to the St. Regis, but he promised me we could move in the very next week as long as I was okay with his interior designer decorating the place for us to expedite things. I'd never had my own home before, so I was eager to leave my stamp on things, but I understood Sin's desire to rush. Having a permanent place of our own lent our precariously placed relationship a stability that we both desperately wanted. So, Sin sent me Emma Meyers' email, and we were already communicating about color schemes and designs. I took a liking to her immediately, especially as she was originally from London and understood my desire for a European-style home.

I looked up from the screen of my phone, drawn by the feeling of Sin's eyes on me. He stared at me from over the thin sheets of *The New York Times*, his eyes aglow with love and the morning light filtering in through the windows. Even though we were in the States again, we still tried to have a coffee together every morning before heading our separate ways.

"What are you staring at?" I asked, playfully annoyed.

"The love of my life."

Heat suffused my cheeks. "Has anyone ever told you that you're almost unbearably romantic?"

He reached across the little table and brought my hand to his lips. I gasped when he bit one of my knuckles and then gently laved it. "I am unbearably greedy. I have finally captured my siren, and I have no desire to let her go."

I laughed, my heavy heart lightening under the bright light of his attention. "Careful, or you will spoil me."

"Count on it," he said with a wink as I got up to rummage through my tote bag for my birth control.

He watched me intently as I popped one in my mouth and swallowed it. I narrowed my eyes at him in question, but he only shrugged one shoulder before returning to the paper.

It wasn't until I sat down again and plopped my feet in his lap that he asked, "You really like the apartment?"

"I love it. In fact, I'm going to spend the morning at the gallery and then head over to meet Emma this afternoon. Are you sure you want me to go full steam ahead on the decorating?"

"Absolutely. Carte blanche as well."

"Sin..."

"I won't argue about this. It will be the home of our future children one day, yes? So, it must be perfect. I'll leave my card on the counter, and I insist you use it for everything. Later today, I'll arrange it so you can have a card in your name on the account."

Something fluttered in my belly, but I bit my lip to quell the questions that bubbled up inside me. I had been so certain Sin didn't want kids. Wasn't it one of the reasons he and Elena were so ill-suited?

The buzz of Sinclair's phone disturbed me from my thoughts, and I watched distractedly as he answered. My Frenchman never really stopped working. It wasn't unusual for him to take calls at all times of the day and spend extra hours on the site of his new project. It was no wonder that he and Elena had made such a good pairing when she spent eighty-plus hours at the law firm each week. Sinclair was sensitive to my mood, and I could sense his apprehension whenever he took a call or came home too late for dinner, but there was no reason for it. I enjoyed his work ethic and single-minded intensity; they were two of the qualities that he had applied so ceaselessly to his relationship with me. My showing was in less than a week, and though I was close to completion, I still had two pieces to tweak before I felt secure in the collection, so I was busy as well, especially with the time we had taken off in Paris.

I *was* lonely, but it had nothing to with the amount of time I spent with

Sinclair. I missed my family with an acuteness that echoed like church bells from my heart throughout my body at every hour of the day. It seemed as though I had been chasing after the dream of a complete and perfect family since I was a child, poor and lonely in a dirty house abandoned by my father, sister, and brother, left only with a broken mother and a hostile Elena. But even then, there had always been hope, the belief that sometime in the future we would be reunited and peaceful again.

I'd eradicated that future like a bug beneath my heel.

"Stop with the baseless accusations, Paulson," Sinclair bit out, standing up abruptly and slamming his hand down on the table.

My head snapped toward him as he began to pace through the small living area of the suite.

"I did no such fucking thing, and you know it. We have been business associates for years. I have known about your proclivities, and you mine for *years*. I would have nothing to gain and everything to lose from telling the press—"

He cursed under his breath in French and tugged a hand through his overlong hair. I bit my lip as I watched him, apprehension crawling over my skin like a dozen spiders. Suddenly, he stormed back toward the table and slapped open the paper he had been reading to the society section. I caught a glimpse of the name Paulson, and a portrait of both husband and wife before Sinclair's hand crumpled it up under his fist.

"Believe me, Paulson. I will get to the bottom of this. Give me forty-eight hours." He gritted his teeth and hissed an exhale through his clenched teeth. "Fine. Thirty-six hours then."

He shut off the phone, threw it to the table, and watched as it skittered across the glossed surface before falling to the floor.

"Fuck," he roared, roughly pulling both hands through his hair.

I remained quiet while he reined in his anger. I'd never seen him so frustrated, and I wasn't sure how to handle it. The relief I felt when he finally turned to me with anguish, and not anger, in his eyes, surprised me.

"Someone leaked the Paulson's BDSM lifestyle to the press."

My mouth fell open in a horrified O.

He nodded and dropped down into his chair with a loud sigh. "He's blaming my camp and threatening to pull out of the Dogwood Hotels deal.

It's a multimillion-dollar contract that I've spent two years securing. It means constructing hotels in four countries, including a casino in Vegas, over the next five years." He closed his eyes. "It would have secured Faire Developments as one of the leading development firms in North America."

My heart stuttered. "Who do you think could have done something like that?"

"Honestly? Not many people. I want to be furious with Paulson for accusing me of doing something so unscrupulous, especially when it's crippling to me as well, but I'm one of only a handful of people who know about what goes on behind closed doors in that house, so I can't blame him for not thinking clearly at a time like this. The man's entire reputation is built on frankly puritan values. This is devastating for him."

"And for you," I reiterated, reaching forward to grab his clenched hands. "What are we going to do?"

A slight smile pulled his lips to the left. "*We* aren't going to do anything, my siren. You are going to continue your day, spend the morning at our home, work on your art, and visit your sister, and I promise to be in a better mood when I next see you."

I pursed my lips, but I understood. "Probably not tonight."

"No, probably not. I can't rest until I figure this out." His eyes pleaded with me to understand, and I could see by the grinding of his teeth that he was anxious to be off on the hunt.

I cupped his tense cheek, leaning forward to kiss the muscle jumping in his jaw. "*Bonne chance, mon chasseur.*"

He smiled tightly but pressed a firm kiss to my lips before he took off, his phone already to his ear as he barked orders to Margot.

I tried not to despair of our run of bad luck as I downed the rest of my now cold coffee and pushed away from the table to get ready for the day.

I decided to stop at Cosima's apartment first. Hades was still there after all, and the poor cat needed some food and affection. I felt the echo of my sister's vibrant spirit the moment I opened the door. The lingering scent of her, rich honey and warm spices, made my eyes tear but in a good way. I knew she would recover from this, not only because I needed her to and she had never before let me down, but also because she was the best and strongest person I knew. She could pull through anything, even a coma.

Hades squawked at me, tripping me up as I retrieved his food from the cupboard and set some down for him in a clean bowl. While he ate, I sorted through the mail piled up on the kitchen counter, dividing them into urgent and non-pressing piles for both Cosima and myself.

I frowned when I came across an envelope with my name written in vaguely familiar script across the front with no return address, no postage stamp. With a sense of increasing premonition, I extracted the letter folded inside. Most of the page was blank but for a few words written in red pen.

I've found you again, mia cara.

Something gentle pressed against my shoulder and I screamed, the paper falling from my hand as I spun to face the intruder. It took my panicked brain a moment to realize that the person I thought would be standing there, the same person I was almost sure had written the letter, was actually Dante.

It took me a second more to absorb the fact that he was standing in my sister's kitchen wearing nothing but an indecently tight pair of white boxer briefs that fought valiantly to contain a morning erection.

I looked up at him with wide eyes and stuttered, "What, what are you doing here?"

He frowned at me. The left side of his thick head of dark hair was sticking up from sleeping on it funny, disturbing the overall effect of his intimidating stature. I focused on that instead of his absurdly defined body. Lord, the man must have worked out religiously.

"Hades."

"Excuse me?" I blinked.

He gestured at the still feasting cat. "Cosima would have wanted someone to care for Hades. I figured that I would stay here until she was well."

"Huh, you just figured that? And how did you get up here exactly?" There was a doorman, a key fob for the elevator, and another key needed to enter the apartment.

He grinned rakishly. "I have my ways."

I narrowed my eyes at him, absently noting that my primary fear had dissipated. Dante was a big, scary man, there was no hiding that, but after seeing his love for Cosima, it was impossible to think he would truly bring me harm.

He chuckled, rubbing at his bare stomach. I tried again not to notice that he had something like a twelve-pack going on down there. "She gave me a key when she bought the place."

"She trusts you."

I'd had every reason to believe that before this revelation, but Cosima believed her home was sanctuary, and she would never allow anyone less than family to harbor a key. My eyes skirted the long, cut man in front of me with a new appreciation. What had this scary man done to make my sister love him?

"*Si.*"

I shook my head. "I want to apologize for my family yesterday and for my reaction just now. Cosima is just usually so open with us about every-thing. It's difficult to imagine that she would have kept something, *someone*, like you hidden."

Dante stared at me intently, his eyes huge and entirely black. I wanted to shiver, to tear my gaze from his and flee the apartment, but I stayed still, letting him take his measure. Before everything with Sinclair, I may have cowered, but he had made me stronger and now I relished Dante's scrutiny, even if he did see the immoral stain of my affair on my skin.

"Your sister has kept dark secrets from you all your life," he finally said, his voice a beautiful mixture of British and Italian.

He sighed, gesturing for me to take a stool at the counter as if this was his home and not mine. Despite his arrogance, I did take a seat because I could tell he was about to open up to me.

He walked over to the wall where two of my paintings were propped. I watched as he ran a finger down the edge of one canvas, the one of the dark-haired woman bound in a shibari-style by ropes of her own hair.

"Cosima would do anything for you. She has done *many* things for you in the past, things that she would castrate me for telling you, so I will not. But you must know that she has continually sacrificed her happiness for your own, for your family. She always had a special place in her heart for you, though, her *bambina*."

I smiled at her endearment for me even though the fact that he knew it made me shiver. How could he know so much about her, about our family, yet we had never even known he existed?

"Are you her lover?" I asked before I could censure myself.

I blushed when his eyes slid to mine with heated amusement.

"No, I have never been with her romantically." He laughed at my shock, leaning back against the opposite counter as if we were having a normal conversation. "I love her, but because she is *mia sorella di scelta*."

My chosen sister.

"We met when she lived in England. It is a long story, one that I have said before is not mine to tell. The only thing you must know is that she is under my protection." His expression was fierce as a warrior before battle, his posture that of a soldier. I had no doubt he could protect Cosima. The man was basically a heathen.

"Why should you need to protect her?"

He crossed his arms across his expansive chest but didn't answer.

I gritted my teeth in frustration. "Fine. Who are you to offer protection?"

His full lips twitched. "Now, you are asking the right questions. I told you before, you will hear about me. I am Don Salvatore."

Even though I had forsaken my country of birth years ago, there was something in my Italian blood that reacted instinctively to the presence of a made man.

I gasped, scooting back on the stool until I nearly fell over. "You are in the mafia."

He shrugged one massive shoulder. "I am in the business of money and power."

"Do you know anything about Cosima's attack?" I demanded.

His lips thinned. "There is no reason to share details with you. I am working on it."

I shivered at the raw threat in his words. Whoever had hurt my sister would pay brutally for doing so.

"My family won't warm to you, not when you remain so enigmatic," I explained. Not to mention, we all abhorred the Mafia, the men who had so ceaselessly stalked us in Italy. My fear was warranted, and I was grateful for it. A naïve person might have seen the threat of violence, the money, and the power as glamorous, but I knew it only meant death.

I shuddered.

"Your safety comes before everything else. Cosima would want that," he countered.

He was right, so I didn't argue with him. Instead, I decided to trust in his ability to get to the bottom of Cosima's accident. No matter his motivation, it was obvious that he loved Cosima and that he was ruthless, a mafia man with the same soulless eyes I had seen so many times around the house in Naples.

Which reminded me of the letter I had let slip from my fingers. I searched the ground for it, spotting it just beside Dante's feet. My gaze drew his to it, and before I could move, the paper was between his fingers. He glowered at it.

"Who wrote this to you?"

I bit my lip, unwilling to tell him. Even though I had my deep suspicions, I didn't want them to be true. I'd left Paris to escape, and I deeply wanted to refuse the idea that he could have found me so quickly again. I closed my eyes, though, because I had been incredibly incautious about the publicity for my upcoming show. Though I had changed my name to Giselle Moore in hopes of creating a new identity, my cover had been blown when he found me in Paris.

"Giselle," Dante called me back to reality. "Who wrote this?"

"A man," I said, unhelpfully.

A man who has been stalking me for the last four years.

"Christopher?"

My eyes snapped to his. "How do you know about him?"

"Your sister. She told me a little about him. This is the man who abused you, *si*?" His eyes sparked with anger and the hand that held the letter shook with tension.

"I don't like to talk about it."

"Well, you bloody hell should talk about it to someone," he bit out, his British accent more pronounced. "Does your man know that this sociopath is back in your life?"

"It may not be him," I countered, but there was a sinking feeling in my gut as I remembered the odd candid photo of myself that had been sent to me, the feeling that I'd been having of being followed.

When Christopher had found me in Paris, he had confronted me right away. It seemed that now we were playing an extended game of cat and mouse.

I watched Hades pounce on an imaginary foe on the carpet in the kitchen and swallowed thickly. It was only a matter of time before Christopher confronted me again. I couldn't imagine what he was waiting for, but whatever it was couldn't have been good.

Dante watched me while I digested this before finally shaking his head. "You need to tell your man about this, immediately. Call him while I change. Were you planning on going to the hospital today?" I nodded. "Good, I will escort you."

He stalked off into Cosima's bedroom.

I desperately didn't want to call Sinclair. He was dealing with so much already with the Paulson scandal, and I was pretty sure I could handle things on my own. Christopher was a sick, twisted man, but he wasn't a murderer. He wouldn't rape and pillage me. Besides, now that I knew he was back, I would take extra precautions to stay in a group or on busy streets. He wouldn't approach me unless I was alone. There was no reason to make Sinclair crazy with worry over it.

Happy with my decision, I slipped off my stool and had my coat on by the time Dante came out dressed to leave.

"You informed him?" he asked me with dark, narrowed eyes.

The expression was meant to be intimidating, but I'd had practice with mafia men far more scary than him, so I was able to smile casually and nod.

"Good. Let me know whenever you want to go to the hospital, and I will escort you, okay? No need to take unnecessary risks. One Lombardi in the hospital is enough."

I nodded mutely but couldn't help but frown at the contradictory man who opened the door to lead me out of the apartment. Dante was clearly a devoted and passionate man to those he loved, yet he was a self-proclaimed made man, which made him any combination of murderer, thief, and liar. What role could he possibly have played in my sister's life?

Chapter Fifteen

Giselle

I didn't see Sinclair for the next three days.

He had warned me that he was a workaholic, that he often spent weekends and evenings sequestered in his office high above the city. I tried not to remember the part where he told me it would be different once we were together. It wasn't fair of me to be angry with him, not when he was working on saving a deal that he had lusted after for years, not when our relationship was the reason for its currently precarious position.

But I missed him. It was lonely living in a hotel room in a city that had become my home, without my family to comfort me. I had made my decision to put Sinclair first. I didn't regret it, but my isolation highlighted my change in circumstances like a neon pen. Though he texted, I found myself worrying about our longevity, if we could withstand everything coming at us in droves, and about his stance on BDSM, if he would waver without frequent scenes and fall into shame again.

To make matters worse, my pill pack had disappeared again even though I ransacked the suite looking for it. I made an appointment with the doctor to get another one, but I considered switching to an IUD or a contraception shot given my recent bouts of forgetfulness. I didn't worry Sinclair about it because I didn't think it was cause for worry. I had missed one or two pills in Paris without consequences. Sinclair didn't really want kids or marriage or the white picket fence, and I was okay with that. I'd never had the same longing that my sisters did for children of my own, but I was fully prepared to rock the cool aunt role.

I threw myself into furnishing our new apartment to take my mind off everything. Armed with Sinclair's black AMEX, Emma Meyer's professional opinion, and way too much angsty energy, I hit the best of New York's stores. Though we had already purchased a variety of things online or through Emma's connections with auction houses, warehouses, and antique stores, it was fun and somehow mandatory to touch most of what would be in my home before I bought it. We were searching for a French provincial style sofa to match the coffee table we had found at Jung Lee's when my phone rang.

"Giselle," Sinclair said in greeting.

The one word was laden with meaning; his longing and the relief he felt at being able to talk to me, his continued frustration at the collapsing Paulson deal, and his resulting bone-deep exhaustion.

My heart ached for him.

"Sin," I said, infusing the one syllable with the very same love and yearning I'd sensed in his voice.

He sighed gustily. "There, that is better already. Tell me what you are doing so that I can pretend I am with you, where I am supposed to be, instead of here in the office."

"Emma and I are still shopping. I thought it would be overwhelming to furnish an entire, *massive* house, but Emma has this system where she catalogs everything we've bought into folders on her iPad so that we can always refer back to them and make sure everything is copasetic."

"Excellent," he said. "We wouldn't want to live in a mismatched house. I cannot think of a worse fate."

"You're teasing me."

"I am."

"You miss me."

"If you only knew how much, you would be here as quick as a cab could carry you."

I bit my lip. "I've been desperate to do just that, but I worried that I would be distracting you."

Another sigh, this one short and punctuated with irritation. "You would. Especially as it has been three interminable days since I had you. No, the next time I lock eyes on you, Elle, it will be in a private place where I can take you properly."

A little shiver shot down my spine as I sighed in longing.

"That little gasp you make when I've been teasing you, and I finally dip between those sweet thighs," Sinclair continued in a voice that pebbled my skin and drew my nipples tight like a sluice of cool water. "I crave those little sighs and moans you make when you try to keep yourself still under my fingers. Such a good girl."

"Sin," I breathed, my thighs pressed together as I stood, helplessly turned on, in the middle of a furniture warehouse.

"Are you wearing a skirt today?"

I looked down at the dark gray of the raw silk dress I was wearing. It was a cold but snowless winter day in New York, so I paired it with thick black hold-ups and knee-high black leather boots.

"Yes."

"Good, when you get off the phone, I want you to go into the restroom, take off your panties, and put them in your purse. Then you are going to touch yourself until you make those little noises I like so much, but because I am not there to hear them, you will not come. Do you understand me?"

"Yes, sir," I whispered.

"I have to go, but I promise I'll be back tonight. Wait for me naked on your knees by the door at seven o'clock, *d'accord*?"

Emma chose that moment to return. "Giselle, I need you to look at this gorgeous loveseat they have. Neoclassical French. You'll die. And I know you wanted to wait to pick out the bed with Sinclair, but there is this huge black wrought-iron affair that I know you would both love."

"Ugh, Sin, I have to go," I said into the phone.

"Get the bed."

"Excuse me?"

There was a smile in his voice when he said, "Get the bed, Elle. I love the sound of wrought iron. It will be easy to tie you to the headboard that way."

I swallowed thickly as his disconnection cut off his smoky chuckle.

"I have to use the restroom, but when I come back, take me to the bed," I told Emma. "And is there any way we could put a rush on delivery?"

It was early evening before I got the chance to visit Cosima in the hospital, later than I usually went, so I wasn't surprised that someone else was there to visit her. I was surprised, unpleasantly so, by whom it was, though.

Elena sat in a chair pulled up beside the bed with Beau, her best and only friend. I hadn't seen him since my welcome back party in the fall, but previously, we had always enjoyed an amicable friendship. He was very beautiful, proudly gay, and had an insane sense of fashion. I didn't know what he made as a lawyer's assistant, but it was enough to keep him in Boss, Prada, and, on the rare occasion that he dressed 'down,' Lactose.

My lips were smiling before my brain could register that he was glowering at me. Actually, glowering was probably not a strong enough word to describe the absolute hatred that he emitted. It thrummed and throbbed through the room, making me somehow motion sick.

"What are you doing here?" he snarled even though Beau was a smart man, and it was obvious I was there to visit my potentially dying sister.

"Cosima," I murmured.

"Get out." That was Elena, her eyes still focused on our sister in the hospital bed. "You aren't welcome here."

I wanted to get out. I wanted to run out of the room, out of the hospital, out of the state, and across the Atlantic back to France because if I let myself be propelled by the sheer force of her hatred, that is where I would have ended up. Far away from her.

Her eyes cut my way blazing with inner fury, and I readjusted; not just far away from her. Elena wished I was dead.

She affirmed my belief by saying, "It should be your lying, cheating, fat ass in this bed and not Cosima's."

I reeled, my stomach tossed backward, my heart hitting hard against the back of my rib cage. My foot caught me before I fell on my ass, but only just.

The Mean Girls snickered.

I opened my mouth to say something without any idea of *what* exactly to say when a large presence at my back made me stiffen.

"Excuse me," an incredibly posh British accent ordered.

I whirled around to face the man, and my mouth fell further open. The man in front of me was even taller than Dante, some impossible height that was made even more astonishing by the fact that he was perfectly proportioned, not as deeply muscled as the Mafia man but close. That was where the similarities ended, though, because this man was not rugged. His dark blond hair was pushed back from his regal forehead like a golden crown, highlighting the aristocratic features that I honestly didn't think I could have re-created with paint or brush. He was so exactly symmetrical, so beautifully colored in tones of all gold but for the bright glint of steely silver at his eyes. They weren't black, those eyes, but I recognized in them, as they bore down on me, the same ruthless, violent capabilities that lived in the eyes of the made men I'd known in my youth.

This stranger was not a good man.

Elena seemed to have surmised the same thing. She stood swiftly, moving to the front of Cosima's bed to block our vulnerable sister from the newcomer. It was a beautiful gesture that made me feel better about her as a person and worse about her as my sister.

"You have the wrong room."

The blond prince—seriously, he could have been King Arthur reincarnate—looked down his nose at us. "I do not."

"This is Cosima Lombardi's room," I offered.

Elena dug her sharp elbow into my soft side.

"Perhaps *you* are in the wrong room. This is Cosima Davenport's room."

"What?" I breathed.

"Excuse me?" Elena asked harshly.

The blond stranger was completely unfazed by our horrified expressions. In fact, he idly adjusted the gold cuff link at his wrist and said, "The woman you are trying to hide from me is my wife."

Oh my God.

Oh my *God*.

Putain.

Who was this guy?

"Who are you?" I asked, my voice still breathy with incredulity.

"Her husband," he said, standing straighter, proud and so tall even Elena, who was tall for a woman at five foot eleven, had to tip her head back to maintain eye contact with him. "You may call me Alexander, seeing as we are family."

Still reeling, Elena, Beau, and I stood mutely as he walked briskly around us and took the unoccupied chair up against Cosima's bedside. He sat down on the very edge, looking stupidly big for the tiny orange chair, and immediately took her hand.

"My beauty," he murmured, his hard mask collapsing as he took in her lank hair, the deep bruises that were turning yellow over the left side of her face.

"Cosima isn't married," Elena said, the first to recover.

"She is. I was at the ceremony."

"She would never get married without telling us," Elena snapped, moving forward to point a finger in his face. "You are some *freak* stalker who has seen her in magazines and fixated on her. *Get out!*"

Alexander stared at her without expression. Even though I was used to Sinclair's immaculate mask, something was terrifying about this British man's blank face. Sinclair hid behind his propriety, his beautifully honed manners and perfectly enunciated speech both because he been trained to do so by his adopted parents and then because it gave him a degree of necessary separation from others.

Alexander was not wearing a mask. He truly seemed devoid of feeling. So, the way he stared at Cosima with devoted yearning sent shivers of revulsion down my spine. I wouldn't have been surprised if this man was a psychopath. Was this the man who had put those deep bruises around my sister's wrists when she had visited England before Thanksgiving?

His unfeeling gaze cut to mine, and I had my answer.

"I would say your goodbyes," he said quietly. "Visiting hours are over, and I am the only one who has been granted the choice of staying the night with her."

"Like hell you are," Elena snapped. "How do I know that you are who you say you are?"

"He is her husband," Dante said from the doorframe, his voice uncharacteristically low and subdued.

We both swung his way.

"They were married years ago in England. If you press him, I am sure he will show you the marriage certificate," Dante continued.

"What the hell is happening?" Elena demanded. "First you and now, this maniac who claims to be her husband?"

"Stop."

Everyone froze for one eternal second before leaping into action, converging on the hospital bed like a carrion around a scrap of meat.

"Cosima," I breathed out on a sob, reaching out to grasp her calf because Elena and Alexander both had hold of her hands already.

"Bambina," she croaked, her eyes barely slatted open. "Water."

Alexander was already tipping a small plastic cup to her lips so that she could sip. "Just a little bit, my beauty. You do not want to make yourself sick."

"I'll go get the doctor," Beau said before dashing out the door.

"You scared me," Elena breathed in a voice I hadn't heard from her since she was a little girl. "You terrified me, Cosima. What would we do without you?"

"You would survive," Cosima whispered hoarsely.

Elena's hand spasmed against hers. "No, I wouldn't. So much has happened..."

Cosima's eyes darted to me, and I knew she understood just exactly what had happened during her absence.

"You will survive," she repeated, giving both of us a slight smile.

"Everyone needs to leave," Alexander demanded with the kind of authority I had only ever felt before from Sinclair.

"We don't need to do shit," Elena cursed, clearly beyond her breaking point.

"Xan," Cosima scolded softly, tilting her head on the pillow so she could address her apparent husband. "You came."

His face softened, growing so handsome that both Elena and I gasped softly. He leaned forward to smooth her hair out of her face.

"I am the only one who hurts you, remember?"

I shared a look with my sister, completely disconcerted by the entire situation, but mostly by the increasingly-more-likely-a-psycho-than-not Alexander Davenport.

Cosima had no such reservations. She leaned into him and dragged a deep breath in like it was the first and only breath she had ever taken.

"I know," she agreed.

We watched them share an intimate moment before Elena cleared her throat. "Cosima, I know you just woke up, but what the actual *fuck*? You are married?"

"Yes," she whispered, closing her eyes and resting back against the pillow. "I know you are worried, but Alexander cares for me. He is here to take care of me, and so is Dante."

The doctor hustled into the room at that moment, bracketed by a small contingent of nurses who somehow bustled us out of the way as they went about checking out Cosima.

"You need to leave," the doctor, a stern man by the name of—no joke— Kyle Steele, demanded.

"I am her husband," Alexander said, throwing back his shoulders so that he seemed to take up the entire right side of the room.

Dr. Steele stared at him for a moment. "Fine, but stay in the corner. The rest of you, out."

"It's okay," Cosima assured as we stared helplessly at her. "I am awake now. I'll see you again soon, *si*?"

We both nodded woodenly, and though we didn't speak on our way to the elevator and rode down together, I knew we were both more worried about our sister than she had been even when she was in a coma.

Sɪɴᴄʟᴀɪʀ ꜱᴛᴏᴏᴅ ɪɴ ᴛʜᴇ ᴅᴏᴏʀᴡᴀʏ, ᴏɴᴇ ʟᴏɴɢ ʟɪɴᴇ ᴏꜰ ɢᴏʀɢᴇᴏᴜꜱ Fʀᴇɴᴄʜ ᴍᴀɴ, and even though I wondered absently why he didn't come closer, I was happy for the opportunity to soak him in after days apart.

All that thick mahogany hair was pushed back from his forehead but curled slightly around his ears, overlong once more and striking against his dusky skin, his incandescent irises. His suit was one I hadn't seen before, a light, luminescent gray that hugged his tall, lean form like quicksilver. I took a moment to note his expression, its blankness, and then to hunt for his little tells. His eyes were dark under heavy brows, his mouth firm, unyielding, and his stance strong.

A little shudder zipped my spine closed vertebrae by vertebrae until I stood ramrod straight. Because my Dom stood in front of me.

I had called him immediately after leaving the hospital to tell him about Cosima waking up with the strange addition of an honest-to-God husband at her side, and I had assumed that we would table the play for the night and talk about what was happening with her.

Apparently, Sinclair had other plans, and as I had grown wet the moment I set eyes on him after a long three days apart, I was rearing to go.

"When you finish undressing, go into the main room and sit in the chair positioned for you, close your eyes, and do not move until I tell you to do so."

My mouth was dry around the words, all the moisture in my body rushing to between my legs. "Yes, sir."

I shed my clothes on the move, so eager to have his hands on me, his voice in my ear commanding me to please him that my fingers were shaking.

The chair was in the middle of the small living room, and the other furniture had been pushed to the side, isolating the chair, isolating *me*, in the empty center. I took my seat with my pulse already pounding between my legs.

It felt like a long time later, but it was probably only ten minutes when I felt Sinclair's presence behind me. He loomed over the back of the chair, and I could tell his body was curled over mine, not protective and not threatening, just close enough to bear down on me with nothing but his presence.

"I bought you a gift, my siren. Would you like to open it?"

I was surprised, too aroused to immediately respond to the non sequitur. He chuckled as his hand appeared from around my back to offer me a large, flat, black velvet box. My fingers continued to shake as I took it from him and flipped open the lid.

My breath caught as I took in the large, blush pink pearls coiled within the satin. They gleamed dully in the low light shed from a lone lamp in the corner of the room, but I knew they were expensive, utterly beautiful. They perfectly matched the pearl collar I wore at my throat.

"Sinclair," I said, his name full of thanks.

He stayed behind me but leaned forward to pluck the strands from the case, lifting one long necklace and then another and finally, two more. They reminded me of the 1920s girls that dripped with pearls in Paris's hottest jazz clubs.

"I love them."

"Good," he murmured, finally coming out from behind my chair.

He was still wearing his suit pants, but they were unfastened, revealing the tantalizing trail of dark hair that led down from his naval. I watched raptly as he crouched before me, his lean muscles undulating. Gently, he took my left hand and wove one strand of pearls around my wrist while he began to explain to me.

"Really, these are a gift for both of us. You are such a lady, Elle, when we are in public, in your feminine dresses and classy accessories. It's fucking delicious," he leaned forward to breathe against my lips as he wrapped the pearls and, therefore, my left wrist to the arm of the chair. "Do you know how hard it makes me to see you like that knowing that you're mine? All that innocence and purity, mine to corrupt."

I shivered as he bound the other wrist to the wooden arm. There was no room for me to move, but the restraints, being delicate pearl necklaces, would be easily broken if I thrashed or pulled too hard.

Sinclair read my mind. "You'll have to stay very still for me. Can you do that?"

I swallowed hard. "What are you going to do to me?"

His eyes grew cold a second before his palm smacked loudly, though not painfully, against my inner thigh as he spread them in order to bind my ankles to each chair leg. "Is that how you address me?"

"Sir." I panted when he pressed his nose to the curls above my clit as his nimble fingers finished fastening me. "Sir, what are you going to do to me?"

"If you keep very still, I'm going to fuck this sweet pussy with my tongue until you come all over my face. And then, after I do it again, I'm going to make you lick yourself off my lips before I fuck your beautiful face."

A soft sigh escaped me.

"Would you like that, Elle? Would you like to give me your sweet cum?"

"Yes, please."

I was devastated when he stepped away from me, straightening so that he could take me in, bound with pearls to the chair.

"*Putain*," he swore harshly, his hand going to the hard ridge straining his pants.

My mouth dried up as I watched him stroke himself through his pants.

"Let me do that, please," I offered, begging already, and he hadn't even really touched me.

"No."

"*Please*," I tried again after I saw his hips buck into his touch.

God, I wanted him in my hands, in my mouth, even just against my skin.

His face hardened. "I just told you what I had planned, Elle. This is the second time you have asked me to derail my plans. Would you rather have my cock than come on my tongue?"

"Yes," I gasped immediately. "Please."

He stared at me for a long minute, and I was giddy at the thought of him giving in to my desires. I could already taste him on my tongue. His scent dazed me as he leaned over me, hands over my bound wrists so he could lean into me.

"Well, I do not want to give you my cock, and it's my choice, isn't it? What happens to this body? I control that."

A shudder violently seized my spine, but I stared at him through it. "Yes, sir. Sorry."

"You'll be forgiven if you give me that orgasm," he said matter-of-factly. "You have two minutes to give me what I want, Elle, or I'll untie you, leave you wanting, and I will jerk off in the shower alone."

I whimpered as he dropped to his knees and ran the flat of his tongue up the seam of my sex, parting my wet folds. He stroked either side of my slick flesh with his thumbs, his eyes on mine.

"Two minutes," he warned again.

Then his head descended, and his mouth was on me. There was nothing gentle or slow about the way he attacked my pussy. No, he fed from me, sucking up all my juices and driving his tongue deep inside me to scoop up more. When he touched my clit, he didn't play with it. He sucked it deeply into his mouth and even gently grazed the hood above it with his teeth so that I jerked against the pearls.

The only sounds in the suite were my heavy panting and frequent gasps and murmurs, and the incredibly erotic slurp of Sinclair as he fed from me. His dark head between my paler thighs was so sexy. I could have come from the sight alone.

"Sin," I groaned out, long and low.

"Such a sweet cunt," he whispered, his lips moving against me as he spoke.

He pushed his hands under my legs, curling them over my hips so that they pressed into the tops of my thighs, pulling me tighter against his hot mouth.

I gasped and my legs shook when he pressed his nose hard into my clit and fucked me with his tongue. Thirty seconds later, my body was drawn so tight, straining against the pearls so hard that I was certain they were going to break. That anxiety coursed through my pleasure-soaked system like lighter fluid, so when Sinclair reached a hand up to put hard pressure against my womb, and the other descended between my legs to drive two fingers into my drenched hole, I went up in flames, the stress of keeping still ratcheting up my orgasm until nothing else was in my head but velvet black bliss.

"Good girl," Sinclair said as I came down, his fingers sliding languidly in and out of my clenching sex. "Under two minutes."

His praise washed over me, giving me goose bumps.

He reared up from his knees to brush his wet lips against mine.

"Taste how fucking sweet you are," he ordered before his hand came up to firmly pinch my chin, and his mouth slanted over me.

I moaned against the silky, delicious invasion of his tongue.

He was right.

I tasted good.

So good that my pussy quivered with the aftershocks at the dirtiness of having the taste of my orgasm in my mouth.

"What do you think?" Sin asked me as he took himself away from me. "What is sweeter... your cum or mine?"

My eyes practically rolled into the back of my head.

Sinclair grinned wickedly at me, his eyes dark, dark, dark.

He stood and pulled his gorgeous cock out of his pants. There was already a bead of arousal on his crown, making my mouth water.

He stepped closer, and I realized that the chair was low enough to take him in my mouth without him having to bend his knees. My mouth dropped open automatically to catch him as he moved his wet cock like a paintbrush against my lips. I moaned as his hot flesh pressed against my cheek. He held himself there as he stroked a hand down my hair. He smelled so good, musky and male, edible.

"Does my siren want my cock in her mouth? You like the taste of cum, don't you? Yours and mine. Well, you'll have to work for mine. I'm not going to come in under two minutes."

I could tell he was smiling, high on the power he held over me, but I was too far gone to care. We hadn't had this in three days, and the submissive in me had been beyond nurtured since we got together. She had been spoiled. And she wanted his cum in her mouth more than her next breath.

I pushed all that desire into my eyes, into the single lush word from my lips. "*Please*."

His hand ran softly over my crown and then fisted hard in the hair at the nape of my neck. "Open wide."

I did.

He slid in smoothly, right to the back of my throat and down. I gagged slightly around his girth before I remembered to breathe through my nose.

"Now, stay still while I fuck you," he ordered as he began to thrust in a steady but controlled rhythm, using my mouth, using me to get himself off.

My clit throbbed powerfully, and my arousal slid down my thighs and pooled under me on the wooden seat. He fucked my mouth for so long that my jaw began to ache, and my eyes teared up, but I loved it. I loved how the drool spilled down my chin and how I had to fight to accept each thrust down my throat. The effort turned me on because I was doing it to please him, and there was nothing sexier, nothing more rewarding than finally, so many minutes later, taking the prize of his hot release on my tongue.

He kept himself in my mouth as he started to soften, and he looked down at me as he tenderly stroked my hair back from my face.

"*T'es tellement belle,*" *he whispered.*

You are so beautiful.

I smiled when he slipped from between my lips and closed my eyes to better absorb his compliment. They were still closed when he moved away and came back with a glass of cool water, which he brought to my lips so I could drink.

"Uncomfortable?" he asked after a few minutes of petting my head and feeding me water.

I shook my head because even though the pearls were tight against my skin, I liked the way they felt.

"Good," he leaned down again to look me in the eyes, and I found his were still delightfully dark. "Because in about three minutes, I'm going to make you come on my fingers and then again on my cock."

I smiled, so happy I felt high. "Thank you."

His lips didn't even twitch, but his eyes sparkled. "You're welcome."

We shared the moment before he right himself and his Dom mask was back on.

"Now, let's test how strong those pearls are, hmm?"

Chapter Sixteen

Giselle

I WOKE UP THE NEXT MORNING WITH VOMIT IN MY MOUTH.

I scrambled out of bed, kicking Sinclair in the shin as I did so that I could make it to the toilet in time. I emptied my stomach, but my stomach still roiled and churned like the sea during a monsoon. I doubled over the toilet, desperate to vomit and so nauseous it brought tears to my eyes. I groaned, long and low like a bleating cow.

"Giselle?"

I *really* didn't want Sin to see me like that.

"Leave me alone," I called, my voice breaking on the last syllable as bile flooded my mouth, and I finally began to throw up again.

I didn't hear him come into the bathroom, but I wasn't surprised when cool fingers collected my sweaty locks and held them away from my face, and his minty breath wafted across my neck.

"You should know by now that I will never leave you alone, especially when you need me."

I could only groan in reply, wracked by dry heaves. One of his hands rubbed soothing circles on my back. I rested my forehead over my hands on the porcelain rim of the toilet and sighed, exhausted.

"I don't know what's wrong with me," I said shakily. "I've been feeling so out of sorts the last couple of weeks. I think it might be the stress."

Sin was conspicuously silent for a few minutes, running his long fingers through my hair before tying it back in a ponytail. He prepared my toothbrush for me and watched while I erased the gunk from my mouth.

When I was done, I sighed again when he sat down against the wall and pulled me into his lap. His smoky scent surrounded me, as warm and tangible as his arms pressed against my skin. I gripped a handful of his shirt, tipping my nose up into the hollow of his throat to take a large handful of that fragrance into my lungs.

"Thank you," I breathed.

His arms constricted slightly around me. "Don't thank me for something I'm happy to do. It's my privilege to take care of you." He sighed. "I haven't been doing a great job of it lately, or ever actually."

"Hush," I said, mocking his habitual use of the word. "I'm the happiest when I am with you. This life... this life is only good with you in it."

Sin pressed his lips to my forehead and squeezed me tighter.

I laughed at his somber aura. "What is the matter with you, Mr. Serious?"

"A lot is going on in our lives right now."

"*Mais oui, comme toujours,*" I agreed because our lives were always dramatic.

"Elena still hasn't forgiven us and likely never will. Cosima is..." He sighed so heavily that I felt the weight of his breath fall on my face like a stone. "Cosima just woke up from a fucking coma, and now her never-before-seen husband has shown up. Your show is in two weeks and I don't know what the fuck is going on within my own company. It's a lot."

"Yes," I said again. "I'm well aware, Sinclair. What's your point?"

He maneuvered me quickly so that I was straddling him. I locked my ankles around his waist and sunk my fingers into the back of his overlong hair. He needed another haircut, but I wasn't going to tell him that because I liked his roguish locks. I smiled as the silky strands passed through my fingers, but the expression fell off my face when I looked down into his serious electric-blue eyes.

"Sin?" I breathed, nerves fluttering in my vacant tummy.

His beautiful face was perfectly impassive, but those too blue eyes flared with suppressed anxiety. He took a moment to gather himself before saying, "I think we might have another thing to add to the list. I only hope you think it's a blessing and not another tribulation."

"You're scaring me."

He nodded. "*Je suis désolé, ma sirène.* I'm nervous."

"No," I said with faux dramatic shock, "not the ever-unflappable Daniel Sinclair!"

A reluctant smile tipped his lips as he shook his head at me. "You are aware that I'm crazy about you, correct?"

"Correct. Now tell me what has you acting so strangely."

He tipped his forehead down to press it against mine. I swallowed the irrational fear that was building in my chest because I knew that whatever faced us next was no match for the two of us together.

"I think you're pregnant."

The bottom dropped out of my hollow stomach.

Sin leaned back to take my cheeks between his large palms so that he could properly scrutinize my face. My brain had blown a fuse, so I didn't know what he could have been reading in my expression.

"Elle?"

"Mm-hmm?"

The corner of his lips twitched. "How are we feeling here, siren?"

I blew a gust of air into his face. "I'm not pregnant, so I feel fine."

One red brow rose.

"I'm on birth control!"

"Because no one has ever become pregnant while using contraception."

Guilt seeped into my mind as I searched my memories, recalling how many times I had been forced to double up on the pill in the last few months. I wanted to blame the total upheaval of my life or even Sinclair, for being so distractingly sexy...

I choked on my exhalation and looked up at him with wide eyes. "You wanted this."

His eyes were clear and bright, unrepentant. "I hoped."

"Sin!" I shoved him in the chest and scrambled to get out of his grasp, but he only held me tighter to his chest. "You can't just *do* something like that. Did you throw out my birth control in Paris? What kind of person would manipulate their partner into getting pregnant?"

"The same kind of person who fell in love with their girlfriend's sister," he said with exceptional calm. "Before you get angry, let me ask you this; is the idea of having a baby with your hair and my eyes so horrific to you?"

Before I could help it, the image of a toddler with a shock of red curls and cerulean blue eyes appeared behind the screen of my closed lids.

"We would have good-looking babies," I whispered, mostly to myself.

"We *will*," he corrected me, running his knuckles down my cheek so tenderly it made my heart ache. "I want a little girl just like her mother."

I groaned. "So did I, but eventually, not now, not when Elena hates us so viciously, and our family is completely at odds. Not to mention that you and I have only been together for a few months!"

"Hush," he said.

I opened my mouth to protest, but his lips caught my breath, gently crushed against my own in a searing kiss that I felt all the way to my toes. I sighed into his mouth, surrendering to the craziness of our love, the inexorable pull between us. My hands locked in his hair and pulled him even closer.

He smiled against my lips. "Please, tell me you are happy."

I pressed one hand to his cheek, ran my thumb against the prominent ridge of his cheekbone. It still bewildered me every day that somehow this ridiculously perfect man was *mine*.

"You own the lease on my happiness," I murmured, reminding him of the night we had finally succumbed to our attraction and slept together again despite all the things working against us.

Our life wasn't easy, but that didn't mean our love had to be difficult too. As long as we focused on each other, I knew that I would live happily ever after no matter what happened.

"My love for you is greater than the world," Sinclair said, pressing his forehead against my own. "And I will feel the very same about our daughter."

"Son," I said automatically, my hand flying to my stomach. "I think we are going to have a son."

"Want to bet?" Sin asked with a raised eyebrow.

"Are you really going to bet against a mother's intuition?"

He groaned softly. "Is it strange that I am incredibly attracted to you, right now?"

I tipped my head back to giggle. "If I had known the image of me barefoot and pregnant was all it would take to pin you down, maybe I would have tricked *you*."

He scowled at me playfully, so I laughed again.

"I guess I need to make a doctor's appointment," I mused.

His silence was conspicuous enough for me to notice.

"Sin..."

"Mmm?"

"Did you already make me a doctor's appointment?"

He shrugged. "You haven't been feeling yourself for a while. It was just a precaution." When I slanted him a look, his lips twitched. "We have an appointment on Wednesday with the preeminent Ob/GYN in the city."

"Of course we do. Nothing but the best for me, right?"

"Exactly," he agreed solemnly, despite my sarcasm.

"You are crazy. Have I ever told you that?"

"Only a few dozen times in the past four months."

We grinned at each other, our smiles so broad that they folded the skin of our cheeks into hospital bed corners. Then we were laughing, laughing so hard that tears leaked from our eyes and ran down our cheeks. It was the first time I had cried happy tears in much too long, and I clutched Sin tightly, almost painfully, even amidst our mirth because the only thing that terrified me in this life was the idea of losing that, losing him.

It was the weekend, and Sinclair and I were in our new furnished apartment. Emma had worked absolute wonders, and I couldn't believe how beautifully everything had come together. Even Sin had looked pleasantly shocked when she had shown us around the apartment that morning. Everything was absolutely perfect, but Sinclair confirmed it by kissing my breath away as soon as Emma left us alone.

"This is absolutely perfect," he had said after breaking away from me. "The only thing we need to do is furnish the baby's room."

So, Sinclair had called Rossi and Eddie to pick up painting supplies while we laid out spare sheets in the future baby's room. Sinclair wanted to paint a mural together for him or her.

He'd caught me when I had literally swooned at the idea.

"What do you want to paint?" I asked as I came back into the room after changing into an old, paint-splattered pair of overalls and a pink crop top.

Sin stared at me for a second with heat in his eyes. "What?"

I grinned. "What do you want to paint for the baby?"

"I thought we would do a beach scene, like Cabo," he explained unnecessarily as he came over to me and placed a firm hand on my abdomen. "Where it all started."

"You are so poetic," I said with an eye roll to mask the fact that I wanted to cry.

He smiled softly at me before placing a kiss on the tip of my nose. "Should we call over more friends to help us? We could turn it into an impromptu housewarming party."

"That sounds awesome," I said, but he caught the glimmer of despair in my eyes.

Neither Elena nor Mama would come.

We wouldn't even bother to invite them.

I had tried to reach out to Mama a number of times since our conversation, but she remained radio silent, and I wasn't surprised by it. Of course, my understanding didn't soften the blow of hurt I felt each time her phone went to voicemail, each time something new and exciting happened in my life that I wasn't able to share with her.

It was hell, but not having my mother and one of my sisters wasn't the worst fate I could have been dealt with as far as consequences went.

Sinclair and the beauty he infused in my life every single day were a testament to that.

By the time the sun was setting on our Saturday, I had been further proven right.

Cosima had arrived on the arm of her husband, Alexander, both of whom had mostly kept to themselves because my sister was still recovering, and Alexander wasn't exactly a comfortable man to be around. She hadn't divulged much about her relationship with him, only that she cared for him and that she would give us the full story when she was feeling stronger. Still, it felt marvelous to have her alive and well on my new couch in my new apartment while the rest of us, Rossi, Eddie, Candy, Richard, Emma, Duncan, and Sebastian, all painted the nursery.

Sebastian had pulled me aside as soon as he'd arrived because we hadn't had time to speak alone since Cosima's accident.

"I suspected," he began, straight to the point. "It was obvious that there was some serious chemistry between you the moment I saw the both of you in Mama's kitchen the night you finally came home to us. From then on, it just became increasingly more difficult to ignore."

He sighed, his gaze cutting over my shoulder to where I knew Sinclair was arguing with Rossi over the type of music that should be played for a baby in the womb. They had been bickering about it for the last half hour, Rossi for classical, Sinclair for jazz, but they didn't seem to be running out of steam.

"He loves you," he said with another dramatic sigh. "It's always been so fucking obvious that I'm surprised either of you took so long to act on it. We both know that Elena and I aren't particularly close and that you, *bambina*, have always been my girl, but I just have to say, what is happening here, as beautiful as it is for you two and as happy as I am about it, it's a nightmare for Elena. I haven't seen her much, but I know she's hurting. Unfortunately, you did that to her. I hope that you can understand when you see her in the future. She never had any reason to be mean to you before, but now, well, I think you know she has a reason."

"I can understand," I said after swallowing back the acidic taste of guilt in my mouth. "I'm not mad at Mama for taking her side, and I'm not mad at you for saying what you need to say to me. I did a bad thing, and I regret so much that it hurt her but..." I bit my lip, and my hand found my tummy.

I had only known that I was pregnant for a few days, the pregnancy tests that Sinclair had gone out to get for me that morning confirming it, yet I was already so *aware*. My breasts were sore, swollen slightly already, and there was a tight sensation in my womb as it swelled with our baby. Sin and I had both already geeked out and bought nearly every book known to man who was written about pregnancy.

I had never imagined a man like Sinclair loving me, and I had certainly never imagined having a child with that man, but now that it was happening, I was loving every single minute of it.

In fact, part of me was sincerely convinced that I was the luckiest person in the world.

"But I have never been happier," I finished, looking up into Sebastian's burning gold eyes. "And I'm determined to enjoy it."

My brother stared at me, a war raging in his eyes. He had spent his entire life providing for me, protecting me from the real-life monsters that haunted our reality. Sinclair had now, effectively, usurped his role, and he had done it in a way that my brother had a hard time with. He was the man of our family and more a father to me, even though he was nearly two years younger than me, than our own father had ever been. Now, the man I wanted to spend the rest of my life with was also the man who had broken the heart of another one of his charges.

I went on my tiptoes and pressed my hand to his cheek. "I'm sorry to put you in this position."

He closed his eyes, leaning into my palm. "As long as you can tell me, every day, and Gigi, I am going to be calling you every day for a while now, that you are happy, then I will be happy for you."

"Thank you," I said earnestly.

He nodded curtly and cleared his throat. "Now, I'm going to go say the same thing to your future baby daddy." He looked down at my stomach and shook his head. "He sure doesn't waste time when he really wants something, does he?"

I giggled, "No, he does not."

Now, all of us were settled in the sunken living room, having ingested far too much Di Fara's pizza. Brooklyn was a gorgeous miasma of lights and inky blackness outside the massive windows in the clock face that sat in the center wall of the living room. The men were drinking beer, Cosima and I were sticking to tea, and the atmosphere had relaxed a little since Sebastian had his requisite talk with Sinclair, and Alexander Davenport had bent enough to join the conversation.

After hours of fun and work, the mural was shaping up to be extraordinary even though we had non-artistic people helping. At one point, Emma, Eddie, and Cosima had sat beside each other and started a Pinterest board for the nursery that they were determined to turn into a reality.

"I can't believe my *bambina* is pregnant," Cosima said now, her head on my lap so that I could stroke her hair.

She was still pale, and there was a long line of stitches on the left side of her hairline that was still an ugly red.

"I can't believe you are married," I half teased, half scolded her.

She closed her eyes. "Don't bug me about it. Gigi, I told you that I would tell you everything soon. I just want to wait until things are less volatile."

"What do you mean?" I asked with my hand paused mid-stroke.

"Can't we just focus on how beautiful this afternoon has been? Look at all the people who love you," she said, gesturing to the assorted member of my gang.

Warmth seeped into my heart at the sight of Sebastian with his tongue between his teeth as he read one of my baby books. Sinclair, Richard, and Candy were talking about an upcoming event for Romani International,

Eddie and Rossi were bent together over the Pinterest board they had created on my iPad, and Emma was actually flirting with the nerdy but adorable Duncan Wright.

It was a good scene, and it hit me hard that Sinclair and I had created this family for ourselves, this network of good people who only wished good things for us. I wished that Stefan and Odile could have been there, Brenna too, but it was enough to know that they would be there if they could. Cage was out of town for an interview on Ellen de Generes in LA, but I couldn't wait to show him our place and tell him about the baby when he got back.

I closed my eyes to absorb the beauty of having a home, a man, and a family for the first time in my life before I looked down at Cosima. She was staring up at me with pride and satisfaction.

"You just successfully distracted me," I admitted.

She smiled. "Good. You deserve this, Elle. Mama will come around, especially when she hears that you are pregnant. Her first grandbaby? She will be at the door in a second."

"I would rather you didn't tell her," I said.

Sinclair and I had talked about it, and I didn't want the world to know yet. We weren't that far along, and more, I didn't want to take Mama away from Elena. She needed someone in her corner that was assuredly not in mine, and I wasn't ready to take that away from her yet.

"You are too good to her," Cosima said, understanding.

I flinched. "I don't know how you can say that, knowing that I cheated with Sinclair."

Her eyes glazed over with painful memories as she tipped her head up slightly to look at Alexander, who sat with her feet in his lap at the end of the couch. He had picked up one of the baby books that littered our new glass coffee table, and he seemed completely absorbed in it.

"I encouraged you to go for it when you asked for my advice back in Cabo, and even knowing that it was my other sister you were hurting, I wouldn't have advised you any other way. I've known Sinclair longer than both of you, and I have never seen him like *that*," she said, pointing over at my Frenchman as he laughed loudly with Richard and Candy.

He caught my eye and winked.

I beamed back at him.

"See?" she said softly. "That is exactly why I do not begrudge you the affair or the secrets you kept from us for so long. Not only because you have that unspeakably epic kind of love with Sin, but also because, as you now know, I've kept my own secrets too."

She sighed deeply and bit her lip before continuing, "I have to go away from a while now, *bambina*, and I cannot say where I am going or for how long. I need you to be okay with that."

"I'm not," I said immediately.

"Well, then, I'll just disappear."

"That's what you are saying that you are going to do anyway," I pointed out.

She stared at me with those beautifully intense golden eyes until I was lulled by them. "You need to trust that I'm doing what I need to do to be happy, to be better."

I slid a glance over at Alexander. "Does it have anything to do with him?"

"Yes. I know you don't understand, but Xan is a huge part of my life. I would do anything for him just as you would do anything for Sin."

I closed my eyes, overcome with worry. "What do you want me to say to that Cosi? That I am okay with you disappearing with a man who I don't know anything about except maybe for the fact that he likes to seriously cause you pain?"

"I know that you and Sin don't exactly have a normal relationship," she pointed out with flashing eyes.

"He would never leave deep purple welts on my wrists," I countered.

Cosima lay stiff as a board in my lap, but her voice was soft, pleading as she said, "You won't see me again after tonight for a while. I'm not even telling Sebastian."

"He wouldn't let you go," I interjected.

"No, he wouldn't because he can't understand. I thought, hoped, you would at least try to," she said.

I sighed heavily because there was nothing else I could do. Cosima was her own woman, and she would do what she wanted.

"Okay," I said. "As long as you can promise me that you'll be happy wherever you go and that *eventually*, at least, you'll come back to us."

"I promise," she said solemnly, turning her cheek so that she could kiss that hand that I rested at her hairline. "Thank you, Gigi."

I leaned down to press a kiss to her forehead as there was a knock on the door. Sinclair and I locked eyes before he got up to answer it, but we both had a bad feeling about who may be on the other side.

We were right.

"You *fucking* adulterer," Elena screamed as soon as the door was open.

I closed my eyes for a brief second to gather my wits before I gently pushed Cosima's head off my lap and scurried to the door to be by Sinclair's side.

Elena's red face turned to me, and she shrieked so fiercely that spittle flew across my face. "You are the biggest bitch I have ever met! I cannot believe you are my sister, you spiteful, hateful shrew. You think that you can just take whatever you want, don't you? First, you take all of Mama and the twin's affection because you are so fucking fragile and pathetic that they need to waste all their time taking care of you."

She had stepped through the door and was stalking me, forcing me to move backward until I hit the glass wall of the elevator in the middle of the room. Sinclair was beside me, keeping a wary eye on Elena, but he let her get it out, and I thought that was good of him.

"Then you took Christopher and turned him into a fucking psychopath. He was good to me before you corrupted him. He took me to museums and festivals, he read to me, and so patiently taught me English even though I sucked at it. Then you grow those goddamn tits, and suddenly, he only has eyes for you," she sneered at me. "You practically begged for his attention, yet you go crying to the twins as if he raped you. Do you know what that made him do? Do you know what a man goes through when he is accused of rape? It turns him into that fucking animal."

"Elena," I breathed because she was confirming my worst imaginings.

"Yes, Giselle. Christopher couldn't have you, but he could have me, even when he didn't want me, and he *raped me for six goddamn months*."

My heart was beating in my throat, and my sensitive stomach was thrashing against my other organs violently. I needed to throw up so badly that my entire body shook.

"Elena," Sinclair said quietly, authority still clear but calm in his voice. "Please, take a deep breath, and let's talk about this privately."

I had forgotten that we had an audience.

Apparently, Elena didn't care.

"Finally, years later, I find a man who I care about, that cares about me. I get out from under the weight of Christopher, of that stinking fucking Naples and all that poverty, and actually make a life for myself. And what do you do? You show up and fucking. Ruin. Everything. *Again!*"

Elena moved forward so quickly that Sinclair couldn't stop her. She grasped my shoulders and brought my head back sharply against the glass wall as she shook me.

"He leaves you for me, and now Margot tells me that you are GODDAMN PREGNANT?"

"Elena, please," I said, trying to ignore the ache echoing out from the base of my skull. "I am so, so sorry."

"Elena," Sinclair said, his voice cutting into her so hard that she flinched a full foot away from me, releasing her grip before she could even consciously be aware of it. "You will not touch Giselle like that. I understand that you are angry, and rightfully so, but you do not touch a woman, your sister, or a pregnant woman like that, for *any* reason."

"Fuck you, Daniel. You are just as bad as that slut, and everyone is going to know it."

Sinclair vibrated with fury, and it was Elena's turn to retreat as he moved closer. She might have played at being a predator, but Sinclair was the ultimate alpha wolf, and her manhandling of me had caused him to shed his thin veneer of civility.

"If you think that you can come into my house and hurt my woman, physically, mentally, or emotionally, then you are just fucking stupid. We hurt you. Fuck, if we don't feel that regret every day. There is nothing to do for it but apologize but empathize. We have kept as far away from you as we can and allowed you to treat us, particularly Elle, with absolute cruelty. That is done now. I hurt you, Elena. It was me who did this and me you should be angry with just as it is Christopher that you should be angry with and not your little sister. Have you ever thought that treating her like shit for her entire life may have led her to this? Maybe she would have tried harder to resist if you'd given her any kind of love or warmth over the years.

"As it is, I'm fucking glad she didn't because she is *mine* now, and no one messes with her, not even you, not even if you think you deserve to. So, get out of our fucking house and stay away unless you can pretend to be fucking civilized."

His voice was not loud like Elena's had been or coarse with an excess of emotion. Instead, it was stripped of anything but cold, cold malice, and I watched as every word hit Elena like a physical blow. In the end, she stood shaking in the doorway, her eyes skirting over the entire space, over our collection of friends, including Cosima and Sebastian in the living room, before they landed on me again over Sinclair's shoulder.

"You took everything from me," she breathed, so broken that it was painful to look at her. "And somehow, I'm the bad guy."

I wanted to say something, but the bile in my stomach had finally flooded over, and when I went to open my mouth, I threw up all over the floor.

"Dammit," I heard Candy curse as she dashed over to me, holding my hair back as it came flooding out of me.

Sinclair appeared a moment later with a small copper trashcan for me to heave into.

"I think it's time everyone went home," Eddie said softly over the loud sounds of my sickness.

By the time I finished dry heaving minutes later, everyone but Cosima, Candy, and Alexander were gone. Sinclair scooped me up, vomit-stained clothes and all, and strode with me up the glass staircase two steps at a time until we reached the master bathroom. Candy had followed us up and immediately turned the bath on while, surprisingly, Alexander, turned the shower on.

Sinclair was busy undressing me, his jaw ticking like a countdown to another explosion.

"Sin," I croaked through my sore and dry throat. "It's okay. She needed to do that."

He paused after stripping me naked to look me in the eyes, his utterly haunted. "I am so sorry."

"*Mon amour*," I breathed, placing my hand over the thudding heart in his chest. "Please, don't be."

"Get in the shower, honey, then the bath will be ready once you've rinsed off," Alexander said softly.

He looked me in the eyes, not once at my bare flesh. I was too hollow to thank him for that, but I noticed it all the same. I nodded and stepped through the open door to the walk-through shower. Surprisingly, Sin came with me, clothes and all. I hiccoughed as he tugged me into his arms and pressed my cheek to his chest. I burst into tears when he stepped us both under the hot spray.

"Let it out, my siren," he cooed over and over again as he gently gathered my vomit splattered hair and lathered it with my honey-scented shampoo.

He moved me like a precious doll as he tended to me, washing and conditioning me before picking me up in his arms to transfer us both into the waiting bubble bath. He arranged himself behind me in the huge white tub and tucked both his arms and legs around me.

"I've got you," he whispered into my hair once we were settled.

"We hurt her so badly," I breathed, completely wrecked by my puking and the crying jag.

"We did," he acknowledged. "It was awful, but it is over now. You let her have her freak out, and she doesn't get any more. This life we've fought for does not include her bullying or her bitterness."

"Sin," I protested, but he stopped me with a finger to my lips.

"No, Elle. We didn't fight for this relationship only to have it poisoned by her every single day. We did a bad thing, a really fucking horrible thing to someone we both cared for, but *it is done*. We cannot keep retreading that path, or we will never be happy."

God, he was so right. I knew it, but it didn't seem right to be so incandescently happy when she was so miserable.

"We aren't good people," I said because I needed to acknowledge it.

"We did a bad thing," he repeated. "So, maybe we aren't the best people, but I do not really fucking care. I would rather be a villain with you than a good person with anyone else."

We sat in silence for a long time after that. Distantly, I could hear Alexander, Candy, and Cosima cleaning up in the kitchen.

"Where did Seb go?" I finally asked.

"After Elena," he explained.

"Good."

"We're going to be fine, my siren. Even if it was just you, me, and this baby, I would make sure that we were the happiest family in the world. But we are not alone. We just had a whole group of people happy to congratulate us on our new house, on our baby, and our new life together. We're going to make it through this, and I am going to give you a happily ever after. *D'accord*?"

"*Je te crois*," I murmured back because I believed him, even if it was hard to imagine it at the moment.

Chapter Seventeen

Giselle

I was beginning to wish that Sinclair wouldn't read *The New York Times* anymore.

"Fuck," Sinclair cursed as he slammed the paper down and reached for his phone. "Fuck!"

"Sin?" I asked, uncurling from the deep chaise lounge we had on our upper level deep.

We were drinking our morning tea—Sinclair had decided to forgo coffee as well in a show of moral support—and enjoying the beautiful late winter morning sunrise over Brooklyn. We both loved the dual view of the Brooklyn and Manhattan bridges, and it was the perfect way to begin every morning. Sinclair had made the pot of herbal tea, wrapped me in a blanket, and brought me up the stairs to present me with the only breakfast I could stomach, a thin slice of extremely toasted bread.

I had just finished, and we were idly discussing the party he was planning in celebration of my gallery showing in two weeks when something in the paper turned him instantly on to beast mode.

"What the fuck?" Sinclair bit out into the phone. "How the hell did this happen, Margot?"

I listened to the one-sided conversation with my lip between my teeth.

"And I'm supposed to believe you? Was it you who tipped them off about the Paulsons too? Bullshit, M, Elena showed up here last night fucking livid, putting her hands on Elle, who is fucking pregnant, as you well know, saying that you told her about the baby. So forgive me if I don't believe you when you say that you had nothing to do with the Paulsons or this new article."

I zoned out after that in favor of leaning forward to snag the offending paper of the little table it lay crumpled on.

Faire Developments CEO and son of Mortimer Percy, New York State's governor, has a torrid affair with longtime girlfriend's sister.

Okay, yeah, I could understand why Sinclair was furious.

The article went on to state some of the intimate details of our affair; how we met in Mexico, the subsequent reveal that Elena and I were sisters, our continued affair, and finally, how we were now living in sin in Brooklyn. It also mentioned that I was an upcoming artist with a gallery showing in two weeks.

"Fuck," I echoed.

"I'll deal with this," Sinclair said, suddenly crouching in front of my chair. His face was harsh with contained fury, but it was his eyes that slayed me, filled with panic. "Fuck, this is too much for you to deal with right now."

I reached out to take his head in my hands. "Sin, please, I am okay right now. It sucks that someone felt the need to out us to the press as if we are some reality program, but at least everyone knows now, right?"

Sinclair did not laugh at my lame joke.

"Honey, seriously, I am okay. It might mean that some people might not come to my showing, but I can live with that. I'm worried about what it means for you."

And I was, the Dogwood deal was hanging by a thread, and Sin still hadn't found the person who had released the information about Mr. Paulson to the press.

He sighed. "I think this will be the end of that."

"No," I said immediately. "You can't be serious? Paulson would really pull out of the contract because of *gossip*? Can he even do that?"

"It isn't only Paulson, but the investors he brings to the table, and they all follow him because they share the same sensibilities," he explained.

"I'm sorry," I said.

He leaned forward to press a hard kiss to my lips. "Enough of that. We aren't doing this to each other. I do have to go, though. I know it's a Sunday, but I need to manage this."

"I understand."

He nodded again and gave me another kiss, this one with tongue so that I was panting slightly when he moved away.

"Later," he promised.

I nodded and watched him walk away. I stayed in the chaise until I was sure I had given him enough time to get ready and leave before I got up to do the same myself.

IT WAS HARD TO FORGET HOW OPULENT THE PAULSON'S APARTMENT WAS, BUT the massive chandelier in the foyer seemed even bigger than the one in my memories. I waited there while Gus, the butler, went in search of his mistress.

I was nervous. It could turn out to be a massive mistake to show up unannounced and somehow beg for them to continue to honor Paulson's deal with Sinclair, but at this point, when Sinclair was so uncharacteristically resigned, I knew I had to risk it.

"Giselle, what a surprise," Terry said as she swooped into the room.

I couldn't help but smile at the sight of her. She wore her signature hoop earrings, and her huge hair was out to *there* in teased curls. It was still midmorning, but she was already decked out for the day in a leopard print blouse and black cigarette pants. She looked like one of the Pink Ladies from *Grease,* and I loved it.

"Terry," I greeted, still smiling. "I hope I'm not intruding, but I brought you and Paulson a gift."

Her eyes widened with joy before she could subdue herself. I watched her bite her red-painted lip and struggle with what to say.

"Oh fudge, I can't be mad at you. It's not like you're involved in this whole sordid mess anyhow, right? I mean, I told Pauly right from the get-go that Daniel Sinclair was not the type of man to play in gossip, but you know men. They get so *angry* and so *stubborn* that it's hard to convince them of anything."

"Trust me, I know."

She laughed her awesome hyena laugh at my dry tone and came forward to wrap me in her heavily perfumed arms. "I missed you, girl."

"Same here, Terry," I murmured into her cloud of hair.

"Okay, okay, before I get mushy and ruin my makeup, let us go get Pauly. He is just about to go into the office, so you have good timing," she said as she linked our arms and led us down the vaguely familiar hall to her husband's office.

"I read about the whole affair thing in the paper this morning. Horrible stuff having your personal life displayed like that." She wrinkled her nose at me. "Anyone who sees you two together, though, will know that it was no tawdry thing. Don't you worry, hon."

"Thanks," I muttered as we pulled up to the door, and Terry knocked perfunctorily before leading us inside.

When we entered, Paulson was sitting behind his palatial desk talking on his Bluetooth, and I had a *déjà vu* moment. He immediately hung up and glared at his wife.

"What is she doing here, Teresa?"

"Don't Teresa me, Pauly. Giselle is our good friend," she warned.

"A good friend who is dating a man who I am not certain I should trust at the moment."

"Excuse me, Paulson, but Daniel Sinclair is not the kind of man to play games, especially when they would hinder more than help him. He is intelligent and fair. You know him well enough to know that as fact," I said, my voice strong despite his glower.

When he didn't respond, I squeezed Terry's hand and let go in order to take the awkwardly large brown wrapped canvas out from under my other arm.

"I came here to remind you of his goodness but also to remind you that we are just as vulnerable to gossip as you, as evidenced by the article in the paper today about us. Sinclair and I live a BDSM lifestyle too. We understand and accept the sanctity of that kind of relationship, especially how easy it is to misconstrue. I'm sorry that happened to you, Paulson, but if I may, I have some advice. People know your secret now. The only thing you can do is hold your head high and *own it*. Otherwise, people will always judge you and do it easily because you let them shame you."

I waited a beat for my words to sink in before I placed the canvas before me and ripped off the front of the paper. "This is my gift to you, regardless of how you choose to proceed with Sinclair."

They both stared at the large-scale painting I had revealed to them. There were no faces, only the broad chest of a man sitting behind his kingly desk, his legs spread beneath it to accommodate the woman on her knees under the desk, her pert ass balanced on the knife-like edge of her high heels.

It was a subtle rendering of a bold power exchange. There was dominance and affection in the hand that lay on the women's shining dark curls and power in her submission as she serviced him, knowing she was giving him pleasure.

I loved it. It was one of my favorite paintings in my collection, but I wanted them to have it.

Finally, Terry cleared her throat and looked up at me with shining eyes.

"I always admired your work, knew you were freaking talented, lady, but this is beyond perfection. I couldn't love or appreciate it more."

I smiled slightly, but my eyes moved to Paulson when he cleared his throat.

"You understand that there is grace in such a thing," he said gruffly. "Beauty in it, even though I'm not a man who gets beauty much, 'less it's Teresa. This is a gift of beauty, and I will honor it, Giselle, just as I will honor my deal with your man."

Relief passed through me, making me shudder from the surreal thrill of it.

"Thank you," I breathed out.

"*Thank you*," Paulson boomed in his usual radio announcer voice. "Now, should we call that man and get him over here to share a celebratory drink?"

"We should," I said as Terry jumped up and down, clapping.

When Sinclair arrived, I was sitting on a gold brocade couch with Terry drinking sparkling apple juice while she had champagne. Paulson sat straight but oddly comfortable in an antique wooden chair that looked like something from a torture chamber.

Sin came immediately to me, lifted me into the air and planted a deep, long, wet kiss on my lips. By the time he pulled away, my legs were wrapped around his waist, and both of my hands were twisted in his hair.

"Hi," I breathed against his mouth.

His hands flexed on my bottom. "I love you so much. You have evolved into such a beautiful, fierce woman, Elle. Exactly like a swan."

I blushed like crazy under the praise and butted my forehead lightly against his. "I can be fierce for you."

"Evidently." He chuckled.

"Care for a drink, Sinclair?" Paulson asked, his voice tinged with humor.

Sinclair pressed one more kiss to my lips before he swung around to sit on the couch beside Terry with me in his lap. "That sounds about right, Paulson. I'll have what you're having. We seem to have similar tastes."

They shared a moment of meaningful eye contacted before they both laughed, Sinclair more subdued than the other man's bellowing chortle.

"So," Terry said when they had recovered, and Sinclair was nursing scotch on the rocks. "Who do you think leaked your story?"

"Unfortunately, it's not much of a mystery," Sinclair said with a wince. "Elena showed up at our new place last night because a colleague of mine discovered that Giselle is pregnant."

Both of the Paulsons gasped and then expressed their heartfelt congratulations, which we both accepted with a smile.

"She was less than impressed, and it wasn't the first time she threatened to tell the media about us, but I think it was the final straw," Sin continued to explain.

"Well, damn. I know it must be hard on her, but love is love, things happen, and family is the end all be all right?" Terry said, her nose scrunched again in disapproval.

"It could be argued that if family is the end all be all, then I wouldn't have done what I did," I pointed out softly.

I was willing to move past our indiscretions and wrongdoings, but I didn't want to forget them or underplay them.

Sinclair placed a kiss on my hair.

It was Paulson, though, who offered the best advice I had heard so far. "She comes around, or she doesn't. She's hurt, but if she had handled things differently, you all could have healed together, found a way through that didn't ruin your family. She chose differently, and that's on her."

His words settled the last pieces of sharp-edged grief digging into my happy heart, and I closed my eyes as they shift and smoothed out.

"Happy," Sinclair both asked and reminded.

"Happy," I agreed, nestled on his lap with people we admired, his business deal saved, and a baby on the way.

Yeah, I was definitely one of the luckiest people in the world.

Chapter Eighteen

Giselle

AFTER WEEKS OF NO COMMUNICATION, THE ESTEEMED GOVERNOR OF NEW York and his wife invited Sinclair and me for a formal dinner at their estate upstate.

To say that I was nervous would have been a gross understatement. My stomach rolled and bucked like a rabid stallion as we made our way through the beautiful country roads of Suffolk county. There wasn't anything left in my belly but a few saltine crackers Sinclair had forced down my throat that morning, but it was just enough to make me gag a few times behind my hand, hoping he wouldn't notice.

He did.

"We can still cancel," he offered for the twelfth time that day.

"No, we can't."

I didn't want the Percys to have any more reason to hate me. Yes, I had stolen their son from a perfectly adequate mate while I myself was just a bohemian artist with loose morals whose greatest asset was her breasts, but no one would ever love their son more than I would, and I was determined to make them see that.

"So stubborn, my siren," Sin scolded, but his hand squeezed my thigh tenderly. "I just don't want you to set unrealistic expectations. My father is a kind man, but he doesn't take an interest in anything outside of politics, so he will probably leave you be. You know my mother. She will be looking for any reason to speak down to you, to belittle our relationship."

My heart clenched. I knew he was right, but our love was still so new, so unbelievably unbelievable that I didn't have the emotional fortitude to weather much more censure. It was impossible for me to reconcile the moral *wrongness* of our relationship with the absolute *rightness* of our connection.

Everyone wanted to condemn us, and as a person who had spent her life trying to avoid conflict, to stay firmly out of any kind of spotlight, it was wearing thin on my soul.

I linked my fingers through Sinclair's and immediately felt soothed.

"We can do this," I said.

He ran a thumb over the back of my hand. "We can do anything."

"You are so cheesy," I teased, even though his words warmed me.

"Only with you." He shot me a small smile before looking back out the window. "I want to tell them that you are having my baby."

My tumultuous stomach heaved painfully. "What?"

"I don't want to hide," he said, mulishly. "We've done that. I want the world to know I own you, my siren. I've told you this before."

"Sin, I really don't feel comfortable telling your parents." I felt more than uncomfortable. I was terrified by the thought of it.

"When do you plan to tell them? When our child is two, twelve or thirty-six?"

"Don't be deliberately cruel."

"*Et toi?* I am not the one who refuses to acknowledge our unborn child."

Guilt and anger coursed through my veins like hot lead. I opened my mouth to say something but the sight of an enormous brick mansion secured behind beautifully constructed wrought iron gates distracted me.

It was exactly the kind of place I expected the Governor of New York and his socialite wife to live in, from the gabled windows to the perfectly symmetrical hedges lining the drive. As if I wasn't nervous enough already, my heart leaped into a sprint.

"*Putain*," I cursed under my breath.

Sinclair chuckled softly before parking in the cobbled driveway that looped around a central water feature. I waited, mostly because I was frozen with anxiety, for him to open the door for me.

"Giselle," he said, after gently helping me out of the car and pushing me back against the closed door.

His voice came to me like I was underwater.

"Giselle."

It was the warm stroke of his thumb across my cheekbone that stirred me. I blinked up at him owlishly.

He smiled tenderly. "You look beautiful, and I am very much in love with you. Have I told you that today?"

"No," I couldn't help but pout, drawn in by his unusual playfulness. "Not for at least twenty-six hours."

"Well, that won't do at all."

He pressed his body flush against mine. Even with the layers of silk and cotton between us, I could feel his heat.

"What I wouldn't give to take you back home and leave this godforsaken place. I would tie you spread eagle to our bed and worship you for hours."

"Why don't you?" I breathed, completely forgetting where we were and why.

A smile ghosted along his firm lips. "I cannot run away and hide between your thighs every time I am afraid of losing you."

"It's impossible."

"I know, I own and operate my own company. As enjoyable as it would be, I can't afford to go bankrupt," he teased.

"No," I insisted, hauling him even closer by the lapels of his ludicrously expensive suit. "*C'est impossible que tu passes ne serait-ce qu'un jour sans moi à tes côtés.*"

It is impossible that you will ever be without me.

That was my truth. As long as Sinclair wanted me, I was his.

He softened, wrapping me up in my arms so that my cheek was pressed to his chest and his nose was in my hair. I smiled while he drank in a deep lungful of my scent.

"Okay, my siren, are you ready for the den of dragons?" he asked.

I threaded my fingers through his and looked down my nose at him. "I was born ready."

I WASN'T READY.

The Percy mansion was the American equivalent to a French chateau or an Italian villa but without any of the serenity or warmth. It was like a mausoleum.

A real-life butler with a large mustache answered the massive oak front door. He immediately gave us a cordial greeting and seemed delighted to shake hands with Sin, but I was too intimidated to smile at him.

Sinclair smoothed his thumb over the back of our joined hands as we entered the main hall. Dark wood glistened beautifully from every corner, swooping down in a double curved staircase that framed the entryway. My heels wobbled on the plush Persian carpet we stood on as I took everything in.

I caught my reflection in a large gilt mirror to the left after I woodenly handed my coat to the butler. My cheeks were pale under wide anxious eyes, and my curls spilled like dark blood over my shoulders in the dim light. I was wearing a demure dress, thinking that the black satin and the high-necked halter would read as sophisticated. Instead, it flowed down my curves like an oil slick, highlighting the nipples that had hardened immediately from the cool air outside and the arrogant curve of my ass. The black made me look like a slut, not a lady, and even the pearls at my ears and the elegant pearl collar at my throat could do nothing to elevate my class.

Sinclair's hand found the skin of my bare back, his fingers toying with the long silky ribbon holding my dress together at my neck. "The only thing that will get me through this is the thought of unraveling you like a present at the end of the night."

I shivered and blushed fiercely while the butler pretended not to notice. It took me another moment to notice the faint murmur of voices floating from a room further down the left hallway.

My gaze flew to Sinclair.

It sounded like more than just his parents were there for dinner.

"Hainesport?" Sinclair asked in his dangerously mild tone. "I was under the impression it was just my parents, my girlfriend, and me for dinner tonight?"

The mustached Hainesport cleared his throat awkwardly. "You are mistaken, Mr. Sinclair. Your parents are having a small gathering to celebrate your father's announcement."

Sin stiffened. "Announcement?"

"Yes, sir."

"*Putain*," Sin swore under his breath.

He looked down at me, a muscle ticking in his jaw. I reached up to press the spot with my fingers, offering support even though I had an awful feeling that this night was already taking a turn for the worse.

"They are waiting for you in the dining room," Hainesport said, already making his way toward the party.

I looked up at Sinclair without masking the panic in my eyes. His own flashed with protectiveness, but he only reached down to press a hard kiss to my lips.

"Bigger than the world, my siren."

For the first time since he had uttered that phrase, I didn't take comfort from the words.

I followed after him with my heart in my throat, beating so strongly it threatened to choke me. The sense of doom I felt stalking after us made me want to pick up my skirts and run away, but I reminded myself that this was important. If I wanted to be with Sinclair, I had to accept this part of his life, the elevated, refined society he had been transplanted into upon his adoption. I wished fruitlessly that Cage could be there, but I knew he neglected his foster parents as much as they did him.

When we rounded the corner, we were greeted with the sight of over two dozen elegantly dressed guests. Sinclair cursed softly again.

As if drawn by the sound, conversations fell quiet, and eyes swiveled loudly to look at us. I watched with grim fascination as they cataloged my wanna-be-classy-but-still-slutty dress, the harlot red of my hair, and the hand clasped within my own.

For one half of half a second, they seemed perplexed. They were trying to reconcile past meetings with Elena and what they remembered her as with the woman before them now. They wrinkled their collective noses.

Had Elena always been so... garish?

Another second and they had their answer. I saw it in the tightening of their eyes, how the women searched subtly for their men and how they, in turn, searched my body subtly for further evidence of my curves.

This wasn't the up-and-coming New York City lawyer they had met and admired. This was someone else, and she was considerably *less*.

I tried to tell my insecurities to give it a rest, but their combined gaze was the definition of judgment.

"Daniel," Willa separated herself from the crowd, gliding forward in an exquisite icy blue dress that Elena might have worn. "We worried you wouldn't make it."

Sin's lips tightened at the passive-aggressive comment. "It's nice to see you too, Mom."

He kept my hand in his as they exchanged cheek kisses.

She frowned up at him. "You need a haircut."

I saw the smile try to claim his mouth and took pleasure in knowing it was because of me.

"I like it this way."

"It looks unkempt."

"I prefer to think it looks piratical," he retorted before turning slightly to wink at me.

I giggled softly.

Willa finally deigned to look over at me, her eyebrows prematurely raised in condescension.

"Giselle Moore, I wish we were meeting again under different circumstances."

"Oh? Are we commiserating or celebrating tonight?" I asked, deliberately obtuse.

Her eyes narrowed, trying to discern if I was being smart or not.

"I'm speaking, of course, about the fact that you are here as my son's date and not, as you are meant to be, as his future sister-in-law."

Wow.

I blinked, stunned that she had the audacity to just come right out and lay battle lines. My anger warred with exhaustion; I was so tired of fighting.

Sinclair, apparently, was not.

He stepped forward with his hand wrapped securely around my waist, and though he spoke quietly, his words were forceful. "This is the woman I love, Mom. If you love me or respect me in any way, you will treat her with the kindness she deserves."

Willa stiffened, a muscle ticking in her strong jaw. Sin might not have been her biological son, but I could see where he had inherited his arctic freeze temper.

"I mean it," Sinclair warned.

"Oh, I know," she said softly. "Hence my shock."

She studied me out of the corner of her eye, cataloging everything about me with the precision of a 3D scanner. I stood straight and tall before the scrutiny, secured in my confidence by the feel of Sin's hand on my hip.

"And my begrudging approval," she added.

My head snapped around to look at Sin's reaction, but he seemed just as mystified as I was.

Willa laughed. "I may not be the most maternal woman in the world, and I certainly cannot approve of the inception of your relationship, but if you rebelled against every single thing I taught you about morality and success in order to be with this woman..." Her nose scrunched delicately. "In order to be with you, Giselle, then I won't waste my time and alienate my only son."

The words '*Cage is your son too*' pooled on my tongue like excessive saliva, but I refrained from saying anything.

"Welcome to the family, dear." She smiled again, but it was wooden as she leaned in to whisper conspiratorially, "Next time, we'll go shopping together before an event."

Bitch.

I smiled demurely, ignoring the huff of amused breath from Sinclair next to me.

"Thank you, Willa."

She inclined her head regally. I could see clearly how she would have liked Elena. They both wore their artifice and insincerity like a string of highly polished pearls.

Without another word, she turned and made her way over to a small group that I recognized as a congresswoman, a prolific political advisor, and a journalist from the *NY Times*.

"*Merde.*"

"Careful, most of the people here speak French," Sinclair reminded me.

"As if I wasn't intimidated enough already," I muttered under my breath.

Sin smiled at me, but before he could say anything, a short man in a suit with his sparse hair carefully arranged around his bald crown approached us.

"Daniel Sinclair, it has been a very long time," he said while stabbing his hand toward us.

"It has. How are you, Mr. Carroll?"

My eyes widened before I could curb my reaction. Mr. Carroll was one of the most famous defense attorneys in the country. I knew this, of course, because Elena had been obsessed with the little man/big lawyer for years. It was her dream to battle against him in court one day and beat him. She had mentioned once that whenever she went into court, she pretended Mr. Carroll was her opposing council.

I imagined the shrill sound of my self-esteem rushing from the puncture hole in my confidence. How in the world was a poor artist from Naples supposed to converse with such a man?

Happily, Mr. Carroll took care of the job for me. He turned my way with a small but genuine grin that made him fair more comely.

"Miss Moore, it is my absolute pleasure to meet you. My wife and I have been deep admirers of your work since your second exhibition in Paris. I believe it was in 2013?

"Oh yes," I said, miraculously harnessing my shock. "It was my first nude collection." And this esteemed man had bought some of that work.

I tried not to freak out, settling on what I hoped was a demure smile instead.

Sinclair squeezed my hand in support.

Mr. Carroll chuckled. "Yes, I remember well. My wife is a good friend of Terry Paulson. It was she who turned her on to your art. I must admit, we bought one of your pieces at your last showing, and my wife was incredibly disappointed she didn't get to meet you. She will be furious that she missed dinner tonight."

I laughed, charmed by this innocuous-looking yet charming man. "You must give her my card and tell her to call. I left a few pieces out of the collection if she would be interested in a private viewing?"

His eyes widened comically. "I would have brownie points for *years* if I could secure that. We were looking at the preview catalog for your next collection just the other night and already put a hold on one of the pieces."

This time, we all laughed.

"Well, I'm happy to do it. May I ask which piece you bought?"

To my delight, he blushed faintly. "*Candy*."

He'd bought the painting of Candy Kay sucking salaciously on an over-sized red lollipop. I was proud of both Sinclair and myself for remaining sober.

"One of my favorites too," Sinclair said with a wink.

God, I loved that man.

Mr. Carroll grinned. "Of course, you must be incredibly proud of her, Sinclair. A man has to wonder what a gorgeous artist is doing with a workaholic, fuddy-duddy like you, eh?"

I snorted before I could help it.

Sinclair looked bemused by the comment but shrugged good-naturedly. "You can understand when I say she brought color to my life, Isaac."

He nodded. "I can, I can. Now, if I may insist, I would love your card, dear girl."

I opened my mouth to explain that I had left my cards in my coat, but

Sinclair beat me to the punch, pulling out his slim leather wallet to retrieve one of my cards. He chatted briefly with the man before he handed it over, but I was oblivious to the conversation. I was focused on the man who kept my business cards in his wallet and happily shared his love for me with almost strangers.

Everything awful in life was worth having this man by my side.

When Mr. Carroll had excused himself, Sin looked down at me with a broad grin. The expression slipped slightly, replaced by passion-narrowed eyes and tensed lips. His hand tightened in mine.

"Do not look at me like that in public, siren, or you may not like what I will do to you in front of these many eyes."

I swallowed thickly, tilting my head back to expose my throat, like a beta wolf before her Alpha. "I think I would like it."

Sinclair smiled down at me wickedly and whispered, "If you are a good girl, my siren, I promise to reward you for the tedium of this party."

A shiver coursed down my spine. I couldn't understand how deeply attracted I was to this man. Though, of course, he was absurdly handsome, and his tightly leashed control only served to emphasize the depth of his hidden passions. At first, I thought maybe the taboo nature of having an affair added an extra explosive element to our chemistry, but my theory was contradicted every time he touched me. We had been living together, however unconventionally, for three months, and the kindling that he had ignited within me in Los Cabos was only growing, now a raging inferno that threatened to devour all other rational thought.

Sin turned slightly in front of me, shielding me from the majority of the curious onlookers so that he could gently pinch one of my tightly furled nipples between two knuckles. "Would you like that?"

"Yes, sir. I promise to be a good girl," I breathed.

He smiled sharply and abruptly twisted my captured nipple so that sweet pain radiated through my chest.

"I know you are self-conscious with these people, but you are the color amid all this black and white bullshit. Do not let them take that away from you."

I bit my lip. As punishment, he pulled hard on my nipple, making me gasp.

"I am so out of my league here," I murmured.

Sinclair's soft chuckle stirred my hair as he pulled me against his chest. He gently kneaded my hips with his fingertips, every press of his fingers against the silky material of my dress made my breath catch. Even though I knew we were in the corner of the room and that most people could say we were inappropriately close to each other, my slight worry over what the guests would think only heightened my arousal.

"Do you remember that second night in Mexico?" He breathed against my ear.

"Mmm."

"I was hard the entire night thinking of all the things I wanted to do to you after Iago's party."

I panted slightly as his grip suddenly tightened, pressing me tightly to the arousal tenting the front of his trousers. I pressed a hand to his chest and felt the heavy thrum of his pulse. It was intoxicating to know that his heart beat for me.

He dipped his head low to lick a path around my left ear before blowing on it. "I want you to focus on all the wicked ways I will pleasure your body later tonight. How I am going to bind you to our bed and spend hours between your sweet thighs while these pert nipples strain beneath those painful metal clamps."

Fuck, I was panting now.

"I want you to focus on how you will beg me to let you come on my face, how wet your sweet little pussy will be when I finally slide into you from behind, your ass red from my hand."

"Sinclair," I moaned.

I swear I could have orgasmed just from listening to him speak to me in that voice like smoke and leather.

He chuckled darkly and pressed a sweet kiss to my nose. "Focus on that, my love. Now, are you ready? I believe dinner is being served."

A ragged groan tore from my throat, aroused and enraged by his flippancy. He only chuckled again and tucked my arm firmly in his to escort me to the dining room.

The room was absolutely gorgeous with vaulted ceilings that sparkled gold in the light from three delicate chandeliers.

"Wow," I breathed as images of *Beauty & The Beast* flooded my head. "I can't believe you grew up here."

"I didn't really. Boarding school, remember? In the summers, we usually went traveling. I still have a designated bedroom here, but I can count the number of times that I've actually used it."

"Still..." I drifted off, overwhelmed by the splendor.

Sin chuckled under his breath while he settled me into my seat before taking the one beside me.

"Daniel, darling, your place card is up here next to your father," Willa called lightly from the head of the endlessly long table.

Sin stiffened midway through sitting down. I watched him with curiosity as he moved away from me toward his mother. He stopped beside the empty chair at her left, dipped down to place a chaste kiss on her cheek, and plucked the place card from the table. Willa watched with vague surprise and amusement as he reclaimed his place beside me and switched out the name cards.

There was a rush of whispers across the table, but Sinclair ignored them. Without looking at me, his gaze sweeping across the startled guests, he lifted our clasped hands to place a lingering kiss on my knuckles. I blushed, but thankfully, everyone became distracted by the beautifully presented first course that arrived before us.

Sinclair was quiet as we ate despite the numerous attempts by other guests to chat with him, but I was happy to engage with the middle-aged matron beside me, a Mrs. Hastings, who regaled me with tales of her youthful glory days. I was laughing at one such story when I noticed Sinclair had stiffened beside me.

"It was the idea of children, wasn't it?"

I turned to face the young man questioning Sin. He was around the same age as my partner but boyish looking with his floppy curls and dimpled smile. I remembered his face from the news and magazines. He was the son of the New York senator and one of Sinclair's friends from boarding school.

"It's nothing to be ashamed of Sinclair. God knows, I don't see the appeal in spawning little brats," Liam Reed continued to say. "Deal breaker for Elena, though, huh?"

"Don't be stupid, Liam," a beautiful blonde said from the other side of him. "Everyone knows he left Elena for the sister." She inclined her head toward me with pursed lips. "Didn't you read about it in *The Times*?"

Liam looked vaguely surprised before he threw his head back with laughter. "You dog. I never would have guessed you for a cheat."

Sinclair was still and cold as an ice sculpture, his jaw so tight that I wondered if his teeth would crack under the pressure.

"Don't get me wrong..." Liam leaned forward to wink at me. "This one is a lovely little thing. But you can't tell me kids didn't play a role in it?"

I clenched and unclenched my sweaty hands in my lap, worried that Sin would say something and worried that he wouldn't.

I was right to worry.

Sinclair leveled his freezing glare on both Liam and the blonde, staring them down until they looked away nervously. "Marriage and family were never the problem, at least not with the right woman. Giselle, *the lovely little thing*, who has done me the greatest honor by consenting to be with me despite the havoc I have wrought on her life, is that woman for me. In fact," he paused dramatically, and I realized that the entire table had quieted to listen to his little speech, "we're expecting, and I could not be happier about it."

The silence that blanketed the room was so heavy that it crushed the air from my lungs. Sinclair reached for my hand under the table and took it in his, rubbing his thumb comfortingly back and forth. I tried to take reassurance from it, but the anger and shame that warred inside me beat it back.

"Sinclair?" Willa asked, her voice uncharacteristically soft. "Is this true?"

"It is," he confirmed.

I watched his face transform with a glorious smile, his cobalt blue eyes alight with pride and joy.

Damn, it was going to be hard to stay angry with him.

Willa struggled for a moment with the news. She stared down at her plate, blinking rapidly, before she looked over at her husband at the head of the table. He inclined his head at her, his smile gentle.

"Well," she finally said, "I cannot believe it. I'm finally going to be a grandmother!"

It was my turn to blink rapidly as tears rushed forth and spilled over my cheeks before I could help it. Sinclair tugged my chair closer and put his arm around my shoulders as he began to accept everyone's congratulations.

I decided to rest my head against his strong shoulder, smiling weakly at everyone as they beamed at us. Apparently, procreating trumped the shame of adultery, at least in the high circles the Percy family ran in. I was both relieved and repulsed by their congratulations, but after months of antagonism, I was willing to take whatever niceties I could get.

"*T'es fâchée?*" Sinclair murmured into my hair when we had a moment to ourselves.

"I'm not angry even though that would be justified." I scowled up at him. "How can I be angry when you are so excited for this baby?"

His fingers skimmed over my satin-clad belly and rested there, but it was his eyes, brighter than I had ever seen them—so blue that they were almost neon—that captured my total attention.

"I have never been happier."

I swallowed the sob that rose in my throat. "Me too."

"Sinclair, I would like to speak with you," Mortimer Percy said, suddenly appearing over our shoulder.

He frowned at his father and then me before nodding. "Okay, but Giselle is coming with me."

Mortimer stared at me for a moment before inclining his head in consent.

I puzzled over him as I followed them both from the room. He was a mystery to me in a way that Willa was not. I understand that the woman lived for her role as a matron of New York society, that she loved the power bestowed upon her as a governor's wife, and that, in her own way, she loved the son she had found and molded in France.

But Mortimer was a different entity, one that Sinclair didn't talk much about. I knew that he wanted Sin to follow in his political footsteps, and that he was charismatic and generous. But whatever his qualities, I knew that he too had used his adopted son for his own gains, and I would never forget my Frenchman's sadness as he related that to me in that little cove in Mexico.

So, I was wary as we all settled in Mortimer's office, a place of cedar, leather-bound books, and manly red walls. Sinclair had me sit in a chair in front of the desk beside Willa, who had followed us in, but he remained standing even when his father took his place behind the desk.

"It was you," Sinclair started.

I couldn't see his face, but I knew from the tone of voice that he had discovered something horrifying.

It took me about two seconds to clue in, so I was gasping when Mortimer nodded. "Yes. I was the one who told the press about Paulson's unique... tastes."

"How did you know?"

"You forget that I am the one who introduced you," Mortimer said simply.

"Daniel," Willa interjected when the two men just continued to stare at each other. "We didn't mean to cause you real problems. We just wanted to... give you a push in the right direction."

"Meaning?" he growled.

"Meaning, we wanted you to take your rightful place in politics," Mortimer explained calmly.

"You are kidding me, no?" Sinclair asked in his glacial way.

Willa froze over accordingly, her eyes wide with fear. I wondered if she was worried about what other people would think if they found out or if she truly regretted crossing the line and the risk doing so now posed to her relationship with her son.

"Unfortunately, no," Mortimer said before heaving a huge sigh and focusing on a point over Sinclair's shoulder. "I know we didn't go about it the right way, trying to manipulate you into following my path. It was wrong of us. I can see that now. But you have to understand; every single Percy since we settled in this country from England has been in government. You are my son. I don't care if we don't share the same blood. I wanted that legacy for you."

"That's so fucked up," Sin breathed out.

It totally was.

To his credit, though I didn't really give him any, his father nodded sadly. "Agreed. I know we haven't been the best parents—"

I snorted, unable to keep quiet anymore. "You have been *abysmal* parents as far as I can tell. And before you say that I have no business in this conversation, you are wrong. If it involves Sinclair, it involves me. You two made the deliberate choice to be his parents, and you have never done right by him."

"We gave him the best education money could buy, the tools to succeed in this life," Willa snapped, aghast at my audacity.

"I have no doubt that Sinclair would be successful even if he had remained an orphan on the Côte d'Azur. What he needed, what you promised to give him by adopting him, was love."

"We love him," Willa mouthed, her voice lost to the grief those words stirred in her. She turned to Sin with both her lips, and her eyes opened wide, punctured with remorse. "We love you. You know that, Daniel."

He cocked his head to the side as he studied her. "I do. But Giselle was the one who taught me how to love properly with my whole heart. You don't use your loved ones to better yourself in society."

"That is not what we did," Willa objected sharply.

"It wasn't what we meant to do," Mortimer amended quietly.

The two of them shared a long look before Willa turned to Sinclair with wet in her eyes. "Sinclair, my darling boy, I've always loved you. Since the minute I saw you on the streets in Nice, I loved you."

I watched Sinclair swallow hard. "Honestly, I don't really care anymore. I'm done with family drama. I have Elle now, and we are going to have our own family. If you want to be a part of it, you will do what you can to rectify the mistake you made in contacting the press about the Paulsons, and you will start treating both of us like family."

He looked down at me, and despite his little speech, I could tell he was rattled—both by the betrayal he felt and by their sincere remorse for it.

I took his offered hand and followed him to the door, but we paused when Willa called out to us.

"I just want you both to know that we are going to do better." She shot her husband a look and gathered her composure so that when she looked back at us, she was once again the immaculate society lady. "I want to be in my grandchild's life."

"Do better, and you will be," I said.

Sinclair squeezed my hand, and together, we left.

Chapter Nineteen

Sinclair

I WANTED TO MARRY HER. THE THOUGHT CONSUMED ME TO THE POINT THAT IT was affecting my work. Margot had caught me browsing Tiffany's website for engagement rings when I should have been in the Town Car on my way to the construction site on the Hudson River. She'd paused dramatically before suggesting that Giselle might prefer something more unique, an antique or something custom made. She was right, and the fact she had warmed up toward my relationship with Elle was enough to make me cast her a massive grin. Her shocked but happy reaction made me realize that Giselle was right. I didn't smile enough.

I knew I had to wait, though. Giselle wouldn't appreciate me asking when we were already going through so much, moving at a pace that would have scared the fuck out of me even six months ago. I took immense comfort from the fact that she was pregnant, though. The savage in me rejoiced in knowing that a part of me grew inside her. I'd worried she would be mad about the pregnancy, but the look of confusion giving way to the pure joy that eclipsed her face when I'd convinced her of it would remain with me forever. She had never been so beautiful.

I hated that she wouldn't let me tell anyone, though. It was fucking ridiculous to keep it a secret, especially given that she was probably three months along. I hoped that after our appointment with Dr. Adams that day, she would change her mind.

When I arrived at the office, Giselle was already there, curled up in a small chair with her travel sketchbook in her lap. I took a moment to watch her gently bite the end of her pencil as she stared into the distance at a place only her vivid imagination could construct. Her fiery hair curled over the cleavage exposed by the long wool dress she wore. My dick twitched in my pants even as my heart warmed at the sight of her.

She was so fucking pretty and so fucking mine.

As if she could sense my predatory thoughts, her eyes snapped to mine, clicking in place like magnets. A slow smile claimed her features, and I couldn't help but beam back at her. There were other people in the waiting room, but I paid them no mind as I strode over to my siren and fell to my knees before her, first planting a gentle kiss on her tummy before claiming her lips in a possessive kiss. My hand found her throat, my thumb at her pulse, and I squeezed gently just to feel her heartbeat throttle before I moved away to take the seat beside her.

She blinked dazedly at me before breathily saying, "Hi."

I grinned in pure masculine satisfaction. "Hi."

"I know I just saw you this morning, but I've missed you," she admitted with a faint blush.

Her words liquefied me. I reached out to gently cup that pink-stained cheek. "I missed you too. How are you feeling today?"

"The nausea is pretty bad. I thought I had a handle on it this morning, but I ended up puking in the Paulson's gold plated toilet." She made a face that had me laughing. It was one of my favorite things that she didn't take herself too seriously.

"It's normal," I assured her because I might have gone a little crazy with worry when she wouldn't stop throwing up one morning last week.

"I know, I know. I guess..." She looked off into the distance so that I couldn't see her expressive eyes.

I tapped her chin lightly with my knuckles. "What is it, love?"

"I guess I wish that I could talk to Mama about this. She's done it three times, so I'm sure she knows what to expect."

Fuck, she had the power to absolutely gut me. It was like my heart lived in her small hand, and her moods dictated its every beat.

I simultaneously wanted to kill Caprice for turning her back on her daughter and sell her my soul in order to bring her back to Giselle.

This love thing was so illogical.

"I'm sorry," I said because, at that moment, I really was.

"For what?"

"For being such a selfish bastard. I did this to you." I pressed my hand to her slightly swollen stomach.

"It takes two to make a baby, Mr. Sinclair," she sassed me.

She was so sexy when she sassed me.

"And thank God for that. What I meant specifically was that I deliberately hid the pills from you, tried to make you forget to take them... I really wanted this despite the timing and what it might mean for you."

I wasn't feeling guilty for getting her pregnant—no part of me could feel anything other than pure jubilancy at the thought of our child—but I hated how much pain my love brought her and how she had to choose me over everyone else she loved.

"Hey, hey now," she said, taking my chin in her hand this time. Her eyes were huge, a crystalline gray brighter than pure silver. "I won't argue with you about some of that. You should have just talked to me about having a baby; I had no idea that was even something you wanted in the future, let alone right away. And it is pretty bad timing. We just moved in together, and we are still so new..." She trailed off at the look on my face, and I quickly tried to resurrect my cool façade so she would continue her honestly, but it was too late. "It feels like you and I have been together for years, like we were always meant to be together. As crazy as it sounds, I think you and I are ready to be parents. We will make a perfect nuclear little family. It's the extended family that I'm worried about. I don't think Elena will ever forgive me for also getting pregnant with you, especially so soon after you ended things with her."

"Elle." I pressed her palm to my face with my hand. "I hate to break your heart, but Elena was never going to forgive you, regardless of this."

Tears welled in those beautiful eyes, but she bit her bottom lip against shedding them and nodded a few times to shore up her strength. I kissed the inside of the wrist holding my hand, then dropped our linked hands to my lap so that I could lean forward and kiss her sad-softened mouth.

She sighed gustily when I retreated. "I'll have to tell Mama and the twins at some point."

"You will, but you can decide when that is. We can keep it quiet as long as you'd like." God, but it hurt me to say that.

She side-eyed me before smiling. "How much did it cost you to say that?"

"Just don't make me say it again." My dry comment was rewarded with her laughter. I soaked it up like sunshine.

"Miss Moore?" We turned to a nurse in pink scrubs that stood with a clipboard before us. "If you could come with me, the doctor is ready to see you now. Mr. Sinclair, I'll come out to get you if you want to be part of the ultrasound."

"Of course," I bristled, annoyed she would even ask, that she would even consider barring me from the process.

Giselle placed a calming hand on my arm before getting to her feet to follow the nurse. "Be calm. I'll see you in a few minutes."

I watched her disappear through the door before I opened my phone.

"*Mon frère, ça va?*"

"What's with all the noise?" I asked Cage, wincing at the cacophony of sound in the background.

He laughed. "Give me a second." I waited while he moved somewhere quieter. "There, that's better. How is my favorite redhead?"

"We're at the doctor's office."

There was a long pause while he digested that.

"Okay, I am going to guess that she isn't sick. Otherwise, you'd be going berserker on me. So..." He burst into ruckus laughter. "You old fucking dog, you knocked her up."

I couldn't help my grin. "*Mais oui.*"

"Just when I think you've completely turned your back on the French, you do something so quintessentially francophone like knock up your mistress."

"She is not my mistress."

"Whoa, ease up. I was just teasing. If you tried to make Giselle your mistress, I would happily cut off your balls."

"You're a good friend, Cage," I said dryly, which only elicited another chuckle from him.

"How is she dealing with it?"

"It was a surprise, but she seems happy."

"*Bon.* I am very happy for you, Sin. You've got yourself quite the woman."

Pride sluiced through me; Giselle was the ultimate woman.

"Listen, I need your advice." I waited for him to stop laughing before continuing. "I agree, you're an idiot, but I need someone to talk to, and apart from Elle, you're family."

Cage cleared his throat roughly. "Any time, *mon frère.*"

"I want to marry her."

There was a loud whoosh as Cage exhaled in shock.

"This is a joke?" When I didn't respond, he blew a raspberry into the phone. "Wow, I am shocked. Daniel Sinclair wants to get married."

"He does. Tomorrow wouldn't be early enough."

He chuckled. "Okay, then I don't really understand why you need advice. Marry the woman."

"Her mother has basically disowned her, one of her sisters hates her, and the other just came out of a fucking coma, her brother is on location somewhere in the California desert, we have only been dating for a few months, and we just discovered that she's pregnant."

There was a long pause.

"Seems like a bunch of excuses to me. You want to marry her, then do it. When a man finds a woman like that, he does everything he can to tie himself to her."

Fuck yes. I knew if anyone could understand my primitive need to claim Giselle, it would be my best friend and brother of choice, Cage. Unlike me, he had never tried to civilize himself. He was happy with being a blunt, gluttonous badass even when people turned their noses up at him. Even when our parents did.

The guy had balls of steel, and finally, I felt like he wasn't the only one who did.

"I'll need you to help me pick out a ring," I said. "And I have an idea. It's crazy impulsive, but I don't think I wait to make her mine, legally. I'll need you to help me organize it."

"Done. I'm busy with the new album, but any time, man, I'm there."

I tipped my head back against the wall and let out a massive breath that I wasn't aware I'd been holding in. "*Merci, mon frère.*"

"She brought you back to you, Sin. There isn't a hell of a lot I wouldn't do for her, and you know there is nothing I wouldn't do for you."

I swallowed the stone lodged in my throat just as the nurse appeared in the waiting room again to beckon me forward.

"I'm about to see my baby for the first time."

"Damn," Cage said. "You're a lucky man."

I got up and followed the woman into the hallway. "Trust me, I know."

When I entered the small room, Giselle was reclined with her legs propped up and open over stirrups and covered modestly in a blue blanket. Her eyes were wide with nerves and excitement as they caught on mine. Wordlessly and instantaneously, she reached out her hand to me.

I tried once again to force that stone out of my throat and made my way to her side, linking our fingers.

"Mr. Sinclair, I'm Dr. Madison Adams," the older woman situated between Elle's legs smiled kindly at me after I sat down. "The physical examination showed that Giselle is approximately nine weeks along, but we will be better able to determine the exact date of conception with the ultrasound."

"Excellent," I said, giving Elle's hand a squeeze.

She was fidgeting in her seat, uncomfortable with her exposed position and very nervous. It was her nerves that concerned me. I'd been fairly certain that she was happy about the pregnancy, despite the shock of it, but seeing her now seemed to contradict that.

Before I could ask her, the doctor was gently telling us about how she was going to proceed. She lubricated the end of a vaginal ultrasound wand

and disappeared under the blanket. Giselle squirmed against the intrusion, her fingers cold between my own.

I leaned forward to press a kiss against her hair, and she immediately turned her face into it, searching for more comfort.

Two seconds later, there a percussion noise filtered throughout the room. I watched Giselle look at the monitor beside the doctor, wanting to see her reaction before I looked myself. I was thrilled that I did. Softness descended over her features, smoothing the frown from her brow and setting her lips into a trembling smile.

"Sin," she breathed. "Look at our baby."

My heart was beating so hard that I thought I might die, but I did what she asked and looked at our baby.

It was just a little thing, etched like a pencil drawing in black and white. I had been expecting it to look like a little peanut, not really human, but there was a little head, tiny fisted hands, and two little feet curled up underneath it.

"It looks just like you," Giselle decided firmly.

I blinked then threw my head back to laugh.

When I settled down a bit, my siren was smiling softly at me, awe in her eyes and love tucked into every curve of her beautiful face.

"I'm serious," she said.

"Okay," I agreed, because she was being ridiculous, but I was ridiculously happy, so it seemed fitting.

"It looks like you are eight weeks and four days, which puts the date of conception at November 26th." She smiled kindly at us. "Any special significance for you?"

"Yes," I said.

The good doctor frowned at me, and I realized I might have snapped at her. Giselle gave me a squeeze because she understood my gruffness was a product of emotion, *fucking great* emotion, and not anger.

"It was the first night we officially got together," she explained softly.

Dr. Adams beamed at us.

She was a nice enough woman and the best damn woman's doctor in the city, but I was done sharing the moment with her.

"Is it possible to have a moment alone?" I asked, even though it was stated more as a demand.

I'd found people reacted positively to thinly veiled orders. The trick was to underlay the suggestion with casual authority so they responded automatically before ego kicked in and they remembered to argue with you.

It worked beautifully on Dr. Adams, who smiled again at Giselle before moving swiftly out the door with a murmur that she would be back in a moment.

As soon as the door was closed, I moved into Elle. I pressed my forehead to hers, sinking one hand in all that red hair at the back of her neck so that I was cupping her to me. The other hand, I pressed gently but firmly on the minuscule swell of her abdomen.

"I never wanted my own family," I began, working the words through my irritatingly tight throat. "After my parents died and I went to the orphanage, I met Cage, we become brothers, but I knew in my heart that I would never have a real family again. Not even for an instant when Willa and Mortimer adopted me did I think we were a family. They were good to me, they liked my looks, my intelligence, but they eschewed Cage, fostering him for years with their housekeeper in Paris instead of keeping him with us."

They had been lonely years, that handful of years I had spent studying hard at Trinity's to make up for my deplorable lack of early education, trying so hard to impress my new guardians. I'd always been a fairly serious child, but Cage had brought levity to my world, reminded me to relax and smile. With him gone, I realized now, I'd begun the slow but sure process of becoming the man Elena had met and loved, an automaton replica of the man I wanted to be.

"When Cosima came into my life, she settled herself in it, dragged the rest of your family into my life in a way that was intimate and permanent. I met Elena, but by that time, the idea of family had disappeared and in its place was obligation. We were suited; we shared the same interests, enjoyed each other's conversation, and I found her attractive. But my heart wasn't truly in it because I had stopped using that muscle when my parents died. Honestly, I was happy never to use it again."

I watched Giselle's lips tighten. It could have been discomfort at the thought of my feelings for Elena, or more likely, it could have been because those very feelings made her soft heart sad, that I had thought love was made like that and that Elena had too.

"So, still, no family."

Elle's silver eyes were wet with tears.

"Then you." I paused because how could I properly explain how profound her entry into my life had been? This was why people recited poetry. It was easier to steal words than come up with my own. "I fought it. We both know, I fought it. But I knew from the moment I said goodbye to you on the plane that even if I never saw you again, my life was no longer enough. I needed a family. I needed love and a woman who was wholly mine. Now, in the span of five months, against so pretty impossible odds, I have one. You gave that to me, Elle, and I cannot express how fucking grateful I am of that."

I smoothed a thumb over the tears that slid down her cheeks and into her hair, watching as her lips trembled and her eyes shone. She was so pretty I felt it in my chest.

"I don't know what to say to that," she admitted. "It was so beautiful. Anything I say will just sound stupid."

I grinned at her. "Don't say anything. I just wanted you to know. This baby you're giving me means the world to me."

"Me too. And obviously, I will love him or her no matter what, but I really hope we have a Sinclair lookalike on our hands."

Then I kissed her because there was no other thing I could do.

Chapter Twenty

Sinclair

THINGS WERE MOVING QUICKLY.

Thank God.

I was tired of the subterfuge, of the games and the back and forth over something I knew in my fucking bones was eternal. Everything was falling into place; Giselle was pregnant, and her showing at my own art gallery was just around the corner. The nonsense over the Paulsons sexual proclivities and my affair with Giselle had ceased to matter to the crème de le crème of New York City society (not that I cared when it had). There were only three things that needed to get in line in order for me to deliver Giselle her happily ever after.

One of them, the question of our legal union, I was already orchestrating with the help of Cage and Candy. I wanted to include Cosima, but as she had promised Elle at our pseudo housewarming party, both she and Alexander Davenport had disappeared without any way to contact them. It was hard not to feel anger that she would put the family through that after everything they had been through with her accident, but the crushing worry we all felt, myself included, dominated the irritation. I hoped desperately that she was safe and was using any means necessary to secure the information, both for my own peace of mind and Giselle's.

I hoped I wasn't overstepping by essentially planning everything about our wedding. Most girls dreamed their entire lives of their wedding day and all of its details, but I figured my woman wasn't one of those girls. She was too busy surviving to think about her future, too busy dreaming of the fantastical to focus on her own desires.

So, I was a man planning his own elopement. As unconventional as it was, it was also surprisingly fun. Especially picking out her wedding dress, a creamy collection of lace and weave that would look astounding on her generous curves against all that flaming hair.

I had called Sebastian, who was on location somewhere in the California desert to film a movie about outlaws, to ask his permission. It was an outdated practice and one that I personally found fairly misogynistic, but I knew the Lombardi clan was close-knit and old-school enough to find my gesture both charming and necessary.

Our conversation went something like this.

"Hello?"

"Sebastian, I hope you are well. I'm calling to ask you a rather serious question, if you have a moment."

Pause.

"I have a moment."

"Good. I would like to ask for your blessing to marry Giselle."

Another pause.

This one longer.

Then quietly, he asked, "Are you sure you have the right sister now?"

It could have been a passive-aggressive statement, but the way he spoke softly, carefully, let me know he was just acknowledging the differences here; between Elena and Giselle, and between me with each of them. I didn't blame him. Elena's Daniel had delayed marrying her for four years, and now there I was, asking to marry her sister after only six months of knowing her.

"I have the right woman now."

"She would be happy to live with you in sin forever. She doesn't need marriage," he said because I'm sure he felt that he had to.

"I wouldn't be."

Another dramatic pause. I was used to them. Sebastian was an actor both on and off the screen.

"I'll walk her down the aisle."

She would love that, so I said, "Thank you."

It was a much easier conversation than I had planned for, but I had always liked the only male Lombardi, and I found that he was often surprising.

So, one thing down and two more to go before I could rest easy in my new life.

Those two things were Caprice and Elena Lombardi.

I started with the easier of the two.

Osteria Lombardi was only two blocks away from my office, so I stopped by after work to duck into the kitchen. They were used to me there, the staff knew that I was dating one of the Lombardi women, probably the wrong one, but they let me back without protest, so I didn't care to check.

Caprice was arguing with her head chef over something on the menu, but it wasn't yet busy with the dinner rush. She caught my eye immediately and continued to look at me as she finished her conversation. Without a word, she flicked her finger at me to follow her out the swinging doors and into her cramped office.

She sat down and gestured for me to do the same. Her face was set in a fierce scowl that rivaled Cosima's, and that girl could level a grown man twice her size with one of her looks. I reminded myself that Gisele had gone to bat for me twice now, with Paulson and my parents, and it was my turn to do the same.

"I'm marrying her, Caprice," I started because I wasn't one to beat around the bush and because I knew she would flinch the way she did. I was angry with her for causing Giselle pain, so I enjoyed it.

"You refuse to marry my Elena for years, and now you want a union with my *bambina*?" She snorted. "I do not think she will have you."

"You are wrong. Giselle loves me more than anything," I said, never confident of anything more in my life. "I know this because I feel the same, if not more, toward her. She is it for me, Caprice. I am sorry that Elena was only a step, a necessary one, along the way. I am sorry she was hurt because I found my soul mate through her, but a man doesn't throw away a gift like that just because it causes someone else, of frankly even himself, pain."

She blinked slowly at me. "So, you don't throw her away. You marry her before she can realize what a *stronzo* you are?"

I smiled slightly, but it was sharp, mean. "I am certain that Elle already knows how stupid I can be. She has stood by me through some of my worst decisions yet, and I know she would stand by me still. I am going to marry her, Caprice, and treat her like the queen of my fucking heart for the rest of our lives because that is what she is to me. I am not here to ask your permission. I am not even here to ask your forgiveness. I am here to tell you that I unequivocally love your daughter, Giselle, and I am going to make her my wife."

I wanted to tell her about the baby so badly that the words burned in my voice box, made it hard to swallow and breathe without uttering the news. I resisted. That moment was for my siren to share with her mother if she chose, and I knew that for now, she was sacrificing that comfort in order to give it to Elena.

God, my girl was selfless. It was both beautiful and hard for me to bear.

Caprice's lips were thin with strain as she stared at me. "I have known you a long time now, Daniel Sinclair. I was happy to meet you and give you one of my daughters. You chose wrong, it seems. I know that happens because once upon a long time ago, I chose wrong too, and I hurt my children in doing that. I do not like to see them hurt more."

"I understand that," I said slowly. "But you are hurting Giselle by blindly siding with Elena on this. I get that Elena needs you, and I still care for her, still want her family for her. But Giselle loves her mama, and you've taken that from her. I just wanted to let you know that we are creating our own family. If you stay away too long, you might find that she doesn't need you when you deem her worthy again."

I stood and buttoned up my blazer again as I tilted my head to her. "Despite your bad choice, you made beautiful babies, Caprice. Thank you for that."

Then I left, leaving the matriarch of the Lombardi clan feeling as if she had lost her daughter, and I was glad for it because if she continued to hurt Giselle, I wasn't going to let her have her back.

IT WAS STRANGE TO WALK UP TO THE APARTMENT I HAD SHARED WITH A woman for years and have it not be my own, have no desire for it to ever be again. Giselle thought that I was unnecessarily cruel to Elena when we had interacted since the breakup, but I didn't have it in me to fabricate kindness when she treated the woman I loved like dirt and me not much better. It killed me to draw the parallels between Willa and Elena, but as soon as I did, it was impossible to stop. They both loved me, but the way one loved their show pony or Best in Show breed. They loved me for what I could give them.

The world would have to forgive me if I was tired of that shit.

Still, when I knocked on the door, I did it without anger. I wasn't sure exactly what I wanted out of the exchange, but I hoped it would bring Elena some closure.

She answered the door in her lounge clothes, a long cashmere cardigan over a matching silk short and camisole set. Her hair was pushed back from her face with a velvet headband, and she had her black-framed reading glasses on her nose. She looked absolutely beautiful, yet not a part of me wanted her.

Good to confirm.

"Elena," I greeted, holding up a bag of Sushi Yasaka take-out and a bottle of her favorite sake. "May I come in?"

She hesitated sweetly for a moment before opening the door further. I swept in, went to the kitchen to gather plates, chopsticks, and napkins and met her at the coffee table where she had her papers laid out.

"Put those away, and let's eat," I ordered as I pulled out her favorite rolls and set them in front of her before pouring out the sake into the little ceramic glasses we had bought together a few years ago.

"Why are you here, Daniel?" she asked in an aberrantly soft voice. "To yell at me again?"

"No, darling," I said, softening toward her when she curled up into a ball on her side of the couch with her tray of sushi propped up on her knees. "I'm here because we haven't really talked since the breakup, and I wanted to give that to you."

Her lips twisted. "I can't decide if that's really nice of you or kind of douchey."

"Probably both," I said before popping a spicy tuna roll into my mouth.

We ate in silence for a while because I didn't really have anything to say. I just wanted to be there for her one last time in case she had something she wanted to say.

Finally, she spoke, "You really love her, I guess."

"I do," I said, firmly even though I felt a brief flare of guilt.

I loved Elle so much more than I had ever loved anything.

As if I had said those words out loud, Elena flinched then sighed. "Yes, I guess I could tell that."

"Yeah?"

She nodded. "You were so weird when you got back from Mexico. Moody. Happy one day and so sad the next. It was so out of character that I should have known it was someone else making you feel that way. You were never moody with me."

"It's called emotional, Elena. You should try it sometime," I said, joking but completely serious too. "Maybe not as explosively as you did at my house the other day, and maybe not so much it makes you vindictive enough to go to the press…"

She blushed furiously. "That was terrible. I still can't believe I did that."

"You were angry."

"I was. And," she hesitated, "I've hated her for so long. You know a little bit about that. I never really said anything kind about her to you. Christopher, he, well, he pitted us against each other from a young age, and I was never strong enough to get over it."

"Maybe it isn't too late," I suggested even though I knew it was.

"It is," she confirmed softly. "She has everything I ever wanted."

"I truly believe that you will find something that you want more," I said, facing her fully so that she was forced to witness my intensity. "We were not right for each other, and that's okay. Not just for me because I have Giselle now, but for you, because now you can find someone who will truly make you happy. I never did that for you."

She didn't protest, but I knew she wanted to.

We finished our meal in more silence.

"I have these for you," I said after I had cleaned up. I handed her the documents that I had my lawyer draw up. "This legally gives you the apartment."

She stared at the stack of papers in my hand before taking them with a hard nod. "Thank you, I love this place."

I never really had because I hadn't spent much time in it. I already loved my house in the clock tower so much more; the mural on the wall of the nursery, the studio I'd had installed on the top floor in a room full of windows, the bed I shared with Giselle.

I wanted to get back there.

"I'm leaving," I said, crouching in front of her. "I won't be back again, but if you ever need me, you can call me, yes?"

I meant it. Elena was the kind of woman who was really a queen. She deserved knights and footmen and kings bowing at her feet, taking care of her every need. I thought that was one of the reasons I was drawn to her in the first place.

I didn't want to leave her alone.

"Promise me," I said, looking into those big gray eyes, so much darker than Elle's but still so familiar to me. "I know it seems like a poor consolation, but I will always be here for you."

She swallowed hard twice before she nodded. "You can leave now."

"Okay," I said, staring at her for a second more before I did just that. "I don't blame you for the anger, for the scene at the house or the article in the newspaper. I have to live with what I did to you, and it won't ever get easier."

"Good," she said without fire.

"Good," I echoed before casting one more look at the place I had called home for almost half a decade and the woman I had thought was mine.

Good, I thought as I closed the door behind me and set out with a clear mind to get home to Brooklyn as quickly as my Porsche would carry me and the traffic would allow.

When I told Giselle that night, holding her in my arms after taking her hard in our bed, about my visit to Elena, how it had felt like closure, she too had murmured *good,* and I knew she felt clear of it as well.

Chapter Twenty-one

Giselle

IT WAS FINALLY TIME.

My life had taken on the quality of an Italian soap opera since meeting Sinclair, with so many incredible highs and lows that it felt we would never settle in to our life together. I hoped that the excitement of the gallery opening would mark the end of the many consequences we reaped from being together and herald a new, calmer beginning for us.

But calm, I was not.

"Are you serious?" I asked, my voice shrill as a teakettle whistle.

Rossi laughed kindly. "I am. *The New York Times*, Robin Cembalast from *ARTNews*, and Jerry Saltz from *New York Mag* have all confirmed their attendance tonight."

"I can't breathe," I said with the last of the air left in my lungs.

"Yes, you can," Eddie said, rubbing soothing circles on my back. "You have to breathe so that you can answer all the lovely people who are coming to see *your* exhibit tonight."

I shook my head manically, my hand over my tripping heart. Stars and black spots flashed before my eyes.

"Giselle, darling, people are going to begin arriving in half an hour. You need to calm down," Rossi scolded.

"Can't," I squeaked.

Everyone was going to hate my work. It was the edgiest I had ever been. The most subdued of all the paintings was the one of Mama with a deep swatch of sweaty exposed bosom in front of a stove. I was already mildly notorious for my affair with Sinclair. What was my flagrantly sexual display going to do to his reputation? I tried to inhale and choked. How had I been so selfish?

I looked around frantically, trying to find an escape from everything, when I felt two cool hands descend on my shoulders, stilling me immediately.

"Ladies," Sinclair's cultured, slightly accented voice crooned over my shoulder. "What seems to be the problem here?"

Both Eddie and Rossi slumped in relief at the sight of him.

"She's having a mental breakdown," Eddie said candidly.

"Eddie," Rossi rebuked, but it was okay. It was the truth.

"I think I'm dying," I told him, leaning back into his strength so that I didn't collapse.

"Well, we can't have that, can we?" There was amusement in his voice, but the arms that wrapped around my waist and the hand that subtly covered my slightly swollen abdomen were kind and supportive. "If you'll excuse us for a while, I think I'll take Giselle into the back to calm down."

Rossi looked at him critically. "Fine, but don't mess her up too much, and she needs to be out on the floor by the time the doors open at seven."

"Of course," he said somberly, but I could sense his amusement as he gently led me into the small kitchenette off the gallery rooms.

He placed me in a chair and set about making me a cup of tea. I didn't particularly like tea, but ever since we'd found out about the pregnancy, Sinclair was a stickler for sticking to health guidelines, which, unfortunately, included banning me from coffee.

Only when the kettle was set on the stove to boil did he come and kneel between my legs, both his strong hands braced on my thighs so that his face hovered just in front of my own. I stared into his cobalt blue eyes, searching for a safe place to anchor myself amid the turmoil in my own mind. He let me stare at him for a long, silent minute while his thumbs rubbed gently across my thighs.

"You are scared," he began, his voice as cool and refreshing as spring water. "I understand that this is a nerve-wracking endeavor, your first show in New York City. As a patron of the arts in this ruthless city for years, I do not take that lightly. But you must also understand that as a man who is your partner, who has grown as you've grown and witnessed you blossom with confidence, that I am nothing but excited for you tonight. This evening the world will be introduced to my siren, a woman of skill, sensuality, and a keen observation of the dark side of the human psyche. They will find your artwork stirring and visually appealing, as those are facts, my love, and not a matter of opinion. So, whatever nerves you are feeling, feel them, but know that when this is all over, and you are lying in our bed tonight, you will do so with pride and satisfaction at a job well done, d'accord?"

His powerful words lingered in the air, and I greedily sucked them in through my mouth to better absorb their potency. The trust and respect of a man as powerful as Sinclair was not something that could ever be taken for granted. If he believed in me, it was impossible not to believe in myself.

"I love you so much," I breathed, weak with relief.

He smiled as I pressed my forehead to his shoulder. "And I you, toujours."

"Do you think she'll come tonight?" I asked after a moment.

He didn't ask who I spoke of. "I can't say. She was always prideful, and given that she is in the collection, I'd imagine she would at least come to see that you didn't do her a disservice."

"Do you think I did?" Worry had been eating away at the lining of my stomach since I had completed the last piece of the collection, the one of my sister wrapped in melting ice sculptures.

"Enough worry," he said, shifting away from me to look into my face. His eyes were cold and shuttered, and I knew even before he spoke that his next words would be an order. "Get over my knee."

Instantly my core clenched. I hesitated briefly before settling over his lap, not because I didn't want the spanking but because I had been secretly craving such a release all day. Nothing could eradicate my demons like the glowing space I occupied when I submitted to my Frenchman.

"I can feel your eagerness," Sinclair murmured darkly as he caressed my bottom through the silky material of my skirt. "This is not a punishment, siren, so I do want you to enjoy it. This is about release."

I let out a shaky sigh when he pulled up my dress and hoisted the edges of my half-bottom panties so that they slid deeply between the crease of my ass. I squirmed against the pressure it put on my already sensitive clit, but he stilled me with a firm hand to my lower back.

"Still, I expect you to thank me for each one," he said, in that unflappable voice.

I shivered in anticipation, moaning when his hand smacked against my skin.

"Thank you, sir."

He rubbed the sting hard with his fingers. "Mmm, you are welcome, siren."

The next hits came one after the other, alternating between one cheek and the other. Each stinging pain lulled me further into subspace. I could hear my breath panting loudly in the space, punctuated only by the harsh slap of his palm against my flesh.

Somehow, I remembered to thank him each time.

Eventually, his hand moved from my lower back to the sopping wet place between my legs. His fingers slid through my folds, barely dipping inside me. I wriggled and moaned, wordlessly begging him to finish me off.

"Use your words," he reminded sharply.

"Please, sir, may I come?"

"I don't think so," he said, boredom dripping from his words like my arousal was from his fingertips.

"Puh-please," I begged as he swiftly pressed two fingers inside me and curled them toward my front wall, pressing against the small patch of tissues that always made me detonate.

"Tell me what you are thinking about," he demanded.

Thoughts swirled around my head before disappearing too quickly to verbalize.

I groaned.

The next spank was especially brutal. I hissed through my teeth and teetered closer to orgasm.

"Not good enough. Tell me; are you worried about the show, about what anyone may think of your art, of yourself? Or are you thinking about me, about my fingers inside your sweet, wet pussy, and my hand branding your ass a nice, scarlet red?"

"Your hands, your fingers," I panted, pressing harder into the erection I could feel poking my stomach. "Want your cock."

He chuckled wickedly. "Good girl. I should be the only thing on your mind. I am the master of this body, the owner of your thoughts. When I touch you like this"—he plunged another finger inside me while circling my asshole with his arousal-dampened thumb—"you know who you belong to."

"You, sir," I cried out, so close to climaxing that my vision was growing dark at the corners.

"Yes, *me*. Come for me now," he ordered.

A second later, I was lost. Blackness surged toward me, hot and cold, a swirl of sensation that pummeled my body and made my skin sing from the inside out with sensitivity. Every negative sensation that had weighed down my body was obliterated by the welcome darkness, and I think, for a least a moment, I blacked out.

When I came to again, Sinclair was cradling me to his chest, and my clothes were righted. He smiled against my hair as he stroked it, satisfaction oozing from him even though he hadn't been the one to orgasm. I loved that as a Dominant, he got off on orchestrating my pleasure as much as I did from experiencing it.

"I'm going to keep your underwear in my pocket, and you are going to walk around this gallery tonight knowing that I own you, feeling that and only that between your thighs." He paused to let the words sink in. "Are you ready now, Elle?"

I tipped my head back and beamed up at him. "Let's do it."

THERE WERE DOZENS OF PEOPLE. EVERY TIME I WAS INTRODUCED TO SOMEONE new, another person over my shoulder was waiting for an introduction. Some of them I knew immediately, like the art critics Jerry Saltz and Holland Cotter, Jace Galantine, the famous movie star that Sebastian kept a wide berth from, and Louis Vuitton Foundation's CEO Bernard Arnault who had first championed my work in Paris. They *all* had something nice to say about my paintings. I tried and probably failed to be cool about it.

Of my family, only Sebastian was there, having flown in from filming his new movie in Los Angeles just to be a part of opening night. He apologized on behalf of Mama, who was at the restaurant managing a private party, but I knew that she wouldn't have missed it for the world if she had wanted to be here. It made me sad for a moment, Mama's continued distance and Cosima's inexplicable absence, but I had reason to be happy still. All the friends I had in the world were there to support me, including Stefan, Santiago, Kat, Richard, Duncan, Robert, and even Odile, who Sinclair had flown over as a surprise for me.

The Paulsons were there too, their first public outing since the scandal. Mr. Paulson looked mildly uncomfortable, but after their experience being ground through the rumor mill, he seemed lighter somehow and was less careful about his gestures of affection and dominance over Terry.

Even Brenna showed up.

"*C'est une blague*," I exclaimed in French when I found her lingering by a portrait of Sinclair.

She laughed, but her expressive face didn't light up the way it usually did. "Not a joke."

I leaped at her, completely oblivious to the persona I had tried to cultivate throughout the night. She caught me, staggering backward under my weight as I squeezed her roughly.

"*Je te déteste,*" I told her over and over again, as I rained kisses down on the top of her golden head.

Her shocked laughter quickly dissolved into silent tears as she brought me closer still.

"I missed you too," Brenna whispered.

"I was always right here," I reminded her gently.

She nodded and squeezed me once more before taking a step back. I watched her wipe the tears from under her eyes and noted that she was healthier looking than the last time I had seen her, depressed on the arm of her famous husband.

"What has happened to you?"

Her smile was shaky but bright. "Almost as much as has happened to you, it looks like. I'm sorry I didn't respond to your emails and calls, but I had to go off the grid for a while. When I logged back into reality last week, I devoured all of your notes, but I still feel like I've missed so much."

I followed her excited gaze over my shoulder and saw Sinclair standing across the room speaking with Cage. As soon as he felt my eyes on him, he turned unerringly in our direction. My breath hitched at the quiet possession in his eyes as they dragged over me, checking in on my state of mind and my companion. Finally, his lips twitched into a slight smile and he dipped his head to acknowledge Brenna's presence.

I bit back a smile.

"Let's start with *him.*" Brenna laughed, linking my arm through hers. "And then move on to what possessed you to create this amazingly provocative art. The Giselle I knew didn't know anything beyond the practical value of rope, chains, or handcuffs, and now I find you exploring BDSM?"

It was my turn to giggle as we paused in front of the portrait of Madame Claire using Dominic as a footstool, her face hazy behind a cloud of looping cigarette smoke. The oil painting was done in somber hues but for the brilliant red soles of her stiletto heels crossed over the corded muscles of his back.

Brenna licked her lips as she stared at it. "This is deeply titillating stuff, Elle."

I grinned. "I have you to thank for all of it. If you hadn't sent me to Mexico in your place, this would never have happened."

I frowned, though, because I had never really thought it through. If Sinclair and I had met as future in-laws, would the sexual chemistry between us have remained dormant?

Awareness pulled my spine straight like a zipper, locking my posture in vertebrae by vertebrae. I shivered as Sinclair took the final step forward to stand beside me and discovered that I had the answer to my question; no matter the meet-cute, Sin and I would have eventually ended up together.

"Brenna Buchannan, I'm a fan of your work, both as an actress and Giselle's best friend," Sinclair was saying when I clued back in to reality.

My best friend grinned and giggled like a little girl. "It's always nice to meet a fan. I'm sorry it has taken us so long to be introduced."

"She was worried," he admitted with a scolding frown as he tucked me into his side.

Brenna blushed, but I stepped in to save her from Sinclair's scrutiny. "She wouldn't have disappeared without reason. I understand." I tilted my head up to stare at my handsome boyfriend. "Sometimes, we all need to disappear."

His eyes sparkled at the reminder of our trip to Paris. I swallowed audibly when one of his large hands wrapped around the back of my neck, his fingers running lightly over the pearl choker. It was a subtle cue to remind me that I belonged with him.

"I'm hosting a little after-party to celebrate Giselle's success after the gallery closes. I hope you are free to join?" Sin asked.

Brenna beamed at him, but I was distracted by the rest of their conversation by the sight of my sister standing frozen in the entryway.

Elena was dressed impeccably, as always, the cashmere backless black dress contrasted beautifully with her clear skin and dark red hair. A number of people had stopped staring at the art in order to evaluate her.

I swallowed thickly before excusing myself from the conversation with Brenna and Sinclair. He had no doubt noticed her too, but after a quick caress, he let me move forward to handle it myself.

"I didn't think you would come," I said as I approached her.

She didn't look at me, caught up in the massive canvas of Sinclair that dominated the small front wall that immediately faced the entryway.

"I didn't think I would either."

I nodded even though I was aware that she wasn't paying me any attention. So, I stood there beside her, staring at the portrait of a lover we had both shared at some point. The three of us hadn't shared the same space since the day Sinclair and I had returned from Paris to see Cosima in the hospital, but it was somehow more intimate to be staring at my image of him with Elena by my side. She was staring at the heart of the man I loved and, therefore, at the very heart of me. If she said something cruel now, as would have been her right, I knew it would eviscerate me.

"It looks just like him," she finally said, her voice softened by the Neapolitan accent she usually tried so hard to hide. "Yet, I've never seen him like this. Does that make any sense to you?"

I was careful to shrug casually even though it did make sense.

"It would have been hard not to notice how much you love him if this was the portrait you were planning on painting for me."

I cocked my head as I stared at the beloved lines of his form spread over nearly three meters of canvas. There was nothing overtly sexual about the image, it was just a very beautiful man in a very commanding position, but if you looked closely, there was no doubt about the sexual power that emanated from him; the way his fingers curled around the edges of the broad throne, how the veins in his corded forearms bulged and in the slight but provocative tilt of his full, firm lips. There was a glittering menace, a calculated coldness in his eyes that spoke to sexual deviancy instead of violence, at ruthless pleasures to be had if only you had the courage to let him exploit them.

I knew this was the man who I loved, the man who I knew him to be, but I had been worried about the subtlety of the image in the critic's eyes. Would they see him in all his constrained glory?

"It makes me realize how much I made him keep from me," Elena said quietly.

I shivered at the depth of remorse in her tone.

"I saw this in him at first, all the sex wrapped up in this controlled, intellectual gentleman. I think maybe a part of me was even intrigued by it, the fucked-up part of me that never got over Christopher's abuse." She sighed, crossing her arms tightly under her breasts as if she could physically restrain her emotions. "I can confess that I didn't love him the way I should have. We could have been right together if either of us had been willing to be brave, to stand up to the other and actually talk about all the things that made us broken." She shrugged. "I can admit that I could have loved him better, but I will never forgive you from exploiting that flaw, for taking him from me so goddamn ruthlessly."

I sucked in a deep breath, wanting to say something but having nothing to say.

Finally, she turned to face me. Her eyes raced over every inch of my being, setting me on fire with her condemnation.

"I always knew you had it in you. Mama, Seb, and Cosima saw this fragile little girl with her head in the clouds and thought you harmless. Only I knew how dangerous a girl made of fantasies could be." She laughed darkly. "Apparently, even knowing that wasn't enough, even avoiding you for years, you made your way back into my life and made it a fucking nightmare just so you could have your bloody happily ever after."

"Elena," I began, but she shook her head.

"No, don't. I came to say this stuff to you so that our family doesn't suffer. I don't love you, Giselle, and I think we both know that I haven't in a very long time. I don't forgive you either. You knowingly ripped my life apart. Our family will forgive you, society will forgive you, and I think you've already forgiven yourself, but my hatred is one consequence you will have to live with forever."

I nodded, too busy swallowing back the urge to cry to respond to her.

She nodded curtly and turned on her heel to walk away to another painting across the gallery.

I saw someone approach me out of my periphery, but I knew if anyone talked to me before I got a handle on the emotions wreaking havoc with my system, I would dissolve into tears, and the critics would have more drama to speak about than the scandalous nature of my art. With my head down, I sped toward the small back room, only stopping when I had slammed the door shut behind me. I cupped my hands to my mouth, trying to stuff the sobs back inside fruitlessly. Giving in to the misery, I curled forward into the only uncluttered corner of the room and squeezed my eyes shut.

Chapter Twenty-two

Giselle

"I've missed watching you."

I froze mid-sob, my chest expanded in a shuddering breath even as my heart constricted inside me. There was no other voice that could make me feel so afraid, so instantaneously. It was a voice that had haunted my youth and eventually, chased me out of Paris.

Slowly, drenched in paralyzing panic, I straightened.

Christopher stood across the tiny, darkened room. He wasn't a large man, average height and build with an open, engaging face that was somehow quintessentially British. He had large, round eyes that were the soft blue of faded denim and that lulled you into trusting before he had even opened his mouth to speak. There was absolutely nothing threatening about Christopher's appearance, which made him all the more frightening.

"You are so beautiful with tears across your face, Giselle," he murmured, cocking his head slightly to the side in a predatory way that made me take a step back even though I was already pressed against the wall.

"You found me."

He nodded. "As I always do. I would urge you to stop running, as it inevitably leads to this moment, but I have to admit..." His grin was sharp. "I've grown to love the chase."

I was silent as I waited for my limbs to thaw free of the shock. There was a tingling in my toes that I took as a good sign.

"I think you like it too, sweet girl. You know that we are meant to be together, but you run for both of our pleasure. Well, I forgive you for making it more interesting, but now is the time to come together. I've searched for you long enough." He laughed. "It took me too long to realize that you had reunited with your family. I never thought you would do such a thing."

I bit my lip, trying to calculate if anyone would hear my screams. Running for the door wasn't an option when his position put him closer to it. The sultry music playing throughout the gallery had a deep bass, so the chances of being heard were slim unless someone was right beside the door.

Christopher's face darkened as he stepped toward me, stalking so slowly that it would have been comedic in any other situation.

"I've seen you with that man. It seems your taste for your sister's men hasn't waned, but we both know that Daniel Sinclair isn't right for you." He stopped right before me, looking at me for a long moment before his hand snapped forward and tugged brutally at my hair. "He may give you the pain you like, but he isn't me."

"No," I finally hissed. "Sinclair is *nothing* like you."

"What is the difference between us? He hurts you too." Christopher pulled tighter on my hair until my neck was bent back at an excruciating angle. When he was satisfied with my position, he thrust his body against mine brutally. "You love to be painted just like your canvases, all this lovely white skin colored with mauve and yellow and black."

To illustrate his point, his hand curled over my wrist and pressed. I bit back my whimper of pain because I knew he would enjoy it.

"You love the pain. You get off on it just like me."

His words stirred the rage sitting at the bottom of my gut labeled with his name. I had hated him for so long, but I had feared him for even longer, and the depth of my childhood trauma had overtaken the wrath but only for so long. Heat traveled through my previously frozen limbs until I vibrated.

"I get off on the control. And you have absolutely no control over me, not anymore," I practically spat at him.

His smile was disturbingly soft as he leaned back slightly to look over my face. "So beautiful. It's good that we are together again."

"Fuck you!" I yelled, spittle flying in his face.

He licked it from his lips, leaning closer to whisper, "Oh, I intend to."

Before I could move, he stood on my feet, anchoring me to the floor while one arm latched over my arms, constricting them against my torso. With his free hand, he quickly undid his belt and tucked the hem of my skirt into the collar of my dress, exposing my bare sex to him. I sobbed when his fingers brutally pinch my clit.

"I never had your cunt. I wanted to save it for a special occasion, for when you were truly mine, and now some other man has been inside you first." He bit my ear so hard that I could feel his teeth break the skin. "I will have to punish you for that."

I squirmed violently against his hold and opened my mouth to scream. He didn't try to stop me, even when I drew breath again and again to shriek for help. Instead, he laughed cruelly and pierced his fingers inside me in time with my screams. I was still wet from my previous interlude with Sinclair, but I quickly dried up, and his fingers chafed brutally against my delicate flesh.

"Don't fight this. We are meant to be together. I have always known that. Your mother wanted me to marry your sister, but we both know she would never do. Even that gorgeous slut Cosima wasn't good enough for me. I needed your purity. I needed to watch your corruption."

My throat was in agony as I continued to scream, the sound even lesser than it had been a minute ago. I was losing steam quickly. Christopher's erection bounced wetly against my hip. He was small, turgid, and an angry red that disgusted me, but it also gave me an idea. I wasn't strong enough to fight him, but I was strong enough to seduce him.

I reduced my screaming to yelling, interspersed with a reluctant and totally fake moan and groan. Christopher watched me in rapture as I pretended to give in to his touch.

"Yes," I breathed, sagging in his arms. "Oh, I forgot how good this was."

Nausea rolled through me, but I needed to be smarter if I wanted to get the baby and myself out of there.

"You love it," he groaned into my ear. "Tell me you want me."

"I want you."

"Say my name."

"I want you, Christopher," I said. "But I want you properly. I want you to take me for the first time in a bed, not in the back of the supply closet."

He pulled away slightly to look at me suspiciously. I tried to widen my eyes in earnest and ground down on his fingers.

"As much as I want you, I want our first time to be right. Please. There is no rush. You found me, so we have forever now."

I prayed to God that I had been gone long enough for Sinclair to start looking for me.

"You should never have run from me," Christopher said, his face softening as he brought me into a hug. "I would have taken care of you properly. I would have sent you to whatever art school you wanted to go to. You know I love you."

I shivered but clung to him tightly to mask my revulsion. That was the thing about Christopher. He really did believe he loved me, and he had never been physically violent toward me. The bruises and bite marks he had left me with were more a result of his desire to devour me whole, mark me as his, than from brute physical abuse. It was his sweet persuasiveness, and sometimes, when I was being particularly obstinate, his absolute authoritarianism that had made me succumb to his sexual advances. I was fifteen, the first time he had told me to get on my knees and show him how much I loved him with my mouth. It wasn't something a fifteen-year-old girl, sheltered as I was, knew how to refuse.

As if prompted by my thoughts, Christopher smoothed a hand down my hair before gently pressing on my shoulders.

"Be a sweet girl and get on your knees."

My stomach roiled. It was extra sensitive because of my morning sickness, and the thought of giving him head amplified it threefold.

"We should go before someone sees us," I urged.

He smiled softly, petting my cheek. "Don't worry, sweetheart. I have protection."

"What?"

I watched him reach behind his back and pull a small handgun from his waistband. I didn't know what type of gun it was, but it struck me that Cosima would know. She had been the one so well-versed in the Mafia men who came to visit our house in search of Seamus.

"Why would you bring a gun?" I asked, anything to keep him talking but also because he had never been a gun carrier before.

"Nothing will get in the way of me having you again, Giselle."

There was a calmness in his eyes, a surety that spoke of absolute conviction and total insanity.

"Get on your knees," he repeated, pushing harder at my shoulders this time.

I swallowed painfully and did as he asked, hoping even as I undid the zip on his pants tooth by tooth that Sinclair would find me.

His pants dropped to the floor, and his hand was wrapping one of mine around his shaft but still no Sinclair.

Minutes later, when more things, not the worst that could be happening, but *bad*, were happening, still no Sinclair.

Christopher's gun was the hand that held my head to him.

I counted to sixty.

Still no Sinclair.

Christopher was moaning when finally, I heard the door open.

I was pressed to the wall with him in front of me, but I could see sudden movement as the newcomer moved swiftly toward us. I braced myself against the wall when a scream tore through the air. Christopher stumbled, falling against me so I was brutally smashed against the wall. But I didn't care because someone was attacking him.

I rolled to the side when there was enough space and whirled to face the commotion.

Still, there was no Sinclair.

Instead, the body that clung to Christopher's and pummeled him with furious fists was my sister's.

Elena continued to yell, a warrior's cry that pierced the air better than any of my previous screams. She was wrapped around his upper back, landing punches to his neck as he tried to pull her off. She leaned forward and bit savagely into his earlobe, ripping away with her teeth still clenched. Christopher shrieked in pain as she pulled a large chunk of flesh from him and spat it over her shoulder. He tried to dislodge her by slamming her back against the wall, but she used the moment to push off and heave her weight the other way, which disrupted Christopher's balance. He almost recovered, but I scrambled to my hands and knees and threw myself in the way of the foot that sought to secure his equilibrium. I watched as they fell hard to the floor, terrified that she had taken the brunt of the impact before she scrambled over him, straddled his chest with her knee pressed into his neck.

Then she beat him.

And I mean, she brutally laid into his face with her fists, rearing back with her whole body to put ultimate force behind each exact blow. I watched her, hypnotized, as she turned his face into a bloody, pulpy mess.

I was vaguely aware of chaos at the door to the room, of yelling and people rushing forward to pull Elena, screaming and thrashing, off the comatose Christopher. People came to crowd me, but no one touched me. They were talking to me, but I couldn't focus. I couldn't take my eyes off my sister.

Elena finally settled in the corner, panting in Cage's restraining embrace. Her eyes were, surprisingly, on me.

Something passed between us, through that momentary connection forged over threats and violence. The man bleeding on the floor between us had groomed us both. It had never brought us together, mostly because the similarities his influence had formed in us were too damaged for us to connect over. Besides, from the very beginning, he had pitted us against each other, and even when he had gone, we had continued to live out the competition he had constructed for us. He had fucked us both, mentally and physically and in every fucked-up way a person could fuck up two people. It was Christopher, not Sinclair, who had torn us apart. I'd always known that, but it became clear, at that moment, to both of us, I thought, that since the moment Christopher had entered our lives, we were doomed. Our sisterhood was dead.

But at that moment, when her eyes, so similar but darker than mine, bore into me, they were filled with a protective fury for me as well as her own righteous wrath.

No one fucks with you, but me. Her eyes seemed to say.

I tilted my chin to her. I'll take whatever you have to give me.

I meant it to. She was allowed to hate me. It made sense, and I was happy to give her a villain. We would never be friends. We would never be anything but sisters by blood, not by choice. I knew it, and I accepted it. But she had attacked Christopher, and it had at least a little something to do with me.

So, no matter what I'd done, no matter how she might act, I knew that Elena loved me. Not a whole lot, not in a way that she had chosen. But she loved me.

I'd never known before this moment that she did.

"Giselle." A familiar voice pulled me away from our moment of clarity, but I let it because I could hear the panic there.

"Giselle," Sinclair said again.

He was crouched in front of me, between me and the prone body of Christopher. He had one hand on the man's throat, checking his pulse maybe, and the other was busy righting my clothes. He was on lockdown, his eyes cold and hard like marble, inhuman. His hands were perfunctory against my skin as they checked to make sure I was unharmed, but there was a haste to his movements that belied how fucking terrified he was.

"Sin," I murmured.

He ignored me.

"Sinclair," I repeated.

He paused, his eyes doing an intense sweep of my face but skirting past my gaze. I grabbed his hand and put it to my cheek.

"I'm okay," I whispered because there were tons of people in the room now, and this was a private moment, an important one.

I watched his Adam's apple bob once, twice. He struggled, and I watched the fury, the pain, and terror roll through him. I drew strength from it, from his obvious love.

"Nothing happened, not really. I'm okay," I repeated, meaning it.

Christopher had violated me again, but for the last time, I was sure of it. I had evidence of his stalker tendencies and witnesses to collaborate his sexual abuse. The law would deal with him, and if they didn't, I knew Sinclair would find a way to.

"Sinclair," I said again, "I'm still yours."

A vicious shudder wracked his frame before he allowed himself to sag forward, resting his forehead against mine.

"Thought he took you," he whispered brokenly.

My heart stuttered. "Oh Sin, he didn't. I'm okay."

"The baby?"

I had no pain in my womb, and he hadn't hurt me. "Just as fine as his or her mama."

"He is your nightmare," he said, his eyes closed. "Worse than that fucker in Mexico. He is your nightmare."

"Elena and I beat him."

His eyes flashed open, blazing so blue, and he pressed a soft kiss to my lips. "I'm taking you away from here."

"Okay," I whispered because I wanted to leave and because he needed us to.

"Now."

"Yes, okay."

"Brenna?" he said, and my friend appeared over his shoulder. "Take care of her for a second."

My grip on his hand tightened in panic. "Please don't leave me."

His face gentled, and I knew he was remembering how he had left me to Candy so he could beat the man who had assaulted me in Cabo.

"You aren't allowed out in society without me, siren, d'accord? Or I'll need to hire a full-time bodyguard."

My lips twitched because even though it was funny, he was being very serious. "Okay."

"I'm not leaving you. I just need to talk to the police when they arrive and check on Elena. I want Brenna to sit with you, but I'll be right over there." He pointed to just outside the supply room doors where Sebastian was keeping most of the guests away.

I nodded. "Can you bring Elena over here to sit with me while we wait?"

He stared hard at me for a moment, his thumb running back and forth over my cheek. "I owe her a debt I will never be able to pay for saving you from him."

My throat closed up.

"So, yes, of course, but only after I thank her myself."

He pressed a kiss to my forehead before straightening and walking off into the crowd. I leaned into Brenna, who wrapped an arm around my upper chest in silent support.

Together, we watched Sinclair crouch in front of Elena. I could tell from his profile that those glacial features were thawed with gratitude as he thanked her. She flinched against Cage's hold but didn't take her eyes off him. Pain and lingering anger contorted her features, but when Sin reached out to tuck her hair behind her ear, leaning close to press his forehead to hers and cup the back of her head to him, she closed her eyes and sagged into him.

I felt no jealousy witnessing the intimate moment because I knew Sinclair was mine as much as my name was my name and my hair was red. After all this time and all these trials, his love for me was just that irrefutable. So, I felt only warmth watching Sinclair reach out to my wronged sister, only happy that he offered her thanks *and* comfort because she deserved it.

"And I thought my family was complicated," Brenna murmured into my hair.

I laughed softly and leaned back into her. "The Lombardi clan has cornered the market on complicated, I think."

"You're pregnant?"

I froze against her as panic seized me. People knew, our Mexico crew, the Paulsons and the Percys, but not Mama and not the general populous. There was no way I was going to throw that grenade into the already volatile situation.

"I won't tell anyone, Elle. You're my person, my best friend. Besides, I'm well-versed in secret-keeping," she finished in a soft, sad voice.

"I'm pregnant," I confirmed.

Her arm gave me a hard squeeze. "Good, I've always wanted to be an Auntie."

Tears tickled the backs of my eyes. I let out a deep breath to curb the impulse to cry and watched Sinclair kiss Elena's cheek before he moved to the newly arrived police officers crowding the doorframe.

"Are you okay?" Brenna asked.

I was.

In fact, in a bizarre way, I felt better than I ever had. The threat of Christopher, his stalking presence throughout the entirety of my life, had been brought to an end. I felt good that I had figured out a way to avoid his rape. Yes, I'd still been sexually assaulted, but as long as I could wash my hands with industrial-strength soap for the next hour and a half, I knew that I could recover from it because I had recovered from worse. Sinclair had taught me to move past the memories. He had moved me through each sexual act that had been taken from me by Christopher and reclaimed it as our own. I knew he would do the same thing now. And even though I had him to help with this, I also knew that he had given me the tools to do it on my own, and that was somehow even more precious.

"Honestly, I am," I said and meant it.

Chapter Twenty-three

Giselle

"I'M FINE," I REASSURED SINCLAIR FOR THE THIRTIETH TIME.

"I still think we should have gone to the hospital," he repeated for the thirty-first time.

"The paramedics on-site said that I would be fine, the baby is fine, and there is no lasting damage. I told you, Christopher didn't beat me."

We were in the back of Sinclair's Town Car. I was wrapped in a blanket Eddie had unearthed from somewhere in the gallery and cuddled up against Sinclair's side. My adrenaline had burned off, so I was finding it hard to keep my eyes open, but I didn't want to fall asleep with my Frenchman still so riled beside me.

"I wish it had been me to beat the bastard," Sinclair muttered.

I curled closer to him. "Elena needed that more than you did. I think it was closure for her."

We had sat beside each other while the police took our statements, close but not touching. At one point, she leaned close enough to press her shoulder to me as we watched Christopher taken away on a stretcher in handcuffs, but she didn't say a word to me until after the police had left and the guests had been ordered to leave for the night.

"Sorry about your show," she had said, surprisingly.

I shrugged. "Things happen."

"Don't we know it," she muttered.

I snorted, startled, before sliding her a sidelong glance. Her face was soft, softer than I had seen it in years. Our friends and family kept looking at us, waiting for a breakdown, but I knew that she and I felt the same. It hadn't been traumatic as much as it was cathartic to hurt and overcome our very own boogeyman.

"Thank you."

She tipped her head back against the wall and brought her knees to her chest. "No one deserves to be raped."

Not even you.

I nodded.

She sighed into the quiet after a few minutes. "It felt good."

"Yeah."

"Glad you're okay," she whispered, so quietly that I thought I imagined it.

Before I could question it, she had sprung to her feet and stalked off, tagging Sebastian to take her home as she went. My brother shot me a concerned look over her shoulder, but I nodded at him. She needed him more than I did.

As if to prove my point, Sinclair had returned to me and swung me up into his arms.

Now, we were in the car on our way home, and Sinclair was vibrating with fury.

"I'm happy, Sin. It's over. He ruined my childhood, forced me to leave Paris, and took a bunch of things from me that I never offered. It sucks." He growled at my understatement, so I amended, "Okay, it's horrible. But it is *over*. Now, I can forget the fear and the past and focus entirely on the love of my life."

He looked down at me so I could watch the ice in his eyes thaw and turn into liquid love. "He ruined a night that you've been working toward for months."

"True, but he isn't going to ruin anything else ever again, so I'll accept that."

The police had assured us that he would be deported, and Elena was filing a restraining order for me in the morning.

"I didn't protect you from him," Sin muttered, staring into my face as if he might never see it again.

I pressed my hand to his cheek. "You did. You gave me the tools to face him unafraid. You taught me how to love myself, how to be strong and survive. He wanted to abduct me, he had a gun, and still, we beat him. When I was a teenager, he wouldn't have needed the gun. I would have been on my knees because he loved me and perverted me, and I would have thought obeying him was right. Instead, I outsmarted him, and I *won*."

His eyes flashed.

"I need you to let this go and focus on everything good in our lives. I need you to do this because I'm living my dream, and I don't want to live it alone, or it's no dream at all."

"Elle," he breathed on a heavy exhale. "You are so exquisite. I don't deserve you."

"I don't deserve you, which is good because I'll never take you for granted."

"I'm falling in love with you," he said strangely.

I moved back a little to search his face, but he was very serious. "Um, I was kind of under the impression that you loved me already."

I watched laughter eat away at the anger in his eyes. "It's still happening. I fall further and further into you every day."

Okay, wow.

"You are so romantic."

His lips twitched. "I'm just being nice."

I laughed. "You don't have time to be nice, remember?"

He smiled gently and cupped my cheek. "For you, I can find the time."

Swoon.

I snuggled deeper into him.

"I know you have just been through an ordeal, but I had this planned before everything went to hell. If you want to just go home and rest, I completely understand."

"What are you talking about?"

His eyes danced. "How would you feel about a little celebratory vacation?"

"Sin! Are you going to make it a habit to whisk me away on a moment's notice?" I teased, but I definitely wasn't complaining.

"Yes, absolutely."

I laughed again. "Where are we going this time?"

"Cabo."

He watched me clap my hands and jump up and down in my seat, filled with childish delight and unashamed to show it. I smacked a loud kiss on his cheek.

"You spoil me."

"It's much more selfish than that. I like nothing more than to see you happy."

"Sin," I said, overwhelmed by him, by my life and my luck.

"You're up for it? Because we're on the way to the airport right now, and Candy packed a suitcase for you. It's in the trunk."

"Where it all began," I murmured, pressing my mouth close to his. "Of course, I want to go."

"Good, because no wasn't really an option."

I rolled my eyes.

Chapter Twenty-four

Giselle

THE SOFT, FRAGRANT BREEZE WOVE THROUGH THE OPEN FRENCH DOORS TO the balcony and wafted across the sweat cooling on my skin. Sinclair and I had finally ended up in the bedroom, the blankets pooled on the floor, and the sheet twisted around my torso, his legs, like some kind of toga. The air smelled of sex and lavender and that indefinable tropical scent combined with ocean brine, hibiscus, and almost metallic heat. My head rested on the mattress facing Sinclair so that my hair pooled in bloody tendrils over the white sheets where he could draw his finger lazily through the curls, and I could watch the way the pulse jumped in his brown throat.

I could have stayed exactly like that for eternity.

We had arrived at the Westin just after noon the day before and immediately proceeded to the very same suite Sinclair had stayed in all those months ago. There was champagne chilling on the bar, rose petals laid out over the huge canopied bed, and acoustic Spanish music filtered through the room from hidden speakers. I only had a moment to take it all in before

Sinclair had me pushed up against the wall, his hands all over every inch of my body. There was passion in his haste but also a need for reassurance. Christopher had tried to claim and my Sin seeking to eradicate even the notion of such a thing.

He didn't have to work very hard to do it, but I appreciated the effort to brand himself on me against the door, then again that evening on the couch and after a delicious room service meal of *aguachile* and chicken *mole*, on the padded lounge chairs on the balcony.

Now, the morning after, my mind was so saturated with pleasure, with such a deep-seated contentment that I found the demons Christopher had plagued me with my entire life were laid eternally to rest.

"I have never been so happy," I told Sin because it was true and because it was all because of him.

Sin didn't open his eyes, but he hummed his approval and said, "Mission accomplished."

I laughed. "You are awfully smug."

He shrugged one shoulder in that French way of his, and even though he was lying down, his big body spread inelegantly across the breadth of the bed, the movement was somehow graceful. "I am a successful businessman with a gorgeous woman who is carrying my baby lying beside me after a pretty fucking amazing bout of sex. I think my smugness is justifiable."

I smiled so wide that it cut into my cheeks. He opened his eyes as if he could sense my expression, and they warmed until they were as blue and bright as the Pacific Ocean outside our window.

"You have that glow of a pregnant woman," he said, traveling his fingers through my hair until they brushed against my cheek. "Every time I look at you, I cannot believe you are mine."

"If you weren't so dignified, I think you would have your name tattooed on my lower back so everyone would know it," I joked.

His eyes darkened, his tone grew serious. "I do not have to do that for everyone to know that you belong to me. It is written in this tilt of your beautiful mouth," his thumb pressed to the smiling corner of my mouth, "in the way your eyes turn to liquid silver when I'm near. It's in how you turn yourself into my body whether you are standing beside me or across the room, like your body is a compass and I am your true north. And as you grow bigger," his calloused fingers swept down my side until they came to rest over my slightly swollen abdomen, "they will see what belonging to me has done to you."

Tears pricked at the backs of my eyes. I didn't think I would ever get used to the poeticism that lived inside my normally stoic and reticent Frenchman. Crying was a hazard of pregnancy, I knew, but I didn't want to ruin the moment with tears, so instead, I said, "What? That it makes me fat?"

His lips thinned in mock severity before he shifted, quick as a flash, to move fully on top of me, pressing my body, still pliant from his earlier caresses, into the bed. One hand plunged into the hair at the nape of my neck, holding me fast as he dipped down to speak against my lips.

"That it makes you wanton, incapable of keeping your legs closed against my virile charms."

I laughed into his face, but his lips closed over my smiling mouth, eating away the humor until I was writhing beneath him. I moaned in protest when he pulled away.

"I take my virility very seriously, Elle. It's nothing to joke about."

"No, of course not." I nodded, my eyes wide with faux sincerity, and my lips compressed against the monumental urge to laugh at him again.

His eyes narrowed further as he tried to read my solemnity, but there was my favorite kind of smile in his eyes as he nodded and pressed a kiss to the tip of my nose.

"I'm glad we've got that sorted. Now, get up and get moving," he said as he rolled off me and walked into the bathroom.

I spoke loudly over the rush of the shower as he turned it on. "Can't we just spend the rest of the day in bed?"

His head ducked back out of the bathroom; his face creased with boyish excitement. "I have a surprise for you. Now, be a good girl and get your gorgeous self in the shower before I lose control and take you again."

I stretched languorously across the bed, rolling my spine up so that my breasts rounded and presented themselves to him. His face tightened with desire as I got up and slowly sauntered over to him, my hips swaying like a pendulum, hypnotizing him. When I finally reached him, his eyes were dark as midnight and still trained down my body, taking in the heavy slopes of my breast, swollen even more with the pregnancy, and the faint tilt of my belly as it arrowed into my bare sex. I was sure that it was the swell of my belly that turned him on the most. The caveman.

I reached out to wrap my fingers around the base of his once more hard cock and gave it a firm tug. He shuddered and ground his back teeth together. With my other hand, I cupped the underside of my breast, weighing it in my palm before flicking my hard nipple with my thumb.

"Fuck, look at you," he groaned. "You are trying to make me lose my mind."

I grinned slyly. "Is it working?"

"*Desolé*, did you say something?"

My laugh was breathy. "Come shower with me."

"We really do have somewhere to be." He caught my wrist as I moved it over his dick. "It's important, Elle."

I paused because there was an urgency in his voice, and he wouldn't turn down sex for just anything.

"Okay... We'll make it quick." I launched myself at him, forcing him to catch me as he stumbled back into the bathroom.

"Elle..."

"Quit stalling. We have places to be, Frenchman. *On y va!*"

He laughed as he placed us both under the hot stream of water, and he was still laughing against my lips when I took him inside me again.

LATER, AFTER WE FINALLY EMERGED FROM THE SHOWER SKIN WRINKLED AND satiated, I followed Sinclair into the back of a Town Car with no idea of our destination. I watched him as we drove, how his jaw clenched and unclenched rhythmically, and his eyes tracked the blurred landscape flowing out the car window. He held my hand stiffly, but whenever he noticed he was doing so, he made a conscious effort to relax his fingers and throw me a small, inauthentic smile.

For whatever reason, my Frenchman was nervous.

I bit my lip, wanting badly to pester him about it but also deeply intrigued by his uncharacteristic bought of anxiety. This was the man who handled multi-national land deals, who had faced the scrutiny of New York City society without a tremor and survived a childhood in a poor French orphanage.

Sinclair nervous?

I was both giddy and terrified of what that could mean.

When Puerto Los Cabos appeared through the windows, and we came to a stop at the familiar marina, I was even more shocked.

"Sinclair?" I asked as we exited the car, somewhat nervous myself.

He took my hand and smiled down at me, a real smile this time, but the nerves remained in his eyes. "My siren."

"We're going fishing?"

"Not this time."

I cocked my head in question, but he only responded by smiling tightly before he led us forward down the dock. Instead of going to the left, where all the fishing boats bumped quietly against the wooden partitions, we went right. Huge yachts and sailboats gleamed on either side of us as we walked down the planks. I readjusted my grip on my beach bag and wondered why Sin had asked me to bring a nice change of clothes and my makeup.

"Sin?"

"Oui, mon amour?"

"Why are you being weird? You are making me nervous."

He stopped, turning to me with his thick brows raised in surprise. I almost laughed because the expression was so foreign on his face.

"I am acting weird?" he echoed, staring over my shoulder for a moment as if looking through memories of the last half an hour to test the validity of my statement. Finally, he looked back at me, threw his head back, and laughed loudly. "I am. My apologies, my mind was in a different place."

I stared at him suspiciously, but he seemed genuine enough, so my mouth dropped into a pout. "I'm not enough to hold your attention?"

His eyes sparkled so brightly that I blinked against the shine. He took me into his arms in a bear hug and lifted me into the air, laughing. "You are always and, sometimes inconveniently, on my mind."

I grinned down into his face, placing my palm on the creases his smile made in his cheek. My love for him spilled out of my overfull heart and into my chest, pressing against my lungs almost painfully. I couldn't breathe, but I didn't really care.

"My love for you is greater than the world," I told him in English this time.

"*Toujours*," he said.

Always.

I smiled, at ease again, as I slipped to the ground and took his hand again, moving forward. He stilled me, and when I turned around with a frown, he gestured to a gorgeous yacht just over his shoulder.

"This is our ride."

My mouth dropped open.

"*Ahola, buenos dias, Signor Sinclair*," an older Mexican man appeared from around the side of the vessel. He was dressed in a sharp white uniform and captain's hat. "Welcome to *Cuatro Vientos*, I am your captain, Oscar."

I looked over at Sinclair in mute excitement as Oscar led us onto the deck. He grinned at me as we toured the massive ship, taking in the open concept gallery complete with a small grand piano and a gorgeous lacquered mahogany bar the same rich color as Sinclair's hair. There was a master bathroom with an en suite that housed a deep Jacuzzi as well as four other rooms for sleeping and three bathrooms. The kitchen was small but beautifully appointed and currently stocked to the brim with fresh produce and copious amounts of alcohol. There were two men already steering the boat out of the harbor from deep leather chairs, and they took a moment to explain some of the finer equipment to Sinclair when he leaned forward like an eager boy to examine the many panels of tech.

"This is amazing," I breathed as we finally emerged into the open air of the top deck.

The ocean spread out before us, an azure blue unblemished by a single white cap. The sun spilled fistfuls of glitter across the glossy surface like a trail for us to follow into the sunset. My heart seized at the sight, at the thought, because it invariably led me to think about my own happily ever after with Sinclair. Was this it?

I turned back to face him with my heart in my eyes, disorientated when I found him on the ground before me.

"Are you okay?" I asked, deeply puzzled.

His smile was dazzling, fully realized across his hard features. It was so beautiful, from the square edges of his white teeth to the pink stretch of his full lips and the manly crease that cut into his cheeks, that I lost my breath.

"I have never been so happy," he said, echoing my words from earlier that morning. I was distracted by the way the breeze ruffled his overlong hair, how it painted the dark brown with glittering copper and brilliant reds. That was my excuse for not noticing the way his hands cupped a velvet box the way a man might have cradled a baby, with reverence, joy, and a considerable amount of worry.

"Giselle, my siren," he said, drawing my attention back to his face. "Come here to me."

I breached the few feet between us and stared down into his face, cupping it with one hand because I still wasn't used to touching him, to the fact that I was not only allowed but encouraged to.

"Elle," Sinclair's voice was amused as he once again drew my attention back to what he was saying.

"Mmm? I'm sorry, I'm overwhelmed by how beautiful you look." I blushed and rushed on to explain, "I don't think I'll ever get used to being with you. It's impossible not to touch you, not to love you like this."

He made a noise in the back of his throat that was practically a purr. "If you were paying attention to me, you would understand that I'm asking you to spend the rest of your life loving me like this."

My eyes were drawn down to his hands as they presented me with a deep blue velvet box. I was gasping before it was even flipped open to reveal the most gorgeous ring I had ever seen. The large oval sapphire glowed like a midnight sky filled with lightning, glowing from the facets and the exact color of Sinclair's beloved gaze. A thin halo of diamonds surrounded the gem and encased the slim platinum band. My fingers shook as I reached forward to touch the ring, to test its reality.

"What's happening?" I breathed, too shocked to be embarrassed.

"I am asking you to be my wife. I am trying to claim you in every conceivable way so that there will never be any doubt in your mind, in mine or anyone else's, that Daniel Sinclair and Giselle Moore were made to be together and that they will remain together for the rest of their lives." He watched the tears begin to spill down my face, and his eyes warmed, his features softened with a vulnerability that only his love for me could produce. "I told you at our first meeting that I was afraid you would change my life, and you have. Elle, you have taken everything I ever knew and threw it into brilliant perspective with your generous soul and beauty. I have never felt more like a man, more complete and successful, full of fucking life, as I have with you."

"But..." A huge rush of air flew past my lips as I struggled to make sense of this. "You don't believe in marriage."

His eyes sparkled brighter than the sapphire diamond ring. "I believe in nothing as much as I do our love. I want to be able to call you my wife. I can think of nothing better than being your husband, except perhaps being the father to your children."

"Oh God," I sobbed, so inelegant with emotion, so saturated with love and hope and all those emotions that steal your breath away and set your mind to spinning faster than a top. "I love you so much. Of course, I will be your wife. I'll be anything you want me to be."

"*Vraiment? Tu seras ma femme?*"

"Yes," I cried, sliding my hand into his hair and the other over his dear, dear face. "Of course, I will be your wife."

I had never seen anything as wonderful as his face broken open with joy, his eyes so bright and his smile so wide. It almost hurt to know that I was capable of bringing such a man to his knees with elation.

He wrapped his arms around my waist and tugged me even closer so that he could place his cheek against my stomach. "I love you."

"I love you too."

He looked up at me with a slight smile. "Do not take offense, but this time I was talking to our baby."

I laughed, smoothed a hand through his wind-tossed hair. "I will never take offense to that."

He tugged me down to the deck, dragging me into his lap so that I was sitting there, my legs wrapped around his back, my face tucked into his neck and his arms wrapped securely around me. We stayed like that for a long minute, trying to absorb the monumental amount of joy saturating the moment.

"Marry me right now," he said, finally.

"Sin," I giggled, pressed a kiss to the pulse in his throat.

His arms tightened. "Marry me right now."

"Don't kid."

"I don't have time for jokes."

"I thought it was that you didn't have time to be nice?" I teased, leaning back so that I could look into his face.

It was a very serious face at the moment. "I don't have time for a lot of things. This is why I want to marry you right now."

I pursed my lips as I took in his utter sincerity. "Are you asking me to elope?"

The idea wasn't totally absurd. As it was, most of my family would have a hard time justifying attending our wedding, given that Sinclair had been with Elena as little as six months ago. I didn't even know if I was prepared for the society wedding that Willa Percy would want to throw us, and I certainly wasn't prepared for Mama's exclusion in the preparations. My heart panged. No, if I were going to marry Sinclair, as I was suddenly so desperate to do even though the thought hadn't ever really occurred to me, we would have to elope.

"No," Sin was saying, carefully looking into my eyes. "I'm saying that is why I brought you here."

"To Mexico?" I asked, surprised yet again.

He shook his head slowly. "No, here to the place where I knew for sure that I had fallen in love with you."

I frowned as he stood, offered me his hand so that I could get up as well. He led me to the side of the deck, gesturing dramatically to the scene in front of us.

It was the same beach we had spent the afternoon snorkeling at during our weeklong affair. I immediately recognized the huge outcroppings of red rock that acted like parenthesis for the long curve of sterling white sand and the gracefully arching palm trees and colorful fauna beyond that. But I registered all of that with the periphery of my mind because the sight of the people waiting on the shore, mingling amid white chairs before an arbor wrapped in bright hibiscus flowers, consumed me. I spotted Santiago and Kat Herrera, Cage and Candy, and the rest of the original Mexico crew, even Margot and Antonio, the Percys were talking to Eddie and Rossi, who had their arms around each other.

"Sin, what have you done?" I breathed.

His chuckle stirred the hair by my ear as he wrapped his arms around me as if he knew my knees were about to give out and I needed the extra support.

"I've tried to make us both happy by giving you a wedding filled with all the people you love, in a place where we fell in love."

"And how does this make you happy?"

"*Mon amour*, I would marry you in front of dumpster with sewer rats as witnesses if it meant I could marry you immediately. This seemed like a better option."

I laughed, turning in his arms so I could link my arms around his neck and press myself flush against him.

"I promise, I'm going to make you so happy," I murmured reverently.

His hand cupped the back of my head, and his sigh was full of contentment when he said, "Nothing else can but you."

We embraced for a long moment before someone on shore shouted our name, pulling us apart.

"Save that for the honeymoon!" Cage hollered from the beach. "Sinclair, get off that monstrosity so your future bride can get ready."

"Fuck off, Cage," Sinclair yelled back, carefree and full of good humor.

To me, he said, "There is a surprise waiting for you in the bedroom downstairs. Why don't you go ready yourself to be my bride, and I'll meet you out on the beach whenever you are prepared?"

I nodded but felt a tearing sensation at my heart as he moved away from me and began to step down to the lower level. Sensing my yearning or maybe succumbing to his own, he paused and turned back to smile at me.

"Don't take too long, my siren. Thirty minutes tops, *d'accord*?"

I tipped my chin into the air with faux airs. "You cannot rush a woman on her wedding day, Mr. Sinclair."

"Thirty minutes, Mrs. Sinclair, or I'll carry you to the altar over my shoulder."

The witty reply I had prepared withered on my tongue as I gasped at the shock of hearing myself called Mrs. Sinclair. I drifted downstairs in a fog of fantasy and joy, pinching myself a few times to ensure that I wasn't dreaming.

Was it possible for the villain in a story to have a happy ending? Maybe authors just ended the book before they had to explore the potential for the antagonist's growth into someone *worthy* of such a thing.

"I can't believe this is happening," I said out loud as I moved into the master suite, hoping that saying it out loud would make everything more real.

"Well, you better believe it, *bambina*."

I spun around, unable to believe that Cosima could be standing there.

But she was.

My sister looked absolutely stunning, her skin a deep olive-brown and aglow with health, her curves fully recovered from the emaciated shape she had been in over a month ago when I have last seen her. Her long black hair rippled over her shoulders all the way to her waist, and her smile was easy, absolutely gorgeous.

"Cosima," I said because if she was a mirage induced by my happy delirium, then I needed to know.

"Giselle," she said, planting her hands on her slight hips and narrowing her eyes at me. "I hope you didn't think that you could get married without me."

"How?"

Her smile was gentle with compassion as she moved forward to plant a fragrant kiss against my cheek. She still smelled spicy and sweet like only she could.

"Sinclair reached out to Dante, who knew how to get in touch with me."

"Why did you leave?" I had to know. How could she have disappeared after such a terrible accident and left us all to wonder?

Her lips twisted. "I'm so sorry, *bambina*. I wanted to explain things to you, but they are so complicated, and now, well, it is not the time to share my long-winded, frankly horrifying story with you. Now is the time to ready my beloved sister for her wedding day."

I bit my lip as I digested her words. I wanted to press until she broke open under the pressure, spilling all those terrible secrets that had haunted her since she was too young to harbor them, but I also knew that she would never taint my day with her horrors, and it would be wrong of me to ruin the surprise of her presence with grim realities.

"Okay," I said, smiling.

"That was a lot easier than I thought it would be," Candy commented from her spot lounging on the bed. "If I ever disappear, I hope you're harder on me, girl."

I laughed as I launched myself at the bed, smothering Candy in kisses. She grunted under the assault even as her hands pulled me closer.

"Darlin', there will be plenty of time to be kissing later, and the person you'll be kissing is a damn sight easier on the eyes than Candy Kay," Brenna drawled as she emerged from the bathroom. "No offense, Candy."

"None taken. Sinclair is a serious hottie."

"Oh my God, I cannot believe this is happening," I said, my hands pressed to my flaming cheeks. "This is a dream."

"No, *bambina*, this is real, and I hope you are sure about it."

I froze, afraid to look over at the bathroom and acknowledge the woman who stepped out from behind Brenna. I hadn't spoken to her in weeks. The possibility of bursting into tears was pretty high if I turned to face her without steeling myself. So, I took a deep breath, reminded myself that I had survived motherless for four years in Paris and the only family I needed was Sinclair.

It was mostly bullshit, but it made me feel better, nonetheless.

Caprice Lombardi was a beautiful woman who looked nothing like me and everything like the twins, the long black waves and deeply olive skin, even the expression of intensity that seemed to arrest their features at all times. We shared the same curves, though, the figure-eight shape that I'd once been so self-conscious of and a similar smile, the way our cheeks dimpled slightly, and our lips stretched.

She was smiling at me now, and those soft arms were outstretched. "Come and give your mama a hug."

A sob rose in my throat. I didn't care that I was already crying by the time I folded myself in her semolina and lemon-scented embrace. Apparently, it was a day for tears.

She hushed me as one hand stroked down my hair, soothing me the way she had when I was a baby, pressing my head to her bosom so that I could take comfort from her heartbeat.

"Mama," I murmured, over and over in a small broken voice.

"*Si, mia bambina, tua madra.*"

"I'm so happy that you're here. I didn't think... I mean, I never hoped you would be at my wedding."

It was Mama's turn to cry. "Oh no, no, I could never miss this. You are my child. You are my *life*."

I sniffed. "You were so disappointed in me." When her face crumpled, I hastened to say, "No, Mama, I understood why you were. It was fair. It just hurt." I didn't explain how her apathy had crippled me; how my heart had skipped random beats, shuddering and clenching in my chest whenever I thought about her, which was often.

There was nothing like a mother's censure to paralyze the spirit.

"I did not like the way you came together, yes? The hurt you brought Elena, it was terrible and great. She deserved someone's loyalty, and I knew this, that she would not get that from the twins. They understand too much about the messiness of love, and they have always loved you almost like a parent loves their child. They would give you and forgive you anything. Elena needed someone, *capisci*?"

It made sense, of course. Elena was so alone, and even though she had played a large part in her isolation, it was my fault that it had become so starkly defined. I'd taken the love of her partner and the support of our family and any friends she had made through Sinclair. It disturbed me in a third-person kind of way that the greatest consequences felt by my affair had landed on my own sister.

"Okay, we are all happy and together, hurrah hurray! Now, let's get down to the business of making this girl into a bride, hmm?" Candy said, flouncing off the bed to drag me into the bathroom. "Wait until you see the dress your man picked out for you."

"It's a bit indecent for a traditional wedding, but I guess this is a beach ceremony," Brenna allowed, her Southern-born conservatism showing through.

Cosima snorted. "You will look like a vision. Sin won't know what hit him."

I smiled at the thought, but I still hadn't absorbed the blow that the presence of the best women in my life had dealt me. How long had Sinclair planned this for? How could he have known that this was exactly what I needed our wedding to be, in Cabo to bring everything full circle, with all our loved ones and no one else to judge what we had? If I hadn't known Sinclair loved me, there was no way to doubt it now. He was the man who turned all my dreams into realities, spun all my fears into golden desires.

He was the man I had always been destined to marry.

Chapter Twenty-Five

Giselle

I KNEW IMMEDIATELY WHY SINCLAIR HAD CHOSEN THE DRESS FOR ME. IT WAS A delicately constructed mermaid-style dress with an open back, a v in the front that exposed a deep swathe of cleavage, and slight capped sleeves that frothed over my shoulders. The open weave, off-white crochet and lace patterned exposed flashes of skin without being indecent and pooled behind me in a slight train. It was bohemian, utterly unique, and gorgeous, but most of all, with my hair tousled in waves over my shoulder, I looked like a siren emerged from the depths of the Pacific dressed in sea foam come to find her sailor.

My bridesmaids and Mama went to shore first in a small motorboat after long minutes of reassurances, tears and embraces. I waited, fidgeting in the other boat that would take me to the beach, nervous as I'd ever been even though it was ridiculous to feel anything but excitement.

When I arrived on the sand, there was an aisle bracketed by small shells and coral leading up to the wedding arch, and Sebastian waited for me in the shallows to help me out of the boat. The cool ocean water kissed the bottom of my dress even though I held it up, but it felt appropriate to meet Sinclair with golden slippers of sand on my feet and salt spray on my skin.

"You look like a dream," Sebastian whispered as he took my arm, gently tucking it into his.

"Seb, you're crying," I noticed, shocked.

We hadn't had an easy childhood, one filled with violence or at least, the threat of it, poverty and fear. Through none of it had my brother—the man of our house since the tender age of seventeen but really, the true patriarch long before our father disappeared—cried.

His smile reminded me that he was a movie star before his words even registered. "I'm an actor, Giselle. I'm man enough to cry, and I'm damn pretty when I do it."

I laughed, the tension that I hadn't been aware of drained from my shoulders.

"I love you," I reaffirmed.

"*Sempre*," he confirmed. *Forever*. "Now, are you ready to become a Sinclair?"

I squeezed his arm and dragged him forward in answer, startling a laugh from him. Sinclair's eyes were on me, had been tracking every one of my movements since I appeared on the horizon, but I took a moment to check out the guests lining the aisle because I knew once I locked eyes with my Frenchman, he would be all I saw.

Cage grinned hugely at me, his arms crossed over his huge chest in a smug way that told me he thought he had played a vital role in bringing Sin and I together. I tipped my head to him, acknowledging the truth of it.

Dante was there too, bigger even than Cage but not as imposing as the man who stood beside him. I recognized Alexander Davenport and as I watched him watching Cosima instead of me, his eyes trained on her with a degree of possession and dark desire that was uncivilized, I knew that he was the reason for her disappearance, that she wouldn't have been allowed here without his permission and, apparently, his presence.

The Percys both smiled at me, Mortimer's was wide and uncensored with pleasure, and Willa's was appropriately bashful. She had tried to derail our union at every turn but now that it was happening, now that I was carrying her grandchild, she had wholeheartedly embraced me.

My Mexico crew, including, even, Margot and Antonio, all clapped as I passed, making me blush even as their approval filled me with joy.

I was ready to look at Sinclair, but his cool French-tinted tones beat me to it.

"Look at your future husband, *ma sirène*."

His words hooked my gaze and drew it directly to his. The blue of his eyes consumed me for a long moment. I would never find the right words to describe the vividness of the color, the shape of his lids, or the beauty of his russet lashes, let alone the ones needed to explain the look in his eyes at the moment. *Worshipful* was the word that came closest to the swirl of love, possession, awe, and gratefulness that seized him. I recognized it only because I could feel the very same thing sluice through my veins.

Inappropriately, I wanted to get on my knees before him and show him how much he was revered with my lips, teeth, and tongue, with long strokes of my fingers and sharp exclamations from my nails.

Sin's eyes flashed as they recognized the dirty path to my thoughts.

Later, he mouthed through the wicked smile pulling his lips wide.

My brother pressed a kiss to my cheek and carefully, appreciating the symbolism of it, placed my hand in Sinclair's.

"I've cared for her my entire life," Seb said, half benediction, half warning.

Sinclair surprised me by stepping closer, clapping a manly hand over Seb's shoulder. "You've done so well, *mio fratello*. Rest easy now. I have her."

Seb closed his eyes, swallowed thickly, and nodded. "*Si, tu sei la sua.*"

Thank God for waterproof makeup because I was crying.

Sinclair smiled brilliantly as my brother stepped away, and he turned to me fully. I laughed when he tugged me indecently close, our hips flush, one of his large hands at my hips and the other on my cheek, fingertips in the hair over my ear. His eyes bored into mine even when he said to the officiate, "You may begin."

I cried throughout the vows, but happily, they were silent tears, and when Sin dipped his finger in one that streaked across my face, bringing it to his mouth where he licked it away with sparkling eyes, I knew that he didn't mind. His voice was hoarse when he declared 'I do' and when the officiator began to say that Sin could kiss his bride, his hands clenched and unclenched on my skin in restless anticipation.

Finally, he hauled me tight against his body, his arm an iron band across my back and the other tightly woven in my hair so that he could angle my head to seal his mouth completely over mine. I moaned into the kiss, sucking at his velvety tongue as it dipped between my lips. Desire rocketed through me, heady like a drug rush and just as inappropriate to be experiencing at a wedding.

"I cannot wait to fuck my wife tonight," Sin said as he took my ear between his teeth and tugged.

I hissed, my knees weakening so that his arms were the only things holding me up. He took my mouth again in a passionate kiss. Vaguely, I was aware of clapping and catcalling from our assembled guests, but embarrassment was drowned out by pure lust.

Just when I thought I was going to have to climb him, rip off his clothes and ride him like an animal in heat, he pulled away to place his forehead against mine. His uneven breath wafted across my lips, heady and smoky as his fragrance.

Our friends and family were waiting to congratulate us, to party in celebration on the absurdly extravagant yacht that Santiago had lent us for the occasion but for now, it was just us, Sinclair and me.

"You look better than any fantasy I could have had."

I blushed.

"And this blush..." His thumb trailed over my pink cheekbone. "My wife has the prettiest blush."

"Your wife," I echoed, momentarily stunned. "We're married."

"Yes, that is typically the result of a wedding," Sin teased, his rare boyish grin appearing.

"Do you think we deserve this, to be this happy?" I wondered out loud for one tremulous moment.

His forehead pressed hard into mine, his fingers squeezed firmly where they clutched me. I knew if he had his way, we would be stitched together cheek to cheek, thigh to thigh, knitted forever as one person. That was how much he loved me, and more, how much he yearned to possess every inch of me. My mind spun with giddiness, pure euphoria.

"There is no way in my mind or in the minds of anyone here today that we were meant to be anything but together. Fuck the consequences, fuck the right or wrong of it."

Whatever the inception of our relationship, we had evolved and grown into something bigger than morality. We had cheated and lied and caused inexorable heartbreak in each other and those closest to us. We were sinners, undoubtedly, of the highest order. There was no way to deny or forget those truths. They just didn't matter anymore. Maybe it was about damn time the villain had a happily ever after.

I pressed my lips to Sinclair's, showing him how much I agreed with him, how much I only really cared about him, about us. How selfish my love was and how okay I was with it.

When he pulled away again, his eyes blazed with glory, an athlete who had trained and trained and imagined the win and who now, finally, held his prize in his hands.

"You are mine," he said in fierce triumph.

"*Toujours*." I agreed.

Giselle

I was nervous.

There wasn't really any reason to be. Either way, I knew Sinclair would be thrilled. After all, this was our baby, his family, and nothing meant more than his new family.

Still, I was nervous because even though we'd spoken teasingly about it, I wanted to give Sinclair the baby he wanted. Obviously, it was out of my hands and in nature's, but that didn't stop me from worrying.

So I was fidgeting when I arrived at Osteria Lombardi and handed Clarabelle my coat to take before I weaved my way through the busy restaurant to the back corner where my Frenchman awaited me at the table Mama always reserved for family.

I knew he had sensed me the moment I'd entered because his head was up, eyes sparkling like faceted sapphires with anticipation as I rounded the corner and appeared before him.

He leaned back against the leather booth and shook his head, his lips slightly tilted as he took me in. I was wearing a sheer black dress and no underwear. Only strategically placed swathes of lace and jet beading kept the outfit from being entirely indecent.

"*Tu es manifique*," he said, recovering enough to stand to greet me. "Come give your husband a kiss, wife."

It had only been a month, and the newness of being Daniel Sinclair's wife had yet to wear off. I doubted it ever would.

I hop-skipped the final step to him even though I was in impractically tall heels, but his smoky chuckle as he caught me in his arms was worth the risk of falling.

"Hi," I breathed, looking into the face that had irrevocably changed my life.

"Hi," he whispered back, his eyes so bright with love they left sun spots in my vision.

"Elle?" he asked after a long moment of staring. "Are you going to kiss your husband, or is he going to have to take one from his wife?"

Immediately, I pressed my smiling lips to his. Sinclair made quick work of opening my mouth under his, slanting my head to the side with a firm hand in the hair at the nape of my neck, and kissing me breathless.

As my oxygen ran low, I thought vaguely that I never needed to breathe again as long as I could have this from him.

When we parted, he kept me close and ran his hands through my hair before bringing his knuckles to my cheek for a soft caress.

"How is my siren and *mon petit choux*?" he asked me quietly.

My belly warmed at his pet name for our baby, his little cabbage.

"We are both blissfully happy," I told him as I had told him every day since we were married.

I'd been lucky that my morning sickness had been tolerable and hadn't lasted beyond the third month. Now, I felt fantastic, and I was beyond proud of the swelling baby bump under my dress.

Sinclair placed his palm flat against my belly and spread his fingers out, his eyes on his hand as he did so. I struggled to absorb the enormity of love and awe in his electric blue eyes. How was it possible that after all I'd done, I deserved such a man?

"I'm still upset that you didn't wait to reschedule the appointment at the doctor until I could attend," he said as he led me to my seat and settled me with a kiss to the forehead before he retook his chair.

"Even you agreed that it was best I didn't miss any appointments after what Christopher did to me," I reminded him softly even though I hated saying that name.

Sin pressed his lips into a flat line and reached across the table with his palm up, demanding my hand. I gave it to him, watching as he gently clasped it between his fingers and began to play with my wedding rings. It was a habit he'd quickly developed, one that I knew brought him comfort. My Frenchman liked to reassure himself often of our connection, and in public, when he couldn't take me or sit with his hand pressed intimately to my belly over our growing child, he settled for touching the rings that legally made me his.

"We are celebrating our one-month anniversary today, not speaking of that man. Let me change the subject. How did the interview with Jerry Saltz go?"

I beamed at him as I thought back on my interview with the art critic from the *New York* mag. He'd written one of the best reviews after my gallery showing and demanded Rossi give him my phone number so he could get an exclusive interview with the woman "who dared to be deviant."

"It went beautifully. He's an incredibly interesting man. I still can't believe he's so interested in my work," I admitted.

A server arrived at our table with a bottle of sparkling apple juice that, after a chin tip from Sinclair, he proceeded to open the way one would a bottle of champagne.

"Fancy," I joked, but Sin's face was set with sobriety.

"Jerry is one of the best in his field, Elle, so it is, in fact, not at all surprisingly that he would champion your work given that it is remarkable."

I stared into his eyes and realized for the millionth time that Sinclair would never rest until I understood my own potential and loved myself at least half as much as he loved me.

I squeezed his hand gently and said softly, "*D'accord.*"

He nodded curtly, which made me bite back a smile.

"Caprice has prepared a special meal for you, if she may?" the server asked.

Sinclair nodded but kept his eyes on me as the other man swept away. He cocked his head slightly, narrowing his eyes at me.

"What is it, my love?"

I sucked in a deep breath and straightened my shoulders to steel myself against the possibility of disappointment.

"I, I found out the sex of the baby today," I admitted.

Sinclair's eyes flashed and crackled like lightning. "Tell me."

"Sin..."

"Elle, tell me now," he demanded, leaning forward with an intensity that vibrated the air around us.

I swallowed thickly but managed to look into his heartbreakingly beautiful face.

Maintaining the contact, I slid the brown paper-wrapped present I'd plucked from my purse across the table toward him.

He stared at me for a moment before opening the present efficiently with one hand so that he could keep his other laced with mine. I was staring hard at his face as he unearthed the frame from within. Otherwise, I might have missed the way his breath stuttered and came to a stop in his chest.

I waited for him to recover, but he didn't. He just stared and stared at the silver picture frame that held the first picture of our child. On the top of the frame was written in cheesy but beautiful words, Daddy's Little Girl.

"A daughter," he finally said, his voice so soft I nearly missed it.

"Yes, a daughter. She's going to have your eyes and your laughter and, I hope, your brain," I babbled on because I was nervous about his lack of reaction. "Basically, I hope she is a mini Sinclair."

"No," Sinclair said, his voice whipping through the air to crack against my sensitive skin.

I flinched, then breathed, "No?"

"No," he said, tipping his face up from the frame so I could see the way his eyes burned beneath the lacquer of tears. "She will be exactly as her mother is, and just as I feel for her mother, no one will ever love her more than I will."

I hadn't realized how tense I was until the starch washed out of my skin.

"Sin," I breathed.

"Come here," he ordered.

I went there, folding myself into his lap even though we were in Mama's gorgeous and sophisticated restaurant. People were staring, but I didn't care because my Frenchman had his arms around me, and he was so thrilled about having a daughter, he was even moved to tears.

He captured my face in his hands and stared deep into my eyes to say, "I love you more than any man has ever loved any woman. I don't care if that's arrogant. It's the fucking truth."

"I know," I replied instantly. "Because I feel the same about you."

"We aren't staying for dinner," he told me.

I pulled back with a frown. "But Mama made us a special meal."

"If they can pack it up, we'll take it, but I'm taking you home now. I plan to have you naked and spread out like my own personal buffet within the next twenty minutes. I think that will be enough to satiate my hunger, and Elle, I can promise you I will feed you enough of my cock that you will forget all about food."

I wriggled in his lap as wetness pooled between my thighs. "Yes, sir."

His eyes flashed then darkened, and as the server walked passed, he ordered brusquely, "Bill, please."

"Show me, my siren, how you kneel so prettily for your husband."

Instantly, my body collapsed like wet clay to the ground, ready for his hands and will to mold me into whatever shape would please him best. My hair swished over my shoulders as I bent my head to assume the proper position, and I shivered at even that delicate touch.

"Such a good wife," Sinclair told me even as his foot came out to kick slightly between my thighs. "Now, spread those creamy thighs nice and wide, and show me how wet I make your pretty pussy."

I whimpered as my clit throbbed to the beat of his words even as I obeyed him. Cool air wafted over my molten core as I spread my legs to the point of pain, desperate to show him how much I needed him.

"Mmm," Sin hummed as he gracefully fell into a crouch before me. I gasped softly when he reached out with two fingers to open my pussy up further so he could run his thumb through the silky wetness at my entrance and over my pulsing clit.

I writhed under his ministrations and begged softly, "Please, sir."

"Tell me what you need."

"More, sir."

The blue of his eyes flashed frozen as he coolly reminded me, "Use your words."

"I need your cock," I panted as his fingers circled my entrance and dipped just barely inside me.

I knew better than to grind down on his hand, but my hips twitched in protest, my cunt clenching against the emptiness.

"Better," my husband praised, then rewarded me by sinking three thick fingers deep into my wet heat.

I tipped my head back, eyes still on his as I groaned. He thrust deeper, lifting me into the air by my pussy so that I was balanced precariously, entirely dependent on his hold to keep me aloft.

My legs shook as my wetness coated his fingers and began to slide down my inner thighs. Somehow still keeping me raised, he pumped his fingers and rubbed against the knot of sensation on my front wall while his thumb skirted delicate figure eights over my clit.

He had been touching me for two minutes, and I was ready to come.

"Keep yourself spread for me, Elle," my Frenchman ordered.

I whimpered, desperate to rub my legs together, to grind down on his talented fingers. Instead, I held myself still as a marble statue. Only my pussy moved, grasping at him as he pistoned in and out.

"Such a greedy cunt you have, Elle," Sinclair said conversationally.

He reached out to pull the cups of my bra under my breasts so that they were indecently plumped up. I watched dazedly as he brought his free hand to his firm mouth, and his tongue flicked out to wet the pads of two digits. Quick as a lightning strike and just as painful, he lashed out to twist and pull one of my nipples.

I gasped loudly, hips bucking against his fingers as the pain burned through my chest and turned into radiating pleasure.

He did it again with the other nipple. I grounded down shamelessly on the steady, slowly pumping fingers in my pussy.

The burn of the pinch contrasted against the cool his wet fingers had left on my skin. It was so delicious, I almost couldn't stand it.

"Please, sir," I cried out softly.

He ignored me, which ratcheted my arousal up another dangerous decibel. Instead, he lazily reached out to give my pebbled nipple a hard flick.

I sucked in a breath between my teeth and rode his fingers hard, my pussy rippling over them.

When my husband spoke, his voice was ice cold, but I could see the deep heat burning in his eyes. Another contrast that twisted me into delectable knots.

"Diamond hard for me," he said, flicking the other nipple. "Should I clamp these pretty red nipples?"

"If it would please you, sir," I managed to breathe.

It was the right response.

Sinclair dropped to his knees, drove a hand into the hair at the nape of my neck, and tugged hard so that my throat was exposed and he was glaring down at me. His face was stern with desire, his jaw a hard cliff's edge, his mouth pressed into a firm line that acted as a dam to his baser instincts. He wanted to let go, ravage me until I was boneless and taken beyond all rational thought. But first, he would dismantle me, thought by thought, until nothing was left in my head but him. His name strumming with each pulse of my heart as it beat strongly through every inch of my body.

"Sinclair," I rasped as it began.

"You please me," he bit out, violent with passion. "Your pussy on my hand, your juices leaking down my wrist, each rebellious twitch of those lush hips."

Impossibly, he added a fourth finger to my heat and drove deeper inside me, bringing me further up on my straining knees so that I was merely an inch from his mouth.

"It pleases me to know that I own this pussy, that you beg to take my cock in your sweet ass, that you love the feel of my cum on your skin because you know you've earned it."

"Yes," I hissed, nearly drooling with want and growing rabid with the need to orgasm.

"Please."

"Such a beautiful word coming from these lips." Sin dipped down to run his tongue along my pouting bottom lip before he swept it through my open mouth, catching my tongue in a wet dance as he sealed his lips over mine.

It was one of the most erotic kisses of my life, and I'd had a lot, given that I was married to Sinclair.

When he pulled away, I tried to follow, but the hand curled through my hair held me fast.

"How much can you take, my siren? If I wanted to plug your ass while I fuck your pussy so hard the chains on your nipple clamps dance, what would you say to your Dom?"

"Please. I want you to do whatever you want to me. I want to please you," I told him, infusing my voice with the potent mix of desire and love he'd cultivated in me.

Immediately, his hands left me. I whimpered at the loss of his fingers and had to clench my thigh muscles tight in order not to fall out of position as I settled back on my calves.

Sinclair strode to the walnut-paneled corner and began to pull out the toys. I shivered as I watched him move with the economy and grace of a large hunter readying for the hunt.

Only, he'd already caught me, shot me through the heart with an arrow dipped in love, and trapped me in a cage built with bars of loyalty and love.

I jolted from my thoughts when he returned. My arms were lax as he lifted them over my head, shackled them in soft leather and fur cuffs, and then affixed them to a bar hanging down from the ceiling that hadn't been there minutes ago.

"Adjustable." Sin's voice came as a whisper against my neck. "So I can take my siren any way I want."

A soft whir sounded as he raised the bar so that I was once again perched slightly uncomfortable on my wide-spread knees.

"Too much?" he asked.

"No, sir." And it wasn't. I loved the burning stretch that bracketed my aching sex.

I felt him move into position behind me and shivered when he wrapped his arms around my torso to pinch my nipples hard. He pulled and released them like taffy until they were as hard, red, and burning as cinnamon candies. Only then did he produce the delicate metal chain that linked together to clamps in the shape of clamshells.

I couldn't help the soft laughter that escaped me at the little reference to my nickname, siren.

Sinclair smiled against the side of my neck, then simultaneously bit firmly into the junction of my neck and shoulder as he clamped one nipple. I shuddered against him. He moved my hair from one shoulder to the other and repeated the same bite/clamping movement.

"Tip your ass for me." When I did as he ordered, his hands came out to smooth over the dramatic curves before one lifted and smacked down hard on my left cheek.

I groaned as the heat radiated through me.

He smacked the other cheek, then spread them so he could run the edge of his thumbs over my puckered entrance. I shivered as one hand left me, and I heard the unmistakable sound of the lube being opened.

"I hardly need to use this to prepare you," Sin said huskily. "Your pussy is dripping onto the floor."

God, that was hot. I loved being that turned on for him.

His thumb returned, wet with lube, and circled my entrance in increasingly firm strokes until I pushed back against it impatiently, and it drove inside.

I hummed my approval even as Sinclair spanked me again.

"Greedy," he chastised, but I knew he loved it.

"Please, sir, I need your cock," I begged.

"If I don't prepare you, it may hurt," he warned.

"Please."

He made a low, rough sound deep in his throat that sent a flurry of fireworks off in my groin. I felt the tip of his hot cock slide through my wetness, then notch at my entrance just as the tip of the butt plug nudged at my ass.

"You'll take what I give you," Sinclair ordered, banding one arm across my hips, ready to rip me apart at the seams.

"Always," I promised.

A second later, I screamed as his thick cock and the smaller plug thrust ruthlessly inside me. Painfully stretched and loving it, I thrust my hips back against both invasions and begged for more.

Sin rewarded me by sliding his cock nearly all the way out and then jamming it back home, grinding his hips against mine so that I could feel him at the very end of me. He kept up that merciless pace for a few minutes until I was sweaty and writhing against him.

"Keep those legs spread for me," he ordered, and a moment later, the plug inside my ass came to life with powerful vibrations that thumped like the beat of a drum against Sin's cock as it pistoned in and out of my sloppy wet pussy.

"Oh my God, oh my God," I chanted unconsciously.

"Take more."

He wrapped his hand around one hip and slammed me back down against him. With his other hand, he dived between my lewdly spread legs and played his fingers in the pool of wetness he found there. I gasped when his fingers slid farther back and cupped my mound, fingers splayed around his cock as it churned inside me.

"This cunt is mine."

"Yes, sir."

"My wife has the prettiest pussy, the greediest ass, and they are both all mine," he growled.

Yes, the savage was coming out to claim me, and I loved it.

"Yes, sir."

"Do you want to come, my siren?" he asked.

"Yes, yes, God, yes," I panted, on edge for so long that I felt stretched thin and ready to shatter at the barest impact.

"Then come for your husband," he commanded as he slid a finger inside my pussy beside his pumping dick and pressed his thumb hard to my swollen clit.

Instantly, I imploded. My womb clenched like a fist, so tight I thrummed with it, and then, just when blackness crept into the edges of my vision, the tension broke, and I melted into a pulsing mass of sex-drenched flesh.

"That's it," Sinclair urged. Then as if that wasn't enough, he quickly undid the nipple clamps, and the blood rushed painfully back into my breasts.

I screamed and screamed until my voice was hoarse as my orgasm continued, wringing every sensation out of every atom until I was disassembled, no longer human but vibrating atoms kept together by Sinclair's cock in my cunt, his hands cupped over my aching breasts, and his mouth clamped gently over the junction of my neck and shoulder.

Vaguely, I heard him groan, long and low and triumphant as he filled me with his cum.

I rested heavily on my shackles as he held me while we came down. His calloused fingers ran tenderly through my sweat-dampened hair, pulling it over one shoulder so he could trail a line of kisses behind my ear to the end of my shoulder. I melted further into him when he slowly pulled out of my aching sex and retrieved the no-longer-vibrating toy from my ass.

I startled slightly when his fingers spread my swollen sex and dived in to play with his cum. I turned my head to watch him watching my pussy as his seed slid from me and slicked my inner thighs.

"I love seeing my cum on you," he told me without taking his eyes off the sight.

I shuddered violently as an aftershock rippled through me.

"I love knowing it made the baby you carry for us," he said even more gently.

"Sin," I whispered, tears tightening my throat.

He looked up at me then with burning eyes that branded me with his everlasting love. "Thank you for giving that to me, my love."

I knew he meant more than my body just then, more even than the baby we'd made. He meant to thank me for our ongoing happily ever after, for giving him a life filled with color and a family worth fighting for.

"I love giving that to you," I told him honestly. "It's the best thing I'll ever do."

Love so fierce it contorted his face for a moment before he controlled it and made quick work of my shackles.

Before I could get cold, he wrapped my body in his arms and cuddled me onto his lap.

I closed my eyes to absorb the loving touch trailing over my cheeks, lips, and breasts, as they trailed down to my swollen stomach and both hands pressed there to frame the bump.

"Mon amour pour toi et notre bebe est plus grand que le monde," he said into my hair.

My love for you and our baby is bigger than the world.

Extended Epilogue

Sinclair

WE HADN'T SEEN ELENA IN YEARS.

I knew Giselle was nervous by the way she kept fidgeting, tugging the short hem of her lavender dress as far down her thighs as she could force it, no doubt wondering if her critical older sister would make some disparaging comment about a mother not showing too much skin. I palmed Elle's thigh in one hand and squeezed, relishing the way she instantly stilled, then softened into my touch.

Years later, and the magic of our love still fucking wowed me.

"Papa," Genny called from her high chair where she was coloring on a page the restaurant had given her when we sat down. "What does tante

Elena look like? Does she have red hair like Mama and me or black like oncle Seb and tante Cosi?"

I tugged on one of my daughter's curls, staring at the way the sun hit the strands and broke them into multitudes of copper and orange threads.

"Red like you, *ma petit choux*," I told her over her little giggle as I tugged at another spiral curl. "In fact, you look a lot like your aunt."

Her big blue eyes, my eyes, widened almost comically, and her pink mouth made a little 'o' of excited shock. "That's good. I like it when we all look like family. Even baby Theo has red hair!"

I smiled at her because she was so fucking adorable I couldn't even believe she was real sometimes. Still, I noticed Giselle squirm again from the corner of my eye and knew she wondered if Elena would act like family when she showed up. It had been five years since I'd left her for Elle. Five years, a marriage, and two children for us, and countless, often dangerous milestones for Elena in her career as a criminal lawyer and her role as a mafioso's paramour.

Who would have thought all those years ago that Elena would end up with one of the most notorious criminals on the planet? Staid, conservative, socially hyperaware Elena had turned her back on everything she knew.

All for the sake of love.

If she wasn't over her hatred of Elle and myself by now, I resolved that this would be the last time we saw her. I wasn't as nervous as my sensitive wife, though. Though we hadn't seen her in ages, our last interactions with the eldest Lombardi sibling had been largely positive.

Not to mention the time she'd saved my wife from Christopher.

"Where is she?" Genny asked, finishing her drawing with a flourish so she could hold it up in one hand and flap it around like a flag for us to admire. "I made her a drawing!"

Elle finally laughed, caught up in our daughter's constant enthusiasm and habit of exclaiming at everything she found exciting or beautiful, which was most things in life. She had gotten her mother's love of art and beauty, and my desire to be heard.

"It's beautiful, little beauty."

Giselle and I both froze for a fraction of a second as the smooth voice sounded over our shoulders. It was the same tone of voice I'd once heard every day for four years, but the intonation was completely different, smooth and rolling with the lyricism of her native Italy. It suited her high, lyrical voice, but not the woman who had forced herself to speak accentless as long as I'd known her.

I adjusted Theo's sleeping body against my chest with one arm so that I could turn slightly to see the woman I'd once foolishly thought myself in love with.

And not for the first time in my life, I was grateful for my cultivated poker face.

Elena was almost a stranger to me then, and I knew by the gasp that fell from my wife's lips that she felt the very same sense of disassociation.

Oh, Elena was still elegant as hell, her posture straight as a ballerina's, her long, tapered fingers tipped red, her dress obviously expensive.

But that was it.

She wore her hair long now, down past her breasts in a messy length of waves that immediately brought to mind the way Elle's hair looked after I'd mussed it in the bedroom. Where she'd always kept meticulously out of the sun to stave off wrinkles and age spots, she was caramelized and baring more skin than I'd ever seen her expose in public before though she was a long way from being indecent.

But it was the expression on her face that rendered her completely altered than the woman I'd once claimed to know.

She was smiling.

A soft curve of her red painted lips warmed her dark gray eyes like sunlit storm clouds and creased her cheeks in a way that brought out a faint dimple I'd never noticed in her left side.

Her eyes were fixed on Genny as she leaned forward toward our daughter and raised a hand to smooth out the drawing she had made for her. She studied it seriously, the way an art critic measured one of Elle's now-famous sensual paintings.

Genny bounced in her seat, her lips rolled between her teeth, her eyes wide as she took in her aunt and waited for her judgment.

"*Bellisima*," Elena declared after a moment before pressing a sweet kiss to Genny's plump cheek. "May I keep it?"

My daughter nodded mutely, a little awestruck by the pretty aunt she hardly remembered. She watched as Elena carefully folded the paper and slipped it into her big leather purse.

"I'll put it on my fridge so I can always see it," Elena told her with a little wink.

I blinked.

The woman I'd dated hadn't even allowed magnets on our fridge.

"I'm sorry we're late," Elena said, finally adjusting her stance to address Giselle and me. Her little smile didn't fall. "You wouldn't believe what it's like trying to corral these two."

"Oh?" Giselle asked, a wealth of questions in the soft sound.

I squeezed her thigh again just to feel her beneath my hand and let her know I was just as shocked as she was.

"They're impossible. I decided not to wait at the front for them to follow because knowing them, it will take them another ten minutes to wade in from the car." Elena rolled her eyes as she moved toward Elle, surprising us both by leaning down in a familiar cloud of Chanel Number 5 perfume to press a kiss on each of her sister's cheeks. Giselle accepted the intimacy with a choked little gasp, her eyes wide as twin silver coins as they caught mine.

When Elena turned to me, she did so with a little frown before extending a hand to me. The many thin gold bracelets on her wrists clinked together as I shook it.

"It's good to see you both," she said, her voice quiet but sincere. "You look well."

"We are," I agreed, instinctively rocking Theo a little as he fussed in his sleep.

"Dio mio," she whispered, catching sight of his little face under his bucket hat. Without hesitation, she leaned close to me so she could trail a finger down his cheek. "I can't believe I haven't met this handsome little man yet. Mama told me his name is Theodore?"

"Theo," Giselle said, her uncertainty drowned in maternal pride. She beamed as she leaned over to adjust his hat. "He's had a long day, and he fell asleep on the way here, but when he wakes up, you'll be able to see just how sweet he is."

"He's my baby brother," Genny informed her aunt solemnly. "If you want, I'll let you hold him when he wakes up."

Elena bit off the edge of her smile and nodded gracefully. "That would be very nice of you. Thank you, Genevieve."

And Genny, who hated going by her full name, didn't even correct her aunt. She was that infatuated.

Giselle made big eyes at me as Elena finally rounded the table to take a seat. I shrugged a shoulder at her.

It shouldn't have surprised us, not really, to see Elena so content and loose with satisfaction. She might not have achieved the dreams she'd always assumed she wanted, but she was successful and in love.

If Giselle and I could evolve in just a week of loving each other on vacation in Mexico, it was only fitting Elena could change vastly after years of loving the right man.

As if summoned by my thoughts, there was a commotion at the doors to the patio behind us, and a second later, Dante Salvatore strutted out into the sunlight.

I'd forgotten how large he was, head and shoulders above the host who was trying unsuccessfully to escort him to the table because he couldn't keep up with the man's long strides. His broad, deeply tanned face was creased at the eyes and beside the mouth, reminding me he was older than my thirty-seven by four years. He wore all black, from his shoes to the sunglasses perched in his ink dark hair. It lent him a villainous presence as he crossed the stone patio, every diner's eyes immediately tracking him across the space.

I looked at Elena, stunned to see the easy, open smile on her face, the beaming contentment I was familiar with from staring at my own face in the mirror every morning when I shaved.

Fuck me, Elena Lombardi in love was a stunning thing to behold.

And it might have been selfish, but it settled something in me I hadn't known still needed tending to. The guilt I'd held on to for years wilted and died at that moment, as the huge mafioso ate over the pavement in his haste to get to his woman.

He ignored us as he bent to cage her against the back of her chair, staring into her eyes for a long moment.

"*Mia lottatore*," he growled almost too low to hear. "Your daughter is impossible."

Elena's laughter was a high, bell-like toll. I'd never known her to enjoy teasing, but she responded easily to his jibe. "Like father, like daughter." She peered over his shoulder at Giselle and grinned. "Am I right?"

Elle nodded, her hand creeping over to my thigh to pinch it. I chuckled a little under my breath at her incredulity, but only because I was feeling it too.

Who the hell was this woman?

"Give me a kiss," Dante demanded next, still not addressing us.

"I don't feel like it," Elena said with a lazy wave of her hand before inspecting her nails as if she had something better to do.

There was another growl from Dante, and then he was lifting her up, up, out of her chair, prompting a little screech of outrage from Elena, before he sat down in the seat and settled her in his lap. Once secured, he roped her hair around one ham-like fist and pinned her still to stamp a rough kiss on her lips.

When he pulled back, he raised an eyebrow. "You should know by now, if you want to play in public, I am only too happy to oblige."

Elena only smiled a small, secret little smile and wiped at the red lipstick transferred on his mouth with her thumb.

When she finished, Dante looked over at us, speaking as if we were mid-conversation. "I don't have to tell you two she's a fucking handful."

Giselle blinked, then burst out laughing, the warm sound flowing over me like sunshine. It made me grin too, looking at the tension leech from her shoulders as she recovered from her giggles and leaned toward them with a genuine smile.

"Honestly, I'm not sure how you handle it," she teased back.

I kept an eye on Elena, ready to scalp her if she snapped at my wife for being friendly.

Instead, Elena only laughed and stroked her hand through the back of Dante's hair as he said with a roguish wink, "A lot of practice."

"Ew, are you guys talking about sex again?" Another voice, this one young and belonging to a preteen girl with long light brown hair nearly the same color as her tanned skin. She strolled the rest of the way across the patio on slow, almost lazy strides until she reached Elena and Dante. "You know I'm already scarred for life, right?"

Dante's huge hand lashed out so suddenly, for a split second, I thought he meant to do her violence, and I tensed to interfere. Instead, he tugged her close so he could plant a kiss on her forehead that she accepted with faux reluctance.

"Giselle, Sinclair," Elena said, her voice bursting with pride as she laced her hand with the girl's. "This is our daughter, Aurora."

Cosima, Caprice, and Seb had all mentioned Aurora at some point or another the past couple of years, but this was our first time meeting Elena's adopted daughter. It was strange to see Elena in her even though they didn't share any blood. Aurora had the same regal bearing, a familiar resting expression of haughty elegance.

"You're family so you can call me Rora," she offered graciously as she tugged an empty chair closer to her parents so she could sit down and keep Elena's hand in hers.

"You can call me Genny," my daughter offered in the same tone, extending a red crayon to her cousin. "And you can color with me too."

"Cool," Rora accepted easily, angling her chair so she could lean over Genny's high chair.

Instantly, the two girls started chattering away in low voices as they worked together on a new piece of paper.

Beside me, Giselle sniffed.

When I turned to look at her, there were big, crystalline tears in those gorgeous grays.

"Hey, my siren," I murmured to her, tugging her chair closer with one hand so I could wrap my free arm around her. "What's going on here?"

"I'm sorry," she said, waving her hand around to excuse her behavior when it didn't need to be excused. "It's just... it's so nice to see you all."

"Thank you for agreeing to meet a little early," Elena said, leaning forward in Dante's lap to reach across the table for Elle's hand. My wife extended hers tentatively. "I just wanted the opportunity to say I'm sorry for everything that has happened between us over the years. I'm not going to say I'm wholly at fault, but I am going to own my part in our broken relationship. I...I had a lot to work through, and it took me years, too many years, to heal enough to realize my own mistakes. We had so many things working against us since we were just kids who didn't know better. It's been so long, but I know now it's never too late to fix a relationship, and I'd like to fix ours. No pressure. I'm not saying I expect us to be best friends, but I'd like us to try to know each other better." She paused, her eyes sweeping to Theo in my arms, then Genny and Rora, who were still coloring and whispering together. "For us, and also for our family."

Giselle blinked at her big sister, then stared down at their hands, the matching tone of olive skin, one with freckles and the other without. When she looked back up at Elena, her eyes were clear and determined behind the lacquer of her tears.

"I can take ownership for my part in it," she agreed easily. "I'm sorry for everything, and I always will, but I am so happy that you've found someone who makes you as happy as Sin makes me."

I wasn't sure how she would react to that, but Elena continued her streak of confounding me, and she grinned widely, her eyes creased at the edges with genuine happiness.

"You can thank him for teaching me that I didn't have to be the villain of my own story."

Dante leaned forward to place a kiss at the curve of her neck and shoulder in silent support. He caught my eye from across the table, and I felt the most bizarre emotion bubble up in my throat.

It was gratitude.

I was grateful for the man who had brought Elena to life as surely as Giselle had done with me. Even though we had never loved each other properly, I'd cared for this woman, known her and lived with her for years. It eased some masculine sense of worry in my chest to know she was cared for by a man who could protect her, even from her most villainous self.

I jerked my chin up him in the universal male equivalent of a back-slapping hug, and Dante? The man the media had dubbed the 'Mafia Lord' and the 'Devil of NYC'?

He fucking laughed.

He laughed because he knew we were the luckiest goddamn men on the planet to have the love of a Lombardi woman.

And I agreed with him wholeheartedly.

So I laughed too.

Giselle

Seven years later

"It's raining like a cow pisses," Sinclair muttered in his mother tongue as we held the wide-brimmed umbrella over our heads in the deluge of water spilling from quilted gray clouds.

Genevieve screwed up her little nose as she translated the rather crude expression, tugging on her father's hand in shock as she declared, "Papa, that was rude!"

Sin chuckled lightly, pulled her closer into the fold of his black cashmere peacoat. "The French are never rude, *ma chérie*. We are blunt. There is a subtle but very profound difference."

I shook my head at my husband, biting off the edge of the smile that threatened to curve my lips. He was incorrigible, but even after seven years of marriage and parenthood, he still made me feel like the nerdy kid in school with a crush on the quarterback. There was magic to every moment I spent with him, even the most mundane of them, like standing in the rain at Charles de Galle airport waiting for our Town Car to arrive.

He caught my eye and gave me a faint, curling grin that spoke of wickedness and want.

This was why we were having a vacation in our favorite city in the world, Paris, because the past year had been pure, delightful chaos. Sinclair had been featured in Forbes Richest Entrepreneurs Under Forty for his success with Faire Developments, and I'd been working around the clock on my largest exhibition yet, a series of erotic paintings done of physically disabled and disfigured people to showcase their unique form of beauty. It had been an unequivocal success. Even the kids were busy. Genny had exhibited an affinity and talent for ballet that had prompted her indulgent father to enroll her in the best dance academy in the city with one of the best instructors money could buy. She was only eight years old, but ballet was her life. Unsurprisingly perhaps, with parents like us, both our children were incredibly driven and passionate about art.

Theo hadn't settled on any one thing like his twin sister. Instead, every few months he cycled to another discipline. At first, he loved any sport with a ball, then he loved music and demanded lessons in piano from his Uncle Cage, then violin and guitar. By six, he discovered painting one day when I forced him to wait in my studio, and now, nearly a year later, he often voluntarily joined me there to experiment with oils, watercolors, the printing press, and clay sculpture.

Overachievers, Sebastian often joked. It ran in the Lombardi blood and had only been amplified by Sinclair's.

After a massive meltdown a few weeks ago, when Genny burst into tears after twisting her ankle and Theo yelled at his teacher because she didn't understand how impossible it was for a young boy with ADHD to stay still, Sinclair had decided a vacation was the only remedy.

As usual, he was right.

Even after hours on a red-eye flight from New York, a contentment blanketed our little family, a stillness I hadn't felt in months.

The car pulled up to the curb with a rippling splash of collected rainwater in the gutters, prompting the kids to laugh as murky droplets splattered their rainboots. Sin organized the suitcases with the driver while I ushered our babies into the car.

I closed my eyes, leaning my head back to absorb the soothing sound of my husband speaking in the rolling, lyrical French of the south where he'd been born.

"I'm happy we're home," Theo murmured from where he sat with his nose pressed to the window, staring out at the dreary, unattractive parking lot as if it was a Monet painting.

I laughed softly, love swollen in my chest. "Me too, *bambino*."

"Will I really get to meet Pasha Morozov?" Genny asked, immediately cuddling into me because my girl loved physical contact. Her wide blue eyes were the same shade as her father's and brother's, that electric blue I could never replicate with paint and brush no matter how hard I tried.

I kissed her soft crown of auburn hair. "Yes, I believe he runs in your *oncle* Cage's circle."

Which meant Pasha Morozov, the new diamond of the Paris Ballet, was a rouge and probably a sensualist. I didn't exactly want my impressionable daughter to meet a man like that whom she already idolized, but Sinclair had reminded me it was hypocritical to judge a man by his sexual proclivities.

My mind wandered as Sinclair and the driver got into the car, and we took off into the lightening dawn of our first day in Paris.

The last time Sinclair and I had been able to have a proper scene was months ago. Yet another reason—one that went unspoken but was implicitly understood—for our vacation in Paris.

I was dying to bloom open under his control again. The itch of submission fizzled under my skin like champagne as I imagined the many ways my Dominant might bend me to his will.

"Ma sirene?" Sinclair's warm, humor-filled voice wafted to me in the back seat, dissolving my fantasy.

I flushed as he grinned at me knowingly.

"How would you kids like to spend tonight with your uncle Cage?" Sin suggested casually.

Immediately, Genny and Theo erupted in excited affirmation. They loved their world-famous uncle even though they often disliked the random women he dragged to our family affairs. To them, he was the pinnacle of success, much more glamorous than their own parents.

My kids were happy and, from the cast of Sin's familiar wicked grin, I knew I soon would be too.

I WORE SILK THE COLOR OF THE INSIDE OF AN OYSTER, THE COLOR OF SKIN under candlelight, so every inch of me seemed indecently exposed, glowing with some inner light. My hair was brushed and curled into a long curtain of burnished red that rasped over the thin fabric at my breasts just enough to peak my nipples into diamond points.

I knew this was what I'd looked like under my Burberry trench coat when I'd left the hotel with Sinclair thirty minutes prior.

But I did not know how I looked now, kneeling on a small stage in the home of our local friend and BDSM community patron, Madame Claire.

My eyes were concealed by the very same shade of silk corseting my torso and barely covering my sex. The world around me was lost to my sight but heightened in my other senses. I could feel the warm touch of air swirling over me as people moved by, admiring me in faint whispers but never touching.

So sweet, they said in French, the language spilling like satin ribbons, smooth and seductive.

To whom does she belong? one man queried with obvious interest.

To Sinclair, I wanted to respond but didn't.

I wore the collar of pearls around my throat that said more than I ever could in the language of domination and submission about the fact that I was intractably taken.

It was exactly this ownership that grounded me while strangers admired my body. I would never have felt comfortable or open to their appreciation if it wasn't for Sinclair's influence, his voice in my ear telling me I was so beautiful, so worthy of worship.

As if summoned by my thoughts, a light touch trailed from the top of my head down the back of my hair, where a hand slowly twisted my long hair into a rope. Using it as leverage, my head was canted back, my mouth parting instinctively as warm lips sealed over it.

I hummed as Sinclair's velvet tongue slid between my teeth and claimed my own.

By the time he pulled back, I was panting.

"*Salute, ma sirène,*" Sin murmured into my air, his hot breath fanning over my exposed neck.

I shivered violently, prompting a dark chuckle from my lover.

"You kneel so prettily for me," he praised, stroking his hand firmly down my hair now. I arched into his stroking like a cat. "So eager to be seen as the perfect submissive for me."

"Yes, sir," I breathed, desperately wanting to squirm as my core started to throb with anticipation, but I knew Sin wouldn't like that.

"Should we put on a show for these lucky people, then?" he practically purred.

"Yes, please, sir."

"Mmm," he hummed as I sensed him stand at his full height again and move away.

There was a soft click of a clasp unlocking that I knew was his bag of toys and implements parting under his questing hands.

A moment later, the cool slide of silk across the curve of my neck and shoulder sent a shiver rippling down my spine. The audience around us hummed with anticipation as Sin sensuously moved the ribbon over my flesh until I broke out in goose bumps.

"I'm going to bind your beautiful breasts," he murmured to me, his hot breath stirring my hair as he bent to trail the scarf around my belly before sliding it up under the crease of my heavy chest. "I want them swollen and pink for me."

I hummed my approval, lost to reasonable sense as I sank deeper into sub space. He was careful only to touch me with the silk tie as he secured it under my boobs, then up over my back and down through the first band so that my breasts were separated and plumped up by the pressure of the bindings. I could feel the dull, warm thud of my pulse in each, my nipple aching for relief as they furled into hard points.

"I know." He hushed me as my breath came faster. "You're so eager already, but we have so much farther to go before I let you come for me."

He ignored my whimper as he finished binding me, and his hand wrapped around me from behind to pluck hard at my nipples. I arched into his punishing grip, gasping at the ceiling, wondering dazedly how I might appear to the partygoers, wantonly displayed for my Dom.

"Gorgeous," Sinclair praised as one hand trailed down the middle of my breasts to the inside of my left thigh.

I gasped as he delivered a sharp slap there and ordered, "Spread yourself wider for me."

I adjusted instantly, so eager to please that I splayed myself open until my thighs ached from the strain.

"Yes," he hissed softly as his fingers trailed along the delicate skin on the inside of my thighs, making passes back and forth but never deigning to touch my throbbing core.

I was shaking after a few minutes of this mindless sensation play, my head lolling back on my loose neck, my mouth open for my panting breath.

"My siren loves to be on display and admired like the work of art you are," he finally murmured as his fingers trail lightly, too lightly, up the seam of my drenched sex.

On cue, another pair of hands landed on my body, jerking me into sudden alertness until I heard the crooning French tones of Cage.

"It's just me, cherie," he murmured lowly as he moved his big calloused hands over my arms up into my hair so he could hold it away from my neck as Sinclair dipped to puncture kisses down the length of it.

"Cage is here as a prop," Sinclair explained in that cold, exacting voice that made me shiver. "He is here to remind you that I am in charge of your body. That I will always give you what you need, even if you don't know how to voice it. He is here to ground you because, Elle? I am going to fuck you so hard you go flying."

"Oh my God." The words rushed from my mouth like air from a punctured balloon as my hips rolled and wetness leaked down my thighs.

Why was this so hot?

Years of play, and I never grew used to the heady knowledge that I was Sinclair's. His to do with what he pleased, what would inevitably please me because he knew me better than I knew myself sometimes.

And I'd needed this.

This worship.

This admiration.

I was a mother to two young, busy, and gifted kids. It was a round-the-clock job that owned most of my life and a considerable amount of my identity, especially in the past six months of my hectic life.

Somehow, Sinclair had read my soul as he'd been able to do since the very beginning on that plane to Mexico.

He'd known I needed a night to be nothing but flesh and bone.

Nothing but sex and sin.

Nothing but my womanliness.

Nothing but his.

"How does that sound, hmm?" Sinclair asked huskily against my neck before sinking his teeth into the column in a way that had me moaning.

He knew I wanted it, but he always loved the sound of my voice soaked in lust.

"Yes, please, sir," I said, loud enough for the voyeurs to hear. "I want to be held down and fucked hard."

He made a sexy noise in his throat halfway between a groan and a growl before he was suddenly standing up, leaving my back exposed to the cool air.

"Cage, take my spot," he ordered implacably.

They switched, Cage sitting behind me, his arms banded over my lower stomach to hold me in place, his strong torso a chair for me to lean on. It was an oddly comforting and asexual hold that only heightened the eroticism of the act. He was just a prop, another means to bend me to Sin's will, and I loved it.

Meanwhile, Sin moved in front of me. I didn't know exactly what he was doing behind the blindfold until suddenly his hands were on my thighs, dragging me closer to his open mouth beneath me. I shuddered violently as his lips sealed over my soaking pussy, unerringly finding my throbbing clit.

My hips tried to churn, pressing down harder for more friction because I was already *this close* to coming, but Cage held me intractably still. I made a keening noise I might have been embarrassed about if I wasn't under the entrancing domination of my Frenchman.

"Please, sir," I begged as I tried to thrash in Cage's hold.

Sinclair ignored me.

Instead, he feasted like a starved man on my sex, sucking on my folds, tongue fucking my clasping entrance, flicking his tongue deliciously over my sensitive clit.

"Please, please," I started to chant just under my breath.

He didn't tell me to be quiet. He just listened to my increasingly loud pleas until I was almost sobbing with the need to come.

"You look beautiful obeying him like this," Cage whispered in my ear, and his praise of my submission just sent me higher.

"Sir, please!" My shouted words punctured the air as I arched as deeply as I could into Sin's magic mouth.

He pulled away just enough to say like a commander in the Navy, "Come for me, siren."

A moment later, his teeth were sinking into the tender flesh at the inside of my thigh, his fingers pinched my clit and then abruptly released, and I was coming.

Orgasming so hard I lost my breath as every single one of my muscles contracted almost painfully around the explosion of pleasure at my center.

"Such a good wife." Sinclair's voice found me in the fog as my orgasm receded, and I was vaguely aware of Cage moving away from me, and Sinclair turning me with strong, sure hands to better face the audience as he moved behind me.

It was only when I felt the hot head of his cock notch at my center that I clued back into reality. Instantly, I tried to thrust down on him.

His cruel, smoky chuckle wound around me like extra bondage.

"No, no, hold yourself still for me while I wedge the head of my cock in this tight little pussy and make you come all down my cock. If you come all over me, I may reward you with a nice hard fucking after," he promised.

My thighs quivered as I held myself poised high enough to take just the very tip of his dick inside myself, but the urge to take him to the hilt made me moan and whine without shame.

"Hush, siren," he ordered as one hand went to my swollen breasts, alternating between pinching and twisting each nipple while the other arrowed straight to my weeping, swollen sex where he gently drew tight little circles over my clit.

"Oh my god," I panted again and again, my hips jerking slightly as I fought the insatiable urge to seat myself to the hilt on his gorgeous shaft. "Oh my god, Sin, please."

"Are you going to show all these lucky people how gorgeous you are when you obey me?" He continued to speak to me as he played me like a maestro, plucking, pulling, and coaxing music from my sucking wet pussy, from my taxed lungs and my panting mouth. "Are you going to show them how hard you come for me when I play with you like this? How sweet your pussy looks leaking all over my length?"

"Yes, sir," I almost shouted, the last syllable fading into a ragged groan.

Sweat beaded over every inch of my body.

My mind was empty of words except those, the "yes, sir" a muscle memory, a submissive reflex more than conscious thought.

Everything I was other than his had faded away into the blackness, and the only light I could see was the beauty of his love and possession over me.

"So fucking beautiful," he moaned into my ear. "Kiss me when you come for me. I want to eat those sweet moans off your tongue. They might get to see you come all over me, but only I get to feel it."

His words triggered the release as a climax shot through me like a bullet from a gun, tearing down my center as I fractured open under the pressure. Vaguely, I was aware of the wet sloshing noise as Sinclair clamped his hands over my hips and ruthlessly thrust me down to the hilt on his cock.

I screamed as my release spiraled higher, as he started to fuck up into me savagely, his punishing grip giving me nowhere to run. I accepted his rough fucking the way I accepted harsh criticism as an artist, knowing it made me better, wanting to be driven farther, harder.

I gasped and groaned and yelled Sinclair's name like it was the only word I'd ever known.

And when his voice rose to call my name to the heavens a moment later, the sound of them together, Sinclair and his Elle, settled something in my soul I hadn't known needed ironing out.

Even though we'd been busy, with little time for intimacy, even though we'd been together for ten years and had two kids, this was the truth of our lives.

The truth of us.

Sinclair and Elle.

Our love for each other was bigger than anything that might come at us, try to separate us, test us.

And as I came down from that physical high, Sinclair read my mind again as he held my damp, lax body close and brushed a tender kiss over my throbbing pulse before whispering, "*Mon amour pour toi est plus grand que le monde.*"

"Forever," I murmured back, knowing in a way I didn't think I ever could have comprehended before that our love was the backbone of our lives, and nothing and no one would ever change that.

Le Fin.
The End.

Thanks etc.

I first started writing about the Lombardi family when I was sixteen years old. The idea for Giselle and Sinclair's story (The Evolution of Sin) came to me like a lightning strike. It all started with the hypothetical question I asked my best friend at the time, "what would you do if you and my boyfriend fell in love with each other?" Immediately, she responded, "We would be together." After I got over my initial shock, I realized that two people's happiness could be worth more than one person's happiness and Sinclair and Giselle's love story was born. I loved the idea of pitting loyalty and blood against passion and true love. Sometimes, people are too obsessed with what is right and wrong instead of what is best for them. I admire both of these characters for having the chutzpah to face the consequences of their love and their actions; I hope you do too.

Annette, my feisty, loyal PA and loving friend. Thank you for keeping me organized, sane, and healthy. I really don't know what I'd do without you and I never want to find out.

Allaa, my friend and writing confidante, thank you for always being my sounding board and cheerleader.

To my #dirtysoulsister Michelle Clay. I love that you have their words "my love for you is bigger than the world" tattooed on your skin. It means so much that you love their love enough to identify it with your own beautiful love story.

Jenny from Editing 4 Indies, you are my saviour. Thank you for polishing this manuscript from a diamond in the rough into a polished gem.

Najla Qamber from Najla Qamber Designs is my cover and graphics magician and she did an amazing job of this new cover!

I love thanking my gorgeous Review Team for the amazing passion for my work. I can't tell you how much it means to me that I have you ladies in my corner always cheering me on.

Giana's Darlings, you are the best reader's group on the planet and my safe, little happy place on the interweb.

As always, to the Love of My Life. You were the first person I told months after I published The Affair. When I asked you if I should pursue writing inside of being a lawyer, even if I was poor and unsuccessful at it, you said I should follow my dream and you'd support me no matter what. Thank you for being my pilar of strength and support. I love you from the depths of my soul.

About Giana Darling

Giana Darling is a *USA Today*, *Wall Street Journal*, Top 40 Best Selling Canadian romance writer who specializes in the taboo and angsty side of love and romance. She currently lives in beautiful British Columbia where she spends time riding on the back of her man's bike, baking pies, and reading snuggled up with her cat, Persephone, and dog, Romeo.

Join my Reader's Group
Subscribe to my Newsletter
Follow me on IG
Like me on Facebook
Follow me on Goodreads
Follow me on BookBub
Follow me on Pinterest

Other Books by Giana Darling

The Evolution of Sin Trilogy

The Affair

The Secret

The Consequence

The Evolution Of Sin Trilogy Boxset

The Fallen Men Series

Lessons in Corruption

Welcome to the Dark Side

Good Gone Bad

After the Fall

Inked in Lies

Dead Man Walking

A Fallen Men Companion Book of Poetry:

King of Iron Hearts

The Enslaved Duet

Enthralled (The Enslaved Duet #1)

Enamoured (The Enslaved Duet, #2)

The Elite Seven Series

Sloth (The Elite Seven Series, #7)

Coming Soon

Fallen King (A Fallen Men Short Story)

When Heroes Fall (Anti-Heroes in Love, #1)

When Villains Rise (Anti-Heroes in Love, #2)

Made in the USA
Columbia, SC
13 November 2021

48905520R00452